COAST: A Test Of Faith

Sequel to 'COAST: An Act Of Burial'

"Contra omnes dissident"

ISBN: 978-0-9948602-0-0

Edited by Jon Bowser.
Cover art © Jonathon Earl Bowser, 2015, used by permission.
Purchase fine art prints of the cover painting at www.jonathonart.com
Website by Brian Loewen and Steve Pashley, content © 2012-2015 by Xander Richards.
Tactical and medical consultant Gary Taylor.
Printed by CreateSpace.

BARRETT'S PRIVATEERS
Written by Stan Rogers © 1976 Fogarty's Cove Music. Used by permission. All rights reserved. With grateful thanks to Ariel Rogers. www.stanrogers.net

A Note About Sentence Structure And Speech

As I write, I like the narrative to embody a realistic, speech-like rhythm where appropriate and thus I have adopted the somewhat unusual practice of including fragments of speech as part of the surrounding sentence where appropriate. Few authors do this and even fewer editors accept it, but it is becoming a more popular device as our language evolves. Thus, instead of the typical form:

Joe said, "Thank you," and walked away.

I would tend to use:

Joe said "thank you" and walked away.

Stylistically, this method seems much more natural, mimicking the cadence of spoken narration. After 'COAST: An Act Of Burial' was released some questions were raised concerning this practice, so I want to forewarn my readers about this approach to conversational grammar; I believe that you'll quickly get used to this stylistic choice and that it'll help you to enjoy 'COAST: A Test Of Faith'.

A Note About Derogatory Language And Racial Slurs

In this narrative inappropriate terms and ethnophaulisms are sometimes employed. It is not the author's intent to cause offence, but to convey realism in the characters' speech. They are, after all, imperfect creatures like ourselves.

COAST:
A TEST OF FAITH

www.SpyNovels.org

www.facebook.com/AuthorXanderRichards

www.twitter.com/XanderRichards

Gratitude

THANK YOU to Brian Loewen and Steve Pashley for their website work; Gary Taylor for three decades of friendship and his insights into forensics, weaponry and field medicine; Hannu Tiainen, marketing manager of Mobimar Ltd., for the excellent information on their submarines; Bruce Gemmill of Project North Star and Dan Rawlyck of Air Canada for the aviation help; Kelly Chen for her help with Mandarin names; Hans Rosén for the Swedish translation; Andy Burton for immersion-testing a twenty Euro bill; Jake Finnigan for help with the Australian slang; Tommy Chia for his information on the Port of Singapore; Wes 'Big W' Funk for being a great pal and crusader for literature in Saskatchewan; and to beta-readers Orion Croteau, Nael Glenister, Paul Goodwin, Brian James Hildebrand, Donna Miller and Shawna Roberts.

It would be remiss of me not to give special mention to and express my gratitude for the contribution that Jonathon Earl Bowser has made to the COAST project. Not only has Jon created artwork that brings the covers wonderfully to life but his meticulous editorial skills and critique of the work have been a great blessing to me and by extension to you the reader. His friendship and our mutual appreciation of fermented malt beverages have also proven enjoyable as together we discuss the mysteries of life, the universe and everything else, especially art in its many forms.

As always I'm grateful to my dear old friend Brian 'Birdie' Matthews, in collaboration with whom this vision was born twenty eight years ago.

Thanks to everyone who read 'COAST: An Act Of Burial' and to the reviewers who were *much* kinder than I deserve. Thank you again to my wonderful wife Mindy, who really is the most remarkable human being.

Thank **you** for reading this novel.

Dedication

This book is dedicated with heartfelt and affectionate gratitude to the memory of my mother Yvonne (1925-2012) who served in the Women's Auxiliary Air Force during the Second World War, and died shortly after the release of 'COAST: An Act Of Burial', never having seen a copy of the finished book.

It is further dedicated to all those whose duties place them in harm's way for the sake of others. I thank you for your service. In particular I want to extend my gratitude to all the ATOs (Ammunition Technical Officers) and bomb disposal experts, who I consider amongst the bravest human beings on Earth.

Contents

6

001: The City

"I think it will be nasty way to die, having throat cut by saw."

The Slavic accent was as pronounced as ever, but just about intelligible. Waving his empty cigarette holder like a wand, the speaker's sharp little eyes scanned the men at the table, flicking occasionally to his bodyguard who was perched atop a stool at the bar, nursing a drink that he obviously didn't like.

The broken English continued. "He will kill you, he will kill me. We will all lose head."

Vladimir Kholitczyn looked odd minus the beard that usually encircled his weatherbeaten face and with his greying ginger hair dyed black, because there wasn't enough of it left to do justice to the strong shade. His regular leather jacket was accompanied by new jeans and an expensive lightweight shirt for which the British autumn was a poor match. Another questionable combination was the pair of Indian red alligator patterned cowboy boots which projected from beneath the table and beat time with his speech.

Ian McKinley took a gulp of orange juice and considered the threat as relayed by the worst dressed arms broker he'd ever met. Following a bad deal earlier that year, Kholitczyn had pissed off weapons dealer Süleyman Erbakan by grassing him up to their unit, leading the Turk, renowned for beheading his enemies, to seek revenge, apparently not just on the wily Russian, but on TDR.12 as well.

Next to Vlad 'the Inhaler' sat Kyle Bacon, a thin faced, blond-haired north London tech dealer whose intel had, on this occasion, proven better than TDR.12's, having been the only person in their network to come up with a lead on Kholitczyn's whereabouts and having offered to arrange this meeting. Bacon was a native Cockney who claimed to have gypsy blood in his veins and portrayed a peculiar but passionate sense of patriotism about it. He was also a friend of Ian McKinley, who uncharitably referred to Bacon as 'the only camel in the western world with a center parting'.

Kholitczyn continued. "In my country we kill; he is same. But now is looking for me, and also for your guys." He shrugged, displaying the leathery palms of a hard worker that had placed the fields of his native Ukraine firmly behind him for a late Cold War career in the GRU, Russia's foreign military intelligence service. Kholitczyn lifted the cigarette holder to his mouth but stopped short of inserting it. The British smoking ban clearly didn't sit well, and he scowled at the unoccupied end of the antique Bakelite tube with disdain before finishing with a profound nod and eyes wide. "We will be brown toast!"

Chris Carter smiled broadly. "Bread," he amended, cheeks dimpling beneath his patchy mouse brown stubble.

"Da," affirmed Kholitczyn, hoisting a sanctimonious finger as though his error had been a deliberate test. "Bread toast."

"No, brown..." Carter started, then shook his head. "Doesn't matter."

McKinley couldn't help grinning, the expression tugging at the corners of his youthful face in several tiny jerks. "Well," he said, leaning back. "Being someone's target isn't exactly a new experience."

"Da." Kholitczyn wagged the finger again. "But Erbakan, he will not stop till we are dead. He is *Byesposhudnyi*. Is dangerous man but not... What is your word? *Dovkiy*."

"Cunning," stated Carter flatly, as though the purpose of his presence was to make up for the Russian's limited English.

"What's the other word?" interjected Paul Wilson with a nudge to Carter's forearm.

"Relentless," answered Carter, lifting the brim of his cap and scratching his hair, "or ruthless." He smiled and turned back to Kholitczyn. "You were saying?"

"*Herashaw.* Cunning; is not *cunning.* Smart with business, yes, and dangerous. But this is why I come here. He will not look for me at Britain, I think."

Wilson pointed at the Slav's head. "But you changed your hair anyway?"

Kholitczyn smiled warmly, his eyes projecting assurance. "Is... in case of surveillance."

Carter put his elbows on the table, knocking a couple of his Cheese Flavoured Moments out of their packet and clasping his hands together. "So, if you don't mind me asking, what are you planning to do about him?"

The arms dealer nodded wisely, his lower lip protruding slightly. "I am careful. This is problem that can be fixed, but carefully. I have not killed friend before; they say first one always hardest." His telephone buzzed and he lifted it, tilting his head back. "Da."

As Kholitczyn embarked on a torrent of Russian, Wilson leaned toward his colleagues. "Erbakan knows about us through Heinmarsh?"

"Or Vlad," answered McKinley, nodding toward Kholitczyn. "Well, he probably knows *of* us. I'm not worried. Are you?"

"Erbakan," interjected Bacon, his thick London accent making him sound like the archetypal British gangster movie but without the incessant profanity, "'e's bad news innit? Don' mess with 'im."

McKinley looked up with raised eyebrows. "But you *deal* with him."

"Only 'cause o' me dad," answered Bacon. "'E's an existing customer. Sometimes I get 'im tech, sometimes I'm buyin' it."

"Just tech?"

Bacon shook his thin head. "You *know* I don't do shooters." Having disarranged it, he carefully restored his flaxen hair to its former position as he continued. "And I ain't met Erbakan either, just 'is first mate."

"It's not really an issue for *us,*" said Carter. "He probably doesn't know shit about The Team. But I'm concerned for him." He nodded his head toward their Russian colleague.

"He can look after himself," answered McKinley, glancing round to the bar. "Besides, he's got Egor."

"His name *Leonid,*" corrected the Russian as he finished his call.

"Leonid, Egor, Mikhail, Ivan... all the same to me," said McKinley with a sarcastic grin. The smoking ban was getting to him as well, and the more he thought about it the more he felt like going outside and satiating the cravings.

"Where is your man Plugger?" said Kholitczyn to Bacon.

"He don' like being sociable innit? No good wi' people, 'e ain't."

"Excuse me," said Carter, rising to his feet. "Gotta go turn my bike round." He placed a hand on Wilson's shoulder and pushed past his chair, heading for the other side of the room.

"Why he is turning round bike?" asked Kholitczyn. "I thought he is driving car."

McKinley grinned. "It means going to the bog."

Kholitczyn looked none the wiser. "*Toulyet,*" added McKinley.

"Ah," nodded Kholitczyn. "Is well known that British are best at wrecking English language."

Wilson slurped his coke, casting his mind back to the journey he'd been on since early August when he'd been promoted to Tactical Deployment and Response Team Twelve. That had been an insane month of action and danger after which they'd enjoyed relative inactivity, and Wilson was ready for some momentum. His fractured ankle was to all intents and purposes healed and, through physiotherapy, he could run as fast as usual without it bothering him. His team-mates were similarly recovered; McKinley's lacerated leg was fine and the shrapnel wound to Carter's belly was no longer causing anything worse than jokes about him having two navels.

Using time off to meet with Kholitczyn in London would perhaps have been frowned upon by General Sutton but they'd all agreed that it was necessary and the CO's rare absence from base presented an ideal opportunity. Despite the Joint Intelligence Committee's frustrating sluggishness, it was imperative that their ultimate quarry, Heinmarsh, whose machinations had led to the inception of *Operation Copper Burial*, be located. Erbakan, the infamous *silâh tüccarı,* was a reseller of the treacherous American's highly advanced rifles and the only known lead through whom their investigation might be advanced.

Bacon glanced up at one of the television screens. He pointed and said "looks like some protester bird chained 'erself to the railings at Number Ten."

"Really." McKinley could live without it. He hated London so he wanted to get any information they could on Erbakan then head home.

The Londoner rolled his eyes. "What's she think this is? Bloody Greenham Common?"

Wilson rotated in his chair, resting his arm on its back and looking up at the big TV. Right now the news feed was a shaky-cam view of Downing Street into which shoulders and necks intruded. It was hard to see what was going on and there was no discernible audio. Then the view cleared momentarily, allowing him to make out a pregnant woman in a white blouse who was shouting something wildly. She appeared not just handcuffed to the railings outside the Prime Minister's official residence with one hand, but to a man in a charcoal grey suit with the other. It was the same few seconds of footage repeating and it looked like it had been captured with a phone camera. Wilson turned back to their table with the opinion that it was some stupid political stunt going down. Animal rights, nuclear disarmament, the Flat Earth Society... Whatever the protest was about, Wilson didn't care.

McKinley's new smartphone trilled and the team leader took it, pushing himself up and away from the table to find somewhere a bit more private. Wilson turned his own device in his hand, admiring its sleek lines and shiny faceplate. He and McKinley were taking to the new phones well, but Carter had thus far refused to upgrade, arguing something about 'non-matured technology' as well as the usual bunch of indecipherable tech-talk. It was weird that Carter the gadget-geek wasn't embracing the new gear, but Wilson and the team leader were liking their new toys.

Bacon was still watching the news whilst Kholitczyn seemed caught up with inserting an exploratory pinkie nail in his cigarette holder. Wilson picked up his coke again and was about to take a swallow when he was struck by an odd thought. Putting down the glass, he swivelled his head back to the screen just in time to see the view change in a blur of confusing images to a policeman gesturing urgently for people to move away. A caption scrolled onto the bottom of the screen; 'Breaking News: Suicide Bomber in Downing Street'.

Suicide bomber?

Holy SHIT!!!

Wilson jumped up like he'd been bitten by a snake, rocking the table and sending drinks toppling. At that moment McKinley appeared next to him.

"We're going!" snapped the Scotsman. "Grab his phone!"

Wilson scooped up Carter's device as McKinley made for the corridor where the bathrooms were. He barged through the first door and kicked open the gents, shouting "Chris head for the car, we've got trouble!" With this he charged past Wilson and out of the pub, shoving patrons unapologetically from his path. There was swearing and the sound of breaking glass.

Wilson turned back to their two companions, shouted "we'll be in touch!" and also headed out at high speed.

"*Oi!* Bung for the drinks you gorger bastards!" demanded Bacon aghast, but the COAST operatives were gone.

"See, they have business," offered Kholitczyn. "Now," he said, giving Bacon a wide, ingratiating smile and pushing the tech dealer's drink toward him, "why don't *we* do some?"

Wilson caught up with McKinley, running the quarter mile back to the car park and Carter's Range Rover.

"Is it the suicide bomber?" he barked as their feet beat an insistent rhythm on the pavement.

McKinley didn't look round. "We're the closest team. HQ wants us in there!"

They ran across a busy street. There was a squeal of brakes and an angry horn blast from a black taxi. Wilson waved an apology behind him. The unforgiving horn sounded again.

Less than a minute later they both slowed upon entering the multi-storey car park, where their transport was on the fifth level. Thudding up the concrete ramps, they started the climb. Here they could continue running rather than clomping up stairs or waiting for an elevator. It was Wilson's first opportunity to really test his ankle and he was vaguely concerned that at any moment it might let him down.

McKinley forged ahead but not at full throttle. Carter was a decent runner, but not as fast as them. It would take him a couple of minutes longer.

The spiral ramp of the car park seemed to surround them in an endless uphill circle, each rotation as uninspiring as the last, like running inside a giant Nautilus shell. They pushed on, expecting to hear Carter coming up from the rear. Finally they rounded the curve where his vehicle was parked and stopped next to it, McKinley breathing hard and spitting phlegm. Cars stood in uniform rows retreating into the depths of the building and where parking stalls were empty the dusty concrete floor bore evidence of leaking sumps. The vehicles were a mixture of expensive saloons and smaller, more modest economy models, but there wasn't an older car in sight after Carter's beloved Range Rover.

"Can we get there quick enough?" Wilson knew that their team-mate was a fast driver, but this was central London. Not the easiest city to navigate in a hurry.

"You could send him down the road for a pack of fags and he'd arrive ahead of The Stig," answered McKinley, his breath starting to decelerate to its normal tempo. "His speedo *starts* at sixty."

Wilson raised an eyebrow. "Is that good or bad?"

"If you want to bab your pants every five minutes, put him behind the wheel. But if you need to get somewhere really fast, let him drive."

Wilson raised and eyebrow as Carter ran up, panting. "I appreciate your confidence."

"You'll earn it today," answered McKinley. "Let's go!"

Not thirty seconds later the Range Rover hurtled around the circular ramps like a model slot-car on its track. They bounced onto the lowest level and Carter rammed the gate. With a massive jolt and a crash the fibreglass and aluminium barrier parted into fragments. Carter winced at the damage to his vehicle, knowing that he'd just have to fix it yet again.

They charged onto the street with squealing tyres, causing several near collisions. A bicycle courier took a tumble, winged by the Rangey's left mirror.

"Sorry!" shouted Carter to no effect whatsoever. He hung a hard left.

"Where the hell are you going?!" demanded McKinley, pointing to their right. "Downing Street's that way!"

"Through all the traffic!" snapped Carter. "I'm going south side."

McKinley looked round at Wilson, who nodded. Both the new boy and Carter had spent a lot more time in England's capital city. "London Bridge?" he asked.

"Right!" Carter's eyes momentarily widened with a worried look, as he swerved around a lorry. Wilson swore.

They hit the bridge going at least eighty miles an hour along the pavement, Carter hammering the horn to send numerous pedestrians scrambling for their lives to either side. Suddenly, he reached down and flicked two of the many switches on the Range Rover's panel. A siren blared into life.

McKinley was shocked. "You...?"

Carter cracked a momentary smile. "Blues 'n' twos."

McKinley turned back to the front. The clever bugger had rigged so many gadgets into the old car that he didn't know what to expect next.

"Never thought I'd actually *need* 'em," added Carter with an upward flick of his eyebrows, arms frantically juggling the wheel.

Traffic was dense as they came off London Bridge and they had no choice but to go through it. McKinley wondered momentarily what on earth the mandatory London congestion charge was supposed to achieve. The siren seemed effective, though, as vehicles started to move out of the way to allow their passage under the railway bridge on Borough High Street. Carter veered right onto Southwark Street, where conditions were clearer, and jammed the accelerator into the floor.

"Willy," said McKinley, "get the news and find out what's going on!"

"On it!" affirmed Wilson, and pulled his phone from his pocket.

The big car rocked and bumped as it wove round vehicles in blatant contravention of the Highway Code, not always missing other road users. Carter cursed.

"You can fix it later," ground McKinley. He went into the mapping application on his phone and called up a GPS fix of their position. Carter had been right on the money; this was definitely the best route. It was slightly longer, but reaching Downing Street from the south side of the river would be a lot quicker.

McKinley heard an electronic chirp and navigated to his message screen. There was the confirmation.

Order CABE10BK/12-01. Urgent RED-RED-RED: proceed Downing Street SW1 stat. Suicide bomber situation in progress. Cabinet personnel in imminent danger. Neutralise threat, apprehend suspect if possible and deliver COAST HQ. Use of deadly force authorised. End.

Yeah, that was about as expected. McKinley looked up for a moment into the cold London cityscape that was bouncing violently around outside, the autumnal cast of the low elevation sun making the place look even more inhospitable than usual. He turned his thoughts to the mission. They had to pile through this pre rush hour traffic and intervene at the heart of Britain's government. Then they had to stop this lass blowing herself to bits *without* killing her if they could. Then they had to take her captive without getting themselves blown up in the process. Great.

Aware of the swiftly diminishing lead time, McKinley started to plan the intervention. Cancelling the GPS track, he switched back to mapping and slid the view over to Westminster. There was Downing Street running roughly east to west. How did she get past security, wondered McKinley, just as an impact with the pavement sent his ass off the seat and his head into the roof. He grunted a couple of choice words.

Bursting from under the railway bridge at the junction of Southwark Street and Blackfriars road, McKinley jumped as the Range Rover clipped a bus shelter and sacrificed its door mirror to avoid a security van in the right hand lane. Carter cursed, accompanied by a chorus of horns blasting around them.

Pedestrians scattered in panic from the crossing near Rennie Street as the vehicle tore like a missile between the opposing rows of traffic on the narrow road. In a canyon of concrete they sped west as the London Eye came into view. The road widened slightly and Carter raced on as though his own life depended on it. Again the front offside wheel hit the edge of a crossing reservation, the Range Rover lurched and McKinley watched the tarmac on his left get uncomfortably close for a split second.

"Can you...?"

"Sorry!" Carter's teeth were bared in concentration. Here the road was lined with both trees and concrete bollards on the left hand side. The basement entrances of the buildings were protected by railings. Passing on the pavement would be impossible.

Suddenly Carter hit the anchors and the big car went up on its front wheels, skidding like a roller skate on ice. Carter roared. McKinley swore, his head thrust forward by the deceleration, and glimpsed an old lady flinging herself from their path. The next instant there was a thunderous crash as her shopping trolley disintegrated in a hail of biscuits, milk and vegetables.

"Bollocks!" screamed Carter and crunched the gears, dropping all the way down to regain speed. He triggered the wipers, sending Brussels sprouts and spring onions flying.

Wilson snatched his phone off the floor and rotated its screen back to where he could watch the news. "Cordon set up," he barked. "Evacuation! No civvie traffic!"

"MOD90s out," ordered McKinley. "Cosplay the SAS."

There was a familiar sound through the wail of their siren; a loud, insistent thudding like a fifty cal MG through a low-pass filter. McKinley looked up to see two helicopters with police markings flying toward Westminster. They would have snipers on board and would cover the street from both ends. McKinley knew he would have to pull some serious rank to get to the girl first. He lifted his phone to make an urgent call to headquarters. But how to stop her from detonating?

The U-shaped valley of stone and glass pressed in again as they neared the big traffic island with its circular Imax cinema vaguely reminiscent of an old gasometer and ringed by browning bushes, oddly lush in this grey urban landscape. Busses and cars squealed to a halt as Carter barrelled ahead, onto the roundabout and through the red lights. A motorcycle courier lost his balance, fell and nearly rolled under their speeding vehicle. Still on the phone, McKinley shuddered at the narrowness of the rider's escape. They entered the constriction of York Road as Carter bounced over the central reservation into oncoming traffic to avoid an impenetrable melee of slow moving vehicles. Horns blaring, cars and vans swerved from their path and he twisted the hurling car left, onto the raised pavement itself, steering like a precision guidance system to keep at least one wheel on the narrow cobbles. Carter's heart pounded and his mind raced as though turbocharged, all the time strenuously working to keep the vehicle straight and trying to think ahead fifty meters or more.

McKinley finished his call to the unit. Yes, they would hold the police sharpshooters back for as long as possible but if it looked like it was going to hit the fan they'd be ordered to fire at will.

Wilson was still glued to the news despite their shaky passage. Suddenly the onscreen caption changed and he gulped, his eyes wide. Could this get any more mental?

"Hostage is the chancellor!" he shouted. McKinley glanced round momentarily, disbelief on his face. The second most powerful man in the British government was chained to a suicide bomber!

Chicheley Street flashed past on the right, level with Jubilee Gardens and the giant London Eye, the tallest ferris wheel in Europe. This meant that they were almost at Westminster Bridge so McKinley drew his pistol and checked it quickly. Traffic was mercifully lighter here, but he expected delays as they reached the trouble spot thanks to all the stationary vehicles which would be held there. Bloody London, he thought.

"Shitty death!" yelled Carter at Park Plaza. "*One way!*"

"Damnit!" answered McKinley. In his urgent plotting he'd neglected navigation. He instantly scanned the traffic stream to their left. It was blocked like a coconut in a sock.

"Straight ahead!" shouted Wilson. "No traffic!"

"Do it!" yelled McKinley, throwing the consequences to the four winds.

With a loud crunch Carter somehow squeezed the big SUV between the railings and the traffic lights, their bones rattling with the collision. But as they entered the wrong end of the bus lane a double-decker appeared at the other. Carter threw them right and onto the sidewalk again.

"Breathe in!" he screamed as the Rangey hurtled toward the gap between the wall of stone to their right and a lamppost. McKinley involuntarily pushed himself back into his seat. With a harsh scraping sound from its right mirror the nearly two meter wide vehicle just made it between the obstacles. Passing the bus, Carter yanked her hard to the left, just missing the railings which would have probably ended their ride. He pushed the ageing car to its limits, slamming her across another central reservation, past Saint Thomas' hospital and, finally, onto the Westminster Bridge approach. Big Ben loomed ahead showing twenty to five, a monumental reminder of how short the time was.

They screamed into the bus lane then with another jolt onto the south-western pavement, passing the numerous parked cars and seeing the roadblock halfway across the famous landmark. The parapet's trefoil pattern flashed past like the viewing slits of a zoetrope. On reaching the cordon line, Carter hit the anchors and they skidded to a halt right by the police vehicles which were back-to-back across both carriageways. Carter killed the siren. An officer trotted over, an older man with unusually broad shoulders and thin legs. His eyes bore a lamentably weary look which made him seem nearly as ancient as the hundred and fifty year old bridge.

McKinley jumped from the vehicle, flashing his MOD90 at the man. "SAS," he announced. "Got orders to intervene."

A bit taken aback, the officer said "I'll have to check with my superiors" and made as though to turn away. "Wait here."

McKinley jumped in front of the man angrily, holding his MOD90 right in the officer's face. "Read the badge Sherlock! We can either waste time pissing about or I can go save the bloody chancellor!" Without an answer he turned and dashed for their vehicle.

The cop was stunned but managed to shout "stay—!"

"Stay yourself," snapped McKinley. "I'm going to intervene!" With this he threw himself back into the Range Rover as Carter accelerated along the pavement again. McKinley looked back to see the cop lifting his walkie-talkie. Screw him, thought McKinley, I've got bigger fish to fry.

Beyond the roadblock Westminster Bridge was as clear as though it was the location for an apocalyptic movie. The absence of their raucous sirens accentuated the perceived emptiness, and the engine's dual turbochargers whined like dentist's drills as they passed the towering Big Ben. McKinley turned and looked downstream to see that one of the police aircraft was in hover near the London Eye, covering the eastern end of Downing Street. Its twin would be to the west.

Wilson caught his eye. "Radios?"

"Yep." McKinley gave a sharp nod. He took out the tiny transmitter-receiver that every COAST agent carries and switched it on, connecting his earpiece. It didn't have a massive range, but for an interdiction of this kind it would work.

From Bridge Street there was no official right turn but Carter threw it into the opposing lane of Parliament Street without concern in the absence of the usually thick traffic. He had to hand it to The Lilly; they'd done a great job with the evacuation although there were still civilian stragglers heading away from the danger zone. Union Jack flags hung from poles on either side of the street and to their left the Palace of Whitehall stood proudly with noble countenance. They saw news crews being shooed away by stone-faced constables and came to a sudden halt by the secondary cordon at Derby Gate. TDR.12 leaped from the vehicle, McKinley and Wilson with weapons in one hand and IDs in the other as Carter fiddled his radio into place.

Again it seemed the oddest thing that central London should appear almost deserted, especially at this time of day. But apart from some obvious specialist cops and several Metropolitan Police BMW Armed Response Vehicles there wasn't a soul about. The evacuation had been both thorough and staggeringly fast, although the latter was hardly a surprise in this critical location. Even the constant murmur of England's busiest city was almost absent, relegated to the background by the thud of distant helicopter rotors, their brisk drumming reverberating from the many buildings. The only other sound was a female voice shouting crazily, but the suicide bomber was too far away to be intelligible.

A Metropolitan Police officer whose badge identified him as Chief Inspector Hart stood there surrounded by several men in the outfits and helmets of Specialist Firearms Command. The chief, a tall, square-jawed man with short, paper white hair, looked down his nose in a curious mixture of umbrage and uncertainty as McKinley approached.

"SAS," announced McKinley again. "I've got orders to intervene. Run it for me, please sir."

The inspector's expression instantly switched to one of professional relief. Blimey, thought McKinley, I didn't even see the buck *slow down* then. Carter and Wilson came up, dutifully displaying MOD90s. A special forces operative would never carry a real one, but the policemen wouldn't know that.

With a pronounced Oxford accent the officer dismissed his men, who dashed to covering positions on the opposite side of the street. "Right then," he began, "we've got one female; early twenties, Caucasian, appears pregnant, claims to be wearing a bomb. Two hours ago she snagged the chancellor and handcuffed herself to the railings outside Number Ten. Been spouting a bunch of religious twaddle since then; refuses to surrender. She was in a tourist group and passed security without a hitch, so we don't know if it's a legitimate threat but that's how we're handling it."

McKinley frowned sceptically. "No metal on her?"

"Certainly not enough to set off the detectors."

McKinley turned to his team-mates. "Willy, get a sniper rifle if you can; Chris and I'll come round from behind. *Try* not to waste her, but if you have to, then—"

"Got it."

"We've got rifles," interjected Hart.

"What type?" asked Wilson.

"Heckler and Koch G3SG1."

McKinley raised an eyebrow at Wilson, who nodded affirmatively. "It'll do."

"Get him one." McKinley gestured to Carter and himself. "We'll need access to the rear entrance of Number Ten."

The cop nodded, lifting his radio. "You'll have it."

"Let's go!" barked McKinley. He and Carter set off running as Hart transmitted his orders.

They sprinted up King Charles Street with the milky italianate façade of the Foreign Office on their right and its newer, Edwardian baroque cousin—the Cabinet Office—opposite.

At the end they sprinted to the right, flashing their MOD90s at another high ranking police officer, and started running north along Horse Guards Road. McKinley vaulted onto the five foot high wall surrounding the lawn at the base of the offices, pulled out his pistol and headed for the corner with Downing Street where he would be able to scramble over the railings.

Carter joined his friend at the corner of the ornate grey edifice. McKinley gestured past Earl Mountbatten's statue with a nod. "You go through the building; I'm going up the street."

"Roger." Carter ran to the wall again and jumped down to the road.

Now carrying a rifle, Wilson ran along the western side of Parliament Street until he drew level with Downing Street and Richmond Terrace. A small gaggle of armed police in flak jackets and visored helmets surrounded the familiar black gates, hunkered down by their vehicles. It was hard to see what was going on behind the ironwork, but the girl's voice could be heard yelling something about judgement. She sounded like a grade 'A' lunatic. Wilson vaguely wondered if she was part of a sect or some kind of lone wolf. Likely the former in view of the skills required to build a viable bomb that could fox a metal detector.

Suddenly a loud bang clattered from the buildings around him, causing a reflexive drop to the ground and making his ass twitch like a rabbit's nose. Wilson propped himself up on his palms and looked around carefully. There was no way of telling from where the report had come, but the Chancellor of the Exchequer was, thank God, still in one piece. He chided himself; that was a gunshot, not an explosion. But who the *hell* was shooting?

At the rear of Number Ten, Carter stood agape as the helicopter covering the western end of Downing Street started to rotate uncontrollably about half a mile away, just visible through the trees of Saint James' Park. Carter found himself unconsciously stepping sideways to maintain his view of the aircraft's fatal dance. That shot must have been a sniper! The spinning chopper disappeared below the treeline and a few moments later a dull boom reached Carter's ears. A rolling ball of dark grey smoke rose from the direction of Green Park. Carter turned away in near disbelief at what he'd just witnessed. A suicide bomber with sniper support? And damn, they've got some *serious* hardware if they can bring down a helicopter! What the bloody blazes?

McKinley heard the shot but missed the crash as he crouched by the railings which formed the boundary between the lower and upper parts of Downing Street. The narrow western end of the thoroughfare lay about six feet below the famous and more public end, giving McKinley a pillbox from which he could observe. The two were separated by the ubiquitous black railings but a staircase to McKinley's right, though its gate was locked, would provide access for a nimble man. The cops were unconcerned with his presence and, like their inspector, seemed relieved that Special Forces personnel were there.

The shot surprised him as much as his colleagues. Head raised just above the stones into which the railings were mounted, McKinley scrutinised the scene. He saw Wilson's group at the other end of the street, lifting themselves back to knee level and looking around. Whoever fired, it must have been somewhere beyond them. McKinley peered into the distance. Visible beyond the eastern end of Downing Street were trees and just two structures; a tall building on the right at the far end of Richmond Terrace and the enormous London Eye beyond the river. Behind him came a rumbling explosion which he barely noticed.

A tiny crackle in his earpiece preceded Carter's voice. "Hazard to Tripod. Did you see that?"

"Tripod returning. See what?"

"The chopper. Whoever was shooting nailed one of the choppers!"

McKinley's jaw dropped for a moment. "She's got a friend?"

"A friend with pro-grade firepower."

McKinley spat angrily. Some bastard wanted to make sure the girl succeeded and would doubtless snuff her if she didn't. This was a whole new ballgame.

At the back of Ten Downing Street, Carter rapidly scrolled through maps on his smartphone. He located the triangulation application and started to move vectors about, hunting the sniper. He thought for a second, using educated guesses to narrow the search. For the shooter to be able to observe Downing Street they'd have to be high, and that shot had undoubtedly come from the east. Carter toyed with angles and measurements. The Ministry of Defence building was too far north to cover the Prime Minister's front door leaving only three possibilities; somewhere on Downing Street itself, the London Eye or the Whitehall Police Station near the junction of Richmond Terrace and Victoria Embankment.

With Carter were four police officers armed with MP5s. They looked determined yet worried, perhaps uncertain what to do.

"Hey," said Carter to the closest, "I got three possible positions for that sniper."

The man studied the tiny phone screen and listened to Carter's instructions. After a moment he scurried away, talking rapidly into his radio. Carter passed the information to his team-mates.

Carter's voice cut off in McKinley's ear and he mumbled a brief acknowledgement. As he carefully negotiated the steps up to the main part of Downing Street, McKinley could hear what the suicide bomber was yelling.

"This world stands in judgement!" she hollered. "All your guns, your politics, all your wars'll come to nothing! You have been weighed and found wanting!"

"Let the Chancellor go!" barked a police negotiator through a megaphone. "Do it now!"

"I'm not afraid of you!" she roared back hysterically. "I'm not afraid of dying! You can't stop the Kingdom! This is *divine justice!*"

Great, she's a career martyr, thought McKinley as he came to rest on one knee behind an elegant Jaguar XJL in British racing green. He lifted his head and peered through the vehicle's windows. There she was at the world famous doorway, shiny steel handcuffs stretching from her left wrist to the railings. On the other side her hand encased what must be a trigger switch, its thin cable swinging between there and her waist, where it disappeared into the fabric below her protruding belly. No prizes for guessing where the explosive is, thought McKinley, but how the hell did she sneak it through? Beyond the girl's arm, facing McKinley knelt the Chancellor of the Exchequer, his right hand cuffed to hers and head drooping into his left, doubtless in expectation of death.

Despite the chancellor's weight, she lifted her arm as far as it would go. "When I let go of this, we'll all die!"

It was a dead man's switch. Damn! They couldn't shoot her. They couldn't rush her; she'd just trigger the bomb. And what if her friend decided to intervene and conclude their mission? Shit... They were stuck between a rock and a hard place. The only way out would be to talk her down if possible, but she sounded way too crazy for that to work. But why *hadn't* she set off the bomb yet? She'd been ranting for a couple of hours already. Could she be having second thoughts?

McKinley went to radio. "Shadow, report!"

Wilson's reply was instant. "Got eyes on her, ready to take the shot."

"Hazard, report!"

"I'm inside by the front door. What's the play?"

"Listen carefully lads," said McKinley. "I've got an idea."

Wilson transmitted his "roger" and gave an involuntary sigh. What McKinley was asking was going to be hellishly difficult. It was also bloody dangerous and that damn sniper wouldn't help at all. But this was the way it was going to go down.

Wilson brought his eye up to the scope and deliberately slowed his breathing. The rifle was resting on one of the black metal bollards which surrounded the gated entrance to Downing Street, cushioned on a policeman's cap. He was crouching near a police BMW which was too low and too far away to offer any protection, but this was the only choice he had if he wanted a clear shot. The cops next to him had their heads on a swivel, looking out for the sniper. But if Wilson knew *anything* about the art of sharpshooting, he knew they'd never see their opponent. There were police squads heading at high speed for the locations Carter had picked out, but would they find anything? Would they even get there in time?

The telescopic sight was good for a law enforcement model, and Wilson hoped the weapon's owner had calibrated the rifle carefully. If it was off by even a hair, they were bloody well screwed.

One of the cops, the donation of his cap revealing a shock of black hair atop a long, angular face, dropped down to Wilson's right. "You're just gonna shoot her? That's it?!"

Wilson didn't have time to explain. "I've got my orders."

The policeman grabbed Wilson's arm, knocking the rifle off the bollard. "She'll blow up the chancellor!"

Wilson got angry. "Look, we've got—"

"No!" snarled the cop and shoved Wilson, who swung the rifle to clout the man with it when there was a sudden loud impact like a balloon bursting in one's face. Wilson lost his balance and tumbled to the ground just as a gunshot rattled around him and the cop's colleague starting screaming profanities. Wilson looked up into a warm red spray as he felt strong hands dragging him to the vehicle.

The other cop was retching and still swearing between heaves. Wilson shook himself; *thank goodness* the man had the presence of mind to drag him back to cover. He wiped his face and his vision cleared. Not six feet away lay grim evidence that the other cop wouldn't be needing his hat back. Blood and brain matter were dripping from the railings. Wilson's guts chilled at the realisation of how close it had been, sickened that an innocent policeman had taken the deadly round which was meant for him, yet coldly, horribly relieved.

McKinley had ducked at the bang but was back up instantly. Holy shit! That sniper had tried to peg Wilson! One of the cops was down. McKinley knew they had to act fast or get blown to bits.

"Hazard, are you able to rush her?" he asked his radio as the unnatural calm of training spread from his brain to his body.

"On your order, chief," replied Carter, "but there's no way I can make it in time to stop her."

McKinley thought for an intense second. That bloody door opened inward. He was about to order Carter to certain death.

A railing that was level with McKinley split with an ungodly noise as another fierce *crack* bounced from the stonework. Sharp fragments ricocheted around the street, twanging and whining from all angles. McKinley hunched down and there was another loud report.

He raised his eyes above the Jaguar's hood to see the figure of the chancellor slump to its right, chest pulverised and mostly gone. In front of the body, a ghastly swathe of innards was painted onto the asphalt for at least three meters. McKinley swallowed involuntarily, dreadful fatalism gripping his heart at the politician's death, unable to accept that he couldn't have prevented it. The suicide bomber screamed at the carnage as the remains of the chancellor flopped on the ground, dragging her down and forcing her to prop herself up on her trigger hand.

"Now!" yelled McKinley into the radio.

Carter yanked the door, flying out with inhuman urgency and all the force he could muster. The bomber looked into his eyes with terrible, remorseless conviction and lifted her right arm, causing her body to fall prone. She opened her right hand.

A percussive blast erupted from Downing Street, tearing through the air all around and reflecting chaotically from the buildings in a pandemonium of echoes.

Carter landed on the girl, catching her right arm and pulling her left so tight as to render it useless. The trigger, cable neatly severed by Wilson's rifle bullet, dropped onto the ground, inert. Carter's insides shook coldly; it had been fifty-fifty whether that switch was push-to-make or push-to-break.

McKinley broke cover and charged, covering the woman with his pistol.

"You got this?!" he yelled at Carter.

"Got it!" Carter pinned the young woman down as she screamed her angst like a banshee.

Without breaking stride McKinley sped east. It was a hundred meters to the entrance of Downing Street and speed was the only method by which he could avoid being sniped. But he had to present a viable target in the hope of diverting the shooter's attention from Carter and the girl. Cops ran toward and past him.

Another sharp bang blasted his ears and he turned momentarily. Carter was still covering the bomber with his body, tensed as if stung by myriad insects. The woman yelled a blood curdling cry in obvious pain. Holy shit!

Wilson had turned and was firing in the sniper's direction from the relative cover of the police BMW. With Downing Street itself eliminated, the only two possible locations for their opponent were the London Eye and the Whitehall Police Station. With the Eye's proximity to the second police helicopter, it wasn't viable as a gun platform because the shooter would be visible. There remained only the police station.

SNAP! A sound like a whip cracking slapped McKinley on his left cheek and he felt an impact from behind. The sniper was taking the bait! McKinley zig-zagged as he ran, storming through the gates as Wilson picked himself up and ran ahead, blasting rounds toward the top of the Whitehall Police Station. Another sharp crack passed McKinley and there was a scream of agony behind. Several police ran with them, including Hart, who shouted "there's a squad on the top floor!"

McKinley, Wilson and the cops galloped across Whitehall. They had to find and stop that sniper!

The gates to Richmond Terrace had already been opened and they dashed into it. Wilson was firing through the trees, trying to dissuade any response. McKinley looked up to see the second police helicopter above the river, manoeuvring to cover the police station's roof. Just as he realised what a bad idea this was there was another resounding shot. The aircraft suddenly lost height and tipped forward, pieces dropping from its cabin. The sniper had killed their second chopper of the day.

With a yell, Hart ran off the street to make cover as the dying aircraft plunged. McKinley stopped dead, trying to gauge which way it would fall. The chopper disappeared behind the police station and there was a second of silence followed by the sound of an enormous splash from beyond their view.

Stunned into inactivity by the copter's fate, the police stood aghast. Before McKinley could shout a warning, one was burst like a tomato by a round from above. The sniper was getting desperate!

"MOVE!" shouted McKinley as another shot pulverised a nearby car, sending a shockwave through his feet. "*Take cover!*"

He landed close to the railings where Hart lay, propelling orders into his walkie-talkie at high speed. McKinley crawled up next to the cop and barked "where's that squad?!"

Hart rotated, his eyes conveying a feverish edge. "They're at the door—!"

With a flash like lightning the top of the police station erupted in a monstrous explosion. The huge *CRACK* of the pressure wave slammed McKinley painfully to the ground and made his ears sing. Instinctively he looked up, horrified, as an incandescent mushroom of fire gave way to an expanding chaos of debris that plunged toward them. McKinley slapped his hands desperately around his head as the grey London sky pummelled them with masonry, steelwork and shattered glass.

Wilson handed the Heckler and Koch back to Hart, who gave him a worried look and turned away to converse with the other high ranking police officers that had gathered like carrion crows around a dead beast. He tuned in for a moment, picking up that they were ordering a total news blackout for twenty four hours. Standard procedure, he thought, but it's out there anyway and there's nothing they can do. This would make the headlines in every territory big enough to have a newspaper. McKinley caught Wilson's eye and tipped his head back toward Number Ten.

They walked up the famous street toward Carter, who was surrounded by armed police. He was kneeling over the girl, starting an examination. A thin trickle of blood ran from just beside his left eye.

McKinley saw that the woman wasn't moving. Her eyes were closed and her body seemed lifeless. The girl's head lolled inertly to the left as Carter checked her over. McKinley asked the cops to step back, then crouched by his colleague.

"She's gone?"

Carter answered tersely. "No, I had to shut her up." His face took on a more apologetic look. "Sleeper hold."

Well, thought McKinley, at least the day's not an absolute, total loss, but it *is* a bloody disaster. The bloody Chancellor for goodness' sake, two helicopters, the top floor of Whitehall Police Station and several cops notwithstanding. Could it look any worse? He blinked and grimly forced his thoughts back to business. They'd have to get her back to headquarters now, at least a three hour drive. He should probably commandeer an ambulance.

A deep, dirty gouge in the girl's right calf showed how close the sniper had got, and Carter had applied a tourniquet. Many smaller punctures encompassed the furrow, indicating the fragmentation of the projectile which was doubtless the cause of Carter's facial wound. The tarmac beneath her leg was striated and deformed surrounding a disquietingly big crater with a deep central pit. That's a bloody big round, thought McKinley.

He looked at the young woman's face, placid in its enforced unconsciousness. She was strikingly childlike with full cheeks, lips a perfect Cupid's bow over a slightly prominent chin and a small, rounded nose that looked like an afterthought of the designer. Her uneven hair, a slightly deeper fair than McKinley's, spilled down her face across long, thin eyebrows that seemed to reach almost to her temples. There was a slight redness, an indentation in the skin on the bridge of her nose, indicating that she often wore glasses, and the lobes of her ears looked as though they'd been pierced some time ago but allowed to heal. Even in these dire circumstances McKinley found her amazingly beautiful and something deep inside him was profoundly relieved that she hadn't exploded.

Carter took out his knife, snapped the blade open and cut the fabric of the woman's blouse to reach the only place she could carry explosives.

"Bloody hell," he stammered.

McKinley and Wilson looked down in disbelief. There was no bomb, just soft, perfectly normal flesh stretched about her enlarged midriff. McKinley raised himself and stepped back a bit.

"She's actually bloody pregnant?" breathed Wilson as though stating the obvious would offer some kind of catharsis.

Carter bit his lip, then looked up at his friends. "No. There's no *linea nigra*, no stretch marks... This ain't right." He turned back and moved his hands skilfully over the mound, pushing slightly with his fingertips and making the occasional hum as though starting to understand something.

"What?" urged McKinley.

Rather than answering, Carter took his blade again and sliced through the woman's belt and the top of her jeans, revealing her underwear, just above which a long, jagged and obviously fresh surgical wound was bisected by the remaining length of trigger cable.

"Oh shit that's rough!" gasped Wilson, involuntarily backing up slightly.

Carter remained silent, but his eyes were afire with thought. He gently probed the gash, bowing his head to get a better look at the amateurish surgery. Finally he sat back, ass on the tarmac, and wiped his bloodied hands on his jeans.

"She passed the detector 'cause there's almost no metal. It's sewn inside, to make her *look* preggers. It's not the first time they've done this."

McKinley could hardly believe what his Weapons and Equipment Technician was telling him. "Holy crap that's bloody horrible," he breathed, his normally cynical eyes unusually wide.

"Yeah," nodded Carter, a humourless grin tugging at his face. "But who's the father?"

002: The House

Soon, thought Sister Damaris, I will pass from this world into the next.

The sheer *gravity* of this concept threatened to overcome her trained serenity as she pondered the glorious mystery. She repeated the necessary words in her head like a mantra. Calm, peace, obey the call. Her heart slowed a little and she breathed easier. She was on a mission. *Her* mission.

She turned to observe the retreating vehicle as it passed beyond the mini roundabout at the top of Spring Lane, but held herself back from waving. She'd been instructed not to. The car glimmered for a moment in the lights of the filling station then disappeared over the rise, heading south-west toward the city. Damaris didn't know where they were going; she knew only what she must do.

Traffic was sparse, but as she crossed to the central reservation a black Ford Focus slowed and a raucous voice shouted "'ello darlin'!"

The vehicle passed so close to Damaris that she could see their lustful eyes raking her body and hear their mocking laughter as the wind of the vehicle's passage stirred her filmy garments like a bunting of flags. The Ford sped away and she watched it dispassionately. For an instant there was an echo in her mind: *forgive them, for they know not what they do*. But the voice of her leader took over, firmly asserting that there was no place in the Kingdom for reprobates such as *those*. For a moment she felt a deep sadness; it was horribly disappointing that she wouldn't see the inception of the Kingdom, but her glory was in helping to usher it in.

Damaris surveyed the large house with disdainful eyes as she crossed the Mapperley Plains road. So *this* was what the feeding of a relentless global war machine could buy you. This dwelling was built on foundations of death, each brick a memorial to a precious life taken. But for just a flickering instant it appealed to her natural self. Were she still of this world she could easily have loved all that the house represented; security, comfort, perhaps a growing family. But the sheer delight of obeying her leaders prevailed. She was of another world now, a spiritual world, and one with diametrically opposing values.

The trees, though, were *beautiful*. As far as she could remember she'd always loved trees. Their arching boughs framed the house in dusky grey and, above, the remaining leaves were golden brown, visible even through this darkening English twilight. The driveway's gate was open and the tarmac wound from the front of the house like a snaking tongue protruding from its mouth. There were lights on and an expensive car out front – another worldly trapping.

This was it then; this was the place, her final destination in this world, the conclusion of her earthly journey. Here she would accomplish her divine mission. *Kill them wherever you find them*, she remembered as she considered what lay ahead, feeling a deep a shiver of anticipation. Her heart was still beating fast but not so much that she couldn't just about contain her excitement. It wouldn't be long now before her prophesied fulfilment; there were just minutes left. She was treading her final steps before eternity.

She looked around again at the wooded grounds, feeling somehow stronger through the presence of those princely trunks, noticing the gentle whisper of wind in the leafy canopy above as a single tear caressed her cheek. Wiping it away she breathed deeply and set her heart resolutely to the task. Damaris walked onto the driveway, knowing that she would never make the return journey.

His freshly lit fire was invitingly warm and Pogo, the Maltese Pomeranian who mostly lived with his sister's children, was snoozing next to the hearth. He kicked off the slippers and stretched out his legs on the ottoman.

The works of Beethoven were drifting from a handsome Cambridge Audio hi-fi system. He wasn't in the mood for Bach or Vaughan Williams tonight and he felt the need to hear something pastoral. He seldom got the chance to relax with decent music on in the background. His work mandated the absence of entertainment and demanded the presence of full concentration. So it was here, in the rare privacy of his own dwelling, that he could ease off and indulge himself a bit. The music, the fire and the peaceful atmosphere were a welcome change from the businesslike and often frantic tempo of his work. To ensure that his R&R wasn't ruined by fielding countless questions from there, he'd issued strict instructions that he mustn't be disturbed under any circumstances. But now his short vacation was drawing to a close and he felt like he might as well get used to the idea.

The lounge was the largest room in his house and, although refurbished during the last two weeks, was suitably vintage in tone. Classy wine barrel coloured paintwork matched dark cherrywood, offset by earth tone furnishings of a dark grey-green. Only a few years ago this room, indeed the whole house, had been a wreck: crumbling plaster had been piling up at the bases of the walls whilst mouldy wallpaper hung in forlorn and yellowed strips. Rotting floors had given way in places and windows had been smashed by little vandals wielding stones dug from the overgrown garden. But he'd seen the potential in this shell of a house and therefore paid just a little more than he hoped to at auction. The renovations had cost an even greater sum but had resulted in the home he'd always desired for his retirement, now less than twenty years away. The other indulgence—his splendid car sitting outside on the driveway, all deep black and attitude—would one day give way to a more sensible vehicle and he would relax in this peaceful home to write his memoirs under a well chosen pseudonym, creating a riveting story born during his leadership of Britain's most secret service.

General Clive Sutton, commanding officer of the Covert Operations And Surveillance Team, sat in his leather armchair trying to focus on the reports he had to read before the end of his long overdue break. There were a number of dossiers that he had to get through, but one in particular had gained the upper hand in a struggle for his attention.

Sutton sighed heavily, his eyes almost trying to avoid the content. *A locomotive haircut.* How he wished that he'd never even heard that vulgar saying, callously coined by TDR.12's Corporal Carter. Sutton shook his head at the brutality of describing the death of a friend with such casual insensitivity. It was just such an ugly turn of phrase that it had stuck with him, unwelcome though it was.

Andrew Lucas, formerly the Combat and Survival specialist of TDR Team Ten, had driven to the level crossing at Burton Joyce—just three miles south-east from where Sutton now sat—and had thrust his head under a train. Sutton was both disgusted and deeply saddened. A talented young operative in his prime, Lucas had suffered horrendous burns in the Canadian phase of *Operation Copper Burial.* During his convalescence, Lucas had been given the nickname 'Crispy' by other members of The Team and, surrounded by such good-natured ribbing, seemed to be recovering well. Despite the severity of the man's debilitating injuries, Sutton had let Lucas stay on at the base and attempt to rebuild his career. He may never have made it back onto a TDR team but Sutton had hoped that Lucas would find a niche on the base itself, make himself useful and, perhaps, rediscover a sense of purpose in The Team. But no-one had foreseen this horrible outcome.

Sutton frowned, mentally kicking himself. That wasn't strictly true. Carter, who himself had recently been assigned to an anger management course following an incident in Canada, had tried to sound an alert. Despite his usual lack of subtlety, Carter had confided to Major Maddocks, Sutton's XO, that he was concerned for Lucas. Maddocks, knowing Carter as he did, had certainly not paid enough heed to this warning and it was just a couple of days later that they'd received an early morning report from the British Transport Police regarding what they referred to as a 'sudden death incident'. Train-loads of commuters from Newark were late for work that day. Sutton closed his eyes for a moment, feeling sick to his stomach. It was such a *senseless* waste of a life and the loss of another excellent soldier. What on earth leads a person to do that to themselves, he wondered. Lucas had checked out for Post Traumatic Stress Disorder. Yes, the things he'd been through in Canada were horrific, for sure, and those burns disfiguring. But to want to escape yourself so much as to willingly put your head on the railway track in the path of an oncoming passenger train? Sutton shuddered.

The grievous loss of Andy Lucas meant that another whole TDR team had been eradicated and this pressed the issue of its replacement. Sutton had initially held back, not wanting Lucas to feel sidelined, but upon the report of the corporal's suicide Sutton had forced himself into a quick review of advancing Basic Commandos from the regiment. It was less than ideal to throw another virgin TDR team together; Five and Seven were already composed of entirely new people. So, not wishing to appear overly invested in the dourness which pervaded the base, Sutton had picked Geoff Massey, Kathy Steer and Colin Bowskill to be, respectively, the new Tactical and Surveillance, Weapons and Equipment and Combat and Survival specialists of TDR.10. The loss of their predecessors Ward, Briggs and Lucas along with the previous members of Five and Seven was a real bite out of the pool of experienced operatives, but Sutton had no option. If only that damn train had never arrived...

Sutton shook his head to clear his mind a little. Rather than dwell on that unpleasantness, he moved the folder to the back of the pile and expanded his thoughts to the same important question on a wider level, that of replenishing the ranks of COAST as a whole. A lot of good people had been lost in *Operation Copper Burial* and now Sutton had the daunting task of recruiting new operatives, which was one of the most challenging aspects of his job. Long hours would be spent examining service records, psych evaluations, medical reports and other data, trying to spot the unique qualities that could be forged, via the Basic Commando regiment, into an effective COAST operative. This difficult process involved guesswork, gut reactions, a great deal of experience and, in Sutton's fanciful estimation, some of the extrasensory perception in which he resolutely did not believe. It was impossible to formularise what would make a good member of The Team but there was just an indefinable *something* about the occasional military record or personality profile which stood out and caught his attention. It wasn't so much that the candidate was a terrifically good soldier – indeed some COAST operatives hadn't even been in the forces. It was the vaguest hint of a quality intrinsic to the man's character: a determination, a craftiness, an ability or idiosyncrasy that somehow hit the target. Many of Sutton's subordinates were morally dubious yet fitted perfectly into The Team's loyal ranks. Some had even come from *questionable* backgrounds but were outstanding agents. Some were expert in a particular field; most were Jacks-of-all-trades. They were teachable and eager to learn, but one thing they all seemed to understand clearly was the need for a top secret and highly adaptable unit that could defend the interests of the United Kingdom and in which they all played a vital role. COAST—hovering in an administratival sense between civil and military—was neither troop, squadron, battalion nor regiment. It was a *team*, a company of wily buggers who neutered threats, diverted disasters, saved lives and in general made the world a safer place in which to live. Sutton was proud of his team; although only forty eight himself, he looked upon each one as a father would on a son. He hated the times when he had to give orders that sent men to their deaths; he loved the times when they came home *Contra Omnes Dissident*—against all odds—with the bad guy's ass in tow. But now one of his men, rather than die in the field because of orders, had chosen to end it himself. Sutton clenched his eyes tightly for a moment, wilfully resisting the urge to reach for the brandy.

Forcibly turning his thoughts away from Lucas, Sutton started to scan the other reports: Piracy of interesting materials in the Baltic and the Indian Ocean; two SIS agents missing in Iran; a note about the electrical infrastructure on Mallory Island; satellite imagery of Turkish missile sites being dismantled on the shore of the Black Sea – that was a strange surprise. His eyes passed over an analysis of rocket fuel samples smuggled out of North Korea, accompanied by fervent denials of espionage by a prominent German businessman. Perhaps strangest of all was the alleged reconnaissance of a Russian *Akula* Class sub in the Indian Ocean. Sutton huffed; what on earth would a Typhoon, in NATO parlance, be doing down there? As far as he knew—and he knew a lot—the enormous *Akulas* were being decommissioned in favour of *Borei* Class boats such as the *Yury Dolgorukiy* and the *Aleksandr Nevskiy*, much more modern vessels only five meters shorter than their enormous predecessors, the largest submarines ever built. Sutton reminded himself that the UK wasn't the only nation operating vessels that didn't officially exist.

Something occurred to Sutton and he glanced again at the piracy report. Tom Maddocks, with characteristic efficiency, had completed a preliminary read-through of the article and highlighted some of it. There were three notable examples in the cargo manifest of one of the hijacked ships, across which Maddocks had wiped his fluorescent marker: *Titanium alloy*, *Ammonium Perchlorate* and *Radar Altimeter Parts*. The major had made an additional note below, simply scribbling 'rocketry components?'

There was a soft buzz and Sutton glanced up, suddenly wary. As he did so, his television automatically powered-up, displaying a view from one of the security cameras hidden in the garden of his house. At the same time, he knew, that feed would be relayed to the base and the duty personnel alerted. Sutton reached for a remote and zoomed the image in, hoping it wasn't another futile attempt to proselytise him by the local Jehovah's Witnesses. Then he corrected himself; he'd never known them to arrive this late.

A willowy young girl, heavily pregnant, was walking slowly up the driveway toward the house. The first impression that came into Sutton's mind was that she must have been cold. Those flowing, diaphanous garments appeared more suited to life in a hot country, and one without curious onlookers at that because they left little to the imagination. The general judged her to be between eighteen and twenty three years old, about a hundred and sixty centimeters in height with shoulder length light brown hair. She walked with a slightly clumsy gait, her distended belly betraying the maturity of her expectant condition.

Pogo raised his head sleepily and gave a half-hearted bark, shuffling in his basket.

"Easy boy," said Sutton gently. "Stay." The dog laid his head back down but his big, dark brown eyes remained on his master.

Sutton almost laughed. This could only happen to me, he thought. The lateness of the hour, the peculiarity of this visitor and his tiredness were more than he needed. Nonetheless his intelligence officer's instinct kicked in. What was the girl doing there? Was she a neighbour? He didn't recognise her from their files. Was she simply a hard luck case whose car had conked out on the way to the delivery room? Or was there a more sinister purpose to her presence? Sutton's instinct was always to play the Good Samaritan, to go to bat for those in need, but he was also acutely aware that his important position qualified him as a target.

As he watched the young female approach the front door Sutton took his side arm, a Beretta Px4 Storm subcompact, from his desk and checked and cocked the weapon. He would hide it in the back of his trousers where it would be held in place by his belt. He got up and pushed his feet back into the slippers.

As expected his telephone rang and he answered immediately. "Yes?"

The voice on the other end spoke quickly. "Sir this is Basic Commando Penner. My authorisation is 'avocado'. Your security system's alerted us to an intruder."

Sutton replied, also speaking fast. "My authorisation is 'bonanza'. I've got a young woman on the driveway, looks about twenty, average height, medium length brown hair, pregnant. Open the video feeds and start recording."

"Yes sir, already rolling."

"Good. This is the code to release my address details." Sutton punched a numeric sequence into his phone. "If I'm in immediate danger I'll hit the alarm but get a team up here just in case."

"Yes sir!" Penner hung up.

McKinley's head was bobbing in an uneven rhythm, eyes closed, as Wilson negotiated the westbound A52 just four miles south of Long Bennington, his home town. He was a little unhappy with their choice to take the A1 from London. The M1, which also linked the capital with Nottingham, was a major motorway and in Wilson's opinion much better for ferrying a disarmed, drugged and restrained suicide bomber back to base in a commandeered ambulance. They'd have been home by now, he thought, but he didn't disagree with McKinley's reasoning. If there was any chance of an accidental explosion, it was marginally preferable for it to happen on the less busy road.

Not far ahead, Carter's damaged Range Rover wove in and out of traffic with seeming disregard for anyone's safety. Wilson grinned. For Carter to have restrained his right foot enough to keep the ambulance in sight was in itself unusual.

Suddenly, the Weapons and Equipment Tech's voice burst from Wilson's radio, his tone sharp with urgency.

"Hazard to Tripod, over."

Wilson lifted his device lazily. "Shadow here. Mickey's dossing."

"There's something kicking off at base. Just got a general call."

McKinley yawned, lifting his head and blinking several times. "What's up?"

Wilson chanced a look to his left. "Traffic from HQ. I dunno."

Reaching alertness rapidly, McKinley thrust out a hand. "Give."

Wilson passed his radio across and McKinley called back. "Tripod here."

"Mate," responded Carter, dropping any semblance of correct radio procedure, "something's going on at base. They've ordered any available personnel to Uncle Victor's house."

McKinley took the little radio away from his face for a moment to think. Obviously there was a threat condition of some sort, but there was no way they could respond. The ambulance was far too sluggish for that kind of dash, and they had to get their prisoner to base. He keyed the radio.

"Chris, take off. Fast as you can. A46 at Bingham, Gunthorpe Bridge, Lowdham, Lambley. You'll be in the pipe."

"I know the way," responded Carter.

"You got the address?" McKinley didn't know the details, just the area; somewhere on Mapperley Plains. Such a thing was usually an extremely well kept secret.

"Coming through now." The was a pause. "Oh. Just up the road from my gaff. Who knew?"

"Get moving."

"I'll keep you posted." With this the radio clicked off and they watched the big car accelerate hard until its tail lights were no longer visible. If anyone could get there fast it would be Carter, but at this distance he wouldn't be the first. McKinley passed the radio back to Wilson and took out his phone.

"What d'you think?" said Wilson.

"Dunno," growled McKinley, dialling, "but I don' like it."

As Sutton placed the telephone back on its cradle, the doorbell chimed.

Putting the Beretta pistol down the back of his trousers, Sutton strode quietly to his front door. A quick look through the peephole confirmed what the camera had told him. The girl was pretty, an expression of innocence on the childlike face which framed those big, tender eyes, but Sutton was not the kind of man to be taken in easily. Not wishing to blow a hole through his buttock he carefully clicked the safety off the Beretta, put his left hand in his pocket according to procedure and unlocked the large oak door.

A draught of chilly air brushed his face as he pulled the door open a few inches. She stood there smiling yet shivering a little. Her smile widened and her eyes took on an empty, far away look.

"May I help you Miss?" asked Sutton, trying to appear friendly but not too forthcoming.

"I'm Sister Damaris," said the pregnant woman. "You're General Sutton, aren't you?"

Sutton stepped back involuntarily. Other than his own people no-one should know who or where he was! Immediately his pulse started to race and he felt ice cold spread down his back. "What do you want?" he asked suspiciously, retreating another step.

"I've come to bring judgement from the Universal Spirit," she replied with her delightfully feminine voice, eyes transmitting both resolve and *unearthly* fear. "Please forgive me."

In less time than it takes a heart to beat Sutton was pressing madly on the panic button in his pocket and running from the door, his slippered feet barely gaining traction on the polished wood floor. Stumbling, he caught sight of Damaris lifting a cable from beneath the folds of her translucent dress. An instant before she was obscured Sutton saw that beautifully innocent smile quiver as she determinedly pushed a switch.

A searing flash more intense than nearby lightning illuminated the hallway, combined with a hideous hammer blow of pressure which tore the air from Sutton's lungs as pieces of his house flew past him in a melee of debris. He tumbled back along the hall propelled by the blast as vivid orange flame filled the area. Sutton slammed into the doorpost of the kitchen with stabbing pain. He fell onto his side and blacked out.

The next thing Sutton knew was the hound's whimpering as faithful Pogo licked his face, the dog's world invaded by violent destruction and his beloved master harmed. There was unbelievable pain coming from his right shoulder and the rest of his body wasn't far behind. His face smarted like sunburn and his ears felt like someone had slapped him hard on the side of the head. Sharp, piercing pains like insect stings assaulted him from every member.

Sutton tried to move but a wave of nausea swept through him and he puked a bit. The dog came around to sniff at the vomit but Sutton croaked "no Pogo, sit down boy" in the weakest voice he'd ever heard from his own mouth. A short but extremely painful coughing fit brought up what appeared to be blood.

His ears ringing like faulty audio gear, Sutton blinked to clear his vision. He was lying on his left hand side across the threshold of his kitchen door, facing the bottom of the freezer. His eyes came to focus on the nearby floor, strewn with fragments of debris. He moved his head slightly, painfully, so that he could see the hallway. The front of his house was on fire, but that armoured blast barrier had served its purpose, shooting up from its housing in the floor and protecting him. It was leaning over, gruesomely deformed by the explosion. Pogo, erroneously satisfied that master wasn't too seriously hurt, retreated to his glass-strewn basket where he lay making unhappy little growls.

Sutton allowed his eyes to close for a moment to try and think but his mind seemed to be working in slo-mo. Someone who wanted him dead had tracked him down to his home. He vaguely recalled a recent mention of something to do with suicide bombers but his shaken brain couldn't organise the details. He was alive but wounded—perhaps seriously—and the only real evidence had vaporised itself. Out of the many enemies of Her Majesty's realm that Sutton had deployed forces against, who was behind this?

Another horrible suicide, thought Sutton as consciousness started to fade again. It must be the season.

003: The Parent

"You know," announced Carter quietly, nodding as if the forthcoming idea would be profound, "I'd have gone a different way."

"What the heck d'you mean?" asked McKinley, following Carter's gaze to their boss's car.

"Red on black. *So* eighties."

The normally immaculate, lustrous finish of the expensive Jaguar was pocked with dents and spattered with grotesque particles of suicide bomber. The blast had shunted it slightly and the windscreen was a crazy spider's web of cracks. Some vehicular bodywork expert would be earning his pay that month.

Wilson joined them by the vehicle, having overheard the exchange. "You're a callous bastard sometimes," he told Carter, shaking his head.

"Most of the time," corrected McKinley, scowling at the bloody mess.

Carter turned to his friends. "So it wasn't a very powerful bomb."

Wilson looked up at the wrecked frontage of the house, then back to his team-mate. "Powerful enough," he stated. "How d'you know?"

Carter flicked his open palm at the car. "She got gibbed. Explosive overpressure at extremely close range would turn her into a mist. Well, she was *wearing* the bomb, *so* military grade stuff wouldn't've left enough to fill Barbie's bra cup. Now she has the tactical advantage."

That one went right over Wilson's head so he just looked at Carter.

The weapons tech smirked. "She's got us surrounded."

"Thanks," replied Wilson. "Another lovely image."

"And this," continued Carter, indicating the Jag, "would be steel cornflakes. I'm guessing ANFO or some pyrotechnic mixture." He paused, frowning. "But both those theories have problems."

They stood on the driveway of General Sutton's house at Mapperley Top. McKinley and Wilson had just arrived with some other staff after rushing from their headquarters deep below the city, where the other suicide bomber was undergoing surgery in the medical section.

With nearly as great an elevation as nearby Dorket Head, the highest point in Nottingham, Mapperley was a moderately prestigious suburb, largely developed during the early twentieth century, where many wealthy families, enterprising landlords and businessmen owned property. The area was bisected by the well travelled B684 north road, either side of which 'brick basins'—large concavities once quarried for Nottingham's abundant clay deposits—were now occupied by housing developments, retirement homes and light industry. The area's residents enjoyed the proximity and relative serenity of farmland that surrounded the old Gedling colliery while benefiting from the utility of the sprawling city below and to the south-west. Now their peace had been suddenly and dramatically shattered by a mysterious young woman with a bomb in her guts.

"D'you think that's how he survived?" asked Wilson.

"Yes definitely," nodded Carter. "Real, *serious* explosives would've deleted the house."

McKinley shook his head slowly. "Nasty."

"We'll be good for DNA," said Carter, taking a forensics kit from over his shoulder, "as soon as I can get this stuff back." He set the pack on the ground, opened it and started fishing for the necessary items. "I'll see if I can get some trace on the bomb, too."

"Okay," replied McKinley, turning away from the ruined vehicle. "We'll check inside." He cleared this with the Basic Commando guard that was stationed outside the ruined entrance.

As McKinley and Wilson went to the house, Carter plucked a sample tube and swab from the kit, then stood and looked around for a moment. It was easy to see that the front steps were ground zero. Blast striations radiated from the stonework, fading as they retreated. It would be hard work to find all the fragments at this time of night, and Carter predicted that their people would be on the case into daylight and probably much longer. Around him, the garden's nearest shrubs and bushes were knocked about and torn, defoliated by the shockwave, whilst the trees stood aloof as though bearing dispassionate witness to the event. General Sutton's front garden had more than its fair share of timber, useful both for discouraging the curious and hiding the cameras which had recorded the explosion and subsequent fire.

The blaze had been extinguished with admirable promptness by the local fire brigade, the members of which were then ushered beyond the cordon under some rapidly concocted pretence. They were joined by the occupants of the surrounding homes, who had been evacuated through what was presented as concern for their safety. Also thronging there, several hundred feet away, were television news crews from the local stations accompanied by a gaggle of press and radio reporters. Even the local cable company had sent people, although no-one could get usefully close thanks to the temporary closure of the B684 road. Carter watched them out of the corner of his eye as he dabbed at the Jaguar's crumpled bodywork with the swab and considered how much trouble the newspeople could potentially present to a covert unit as secret as COAST. The official story so far was a gas explosion, but it was highly unlikely that such an obvious fabrication would fly. An armed forces figure nearly blown up and his house surrounded by military types whilst the police, fire and ambulance services were kept at bay? Not very plausible, thought Carter, kneeling down by the kit. He placed the specimen carefully inside and extracted another tube.

The building looked bad but was unlikely to be irreparable. There wasn't a single window left intact in the front and most of the back ones had broken as well. The guttering and a lot of tiles had fallen from the roof and there was extensive damage to both the entrance and the lounge's bay window area. The massive slab which normally sat atop granite columns above the front door lay in four pieces around the steps, its two supporting pillars reduced to several uneven cylinders and cast around like dice. The heavy oak front door and its frame were splinters and the automatic blast barrier was knocked askew. Despite Carter's underestimation it must have taken a fair sized explosion to do that. No wonder the car sat at an angle.

McKinley and Wilson pushed themselves through the gap around the bent blast shield, which would never again retreat into its housing, and stood in General Sutton's hallway smelling wetness and burnt wood. Neither had previously known the exact location of their CO's house—never mind actually visiting it—and there was a certain feeling of standing upon hallowed ground despite the surrounding chaos. The general himself was also in The Team's medical bay where he was undergoing treatment for a broken collarbone, puncture wounds, flash burns and concussion. His excellent physical fitness would aid his recovery but no-one would dare to claim that the attack had been anything other than a very close call indeed. They were thankful for that blast barrier because it had served its purpose and kept their CO topside of the grass.

The hallway was dark now whilst a couple of BCs were working to rig up the electricity. The circuit breakers were in a cabinet by the disintegrated door and had been trashed by the blast then thoroughly soaked by the fire brigade. The staircase, to their right, was still in one piece but its banister of carved wooden uprights and polished handrail was mostly fragments. McKinley and Wilson pulled out flashlights and swung the beams around, illuminating particles of floating dust which circulated like microscopic fireflies. The damage to the walls and ceiling wasn't severe and the structure seemed safe enough despite the pounding it had taken, so they advanced down the hallway.

McKinley looked at his colleague, his youthful face barely visible in the reflected torchlight. "What do you reckon?"

"I reckon Uncle Victor got off light."

"No shit," nodded McKinley, sweeping the smashed hallway with his torch. The term which came to his mind was *caramelised*. Everything seemed to have been burned a shade or two darker, even in the gloom. Countless tiny projectile impacts pitted every surface. He looked down at the kitchen doorway where Sutton had landed and where the floor now bore a sprayed outline. Could have been a lot worse, he thought. Only a combination of the general's rapid reaction, the blast shield and the kind of low grade explosives that Carter mentioned had saved the boss.

"Heinmarsh," announced Wilson.

McKinley paused, shaking his head. "Or not."

"Come on, I heard it from her own mouth."

"So, like I said before, why didn't she say anything in de-brief?"

"Drugs mess with your memory. We've been through this."

"Aye, so she could've hallucinated it, right?"

"No! That's—"

"She was so out-of-it she might've said any old bollocks. Not what you'd call reliable intel, is it?"

Wilson tried not to let himself get wound up. For someone who'd previously been more than enthusiastic to see the end of Heinmarsh, McKinley was being unbelievably obtuse – or maybe it was his barely disguised disdain for the new boy. Since the honeymoon period of his promotion and their escapades in Wales, Canada, and on that blasted island, McKinley's approach to Wilson seemed to have changed. It had been good at first; new rank, new privileges, new guys to get to know, but now it felt like McKinley resented Wilson, and the new Tactical Corporal couldn't understand why.

He sighed. "She wasn't *that* stoned. Anyway the drugs were out of her system for ages by the funeral; you *know* that."

McKinley raised his palms. "Doesn't mean she remembered it accurately."

Wilson stabbed his finger in the direction of the floor for emphasis. "'An army of suicide bombers'. Jules' *exact* words."

McKinley frowned cynically. "*Jules* now is it?"

Wilson ignored the diversion. He waved his hand in an encompassing gesture. "Look around you. *Suicide bomber.* I thought you don't believe in coincidence?"

"Aye and he's got," his fingers formed air quotes, "'*more warheads*', which is sketchy don't you think? North Korea and Iran can only scrape together enough Uranium for maybe a couple. Plus you need a whole flock of boffins; so he stole our bombs and snatched her dad, remember?" McKinley shrugged. "Look, let's cut to the chase; has she even mentioned it since?"

Wilson hesitated for just a moment but he had to admit the truth. "No," he muttered.

"Well then just ask. Can't hurt, right?"

Frowning, Wilson said "if I can get a word in edgeways."

McKinley cocked an eyebrow and Wilson continued. "She's always going on about bloody Kenny."

"I thought that was water under the bridge?"

"It *is*, but he's, like, a stalker or something. Won't let go, and his dad—"

"The Secretary of the Treasury," interjected McKinley, raising a finger.

"He just encourages him." Wilson shook his head. "You know what he did yesterday?"

McKinley didn't want to, but because of his interest in the political angle he couldn't help being intrigued. "Thrill me."

"Got a shrink to call. Can you believe that? Told her she's got PTSD and in shock 'cause of her dad dying, and she'll get over it. Bloody nonsense."

Suddenly Wilson felt like he'd said too much. Certainly Kenny was an obsessive jerk who couldn't grasp the meaning of 'dear John', but Wilson had allowed the matter to take up too much of his attention. Here they stood in the partially destroyed home of their CO, yet he was beaking-off about his rival for Julia's affections. The events of *Operation Copper Burial* had mostly derailed Miss Bridgewell's long distance relationship with Kendal Gundersen and now she was stuck between a British covert operative and a high ranking American politician's son who wouldn't give up and whose dad was a control freak that the son dutifully obeyed. The old man was propelling his boy to fight for the relationship.

McKinley picked up on the pause and said "you need more beer."

"Yeah, it's not like *you'd* understand."

McKinley's face clouded over. "Don't lecture me about relationships!"

"But, mate," said Wilson gently yet without wanting to appear as though capitulating, "you don't *have* relationships. You have *one night stands*."

"Aye, well," ground the Scotsman, shrugging defensively. "I got burned."

"Can't've been *that* bad."

Being all too aware of their current circumstances, McKinley's expression passed through several cycles of 'answer' versus 'don't answer' before he finally spoke. His voice seemed softer as he drew deeply on the well of not-very-good memories.

"I was in love." He shook his head. "Five star, platinum plated, full-on with room service. Bought a ring out of my measly pay. It cost fifty three quid; a wee, tiny diamond lost in its bezel..." He trailed off for a moment but quickly regained his focus. "Anyway she weren't impressed. A week later she was bonking my best mate. Bloody *hell*, I really thought she was *the one*, and I was SO wrong. My heart looked like eighties border trouble in Northern Ireland; all Land Rovers blown to shit, craters in the road and body parts hangin' off the barbed wire. *Never again*."

"I don't understand," ventured Wilson, "why you let that pain control you."

McKinley glared at Wilson in the torchlight for a long moment before answering. "No," he said slowly, "I guess you wouldn't."

"Sorry. Anyway," Wilson jerked a thumb back at the doorway, "close bracket. The point is this stinks of Heinmarsh and you know it."

McKinley regarded his friend for a moment. "I'm not making that call. Back burner, for now."

He turned to observe the BCs who were working on restoring the power, then back to surveying the hallway, but his thoughts remained on Heinmarsh. Much as he wanted to resist the conclusion, both Wilson's argument and the evidence around him were more than provocative. The absence of corroboration over Julia Bridgewell's assertion was worrying though because it made a member of McKinley's team look stupid, which made TDR.12 look stupid and, by extension, himself as team leader. The simple truth was that the woman had made a one-time claim and never said anything about it again. That claim was based on a memory retained from when she was under the influence of goodness-knows-what drugs and was therefore highly suspect if not downright untrustworthy.

But Heinmarsh had gone to ground with style and there was not a trace of him on the planet as far as their sources—who were many, various and well informed—could tell. A more thorough vanishing act by anyone other than an accomplished illusionist would be hard to imagine. If there was the slightest merit to the Bridgewell girl's reportage then it was something McKinley was keen to pursue. Which begged the question of her subsequent and complete silence on the matter.

Could this incident be Heinmarsh's work? McKinley considered alternative scenarios. A rogue state perhaps? Some employed suicide bombers, usually the religiously insane hunting for a spiritual promotion. McKinley's mind flitted from one country's name to another, then to known radical factions. Perhaps it was the action of a specific terrorist group; McKinley could name several who would love to see the end of General Sutton. But there McKinley's train of thought came to something of a roadblock; how did anyone even know where Sutton was? His identity was one of the best kept secrets on earth. The idea that someone outside the British secret services knew enough about General Sutton to locate him at his own home was troubling indeed.

There was a looming probability, one that unsettled McKinley at a deeper level than he would have admitted. Their own former colleague Corporal Martin Brook had turned traitor earlier that year, nearly bringing The Team to an end and causing all manner of chaos. Moreover, he'd somehow hacked into their computer system using information tortured out of the late Corporal Stevenson. Who could tell what Brook had learned and passed on? Even though McKinley hated to admit it, the rogue billionaire Kurt Heinmarsh *could* have known where Sutton lived.

During the last six weeks McKinley had tried to forget Heinmarsh even existed. He'd taken some time off, part-exchanged his Vauxhall VXR8 for a new vehicle—which had yet to arrive—and generally enjoyed a period of relative ease. The long overdue work on his house had been completed. A bit of Jack Daniels had been consumed and a few comely maidens had been chased. All in all it had been the R&R that McKinley felt entitled to. But, lacking stimulation yet without current information to work on, he'd drifted back to base in nostomania. Discovering that his team-mates had also gravitated there, McKinley had elected to put his crew on standby and await orders from their general. It was therefore ironic that they'd been in London trying to court Vladimir Kholitczyn's connivance when all this stuff had hit the fan. Who could have guessed this would happen? Two suicide bombers in a single day, and one of them targeting his commanding officer? McKinley shook his head. This was unbelievable, and all the more provocative for it.

A droplet touched McKinley's ear, sharp with liquid cold. He cast his beam upward and saw where water from the structure's dousing was making its way to ground level. Blimey, he thought, what a mess. Wilson was looking around the spot where Sutton had fallen, taking pictures with his smartphone.

Swinging the torch through an arc McKinley noticed Carter approaching from the back of the house, forensic kit swinging from his right shoulder, stepping carefully around pieces of debris which could embody particulate evidence.

"I've got enough samples," declared Carter. "We staying or going?"

"You need to get them to the lab quickly don't you?"

"DNA? Yes."

McKinley prodded Wilson's arm. "Anything else you need to see?"

Their Combat and Survival Specialist turned up the corner of his mouth. The house wasn't telling any more stories for now. "I don't think so."

"Okay," concluded McKinley, starting in the direction of Carter's Range Rover, "let's boogie."

The telephone rang several times before a tired but businesslike voice answered. "Yes?"

"Secretary Gundersen?" The caller's accent sounded vaguely Texan, but there was something a little odd about it. It didn't sound perfectly natural, making the Secretary wonder.

"Yeah. This'd better be important."

"Sir, I'm sorry to call so early, but I need your co-operation in a certain matter."

There was a pause, then a stern question. "Who is this?"

"Sir, what you should be asking is whether your Faroese cousins ought to remain involved in the *Grindadráp.*"

The Secretary of the Treasury was blindsided for a moment, cold fear entering his gut. The whale cull? That was... But if it got out that his Danish relations were helping to slaughter dozens of Pilot Whales every summer... Holy SHIT! The press would *destroy* him! The fear made an abrupt about turn and became fierce, burning anger. He blasphemed, then he was almost shouting. "Who the hell is this?!"

"What about your collection sir?"

"*What?!* What the hell are you..."

There was more swearing and blasphemy. The politician was angrier than a bag of wasps but the Texan voice persisted. "Your *private* collection sir, in the passworded folder on your laptop."

"*Do you know who I am?!*" raged the secretary.

"Your password is *tomahawk seven eight nine.*"

Suddenly the swearing stopped. Its ferocity was immediately subsumed by a fearful tone, almost a breath, grinding from within. The secretary was protecting the mouthpiece with his hand to ensure that he wasn't overheard. "By thunder... *how* do you know *that*?!"

There was no response, so the Secretary spoke in a more controlled manner even though he was breathing hard. "Who... what the hell do you want?"

"You must end your son's relationship with the British woman."

Silence reigned for more than a few moments, giving the impression that the American had passed way beyond what he was comfortable with. When Gundersen spoke, his voice was forcibly calmer, his words uniform and deliberate, conveying a frosting of momentarily gained but unwitting humility over an inferno of fury.

"And if I do, you'll keep your trap shut?"

"Yes sir, of course."

Again a couple of seconds ticked by.

"Deal," hissed the voice of the fifth most powerful man in America. "Now listen asshole, who in the hell are you?"

"A friend, sir. Thank you for your co-operation."

The caller hung up and clicked the tab which would sever the connection, eradicating any trace of its path through the various exchanges, distribution frames, fibre optic cables and satellites on its transatlantic route. He sat back in the chair, calming himself. It's never easy, he thought, but at least it'll help out a friend. It was worth it.

The COAST base deep beneath the streets of Nottingham was a vibrant mess of activity when McKinley returned at 07:00. Officers, administrators and BCs were dashing hurriedly around the corridors. The atmosphere was electric and an unspoken thought seemed to charge the air: someone hit us.

Before he could even get to their office an order barked from the Tannoy, summoning McKinley to one of the large briefing rooms where he joined all the TDR corporals who weren't on missions elsewhere and a brace of captains. It was a wide, low semicircle, the straight wall of which was adorned with five massive LCD screens, each the size of most people's living room wall. In front of these a long officers' console faced the eight chevrons of seats as they ascended in steps toward the back wall.

McKinley lowered his lean form into a seat by the even leaner Wilson, remembering long hours spent in the same room listening to lectures of varying interest during his tenure as a Basic Commando. Next to him, the recent addition to TDR.12 was paying polite attention in readiness for the briefing whilst Carter was tinkering with the new smartphone that he intensely disliked. McKinley grinned to himself. Out of all the tech-savvy geeks on the base, Carter was predictably the outstanding Luddite.

At the front desk were seated several higher ranking figures, notably Captain Chrimes, head of Operational Support, who was typing furiously into his laptop, their friend Captain Mike Dexter from Wales, and Major Maddocks in the central chair. He didn't look happy.

Thomas Maddocks, General Sutton's executive officer, was a slightly dumpy middle-aged man with a reddish, pock marked frontage and a pomade comb-over like a miniature crude oil spill. Maddocks had a friendly face on which laughter lines had carved tiny ravines between the blemishes, and which was partly imprisoned behind slightly oversized spectacles with rims of deep, glossy black and lenses as thick as medieval glassware, resting on his unusually long, thin, crooked nose. Were his nickname not the predictable 'Major Tom', it would probably have been some reference to a pigeon.

Maddocks was an officer with more grasp than most of his defined role in COAST, slotting in as though precisely crafted between the CO and the various departments which comprised the unit. The Yorkshireman was an accomplished administrator, operating from within the ecliptic shadow of General Sutton and able to serve those beneath him with humility and efficiency. In The Team he was regarded with good humoured respect as both a mentor and the man to talk to if something needed to get done. He was also the butt of many jokes, not all of which were friendly fire.

The stocky major rose and called the meeting to attention. He gave the order to sit, waited for the assembled operatives to settle, and began the briefing.

Maddocks ran his hand back over his mostly bald cranium, being careful not to disturb his pedal-bin. "Well, you all know what's been happening," he began, his Yorkshire accent as obvious as a third eye. "Point bein', we've got two almost simultaneous suicide bombing attempts—*never mind* this bloody business with the Whitehall Police Station—one o' which led to the death of the chancellor. The girl's in custody here on base and you can bet we'll be asking 'er some serious questions.

"Now lads, I want you to know General Sutton's okay. Much better 'n y' might expect considerin' what 'appened. He's broken 'is collarbone, got some burns and lots o' small fragment injuries. Eardrums both ruptured. He'll be in t' medical section for a week, then physiotherapy and the like. But I think we can all be glad 'e's going to make it."

Without being prompted the men started clapping, every single one relieved that it wasn't worse.

Maddocks grinned slightly and held up his stubby hands to stop the noise. "Now," he continued, "we got the DNA." He shook his head in disbelief. "Turns out the bombers were sisters."

McKinley, Carter and Wilson looked aghast at each other, as most of the room's occupants were also doing. A subdued murmur filled the air.

"Furthermore," continued Maddocks, cutting right across it, "we've got a DNA trace to their family in London. They're British."

A hand shot into the air across the room and McKinley looked over to see that it was Justin Pell, his opposite number from TDR.4.

"Sir," said Pell, "from which database?"

"Criminal actually," replied Maddocks. "A close relative is a known offender."

McKinley saw that Pell was about to voice another question when Maddocks overrode him. "Now, now, there's work to be done. Your orders will be in your offices. If you don't 'ave a particular set of orders, carry on wi' your regular duties. Everyone except TDR.12, dismissed."

Not again, thought Carter, as he felt numerous pairs of eyes upon him. But it was obvious why they'd been singled out.

When the room was about empty they approached the desk and saluted Maddocks, who returned it with a flick of two fingers at his brow.

McKinley normally got his orders from the chief and didn't much like Maddocks, despite respecting the major's professionalism. He saw Maddocks as a bureaucrat who'd spent too long flying a desk and was therefore out of touch with the day-to-day life of a COAST operative.

Similarly, Maddocks saw the sarcastic, wise-cracking Scotsman as a square peg which performed inexplicably well in its round hole. If there was any exception to the rule by which most COAST personnel found Maddocks to be helpful and approachable in an almost motherly sort of way, McKinley was it. Their mutual discomfort in this situation was something never verbalised but which was as invisibly awkward as gaseous indigestion.

Maddocks looked up at them with a keen expression, his wide mouth making him appear like a cartoon frog.

"So then, how d'your meeting wi' Coral Butterfly go?"

"Cut short, sir," replied McKinley. "I'd like another kick of the cat."

"Aye lad," nodded Maddocks. "You'll be goin' down London anyway t'ave a talk to the dad."

McKinley raised an eyebrow.

"Oh aye," affirmed Maddocks, "'e lives in the east end. Registered sex offender. Not the kind o' person I warm to, but see what you can find out about them girls. Once you're done wi' 'im, go finish your business wi' the Russian. Get me something to work on."

"Sir," said Wilson, "I don't mean to labour the point, but Heinmarsh spoke about suicide—"

"What?" drawled Maddocks, irked. "Too coincidental? D'you think I can commit resources to something that tenuous?"

Wilson felt chided, but Maddocks was right. "No sir."

"For the record, laddie, it's not *your* recollection I question, it's 'ers. Just 'cause she said it don't make it true, even though it looks like a big bloody coincidence. As for me, my 'ands are tied; orders from the JIC. So when General Sutton's back on 'is feet, we'll talk to 'im, and then, *if* there's enough support for another look, we'll see. You got it?"

"Yes sir."

"Right then, on your way now. Dismissed."

"Yes sir," answered McKinley. They saluted and made their way to the corridor.

Staring passively at the ashen streets through the Range Rover's rain-spattered windows, Wilson decided that if some cosmic being had wanted to give London an enema, the East End was undoubtedly where the tube would have gone.

The sky couldn't have been more dismal, he thought, perhaps reflecting the enormous amount of vehicle exhaust it had taken to stain it that insipid grey. The colourless cloud base was mirrored by the pallid cityscape below, a suburb of east London seemingly devoid of cheer. Though varied by different architectural styles, the wall of shops, banks, uninviting restaurants, pawnbrokers and the occasional pub was unrelenting. Garish advertising and shop frontages counterpointed the dejected ambience, an artifact maybe inherited from half a century ago when the Docklands were disgusting slums and familial gangsters enjoyed the benefits of unlikely celebrity status.

But this was a new, modern East End into which prosperity was supposedly creeping apace with the steady influx of immigrant families bearing high hopes and a will to work. The officially sanitised public face of this ostensibly rejuvenated neighbourhood was one of optimism floating on a tide of National Lottery money and government grants, whilst beneath the veneer of Audis, MPVs and cute but impractical hot hatchbacks a depressive undercurrent of residual hopelessness was nonetheless almost tangible. The rows of gothic sixties modernist flats were still the same, facing the smog-encrusted and poorly attended churches, bounded by their neighbours of rundown warehouses and rows of terraced houses stretching into the distance. *Joyeux de vie* was far more alien to this environment than were the countless foreign migrants with their delicatessens, discount jewellery stores and barbershops. If the sun *ever* shines here, thought Wilson, someone should take a photo as evidence.

They were still within the time limit of the news blackout and an official announcement was anticipated for later in the day, but as usual the press were on their game. Aside from that few seconds of pre-evacuation footage which was running constantly on television worldwide, news stands were emblazoned with headlines like 'Number Ten Suicide Bomber', 'PM Under Attack' and 'Downing St News Blackout: Why?'

Carter's mouth turned into a frown as they passed along Kingsland Road and he spotted a rapidly posted billboard which, under the name of the newspaper, went into more detail. 'Suicide Bomber in Whitehall, Helicopters Down, Shots in Downing Street: What Aren't We Being Told?'

"This is gonna kick off big time," he observed.

McKinley huffed. "Tell me something I don't know."

"They'll play it down," said Wilson. "Downing Street's overshadowed Uncle Victor. I think that's a good thing."

"How is any of this shit remotely good?" asked Carter flatly.

"You know what I mean."

Shortly they turned into a street that probably hadn't changed much since the coronation, with opposing pairs of terraced houses filing in a regimented sequence toward the horizon. A hundred yards along, Carter gave a grunt and slowed down.

"This is it," he announced, reversing the big Rangey expertly into a space which might have been better suited to a Mini. "The kiddie-fiddler's lair."

"Don't say that to his face," scowled McKinley, flicking his cigarette butt out of the door.

They exited the vehicle, observed by a sickly looking black and grey mongrel dog. The house outside which they stood was a little two-up, two-down box of dirty yellow brick interspersed with accents of conventional red, precisely the same as its neighbours on each side, a pattern of which the iterations numbered in the hundreds. The stone sills and lintels of the windows were daubed with a tough semi-gloss white which did nothing to suggest that any hint of sentiment might be hoped for within. It was one of the most depressing places Wilson had ever seen, diametrically different than the beautiful countryside in which he'd grown up.

McKinley rapped on the dirty blue door just above where the word 'pervert' had been sprayed in silver paint from which the runs reached all the way to the step. They waited for almost a minute, then McKinley noticed a changing glint of light from the peephole.

The door creaked open and the figure before them appeared an order of magnitude more run down than the neighbourhood. He was a stooping, thin man with grey hair and complexion, standing in greyer clothes that looked like they'd barely survived their most recent engagement with the tumble dryer. His eyes were dark and sunken beneath a pronounced brow that crowned a stubble-encrusted face of loose, uncared-for skin around which long, lank strands of thinning hair hung like dying vines.

"Are you McKinley?" growled the householder, looking his visitor up and down.

"Aye," answered McKinley, holding up his MOD90 identification.

Fox eyed both directions along the street suspiciously and croaked "you'd best come in." He shuffled back into the darkness of the front room.

McKinley didn't bother offering his hand as they followed inside. "Thanks for agreeing to meet, Mister Fox. Geoff? D'you prefer Geoff?"

Fox shrugged indifferently. McKinley said "these are my colleagues Carter and Wilson."

At Fox's nodded invitation McKinley sat on the sagging sage green couch whilst the others remained standing near the front door. Fox lowered himself onto a donut cushion diagonally opposite McKinley in a worn, brown leather chair from which he obviously seldom rose, an old red 'Viscount' telephone balanced on its arm. A bulky television, which looked almost ancient enough to remain switchable between Marconi-EMI and PAL broadcasts, glowed silently in the front corner, topped with cheap plastic boxing trophies and the faded photograph of a smiling woman, attired for twenty years ago, in a heart shaped frame. To Fox's right a small table held several plates stacked unevenly with utensils sandwiched between them, a well used yellow ceramic ashtray, a couple of crossword magazines and an archaic TV remote nearly the size of a paperback book. To the man's left was a narrow fireplace of beige tiles above which hung a gaudy picture of the Swiss Alps with a clock face in the sky showing the wrong time. Across the front of the room, under the window, an ancient dark brown radiogram with Bakelite controls, fabric frontage and cracked veneer sported a layer of dust as thick as a sheet of lasagne. The place smelled of stale tobacco, overused cooking oil and downright neglect.

"Now," began the man, "you're not cops? You swear?"

"Military intelligence," replied McKinley. "Nothing to do with the police at all. Don't be concerned."

Fox nodded warily, his eyes narrowed. "So what's this about then? Why're *you* here?"

McKinley replied "your daughters" and, as though an invisible switch had been thrown, Fox seemed to shrink at the words and his demeanour darkened still further. He looked down and seemingly through the threadbare carpet.

McKinley would have to have been blind not to have caught the weight of Fox's reaction, so he proceeded carefully. His question almost caught in his throat in view of the incident on Mapperley Top.

"You just have the two? Melissa and Jemima?"

Fox nodded mournfully.

"How long is it since you've seen them?"

The man raised his eyes, a sadness of disturbing depth in them. "Nothing since they joined that church 'n' got all righteous, like, but we talked on the phone. Before that, couple of years. They kept away 'cause of... what I did."

Carter knew what Fox had done; he'd read the file. His initial reaction had been of anger, of wanting to tear a strip out of the man who'd ruined a young girl's life. But now, here in the fellow's house, he felt pity for the dishevelled figure in the chair. It was seldom indeed one saw a person under such a massive weight of guilt. The torture of Fox having to live with his conscience was in essence a life sentence.

"Are you in contact with them?" asked McKinley, also impacted by Fox's remorse.

"No... only, I got this letter," said Fox, lifting his head. "'ere, I'll get it."

Clumsily, he raised his body from the armchair using his other furniture as support and moved behind to where an antique writing desk sat snugly against the wall. The hinges squeaked as Fox opened the dusty lid, then he rummaged inside for a moment and pulled out a wrinkled airmail, handing it to McKinley before allowing gravity to pull him back into his chair.

McKinley turned it over in his hands, taking in the details and noting the postmark, which said 'HARBOURFRONT CENTRE' around the top edge and 'SINGAPORE' underneath. It was dated eight months previously.

"Mind if I read it?" he asked, not wanting to appear presumptuous. Fox tipped his head in assent, so McKinley unfolded the light blue paper and read the few handwritten lines within.

Dad,

I want you to know Sister Patricia (Jem) and I are safe and well and we are happier than we have ever been. We found the truth about the Universal Spirit, the Cosmos and all the Earth changes that are coming. We have taken our places in a new Kingdom not of this world and you should be really pleased for us. Mum's spirit is watching over us and she is rejoicing in paradise.

I know you don't understand but we will pray for you. Pray to the Universal Spirit for understanding so you can join us in heralding the Kingdom. This unbelieving world is passing away and you can be part of the new one if you believe.

We can't see you again because of your past but please know that we forgive you. Please don't try to contact us because it will only make things worse. Goodbye dad and may you be blessed to see the Kingdom.

With love,

Sister Damaris (Mel)

Passing the letter to his team-mates, McKinley was torn between emotions. On one hand he could understand why the Fox sisters had wanted to steer clear of their dad after his conviction as a nonce. On the other he was taken aback by the arrogance and finality of the letter. McKinley's own family enshrined somewhat traditional values concerning the domestic hierarchy and it rubbed him the wrong way to see a girl barely out of her teens address her parent thus. Either way he didn't like the language, which reeked of Heaven's Gate, Jonestown and everything he hated about religion.

It also disturbed him to know that the hand which wrote those lines had been blasted to atoms. Why the hell would someone do that to themselves? Like a kick in his guts came the realisation that Melissa's sister had been moments from the same self inflicted obliteration. Wondering momentarily how the procedure to remove the bomb had gone, McKinley pushed the difficult feelings away and looked up.

Fox shrugged miserably, at a loss to say anything about the letter.

McKinley already knew the answer from research and background checks, but he asked to demonstrate his comprehension of the airmail's content. "What happened to your wife?"

Fox blew out a long sigh. "She's gone. Long time ago. I mean... after the divorce, she met this fella who liked his fast cars, only he weren't that good of a driver. Killed 'em both."

"That's tragic," said Carter, passing the airmail to Wilson.

Fox regarded him with eyes of deep, dark hopelessness and his voiced grated like stone on gravel. "Not like what I've done."

"Well," said McKinley without skipping a beat, "we're not here because of that. We just want to know if you have any idea of your daughters' current whereabouts." Damn, it was *bloody rotten* having to say that, knowing not only where they both actually were, but that one was all over their CO's front garden.

Fox waved a hand in the direction of the letter. "Singapore? I dunno. I couldn't afford to get there even if I wanted to."

Wilson took the airmail away from his face. "Aren't you concerned?" he asked.

Fox erupted with unexpected vigour, his hands flailing. "*'Course I'm bloody concerned!* I'm worried sick! Those are my girls. I love 'em to death." He started to calm a little. "But I done a *terrible* thing, see, so I understand. I don't want to make it worse so I ain't callin' the Bill or nothin'. I don't blame 'em... but it hurts..." He let his head droop again. "It hurts like hell."

Carter and Wilson looked at each other, thinking the same thing; this was the most dilapidated and hopeless human being they'd ever met.

Fox blinked away tears and raised his head, clearing his throat. "What they done, Mister McKinley? Military Intelligence ain't no joke. I want to know why you're here."

McKinley thought for a moment. There was so much he couldn't say, but he wanted to answer the dishevelled man. "You understand I can't go into detail, right?"

Fox nodded, his eyes drifting away to some undefined point in the opposite wall.

"I can tell you we're not investigating your daughters *personally*. We're looking into something they might be connected with."

"You mean that church? *Cult*, I call it."

"Geoff," said McKinley, "how much do you know about it?"

"Not much," responded Fox to the carpet. "They said something about being ambassadors for this bloody *kingdom* business." He looked up apologetically. "Before the letter. All I know is it's some island; tropical place, like. Might be *near* Singapore... I dunno."

McKinley glanced at his mates. If that was all they had to go on, it was going to be a long investigation.

The dour east London street seemed almost uplifting compared to the gloom within the little house as they drove away. Fox was such a pathetic case that they were glad to put the visit behind them. He'd agreed to let them take his precious airmail letter on condition that it would be returned to him, but McKinley didn't think forensics would be able to come up with much.

A message to their smartphones told them that Border Force, the government's immigration and border control agency, had confirmed both girls' identities. The sisters were definitely Melissa and Jemima Fox, and both had used their authentic British passports. Surveillance from airport security cameras was still being requisitioned, but it would be interesting to find out whether the women had entered the country seemingly pregnant or not. Given the almost impossible odds against successful subterfuge in this case, McKinley was betting the latter, giving rise to the further question of where and by whom the explosives had been implanted.

The weather started to cheer up as they made their way through the busy city to the same pub as before. Apparently Bacon was treating Kholitczyn as his guest and showing him some uncharacteristically good London hospitality.

Within spitting distance of Foster's famous 30 St. Mary Axe—perceptively nicknamed *Crystal Phallus* and which, to McKinley, looked like an upended Zeppelin—the Old Cock Linnet was a traditional London pub that had fought tenaciously to keep up with the times and had, to some extent, succeeded. This triumph, though, was not without sacrifice as the superficiality of the decor affirmed. Now arrayed in black, chrome, and imitation oak panelling, it had been the kind of watering hole where veteran journos would have congregated before the digital revolution wooed Fleet Street to Canary Wharf with its seductive towers of steel and glass. In those days journalistic communication mostly travelled at the speed of rumour and many world-weary hacks would have spent the morning here over their G&Ts discussing whether a story merited further attention. By one o'clock, those left behind would have been the few that didn't cling to an uncertain income at the dailies and would stare out over the remains of their jellied eels and steak and kidney pies, composing opinion pages and compendious weekly round-ups. Nowadays, news travelled at the speed of Android, Blackberry and TCP/IP via a galaxy of satellites, and any traditional reporter would have been horrified that a story could be played out live on the big flatscreens—from whose digital countenance not a single inch of the bar escaped—before he'd even heard about it, never mind got out his notebook and licked his pencil.

McKinley looked up at the ostentatious televisions and wondered how severe the reaction would be when the official announcement came. The media at large had geared-up for the story and all over the country staff would be preparing themselves for whatever it was and however it might line up with the known details. Around him, Londoners read newspapers, supped on a pint or speculated over the rumours, shunning the stock market oscillations in deference to topicality. The vapours from the kitchen, blended with new shoe leather and expensive aftershave, floated around them producing a mellow, sweet ambience that seemed to insulate them from the outside world. Through the high windows poured huge, distracting spotlights of the low autumn sun, tinged as it was a dirty yellow, declaring autumn's firm grip on north-western Europe despite the unseasonably decent temperatures.

After the usual round of small talk that eastern Europeans seemed to regard as necessary, Kholitczyn refused to be dissuaded from further hospitality and ordered food. McKinley and Wilson went with ham sandwiches whilst Carter chose turkey, and Bacon asked for egg salad. Having sucked noisily on his inhaler, the Russian took some time and much gesturing to make the pretty barmaid with her tight skirt and bemused smile comprehend his strong accent, then rejoined them. Their conversation turned to business.

"So," started McKinley, "we still need your intel on Erbakan. We've gotta find him."

"*Da*," said Kholitczyn, "but I want word that I am not involved. You will do?"

"Of course," answered McKinley, picking up his glass. "Our interest in him's got nothing to do with you. Maybe not much to do with him either, but we've got to find out. I *hope* he's a stepping stone to locating Heinmarsh."

"This Heinmarsh, he is causing all this trouble a few months ago?"

McKinley was swallowing some of his drink but nodded, gurgling "I'm sure you knew that."

Kholitczyn shrugged, frowning as though whether he did or didn't know was an irrelevance.

"Them advanced rifles," interjected Bacon. "That's the name right? 'Einmarsh. You wanna find 'ow to make them guns. I don' blame ya."

Wilson said "Vlad, I don't suppose you have anything on *him* do you?"

"*Niet*," replied Kholitczyn through a humourless grin. "If I would, I would tell."

"Okay," said McKinley, "then how do we find your friend?"

"Is not friend now," corrected the Russian, a most unhappy look coming to his face. "But is difficult. Even I do not know where he is ever."

"Me neither," interjected Bacon.

"He keeps secret, but he travels on boat... *roskoshnoy yakhte*."

"Luxury yacht," monotoned Carter without looking up.

Kholitczyn gave a tiny nod of acknowledgement, as though to a lower class citizen who'd just cleaned his shoes. "There is woman who will make meeting with contact."

"Contact?" queried Wilson.

"Is his man who you have to meet. You cannot knock on door to see Turk." He shrugged. "Unless is very big deal. Bigger than I have made before."

McKinley glanced at his team-mates. "How big?"

Kholitczyn's eyebrows knitted for a moment, then he thrust his jaw toward Carter and spoke in Russian.

McKinley had already got it as Carter translated. "At least two million Euros."

"Blimey," said Wilson, "how're we gonna tag him with that door price?"

"We've gotta find him first," said McKinley. "How do you contact this woman?"

"It is by phone," frowned Kholitczyn. "Satellite phone, so you do not know where is."

"That's what I was going to say," added Bacon.

McKinley smirked humourlessly. "Convenient."

"And it's impossible to tap without being right next door," added Carter. "It's complicated."

"You have to call when is night," said Kholitczyn. "She does not answer in day. But!" he exclaimed, waggling the cigarette holder excitedly, "it is island, I know this." The arms broker finished by grinning smugly, as though this mundane fact elevated him above present company.

McKinley nodded. The same island as the Fox sisters had visited, he thought, or another? "Interesting. I wonder if she's in this hemisphere."

"Why's that then?" said Bacon.

"Night," answered Carter. "You have to call at night. Maybe our night is their day."

The barmaid, smiling though her eyes projected wariness, delivered their sandwiches as Kholitczyn made a big deal out of his generosity for her. She retreated, looking over her shoulder as though having effected a narrow escape. Maybe she found it odd that a man so enthusiastic about his own munificence didn't offer a tip.

The sandwiches were heavy on the bread and vegetables whilst light on the meat, but nonetheless they thanked their Slavic friend and dug in. Carter, though, pulled the wedge away from his mouth, looking at it suspiciously. It was ham.

"Umm, Vlad," he said, "what's in this sandwich?"

"You ask for turkey, I give turkey. You do not like? You are sick?" Kholitczyn's visage darkened, his hospitality offended.

Carter regarded the meat, an eyebrow cocked. Turkey doesn't contain big streamers of fat, he thought. "You sure it's not ham?"

The Russian's face reorganised itself into an expression of deep affront mingled with an exaggerated plea as if for redemption. "Is *bird!*" he declared.

Carter spat a stream of what sounded like derogatory Russian, though neither McKinley nor Wilson understood. It caught the arms dealer out for a split second, then his eyebrows hopped like the upward cycle of a skipping rope.

"*Blyad!*" he exclaimed, apparently pleased. "*Vy gavarite Fenya!*"

Carter smiled, his thumb and index finger slightly apart. "*Nemnogo.* Some *Surzhyk* too," he nodded.

"What's Fenya?" asked Wilson out of the right side of his mouth as the left was occupied with sandwich. Apparently it was a language, and Carter spoke a little. Kholitczyn, Carter and McKinley regarded him curiously whilst Bacon nodded knowingly as if he'd been conversant with Fenya since childhood.

"It's what Russian crims speak," answered McKinley.

"Subset of Russian, if you like," added Carter. "Underworld lingo. Londoners have Cockney Rhyming Slang, Muscovites have Fenya."

"Wow," responded Wilson. "How d'you pick it up?"

Carter grimaced. "Infiltrated a gang... in Smolensk actually."

"Ah," said Wilson, wagging a finger in realisation. "That's where you two met. The pieces are falling into place." The finger made a last flourish like conducting the resolving downbeat of a symphony.

"I rescued his ass," said McKinley bluntly.

"Also, we meet there *first*," added Kholitczyn, not to be outdone. "You know, speak Fenya is good for business." He shook his head with a sour expression. "Why you not work for me? You think I am *zhestokiy*? You do not trust?"

"*Of course* not," replied Carter with a grin. "You definitely can't trust a man who's willing to lie about the contents of a sandwich."

Bacon laughed hoarsely for a second then, realising that he was alone, shut his mouth.

Kholitczyn brushed off the assertion. "You will do," he nodded, waving his cigarette holder as if casting a spell on Carter. "One day you will do, and I pay good *kapusta*. You will make better living than you now work. Very better."

Carter was enjoying this turn of conversation and asked "does the offer of big Russian girls still stand?"

The arms dealer's eyes widened and he stammered. "You... we... I will find you *beautiful* big *lyubovnitsa!* You will see."

Smiling, Carter lifted his glass, giving McKinley and Wilson a cheery wink. "A mistress? I'll think about it," he murmured.

"Hey, Trollhunter, can we get back to business?" asked McKinley sarcastically. Carter chuckled.

"Erbakan's online sometimes," pronounced Bacon through a mouthful of egg and watercress. "Not, like, social networking; 'e posts photos 'n' stuff."

Kholitczyn's lower lip turned down. "I think this is not Turk," he said, shaking his head.

"Photos of where he's been?" asked Wilson.

The Londoner shrugged. "I s'pose. But it'd take a bloody long time to track 'em down, innit?"

"Right," said Carter. "Facial recognition's one thing, but identifying geographical features is still mostly down to manpower. It's not easy."

"Aye," said McKinley. This was starting to sound more involved than a regular manhunt. Whilst the Turk's name had been on The Team's radar for a while, little was known about the man himself, his whereabouts, or his lifestyle. Yet if it led to Heinmarsh, or even pointed them in the right direction, it could be worth it.

"Don't suppose you've got the phone number?" asked Carter.

"'Course I 'ave," answered Bacon glibly, cutting across Kholitczyn's attempt to reply. "It's an anonymous account though: untraceable. I already tried."

"It's a start," nodded Carter.

Bacon grinned, winking. "If you gorgers spoon for the next round I'll give it ya."

004: The Woman

Headquarters was quiet by the time Carter sat down in their office. Wilson had gone home for the evening, unintentionally reinforcing the team leader's cynicism about him. McKinley dropped Geoffrey Fox's airmail into the forensics crew to let them do their stuff, but he wasn't optimistic.

The TDR group 'D' office was a twenty feet per side square, disappointingly beige, with a number of desks, filing cabinets and computer terminals, a communications set, and an eighty inch plasma display dominating one wall. A partition with panes of patterned glass adjoined the corridor, causing traversing figures to ripple as though televised with a distortive video effect that would have been cool in the eighties. Nine big lockers, shared between the trio of TDR teams that occupied the space, stood against the wall opposite the corridor.

McKinley returned to the office with a sealed sample beaker in his hand and some papers.

"MDTs already?" frowned Carter. "You're not gonna do it in here are you?"

"Get stretched. I'll do it tomorrow."

Carter looked relieved. "Thanks. I hate MDTs."

McKinley sat and hunched over the desk while Carter tilted back in his chair, slurping on a mug of Earl Grey and portraying a casual nonchalance that would have raised a disapproving eyebrow from General Sutton.

As the Weapons and Equipment Technician of TDR.12, Carter was responsible not only for the scientific investigation of evidentiary materials, but for medical expertise in the field, maintaining the weapons, demolitions, and the now mandatory computer disciplines, including those which would make a network administrator really unhappy. This last category came under the abbreviated unofficial heading 'tech', and also meant all kinds of gadgetry, bugs, clandestine weapons and surveillance equipment. In short, a Weapons and Equipment Technician was a jack of all trades in anything which required a screwdriver, wrench, soldering iron or alphanumeric keyboard skills. Out of The Team's three disciplines, the tech boys studied the hardest and were commemorated the least. Each TDR team was led by a Tactical and Surveillance Specialist like McKinley, while Wilson was the Combat and Survival man, completing an autonomous trio of which there were fifteen in COAST.

"Come on then," said McKinley, bringing the computer terminal online. The big screen faded from black into the COAST logo and their motto 'Contra Omnes Dissident'.

Slopping tea onto his trousers, Carter wheeled his chair up to the terminal and typed the URL that Bacon had given them for the photo sharing website. He took a couple of minutes to create his own login and they found Erbakan's page under the username *Fena_Oglan1962*. Carter opened a translation window and selected Turkish to English.

"Huh," he smirked. "*Bad Boy 1962*."

"No shit. What we got on file?"

Carter called up another window and entered the Turk's name. A pair of vague images appeared with a panel of text. Carter's finger rubbed his lips for a moment in thought. "He looks like Dracula after a month dining on druggies."

The pictures were less than clear but showed a bald head with pointed chin and nose, between which slithered a thin snake of a moustache. Apparently this arms dealer liked to keep away from prying cameras.

"Is that all?"

Carter lifted a crooked finger to the list of details. "Yeah. Bit of a wandering Jew, this one."

"Not like his American pal."

Carter huffed a short laugh in agreement; Heinmarsh's overconfidence and egotism had led to their operation against him.

McKinley shrugged. "So what about this photo site?"

Carter pushed himself back from the desk and drummed on his thighs. "Yeah; need to do some hacky."

McKinley knew that the next phase of the process would be geeky in the extreme. He was about to leave when he remembered something about hacking that he'd been meaning to address.

"Talking of which, you know last Christmas?" he started. Carter's eyes rolled slowly toward him.

"The phones all played '*Jingle Bells*'," continued McKinley. The incident had been an impressive piece of work by whomever was responsible, with every mobile telephone in the unit simultaneously blasting out the hackneyed tune. General Sutton, whilst seeing the humour in it, had been somewhat concerned and this had led, after extended testing and evaluation, to the new phones they'd recently been issued. "Was that you?"

"'Course not!" Carter looked affronted.

"You gonna do it again this year?"

Carter shook his head, frowning. "No. Boring."

"Back in ten," said McKinley, rummaging for his lighter as he exited the office.

Carter linked his hands, inverted them and pushed away from himself, popping his knuckles. Then he wriggled his fingers in the air as though about to launch into a complex piano sonata. If he could crack the website's main server he'd be able to locate Erbakan's details. A terrestrial telephone number would be perfect, but an email address would still be a great starting point. The name or even the IP address range of the arms dealer's service provider would be useful. Carter opened several utility programs, took a fresh mouthful of his tea and set to work.

He barely noticed when McKinley re-entered their office, half a cheese and onion cob in his hand. "Any news?" the Scotsman asked.

"Ugh," grunted Carter. "Irritatingly intelligent programming, encrypted files... can't get into his details." Suddenly Carter exploded angrily. "Bloody *eff pees!*" He banged his fist on the desk, rattling pens.

"Steady on mate," said McKinley quietly, not wanting to exacerbate Carter's furore.

"Sorry," said Carter, shaking his head.

"Anger management's going... alright?"

"Hate it," Carter grated. He'd been attending counselling sessions at General Sutton's behest. Their CO felt that the course was an appropriate response to an ugly incident at the Bristlecone Lake Mine in Canada.

"What's it like?" asked McKinley.

Carter shook his head. "Tedious. I sit there twice a week with this bloomin' woman and figure out things that make me angry. Then I've got to learn to defuse 'em with logic before they piss me off. It's bloody 'orrible."

"She's a psychiatrist?"

"Psychotherapist actually. *Psycho-the-rapist.*"

McKinley put voice to the question that always floated to the surface of his mind when discussing a female human being. "Is she fit?"

Carter's face assumed a look of disgust. "Face like a bag of spanners. Old enough to be your mum."

McKinley took note, his level of interest plunging to zero. "Well... is it helping the anger?"

"If you mean *making me* angry, then yes." Carter nodded. "It's frustrating."

"Oh."

"Anyway," snorted Carter, turning back to the computer, "I'll try his upload folder."

McKinley dropped his ass into the chair and loaded the rest of the sandwich into his face, watching as Carter alternately typed and scribbled notes on a pad. The Weapons Tech hummed as his fingers skipped to the rhythm of rapid keystrokes and different windows flashed up on the screen, all appearance of his rage having subsided almost as quickly as it had surfaced. Suddenly his hands leaped from the keyboard as though shocked by static electricity and he rasped an acknowledgement. "Ha! You're *my* wife now, Dave! Look, there's his email."

McKinley peeked sideways at the big display, up which lines of green text were scrolling. "We're in?"

"Like a rat up a drainpipe."

"What do we know?"

"Well—"

"Where is he?"

"Umm... yeah, except that. The IP range belongs to this satellite internet provider. Can't pinpoint him, just the footprint he's in. Too ambiguous to be any good."

McKinley grunted sourly. A satellite's terrestrial coverage area could be as big as a continent. But he was quietly pleased because Carter's techno-voodoo had once again swerved past the checkpoints and prised open someone's life. There were Erbakan's personal uploads. Of the private secrets he'd committed to hard disk, some would become neither secret nor private anymore.

"Oh," exclaimed Carter, leaning forward to peer at the terminal, "that's interesting."

"What?"

"See these files? They're the originals from his digicam. You know; EXIF data." Carter swiped the mouse cursor around a list of files and dragged them to a local folder. The illicit download started.

McKinley felt for a second like there was a piece of information that Carter wasn't telling him, but about which he was somehow supposed to know. He knew that pictures from someone's phone would provide an insight into their location and movements, but could a camera do the same?

Carter, though, rubbed his hands together like a gleeful adolescent as the progress bar lengthened. "Come on baby," he grunted.

McKinley was watching over his team-mate's shoulder as the download finished. Carter brought up mapping software, selected a few options and dragged the new files into the window. In a second, scores of tiny yellow flags appeared, each initially bulging elastically but immediately settling down to its usual size.

"Cutting the line," announced Carter and switched back to the terminal window. He pecked in a series of key commands and lines of text appeared as each server in the long chain to the website relinquished its connection. He looked up at McKinley. "No-one will ever know."

"You hope," McKinley grinned.

The map background was completely blue, but Carter zoomed the image out using the mouse wheel. A clear pattern was immediately apparent.

McKinley raised an eyebrow. "Educational," he murmured.

Carter nodded enthusiastically, prodding the monitor. "There's your island."

The yellow flags stretched from the Turkish south coast all the way through the Mediterranean, then south-west paralleling the north African coast and into the Canary Islands; an intermittent chain of geographically tagged digital photographs stretching three thousand miles.

McKinley was mentally calculating the distance. "He does this regularly? On his *yacht?*"

"Creature of habit, eh?" said Carter. "See, he's been uploading from his GPS enabled camera, daft bugger. Innocent hobby for him, peek into his life for us. Can't believe he's that careless."

McKinley smiled. "I like his careless."

"'Course you do." Carter probed the sticking plaster by his left eye, blinking as though it wasn't a good fit.

"Crete to Malta's about six hundred miles," observed McKinley. "That's a very long way for a small craft."

"Right." Carter dotted around the map with a fingertip. "But apart from that he could bunker just about anywhere."

"Could be trading too. He could sell into Greece, Italy, Tunisia, Algeria... anywhere on the Med coast really. Looks like he's got it figured out, eh?"

"*If* he carries product, and I wouldn't. Keep your own hands clean, right?"

Grunting an acknowledgement, McKinley said "so he's just making deals?"

Carter shrugged. "For a guess."

"In Gran Canaria."

The yellow flags were concentrated on the southern tip of the island of Gran Canaria. "Puerto Rico," read Carter. "Same name as that Caribbean place; Port Of The Rich. Looks like a resort town. We don't know anyone there, do we? Other dealers? Terror cells?" He opened an additional window which would access the COAST database and several others. Typing in the name of the resort, several listings started to appear with colour codes matching either their level of interest or any known threat.

McKinley had a feeling they *did* know someone there, that familiar tingling in his brain which indicated that he was one step away from something interesting. He thought for a moment. He'd heard about Puerto Rico, but he wasn't sure where. The name had a familiar ring to it and, as the memory surfaced, it wasn't a happy feeling.

"What?" asked Carter, noting his colleague's pensive expression.

McKinley gave a slight nod as though confirming his internal monologue. "Padget," he said. "BC Darren Padget. On holiday with his rellies. Murdered because of TDR.7, stopping their information from Kholitczyn reaching us. More of Brookie's shit."

"You don't think—?"

"I bloody well do think."

Leaning forward, McKinley took the mouse from Carter and zoomed out again. "Look, he travels this line consistently. There could be lots of other stuff he gets up to along the way; we don't know." McKinley reached to the screen and encompassed the echelon of flags with his thumb and middle finger. "But it seems to me his bases are Antalya and this place. Padget died *right here*. We think Erbakan does business there, and he's selling Heinmarsh's weapons; who's to say he didn't do it?"

"Interesting," ruminated Carter, one eye half closed as if it might expedite the mental processes, "and maybe a little too obvious. I'd love to be able to prove it." He turned back to the terminal and clicked the report on Basic Commando Padget's fate.

"Aye, another mystery solved," nodded McKinley. "Possibly."

Carter frowned, his eyes still scanning the screen. "Here we go; the CNI didn't get much out of the forensics beyond proving the bomb was a McCulloch design. We'd have to produce more evidence that links it to Erbakan... and that trail's *really* cold."

"I know." McKinley shook his head. "But if we *can* link Erbakan to Padget we can get things moving, maybe go after Erbakan himself. What's the date on the latest photo?"

Carter worked the mouse then smiled, his eyebrows raised. "Six new uploads yesterday."

"D'you think his contact woman's there too?"

"Presumably. So we interrogate her to find Erbakan?"

"Not necessarily, but she's the first call either way. I know the account's anonymous, but you can sniff out her phone if we're close, right?"

"Not just that," smiled Carter, "we can triangulate it." His finger span like a falling Maple seed.

McKinley nodded. "Right. Let's get Willy and fly out there tomorrow. I'll bounce it off Major Tom. We'll need Bacon for the introduction *and* he speaks Spanish. What's yours like?"

"¿Español?" replied Carter. "No es un problema."

Before heading home, McKinley had one more thing that he wanted to do, an itching curiosity that he couldn't leave base without scratching. He made his way over to the medical section.

Here the corridors of the COAST base became like those of a hospital, with protective rails secured to the walls at the height of a stretcher's widest dimension and tough linoleum floors in a mottled taupe rather than the hard, grey rubber of the TDR offices. The ubiquitous fluorescent lighting seemed even less inviting than usual, as though the sterile rays disinfected the air of warmth. The soles of McKinley's boots clicked on the floor while the surrounding corridors answered with reverberation.

The Team's medical section wasn't a large facility, perhaps only twice the size of a regular hospital ward in total, and speckled with security features never to be seen in its civilian equivalent. Its rectangular perimeter was formed of smaller cubicles with examination rooms and theaters on one side and a handful of multi-purpose rooms on the other. Between this outer enclosure and the large central workstation there was an open ward of sorts with twelve beds surrounding the island in four groups. Unlike a civil facility, the COAST medical section paid heed to neither privacy nor patient convenience. It was built for function and enviably well equipped.

McKinley approached the workstation as Doctor Manning looked up at him over rounded glasses, his pudgy double chin obscured by the edge of the counter. The top half of Manning's head was tonsured and shiny, with short veils of dark grey hair draping over his ears. He was a man of outstanding medical expertise whose bedside manner varied massively between rudely stern and dotingly humane, depending on the degree to which he sensed deception from his patients. The doctor could be hard at those times, but was always fair and thoroughly concerned with the wellbeing of those whose convalescence he oversaw.

"Corporal McKinley," announced Manning, leaning back in his chair and plucking off his specs, which he wiped on the corner of his perfectly white gown. "I presume you're here to see our young guest."

"Aye. She awake?"

Manning frowned, holding his eyewear up to the light and peering through it. "She's conscious. I wouldn't necessarily call it awake."

Not understanding, McKinley shrugged and Manning clarified. "She's clearly not in her right mind. I'm sure drugs are a factor. Not the recreational sort."

"You haven't got the toxicology?" McKinley glanced at his wristwatch. Considering the hour, tomorrow might be a better bet.

Manning shook his head. "Not yet. Just be nice, okay? You catch more bees with honey, you know."

"I know."

"She's been through a lot. Whoever stitched that thing into her didn't give a shit. Bloody amateur." Manning grimaced angrily.

McKinley frowned. "Recovery wasn't the plan, was it? She gonna be alright?"

"In time," nodded Manning, as though it was a relief to give it voice. "But I'd advise her against ever trying to have children."

Heck, thought McKinley with a shudder, that's horrible, but ultimately it was her choice. "Well," he said, "where she's headed that's not going to be an option. Can I go in?"

"Go ahead."

McKinley jabbed his finger toward the video screen on Manning's desk. "You recording?"

Manning hummed his acknowledgement, indicating the private rooms with his eyes and outstretched glasses. Outside one of the cubicles' double doors were two Basic Commandos standing guard. McKinley nodded to them, eliciting beautifully executed twin salutes, and entered the room.

Strapped to the bed, the suicide bomber had her eyes tightly shut but her mouth was working both hard and silently. The girl's arm was connected to an intravenous drip and a frame held the sheets away from her surgery. She appeared pale and terribly fragile, but was still undeniably attractive.

McKinley grabbed a chair, turned it through a half circle and sat, his chest against its back and his legs straddling the seat.

The prayer stopped and her eyes opened, swivelling toward him. Bloody hell, thought McKinley, she's drop-dead gorgeous. In another time and place he'd gladly have considered buying the first drink in an attempt to woo her. Her eyes were of dark brown, deep and inviting but filled with suspicion. She turned her gaze fixedly to the ceiling as McKinley moved his chair a little closer.

"Well kid," he began, "you're in some right sticky shit. Seriously, *seriously* deep shit."

She continued to stare through the roof, not moving a muscle. McKinley went on.

"If you answer my questions honestly I can help you. If you don't answer, or you try to deceive me, things can get more unpleasant. It's your choice; I can be your friend or your enemy."

He detected a tiny movement in her face, then she spoke. Her high voice was soft and tremulous but forthright. "You're already deceived," she murmured. "You all are; you just don't know it."

"Aye and how's that then?"

"This world has spun a web of lies around you."

Inside McKinley groaned. Whilst her asseveration was true from a certain perspective—and particularly in his profession—it was jargon; religious jargon. What a load of shit, he thought, and something I can definitely do without. "I'm better informed than you think," he replied.

"And who are *you*?" she asked belligerently.

"The name's Ian. You won't remember me but I was there in London."

"Oh." She kept studying the pipes and conduits above, her face perceptibly hardening. "You robbed me of my reward! You haven't stopped us."

McKinley nodded thoughtfully. "'Us'?"

"We are the Ambassadors Of The Godhead," she proclaimed weightily, as though expecting to be heralded by a fanfare.

Great, thought McKinley, not remotely impressed, more god squad crap. He prepared himself for a pointless few minutes and asked "is that your church?"

"We're not a church," she snapped. "We are an *ecclesia*, an assembly of divine warriors. We are the many-membered manchild."

With the terminology being alien to him, McKinley decided to try a slightly different tack. "Okay then, what denomination?"

"We're not a denomination."

"Right," scowled McKinley. He could already feel himself getting irked. "What flavour of Christianity?"

"We are not Christian!" she scoffed exasperatedly, as though it was the most elementary fact in the world. "Or Catholic, or Buddhist, or Muslim or any this world's totalitarian religions! We draw truth from the spiritual traditions of *all* faiths. We are the *elect*."

In his frustration McKinley wanted to get angry, but he was willing to play 'good cop' for a little longer. He calmed himself and tried another approach.

"What's your name?"

"Sister Patricia," she deadpanned as though the conversation was over. If her arms hadn't been held by the restraining straps she would undoubtedly have crossed them in annoyance.

"How about Jemima Fox? That's what it said on your passport at Heathrow. We know—"

She laughed derisively, a harsh falsetto which seemed far too loud for the small room. "It's my old name of course! I'm Sister Patricia of the Divine Wind."

That's appropriate, mused McKinley, knowing that 'divine wind' was the common translation of *Kamikaze*. Again he adjusted his line of inquiry. "Why did you try to blow up Downing Street?"

"To usher in the Kingdom." Her eyes widened and the ghost of a smile flitted across her face. She gazed as though into a brilliant future that was veiled from McKinley's sight. "A new kingdom, not of this world!"

McKinley lifted himself from the chair in resignation. Enough was definitely enough for now. "Thanks," he said absentmindedly as he left the room.

"She's all yours Doc," he told Manning. "Keep me posted if she, you know, wakes up."

The subtropical Canarian air enveloped them with delightful warmth as McKinley, Carter and Wilson disembarked the Boeing 757 and walked into the Aeropuerto De Gran Canaria terminal to collect their luggage. The temperatures were in the twenties and the sun was an impossibly bright ball of intense radiance, contrasting the conditions they'd left back home even though it was an unusually warm autumn for Britain.

Via an arrangement that had been quickly facilitated by Maddocks, McKinley contacted the airport police and hitched a ride to the southern end of the apron, the Gando Air Base of the Spanish Air Force. There he got their secured items released before heading back to the terminal with a couple of SAF personnel. Whilst he and Carter checked their equipment in a spare office, Wilson rented them a vehicle, a white Nissan Evalia minibus.

Once heading south-west on the GC-1 highway they were able to get a much better look at their surroundings and observed that Gran Canaria was essentially a towering, thirty mile wide volcano that had long since stopped issuing pyroclastic flows and other ejecta. The almost lunar landscape was harsh and rugged, comprised of aeons-old basalt formations that looked like a giant child had been playing with mud pies. The colour of the island varied between a dirty grey and a rubicund terra cotta, interspersed with cacti, palm trees and occasional patches of more luscious green, the incidence of which visibly increased with altitude. They drove past fields of greenhouses on the left, their glass and vinyl glinting fiercely in the strong sunlight, whilst on their right the terrain ascended toward Pico de las Nieves, nearly two kilometers above sea level. Electricity pylons and wind turbines strode side by side toward the sea, down bone dry gullies that were only nourished by rain on an average of just twenty one days a year.

Reaching from the back, Carter switched on the vehicle's radio and hunted for an English-speaking channel. When the receiver's RDS display came up with 'Coast FM' he grinned. "Hey look lads, we're famous!"

"I bloody hope not," replied McKinley, chuckling.

Their destination lay to the west of the island's southern tip and they made the journey in just over half an hour, skirting the coast and descending into the town via a tunnel through the hillside. Puerto Rico de Gran Canaria had been constructed in the valley as a holiday resort, with clusters of Pueblo-like whitewashed apartment buildings, hotels and condominiums perched on the rising terraces of lava rock, looking like rows of seats in a V-shaped sports stadium. Recent construction was higher up, overlooking the valley floor where clubs, restaurants and all kinds of shops formed the urbanised center of which a more germane description than 'tourist trap' would have been hard to imagine. Seaward, the beach was a full quarter kilometer wide, infested by human beings on blue and yellow *chaise lounge* chairs, and bounded by two harbours, the smaller of which, on the western side of the town, was clearly aimed at foreign visitors whilst the eastern harbour had a look both more serious and more prestigious with humble wooden fishing vessels moored alongside glittering yachts. Presumably one of the latter was Erbakan's, although several of the larger boats were moored further out in the bay.

TDR.12 made their way to a holiday apartment high above the beach which they'd secured in advance. Like nearly all the other suites in their angular clusters it was a bright white box with a set of glass doors forming the front and a single small window on the side, this basic architecture varying little between complexes. Above and below were identical apartments in stacked, geometrically staggered rows, the little painted concrete patio of each forming the roof of the one over which it was built. Between each column of five suites, covered stairwells connected by long horizontal hallways cascaded to the lowest level of the building where there was a communal swimming pool. Behind the complex a wide circle of tarmac ringed by parking spaces marked the end of the road. Beyond this a narrow dirt track rose quickly until it was no more than a lofty footpath with a spectacular view across the bay.

Inside, the layout was open plan and the furnishings modest. The sliding patio doors led into a square lounge with two cheap wicker chairs and a yellow couch arranged in a tight arc from which the unknown brand TV high on its bracket in the corner could be viewed, and surrounding a little coffee table on which stood a sad looking plant in a china vase. Behind this were a pair of single beds, one each side of the central access to kitchen and bathroom. The little kitchen was decently functional with a moderately sized pine dining table below the window and opposite which was the bathroom entrance. Next to this the back door led to the narrow, dimly lit concrete stairwell replete with countless insect corpses. The suite was floored throughout with polished, speckled grey stone tiles which would be bloody cold for sockless soles first thing in the morning, although nights had the potential to be particularly unpleasant if a foot came down on a cockroach.

Following the mandatory coin toss over sleeping space, by losing which Carter was relegated to the couch, they set up communications on the kitchen table and prepared for their surveillance. Carter got online and checked the photo sharing website.

"Huh," he grinned. "He uploaded another picture a couple of hours ago."

"This place?" asked Wilson.

"He's definitely here."

"Good," said McKinley, pulling out his smokes. "Now we wait. Anyone hungry?"

In Puerto Rico it seemed that the night was almost as bright as the day, and decidedly more colourful. A million brightly-hued lightbulbs electrified the darkness between roof mounted air conditioners and an abundance of satellite dishes resembling a high-tech fungal colony. Signs in every chrominance imaginable broadcast their luminous message across the shopping center, adding to an overall glow that encompassed the mall like iridescent fog.

Wilson took the binoculars from his eyes, seeing a lurid green afterimage against the dark ground at his feet. Goodness knows what the electricity bill for this place is like, he thought.

"You see Mickey?" asked Carter.

"By the trees at the south end. Just lit up."

Carter chuckled as he reached for the bins. "That's him."

Wilson passed them over. "So you send me the code, I point this about until I get the strongest signal and give you the bearing, right?" He regarded the device in his hand. Wilson had seen microphones for capturing wildlife sounds with their parabolic reflectors, and this was similar. It looked like a baby radar dish with pistol grip and a cable leading to his smartphone's USB socket.

"You got it. We won't have diddly till Bacon calls. I'll know the exact moment he connects and I can detect which sat-phone answers as long as she's here somewhere. Once I've got the IMEI we can triangulate it."

"And these things are sensitive enough?" Wilson held up the dish and looked along its axis as though taking aim.

Carter scowled. "They're not designed for satellite signals, but the theory's solid. I'd better get shiftin'. Got to call Bacon at 20:30."

Wilson lowered the dish-gun and looked down at his watch, its minute tritium tubes indicating just after ten past. There was no need to ask whether Carter would reach his position fast enough.

"What if she's not here?"

"Well, then we're wrong, aren't we?" Carter slammed the Evalia's door and rolled down the window.

"Seeya," said Wilson, not entirely satisfied with that answer, as his colleague drove away scattering dust.

Carter threaded his way down the twisting, narrow roads to the valley floor past countless single room holiday apartments just like theirs. Nearly the only other vehicles abroad at this time of night were the ubiquitous white and green taxis, but pedestrians were plentiful, out chasing nightlife, off to try an unfamiliar cocktail in one of the many bars or just taking a romantic walk along the foreshore. It was a gaudy, superficial excuse for a genuinely exotic location but, Carter surmised, not bad for a short stay. The massed crowds of Europeans were evidence of its popularity, perhaps especially at this time of year; not many of their home countries could match the Canaries' pleasant climate.

That afternoon had been spent investigating the locale. McKinley had disappeared into the surrounding towns with the vehicle leaving Carter and Wilson to peruse the area on foot. Wilson had opted for the docks whilst Carter took the town, wanting to check out the site of the holiday apartment where Padget and his relatives had been blown to bits. During his walkabout, Carter had perceived the voices of many nations. There were plenty of Brits, lots of Germans, Italians and French folk – even some Finns and Norwegians. There were plenty of much darker faces too; some would be tourists yet others probably short-stay migrant workers from Morocco or Western Sahara, the coast of the latter being only a hundred and forty miles away. The curious exception was the native Canarians themselves. Carter had only heard a few Spaniards amongst the crowds, leading him to the conclusion that Puerto Rico was far more about tourism than anything else.

He drove past the shopping center, cursing the pedestrians who brazenly stepped into the road with neither thought nor care. For them it was a relaxing holiday environment but Carter was at work, as were the cabbies whose vehicles swarmed the resort. At least they're used to it, he thought.

Also still at work were many foreign nationals for whom Gran Canaria's nightlife was their stock-in-trade. During his explorations Carter had been accosted several times by Brits and others offering colourful but cheaply printed flyers and hoping to attract his patronage to this-and-that bar, pub or club. For this they were apparently paid a small commission and, through conversation, Carter had learned that this practice was a popular means to earn oneself a cheap holiday on the island. After a handful of encounters though, Carter had become weary of the constant invitations to a good time, and had started speaking in Russian to discourage the advances.

He saw the dark figure of his team leader on the right, under the trees between the mini-golf and a fast food franchise, a tiny orange glow at head height signalling the continued intake of nicotine. Carter grinned to himself, entertaining the idea that the Scotsman would smoke in his sleep if he could.

With his smartphone perched on his knee displaying a map, Carter crossed the valley floor near the *Oficina de Turismo* and started to ascend the western slope past restaurants, parked vehicles and carefree holidaymakers. The winding roads were steep with sharp turns, offering alternating views of humble rock and scrub juxtaposed with what seemed to be the Canarian version of Blackpool as Carter's altitude increased. Presently he arrived at the predetermined vantage point, stopped the van by some rusted metal railings and got his gear ready; he set out another dish like Wilson's, some electronic modules and his laptop. The view, even at night, was impressive. He could see the whole valley of Puerto Rico laid out before him, its myriad accommodation complexes stacked like egg boxes against the dark cliffs.

Squatting by the computer, Carter went to radio. "Hazard to Tripod."

McKinley's reply was immediate. "Tripod here. Shadow, you ready?"

"This is Shadow," reported Wilson. "Ready."

"Hazard, make the call."

"Roger." Carter lifted the phone and hit the button. Bacon would take it on his mobile whilst using the landline to call the contact, giving them an additional ear.

"'Ello boy!" Bacon's cockney tone once again assaulted Carter's eardrums. "Did ya think I weren't gonna call?"

"Can you just get dialling please?" replied Carter.

Bacon huffed some unintelligible insult but Carter could hear him pressing keys. "Ready on the last number," reported Bacon.

Carter looked down at the screen of his laptop. "Hit it," he said.

"Done."

Carter took the phone away from his ear, mentally noting the interval. He knew about how long it would take the call to connect. The scanner display on the laptop was passive, but at any second the signal should appear as any satellite phone in town responded.

"What's happening?" came McKinley's voice.

"Nothing yet," whispered Carter. He heard a faint noise and picked up the phone again. "What?"

"I've got ring tone," reported Bacon.

"Bollocks!" spat Carter. There was nothing on the screen. Their own devices were probably the only satellite phones in Puerto Rico.

"So she's not in town," said the team leader grimly over the radio.

Suddenly Carter's screen flashed. A tiny green curve appeared on the graph, indicating activity. "Hold on!" he said excitedly, "I've got signal!"

He fell to his knees and started working on the computer, using his shoulder to hold the phone against his ear. The outgoing satellite signal was fluctuating madly, making reception difficult. Carter swore. The built up nature of the resort town meant that the radio waves were bouncing around like balls in a bingo machine. He could hear Bacon talking in Spanish after an English greeting.

"Get the code!" ordered McKinley.

"It's getting scrambled by interference!" snapped Carter. "We'll have to do it by frequency. Shadow, I'm sending you a frequency instead. You'll have to tap it into the detector manually."

"Roger," replied Wilson. Bloody hell, he thought, now I have to figure this out. He called up the application on his telephone and started hunting for manual frequency entry.

Carter was busy calibrating his end as Bacon's call was progressing. He isolated the frequency and started to track with his dish along the valley, starting at his left and moving south toward the sea. As the shopping center came into range the meter reacted noticeably, but Carter knew there were still problems.

"Hazard to Tripod. She's in the buildings. I'm getting multi-path reflections. Shadow can you copy? She's somewhere in the shopping center."

Wilson had just put the figures in and started to track his direction finder to the middle of the resort. As expected the meter started to register.

"Keep her talking," barked Carter, knowing that Bacon would have a phone to each ear, but he could hear that the call was winding up.

Bacon started to stutter, losing the plot a little in his confusion between the two phones and switching randomly between English and Spanish. Suddenly Carter heard him say "ciao" and the call was over. The meter stopped flickering a second later and the laptop's readout went dead.

"Shit," said Carter.

"You've got the frequency?" came McKinley's voice.

"Yes," said Carter, "but it'll switch on the next call. That's how it works."

"Damn. But she was in the shopping center?"

Carter huffed. "Near as I can tell."

"Yes or no?"

"Yes! In the shopping center."

"Okay," replied McKinley. "Get down here, both of you. Chris, call her. We'll do it the traditional way."

McKinley's voice clicked off as Carter and Wilson said "roger" together.

Taking off from the trees, McKinley was glad that he'd chosen a position so near to the shopping center. He jogged across the road just shy of the pedestrian crossing, eliciting a squeal of brakes and rasp of horn from a taxi, and quickly ascended the four widely spaced tiers of steps up to the shopping center's main level. He was surrounded by the crowd, making it hard to pick anyone out. Many already had phones stuck to their heads.

Why hadn't that idiot drawn the conversation out longer? McKinley scowled as he looked anxiously about. If Bacon called again Carter would have to recalibrate and the contact would probably get suspicious, so the opportunity had been wasted. It was intensely frustrating that this woman who could lead them to Erbakan was probably nearby yet remained incognito.

Wilson set off running, the gear stashed in a madly bouncing shoulder pack. From his position, perched on the eastern ridge, the route was straightforward and gravity was on his side. He just had to pass between accommodation complexes, then down two lengthy flights of steps and he'd be there.

Again holding the phone between ear and shoulder, Carter took the Evalia down the considerably more complex route of vehicular thoroughfares. Sweeping around a counter-clockwise hairpin bend, he heard ringtone. On his right, the golden sand of the beach reflecting the amber floodlights made it look as though the volcano had come out of retirement for one last hurrah.

"Hazard to Tripod, got ringtone," coughed Carter as he wove rapidly down the serpentine road.

"Roger."

Suddenly a human shape flashed into the headlights and Carter slammed on the brakes with a screech. There was an impact and a wail. Shaken, Carter looked up to see a man lolling in the road, clutching his left thigh and yelling what must be obscenities. What the hell language was that? Swedish? The man started getting up, not seriously hurt but seriously pissed off. Carter searched his memory for a moment then yelled "*jag är så hemskt ledsen, förlåt mig!*" out of the window before steering around the staggering pedestrian and accelerating again.

In the shopping center McKinley's eyes darted about. So many people were thronging the mall that it would be hard to locate one person on a satellite phone, and the only giveaway would be that most such devices were a bit bigger than their terrestrially networked counterparts. Above him, signs boldly announcing pizza, cosmetics and cocktails flooded the area with a sickly sweet glimmer as his head swivelled.

"She's not picking up," crackled Carter's voice in his ear.

"Roger that," said McKinley mechanically. She probably wouldn't answer an anonymous caller with a blocked number. That was a setback, but at least he'd be able to see someone looking at their phone and going through the actions of rejecting the call. Girls of every nationality swam around him in revealing bikinis whilst their drunken boyfriends laughed raucously in shiny soccer shorts, their surplus tops tied around their necks or hanging from their elastic swathed waists. The more mature walked around the periphery, letting the exuberant teenagers do their boisterous thing down the middle of the esplanade.

"Bollocks," he heard Carter exclaim. "She don't wanna talk."

McKinley swore under his breath, turning again and seeing Wilson start to climb the steps.

"Hi there big fella," came a Scottish accent from behind.

McKinley half glanced at the woman. "Push off," he grunted dismissively, turning away.

"You looking for—?"

"Piss off!"

"Hey, I'm just trying to help!" she bleated.

Both accent and phrase caught his attention. Who or what did this woman imagine he was looking for and how could she possibly help? McKinley looked again. "I'm sorry?" he said, eyes narrowed.

"No worries," she shrugged, offering her hand and a toothy, apologetic smile. "I'm Annie. Annie Grainger." She was tanned and statuesque, yet with almost no figure. Built straight up and down, thought McKinley. Her eyes seemed a little too big for her almond-shaped face and had a half asleep look to them, whilst her brown hair was a mess of blonde highlights and cropped short, encircled by a headband that matched her dress. McKinley judged her to be in her forties and a midriff bulge on her strikingly skinny frame suggested motherhood. A tattoo on her left shoulder read 'Live Fast, Die Young', whilst on the opposite side a long, sinuous snake spiralled down her upper arm. Annie carried a denim blue leatherette purse like a baby ball-and-chain, its single strap tethering her left wrist and her telephone snuggled into an elasticated pouch at its side. She was about the same height as McKinley and wore a diaphanous wrap-around garment of pastel shades that looked like a bed sheet yet was without doubt fashionably expensive. McKinley grinned internally; someone somewhere was lying on a bare mattress laughing their ass off.

"Hi," repeated McKinley a little warily, withholding the customary grip. Hopefully she would think his earpiece was simply a Bluetooth model as its designers had intended. He watched out of the corner of his eye as Wilson casually joined a group smoking outside a nearby bar, where he started to peruse the colourful society magazines on a rotating stand outside the next shop. He obviously thought that this Grainger woman was the contact.

"You just look like you're searching for something," she said hopefully. "Hey, what about this suicide bomber thing in London eh? You seen it?"

"I know, right?" answered McKinley as though it was shocking. He smirked at the irony and shook her hand. "I'm Ian. That's a familiar accent you've got there."

Annie smiled again, cranking the flirt level up a couple of notches. "Yours too. Where are you from?"

"Kirriemuir," replied McKinley. He'd have preferred to rush the woman away and get on with business, but he didn't want to act suspiciously. "You?"

"Lossiemouth. Know it?"

McKinley had flown missions from RAF Lossiemouth. "Near that big airfield with all the jets?" he asked innocently.

"Yeah, we're practically neighbours," beamed the woman, touching McKinley's chest nonchalantly as though removing a foreign particle. "You looking for a good time?"

If by 'neighbours' you mean more than seventy miles, and if by 'good time' you mean the contact for one of the most notorious weapons dealers in Europe, then I guess we are, he thought.

The nagging disappointment that the night's investigations were going to be a bust had goaded McKinley since the first call attempt had fallen flat. If they tried again to trace the Turk's ladyfriend it would require another call from Bacon and that would look mighty suspicious. So would another attempt from one of their own phones. It could blow the whole deal before it was even off the ground. McKinley thought fast. What to do? They had port records to fall back on in the hope of tracking any Turkish registered traffic, but that wasn't going to happen at this hour. Tonight's efforts were wasted. Better get the gear back to the apartment and lock it down, thought McKinley. I suppose we can see if there's any gossip going round. Open Source Intelligence, he pondered. I really hate that term.

McKinley smiled quizzically, an eyebrow raised. "What kind of good time?"

"Anything you like," Grainger said with a cheery wink. "We've got some great clubs here. Girls, boys, booze..." She looked about, not wanting to be overheard, then lowered her voice. "Snow, mandy, percos; whatever you're into." She shrugged, her eyes rolling playfully, and repeated "anything you like."

Blimey, thought McKinley, she's a bloody pimp, and I probably shouldn't tell her how many international drug traffickers I've busted.

Observing his facial response, to the like of which she was clearly no stranger, Grainger quickly added "I'm a *club promoter*. I match people with the kind of clubs they'll enjoy."

"Oh right." McKinley stepped over to where Wilson was trying to appear interested in the people pages. "Willy, this is Annie, she's going to show us where to find some nightlife." Dipping his head subtly toward his team-mate, he whispered "stand down."

Wilson looked up dubiously and said "hi", fingering the corner of a magazine, the cover of which featured a glamorous female celebrity who couldn't have appeared more different than the lanky club promoter.

Grainger looked down at the flashy periodical. "You a fan of the Kardashians?" she asked pleasantly.

Wilson smiled politely, shaking his head. "I don't watch Star Trek."

She turned back to McKinley, conveying bemusement with knitted brow and curled lip.

McKinley shrugged. "Well Annie, fit us up," he said.

Carter was slightly miffed at having to ferry the gear back to their apartment but as usual he did what was required without complaint and made his way on foot back to the center of town. The inevitable walk back up those endless flights of concrete steps would sober him up if necessary.

He found his team-mates seated outside a sports bar where the British soccer fans within were cheering Liverpool's match against Aston Villa. Their new friend was regaling them with all the carnal temptations that Puerto Rico could offer, trying to establish where their interests lay. Bloody hell, thought Carter, this could get us into some *right* trouble.

He walked up as McKinley and Wilson simultaneously finished their beers and Grainger got to her feet.

"Look," she said, "I've got to do my rounds eh? Meet with the owners. Why don't you tag along and see if you find somewhere you like?"

McKinley looked up at Carter, easily detecting his friend's subtle frown at having missed out on the first *cerveza* of the night. "Sounds good," he said. The four of them set off, leaving payment on the table.

The first venue was a passable attempt at a traditional British pub owned by a burly lad called Lee, who didn't seem to welcome their guide with any enthusiasm, although the Birkenhead native shook their hands courteously and spread a brace of thimble glasses on the bar before them. He liberally poured a dark red liquor. A lot of the drink fell outside the glasses but Lee didn't seem at all concerned, telling them in bad Spanish to drink up while he and Grainger went to talk business in an office at the other end of the bar.

"Cheers," said McKinley, hoisting the tiny glass to his lips. "Down the hatch."

"Bloody hell this stuff's strong," exclaimed Carter. "It's got to be what? Fifty percent? No more for me, thanks."

"I like it." McKinley replaced his glass. "What about you?" he asked, looking at Wilson.

Wilson touched the drink to his lips and was pleasantly surprised. It was lusciously sweet with an orange tang, tasting like a mix of marmalade, chocolate and honey. He tipped the rest into his mouth and his senses came alive. It was one of the most amazing things he'd ever savoured.

He smiled broadly. "Delicious!"

The sweetness of the moment was shattered by Lee swearing aggressively at Grainger and telling her to leave in thoroughly misanthropic terms. They filed outside, but not before Wilson had polished off the rest of the miniature shot glasses.

The story was the same at the next three venues: a noisy dance club with smoke machines and lasers, a sixties and seventies disco for the mature-but-lively crowd, and a Mexican styled bar. Grainger would introduce them and out would come the cluster of tiny glasses and the strong liquor – obviously a Canarian tradition for greeting newcomers. McKinley and Carter seemed disinclined to imbibe but, whatever the drink was, Wilson loved it and couldn't get enough. Again, Grainger's meetings with management ended tensely and they started to wonder what kind of promoter she could be.

When they arrived at The Pink Puffin the music consisted of danced-up cover versions of chart songs whilst pictures of icons such as Lady Gaga, Madonna, Freddie Mercury, Cher and Boy George shared the walls with shirtless male models and rainbow banners. The light blue suited owner, an overly tanned, blond-dyed New Zealander by the name of Brent, welcomed them kindly and strew thimble glasses in front of them just as the others had.

"Drink up boys," he adjured them pleasantly.

"Brent," ventured Wilson, "what's with the name?"

"Huh?"

"The Pink Puffin. How d'you come up with that?"

Brent's top teeth projected over his lower lip as he giggled like Betty Rubble. "Dope it out, dag," he grinned, giving Wilson a hearty slap on the shoulder before waltzing into a back room with Grainger.

"Yeah, go figure," murmured Carter.

"Is this a gay bar?" asked McKinley, looking concerned.

Carter rolled his eyes. "Oh you think?"

Wilson was again tipping the delicious alcoholic nectar between his lips.

"Hey big lad," said McKinley, "steady on."

Wilson blinked hard. Honesty propelled him to admit that McKinley was offering good advice. He was getting more dizzy than he'd have expected.

"'M okay," he replied, slurring a little.

Alerted by a gentle buzz, Carter pulled out his smartphone. "Bacon," he said.

McKinley looked over. "What's he want now?"

Carter shrugged, pushing his chair back.

"How d'you live with that old brick?" lambasted McKinley with a sneer, taking out his own phone and wobbling it between thumb and forefinger. "It's the size of a house. My phone's new... slim... *sexy.*"

"Mickey," grinned Carter, "*you know* any line of reasoning with 'slim' and 'sexy' in the same sentence ain't gonna work on me." With this Carter rose from the table and went out to take the call without having to compete against the club's booming sound system.

No sooner had their weapons tech vacated his place at the table than it was filled by another man who seemed to slide onto the stool as though on rails. He was moderately tall with an impressive but tidy mop of dark brown hair and striking features. His gaze shone beneath the well defined eyebrows of an elegant A-list actor from a handsome face that appeared both youthful and thoroughly lived-in at the same time. He was smartly dressed with a short-sleeved mauve collared shirt and black jeans that looked fresh from the shop. His left wrist bore a small black watch with narrow leather strap whilst a gold chain encircled his right.

"Hi," said the man in a North American accent. "You're new here."

"Just visiting," answered McKinley bluntly. They didn't need a spare.

"I'm Jimmy. I live here."

"You from America?" asked Wilson, still blinking.

"Canada," replied Jimmy.

"Canada!" repeated Wilson a little incoherently. "We were in Canada a few weeks ago."

Oh bloody hell, thought McKinley, the drunken idiot's going to get us in shit somehow. He was about to censure Wilson when Jimmy burst out in delirious surprise.

"No freakin' way! Whereabouts?"

"Sasquatch... ewan," said Wilson.

Jimmy lit up like one of the gaudy neon signs adorning The Pink Puffin's exterior. "You're shittin' me!" he squealed with even more emphasis. "I'm from Saskatchewan!" He put his hand gently on Wilson's back. "Oh, you've got the build of a forces man." He looked for a moment at McKinley, then in the direction of Carter's exit. "In fact you've all got that look."

Wilson's face registered intoxicated surprise. "We've what?"

McKinley was getting pissed off with this overly affectionate Canuck who was in imminent danger of getting his lights punched out. "I guess you've got some experience with sailors then," he sniped.

Jimmy brushed it off with ease, his defences not even remotely dented. "Oh yeah," he replied airily, "I'm a cruising missile." With a grin and wink at McKinley he patted Wilson's back, although it was more of a rubbing action. He leaned and spoke into the combat specialist's ear. "You need a drink. BRB."

"Well that's, sure, yeah, thanks," said Wilson, avoiding McKinley's dog-eye.

As Jimmy went off to the bar, Carter dashed back in. He gave a quick, puzzled glance in the direction of the retreating Canadian then spoke to McKinley.

"Bacon!" he hissed. "The bloody idiot's calling her back."

"What? Why?!"

"Stupid bastard wouldn't be told. Thinks he's helping."

McKinley winced, growling "he's gonna wreck this!"

"Here, you talk to—" Carter's mouth slammed shut and he looked up as Annie exited the back room followed closely by Brent, who seemed no happier than her other clients but wasn't making such a song and dance about it. She stopped briefly at the bar and exchanged a couple of words with Jimmy. Then a telephone rang and Grainger reached for her purse. She fiddled for a moment to extract the gadget then eyed its display.

McKinley and Carter looked at each other nervously as Annie answered. "Kyle?" they heard her say. "What's up now?"

McKinley squinted as though in pain, his lips drawn wide in a grimace. "Shit!" he whispered.

Annie walked out into the concourse, the telephone glued to her ear, talking Spanish. Mentally, McKinley kicked himself up the ass. They'd been hunting for the bloody contact but *she* had found *them*.

Carter leaned across the table and said "damn it! We are *so* blown!"

"She's the contact," mumbled Wilson, blinking too much and licking his lips.

Both McKinley and Carter glanced at him contentiously. Wilson took the hint and rotated his head back to the projection screen with its distracting music video. Bloody hell, was that liquor *ever* strong, and he was really feeling it. Where did that friendly Jimmy go?

Thinking hard, McKinley hissed at Carter. "She'll know something's up. And she can ID us. We've got to change the game."

"How?"

McKinley gesticulated in emphasis. "She's not going to lead three *tourists* to a bloody arms dealer is she? If we try to question her she'll rumble us and leg it."

"We could remove her," said Carter without thinking.

"You mean like those poor... two poor bastards in Canada?" slurred Wilson far too loud. "You'll just kill anyone, won't you?!"

"Hey, he pretty much saved the world a few weeks ago," snapped McKinley. "You wanna shut up?!" Wilson was so caked that he was in danger of ruining everything. McKinley turned to Carter. "And you!"

Jimmy seemed to materialise by the table, an ornate glass in each hand. Looking at Wilson, he trilled "I think someone needs a little pick-me-up."

The last thing he needs, thought McKinley, looking intently at the drinks, is to be picking you up.

Jimmy put a glass in front of Wilson and placed his hand on the young man's neck. With a friendly squeeze and a raised eyebrow at the others, he said "this'll help."

McKinley was getting mad. "Piss off Liberace!" he snarled.

"Someone's got a frownie face," cooed Jimmy, eyes rolling.

"You'll get a bloody *smashed* face if you don't get lost!" retorted McKinley, rising from his chair.

Wilson looked angry, the drink stopping in the air just in front of his mouth. "Hey, don't—!"

Carter closed his eyes for a moment and shook his head.

"Leave him alone!" glared Wilson as McKinley looked at Jimmy with violence in his eyes.

The team leader lashed out with his left hand, sending Wilson's drink flying from his grip. Wilson swore and jumped up. McKinley strode around the table, grabbing Jimmy's shirt and tearing it away from its collar. The Canadian raised his arm in defence as McKinley drew his fist back to deliver a punishing blow. Wilson pushed himself between them, ready to strike McKinley, whose arm Carter held back.

"*That's enough!*" barked the weapons tech. Everyone in the bar was watching.

"You asshole!" shouted Wilson. "He's just being friendly!"

"With drugs in your drink?!"

"*Bullshit!*"

McKinley got right in Wilson's face. "*Eff you!*"

"Let's go," said Carter firmly, pulling McKinley by the arm he was still holding. A bar-fight and the possible involvement of local law enforcement was the last thing they needed.

Annoyed as hell, McKinley let Carter lead him outside into the warmth and comparative peace of the island night. Around them the crowd chattered, smoked or made their way to the next watering hole. With a pensive expression on her face Grainger completed the call with Bacon and excused herself, brushing past them to re-enter The Pink Puffin. She glanced back momentarily with a very worried look.

Carter let go of McKinley's arm. "I saw the floaties in his drink."

"Could've been *anything*," spat McKinley. "Poison, drugs... *Shit!* Stupid bastard."

"*So?*" Carter was aghast. "We gonna rescue him or what?"

"No!" insisted McKinley angrily. "Serves him right! If that puff wants a bit of Willy he can bloody have it."

"You could've phrased that better," observed Carter, raising an eyebrow. He lowered his voice. "What if it *is* something worse than a roofie colada?"

"He's a big lad," replied McKinley nastily. "He can look out for himself."

Carter's eyes conveyed disbelief. "So you're just going to let this happen to teach him a lesson? *Seriously?!*"

McKinley's expression was the nadir of indifference. "Bloody right."

"What about protecting your team-mate?!"

"Sod him!"

Carter let out a grinding sigh, his shoulders drooping. McKinley's anger was just as blinding to the team leader as drunkenness was to Wilson and, until it dissipated, Carter knew that any argument he made would be null and void. He wanted to grab their drunken team-mate and leave, but at the same time he didn't dare risk a public punch-up. And McKinley had a valid point: allowing your drink to get tampered with was the height of stupidity, *especially* in their line of work.

Bothered by the depth of his rage at Wilson, McKinley turned away from the club and started walking, leaving Carter bemused. He pulled out a cigarette and lit up.

"Let's go," McKinley said through a cloud of exhaled smoke.

005: The Meeting

SLAP!

The chilly liquid hit him like a ballistic impact. Shocked awake, Wilson choked and spluttered, coughing up strange tasting water and shaking his head, then regretting the motion as a severe headache claimed the center of his attention, immediately disenthroned by an enraged shout.

"*Wake up shit for brains!*"

Blinking fluid out of his eyes, he saw McKinley tossing the empty vase onto the other bed and narrowly missing Carter, who was sitting on its edge, ankles crossed and arms folded. Wilson realised that he was lying on his own bed, which was now sopping wet. His stomach seemed to be a dark cavity of nausea and he felt weak. The room continued to come into focus.

"We need to talk!" snapped the team leader, clearly livid. Wilson got his breath back and nodded. Bloody hell, did he ever feel like shit, and now it looked like he was in for a bollocking.

"Never, ever, EVER again!" barked McKinley. "Don't *EVER* get blind drunk like that when we're on mission!"

"Hey, screw you!" croaked Wilson in pique, ready to defend himself. On mission? The bloody mission had been postponed. "You said—!"

"Shut up!" snapped McKinley, jaw set, lips pulled back in a furious sneer and finger trembling just centimeters from Wilson's face. "This is NOT a discussion! This is *me* tearing *you* a new one! I never get pissed out my brains when there's work to do!" He thrust an outstretched finger toward Carter. "Neither does he. You don't see *us* getting trashed and picked up by a bloody queer, do you?! You were so pissed up you didn't even notice he dropped some shit in your drink!"

A memory appeared as if unveiled in Wilson's aching head. *Oh my freakin' goodness*, he thought, did this really happen? Yes it did; he could remember the man's face. His name was Jimmy wasn't it? Canadian fella. The rest of the memories were more of a blur than he was remotely comfortable with and there were worryingly few. What the hell couldn't he remember? He'd blacked out. There was something in the drink? Oh *CRAP*...

"Look, I don't give a shit what you do in your private life, but NOT on mission! Not with some damn cocoa-shunter! If that's your thing just keep it away from me! D'you realise what could've happened to you?! You could've been *compromised!* Or poisoned! When you pull irresponsible shit like that it's no wonder it took you so long to get promoted!"

That was bloody unfair. Wilson lifted his head and was about to protest but thought better of it.

"I bet you don't even know how you got back here! But right now there's just two things I want to hear," prompted the wrathful Scotsman.

Wilson tried his voice. "Sorry?"

"Sorry what?!"

"Sir... sorry, Corporal." Damn it, why was it taking him so long to get used to his new rank?

"And the second?"

Wilson thought for a moment. His guts were churning and the headache was a blinder. He lowered his bonce back onto the soggy pillow. "It'll never happen again."

"Two for two," ground McKinley unpleasantly. "Adequate. You're bloody lucky you're alive. Now get your shit straight. We'll be back in a bit." With this he turned and started for the door.

"Uh, Mickey," prompted Carter, his finger raised, "the other side of the story?"

McKinley span, looking at Carter as though he was equally guilty. "*What?!*"

"That was the shit; how about the sandwich?"

"Oh... aye, right." McKinley moved back toward Wilson, whose prone body he overshadowed as if to threaten. Again the finger sought its target.

"I was gonna kick you right out of this team. Dismissed, gone, demoted, bloody game over. Back to the BC regiment. You don't think this shit's serious? I was gonna make the call. But then *he* found *this* in your pocket." McKinley held up a small piece of folded paper.

"What's that?" said Wilson.

Sneering unpleasantly, McKinley dropped the piece of paper onto Wilson's chest and turned to Carter. "Sort him out," he ordered.

As McKinley shut the back door hard behind him Wilson sighed heavily. He'd thought that Carter was the one with anger issues. He rubbed his eyes for a moment, increasing his disorientation slightly, then propped himself up on his left elbow and took the paper, unfolding it between thumb and forefinger. There were a pair of Canarian telephone numbers on it. The first was accompanied by a line of handwritten text that said '*call me! Jimjam*' after which there was a huge smiley face with hearts for its eyes. Great, thought Wilson, as worry about the forgotten events of the night swelled like an incoming roller on the ocean.

The second set of numerals, though, was more interesting. It was another Canarian number and this time the text—also in what was presumably Jimmy's writing—said '*Annie home*'.

Carter sat forward on the edge of the opposite bed and smiled. "Your lost night wasn't a total loss."

Wilson sighed. "Can you track her?"

"Already done." Carter swivelled his eyes to indicate the laptop sitting on the kitchen table. "Address, personal details, Facebook friends, passport... the works."

"No shit." Wilson was still in turmoil from his rude awakening, the telling-off and the many unanswered questions he suddenly had to consider. He felt compelled to audit the incoming data. "Look, Chris, d'you think he was serious? About getting me demoted?"

"Why're you asking me? It was his rant."

"You didn't discuss it?"

Carter huffed. "I already got ranted at, if that's what you mean."

"Oh. Why—?"

"Anyway," launched Carter, moving eagerly on, "I got something for ya." With this he lifted himself from the bedside and strode into the kitchen area. Wilson blinked, sighed and gently shook his aching head, imagining his liver sitting on the side of the bed smoking a cigarette and asking what the hell he'd done to it.

Carter returned a moment later with a loaded tray holding bottles and jars of diverse shapes and colours. He set it down on the white plastic nightstand and sat on the edge of Wilson's bed.

"I don't have the kit to figure out what that guy slipped you, but—"

"*Oh bloody hell,*" groaned Wilson. How could he have let that happen? But didn't McKinley smash the drink? Did I actually stay and have *another*, Wilson asked himself worriedly. *I am a bloody stupid idiot.* No wonder the haggis hunter's freakin' boiling over.

"Yeah, there was stuff floating it." Carter seemed much less perturbed than their colleague. "I'm guessing it was GHB because it wore off quickly. But this," he indicated the tray, "is for the hangover."

Wilson frowned. It was a full tray.

Carter pointed to the various containers. "We've got paracetamol, honey, brewers yeast, sports drinks, eggs and water – *lots* of water."

Wilson counted two bottles of the latter, two liters each. "You want me to drink all that?"

"Dehydration mate. Plus flushing all the crap out of your system, balancing your electrolytes and so on. Don't worry; it's all good stuff. You'll feel much better."

"Thanks," said Wilson, as there were several horn blasts from upstairs.

Carter rolled his eyes. "He's playing my tune. See ya later." The weapons tech rose from the bed, tucked his shirt into his trousers and opened the back door to leave.

"Chris," called Wilson.

"What?"

"D'you know what happened last night? I mean, d'you think—?"

Carter dismissed it with a wave of his hand. "I don't know, I don't need to know, and if I did I wouldn't judge. Stuff happens."

With a cheery smile Carter shut the door and Wilson heard him climbing the stairwell. Might as well start with the eggs, he thought, then a shower. Bloody *hell* I feel stupid.

The cop's English wasn't very good. McKinley switched to the native tongue.

"We can talk in Spanish if you like. We're both fluent."

He, Carter and the policeman sat in a dull brick walled cubicle in the tiny police station. The room could hardly be described as an office yet bore all the trademarks of one with a desk, two telephones, dual filing cabinets, a computer terminal and a barely used bookcase. A narrow window looked out on the town, its hardly adequate illumination augmented by a double fluorescent tube spanning almost all of the ceiling. The cop himself was visually more interesting, built like a bull with a smooth, bronze complexion and dark brown eyes beneath bushy eyebrows. Whilst he seemed endowed with black hair on almost every square centimeter of his skin, that on his head was tightly cropped to within millimeters of his scalp. Laughter lines around the cop's eyes gave him the appearance of being the kind of man who'd enjoy a joke, but there was nothing funny about today's encounter.

He scowled across the neatly organised desk at the COAST operatives, a pair of tough looking foreigners that were causing him a huge bloody headache. "Which of you is..." he peered at the sheet of paper in front of him. "Peter Webster?"

"That's the third member of our group, sir," answered McKinley. "He's not well this morning. Food poisoning. We left him at the apartment."

"The vehicle was rented in his name."

No, thought McKinley, it's rented in the name on the passport. "That's right," he nodded, "but we're all driving it."

The cop snorted angrily. Were they trying to be evasive? "One of you hit a pedestrian yesterday evening on *Avenue de la Cornisa*. A Swedish tourist. Do you admit this?"

McKinley groaned inside. Well done, Chris, you bloody stupid sod. Having learned they were being summoned to the cop shop he'd already dealt Carter a large dose of grief, but there was an increasing chance of a repeat performance.

Carter nodded to the *policía*. "I was driving. It wasn't my fault. He stepped out in front of me without warning. The vehicle grazed him and I made sure he was okay before leaving the scene."

The officer's face hardened further. "He says you were driving very fast and that you didn't stop."

"That's not true," repudiated Carter, his poker face set to eleven.

"His companions say the same thing."

Carter held up his hands, shrugging. "That's understandable, but it's not true. I suppose he didn't mention that I apologised and offered to help, did he?"

The policeman had heard all this bullshit before and he didn't need it. Damned tourists arguing about who did what to who and how, except that these two and their absent colleague obviously weren't tourists. He leaned back in his chair, angrily considering his response to the *dos extranjeros*. The information that was completely absent from his inquiry with Interpol might have hinted at more than the data itself, and he was prohibited from pursuing their prosecution. But he sure as hell wouldn't let this lie.

"I know that you work for the English government," he sneered, "and that you're here to hunt a terrorist."

McKinley nodded. "That's right."

The cop spread his hands wide, mocking in his tone. "That's all they will tell me. I don't suppose you'd care to fill in the blanks."

McKinley tried to tread carefully. "No sir, I'm sorry; there's a lot that we're not permitted to discuss. But you should understand that we're on the same team." McKinley's finger oscillated back and forth between him and the Spaniard. "You serve and protect; so do we. We've got no interest in causing you any problems."

Fuming, the officer tipped his head slightly to one side and growled. "But you already did! This Swede; he wants to press charges. His *advokat* is bugging me hourly. My superiors are telling me to prosecute you regardless. So you're making me some big problems already!"

McKinley could see where this was heading; the man was a parochial law enforcement officer stuck between a rock and a hard place but wanting to defend his jurisdiction like a castle. "I'm sorry," he said. "It certainly won't happen again."

The cop leaned forward, putting his elbows on the desk and grunting "you're so right." He stood to reinforce his presence, not knowing how thoroughly wasted this gesture would be on McKinley and Carter. Putting on his most magisterial face, he snarled "I'm going to be watching you, watching everything that you do. You put a single foot out of line, you make the smallest mess in my yard and I'll arrest all three of you and have you sent back to England on the first jet. Do you understand?"

McKinley just wanted to be done with this crap and get back to work. "Yes, understood."

The cop, lip still curled in anger, nodded sharply in the direction of the door. "I'm going to get pictures of you and your passport details; then you can get out of my sight."

Feeling guilty, Wilson had thoroughly cleaned the apartment when McKinley and Carter returned. He heard their heavy steps descending the stairwell and tried to appear nonchalant.

Throwing the door open, Carter took a quick glance around and said "you've tidied up. Did you feel guilty or something?"

Great, thought Wilson sarcastically, I'm that transparent.

McKinley pushed Carter through the doorway and looked right at their younger colleague.

"You," he growled, the same accusatory finger as earlier assuming its familiar pose, "time to go to work. Walking involved."

Wilson was both surprised and wary, considering the earlier fireworks. "Me?"

McKinley started opening a bag of gear. "*We* can't; the local plod's pissed off and they're following us." McKinley looked up at Wilson, noting his enquiring look, and thrust the finger at Carter. "His fault." He paused. "But they don't know what *you* look like. That makes *us* a diversion."

There was an electronic chime ringing with distortion like the jingle of an old ice cream van and Annie Grainger rolled over, exposing her naked back and legs to the downdraft of the big ceiling fan. She peered at the clock radio, seeing that it was just before midday. Who the hell was it? She wrapped the unused sheet roughly around her slender nakedness and stumbled over the cold tiles to the door, glancing around for her cigarettes.

The tiny LCD security monitor revealed the tall, auburn-haired young man from last night, the one who'd had too much and left with Jimmy, standing outside. He appeared to be wearing tight brown shorts, a multi-coloured Hawaiian shirt over his impressive physique, and cheap plastic shades. Grainger swore, wondering what the hell he was doing there. She found her packet of *Fortunas* on the kitchen counter and quickly ignited one.

Annie put her head up to the heavy wooden door, the cigarette dangling from the corner of her mouth like a broken twig. "What?"

"Hi, Annie?"

"What do you want?"

Wilson tried to be as pleasant as possible as he stood in the heat, feeling like a twit in the cheerful outfit. "Sorry to disturb you. It's Willy. We met last night. Jimmy gave me your address. I wonder if I could talk to you please?"

"What about?" She didn't need this crap. And why was that maple-sucking bendy-boy giving out her address anyway? She made a mental note to send Jimmy a stinging text message.

His voice sounded sorrowful, like he was pleading for help. "Uh, can I come in please? It's kinda personal."

Personal? Crikey, she thought, what did Jimmy do to you? Smirking at the vulgar idea, she pulled the sheet a bit tighter and unsnibbed the brass-handled cylinder lock, curls of smoke fluorescing in the shaft of intense sunlight as the door opened.

Smiling sheepishly, Wilson stepped into the dark apartment, noting a similarly economical approach to both construction and furnishings that he'd seen in their own. Three quarters of the roughly square space was lounge, bedroom and kitchen, with a double bed in the far right corner by the patio doors and a simple seating area on the left, surrounding a big television on its corner stand made of cheap laminate. To the immediate left was the windowless bathroom whilst the kitchenette formed the nearest corner at the right.

"So what's on your mind?" said Grainger, pushing the cigarette more firmly into her mouth and blinking as the smoke invaded her eyes. She turned away from Wilson, holding the sheet with her elbows.

Wilson brought the compact stun gun disguised as a phone into contact with her back. Grainger gave a pained squeak and collapsed to the floor, her body quaking as her discombobulated nervous system reacted to the high voltage shock.

Wilson brought his radio out of his pocket.

"Shadow to Tripod, I'm in."

"Roger Shadow. We're under the deck."

Wilson walked past the incapacitated woman and approached the floor-to-ceiling glass doors which were just like those installed in their own suite. He pulled back the orange curtains, revealing the small balcony beyond. Grainger's place was built against a much steeper slope than theirs, rendering the typically angled construction of such complexes impossible. Wilson opened the sliding door and gave Carter a hand as he hoisted himself over the railings.

"Thanks," said Carter, pushing past Wilson and making his way to Grainger, who was struggling, squid-like, to raise herself up. Carter lifted her easily and explained that he wasn't going to hurt her. She moaned unintelligibly.

Wilson grabbed McKinley's arm to steady the team leader as his boots found the concrete balcony. "Still being tailed?" Wilson asked, wary of what his colleague's response might be.

"Aye," answered McKinley dryly, leaning on the railing and nodding his head down the incline to where their vehicle was parked by the *taberna* from which their exit had been by the back door. Not far beyond was what appeared to be a car in police livery, but much smaller than usual. The tough thicket that covered the steep slope had obscured their climb.

"That's *never* a Smart Car?" frowned Wilson.

McKinley didn't look up. "Not even. It's a Renault Twizy. You could outrun it."

"Crikey."

McKinley's expression didn't waiver. "Bloody cop's got it in for us. We took every turn trying to lose the prat." With this McKinley pushed past and headed inside. "He's tenacious, I'll give him that."

Wilson saw that Carter had laid Grainger on her bed and was tying her wrists and ankles. He'd taped her mouth shut and covered her with a couple of sheets to preserve what little modesty he might. She was still a bit disorientated, but getting over it fast and yelling in anger through the tape.

Once Carter was done, McKinley sat on the bed next to her and produced his FN Herstal Five-seveN, pushing its sound suppresser hard into her temple. She stiffened with fear and the yelling stopped instantly.

"Don't make a *sound*," ordered McKinley, and pulled the tape off her mouth. She looked back with terrified but somewhat defiant eyes.

McKinley started with instructions, his face like stone and his tone implacably solemn. "First of all, you keep quiet unless directly questioned. Secondly, if you try *anything* stupid you'll just die, so don't. Thirdly," he tipped his head sideways at Carter, "he won't hurt you, but I definitely will, if I have to. You got it?"

Grainger nodded carefully, breathing hard.

"Where's Erbakan?!" barked McKinley.

Shocked again, the woman shook her head.

"Speak up," snarled McKinley. "I can't hear you."

"I don't know!" she pleaded. "I never met him!"

McKinley glared. "Fairy tales."

"*I've never met him!*" she repeated. "I don't know what he looks like, where he lives or anything!"

"Bullshit!" snapped McKinley. "You're his contact!"

"Uh-uh," she disagreed, her eyes wide. "I'm just the first call!"

"So you *are* a contact," said McKinley, his eyes drilling into hers. "Okay. You're going to set us up. Arrange a meeting; two new buyers. Big money."

"I can't!" she said desperately, her eyebrows knitted and biting her lower lip.

McKinley's face tightened into a humourless smile. "You *will.*"

"Please!" she spat, "I don't arrange the meetings, I just call another guy! He'll know something's wrong! He *never* meets new clients!"

"Really?"

"You have to see another man who decides who meets him."

McKinley frowned. "Decides how?"

"You have to be a customer already! Please! You think I *wanna* do this shit?!"

McKinley shared a quick glance with Carter and Wilson. He softened his tone just a hair. "So why d'you do it then?"

She shook her head. Her fear was starting to subside. "No! I can't tell *anyone!* If he finds out—!"

McKinley tapped on her skull with the pistol, bringing her to immediate silence. "Tell me now."

She moaned and clasped her eyes tight shut, swearing. Then she appeared to have a different thought and they snapped open. This time she was coy.

"Hey, who are you guys? Who d'you work for?"

McKinley sneered. "You don't get to ask questions."

"No, I mean... really, can you help me? Are you, like, MI6 or something?"

In the face of McKinley's silence, she took a chance. "Look, you want to get rid of him?" she blurted. "So do I! I hate those bastards! I just want to get out of here! Are you going to kill him?"

McKinley raised an eyebrow. "So, you *want* to help? Is that it?"

"I can!" She pushed herself up a little despite being tied. "Can you make a deal so I don't get put away? And protect my boys?"

McKinley huffed at her boldness, smiling slightly. The threads were coming together. "So he's threatening your kids. Where are they?"

"Back home. They're in a private school their dad pays for. They're okay but Erbakan's got me over a barrel. If I ever turned against him..." Now she looked intensely angry, and no wonder.

"You're not a club promoter, are you?" frowned McKinley sarcastically.

"It's a cover." She rolled her eyes. "I collect his protection money."

"Dual income," observed Carter. "That explains the reactions we saw last night."

"He just put the rates up," she nodded, and her expression darkened. "*Please* can you help me? I've got to get out of here! Please!"

Without a word McKinley stretched the tape back over the woman's mouth. Motioning with his head, he strode over to the bathroom and his colleagues followed.

Once inside the dimly lit, clammy little tiled room, McKinley spoke quietly. "You think she's for real?"

Carter's mouth twisted into a frown. "Probably playing both ends against the middle."

"Hmm. You?" McKinley looked at Wilson, his displeasure still obvious.

Wilson raised an eyebrow. "Back story should be easy enough to verify."

"On it," said Carter, pulling out his phone.

McKinley wagged a thoughtful finger. "Get me something on the kids."

"Rog."

Wilson continued, still keen to get back in McKinley's good books. "Why don't we talk to Bacon? He's an existing customer. He could fly down here and make the introduction."

McKinley's eyes took on a thoughtful look as he considered this. "Aye," he nodded. "As long as he doesn't get himself killed. Chris, any news?"

"Moments away from maximum discomfort."

"Right." McKinley swung open the bathroom door and let his team-mates out. They approached the bed where Grainger was looking more pissed off than afraid now. It was clear from her position that she'd been trying her bonds.

McKinley sat down on the edge of the bed and pointed an outstretched thumb back at Carter. "You should probably know he came first at knotting in the Scouts."

She scowled miserably but didn't try to speak. McKinley leaned over and pulled the tape back, more gently than before. Then, without looking away, he reached into her ashtray and took out a small object. Sniffing at the tiny roll of partly burned paper, he stated "we both know the police won't react well to *this.*"

She glared back defiantly, her eyes dark with suspicion. "I suppose that'll be the least of my worries."

"Aye." McKinley nodded, flicking the roach away. "You said Erbakan's got you over a barrel. That's changed now 'cause *I've* got you over a barrel." With this he angled his head at Carter.

"Benjamin and Timothy Milldean, fourteen and twelve. Rossall School, Fleetwood," read Carter. "Their dad, your ex Graham's the owner of Milldean Coachworks in York. They're both in Lugard house. Tim's good at sports, Ben likes acting and he's rehearsing '*The Thwarting Of Baron Bolligrew*' for Christmas. Their exam results—"

"Stop it!" she yelped. "How d'you bloody know *that* you creepy bastard?!"

Carter rolled his eyes. "Please," he grumbled.

"Doesn't matter," interjected McKinley. "Point is, our people can protect your kids... *or not.*" He paused for a moment to let this sink in, then brought the Five-seveN's silenced muzzle to the bridge of her nose. "I'll give you the benefit of the doubt for now. But if you screw me over, if you try anything remotely stupid, if you warn Erbakan or something... well, you see what I'm saying."

"*Bésame culo!*" she spat.

"You're welcome," said McKinley flatly. "I thought you *wanted* to help."

Bacon refused to travel in anything other than the first class section and insisted on being booked into the most expensive hotel at the resort, asserting that appearances were *so* important. He further asseverated that it was reasonable compensation for the fact that he was just about fouling his Calvin Kleins in fear at the thought of meeting and potentially angering the notorious Turk. However, the Londoner wafted into the airport's arrival lounge as though expecting a crowd of pubescent females to throw their underwear in greeting, and eschewed the proletarian Nissan Evalia in favour of the most ostentatious taxi into which his ego could be crammed.

Although narked at the gadget dealer, McKinley went along with his pretences for the sake of getting the job done. The importance of appearances was indeed a fact, but so was the explanation he'd have to provide later for bending his expense account. After Bacon's taxi had left, though, the team leader shepherded his crew into the island's main city of Las Palomas where they acquired the kind of clothing they'd need to create the right impression with a multi-millionaire arms dealer. This done, they travelled back to Puerto Rico and over a delicious gourmet lunch in Bacon's impressive suite they discussed the subterfuge and planned their moves.

Grainger, in the meantime, was supposed to be setting up the preliminary meeting which would be their next stepping stone to Erbakan, and by early afternoon the call came.

"We'll deal with the engine driver, thanks, not the greasy rag," said McKinley, his face like flint and his tone similarly unmoving. He hoped to hell that the contact hadn't noticed the police car outside, although he had to concede that the cops' presence might serve the notion of these sharply dressed Brits being known bad guys that were looking to source some hardware.

The corner booth in which they sat was large and comfortable, with velvet seating of a blue so dark as to be almost black. The nonagonal table was crystal clear glass a full inch thick with tiny blue LEDs mounted beneath to provide accents.

Were this a London club it would have been all oak and burgundy tufted carpet. The newspapers would have been delivered, the butler would have been summoned with a button and silence would be mandatory. But in the Canaries a gentleman's club so traditional would quickly have been out of business, so this was the local riff on such an establishment, with mirrors, marble bars, little paper umbrellas in the drinks and a somewhat more relaxed dress code. To dismiss confusion it was even named 'The Gentleman's Club', although the meretricious sign did nothing to distinguish it from other, less exclusive clubs in the eyes of potential clientele. The pair of muscle-bound doormen would take care of that.

At the far end of the big venue was a tidy, well illuminated stage on which a semi-clothed man and woman were performing simulated sex acts for the crowd which, with it being siesta time, consisted of just two wealthy looking middle-aged men at the bar, a younger suited man alone at a center table glued to his tablet computer, Bacon, TDR.12 and the man with whom they were meeting.

He sat opposite them, a leathery beast in an ill-fitting dark grey suit of inappropriately shiny material, with twisted, prominent teeth through which a voice like a bullfrog carried oddly generic eastern European speech with good English, making his exact origin difficult to determine. He was thin of face but with flabby features and a balding dome bearing short black hair. The pistol in his jacket could hardly have been more obvious. Already having necked two double shots he looked daggers at McKinley and responded angrily as Wilson—playing the bodyguard—stared back with intransigent malevolence.

"There is no *engine driver!* You deal with *me!*"

"All the same," added Carter firmly, "we're not here to waste time with lackeys. No *offence,*" he simpered, smiling falsely. "Tell your boss there's five million U.S. on the table... if he's hungry."

"I'm not... *hungry*," scoffed the contact. "What's five million? I don't need your business."

"You should," said Bacon a little too enthusiastically. "It's good business."

"Besides," said McKinley, pushing a small sheet of paper across the table, "you wouldn't want Erbakan knowing you turned business away, would you?" He tapped his index finger on the paper. "This is his personal email, isn't it? Gründel would be glad to take our money; I've only got to make the call. Or Kholitczyn."

The guy's eyes lowered to the sheet, rose back up to McKinley, then scanned the others thoughtfully. "You don't know where to find Kholitczyn," he asserted. "No-one does."

Apart from you I suppose, thought McKinley. "Doesn't matter," he replied. "When he smells this pay day, he'll find us."

The Slav thrust his jaw at Bacon and his manner became slightly more polite, obviously unwilling to deter an existing client. "Why aren't you making this deal? You can get anything you want."

Bacon shook his head hard, palms splayed. "I ain't a warmonger, alright? I just do tech; no weapons."

"I think it's a hard distinction to make, sometimes," said the contact, nodding slowly.

"Hey!" snapped McKinley, prodding at the piece of paper. "Are you going to contact your boss or am I?!"

The man's face flinched slightly, betraying anxiety. His eyes raked the four men again, then he nodded slowly. "I'll make a call," he rattled, "and we'll see. There's one question though; if you can deal with others, why come to me?"

"That's for us and Mister Erbakan to discuss," affirmed McKinley in such a patronising manner as to dissuade further inquiry. He admired the intermediary's determination to protect his employer but they weren't going to settle for the guard dog; they wanted the homeowner.

As the contact left the booth to use his telephone, Carter turned to Wilson and said "you're quiet."

"Bloody right," growled McKinley before Wilson could answer. "Stay like that."

Carter tapped quickly at his phone. At this range its inbuilt sensors might be able to pick up the call and prise open Erbakan's security a little more. McKinley, however, thrust his own device at Carter, saying "use this."

Without looking up, Carter took McKinley's phone and went through the process again. "Think I got 'em," he said presently. "Outgoing's a Thuraya—good job it's in GSM mode—the other's prefixed 90-538."

"Isn't that Turkcell?" queried Wilson.

Carter raised his eyebrows in approving surprise. "Good memory."

"His roaming bill must be up there," noted McKinley, reaching to retrieve his phone.

Wilson pointed at the handset as Carter passed it back. "I thought you don't like the new ones."

"I don't," said Carter. "But the receivers are more sensitive."

"You're a berk," snorted McKinley derisively. "You should be all over new tech, but you have to find fault wi' everything, don't you?"

Carter looked up. "I prefer to wait until the technology's matured. Hey, cavē!"

His Latin alerted them to the contact's return. The man strolled over to the table, pushing his telephone back into a pocket of the chintzy jacket. Addressing

McKinley, he said "be at the east pier, *Calle Puerto Base*, at 7:30, by the pirate boat."

Turning to their Londoner colleague, he nodded cordially and offered the valediction "Mister Bacon" before turning his back and leaving.

"Shit! I was hoping we'd meet here," said Bacon nervously, looking around the club.

"Aye, but I think you've got us into a much more exclusive joint," nodded McKinley approvingly. "Good lad."

The pirate boat turned out to be what looked like a small brigantine painted mostly in blue and rufous brown with gold ornamentation, fitted out for charter voyages on which tourists could drink, party, act irresponsibly with plastic swords and say "arrr" with bad Cornish accents and annoying frequency. The *Timanfaya*—named after the national park on the nearby island of Lanzarote—was moored by the long outer pier, a three hundred meter breakwater constructed of stone and concrete with a high wall to the seaward side and lined along the opposite with short mooring bollards and palm trees in stout white, blue-rimmed pots.

McKinley was keenly aware of the tiny Renault that had shadowed them to the harbour. He could only hope that the stupid cop had got it through his head that they were fighting for the same cause. It was a niggling complication and one that he could arrange to have removed—if proven completely necessary—by means either fair or foul, but whichever way it would only lead to more difficulties. The inquisitive cop's surveillance was something they'd have to put up with for the time being. Thankfully, the Twizy wasn't amphibious and the fact that the cop was keeping his distance seemed to suggest that he wasn't going to employ the *Guardia Civil* patrol boat moored just meters away.

Tourists strolled around the four men, their little cameras beeping and clicking as they entrusted the precious moments of their vacations to cheap memory cards. The COAST operatives were wearing shades for the obvious reason of all this photography, whilst Bacon wore his expensive Karl Lagerfelds simply because he could.

The tech dealer was in a fashionable black blazer of lightweight fabric with functionless epaulets, and a similarly dark but patterned shirt. His beige jeans, their material much more sturdy than the high street varieties, were held up by a brown leather belt of such thickness that its manufacture might have involved the demise of several cows. His somewhat teenage outfit was completed by a TAG Heuer *Formula 1* wristwatch and dark grey Balenciaga sneakers.

McKinley looked businesslike in a light grey jacket over a white collarless shirt with expensive black jeans and dark brown leather brogues, his Breitling *Aerospace* wristwatch copy being sufficiently well crafted to fool most observers. Carter's timepiece was a large, leather-strapped Swiss Legend *SL Pilot Chronograph* that appeared considerably more expensive than it was, whilst he was attired more casually in a dark green polo shirt, rust coloured shorts and the most flamboyant gold plated chains they could find on a budget. His feet were planted in Timberland field boots that matched his outfit.

Wilson was still every inch the bodyguard, all in black with impenetrable sunglasses. The obsidian shirt and suit emphasised his musculature and as long as he assumed a taciturn disposition he was unlikely to face questions.

'Shoes'—false passports—had been issued to TDR.12 in the cover names Andrew McKittrick, Craig Carver and Peter Webster, and each had memorised a convincing back story. Now all they needed was for Bacon to remember and stick to his own part of the plot.

A launch with a small forward wheelhouse approached the pier and they recognised their contact and two others in the rear of the small vessel. As the pilot brought it alongside, a younger man jumped onto the dock and his colleague threw him a thin nylon hawser, which he wrapped round one of the bollards a few times and held.

Gallina, barely big enough for the eight of them, came to rest and the contact man waved cheerfully, making it impossible not to notice how much his demeanour had changed.

"Ahoy there," he shouted. "Come aboard, come aboard!"

Ignoring the offered assistance, McKinley jumped down into the boat and thrust his hand toward the contact, wanting to assess whether the welcome was for real.

"So good to see you Mister McKittrick," beamed the big Slav as he shook. "I apologise for my rudeness earlier. I have to vet Mister Erbakan's visitors; I'm sure you understand. He does not normally meet new clients, but we made inquiries, and it seems you are men of some importance."

"Okay," responded McKinley flatly, turning deliberately toward the prow of the small vessel. The hours invested in creating a plausible back story hadn't been wasted after all and apparently, via his network, Vladimir Kholitczyn had followed his instructions to vouch for them.

Bacon was received with courtesy next, followed by Wilson, who made a point of looking nastily at their guide and his crew.

When Carter got on board he said "thank you. *Etoochen' krasivyy vecher.*"

"*Da eto,*" agreed the contact without thinking.

Yes, it is a beautiful evening, thought McKinley as the planned deception played out. Chris, you're a cheeky bastard. Just don't go blowing it by trying to impress him.

"Just testing," grinned Carter, a little amused at the contact's slip-up. "I thought I recognised your accent earlier. But I think you've lived somewhere else than Russia, haven't you?"

"Your knowledge of accents is impressive Mister Carver," growled the man, surprised by his own indiscretion, "and your Russian is *prevoskhodnyi*. I grew up in Krasnodar, but I also lived in Romania and Turkey."

"Oh, said Carter, "so that's how you met Mister Erbakan?"

The contact's mouth worked silently for a moment as though chewing on something horrible. "Let us go. Mister Erbakan's chef is preparing a wonderful meal for us all to enjoy." He snapped orders in Spanish at his crew.

Smiling, Carter turned away as their man on the dock carried the coiled rope back on board. The pilot revved the outboard and the *Gallina* swung in a graceful loop, exiting the harbour and turning west. There were few other boats out at this time, but evening jetskiers circled around them, enjoying the adrenaline hit from riding their aquatic motorbikes.

Once out of port the journey became a little rougher and most of the boat's compliment sat down on the benches which lined its hull whilst McKinley and Carter remained standing to the left of the wheelhouse and Wilson stood with hands crossed and legs apart at the stern

They passed the length of the breakwater, motoring toward the small flotilla of large and impertinently costly private vessels that were moored outside the harbour.

The pilot backed off the throttle and the launch seemed to relax into the swells. The radiant peach glow of the sinking sun bathed them from ahead as Puerto Rico's beach and western pier receded astern. Only the biggest of the private yachts were moored out this far, vessels of sufficient size to smoothen the Atlantic swells although, if the weather turned worse, they would doubtless make for the harbour. All of a sudden it was a different world: one not of arms dealers, deceit and danger, but of having considerable excess money and a surfeit of leisure time with which to enjoy it. Surrounded by the almost tangible luxury of ostentatious custom vessels in this popular holiday resort, there was a strong, pervading sense of the diametric difference between those worlds. Worlds that under normal circumstances—as if there were such a thing—should probably never be allowed to meet. Here, offshore, the gathering of extravagant boats was ideally situated to boldly advertise to the rank and file of Puerto Rico what money could bring to those blessed with plenty of it. There was nothing to suggest which was Erbakan's yacht and, indeed, they seemed to be passing through the moorings rather than heading for one.

With the motor burbling its accompaniment, they gradually left the shoal of yachts behind. An increasing oscillation in the launch's hull indicated their track further out to sea. The lights of the town shrank into insignificance as the sun became uncomfortable to look toward and the shoreline grew dark, craggy and as harsh as coarse grit sandpaper.

Standing next to McKinley, Carter murmured "feels like they're taking us somewhere to whack us."

"You got a map of the coastline?"

Carter spent a few seconds tinkering with his phone, then rotated its screen to face his friend, who murmured an assent.

Wilson took in the golden but bleak scene as the wind flicked his hair back. Since *Operation Copper Burial* he'd let the reddish mop grow a bit and it felt too long for him even though it was still within regulation length. Now the additional inch was easily catching the sea breeze as an impressive vessel hove into view, appearing from a sheltered cove ahead.

Erbakan's big trimaran *Fata Morgana* was the most badass yacht any of them had ever seen and hands down the sexiest. Aggressive angles like a stealth fighter juxtaposed with sweeping curves more appropriate to projectile weapons characterised her owner's intent; she was clearly and assertively built for speed. Her prow was like a tanto point knife blade, ready to slice mercilessly through the ocean, and she seemed poised to leap from her mooring and tear off into the horizon. There was not a square foot of the yacht that wasn't proudly announcing itself full of power, evoking the look of an Independence Class littoral combat ship. The hulls were a rich, resonant black, flashing and sparkling in the sunlight reflecting from the waves. The superstructure, though, was non-reflective, embodying a military style of marine architecture but without straying too far toward function over form. The almost menacing look of the yacht made her seem like a raptorous predator, waiting until their tiny launch was within reach before instantly pouncing to consume her prey. If ever a boat could be described as feminine and deadly at the same time, this was surely her.

McKinley took in their surroundings with interest, particularly the location. The narrow cove, he saw on Carter's map, was about two miles from Puerto Rico, equidistant between there and Puerto de Mogan. It was an ideal sheltered mooring for someone wishing to remain incognito, but there were signs of recent construction near the beach which would eventually bring an end to that.

"Can't be seen from the road," he said quietly, leaning toward Carter.

Their captain, such as he was, muttered something in Spanish and dropped the revs even more. The boat settled into an uneven rhythm as he turned it parallel to the *Fata Morgana* and made for the stern.

The central, longest hull had opened like the mouth of a fish, lowering a huge door to become a platform just above water level. As the *Gallina* turned to moor, the contact got up and stepped over to McKinley and Carter. Bacon also rose.

"If you are armed," he said, "I must ask you to give me your guns."

"Piss off," replied McKinley without looking at him.

"I think I'll sit down," said Bacon, and did.

The contact frowned unpleasantly at McKinley's rebuttal and said "I must insist." With this he looked up at the deck of the *Fata Morgana* and gave a signal with his hand. Four men stood from behind the gunwales, each holding an assault rifle. McKinley and Carter exchanged a look of resignation and McKinley said "Webster," turning to Wilson.

Wilson undid the jacket to reveal their pistols in a well-concealed multiple holster: his own Walther P99, Carter's Desert Eagle and McKinley's Five-seveN.

"Just the clips," ordered McKinley.

"I cannot allow—" began the contact when one of his men tried to grab Wilson's arm.

Wilson gripped the encroaching arm hard and twisted it the wrong way with a *crunch*, at the same time punching another in the face with the ass end of the Desert Eagle. As the pilot made a lunge at him he neatly side-stepped, still holding the first man's arm, and the pilot hit the side of the boat. Moving with unnatural speed, Wilson span on the spot, sweeping the first man's legs from under him and kicking the pilot in the ass, knocking him over the side of the launch. His hands now free, Wilson threw McKinley and Carter their weapons, then he shoved the other man's unbroken arm up behind him and slammed his head down hard on a cleat. The man whose face had been pistol butt-lacerated got up and was about to advance when Wilson's P99 was rammed into his Adam's apple and he froze like a statue. The whole altercation hadn't even lasted ten seconds, precluding the four gunmen on the yacht from finding a target without endangering their own.

The contact had his pistol out and almost pointed at Wilson when there was the click of a large gun being cocked and Carter's voice.

"This is a Desert Eagle fifty cal. If I fire it, your brains'll be dripping off your little gangster boys before they've even heard the bang." Carter was behind the man, his ludicrously big pistol pressed to the base of the contact's skull. McKinley brought his Five-seveN to the contact's temple and the man's face went pale; almost as pale as Bacon had gone. Two guns to his brain box, and he *definitely* wasn't expecting that kind of party.

"Now let's all relax," McKinley suggested, "before this degenerates into the kind of violence only Tarantino can pull off."

"Professionally trained!" came an earthy shout as handclaps reverberated from the *Fata Morgana's* stern. "I like them! Scum, let our guests keep these guns, but take the magazines like he says."

Looking up they saw a man on whom the cartoon Captain Hook could have been modelled without drastic changes except for the shaved pate and extensive scarring on the right of his face. Süleyman Erbakan was standing on the open area at the back of the steel and carbon fibre bridge, actually applauding the way they'd quickly neutralised his men. The four with automatic rifles stood down.

The contact, to whom Erbakan had referred as 'Scum', turned toward McKinley, whose pistol didn't waver. He was now looking right down its barrel. "Deal?" he asked, trembling.

McKinley nodded. "Deal," he said, and ejected the clip, cycling the action once to clear the weapon as Carter and Wilson did the same.

"Lets go on board," said Scum uneasily, looking so shaken as to warrant a hug from his mother. "*Mne nuzhen chertov napitok!*"

The interior of the *Fata Morgana* wasn't as big as they'd expected, with the useful floor space mostly located over the central hull. It did however continue to amaze. The theme of the design was walnut and rich sienna leather, offset by carbon fibre and subtle highlights of oiled beech with lemon chiffon and tuscan buff cushions on the large couches. Touch-screen LCD panels were never far from reach and seemed able to access almost every function of the vessel from anywhere on board. Across the ceiling countless tiny LED lights in all kinds of colours gave the space a smooth ambience which made it look like the set of a television show.

Their host didn't match his surroundings in any meaningful way other than the glittering metalwork he'd had put through his lower lip and left eyebrow. His nose was bent down as though harshly broken by walking into a plate glass window and below its pointed tip a dark handlebar moustache spread along his top lip, diving vertically at the corners of his mouth. He had a goatee beard and full though narrow eyebrows, but apart from these Erbakan's cranium was bald, presenting a tall, shining dome of near-perfect symmetry. His eyes, an intense, deep brown, were lively, darting about and taking in everything without always necessitating the rotation of his head. The most noticeable feature of Erbakan's face, and the hardest to ignore when conversing, was the mass of ugly scar tissue running back from his right cheek. Reddened and taut, it looked as though he'd been caught in a backdraft or some other rapid conflagration. The scarring covered his right ear, which was chewing gum pink and wrinkled as though trying to wear too much skin. Whether from the same incident or not, his right arm had a strong, continuous tremor which could be clearly felt when shaking hands. This was obviously why he preferred to use his left hand whilst its restless twin lay redundant, twitching in his lap most of the time.

The meal was indeed wonderful, although it was clear that it had been prepared by a local chef-for-hire that was brought aboard solely for that purpose. After an apéritif of Raki, the starter was an amazing chicken liver paté with toast and orange sauce. This was followed by a sumptuous buffet featuring Canarian specialities alongside various kebabs and other Turkish staples. In deference to the *Rosbifs* there was even a passable shepherd's pie, although the meat looked a bit pink.

After the dessert course, one of the crew played bartender. The drinks menu was somewhat narrower with a selection of European beers alongside the well known Turkish Efes Pilsen, a couple of wines and a handful of spirits. Once they'd all got a drink, Erbakan conducted a short tour of the *Fata Morgana*.

It was notable that there weren't any crew quarters to speak of. Two bedrooms in the lower central hull—one large and ostentatious, the other cramped but functional with a double bunk—indicated that Erbakan's muscle was locally hired. After these modest living quarters, storage areas, the galley and foredeck, the Turk led them indoors to the lounge again.

"I want to show you something," he said. With this he placed his drink on a nearby table, turned to a small numeric pad on the wall and keyed five digits. The lustrous walnut veneered panel slid back with a hum to reveal a brightly lit display case within.

"Oh *shit!*" exclaimed Bacon, thoroughly disgusted. He turned away, making gagging noises.

Inside the cabinet was a macabre display of bronzed human skulls arranged in three columns of eight. There were empty mounts at the bottom, clearly ready to receive the next phase of this morbid collection.

Erbakan gave a hideous smile. "I show this to my good friends," he crooned weirdly. "It is not a museum. It is a *reminder* that I sometimes have to deal with traitors." He swept his hand down the exhibit as though he was selling it on a television shopping channel. "These came from the wealthiest people who tried to double-cross me. This one," he pointed to a central skull, an obvious bullet hole in its burnished forehead, "Dubczek. Have you heard of him?"

McKinley looked at Erbakan and shook his head. The TDR.12 boys knew exactly whose cranium it had been but could say nothing. Václav Dubczek had been the go-to arms dealer in the former Czechoslovakia, and his disappearance was a long standing mystery. But rather than being forever entombed in a concrete bridge column or nourishing bottom feeders on the sea bed, here at least was his skull. Where the rest of Dubczek had gone was anyone's guess.

"He was moving gear through the Czech Republic into Germany in the nineties. It was good business for us both, but he screwed the numbers, ripped me off. This is wrong."

"I guess he lost his head," ventured McKinley, fascinated by the gruesome exhibition.

Erbakan coughed a small, humourless laugh, wagging his finger at McKinley. It clearly wasn't the first time he'd heard that. "You are a funny man, Mister McKittrick, but yes. It was good for him that my men found him first. Personally I prefer when *hain pislik* is alive."

Carter stroked his finger gently down the glass as Bacon made more retching sounds. "You've turned capital revenge into an art form. It's admirable."

The Turk bowed his head. "Most kind, thank you. But it saddens me that, like all great artists, I will not be truly appreciated until I myself have passed away."

"Can we *please* move on?" begged Bacon tremulously.

The raised wheelhouse was spacious, with the pilot's station—as high-tech as they'd ever seen—on the right. NASA's financial department would never have approved this level of luxury, but the organisation's scientists would have been geeking-out in droves. There was a wraparound console of touch panels, but all the physical switches were illuminated in bright blue and the traditional navigation controls finished with leather and gold. Here the helmsman would have a commanding view of the yacht's surroundings from the plush leather chair on its pedestal. In the corner diagonally opposite and next to the short corridor of steps that led to the lounge was a big chart table with an L-shaped leather couch. Forward of this, a central stairwell descended to the front of the lounge and continued below the foredeck.

Ever the nerd, Carter noticed something intriguing.

"Mister Erbakan—"

"Sully; call me Sully," ground the Turk.

Carter pointed at the throttle controls. "You've got three engines, but the middle one's clearly the most important. How does that work?"

The arms dealer grinned widely, proud of his vessel. "I use engine one all the time. The others only when I need. They are all reversible hydrojets."

"That's interesting," nodded Carter. "But hydrojets are inefficient at lower revolutions, right?"

McKinley rolled his eyes.

"Aha!" laughed Erbakan. "Yes. Engines two and three are an advanced design, for high speed only." He lowered his voice for effect and growled "if I have to outrun the coastguard," smiling.

"May I ask what her top speed is?"

"I have taken her up to seventy eight knots. She will do more."

"Wow," cooed Carter, genuinely awed. "That's about ninety MPH. *Bloody* impressive!"

McKinley wasn't as stirred. "Sully," he said, "I appreciate your hospitality, and this is a fantastic boat, but I was wondering when we were going to talk business."

"Yes, yes," nodded Erbakan. "Forgive my bragging. Let us sit on the deck." With this he held out his hand, ushering them from the wheelhouse and through the lounge toward the stern. The crewman responsible for drinks brought each a refill and they sat on the couches that ringed the upper deck.

The sky to the east was deepest ultramarine, gradually fading to brilliant orange as it crossed the heavens to meet the setting sun, and the rocky coastline was a black as coal. To the south-west, a tiny triangle of the crescent moon was growing at the horizon and, way above, the first stars were becoming visible. The *Fata Morgana* rode her mooring evenly, the slowly rolling waves hardly perceptible on board thanks to the trimaran hull. Barely visible to the east, the little launch *Gallina* was approaching after her hospital run.

Obviously being aware of his accent, Erbakan addressed McKinley and asked "Mister McKittrick, are you an Englishman as well?"

"No," smirked McKinley. "I work for a living."

Erbakan sat back, nonplussed at the humour. "Mister Bacon," he smiled, his shiny piercings glinting as he gestured ingratiatingly from his couch to theirs. "It is so good to finally meet you after all this time."

"You too," said Bacon, raising his glass, which trembled slightly.

"We have done some good business, no? I am pleased with the products I have sourced from you."

"Thanks."

Having concluded this pleasantry the Turk rotated to the COAST lads. He asked humdrum questions and they responded with nondescript answers. Erbakan wanted to know about the kind of business they did and where his products would end up. After a while he seemed satisfied.

"Well gentlemen, you must tell me what I can do for you."

McKinley took a breath and answered. "We've got some interested parties wanting to organise a little unrest in a certain country. We've been authorised to acquire arms of up to five million US value, payable in diamonds and reprocessed fine gold. We need various weapons from handguns to light artillery, and ammunition for a fortnight of intensive combat."

"Do you have numbers?"

"That's negotiable, but at least two hundred rifles and an appropriate selection of the other stores."

The Turk shook his head. "This is a lot to ask for five mill, and it is getting harder to trade diamonds, especially if they are from Africa. I do not think I can do it."

"I understand," nodded McKinley with a knowing smile. "This is the bit where we dance round each other until we've got a deal. But let me offer you a carrot; if you make it happen, all our future orders will go through you, subject to availability."

Again Erbakan shook his head. "But you are not spending your own money. If you were, we could figure out a price." His hands made a juggling motion. "I think you will not get all of what you want. Can you prioritise?"

McKinley nodded to Carter. "Yes," said the weapons tech. "The most important stores are small arms and RPGs. What do you have available?"

"With this budget you are looking at used equipment, of course. I can get perhaps AK-47s, Pindad SS2, Armalites and some pistols. I may have a possibility of getting several hundred units of the Chinese QBZ type 95."

"Right," interjected Bacon, "but they need current stuff, innit? Modern gear: Steyr ACR, IWI X95, HK417, that sorta thing."

Erbakan's face registered something between surprise and suspicion. "For a man who does not deal weapons, Mister Bacon, you know your guns." He looked sad for a moment. "If *only* I could get those items."

"Yeah, well, I keep me 'and in, you know?"

McKinley and Carter exchanged a glance, their expressions remaining passive but their unspoken communication tense. The nervous Londoner was blabbing his mouth off stupidly, stepping way beyond the bounds of his remit. But what could they do? Any attempt to curb his eagerness would only increase Erbakan's distrust.

Bacon continued. "What you got that's similar or better?"

As the TDR.12 men cringed inside, Erbakan's eyes bounced back and forth between them for a moment, like he was calculating a bet. Then he nodded slowly. "I think this is why you came to me, is it not?"

"We've heard the talk," answered McKinley carefully.

Erbakan rose, taking up his glass. "I will be right back," he said, and descended the narrow steps to his living quarters. They heard the glass being put down and five short beeps, then a heavy door opening and shutting again.

Their host reappeared bearing an unhappily familiar object, a weapon that had killed plenty of their colleagues. Thanks to their investigative team they now understood its sleek high-tech lines and operational details, but this particular example was equipped with a lightweight skeleton stock and disruptive pattern finish. It was a Heinmarsh rifle.

"You like this?" asked Erbakan, bearing the weapon forth. He smiled widely, revealing teeth which looked like rows of dilapidated tombstones. "It is just the little one."

006: The Hostage

"The, err... little one?" said McKinley as he took the rifle from the Turk, who looked on like a doting father might watch someone holding his infant progeny. "This is a version of the original," he drawled, "but there is an artillery prototype in development."

Trying to look surprised, McKinley said "what's special about it?"

Erbakan shrugged. "If you have heard the talk, you know it fires caseless ammunition. It is the only rifle in the world which can."

"Interesting," said Carter. "No cook-off?"

Erbakan's thin lips curled into a prideful smile. "That problem has been solved."

"May I have a closer look?" asked Carter. McKinley passed the rifle to him and Carter turned it over in his hands. As well as the skeleton stock, camo finish and lighter materials—presumably advanced composites—there were other minor changes from the examples he'd seen before, little details that told him something important.

Despite the discovery and destruction of Heinmarsh's secret weapons factory near Aberystwyth a couple of months ago, development and manufacture of these weapons was apparently continuing. This led to another probability; Heinmarsh was still alive and kicking. Somewhere, at some remote grid reference on the Earth's surface, the sinister American was still knocking out highly advanced weaponry for profit, the end of which was goodness knows what wretched plan. From what Erbakan had let slip it was further possible that he and Heinmarsh were in direct communication. This would count toward the evidence that TDR.12 needed to mount a bigger operation against Erbakan and his deadly business.

Carter passed the gun back to McKinley who in turn passed it to Wilson. Wilson cycled the action, checking it over thoroughly as though he wasn't on the research team that was reverse engineering them.

Erbakan continued. "Eventually they will build a handgun, but there are many technical problems."

"That's a *nice* shooter," Bacon prattled on. "Reckon I could make an exception; just one, for meself, like. Who builds 'em?"

Erbakan's expression grew darker. He paused for a moment and shook his head. "It is not made by any weapons company you have heard of."

"Where then?" asked Bacon, smiling.

Bloody *moron*, thought McKinley, fuming inside.

"You should not ask, Mister Bacon," muttered Erbakan unhappily. "All I will say is that it is in the Far East."

"Boss?" interjected Scum, prodding at his wristwatch.

"Yes, thank you," nodded the Turk. "Gentlemen I do not mean to be rude, but there are other matters I must attend to and so we will pick this up later."

"No demonstration?" asked Carter, looking affronted.

The weapons dealer frowned. "Perhaps tomorrow?"

"Damn," replied McKinley. "We have to head back to the UK tomorrow. We need to make a deal tonight."

Erbakan was adamant. "I am so sorry, Mister McKittrick, but this is unavoidable. We will meet in the morning yes? Before your flight."

McKinley looked at Carter. "We could do that," nodded the latter.

"Scum will take you back to Puerto Rico," Erbakan said, thrusting forward his hand in such an obvious parting gesture that only blindness could have misjudged its intent. "He deals with the locals. He will take you where you can get whatever you want. Food, drinks, women, pills, you know."

The *Fata Morgana's* crew, who had been congregated on the boat's foredeck, returned the clips from their side arms. Bacon looked very relieved that they were departing.

As the *Gallina* pulled away from the yacht Erbakan waved politely, but spoke in Turkish to one of his men.

"Kill the others, then bring Bacon to me."

Rocked by the Atlantic whilst the cooling breeze stroked their exposed skin, the launch arrived at the breakwater about fifteen minutes later. The sky was now dark and star-speckled but the high standard of illumination at the harbour made navigation easy. *Gallina's* tyre fenders gently nudged the concrete pier as their crew leaped ashore, mooring lines in hand. Scum had called ahead and there was a cab, a Mercedes E-Class estate car, waiting for them. Also waiting for them some distance away was a cop in the little plastic Renault.

The taxi ferried them up the western slope of Puerto Rico's valley, to a point near where Carter had attempted to triangulate Grainger's satellite phone. Here they came to a large, prestigious looking restaurant with a bar and patio. The building seemed mostly glass with tall, narrow windows stretching up to the square roof on which was perched a jumbo air conditioning plant. Inside, lighting of a strong sepia tinge augmented dark décor and furniture. Waistcoated servers wove between glass tables with oak rims, on each of which a small trio of candles provided a comforting glow. Customers whose apparel clearly delineated them from their more humble counterparts in the town center conversed at a modest volume and sipped drinks with tantalising Spanish names. TDR.12, Bacon and their escort grouped themselves on the tall, shiny black stools at the bar, a substantial construction of oiled walnut with a beautifully polished black granite surface.

"Order whatever you like," said Scum as the bartender approached. "We've got an agreement."

"Free drinks or expensive repairs?" suggested Carter.

Scum raised his open palm toward the weapons tech. "Something like that."

"I have to ask," said Wilson, "why on earth they call you 'Scum'?"

The Russian laughed resignedly, undoubtedly having answered this question far too many times. He held out his hand. "Shurik Skumarovsky, at your service."

"Peter Webster," said Wilson, returning a strong but mannerly grip. "Mine's a vodka straight, thanks. Stolichnaya if they've got it. You know that 'scum' isn't a nice thing to call someone in English, don't you?"

Skumarovsky huffed. "Mister Erbakan thinks it's funny." He motioned at the bartender. "I'll get a Stolichnaya too; double." Turning back to Wilson, he added "we drink Lokka on board. It's cat piss."

Bacon got Scum's attention with an outstretched finger. "Those guns," he said. "They're bloody different innit? Think I can get one?"

"I thought you didn't do shooters," McKinley said, but his implied message was 'shut the hell up!'

Scum shook his head. "It's not my department. If another big order comes through we could perhaps get some more, for special clients." He sipped the vodka, looked at the little glass for a moment licking his lips, then tipped the rest into his mouth and swallowed hard. He certainly likes the voddy, thought McKinley.

"They that popular?" asked Carter.

"You're kiddin' aren't ya?" argued Bacon. "Who *wouldn't* want one o' them things?"

Carter looked angrily at the Londoner, who didn't get the hint. "Look, I know you don' wanna be specific, but where they make 'em?" he prodded.

"Oh, you'll get me in trouble," replied Scum dismissively, catching the barman's eye.

"Go on," urged Bacon. "Which country? For real, like. I won' tell anyone."

Their host checked around before speaking. He seemed to realise that the only way to curb Bacon's unwelcome curiosity would be to throw him a bone. "Indonesia. I'm not saying any more than that." Scum shut his trap quickly as the barman delivered his double shot.

"I should go visit the factory innit?" laughed Bacon. "See if they're givin' away samples."

Scum looked horrified as he turned angrily toward Bacon. "*What?!*"

"It's alright big lad," said Bacon quickly, "I'm just kiddin' innit? Chillax." Smiling like an overly hopefully comedian before a tough crowd, he raised his hands in a defensive gesture.

"Kyle," interjected McKinley, "let it go pal. We'll get your popgun, alright?"

Realising that he'd crossed a line, Bacon quickly said "anyway, I'm fadin' out here. It's the jetlag. I'm goin' back to me 'otel, get some doss."

McKinley smirked, knowing that the UK and Gran Canaria lie in the same time zone. "Righto mate. You want us to lift you to the airport tomorrow?"

Bacon shook his head. "Oh, I ain't goin' 'ome yet. Decided to make a week of it, didn' I?"

"Wish *we* could," said Carter.

"You can stay if you want," said Scum. "We can make arrangements."

"Later!" yapped Bacon, walking a little too quickly out of the restaurant whilst dialling a cab on his phone.

"Thanks," said McKinley as he watched Bacon leave. "Appreciate the offer. But we've got stuff to do." He shrugged affably. "No rest for the wicked. Sorry about that, by the way."

Their host shook his head. "He's not very discreet, is he?"

"So what's your job for Erbakan?" asked Carter. "He said you deal with the locals."

"Well, I take care of his business interests here. We have a few things going on. Also if some local guy has a problem with someone, he can come to me and I'll make sure they get hurt. It's good PR for the boss. The yacht crew are my guys; all local. Apart from the engineer."

Scum knocked back his vodka in one shot. McKinley sensed an opportunity and, raising his voice so the barman would hear, pointed at Scum and said "another!"

Half an hour of largely pointless banter and a full seven double vodkas on Scum's part later, McKinley felt like he was ready to start the interrogation, such as it was.

"As I understand it, then," said McKinley, "you're running the girls, the protection and the local hit squad. I bet that keeps you busy."

"Also police," slurred Scum. "So they'll turn the blind eye."

"You ever killed a foreigner by mistake?" asked Wilson, smiling.

"I've killed some *not* by mistake," laughed Scum, waving along the bar for another drink as the current one leaked down his chin and onto his lapel.

McKinley joined in the laughter. "No Brits I hope!"

"Nah," said Scum, shaking his head.

"Wait a minute though," interjected Carter, "wasn't there something in the news about a Brit family getting blown up right here in town?"

Scum lowered his head. "Oh, that. I hope you won't be personally offended, personally."

McKinley raised an eyebrow. "You did that?"

Instead of answering, Scum's hand leaped to his ribcage, accompanied by a muted buzzing sound. "I've got a text," he announced, pulling the phone from his pocket. "Excuse me." He wobbled away from the table.

"Damn it!" whispered McKinley holding thumb and forefinger a centimeter apart. "He was that close to 'fessing up!"

"No worries," said Carter. "He's pretty much said enough already."

"How's the recording going?" asked Wilson.

Carter took out his phone, unlocked it and checked the display. "Good. Zero error rate, decent audio levels... we're good."

Scum appeared a little agitated as he approached. "I'm sorry, I've got to go. Mister Erbakan needs me."

"Well," said McKinley, hiding his disappointment expertly and shaking the man's hand, "it's been a pleasure. I guess we'll see you tomorrow."

"Good, good," stammered Scum as he made to hurry away. "Thank you!" With this he shoved the door open and dashed unsteadily for a waiting taxi.

"*Ey voditel', ty chertov urodlivoy svin'yey i ot tebya vonyayet!*" said McKinley, turning and winking at his colleagues in the back.

Their cabbie produced the expected reaction, which was to continue driving nonchalantly. Apparently the man's knowledge of Russian didn't stretch as far as understanding that he was being called an ugly, stinking pig, so McKinley addressed his team-mates, continuing with the Slavic lingo.

"So what've we got? A *near* admission of Padget's murder, a slightly upgraded design on the rifles, Heinmarsh is back to his tricks and... Indonesia."

"If Heinmarsh's behind our suicide bombers," replied Carter. "And Indonesia's *all* islands."

"Well that really narrows it down," carped Wilson. "There's only what? About ten thousand of 'em?"

"More," said Carter, "but think about it. It's got to be off the beaten track, unpopular with tourists, fair size, needs electricity *at least* for a manufacturing operation. There'll be comms: phone, internet, perhaps radio. That's a start."

"Do you mind slowing down a bit?" asked Wilson, still catching up with Carter's last sentences. Boy, was their weapons tech *ever* fluent in Russian.

"Can I just say," drawled McKinley, "we're going off half cocked. The idea was to kickstart a serious investigation into Erbakan first. I'm sure *he* knows where it is." He looked beyond his friends and out of the cab's back window. "At least that stupid cop's not tailing us."

The taxi pulled into the big, teardrop shaped terminus at the top of their apartment complex. McKinley switched to Spanish and paid the driver, who drove off quickly to find his next fare.

Four figures emerged from the darkness at the south end of the building, carrying knives and baseball bats. Slowly, ominously, they advanced toward TDR.12.

"I wonder if we've been rumbled," murmured Carter, pulling out his pistol.

"No shit," said McKinley as he and Wilson did the same. "Back off!" ordered McKinley in Spanish. The men kept coming.

"Idiots," muttered McKinley and held his pistol up to fire a warning shot over their heads.

Pop.

There was no recoil, there was no bang. The gun made a muted *clack* and nothing else. McKinley looked at Wilson, who tried to fire his Walther in the same manner with the same insipid result.

"They nobbled the bloody guns!" spat McKinley.

"The rounds," said Carter. "The clips!"

As if to reinforce this point, one of the four threw a small plastic bag at McKinley's feet. His first reaction was that they were being framed for drugs and he quickly kicked the bag to Carter.

"What is it?"

Carter retrieved and looked closely at the little packet, holding it up toward one of the streetlights so he could see through it yet keeping one eye on the four men.

"Clever," he hissed sourly. "They took the propellant out of—"

Dressed in a bright red shirt, the first of the men ran at Carter with a yell, brandishing a knife. Carter waited until the last instant and moved as the man fell over with his own momentum. Carter wheeled and said "shit!" as his nimble attacker rolled out of it and up again.

McKinley was expecting the others to attack now. "What?!"

"Four more on our six."

"Aye now it's a fight!" shouted McKinley as a bald, barrel-chested older man ran at him with a scream. Rather than swing down, the muscular man attempted to pivot his bat up at the team leader like a golf club. Dodging deftly, McKinley caught his arm and pushed it back over his head, stamping the guy's instep at the same time. Hurt and relieved of his weapon, baldy turned to get a face-full of baseball bat and dropped like a stone as all their attackers ran at them.

Wilson cast away his shades and took on two at once, using their attack against them; he ducked quickly as a tall black man tried to club him, and dodged again as the other, glinting with lots of facial metalwork, tried to knife him. Rotating, he swept their feet from under them and leaped out of his spin with astounding agility. As they fell, Wilson turned the knife into its owner's throat and his boot came down hard on the other guy's pierced nose, breaking it. Wilson tried to stay on his feet, but he was jumped by a strikingly skinny man and a Middle Eastern looking guy, forcing his body down.

Carter punched a curly-haired man, breaking his bristled jaw with a resounding crack. He then leaped onto Wilson's attackers as McKinley was knocked over them both, creating a mini rugby scrum of ferocious conflict.. The team leader rolled back to his feet instantly as Carter took the stick insect fella's neck and snapped it outright. The red-shirted man grabbed a bat and brought it down hard on Carter's back. The weapons tech exhaled sharply with a groaning, agonised yell, turning over. The man tried again and Carter rolled out of the way.

McKinley saw that Wilson was already breaking the Middle Easterner's arm and span to the last man, who looked younger than the rest and terrified. McKinley yelled a war cry and rushed at the youth, who turned tail and bolted toward the northern end of the building. McKinley gave chase and the man threw the baseball bat behind him. McKinley fended it easily away as the lad jumped onto the whitewashed rock wall and then onto the roof of the building with impressive agility. McKinley followed.

Rolling left and right on the tarmac, Carter was being narrowly missed by the flailing bat. A swing came too close to his head and Carter grunted in surprise. Sensing the opportunity for a decisive blow, Red Shirt raised it once more, and there it stayed.

Wilson pulled back on the bat he'd just caught and the man overbalanced into Wilson's waiting arms, who took his neck in a vicelike hold and with gritted teeth pulled up sharply. There was a sickening crunch and the man's body went as limp as a rag doll, the bat clunking woodenly as it bounced on the road surface. The Spaniard whose jaw Carter had smashed was getting up. Wilson deftly snatched up the bat and span round like lightning, cracking the man's head before he could even make it off his knees.

On the roof, McKinley side-stepped the younger man's punches and grabbed an arm, levering it down with the intent of bending it up behind the guy's back. His adversary, surprisingly agile, pulled a forward roll and his boot collided with McKinley's head, just in time for the Scotsman to realise how close they both were to the edge and that their mutual center of gravity was beyond it. They fell.

At ground level, the metalwork owner whose nose Wilson had broken was running toward the south end of the building in flight. In a swift, flowing movement Wilson span, scooped up a discarded knife and sent it hurtling into the night. There was a cry, but continued footfalls. The guy was hurt but still running so Wilson and Carter turned their attention to the remaining thugs. Three were dead, one out cold and two were incapacitated by their injuries.

"Where's Mickey?!" gasped Wilson.

"Don't know!" yelled Carter, when there was the sound of an engine being revved into next week. A dark coloured SEAT Exeo tore toward them in a cloud of dust. Carter threw himself to the right, out of the car's path whilst Wilson headed left, sprinting along the side of the building to take a better look at the vehicle.

With a squeal of rubber under torture the Exeo drew level with Wilson and swung round as Carter got up and dashed after it. Wilson found himself with his back to the low wall at the edge of a steep drop and the vehicle heading right for him at speed.

Carter tried to shout a warning but in a flash he saw that it was too late.

Wilson jumped on the spot, clearing well over a meter as the vehicle slammed into the wall with a shocking smash of metal and plastic. Wilson landed badly on the edge of the wall as the masonry started to give way. He managed to grab a piece of the car's mangled bonnet to stop himself from plunging down the slope, but the sharp metal cut his fingers. The wall beneath him was crumbling fast, its stones tumbling down the cliff, so Wilson quickly rotated his body and somersaulted into the road to the vehicle's right.

Carter had the driver out on the ground and was applying footwork generously. Wilson yanked open the passenger door to see the man with facial piercings knocked right out, his body hanging limply in the seatbelt, broken nose liberally dribbling blood into his lap and the knife protruding from his upper right arm.

Wilson looked over the roof of the vehicle to see Carter sticking the boot into the driver again and again, apparently drawing some savage catharsis. The driver's guts must have been pummelled to jelly by now.

"Hey!" shouted Wilson. "I thought you were on anger management."

"That's what I'm doing!" yelled Carter between kicks. "Managing my anger!" In went the boot again. "Feels great!"

"He's had enough!"

Carter paused, panting. "Probably." He started to turn away then gave the guy one more brutal kick in the stomach. "Now, where the hell's Mickey?"

Wilson looked around. There was no sign of their team leader. "You don't think they snatched him do you?"

"Not without some public disorder." He pointed at Wilson's right hand. "You're bleeding."

"Duly noted. How's your back?"

"Its problems are all behind me."

"Let's find him."

Trotting in opposite directions, they checked the area's perimeter rapidly and thoroughly. It soon became clear that McKinley was nowhere to be seen and their concern increased.

"Head count," said Carter, indicating the strewn bodies one by one. "Nine with the driver, but there's only eight. Someone's missing and I bet Mickey chased him or something."

Carter easily lifted the broken arm's Middle Eastern owner to his feet and angrily questioned him in Spanish. When the guy's only response was to shake his head fearfully, Carter shouted at him to piss off. The man jogged down the hill as fast as he dared, cradling his injury and grunting with each stride.

Wilson tried his phone. There was no response from McKinley's, not even ringtone.

"That's weird," said Carter cheerlessly. "We'll give it a few minutes. Let's clear up."

They slung the bodies of the red shirted guy, the black fella and the skinny man over the broken wall where they landed in dense bushes between the apartment buildings. The last men, the bald guy and the curly-top who were unconscious on the ground, were laid in some thick shrubs at the roadside were they would be somewhat protected until one of them awoke. Wilson's nose break and knife wound victim might bleed out, and the Exeo's driver could die of internal injuries, so they had to think quickly. They decided to get them away from the scene and then call an ambulance. The vehicle's engine was still running, albeit with some hissing and grinding, so Wilson lifted the driver into the back of the car then drove it about a kilometer down the hill and into a narrow side street where it could be found.

Carter dumped the attackers' weapons in the garbage and was making a sweep of the area when Wilson arrived back.

"I'm off to look for Mickey," he said, and turned as if to leave.

Carter grabbed his arm. "Better we stick together. More of these idiots might turn up."

Wilson was about to argue when they saw a vehicle coming up the hill toward them. It was one of the green and white cabs and they made out a pair of figures within. Carter and Wilson backed into the shadows in case the occupants were more unfriendlies.

The cab stopped nearby and McKinley's bedraggled figure got out, dripping water onto the road, his flashy jacket and shirt ruined. "Sorry about the mess," he said in Spanish, throwing a small handful of damp Euro notes at the driver, who shook his head unhappily before reversing into a turn and driving off.

"Should I even ask?" said Carter.

"We were fightin' on the roof," explained McKinley, tipping his head toward the north end of their building, "and we fell over. I thought it was lights out but then I was tumbling down the top of the stairwell."

"Oh," interjected Wilson. "Down the flat bit between the apartments."

"Aye. Landed in the pool. Scared the shit out of this German couple."

"Ah," nodded Carter. "*That's* why your phone's dead."

McKinley took out the phone, looked at it, shook it and swore. There was a large splay of cracks across the screen and water dripped from its charging socket.

"What about the other guy?" asked Wilson.

"He dinnae have a good landing," said McKinley. "He'll be in hospital for a bit."

They saw the lights of another vehicle approaching, flashing blue and red. "Oh *brilliant*," complained McKinley. "That's all we need."

The cops pulled up and five got out. "I guess the wee Renault couldn't take the strain," said McKinley under his breath.

"Well, this *is* a surprise," said the same cop who'd ordered their surveillance, in Spanish. "I leave you alone for a few minutes and a gang fight happens." He swaggered toward them.

"An *alleged* gang fight," retorted McKinley. "As you can see, we're the only ones here."

"There's a point," said Carter, switching to Russian. "How does he even know?"

"I'll give you three guesses," said McKinley.

"Stop it!" snapped the cop. "You speak in English or Spanish when talking to me!"

"We *weren't* talking to you," retorted McKinley, instantly swapping back to the regional tongue. "But that's fine."

The cop leered unpleasantly. "Don't try to give me attitude!" he snarled.

"Actually," said Carter, "just to avoid the kind of incident you're talking about, we blocked the barrels of our pistols. You can check if you like. I'm going to bring out my weapon now. It's disabled and not a threat."

The other four cops reached for their side arms, but the lead officer held up his hand warily. Carter took out the big Desert Eagle and pointed it at the ground and away from them. There was another small pop, nearly inaudible behind the metallic clunk of the heavy pistol's action.

"See?" he smirked. "Nothing. Now, if I open the chamber, you can see we lodged a round in the receiver. So it's obvious we had no intent to use them."

You clever lad, thought Wilson. With the powder missing from the rounds, the tiny pressure of the primer's detonation would give the bullet just enough kick to leave the shell case and stick in the rifling. It would look like they'd done it deliberately, just as Carter said, but a short repair session would be in order.

The cop glanced around. Apart from a couple of deposits of blood on the tarmac, there was nothing suspicious to be seen. That broken wall looked like some drunk driver could have done it. "Why are you wet?" he barked at McKinley.

"Aye, well, there's a funny story," said the Scotsman, smiling. "I was checking out a party in the valley when someone pushed past me and I fell in the pool."

"I don't believe you."

McKinley shrugged. "So what then? Did it rain this evening? Just on me?"

The hirsute cop ignored the sarcasm. "What's in your pocket?" he asked Wilson.

Wilson pulled out his hand and held it up, fingers outstretched, a near perfect line of cuts spanning the middle three, smeared red and sticky. "I grabbed my penknife the wrong way. Stupid mistake."

The policeman, completely unimpressed, looked around for a few moments, taking in the whole parking area, his eyes lingering on the rubble of the wall. Then he turned to his men. "Get their guns," he ordered.

There was no point arguing. The TDR.12 lads handed over their weapons as the cop continued.

"You'll get those back once we're at the airport." He pointed at the apartment building. "Right now you get in there with my men, you collect all your shit and put it in your van. Then we're going to follow you to the airport and make sure you're on the first flight back to England. If I ever see you again you'll be arrested and charged; I don't care who the hell you work for. Do you understand?"

"Aye, that's okay," snorted McKinley angrily. "That's fine. I'm sure we're done here anyway."

It was impossible to deny that dropping through the clouds over Manchester was a miserable experience at this time of year. The fiery dawn was spectacular from their aircraft at cruising altitude but occluded by a light drizzle issuing from the low cloud ceiling as they touched down. Leaving behind the bright sunshine of Gran Canaria for the brown leaves and grey weather of Britain was a shame.

Once at headquarters they were pleased to find out that General Sutton was back on base and looking to meet with McKinley. Carter and Wilson started to fill in reports of their time in Gran Canaria whilst McKinley went to consult with the boss.

Sutton's office was small for a general's, no bigger than sixteen feet on a side, space being limited on an underground base, particularly one located in caves beneath England's eighth largest conurbation. The walls were imitation wood panelling with daylight-tone illumination supplemented by other colours. The utilitarian furnishings were beneath the level one might have expected for an officer in Sutton's position. The tech, though, was impressive, with bumper size plasma screens on the left and right walls. As the sliding door hissed shut, McKinley approached the desk with its pair of additional monitors, checking out the push-pins on the big wall map behind it, which indicated the global locations of the fifteen TDR teams. The clock above the map read 09:38. He saluted and Uncle Victor wagged a finger at the chair.

General Sutton's kindly face looked weary. Still crowned with a generous mop of black hair despite being at the ass end of his forties, the general sat stiffly in his chair, his arm in a sling to keep it immobile. His beard, meticulously trimmed, formed a perfect additional border of black around his face, and his uniform was as impeccable as ever over his fitness exemplar body. The narrow glasses suggested that he'd been reading.

"Corporal McKinley," started the general, "let's get straight to the point. Is Erbakan linked with the Padget bombing?"

"Not exactly sir," replied McKinley. "He keeps his hands clean. His XO is a guy called Skumarovsky; deals with the local side of Erbakan's business. He pretty much admitted to it."

Sutton nodded, looking oddly relieved. "That's good." He paused and sighed. "I hope this cuts some ice with the JIC."

"Sir?"

The general shook his head, wincing slightly at the pain from his shoulder. "Ian, I'm sorry. This is difficult."

Ian? McKinley had only heard General Sutton use his first name a handful of times. Something was up. Something *difficult?* The commanding officer went on.

"They're asking a lot of questions; about the unit, *Operation Copper Burial*, your leadership."

McKinley started to feel cold inside.

"I'm not going to sugar coat this. It looks like they want someone's head on a plate; probably yours. You're to accompany me to a hearing in London tomorrow morning."

"My team sir?" McKinley was getting worried. There was nothing wrong with accountability but being held responsible was a different matter altogether.

Sutton shook his head slowly. "No... no, it's *you* they're after. They're hunting scapegoat. As for Carter and Wilson, I've got work for them concerning Heinmarsh's supply lines."

"Sir, I—"

"Look," interrupted Sutton, "don't go worrying about it. I'm on your side and so are my command staff. I've got nothing negative to report about either your conduct or record. We'll go and stare down these bureaucrats together, okay?"

McKinley was doubtful, but answered "yes sir."

Sutton closed the folder in front of him and passed it to McKinley. "This is for your team. I want your reports completed and any evidence processed by this afternoon so I've got something to hit the JIC with. Those two can leave as soon as their reports are in. I'll see you in the transport bay at 06:00, alright?"

"Yes sir."

"Have you collected a new telephone?"

"That's my next stop sir."

"Good. One more thing; Carter's late with his MDTs again. I don't care how much he dislikes it; they're to be on time in future. Understood?"

"Yes sir."

Sutton nodded. "Okay then, dismissed."

Aside from the activity going on around him, McKinley's footsteps seemed to echo in the hallways. Despite General Sutton's adjuration to the contrary, he was worried but not entirely sure why. Sutton had exonerated him from all blame and was backing his corner. Nonetheless he couldn't help but wonder what on earth the Joint Intelligence Committee wanted to harangue him for.

Shiny new phone in hand, McKinley was so lost in thought that he almost missed their office door. Inside, both Carter and Wilson were tapping their reports into computer terminals, oblivious to his entry.

"Lads," announced McKinley, and both of his colleagues looked up.

"Hi," said Carter. "How's the boss."

"Aye, he's okay; bearing up I guess. Obviously in pain though. Gave me this for you." He held out the folder.

"Us?" queried Wilson.

"You two. I'm off to London wi' 'im tomorrow. Making a presentation to the JIC."

Carter raised an eyebrow. "Interesting." He leaned over and grabbed the folder. "What's this then?"

Wilson wheeled his chair over and looked at the papers. "Holyhead? Isn't that on the Isle of Anglesey?"

"Yes," nodded Carter absentmindedly. "Requisition shipping logs and manifests for *Thames Sceptre*... interview witnesses... check out satellite records..." He slapped the file shut. "All standard stuff. You wanna sign a chopper out?"

"Beats driving," agreed Wilson.

"*Thames Sceptre*," repeated McKinley with a thoughtful look, "was one of the ships on Heinmarsh's fleet."

"Indeed," said Carter, as McKinley's phone rang for attention.

Lifting the device, the team leader answered "McKinley here." He waited a moment and said it again, then took the phone away from his head and cancelled the call. He shrugged. "Wrong number."

Carter's attention had returned to the file. "This business with the satellite imagery's interesting. Seems there's been some dodgy stuff going on with the shipping manifests too."

"Forging?" queried McKinley, but his phone sang out again. "Bloody hell!" he snorted and turned away to take the call. "Hello?"

Again McKinley waited, but this time there was a murmur on the other end. "Hello?" he repeated. Whoever was calling, they were having difficulty speaking. "Who is this?"

McKinley listened hard and heard "mi... mi... mi..." He put his hand over the mic and mouthed "stuttering" to his colleagues.

"Oh!" Carter almost jumped out of his chair. "Is it Plugger?"

McKinley raised an eyebrow.

"Bacon's XO," continued Carter. "He stutters like a busted CD player."

McKinley realised what Carter was saying. "Right!" He uncovered the microphone. "Is this Maurice Broadwick? Plugger?"

"Ye... ye..."

"Plugger, what's up? How did Broadwick have McKinley's number? Bacon must have passed it across. Was something wrong?

"Vi... vi... vid... video!" Plugger sounded terribly agitated and this was only making his stutter worse.

"What video? What's up?"

"Se... se... sen..." There was a pause while McKinley heard his interlocutor drawing breath. "Send you video!"

"You want to send me a video? What video?" McKinley wasn't trying to sound obtuse, but he was having difficulty.

Plugger roared in anguish and hung up sharply. "What the hell?" said Carter.

"He wants to send me a video." McKinley frowned. "Goodness knows why."

"What kind of video?" asked Wilson.

"Well, if I knew that..." started McKinley when a text message arrived. He touched the screen to retrieve it and wasn't surprised to see that it was from Plugger.

Got 2 send u vid *extremely* serious & disterbing. Need ur *URGENT* attention!!!!! M. B.

"Chris," said McKinley, turning back to his friends, "text him the secure email address please."

Carter lifted his phone. "What's his number?"

McKinley recited the eleven digits and Carter sent the text. They all gathered around the same terminal waiting for the email to arrive. What the hell could this mean?

"Here it is," announced Carter, seeing movement on the tiny status bar at the bottom of the email client. The email appeared in the preview pane and it was impossible to miss the subject line; "PLEASE HELP!!!"

"Play it," ordered McKinley, and Carter clicked the video link. The player logo rotated in the middle of the screen for a moment, then Bacon's face appeared, filling a narrow vertical strip in the middle of the screen. He was close and out of focus, his visage distorted by its proximity to the phone's tiny wide angle lens.

"Hey Ian," he said. "I'm in trouble 'ere. I'm on Sully's yacht an' 'e won't let me leave. He ain't threatened me, like, but I think, well, you know, 'e's got them skulls and I'm shittin' meself. I'm okay at the moment, right, but—"

With a sharp bang and Bacon's cry of pain the picture became motion-blurred nonsense for a moment, then another face appeared: Erbakan.

"Carver, McKittrick, Webster," he growled, "or whatever your names are really. I know you work for British intelligence and you are trying to screw with me. So we will make a deal I think. Your government will pay me the five million that you spoke about and you will get your friend back. The longer you take to pay, the less of him you get back. Hold this."

As Bacon pleaded in the background someone else took the phone and they heard Erbakan's order; "keep him still." Again the image was scrambled by movement, but a couple of seconds later it came into focus, revealing Bacon being held on the floor and Erbakan unfolding a blade.

The next part of the video was indeed disturbing and disgustingly gruesome. It was difficult to watch and hard to listen to the gadget dealer's agonised screams as the barbarous Turk sliced off his left ear. Bacon's yelling started to subside as Erbakan turned back to the camera, his hand covered in repulsive gobs of blood and holding the severed auricle.

"Pay me my five mill!" He shouted in horrible rage, spittle spraying from his twisted mouth. "You pay me my money or you will get him back as a kit! You know where I am." With this he squished the bloody ear into the camera, turning the whole screen dark red. The video's last second or so contained a fragment of Turkish as the arms dealer told whoever was holding the phone to stop recording.

Once Carter and Wilson had left for Wales, McKinley made his way to the transport bay feeling like he was under a cloud. He sat on the loading dock, one hand holding a cold coffee and a cigarette dangling from the first two fingers of the other. With the area's only activity being occasional vehicle movements there was some sense in which he could feel enough clarity to address his difficult circumstances for a short while.

McKinley felt trapped. The JIC wanted to give him a good grilling and he felt like he'd led a friend to their execution. How the hell would he solve that? He'd made the general aware of the Bacon situation and received a somewhat ambiguous, non-committal response. Sutton had other and bigger fish to fry apparently, one of which being the preparation of his arsenal in case the Joint Intelligence Committee proved even more hostile and less supportive than usual.

Carter and Wilson had submitted their reports, the former also writing McKinley's from some rapidly scribbled notes and a short burst of Scottish into a dictating machine. Maybe one day, McKinley mused, he'd get around to penning a whole report on his own. And pigs might fly.

McKinley badly needed a distraction, so he did the only thing he could think of which might address that. He went to talk to someone whose problems were worse than his own.

The medical section was more active than the transport bay and he found Doctor Manning in the middle of overseeing several patients. McKinley noticed Cassius Dunn, Combat and Survival Specialist of TDR.4, face down on a trolley and said a quick hello. Dunn, one of the most handsome West Indians McKinley had ever seen, grinned as he relayed a short tale of ass-kicking in Bolivia which included drug dealers and a pistol round in his right buttock.

Manning noticed McKinley and beckoned him aside, lowering his voice.

"You're here to see the girl?"

"Aye."

Manning nodded thoughtfully. "Good. You're the only person she'll talk to."

McKinley frowned, raising a questioning eyebrow. "You're kidding?"

"Goodness knows why she'd want to talk to *you*," scowled the doctor, "but it is what it is."

McKinley thought for a moment. A little tiny bit of good news, thank heavens. If he could work the girl for intel it would certainly go in his favour.

"We got the toxicology, by the way," continued Manning. "Strange one, this."

"Oh aye?" McKinley raised an eyebrow.

"Mycotoxins and tropane alkaloids, it *looks* like," frowned the doctor, "but there was a whole alphabet of different compounds floating around in there."

"And that means what exactly?"

Manning rubbed his fingers on his forehead. "Well, it's like multiple personality disorder, but drug induced. She swaps between two personalities. One's the suicide bomber, the other's an ordinary British teenager."

"Interesting," said McKinley, not knowing what to make of that. "Thanks." He turned toward the girl's private room. "Just record everything."

"Always do," affirmed the doctor with a thumbs-up, heading for his desk.

McKinley closed the wooden double doors behind him as Jemima Fox looked up. Or was it Sister Patricia? Either way her face transitioned from uncertainty to smile faster than McKinley would have expected.

"Ian, hi," she said, seeming for a moment to forget that she was a terrorist accused of trying to demolish the heart of the British government and imprisoned on a secret underground base, her sister dead and her future blacker than the devil's coal scuttle.

McKinley smiled back. He didn't mean to. He was trained to remain neutral and dispassionate, but there was something so refreshingly contagious about her expression that he returned the gesture before he could stop himself.

He sat down and crossed his legs. "How are you doing?" he asked cautiously.

"The doctor says I'm going to be alright," she admitted, "but my insides are messed up. I won't ever be able to have kids."

McKinley nodded and changed the subject. The Sister Patricia persona seemed to have retreated for the moment and he wanted to capitalise on the opportunity. "You seem to be feeling a bit more yourself."

Her head sagged and her voice was roughened by desperation. "I've been so confused! I'm *so* sorry! I know it was wrong, so wrong! I'm sorry! I just wanted to usher in the Kingdom!"

Her tragic remorse seemed so genuine that McKinley held up his hand to stop her. She calmed a little and said "where am I?"

He tried to speak gently, not wanting to scare her. "Why would you want to blow yourself up?"

Tears abseiled down her cheek. "I... well, martyrs are welcomed into paradise." She shook her head. "I don't know why... I can remember my house now..."

That's interesting, thought McKinley, making a mental note to discuss her confusion and memory loss with Carter. He tried a slightly more direct approach. "You spoke about the Ambassadors Of The Godhead. Can you tell me where they are?"

She nodded, her eyes wary.

"Where is it?"

"The island," she muttered. "I don't know where it is. It's so warm."

McKinley spread out his hands. "Well, you must remember going there."

"No." She shook her head sadly. "We went to a revival service in Singapore. After the Universal Spirit took away our old lives we were already at the village. Wolf River."

Suddenly her expression changed as if an internal switch had been thrown. It was a subtle thing, but her countenance took on a faint hardness and her eyes became vacant, as though the person inside had made their exit via the back door. "Don't *you* want to know the Universal Spirit?" she asked. "Don't you want to be *at peace?* To be a vessel of *love?* You can." She lifted her body toward him, her whole face radiating its petition. "Let me show you the path!"

"If you're trying to appeal to my better nature," replied McKinley, a little blindsided, "you should be aware that I don't have one. As to the rest, how much explosive does it take to cross the line from love to terrorism?"

She turned toward him, her eyes afire with accusation. "You have to break eggs to make an omelette!" she slurred. McKinley knew that something had triggered the re-emergence of Sister Patricia, who was again in charge. The speed and totality of the switch in Jemima's personality was both remarkable and creepy.

"Don't give me that shit," he said, irritated. "You're nay better than any other bloody butcher!"

"Hey," she yapped. "*I'm* a servant of the Universal Spirit! I'm a member of the elect and you cannot talk to me like that!"

"No," snarled McKinley, "you're a terrorist of the universal bullshit!"

"That does it!" she pouted. "I'm calling a holy fast! I'll hunger strike and I'll become a martyr, and my death will be on *your* conscience!"

"Aye, and conscience is something you'd know *all* about, Jemima!"

"My name is *Sister Patricia!*" she yelled, as the door crashed open and Doctor Manning scurried in.

McKinley nodded slowly, his eyes narrowing. "Well I'll tell you what then, Sister *Malnutricia*," he drawled. "You go on hunger strike. Fine. I'll wait a couple of days then set up a camp stove right here and fry some nice crispy bacon. And we'll gauge the strength of your resolve."

The suicide bomber blurted a string of abusive terms, the lewdness of which even McKinley found a little shocking. He giggled, looking sideways at Manning. "Oh that's not very Christian now, is it?"

She rolled her eyes exasperatedly. "We do not follow this world's religions! Why don't you people understand?" She shrugged dismissively, giving up the argument and looking pointedly in the other direction. "You are blind and deaf!"

McKinley turned toward the doors but Doctor Manning gently diverted him to one side.

"Corporal," he whispered, "this business with the camp stove? You were joking, right?"

"No."

Manning made a resigned sigh. "It could be interpreted as torture."

McKinley raised an eyebrow and turned to the medic. "Really?" He pulled his head back as if taking a better look at him. "Well, where I come from, giving a starving person food's considered charitable, and stopping someone from dying's the doctor's job. So, if you'll excuse me, you do your bit," he stabbed his finger into Manning's chest, "and I'll do mine."

With this McKinley turned to the doors and was about to shove them open when he heard a little voice.

"It's Jem."

McKinley turned back. "What?"

"Jem," the girl said quietly, her eyes full of terrible fear and confusion. She looked as fragile as eggshell. "My name's... Jem."

"Is it now?" replied McKinley. "Well *Jem*, you're a rough diamond for sure, but I'll dare to bet there's a polished stone in there somewhere."

007: The Inquiry

The chopper landed on the Isle of Anglesey at RAF Valley, a familiar airbase where both Carter and Wilson had trained on BAE Hawk aircraft to get their jet ratings. After a short taxi ride via the North Wales Expressway they dumped their gear onto the Holyhead quayside at the end of Turkey Shore Road by the Dock office. It was a dumpy little grey building that looked like the poor cousin of a council house and which was surrounded by black bollards and galvanised steel crash barriers, as though someone might accidentally knock it into the depths of the harbour. Beyond it, a number of brightly coloured but sea-worn fishing vessels clung to their moorings as the Irish Sea tried to shake them in its grip.

The harbourmaster was Viv Evans, a jolly old Welshman with a neatly trimmed white beard and the kind of figure that demonstrated more interest in chips than fish. His dark blue cap looked as though it never left his head and his veined, ruddy cheeks gave away a penchant for liquid refreshment. He invited Carter and Wilson into his tiny office which smelled of pipe tobacco, and they sat on old, black lacquered wooden chairs that creaked as though about to lose their structural integrity, whilst Evans pulled out his shipping records for May. His little headquarters enjoyed a grand view of the harbour which would have been better demonstrated by fairer weather than they were having that afternoon. If it gets too much worse, thought Wilson, we won't be able to fly back tonight.

"Well now, you see," said Evans, passing the paperwork to Wilson, "*Thames Sceptre's* been 'ere a few times, takin' on supplies, you know?"

"What kind of supplies?" asked Carter.

"Well it's all 'ere, see, in the record," replied the harbourmaster, indicating columns of writing with his open palm. "Food items, fuel oil, machine parts. She goes to Scrabster and back, but I 'eard they're for some island or something. Bloody awful voyage if you ask me. Anyway, one of my security boys saw them loading something else now, didn't 'e?"

Carter had noticed cameras around the building. "Did you get it on video?"

The Welshman held up his hands. "Well I don't know, see. We didn't check back as far as May yet, did we? I 'ad to let 'im go in June, poor fella, because 'e... well, he wasn't a terribly honest man, you know?"

"Right, so how come this wasn't reported before?"

"Well we only found out this week, see? One of my boys was 'avin a drink with 'im in The Boston—that's the pub just down the road 'ere—and 'e told 'im. So my lad told me and I got onto the coastguard."

"Good call," said Carter, "and thanks for your diligence. How can we check your video records?"

Evans held up a finger. "Well now, they tell me I can see it on this computer, but I don't know 'ow. I'm too old for this tomfoolery. I don' even know 'ow to send a text message now, do I?"

Wilson grinned and Carter asked "well, do you mind if I have a look please?"

"No, no, go right ahead," offered the jovial harbourmaster, raising his bulk. "You'll 'ave it up in seconds, no doubt."

"Thanks," said Carter and moved behind the desk.

"Anyone want a cuppa?"

"Yes please," chorused the COAST lads.

"Righto," nodded the Welshman, "I'll be back in just a jiffy."

Whilst Wilson sat on the window ledge, Carter worked on Evans' computer. It wasn't long before he'd called up the appropriate set of files. "What's the date again?" he asked.

Wilson checked their file again. "May eighteenth. The manifest is exactly what he said."

"Eighteenth, eighteenth... got it," said Carter. "What was the time of sailing?"

"Zero eight hundred. I guess we're looking at the previous night."

"Yes." Carter perused the files, which were time-stamped by hour.

Skimming through the video logs took time and concentration but the harbourmaster, who couldn't seem to do enough to help, kept the refreshments coming. By six o'clock that evening they'd reached the file for 03:00 on May eighteenth and started to notice activity at the dock. They slowed the playback to its normal speed. Despite the low resolution video, they could see that a large truck had pulled up by the side of the *Thames Sceptre* and, although they couldn't make out details, something big was being craned into her hold, something big and entirely absent from the ship's manifest.

"I'd love to be able to check that," said Wilson. "I wonder where the heck she is."

Evans had been falling asleep on a chair by the door but with a grunt he suddenly reached wakefulness again. "Well, she's right 'ere now, isn't she?" he said. "No-one wants 'er any more, poor old girl."

The *Thames Sceptre* looked as run down as Evans' dour epithet had suggested. She was a coastal freighter, about fifty meters long and ten of beam. Her long, squarish hull was a neglected matte black on which spatters of red and orange corrosion had encrusted her like sores, and the windows of her superstructure were dim with dust and water marks. Her deck area was comprised of two massive cargo hatches, painted green, covering the holds below. The fading light of the Welsh evening did nothing to improve her appearance as the increasing wind whipped their hair and touched their ears with chills of ice.

"I don' know what 'happened with 'er," said Evans as though he was their tour guide. "Someone tol' me the owners went bust, you see, so she'll be going to the scrappies' next month. Bloody paperwork's a right 'eadache, don't you know?"

"We only need a few minutes," said Carter. "I suppose we access the holds via the engine room?"

"More than likely," said Evans. "I never been on board of 'er myself, like."

Whilst Evans waited on the quay smoking his filthy old nose warmer pipe, Carter and Wilson entered the *Thames Sceptre*. The wheelhouse was as expected: left in a tidy condition but having gained a layer of dust since last any orders were issued there. They descended to the engine room and forward into the cargo holds, swinging torch beams ahead as the whistling wind stirred the waves, making the hollow sounds of the deserted vessel ring around them.

The aft hold was the longest, and its covering hatch about four meters above their heads. A couple of inches of water sloshed around their feet as the *Sceptre's* pumps hadn't been run in months. The metallic space was dank, smelling of diesel and rusty iron.

"Are you thinking what I'm thinking?" asked Wilson once he was certain that the helpful harbourmaster was out of earshot.

"Of course," smirked Carter, his face looking ghoulish in the torchlight shining from below it. "Don't you know I read your mind?"

Wilson huffed. "Geiger counter."

Chuckling, Carter flicked the power on. The instrument clicked and rattled its reaction.

"Yes," said Carter, "that's the sound of me being not surprised at all. Residual's through the roof."

"He docked at Scrabster? That was a risk."

"I don't think he did."

Wilson raised a single eyebrow, barely visible in the gloom of the hold.

"That boat. At the dock at Mallory Island. Heinmarsh's country retreat."

"I know," nodded Wilson. "It had residual radiation too."

"I'm thinking he took his bomb out to sea in here and craned it onto the other boat."

"Holyhead to Mallory and no witnesses," agreed Wilson. "So are we saying there's still a nuke of some sort there? Surely not."

Carter rubbed at the stubble on his chin. "Probably not; I don't know. They've scoured the place thoroughly. But I think we need to shoot up there tomorrow."

Back on the dock, Evans was sitting on a lobster pot, smoke being whipped from his pipe like rocket exhaust. "Glad you're done," he grunted as they approached, "it's gettin' bloody cold out 'ere."

"We're going to need somewhere to stay overnight," said Wilson. "You know anywhere?"

"Well you can stay at my 'ouse if you want," replied the Welshman. "I just got to lock up the office then perhaps we'll 'ave a couple of pints at The Boston. What d'you think of that?"

"I think that sounds good," replied Carter. "Thank you."

Two hundred feet above him, the largest four-faced chiming clock in the world, colloquially known as Big Ben, had struck half past nine a few minutes before Carter's text arrived. McKinley read the message with interest, glad of anything that would take his mind off the hour that he'd been waiting in the uncomfortable chair. His team-mates had found residual radiation on Heinmarsh's little cargo ship and were flying north to Mallory Island. McKinley made a quick calculation that they'd be there by lunchtime. As to the timing of his own movements, he could only guess. The JIC were taking their sweet time with his boss.

To McKinley, the corridor looked like some poorly managed country hotel that offered overpriced accommodation to the kind of people who firmly believed that Britain still had an empire. But the heart of that former administration was where he now sat, a building that had—at the height of 'the empire on which the sun never sets', and which had covered nearly a quarter of the planet's habitable surface—played a role in the governance of about half a billion souls.

The Palace Of Westminster, informally known as The Houses Of Parliament in deference to its role, was a massive, neo-gothically ornate edifice dating from the late nineteenth century. It was here that both common politicians and lordly peers introduced bills, debated them, politely insulted each other and almost casually determined the destiny of the United Kingdom and the sixty five million citizens therein. McKinley admired the politicians for the difficult job that they had to do, but he hated the politics. In McKinley's political dream team, Jeremy

Clarkson would become the Prime Minister of England and Sean Connery that of Scotland, which would of course gain its independence. Those outspoken characters would certainly cut to the chase, firing all the useless middle management and actually getting the job done. McKinley, whilst being well read on matters political, balked at the idea of becoming involved in politics himself. His disinterest, though, was nothing next to Carter's, who on several occasions had expressed a desire to finish what Guy Fawkes had started.

Bright squares of fluorescence like a ship's portholes lined the dark wooden ceiling every fifteen feet or so, whilst the only source of natural light was a distant stained glass window forming the far end of the arcade. Each doorway was an arch of beige limestone containing a rectangular oak door with glass panels, itself surrounded by clean, white paint that looked fresh. Small, faded artworks and ancient documents in decorative frames lined the walls, each bearing a tiny descriptive plaque.

The bloody balaclava, provided to hide his identity, was itching like mad and, in view of the fact that there was no-one else about, McKinley pulled it up over his face to scratch. He raked his cheeks, nose and neck with his freshly cut fingernails, feeling the sharpness left by the clippers. Hearing a sound off to his left, he quickly pulled the woollen mask back over his face.

A suited clerk came through the door and walked up to where McKinley was sitting, his footsteps producing echoes that rippled up and down the long, bare corridor.

"The subcommittee will hear you now sir," he announced, his hand outstretched away from the door. "It's this way sir."

McKinley got to his feet and fell in behind the young man who opened another, smaller door without glasswork. McKinley walked inside to find himself in a short wood lined corridor with a chair and desk at the end. A black and white television monitor on the desk showed a view of the meeting room beyond, whilst a silver microphone sat on a short stand to its left and a triangular corner shelf on the right held a black monitor speaker with volume control and glowing red LED. McKinley turned as the clerk locked the door behind him, his mind instinctually hunting for a route of escape. Relax, he told himself.

"Would you please sit down, Operative Tripod?" came an unfamiliar voice. It was definitely southern, from the home counties or maybe the south coast. Worthing? Bournemouth? Somewhere like that.

"Yes sir," said McKinley, taking his seat without knowing whether his response was appropriate.

"Now, you can see us on the television monitor," said the voice, and McKinley observed a slightly indistinct figure on the screen, sitting at the head of the long table and gesturing as he spoke. The figure looked rounded, pale and older than the tone of its voice seemed to indicate. To the man's left and right were people he didn't recognise, four men in black or grey suits and a woman in a dark red outfit with black hair. At the near end of the table, facing away from the camera, was General Sutton in his dress uniform yet with his arm still in its sling.

"Why we should protect your identity in this forum is quite unclear to me," continued the speaker, "but rules are rules. My name is Clifton Cambion-Dawkins, Member of Parliament. I've been asked to chair this inquiry subcommittee of the Joint Intelligence Committee. You may refer to any of us as 'minister', with the obvious exception of General Sutton."

"Yes Minister," said McKinley. Cambion-Dawkins sounded like a bit of an ass, but McKinley was willing to give anyone a chance.

"Now then," said the politician, "if I were in your position I imagine I'd be somewhat worried. I wonder whether you could please explain to this committee the debacle of your failure in Canada?"

Oh great, thought McKinley, he's *much* more than a bit of an ass, but General Sutton spoke before he could.

"Minister," came Sutton's clear tone, "as we've already been over this I don't see why it's appropriate to question my officer in such unfavourable terms."

"Of course not," said Cambion-Dawkins, "but I'm afraid I remain unconvinced that the Canadian phase of *Operation Copper Burial* can possibly be seen as anything other than a gargantuan cock-up. This inquiry needs to hear from the officer whose failure it was."

Damn and bugger it, thought McKinley, it's going to be a *bloody* long day.

The chopper descended to a thousand feet above the dirty grey of the northern Atlantic, which looked terribly frigid and uninviting on this bleak autumnal day. They'd spent most of their flight from Wales above the worsening weather but a low cloud base demanded their descent for final approach. Carter, elected by coin toss for the outbound flight, was fighting to keep the aircraft level in these blustery conditions. Buffeted by the same winds that were plucking the tops from the waves and disintegrating them into spume, the Eurocopter EC155 wobbled unsteadily beneath its 12.6 meter rotors as Wilson watched the dismal seascape roll past.

Carter had done some seafaring during his years in Naval Intelligence and was more used than most to unfavourable marine conditions, but nonetheless he was glad to be in the helo. Although this could hardly be called a storm, any trawler working these waters would be tossed about like a tennis ball in a washing machine. Yet people do this every day, he thought, bringing to mind the life of a Scottish coastal fisherman. Up before first light and stuck on a tiny boat for hours in weather like this for little or occasionally no reward was a tough deal even before the European parliament started ruining things. But making sure that their aircraft didn't end up at the bottom of that same sea was bloody tough as well. These conditions were light years from ideal.

Wilson's "hey!" announced their first sight of Mallory Island. It emerged from the grey in the middle distance, thrusting up through the relentless ocean like an excrescent carbuncle. The unsightly little island was formed of two hills on the higher of which was sited the cliff house of Kurt Heinmarsh, the adversary who had caused so much chaos and death during the summer. There was also a large dock on the island's south-western side, and a tiny settlement in the north once inhabited by a mercenary gamekeeper that Carter himself had killed. He put his tongue into the hole where his tooth used to be. That had been a rough fight.

Skirting the southern hill as the aircraft descended, they came into view of the dock where COAST had set up a hamlet of cabins that housed the investigative crew that had been on this forbidding lump of rock since September. Groups of kittiwakes and gulls soared from the guano spattered cliffs while curious puffins watched from the jagged rocks nearer to the shoreline, their big, almost triangular orange beaks rotating upward in synchronism.

Despite the length of the journey, Wilson was cheered slightly by seeing both cliff house and dock in perspective. That wasn't *such* a bad shot, he thought, remembering that it was Heinmarsh's head that he'd been aiming for. He recalled his encounter with the American billionaire, who was undoubtedly insane. At least, that's what Wilson believed, as did his team leader. Carter had on several occasions expressed a different opinion, that Heinmarsh was just as ingenious as he was dangerous, but it was typical of Carter to point out an alternative view, even when he knew that nobody would share it.

Making careful adjustments of the flight controls, Carter brought the chopper into a hover over the main helipad and gently set her down near to another Eurocopter and a pair of black COAST Land Rovers. It felt strange to be back on Mallory Island and to again enter the environment of their last encounter with the corrupt American. There was the massive dock before them, conspicuously large for such a diminutive island because it was built to sufficient size for a submarine. The icy torrent of the stream passed to their left beneath a new bridge constructed for the unit's convenience after McKinley had demolished the original.

It was on this dockside that Wilson's sniping had saved the life of their team leader and, as Carter stepped from the helicopter, the details all came back vividly: the American clutching at his pulverised left shoulder, McKinley falling into the soft mud at the bottom of the iron ladder, Heinmarsh starting the countdown timer for an atomic weapon that had turned out to be a feint. Carter thought about the short gun battle with PLA Navy sailors that had mutinied and hijacked the submarine, even though this was officially denied by the Chinese government. It was the arrival of five COAST helicopters which had decided that round in their favour but nonetheless Heinmarsh had vanished under the polar ice and thence to goodness knows where. Much of the events of that previous skirmish had taken place before sunrise, but the gloominess of this squally North Atlantic day seemed somehow darker, colder and more forbidding than that fateful night.

Standing a short way from the Eurocopter, holding onto his cap as the twin Turbomeca Arriel engines powered down, was Basic Commando Gavin Cottingham, a square faced young man with straw coloured hair whose COAST fatigues betrayed the shape of his impressive physique, leaving no doubt as to his placement in the Combat and Survival discipline. Cottingham had been ordered to take charge of the investigation at Mallory by General Sutton in a last test of his abilities before being grafted into TDR.14 alongside experienced leader Jeff Carrier and another promoted BC, Kevin Hudlin.

Cottingham saluted and they returned the gesture as they approached. The coarse concrete was coated by a driven layer of water to which the rain and sea spray were continually adding. Visibility was reduced to such an extent that it made Mallory Island seem like the only place in the world, hidden within banking, grey mist beneath a featureless overcast.

"Thanks for coming sirs," said Cottingham over the whistling of the damp wind. "Can you give me the details?"

"We think Heinmarsh ferried another bomb here," replied Carter. "They loaded something big in Holyhead and—we think—brought it here. The hold of the boat's slightly radioactive and we've got a bunch of satellite surveillance showing activity here around the same time."

"That's interesting," agreed Cottingham. "Everyone's been wondering why he came here."

"Exactly. Did he collect whatever it was in August? That's the question. Hey, can we find some shelter?"

"This way," answered Cottingham, beckoning with his hand and trotting off toward the biggest of the temporary buildings.

Closing the door and mercifully putting that numbing spray behind them, they found that the hut was set up as a mess, with rows of cheap, white plastic tables, brown PVC chairs and a small field kitchen at which a coffee machine with a fresh brew was a welcome sight. Wilson helped himself whilst the tea drinking Carter continued to speak with Cottingham.

"You had any uninvited visitors?"

Shrugging his shoulders, the young operative replied. "News crews spying on us when the weather improves. We just warn 'em off on the radio." He smiled. "Haven't had to call in the Tornadoes yet."

"Right." Carter changed the subject. "Have you found anything, anywhere, which could *possibly* hide another nuke?"

Cottingham looked as though he'd been squirted this question a few too many times. "No sir, nothing. We did locate a tunnel beneath the cliff house, but it's clean; doesn't look like he even used it."

"No residual radiation?"

Cottingham shook his head firmly. "Not a sausage. It's tiny anyway; hardly even room to squeeze in there."

Carter looked up as Wilson took a seat next to him. "I guess we'll have to search the whole island again." Seeing Cottingham's expression, he quickly added. "Not that your crew haven't done a great job, I mean. It's just that he might have been really good at hiding stuff."

"There is just one thing," declared Cottingham, arching his eyebrows. "The case of the missing power cables."

Carter and Wilson looked at each other. "Huh?" said the former.

"We've been plotting the infrastructure," declared Cottingham.

"Didn't read the report, did you?" said Wilson.

Carter nodded reluctantly. "Right."

The young BC went on. "Thirteen power circuits were routed out of the old generator cellar, the little islet that got blown up. We traced four to the house, four here and two to the cottage at Kishorn Cove. That leaves three unaccounted for."

"You test continuity?" asked Carter.

"Yes sir, first thing we did. Two are dead, but the other's got a load indicating a transformer or something."

"You tried digging 'em up?" asked Wilson.

Cottingham cocked an eyebrow. "We've opened the manholes. We know they pass here," he said, spreading his hands, "but they don't go as far as the cove."

"Okay," said Carter. "I'll get to work."

"Did you want to wait for a break in the weather?" asked Cottingham.

Carter grunted a short laugh, shaking his head. "I checked the met' reports. We're not going to get one."

Bloody *hell*, is that asshole's voice *ever* grating on me, thought McKinley. He'd been sitting in the little wooden box for more than two hours and he was getting extremely fed up. So far, he'd managed to step around some of the difficult questions that were being shot at him, but the chairman's attempts to make McKinley self-incriminate were getting more determined.

"So," said Cambion-Dawkins, "let me get this right. *Knowing* that the target had considerable numbers of mercenaries at his disposal, you sent a numerically inferior force into the Bristlecone Lake mine. Is that right?"

"Well Minister—" started McKinley.

"A simple yes or no will suffice, Operative Tripod," he scoffed.

"But it's *not* simple, Minister," interjected Sutton.

"General, I believe we were addressing the question to your subordinate," continued the singsong voice of the chairman. "You were already given more than an hour of our time this morning."

"Minister, a yes-or-no answer fails to illustrate the complexities of the operation."

Cambion-Dawkins ignored the general. "Yes or no, Operative Tripod?" he demanded.

McKinley could have spat nails. He was getting so angry with this bureaucratic shithead that he was starting to feel that being in a separate enclosure was a very good thing. "Yes, Minister," he ground. Should he have said no? Damn. Too late now.

"Finally an admission," crowed the chairman, pushing himself back in the chair as if relieved. "I think we're actually making progress here." He paused for a few seconds, shifting his papers about in blocky monochrome via the monitor. McKinley imagined for a moment that a first person shoot-'em-up video game based on politicians would be a great idea.

"So let's see what we've got here," said the slimy MP. "Considerable loss of life in both the domestic and foreign phases of *Operation Copper Burial*. Her Majesty's forces base at Bodmin Moor almost wiped out—"

"Minister!" barked Sutton, immediately calming down again so as not to cross a line. "Are you attempting to blame my operatives for the attack on Bodmin Moor?"

"Well General," replied Cambion-Dawkins, "as I read it, the base was attacked and the records office destroyed by our enemies *because* your team was closing in on them. Furthermore your technical division failed to prevent infiltration of your computers by the double agent, thus mandating your team's investigation via the hard copy reports archived at Bodmin Moor. Might I remind you that the same double agent enabled the sinking of the *Fort William* and the loss of the warheads in the first place? If that's *not* cause and effect, then I'm sure I don't know what is."

McKinley could hear the tension in Sutton's voice as the general responded. "Minister, this inquiry is ignoring many facts. We found and retired the traitor, identified and pursued the enemy, retrieved two of the warheads intact and destroyed a third saving North America from a catastrophic EMP attack. We rescued the hostages and generated a massive amount of usable intel. Yes, I agree that the loss of life has been tragic, but *Operation Copper Burial* is not a failure!"

"No General, of course not, of course not," simpered Cambion-Dawkins. "This inquiry is simply trying to establish a balanced view of events."

"Furthermore," continued Sutton, "*Operation Copper Burial* is not over. We are still—"

"We'll see about *that* General!" snapped the politician waspishly. "Now if you'd be so kind as to let me continue?"

"Yes, Minister," conceded Sutton. McKinley was horrified at the general's sudden passive tone, but he recognised that his boss was treading a fine line between defending the unit's actions and pissing off their employers. If McKinley thought he was having a hard time, Sutton was probably having a harder one.

"Well then let's move on to this new fiasco in Gran Canaria," drawled Cambion-Dawkins. McKinley's eyes bulged in his head and he felt as though a swarm of ice cold needles was attacking his upper back. Bloody hell! Did this officious bastard read reports in his sleep or something?

"I understand," continued the politician, "that a British arms dealer is being held hostage by a Turkish arms dealer as a result of TDR.12's interference. Furthermore it appears that three Spanish nationals were killed and several more injured by TDR.12 during an altercation. Could this possibly get any worse?"

McKinley expected Sutton to say something to rebut the MP's accusations, to champion his operatives, but in truth it sounded desperately indefensible. Gran Canaria *was* a bit of a screw-up and they'd been his moves. Bacon was in mortal danger—perhaps even beyond that point already—and it was his responsibility. Without lying to the JIC, there was nothing either he or Sutton could do.

"I've not yet reviewed reports on the matters to which you refer, Minister," said Sutton, "and I therefore cannot comment."

The low res Cambion-Dawkins on the monitor looked down his nose at General Sutton in the same superior manner with which a headmaster might posture before a wayward child upon whom he was about to visit punishment.

"I see. Let's look at the events on Mallory Island then, in which case I have just one question for your operative, General."

McKinley saw his boss nod. They both knew what it would be.

"Operative Tripod," continued Cambion-Dawkins, "I understand that you had the opportunity to execute Mister Heinmarsh *as ordered*, but instead you went after the bomb. Can you explain that please?"

Yeah, thought McKinley, I'll explain it with a brick to your skull. He composed his thoughts for a moment then answered. "My orders were specific, Minister. The warhead was the highest priority."

"But according to your team's reports you had the man at your mercy," complained the politician. "Why didn't you take a moment to retire him?"

"I'm not in the habit of challenging orders, Minister," said McKinley gravely.

Without the slightest shadow of the expression reaching his face, Sutton winced inside.

"Well, I'm afraid I disagree," sneered Cambion-Dawkins, "as does your service record. In fact even General Sutton reported that it was your insubordination which led to the Bridgewell connection." He made pause as though drawing back his fist for the next disparagement to be a harder punch. "I'm sure we're all glad of that but, in the light of your failure to kill Mister Heinmarsh when you had the perfect opportunity, it demonstrates that there's a fine line between the letter and the spirit of the law, and *you don't know where it lies!*"

McKinley set his jaw and clenched his fists, with both of which he yearned to smash the little television screen. There was also a lot he wanted to say or, more accurately, shout, but none of it would be helpful.

General Sutton, thankfully, stepped in. "In this case, Minister, my man followed his orders accurately. Those orders came from me and I expected them to be obeyed. Heinmarsh had started the timer and vital seconds could've been lost."

Even McKinley could see Cambion-Dawkins rolling his eyes. "To diffuse a fake bomb?"

Sutton's voice hardened. "Minister, you know as well as I do that it was believed Heinmarsh had triggered the timer on the nuclear warhead."

For a change, Cambion-Dawkins didn't come back with a deprecating retort. Instead he nodded slowly, lowered his eyes to his paperwork and turned over several pages.

"Very well," he said, making a note. "Now, just one more thing. Are you *sure* there's nothing else you want to bring to light, General?" he asked. "No other incidents from your unit's fiasco in Canada?"

McKinley was already way ahead of Cambion-Dawkins, certain as to which incident the cabinet member was referring. But the fact that Cambion-Dawkins was asking seemed to indicate uncertainty. Would the general back the workers or the shareholders?

"No sir," Sutton replied. "I believe everything is covered in our reports."

Even via the imperfect video feed McKinley could see Cambion-Dawkins' face contort into what would have been a snarl had the expression been audible. "Nothing else about Operative Tripod and his TDR.12 shower? Nothing noteworthy?"

McKinley felt a small sense of satisfaction as General Sutton made his denial. Cambion-Dawkins was fishing for information, trying to draw the general out. It was obvious that the politician thought he knew something about Corporal Carter's indiscretion in Canada and was fishing for a confirmation. But the doubt implicit in his enquiry would be Sutton's escape clause. With that thought came another more worrying: how the hell did Cambion-Dawkins know anything about it at all? As far as McKinley knew, Sutton and his command staff had been extremely careful to whitewash the incident. Had they made a critical error?

The MP's growl brought McKinley back to the moment.

"Well, if you should find out anything more you'd better inform us of it hadn't you General?" Cambion-Dawkins spat Sutton's title scornfully, as though detestable. McKinley almost laughed. The venomous arrogance of this jumped-up cockalorum was close to comical.

Sutton nodded deferentially and said "yes Minister, of course".

The central figure on the monitor leaned forward. It looked to McKinley as though this moment was rehearsed and about to be played out pointedly to an audience of one.

"All that being as it is, then, I propose we take a vote," said Cambion-Dawkins. "I move that Operative Tripod be suspended from duty pending a much more in-depth inquiry at a date to be determined. May I have a second?"

The crimson woman raised her hand and Cambion-Dawkins said "thank you ma'am. All in favour?"

Four more hands rose in the room and McKinley fell inside.

"Motion carried."

Behind the helipad, next to the steep rocky slope, Cottingham held the manhole cover open as Carter worked. The interior was reminiscent of any mains electricity installation with thick, waxy cables held tightly in place by brass grommets. The cables snaked into a watertight plastic compartment, the lid of which was now sitting by Carter's legs as he lay with his head in the manhole, flashlight clenched in his teeth. It wasn't the easiest circumstance under which to make electrical connections, but the destruction of the island's generator had rendered the whole system inert so at least it was safe.

Carter levered himself up, wiping excess wetness from his face. "Right, let's find out where it goes. You want to hit the switch?" He threw a nod to Cottingham.

"Yes sir," responded the BC. He was uncertain how a wire from the walkie-talkie's antenna socket to the mains would help them to locate the power lines, but Corporal Carter seemed sure of what he was doing. He held down the transmit key then pulled a white zip-clip tight, holding it in place. The little radio was now transmitting continuously on an unused channel.

Carter walked several meters north-eastward in the direction of Kishorn Cove. The frequency sniffer in his hand jumped; a line of tiny green LEDs indicating signal strength. He moved back and the line shrank, then multiplied again as he lowered the unit. Carter flexed the fingers of his free hand, feeling the frigid clamminess seeping into his bones. Damn the bloody weather.

"Good signal," he told Cottingham and they set off, following the only road on the island. To their left the grey ocean raged and on their right the silent, ancient slope was a mass of dwarf waterfalls coursing toward sea level. The wind was gusting more fiercely now, leading Carter to wonder whether a trip back by helicopter would even be possible. Wilson was sitting this one out in the mess, knocking back the coffee and talking with some of the other BCs on Mallory. Easy life, thought Carter with grim humour.

Shortly the tarmac came to an end and the road continued as gravel and cloying, ecru mud. Here it dipped slightly toward the beach, the large pebbles of which Carter vividly recalled playing hell with both his ankles and his recent injuries as he and McKinley had forced themselves to run along the shore from the base of Charlotte's cliff to the dock. Thank God their young colleague had come to the rescue near the half way point with a barely serviceable Land Rover that had carried them the remainder of the way to their encounter with the crew of the Chinese submarine.

Carter kept his eye on the signal strength meter, the readout of which was mundanely steady. The tempestuous weather was hurling great splashes of seawater at them and the temperature seemed to be decreasing, but the two kept trudging, entering the small valley where the road veered away from the seafront and was separated from it by a twelve meter rocky hillock.

"Hold on," said Carter momentarily, his extended arm blocking Cottingham's path. The LED ladder had dropped dramatically. The young BC looked closely as they stood in the middle of the cutting.

"Let's walk it about a bit," suggested Carter, making a small circuit around Cottingham. "Interesting."

"It's going into the hill?" exclaimed the BC.

"Looks like it." Carter made some more geometric moves, trying to get a handle on the path of the buried cable. Yes, the signal was stronger nearer the steep slope. He moved to the left and to the right, observing what happened on the readout. "Definitely," he concluded.

By the time Wilson and a group of BCs arrived Carter had made a thorough survey of the rocky scree.

"There's something buried here," he told them. "Something that needs power."

"Let's get digging," Wilson said.

Again sitting alone in the long, quiet corridor, McKinley felt like shit. The inquiry had gone about as badly as he could have feared barring execution.

He was suspended from duty. Holy bloody shit, he was *suspended from duty.*

Worse, he was suspended through the twisted semantics of the worst political bullshitter he'd ever met. Worse still, a good friend who'd simply tried to help was minus an ear and possibly more by now. Yet worse, he'd been kept waiting with nothing to think about but his misfortune for another hour whilst the damned bureaucrats presumably tore his CO a new one in the privacy of the meeting room. McKinley felt like finding some nearby bar and getting so hammered that his rank and privileges would become a long-term irrelevance.

With a sudden click the door opened and out walked General Sutton, briefcase and jacket in hand. He looked at McKinley and tried to smile reassuringly, but didn't quite pull it off.

"How are you doing?" said Sutton quietly.

"Sir, with respect, do you really have to ask?"

"Okay," replied Sutton with another attempted smile. "We'll talk about this some more, but not here. I have other business to attend to, so you can make your way back to Nottingham via public transport. Is that alright?"

I suppose so, thought McKinley, what the hell choice is there? "Yes sir," he affirmed.

A long and soaking hour after finding the end of the power lines, Carter, Wilson and their small crew had uncovered a metal mesh anchoring rocks, soil and grass to what appeared to be an angled hatch over two meters square. The Basic Commandos were amazed but Carter and Wilson simply accepted the find as more evidence of Heinmarsh's furtive activities.

The weather was steadily worsening and the visibility was now so bad that they couldn't see the dock just four hundred meters away. Massive breakers pummelled the nearby beach, but the little valley through which the road passed afforded some slight shelter.

Four BCs had joined them for the digging and now all six had their gloved hands under the edge of the huge hatch, Carter's reasoning being that it had to open upward. With power denied to the island, any operating mechanism would be useless so manpower was the only choice.

"Alright lads, on three," announced Wilson and made the count. He pulled hard and, when the hatch didn't move, gave it a second burst of strength. They were all grunting with the effort, their limbs aching in the horrible damp cold.

Suddenly a metallic crack accompanied by a jerk of upward motion sent them all rearing backward. The hatch was open by slightly less than a foot, revealing darkness beneath. They looked at each other and pulled again. Once the gap had been increased to around eighteen inches, Wilson slid under the hatch and pushed from there. In half a minute the metalwork was horizontal and the space beyond open. They carefully took the pressure off the hatch and it stayed in position.

"Find something to prop this up," ordered Wilson, "and get some lighting!"

A couple of the BCs drove off to fetch the equipment. Carter, in the meantime, had switched on his flashlight and was advancing into the cavity.

Revealed in the beam of his torch was a rectangular space that barely met the description of a room. At about seven meters deep by five wide and with a low ceiling it seemed more like the dilapidated garage of some ruined house.

However, the furnishings in the space were about as far from archaic as they could be. Around the walls were steel benches, cabinets and racks of tools juxtaposed against computer terminals and other electronics. In the far left corner was what appeared to be a heavy isolation cabinet with big windows. The area was dominated by a large central workbench of shining metal, next to which was a trolley containing more electronics.

As he blinked rainwater from them, Carter's eyes were starting to adjust and he was amazed by what he saw, but he needed more light. Seeing that the guys were approaching with lighting rigs and a portable generator, he told Wilson that it was his intention to power up the room's own lighting.

It only took a few minutes to roughly patch the generator into the space's breaker panel, although the hastily rigged workaround would never have passed a health and safety inspection. They started the generator and Carter threw the light switch.

Buried in the island's hillside was a laboratory and workshop. There were no other descriptions that would fit the cavity, arrayed as it was with all kinds of machinery and technical systems.

"Well," started Wilson, striding in and glancing from side to side. "I wasn't expecting this."

Carter was working his way around the perimeter, taking stock of the kinds of tools there. "No," he mumbled, "but I'll give you one guess what he was working on."

"The warhead," answered Wilson. He looked around the room. Surely Heinmarsh hadn't travelled all the way here with his captive physicist *just* to modify the nukes?

He joined Carter at a wide table near the back of the room where there were a number of large sheets of paper laid out. Wilson held one up and they looked at each other.

Carter swore. "Heinmarsh *definitely* told you that he'd tried to build a bomb, right?"

Wilson had a horrible apprehension of where this was going. "Yes. He said *they* tried to build their own and almost got it finished."

"So now we *know* why he came here," nodded Carter darkly.

Wilson's brow knitted. "So is this—?"

"Yes it is," interrupted Carter, index finger tracing a quick circle around the plans. "His home brew nuke was stashed here and he took it on that sub. So he still has *two* potentially viable nuclear weapons."

Carter walked out into the colourless daylight. "Get us patched through to base!" he snapped at the BCs. "We've gotta call this in – and I don't care what anyone thinks about the bloody weather, we're taking that chopper back now."

Refuelling at Edinburgh Airport, they flew south again, pushing the Eurocopter toward its never-exceed speed of 324Km/h.

They were passing near Leeds as Wilson heard his colleague swear. He looked over to where Carter was in the other seat, toying with his phone. The weapons tech looked worried, but glanced up at his friend with a sense of urgency.

"You need to see this," he said over the aircraft noise. Through the headset it sounded as though he was speaking right into Wilson's ear.

"Sure," replied Wilson. Carter leaned over the control panel and connected his phone.

"What is it?" asked Wilson, but Carter didn't answer. He was punching buttons on the helicopter's A/V system. Suddenly the central flat screen monitor flickered and changed to 'Server found'.

"Watch this," said Carter, and clicked something on his phone.

The monitor flickered again, blocky diagonal lines flashing by, then cleared. The image was of a disturbingly familiar scene. In the background was a cream coloured building which looked like a large, square wedding cake with three arched wooden doors above rows of steps. These were mostly obscured, however, by a mass of bodies frantically diving in and out of frame. A policeman could be seen, backing away from the camera, his hand outstretched toward it, urging people to stay back.

"Where is this?" asked Wilson, trying to both watch and fly.

"Bulgaria; five hours ago. See the inscription? It's *'Suedinenieto pravi silata',*" Carter pronounced the motto, "if there's any similarity to Russian. Now watch."

The camera steadied slightly and the cop seemed to be pleading with someone out of shot, obscured by a nearby shoulder. Instantly the image shook again and they saw the cop being jerked backward as though on wires, a nebula of red around his neck.

"Sniper!" exclaimed Wilson.

The figures in the foreground were panicking. Suddenly the picture flashed, the building vanished into a blur of motion and the camera came to rest on its side, pointing along the street as people were running away. They saw an expanding haze of smoke and several more police officers hurriedly trying to herd pedestrians out of the area.

"You see?" said Carter, scrolling the video back. "Check this out."

His finger slid to a halt on his telephone screen, as did the maelstrom of images on the chopper's monitor. Carter scrolled through the video a frame at a time until something became horribly clear.

"Holy shit," breathed Wilson, as the mixture of revulsion, anger and righteous humanitarianism again rose inside him.

The freeze-frame was of a young pregnant woman with black hair chained to a thin, middle-aged man in a suit, presumably a member of Bulgaria's parliamentary assembly. Behind her, the policeman's body was spread on the steps like an unloved rag doll. The girl's mouth was open in a scream and she had her hand on a switch essentially identical to what they'd seen in London. The subsequent frame was a searing ball of light where the young woman had been, and the next total chaos.

"Same M.O.," said Carter. "This shit's getting round."

"Furious doesn't even bloody come close!" barked General Sutton. "Of course I'm annoyed. We've got a murderous nutcase with potentially two nuclear weapons on the run somewhere—one belonging to Her Majesty's armed forces—and we're ordered to stand down?! It's insanity. Bloody insanity!"

Sutton was more agitated than they'd seen in a long time. His good arm was thrashing the air like a whip as he strode back and forth behind his desk.

"I've never encountered more obtuseness in all my career! Absolutely bloody ridiculous!"

"Sir, ventured Carter, "what about Bacon?"

Sutton's turned toward his men. "Damn it! I cannot authorise a rescue mission and the government won't pay the ransom." He paused, shaking his head before continuing in a deeply grave tone. "You may have to accept his loss."

Carter sensed McKinley's indignation rising like a wave and the Scot almost shouted.

"Sir, we *have* to rescue him! It's 'cause of us he's being held!" McKinley was trying to hold back in addressing the general, but his fist was shaking.

"I can't do *anything.*"

McKinley's edge dulled slightly. "Yes you can sir. You can—"

"Against orders?!" snapped the CO. On seeing McKinley's expression he continued. "Yes; we've been *ordered* not to intervene."

McKinley tried one more time. "But sir..."

Sutton held up his hand to quell the corporal's plea. "A civilian presence on a COAST mission was totally unauthorised, and if you'd asked I wouldn't've cleared it. So I'm afraid this is on you. I sympathise, I truly do, but I'm out of options."

Wilson glanced sideways at his team leader, who looked as though someone had kicked him in the crotch. "Sir, these suicide bombers," he started. "What about that?"

Sutton's eye's screwed up in frustration, then he took a deep breath. "As long as there isn't another incident on UK soil, it's out of our hands. The Security Service have got that one now."

"Sir, the evidence is that it's international—!" burst McKinley, but Sutton's bellow shut him off.

"*I know!* I saw that video from Bulgaria and we're hearing unconfirmed chatter about a similar incident in Pakistan. I'd be sending teams out right now if it wasn't for that... that..." Sutton spewed a term so vulgar that all three were surprised, "making his case that we're incompetent fools!" The general slammed his fist down on the desk angrily.

Having got the bluster out of his system, the boss continued. "So here's the dice. We're ordered to lay off *Operation Copper Burial.* We can't even re-open the investigation until there's positive proof of the whereabouts of our warhead. We're ordered not to attempt a rescue mission for Bacon. Which reminds me..." Sutton stopped for a moment, glancing down at his desk. He picked up a newspaper and turned it toward them.

BIG REWARD FOR GANGSTER HOSTAGE

"Yes," said the general, seeing their reactions. "Broadwick went public a few hours ago."

"Blimey," whispered McKinley, understanding the complications this might cause.

"You'd better hope—*if* Bacon's returned—that he's got the sense to keep his trap shut. Anyway," continued Sutton, "we're also *ordered* not to investigate these suicide bombings. You, McKinley, are to leave base by eighteen hundred hours tomorrow and not return until ordered. You two'll be staying on for now and I'll assign you a BC to take up the slack. Carter, your seniority makes you team leader and I expect you to take it seriously. Is this all clear?"

Three voices said "yes sir" without enthusiasm.

"Right then," said Sutton. "Carter, Wilson; dismissed."

McKinley's colleagues filed out. Sutton waited until the sliding door hissed shut then pointed at the middle chair opposite his desk. They sat.

The general was still breathing hard but he managed to behave with the calm of professionalism. McKinley wasn't as successful. His guts were in turmoil and in his mind there was a tape playing of the awful sounds Bacon had made whilst being mutilated.

"McKinley," said Sutton, "you're basically a good soldier. This inquiry, bloody stupid nonsense that it is, it's going to come to an end sooner or later. The cream always rises to the surface. You'll vindicate yourself, I know it."

"Sir?"

"A while ago I told you that you have the luck of the Irish. I don't believe in luck, but I stand by the sentiment."

McKinley's eyes narrowed involuntarily. Where was the boss going with this?

"Like I said," continued Sutton, "you're a *soldier*, a warrior, and this isn't some cosy government office where the politicians can just swan in and do what they like. You know a true warrior never gives up. He's the kind of man who plays roulette on a hunch; he waits for the right moment, throws all his chips on one number and the consequences be damned. So when the perfect spin comes along, as it eventually will, he'll break the bank. Such a man might lose a few preliminary rounds, but ultimately he could take the house."

McKinley sat there, not sure what he was hearing.

"It all depends," said the CO, "how badly you want to prosecute your cause."

"I don't know how I can, sir." McKinley shook his head despondently.

"Well Corporal, for a start, a little faith in your commanding officer would go a long way. I've certainly not forgotten about Heinmarsh, or about Mister Bacon, or about these suicide bombings. Enjoy this break; think things over. You'll feel better in time." The general finished with an ingratiating smile which, under these circumstances, seemed both out-of-place and unnecessary. "Dismissed."

Carter found McKinley sitting on the loading dock in the transport bay, his new favourite spot for me-time. He used McKinley's shoulder to steady himself as he dropped his backside onto the dusty concrete edge beside his friend. It was late afternoon and few people were about. It was unlikely that there would be intrusion to their conversation.

"Penny for 'em," Carter said.

McKinley withdrew the cigarette from his mouth, looked through the ribbon of smoke for a moment, then blankly said "I'm screwed."

"Nah," said Carter, shaking his head and trying to be positive. "This'll blow over. Me 'n' Willy are still with you."

Despite his encouragement, Carter had seldom seen his friend looking so sullen. There had been times when the going was shitty, for sure, and plenty of them. But this was something different. McKinley's ass was about to be thrown under the bus just as he'd unwittingly thrown a friend's to the sharks.

McKinley looked round at the weapons tech. "Bacon," he said, almost stinking of guilt.

Carter nodded, his face now deadly serious.

"I don't know what to do any more," McKinley murmured. "I feel helpless. It's... *so wrong.*"

Carter angled his head thoughtfully. "Mind if I tell you a story?"

McKinley huffed. "Whatever."

"There was a guy my dad knew, name of Barney; self made millionaire. I think he was a pretty clever bloke. Anyway, I was about eighteen I think, and he sat me down and told me to always remember this advice."

McKinley was already losing interest. "So?"

"He said "kid, if you're right, fight. If you're half right, fight until you know either way. If you're wrong, make your apologies and back off"." Carter gave McKinley a gentle punch on the shoulder. "You know what they say," he added. "If you don't like it, fight it."

Unfortunately this seemed to dent the Scotsman even more. "I feel like I haven't got any fight left in me," he said. He took another pull on the smoke, looking at it disdainfully as though it wasn't doing its job.

"Okay," said Carter, offering his keys. "Take the Rangey. Go for a long drive in the country. Clear the fog."

The couple of miles home seemed like more than enough to McKinley, but he accepted Carter's offer nonetheless. "Sure?"

"Absolutely. Willy'll drive me home. Just don't touch any switches that aren't labelled."

You're such a bloody geek, thought McKinley. "Thanks," he mumbled, turning his attention back to the cigarette and his thoughts back to the bleakness of the future.

008: The Challenge

Early evening was upon him and McKinley found himself listless, in want of the long drive that Carter had suggested. The yellow and brown leaves seemed to wave through the reddening rays of low sunlight, beckoning him. Outside the air was pleasantly cool, but indicative of much less pleasant temperatures to come. All of nature was drawing on its winter shawl as overcoats closed in on the human populace.

Carter's Range Rover was there to do with as he pleased—as long as he stayed clear of the unidentified controls—so McKinley pulled on some boots and wrapped a khaki canvas jacket around his shoulders, tossing a bottle of Johnnie Walker Black Label onto the passenger seat and taking off eastwards.

The A52 road was surprisingly quiet as he drove. Behind him the dipping sun silhouetted his face in the mirror so that he couldn't see his own expression, but he knew it was troubled. He knew that there were questions begging for answers and he needed the clarity of solitude. This was not a night to loll around at home, nor shelter from the wind in a pub. This was a night for consideration.

Once beyond Grantham he passed by Folkingham and the hills started to smooth out. The Fens welcomed him with wide, deep cobalt skies, linear drainage canals stretching into the distance and an increasing sense of isolation. The hills to his rear darkened quickly, night creeping over them like a swarm of insects. In the valleys inland, the Earth's umbra truly seems deeper, and householders check their locks twice. The cover of darkness is a necessary evil. In The Fens, the dusk dwells longer as the moon rises from the stark but glittering line of the North Sea horizon. Nightfall is a beautiful thing in the flatlands of east Lincolnshire.

Wide fields, denuded by the harvest, stretched out like a patterned tablecloth around the vehicle as McKinley continued east, still not knowing where he was heading but goaded to find it. Along the way, cheerfully lit diners and garages exchanged themselves at regular intervals with expensive houses and shuttered fruit stands. Farms became fewer and further between, interspersed with pastures of increasing size. McKinley rolled down the window and the big vehicle was imbued with the musty smells of autumn whilst skylarks provided the soundtrack.

McKinley turned south by Kirton and, once beyond Frampton, started to feel the clarity and isolation that he sought. The Lincolnshire lowlands became bleak around the speeding Range Rover and McKinley came into sight of The Wash, a twenty mile wide, almost rectangular estuary carved into England's east coast, dangerous to navigation and which had in times past been used for practice bombing runs by both the RAF and the USAF. The scents gradually segued from woodlands and grass into saltwater and river mud.

On his left, McKinley noticed a small copse that seemed to be calling his name, and he abandoned the Range Rover at the roadside, accompanied only by the bottle. Crossing the dry furrows, he settled down with his back against the trunk of a stately oak and cracked the whisky. Taking just a small mouthful, he felt himself relax a little, trying to recall his point of origin and whatever course he might be on.

In his early adulthood McKinley had started on the same familiar ladder that most tread: the advancement of his career and the accruement of worldly goods.

He'd believed then that such things were part of the human journey simply because it was what all the other human beings were doing. By observation, therefore, his contemporaries laboured under the same belief, and amassed their share of the adornments that the western world provided: a nice car, an audiophile sound system, a house, a better rank, a newer mobile phone. He'd worked his ass off for nearly two decades to advance position, collect material items and accumulate experience.

What he'd forgotten, and what he now realised, was that there was a time when he didn't have any of those things and neither needed them nor cared. Was it possible to get by without them now, or was his internment in the system too much of a habit to break?

Some time ago, before all the appurtenances had adhered and caused an imperceptibly gradual but nonetheless irrevocable diminution of his world, he'd enjoyed the carefree liberty of youth. Only the bare necessities were truly necessary and everything else was either too much of a burden or yet to be acquired. The world was wonderfully free, and McKinley was free in it. But with advancement came responsibility, with responsibility came accountability and, with that, the light of freedom started to recede until it was becoming not so much a light at the end, but at the *beginning* of the tunnel. Liberty effected its withdrawal like viscous honey creeping from a cracked container; like the fragile dandelion which forces its way through concrete.

Having through the subtlety of freedom's egress become encumbered, McKinley hadn't noticed that he'd forgotten who he was before all that advancement. And, being thus forgotten, career, culture and peer pressure ensured that the old person remained no more than a shadow, creeping about in the dark and offering the occasional taunt. Its voice, having become subversive, was then mistrusted and attended by suspicion. Its cries went unheeded because the bricks of the jail were the beautiful trappings of maturity and the imprisonment was both justified and chosen. If anyone had told McKinley then that such things might be comparable to penal servitude, he'd have asked them what they'd been smoking.

The sun's last segment oozed into the distant horizon and McKinley wished he could somehow dissolve and blend into these picturesque surroundings. He wanted to get away from all the idiots, criminals, terrorists and gangsters, away from all the bureaucrats, politicians, nay-sayers, time wasters and accountants. Here, in this place, he could at least feel somewhat disconnected from such things. He could take time, sit back and try to figure out what really mattered.

To his rear, from within the copse, a wood pigeon cooed. Apart from the birds and other natural sounds, there was peace here of a kind unknown in urban areas. McKinley looked to his right. Milk parsley surrounded a nearby pond, above which swallows wheeled and dived, hunting for damselflies and black-tailed skimmers. Further above, a formation of ducks passed over in their habitual migration. McKinley smiled to himself; nature nut Wilson would have known the names of all the flora and fauna. He closed his eyes and turned his thoughts to business, taking an occasional sip of the liquor.

Much as McKinley hated to admit it, like Sister Patricia he felt robbed in some way. But there was no deeper level of personality, no *Jem*, to which he could revert. He was here, this was it, and this was the way it had been all along. It was the hand he'd been dealt. The Joint *Unintelligence* Committee were being magnificently block-headed and, as much as he couldn't understand it, he was driven to fix it and to take care of business like he'd been trained, like

COAST always did. Something was woefully wrong, a problem that he felt compelled at the deepest level to redress.

But what did the future hold? Would all this be taken from him? Would he lose both the right and the ability to act? He looked up, imagining for a moment that the Sword of Damocles was lurking in the arboreal canopy. It might as well be. In their parochialism the JIC were not amused, the target of their disapproval being Tactical Corporal Ian David McKinley of TDR team twelve, codename Tripod, known to his friends as Mickey. They were planning to sacrifice him on the altar of bureaucratic idiocy and political convenience. McKinley took another gulp of the whisky and let his head drop onto his chest as the alcohol warmed his throat.

Everything about his position was bestowed by someone else. Yes, he'd earned it, worked for it and was entitled to it. But whether he liked it or not, he served at the JIC's pleasure. If they wanted to take it all away there would be nothing he could do to keep it.

Yet here he was, in a cool, dark meadow near the North Sea shore, swigging Johnnie Walker and feeling oddly content. The drink was *rented* and, once its useful effects had abated, would return to the planet's hydrological cycle. He didn't own the field or the trees and certainly not the wildlife that he envied for its carefree existence. Heck, he didn't even own the Range Rover. The bank still owned some of his house, and the delivery of his new car, most of which they would also own, was delayed by goodness knows how long. And, looking at it from that perspective, it was all just *stuff* anyway. There was a time when he had none of it, probably couldn't imagine having any of it, and didn't care.

In a moment's luminescent epiphany, McKinley realised that he'd been labouring under an illusion. All of it was meaningless when said and done. It didn't matter that he led a successful TDR team. His previous triumphs in the army might as well be void. He didn't actually need a house, a car, the bottle in his hand or even the last few smokes in his pocket − much as the thought of forsaking the latter was troubling.

Somewhere along the lengthy railway track from childhood to where he was now, McKinley had forgotten himself. There was something he'd stopped believing, by infinitesimal degrees, as the fabric of possession and position was woven around him, largely by his own hand. He'd done years of hard labour to build his own prison cell and was languishing in it. Time to break down the walls.

McKinley was still here. He was still the center of his own universe and the prison was an illusion that he'd accepted. It was a hard concept with which to wrestle, but he was winning now.

The moon was getting brighter on its long arc through the sky. Bombers' moon, thought McKinley, remembering that Lincolnshire was home to many squadrons during the Second World War. There were disused airfields everywhere around here. He wondered how many Lancasters and B-17s had rumbled over this very spot on their way to rain hell on Germany. He thought about the chain of events that had led to that massive global conflict.

The League Of Nations, forerunner to the UN, had willingly ignored the military buildup in Hitler's Germany. Almost the only guy waving a red flag at that time was Winston Churchill. Appeasement, Churchill had said, was like trying to feed an alligator in the hope that it'll eat you last. Then, after their annexation of Austria and the Sudetenland, on the first of September 1939 the Nazis hit Poland, and that became the generally acknowledged start of the most destructive international war mankind had ever known. How had the Allies not seen it coming, mused McKinley.

He rubbed at his chin with his free hand. The bureaucrats in the JIC were doing almost the same thing, heads firmly in the sand or, he thought, somewhere darker and considerably less pleasant. He remembered the famous quote '*all that is necessary for the triumph of evil is that good men do nothing.*' Heinmarsh was still in business and a British citizen was in mortal danger, yet the supposedly good men were indeed doing nothing. Such well-informed politicians should *know* that a character like Heinmarsh would never back down, especially if he was presumed dead. It was foolhardy in the extreme to believe that his ambitions would simply roll over and die, so *someone* had to take the bastard out.

Like grains from a cosmic salt shaker, stars were spreading across the sky. As he sipped on the bottle McKinley considered whether or not his life now was preferable—or even comparable—to that he'd had twenty years ago, before COAST, before the army and before the bloody girl had ripped out his heart and shredded it before his eyes. Arguments and counter-arguments swapped places in his head like some kind of square dance. *Take your partner by the hand, why can't the bureaucrats understand?*

Even if it *was* all stripped away, he was just thirty four and with effort and commitment he could do it again. It would be more difficult, but what mattered was the central component that he'd overlooked: himself. But would it be worth it? He was arguably at the peak of his career now. Could he beat the odds like the title character in the Book of Job, who'd lost everything in one fell swoop then, much later, gained back far more?

McKinley felt his eyes getting tired and he faded into a slumber filled with dreams of endless possibility and duty versus loyalty. His mind roamed here and there, hunting diverse futures for reality and certainty, hoping that he'd find them to be the same, or at least close cousins.

When McKinley opened his eyes his clothes were smothered in myriad tiny droplets of dew, the field was shrouded in dense grey mist from the sea and he was *bloody freezing*. His watch read 05:47. The copse was devoid of bird sounds and had shed leaves on him. He coughed as he lit his first cigarette. His drinking buddy Johnnie was lying by his side half gone, but McKinley didn't have a thundering hangover. Ignoring the protest of his chilled, stiff body he got up, brushing foliage and still-moist bird lime from his clothes, then wandered over to the pond, filling his lungs with nicotine as he added a small amount of urea and other solute chemicals to the watercourse. The mist surrounded him on every side except the inside which, for the first time in ages, seemed perfectly clear.

Turning the Range Rover round, McKinley headed toward civilisation. Again the sunlight, diffused into a nebulous golden aura by the fog, was behind, but he knew that the face looking back from the rear view mirror was much more confident than yesterday's. Some paradigm had shifted during his lost night. He didn't need to find himself. He'd been there all along and he'd taken it for granted. He could be neither bought nor sold, removed nor forsaken. It was only society's hunt for advancement that had derailed him from the obvious notion that no-one would realistically want to be burdened with power or position when there's *life* to be lived.

Certainty seemed to sit personified on the vehicle's passenger seat, affirming him as he drove. He knew what to do. He had a plan.

It was half past eight at COAST headquarters and Basic Commando Louise Cumberland was a fearsome woman. She was a little shorter than Carter with a squarish block of a body and a face that didn't invite argument. Although young, she was highly successful in the Tactical and Surveillance discipline and was on track to running her own TDR team. She took no shit and dealt plenty out. Wilson tolerated her whilst Carter hated her, suspecting that her assignment was connected with General Sutton's adjuration to take his duties seriously. But whether or not they liked it, the boss thought that she would be a good if temporary addition to TDR.12.

The weapons and equipment technician not only felt uncomfortable with Cumberland but in his leadership role. He'd always seen their team like a car with McKinley's engine, his drivetrain and Brook's, then Wilson's wheels. Mixing the order of those components would be a mechanical nightmare, especially if the new component argued a lot and didn't respond well to orders. If Mickey were here, he thought, he'd kick her ass right into line.

Then, suddenly, McKinley *was* there, poking his head round the door of their office.

"Morning chaps," he smiled.

"You're cheerful," frowned Carter. "What happened? You wreck my car? What went wrong?"

"Nothing's gone wrong; I'm just here to collect some stuff. Decided to make the best of it." He turned to their new colleague, jerking his head in the direction of the corridor. "Cumberland, get lost."

Her eyes widened in outrage. "You can't walk in here and give *me* orders! You're suspended from duty. You shouldn't even be here!"

"Cumberland," said Carter evenly but firmly, "piss off."

"*What?!*"

"Are you freakin' deaf or something?" snapped Wilson. "Your team leader told you to piss off! And shut the bloody door!"

Her body language screaming every retort that rank and uncertainly forbade her from vocalising, Cumberland marched out and pulled the door behind her, shutting it with a vindictive bang. They waited until her figure had disappeared along the corridor.

Falling into a chair, McKinley said "nice to be back among friends," a big smirk dividing his mug.

"Come back Mickey; all is forgiven," said Carter. "She's a bloody dragon. I hope to heck she never, ever makes team leader... unless it's in front of a dog sled."

Wilson nodded. "I wouldn't want to meet her in a dark alley."

Carter's eyes widened. "Mate, I wouldn't want to meet her in a *well lit* alley!"

McKinley grinned. "Chris, will you secure the room please?"

"Gimme a sec." Carter went to his locker, opened it and pulled out a ghetto blaster, muttering "here's one I prepared earlier."

Wilson wondered what was going on as Carter plugged the little stereo in and cranked up something that he probably wouldn't have described as music.

"What the hell's this?" complained McKinley over the din.

"Karlheinz Stockhausen. Don't pretend you know who that is."

"I won't," laughed McKinley, shaking his head.

Wilson frowned. "Why am I not surprised you *planned* to hold secret conversations in here?"

"You're one of us now Willy," said McKinley sternly. "Get used to it." He beckoned his friends closer so that he could be heard despite the cacophony. They leaned over the desk.

"Listen lads, this has to stay absolutely confidential. I'm asking you as friends. This is really, really serious shit. You got it?"

Carter and Wilson glanced at each other then nodded.

"You sure?"

They repeated the glance, speaking simultaneously.

"Yes."

"Uh-huh."

So here we are, thought McKinley, this is it. He composed his thoughts for a second and looked from one to the other, making sure of their attention.

"Okay. One, Bacon's gonna die and it's our fault; two, there are still live nukes out there; three, someone—*maybe* Heinmarsh—is targeting government officials with suicide bombers; four, the team leader of the lead team's been suspended," his finger span as though to circumscribe them. "If that don't smell suspicious I dunno what does. Five, the JIC are washing their hands of this whole bloody mess and there's nothing Uncle Victor can do."

"And your point is?" asked Carter airily.

"*Someone* has to do something about it."

"Who?" said Wilson sceptically.

McKinley leaned back, grinning, his eyebrows leaping conspiratorially.

With realisation Wilson's mouth started to open. "Oh—!"

McKinley cut right through it. "We've got to do something *unofficially*. If you're up for it, *if* you're on board, we're gonna go off the grid."

"You... bloody *what?!*" Wilson's eyes just about left their sockets. "No, no, no! You are *so* out-of-line man!"

"Willy! We need—"

"*No!*" Wilson complained. "There's no 'we' about it! You want to stick your job down the crapper? Just like *that?!*"

McKinley's ire started to rise. "I want to *vindicate* The Team!"

This seemed to slow Wilson down for just a moment and McKinley took the opportunity to address Carter. "You?"

Carter's eye's were elsewhere. "Thinking..."

Hands in the air, Wilson said "we could be bloody court-martialled just for discussing this! It's insubordination! I only just got promoted too!"

"We've *got* to rescue Bacon," affirmed McKinley, "or his blood's on our hands. I don't see how we've got a choice." He paused for breath. "I already spoke to Plugger and got some stuff figured out, but the clock's ticking. Then after we've got him back we give Heinmarsh an FGK. If he's behind these suicide bombers like your girlfriend said," he looked pointedly at Wilson, "then we've got to. Don't you wanna prove her right? The JIC's freakin' useless. So *we've* got to *act*."

Wilson blinked as if clearing his vision. "How are *we* supposed to *act* without The Team? I suppose you've thought about that, have you?"

McKinley and Carter looked at each other for a moment. "Planned for it, actually," murmured the latter.

"You've...?"

Carter shrugged. "We... put stuff aside, just in case."

Wilson's brow was furrowed. "What, you mean you saw this coming?"

"No!" mewled McKinley. "But it was always a possibility."

"*'Fortune favours the prepared mind'*," quoted Carter. "Louis Pasteur. Seriously, you think I've got a loud CD player stashed in my locker for fun? You just said you weren't surprised!"

"Willy," said McKinley, "I really need your help. The longer we wait—"

"You want me to piss my job up the wall!" exclaimed Wilson. "On the off chance that you can *maybe* get yours back? You're bloody mental!"

McKinley sighed heavily. "I'm playing the odds, but I can't do it on my own. It's a *massive* risk, I know, but I bet we can do it even without the unit. If we can rescue Bacon we're already winning right? And I already got Plugger on board with that, even though he went public. But I want to hand Heinmarsh's ass to the JIC. Even if we just locate the warhead, Uncle Victor'll back us up."

Wilson was shaking his head hard. "He's in on your bullshit?"

"'Course not!" growled McKinley, stabbing his finger at Wilson. "But *you heard* him say the brakes'd come off if he had *positive proof* of where it is. That's all he's waiting for!" He threw his hands in the air. "I *bet* we can get it. Either way we need to move bloody quick or it won't be a *horse's* head you'll be waking up with!"

"Thanks to you!" snorted Wilson angrily. "It wasn't *my* idea."

Carter patted Wilson's shoulder apologetically. "Actually mate, that turns out not to be the case."

"It *was* your idea," added McKinley.

Wilson's eyes widened as he recalled their conversation in Annie Grainger's bathroom. "Oh... *bloody bollocks!*" he sighed.

McKinley leaned forward, pressing his advantage. "I hope you noticed I made of point of *not* explaining that to Uncle Victor."

Wilson turned away from them, shaking his head. Herr Stockhausen continued his assault on the room. McKinley watched Wilson for a moment, then turned back to Carter.

"You're quiet," he said.

"You're crazy. Kangaroos loose in the top paddock. But it's an intriguing idea."

Wilson turned, eyebrows knitted in consternation. "You're not seriously considering this?"

"Perhaps," said Carter, pulling thoughtfully at the few millimeters of mouse brown growth on his chin.

Wilson thumped his ass onto a seat and rubbed his forehead. "Yeah... well... *I am.*"

McKinley blinked. "You are?" He hadn't seen that coming.

Wilson shrugged. "You're right. We've got to rescue Bacon. We'll get court-martialled or something, but we've got to try. Now, I don't care about Heinmarsh; he's an asshole. But I do care about these kids that're blowing themselves up. I didn't sleep last night just thinking about it. It *has* to stop. If I can intervene when nobody else will, I can't ignore it."

"Admirable," murmured Carter.

"So look," continued Wilson, "I'm up for rescuing Bacon; that's urgent. Then *maybe* we'll see where we go from there."

"Sensible," nodded Carter.

McKinley looked at him. "What about you?"

Carter frowned. "I agree about Bacon, but what *really* scares the shit out of me is freakin' nukes in the wind. That's a major disaster waiting to happen, or worse, like a regional war or something. How can *anyone* let that slide? I'm with you."

"Predictable," muttered Wilson.

McKinley was starting to feel a certain thrill in his guts. "So you're in? As far as rescuing Bacon. You're *both* in? 'Cause we need to get shifting, like, yesterday."

His colleagues looked at each other yet again. "Well," said Carter, "on the upside; no MDTs for a while. On the downside; goodbye job, it's been fun."

Doctor Manning looked up and jumped. "Holy cow McKinley, you scared the crap out of me!"

"Sorry doc," smiled McKinley, his arms crossed on the laminate bridge of the Doctor's station. "I didn't mean to."

"You're not usually this early," noted Manning, looking up at the big wall clock.

"I'm kinda in a hurry."

Manning leaned back in his chair. "Yes, I heard about that business with the JIC. Sorry about your—"

"Doesn't matter," interrupted the Scotsman. "You know I've got to be off base soon," he shrugged, "so d'you mind if I have a quick word with her?"

"You probably shouldn't," frowned the medic, "in view of the circumstances, but you're still the only one she'll open up to."

McKinley pushed himself away from the counter. "Thanks. Won't be long."

"She's improving, by the way," said the doctor to McKinley's retreating back.

McKinley closed the double door behind him. There was Jem still restrained, still connected to tubes and wires, and she looked asleep. He sat on the edge of her bed and she opened her eyes.

"Ian," she smiled, and her voice rang in his ears like fairy bells.

"Hey," he said, "how're you doing?"

"Better, I think." She seemed far more positive.

"That's good."

"I can remember stuff! I can remember my life *before* the Ambassadors..."

McKinley recognised that look. "Hey Jem, Jem!" he said as her eyes glazed over. He grabbed her shoulders. "Come back! It's Ian. You're not in that place any more! You're in hospital, in Britain."

She blinked, shaking her head. "Oh my goodness, I was there! I was back there!" She started crying.

"It's okay, it's okay," soothed McKinley. "It's just a flashback. Try not to think about... that stuff, alright? Think about your old life, you know; mum, dad, Mel. You lived in London, right? With Mel in Chingford."

"I remember," she sniffled. "It... wasn't as bad as they said." She tried to raise an arm to wipe her moist face but was prevented by the restraints. "Why did they lie to us?" she sobbed. "Why would holy men say things that aren't true?"

"Well, maybe they're not actually holy."

Her tears renewed their flow. "They're not! They're liars! All they want to do is make us into robots!"

McKinley grabbed a tissue from the bedside cabinet and did the honours as gently as he could. "How come you didn't remember before? When you were... you know?"

"I don't know. It was supposed to be the Universal Spirit taking away my old, sinful life, but I'm not sure now. I'm so confused."

"Aye," answered McKinley, wary that she'd mentioned religion again, "but you're getting better?"

Her smile reappeared from behind the clouds, lighting up the room. "Oh yes!"

"That's good," said McKinley. Time was short and he needed information. "Jem, tell me about the island. I need to find it."

She peered up apologetically. "I don't know. Somewhere way south of Singapore I think."

McKinley consulted his mental map of the world. The only places roughly south on that longitude were southern Sumatra, Java and the tip of Western Australia. After that, her dad's description of 'tropical' and hers of 'warm' would tend to eliminate Antarctica.

"What can you tell me about it?"

Jem looked worried and reluctant, saying "it's hard to think. I don't want another blackout."

"I understand," nodded McKinley, smiling gently. "But this is really important."

"Why?"

McKinley frowned. "Well, for a start you could be just one of many—"

"Suicide bombers!" she blurted. "That's what they believe, you know? To bring in the Kingdom. We have to be ready to die for it. They want volunteers to 'go to the mission field' when you're there," she admitted, trying to make air quotes with her tethered arms," but I only found out about the... bomb after I come back home..." She looked down and shook her head sadly. "I'm *so sorry* Ian! I didn't realise what I was doing." Suddenly she bawled again. "I didn't want to die! Why did they make me think that?!

For some reason that he didn't fully understand, McKinley hugged her, holding her securely until her tears subsided, whispering "it's okay, you're safe," again and again.

"Everyone there's ready to be a suicide bomber," she admitted. "They just don't know it yet."

"Bloody hell," breathed McKinley. According to Julia Bridgewell, Heinmarsh had spoken of an *army* of them. How many could that mean? But with a glance at his watch he got back on track. "Jem, there are things I can't talk about for security reasons. But I really need to find the place. Please help me."

She screwed up her eyes. "It's all such a blur. It's like a jungle; weird plants and animals. And it's on the ocean. I remember they said "next stop: Hawaii"."

Again McKinley checked his internal globe. If the island was on the Pacific rim, then it certainly wasn't directly south of Singapore. McKinley's thoughts went to Skumarovsky's Indonesia revelation. Indonesia was mostly *east* of Singapore.

"I'm sorry," she said. "I know that's not very helpful. There are loads of islands."

McKinley raised an eyebrow. "What about Wolf River?"

Her expression was emptying again, but it was a different look than her blackouts. This seemed thoughtful, pensive. It was a far away look like watching someone trying to remember the name of an old acquaintance.

"That's the village, where the *Ecclesia* is."

McKinley had done a little homework. "Aye, the assembly. That's Greek, isn't it?"

She grinned, obviously pleased. "Yes, yes it is!"

"What's it like? All mud huts or are there houses and electricity and stuff?"

"Yes, it's actually a modern place, but the rest of the island isn't. There are only roads around the village and the dock. Pastor Makaru drives a massive car. I think it's a Rolls-Royce."

"He's the leader?"

"He's err..." she wobbled her head, trying to find the word. "He calls himself an apostle, but I don't really believe that. He's sort of like a prophet. Yes, the leader."

"Okay, back to Wolf River."

"There's the village—where we lived—and the Citadel, the greenhouses and labs, the beach and the power plant. No-one's allowed beyond there." Suddenly she screwed up her face in frustration. "It's all so vague!"

McKinley leaned toward her. "Take it steady."

Tears of frustration welled in her eyes. "It's like a dream you wish you could remember!"

McKinley went out on a limb. Feeding a witness was contraindicated in every interrogation manual he'd ever read, but he *had* to know. "Jem," he said carefully, "could this be Indonesia somewhere?"

Her beautiful eyes widened. "Oh! Yes, it is! They gave a talk about acting properly in front of the locals because they're Muslims. You know, dress decently and stuff."

Well, thought McKinley, that's understandable. Indonesia's got the biggest Muslim population in the world. He filed the information away, keenly aware that the longer he tarried the more difficult things could become. With regret he moved on, glancing around at the door just in case and lowering his voice to the merest whisper. "Look, I've got something for you. I want you to keep it a secret; our secret."

She lowered her voice to match. "Yes, okay."

"I'm going away for a bit."

Making sure that his body blocked the video camera he opened his hand, revealing an old model of mobile phone. It was small, the kind of thing you could hang on your key ring without injuring your crotch as you pocketed it. He winked at her. "Keep it *absolutely* secret, okay?"

"Yes, yes," she nodded. "But what if they search me?"

McKinley slipped the little phone under the covers. "That's the idea," he winked. "But you tell them it's for General Sutton. Urgent, okay? *General Sutton.* You have to be firm about it."

"General Sutton," she repeated. "I can do that."

He smiled with difficulty. "I gotta shoot. I don't know when I'll be back."

She seemed dismayed. "Where are you going?"

"I can't say."

"You're going there!" She paused for a moment as McKinley didn't answer. "It'll be dangerous!"

"How so?"

"There are guards all over the place with guns!"

"Not to worry," said McKinley with a grin. "I'll take one of my own." That was more than she needed to know. McKinley raised his voice to its usual level. "You keep getting better, alright?"

Their eyes met for a long moment. "I'll try."

"Seeya." With this McKinley lifted himself from the bed and walked out of the room, deliberately not looking back at those amazing eyes. He'd stayed way too long and the lads would be waiting.

Manning rotated his chair toward McKinley. "You have a remarkable effect on that young lady, Corporal."

"It's just for show," said the Scot, and hurried from the medical bay.

In the corridor, McKinley spoke quietly, his right index finger pressed to a tiny earpiece. "Chris, you ready?"

"One mouse click away," came Carter's voice.

"Do it."

There was climbing, and there was *climbing*. This was the latter.

Wilson hung in the ventilation shaft in almost total darkness, ascenders in both hands and what felt like half a ton of gear hanging from his waist. He waited, giving it a few seconds to get his breath back. He was about three quarters of the way up the shaft and starting to get tired. He hadn't done a decent climb since that godforsaken cliff back in August, and he hadn't done a prusiking climb for much longer, never mind the additional weight.

His heart rate having settled slightly, Wilson reached above with the first ascender and locked it, pulling hard and working his way up the less-than-ideal rope. The fluorescent orange nylon was dirty, as though it had been there for a good long time. Why on earth there should be a rope dangling down the number three ventilation shaft and how McKinley and Carter knew about it were matters of some suspicion, but he was glad of it. There would have been zero chance of getting off base with their equipment otherwise.

Nearing the top, Wilson saw in the circle of yellow light from his helmet lamp the steel joist that his colleagues had described. Here the rope was tied, and the top of the shaft was about another eight feet, ending with a louvered grill at its side. Somehow, he had to get their gear out of that.

Wilson tied the heavy package to the girder, then swung his body hard, flipping up and onto the horizontal beam. He wobbled for a second, the rope wiggling like a spastic snake in fast forward, then his hand found the wall and he steadied himself. He looked down. Way below was a vague spillage of light from the bottom grille. It looked horribly far beneath him on the narrow joist. Now came the difficult bit, and there was nothing to which he could secure his rope. Nonetheless he pulled up the bulk of its length and tied it short so that, if he fell, he wouldn't plummet all the way to the bottom. That would mess up their extracurricular activities real quick.

The only ways to reach that damn grille were either to jump—not a great idea—or to brace his hands and feet against the shaft wall and use friction to push himself up. Mindful that the drop was about a hundred and sixty feet, Wilson had already chosen the latter option. Checking his connection to the rope, he aligned himself across the girder and stretched outward with his gloved hands. He could feel gritty dust through the material; not a good sign.

Wilson pushed hard and tried his weight. He lifted his boots just off the joist and held his position for a second. Feeling minutely more confident, he let the weight go to his splayed legs and moved his hands up.

Four more iterations of the same movement later, Wilson was nearing the grille. He could see thin strips of grey light, but could he reach it, much less undo the screws? Making extra sure to brace his legs firmly, Wilson took his right hand off the shaft wall, leaning as far as he could to the left to grab onto the grille. He got a fingertip into one crack and used it to pull the rest of his hand closer.

Suddenly the grille parted from the wall. Wilson's left foot lost its grip and he fell. The girder slammed him in the chest as he landed on it and rolled. Dropping the grille, he hooked his right arm over the joist and swung, his feet slamming into his heavy bundle of cargo, the knot of whose rope started to give way. Hearing the whine of the rope as the grille clattered to the bottom of the deep shaft, Wilson grabbed desperately with his other hand. He caught the rope and the cargo's weight nearly pulled his arm out of its socket. He grunted in pain, teeth clenched and eyes screwed up.

The reverberation of the grille's plunge died away to a moment's silence. Wilson was hanging off the steel strut by his right armpit with the weight of the gear just about pulling him in two. If he let go of the gear he'd be able to get back up, but by now there would be attention from the base's HVAC plant operators, and if he let go of the joist they'd both fall and he'd be left hanging at the end of his rope.

What a bloody mess, thought Wilson, wondering how the heck he'd get out of this. One way or another he'd have to do something fast because the pain was becoming unbearable. He looked down.

There was about four feet of spare rope dangling out of his left hand, so Wilson tried to lift the end of it with his leg. After six attempts failed, he swore quietly. He needed more muscles. Wilson hooked his knee under his left hand and, using the strength of both managed to lift the heavy gear toward him. Now his hand was level with his waist. Being as careful as possible, he tried to flick the end of the rope up and toward his harness. It didn't work.

Suddenly he froze, detecting conversation echoing dully from below. Damn the hell out of it! They'd heard that grille falling. Time was running out. At any moment they might open the bottom shaft and see him. Damn good job he'd had the sense to jam it shut from the inside with a spare screwdriver, but that wouldn't stop them for long.

Flicking the end of the rope madly, Wilson tried to get it into his right hand, which was going numb from the effort of holding himself to the girder. Suddenly he had it! He shuffled his hand like mad to get as much of the rope as possible into a controllable position, then he shook the end again and caught it in his mouth, wincing as the ghastly taste of dust and years of the base's exhaust air assaulted his tongue.

Making sure that his aching right hand could hold the weight of their package, Wilson finally released his tortured left hand, opening and closing it rapidly to increase blood flow. He heard a metallic knock from below. They were starting to open the hatch!

Wilson quickly tied a rough knot in the ropes, wrapping the loop several times around the joist to secure them. Then he hauled himself onto the girder again and straddled it. There was only one thing to do, and he'd better be bloody quick about it.

He started to pull the heavy pack toward him, hearing muted voices and more tooling sounds from the bottom of the dark shaft. Once the gear was just below him, he balanced himself against it and lifted it onto the girder. He made sure it was balanced then carefully stepped up onto the beam. The only way to get the heavy pack out would be lift it from above. He wasn't quite tall enough to force it through the gap from below, even though it was about narrow enough to fit. The first thing to do was to rearrange the ropes. Now he was forced to untie himself from the girder, not wanting whoever was trying to open that panel down there to find the rope.

Wishing desperately for good balance, Wilson stood on the beam, braced his hands against the side walls again and carefully lifted himself onto the pack, feeling its valuable contents shifting under his boots. It wobbled but remained stable. With the ends of both ropes in his hand, Wilson could now reach the edge of the grille's opening. Moving slowly, not wanting to disturb the pack's precarious balance, he pulled himself up to the edge and threw the ropes out as far as he could.

A tarred roof on Nottingham's mildly rainy skyline greeted his eyes, and there was the top of the fire escape that Carter had told him about. Wilson squirmed and wiggled his way through the hole and finally rolled onto the damp roof surface, feeling the minute kisses of raindrops. Not even allowing himself time to get his breath, he undid his own rope and secured the pack's to a nearby chimney. Standing by the open hatch, Wilson took the rope and lifted with all his might. The pack shifted on the girder and fell a couple of feet, nearly tugging him back through the hole again. Wilson braced himself against the shaft's top housing and pulled like mad. Even from outside he could hear the creaking from below as the engineers fought against his carefully placed screwdriver.

With a grunt, Wilson fell backwards and the gear landed on him. It didn't seem as heavy now. He quickly rolled it off and put his head near the ventilation shaft. There was a rattle, a clunk of metal and a deep voice with a northern accent.

"Bloody Nora," it echoed, "the grille fell down."

"Bugger me," responded another, equally reverberant. "I suppose I'll get up there and sort it. You can write the report."

"Righto."

Wilson grinned. He'd made it by a gnat's whisker. Now he could secure the gear in such a way as to carry it on his back. He descended the fire escape to the next roof and from there made his way to street level.

Stepping to the pavement a few minutes later in a narrow alley behind a cinema, Wilson saw Carter's Range Rover at the end. He ran as quickly as he could under the weight and started to stow it in the back.

"You took your bloody time," complained McKinley from the front passenger seat. "We should be half way there by now. What the hell were you doing?"

Wilson paused for a second. What would be the point? "Just hanging around," he said, and shut the tailgate.

After making sure their passports were scanned at Birmingham Airport for a flight to Copenhagen, TDR.12 evaded airport security and travelled at speed to McKinley and Carter's little industrial unit at Hereford, where they consolidated their plans and sorted out which equipment to carry. Again, Wilson was surprised at his team-mates' preparedness. The conspiratorial level of detail they'd put into their 'insurance policy' was remarkable and a little troubling. Much as Bacon's kidnapping was essentially Wilson's fault and weighed heavily on his conscience, he felt caught up in a strong current of uncertain direction.

They headed south to Bournemouth on the English Channel coast, where they chartered a small jet rented in advance by Plugger, in whose mind an advance of twenty eight grand plus fuel was a small price for the safe return of his beloved employer. They logged their destination as Tenerife.

They took turns at the controls of the aircraft, or discussing McKinley's plan otherwise. Wilson took the opportunity to catch up on sleep whilst Carter picked

McKinley's brains about his contention with the Joint Intelligence Committee. They read intel and watched videos from Carter's phone, eager to glean the tiniest crumb of information that could provide an advantage.

After crossing France and Spain they refuelled at Gibraltar, then flew down the Moroccan coast. Between the islands of Fuerteventura and Gran Canaria Carter faked an instrument failure and McKinley declared an emergency situation to Canarian traffic control, requesting permission to land at the *Aeropuerto de Gran Canaria*, where they touched down around half past nine in the evening.

General Sutton rubbed his tired eyes with his good hand. It had been a long day and, not that he'd ever tell anyone as much, he wasn't feeling up to it at the moment. His attempted murder by the suicide bomber had taken a lot more out of him than he'd ever admit, never mind all the stupid paperwork that had resulted from it. His insurance company's bureaucrats were doing their utmost to screw him, and the staff of the Joint Intelligence Committee were haranguing him almost hourly. What a bloody day.

He closed his eyes for a moment, relaxing. The lights in his office were set to night-time levels, providing a somewhat peaceful atmosphere and making the glow from his monitors seem much brighter than normal. He should probably head to the accommodation section, read reports for an hour, and try to get his head down.

His eyes flickered open as his desk phone rang. Noting the display, which said 'Manning, Dr. K.', he answered. "Sutton here."

"Oh, General," came the doctor's voice, "I'm sorry to disturb you. I meant to get through to Major Maddocks or your secretary."

"They've gone home Kieran," replied Sutton with a slight upward twist to his lips. He was usually the only one to have missed how far the evening had progressed. "What's up?"

"I'm unable to access some recent data and I wondered if it's been locked down."

Sutton trapped the receiver between his head and shoulder, fumbling for a pen with his left hand. It felt weird and his writing skills with that limb were juvenile at best. "What data?"

"The video files of Jemima Fox. But here's the odd thing; it's only the bits when she was talking to Corporal McKinley that are unavailable. Has it been classified?"

Sutton frowned, thinking. Neither he nor Maddocks had ordered any data secured.

"General?"

"It's alright. We'll talk about it in the morning. Is there anything else I can help you with?"

"No sir."

"Okay, cheers." Sutton dropped the pen and replaced the receiver on its cradle. He sat for a moment, the fingers of his good hand drumming on the mahogany desk, then logged in to the Internal Security section of the unit's computer system. He navigated to the medical department's information and noted the cross-hatching over several files. Sutton's clearance being the highest in The Team, he had unlimited access to the system and checked the properties of the unavailable data. Indeed, they were absent; not locked down but deleted. There were however transfer records indicating their duplication to a mobile device, the electronic serial number of which had been registered inactive more than a month ago. But General Sutton knew exactly who it belonged to.

009: The Yacht

"I'm asking you to trust me, *amigo*," pleaded McKinley.

The Spanish Air Force duty officer, Valenciano, shook his thin head sadly. He wanted to help these British anti-terrorist officers, especially if there were terror cells on his own doorstep, but his hands were tied.

McKinley would have preferred dealing with the base commander directly, but at this time of night there were only a few staff about. Across the runway, the civil airport was as busy as ever, the constant traffic of its utility vehicles clearly visible from Valenciano's office.

"It's not about whether I trust you," replied the lanky Spaniard. "I'm under orders just as you are. I can't contravene my orders and I *definitely* can't let you off the airfield without going through passport control. Your equipment has all the correct paperwork, yes, but I have *no choice* with your personal identification."

"Would you give me just a moment, please?" said McKinley, wagging his finger in thought. He turned away to his colleagues.

"So then," he started in Russian, his voice almost down to whisper level, "no good choices. Either we use our own passports and get flagged by GCHQ or we use the shoes and it goes straight to that cop, then Erbakan. We're in shit either way. Which flavour do you prefer?"

"Better Erbakan doesn't see us coming," replied Wilson. "Or the cops."

"Hold on mate," said Carter, raising his hand. "Think about it. Even if Erbakan knows we're here, he's on his boat, at sea. He feels safe."

"Aye," interjected McKinley, nodding. "Might give us a slight advantage."

"But the fuzz'll be on our necks in minutes," argued Wilson.

"Right," continued Carter, "but if the JIC get involved then we have all kinds of bigger problems. Our *amigo* here might even get ordered to detain us and we'd be dead in the water."

Wilson shook his head, groaning. "I can't believe we're... What the hell were we thinking?"

McKinley snarled. "Aye, well, we've thought it and we're here now, so let's get this done. False passports, right?"

"I suppose," shrugged Wilson. "But we'll have to get out of here bloody fast."

Wilson pulled the light brown Skoda Yeti into the parking space with a slight squeal of tyres.

"A Skoda?" said Carter, heaving a bergen into the rear seat. "We're really plumbing the depths."

"Oh, you wanted me to wait for a Ferrari?"

"We'll make it work," said McKinley, slamming the tailgate. He looked at the vehicle's badges. "Hey, we said no diesels!"

"It's all they had left," replied Wilson, unfolding himself from the driver's seat.

"Reporters," said Carter with a shrug.

"More than likely," nodded McKinley. He had no doubt that the island was flooding with press and media crews, eager to get the inside story on Bacon. If only that moron Plugger had kept a lid on it.

"But," continued Wilson, "this has more torques and better top end than the petrol version."

That was surprising. McKinley raised an eyebrow. "Four wheel drive?"

"*Yes!*" snarled Wilson impatiently, annoyed at the implication that he couldn't rent an appropriate vehicle.

McKinley muttered "adequate" just as a siren wailed not far away. "Better move!" he snapped, throwing his body into the car. Carter jumped into the driving seat and Wilson landed in the back.

"Reckon we've got about two minutes before they get our plate," said McKinley. "Watch."

They looked south-west as two police vehicles screamed to a halt in front of the brightly lit main terminal building and six armed cops jumped out, racing inside. Once they were out of sight McKinley snapped "go!"

Carter reversed out and took off, shaking his head and saying "never been this popular before."

Knowing that Puerto Rico and anywhere on the highway would be an ambush waiting to happen, they turned north-west and drove inland on the C-812 road, working their way toward the summit of the island.

McKinley lit a cigarette and took a cautious look behind. There were few other vehicles on the winding road and no sign of Gran Canaria's finest in pursuit. "Got your phone?" he said to Carter.

Carter reached into his jacket and gave the device to McKinley, who passed it back to Wilson. "Make the call," he ordered.

Two wasted hours and considerable verbalisations of impatience later, they saw the headlights of the SEAT *Mii* rounding the bend to the car park. Wilson said goodbye and ended his VOIP session with Julia.

"About bloody time!" muttered McKinley angrily, throwing down his cigarette butt.

During the day, the vistas from *Pico de las Nieves*, the island's highest point at nearly two kilometers above sea level, would have been spectacular, even allowing views of neighbouring Tenerife's Mount Teide rising from the clouds, but at this hour the visible half of Gran Canaria that spread out below them was illustrated only by tiny pockets of glittering artificial light. Above the car park, the massive military installation with its spherical radome stood as a sentinel, vigilant across a vast swathe of the ocean including all the Spanish Atlantic territories. The car park was the highest publicly accessible point, fittingly remote, cold and very unlikely to be well attended at this time of night.

McKinley swore. "What the hell's that?!" he exclaimed, arms flailing in frustration. "There's nay room to squeeze a fart in!"

The midget black automobile pulled up by their Skoda and out sprang Jimmy, his toothy smile directed at Wilson like a spotlight. He was dressed in camo pants, black boots and olive drab T-shirt, as though to make some kind of impression on the combat specialist, but he looked more like an extra from an apocalyptic music video. The red Springsteen-esque headband didn't help.

"Hi handsome," he beamed. "I'm so glad you called me!" With this he gave Wilson a manly but slightly longer than usual hug then stepped back, surveying McKinley with wariness. "So let's get this party started," he chirped. "What's up?"

McKinley was pulling out a fresh cigarette, still looking aghast between Wilson and the tiny car, so Carter stepped in.

"We need you to create a diversion," he started. "You see these dummies?"

Jimmy bent to the windows of the Skoda. A pair of roughly fabricated human figures were inside, one in the passenger seat and its brother in the back.

"They're supposed to be us," continued Carter. "You take the hire car, we take yours. You piss off the cops in Puerto Rico when we text you, then leg it toward Las Palmas as fast as you can. Disregard all speed limits."

"Why?" asked the bemused Canadian.

Carter and Wilson looked at each other. "Official business," said Wilson carefully. "When you said you thought we were military men, you weren't far off."

"You're kidding me?" Jimmy's eyes widened in astonishment.

"Deadly serious," said McKinley, turning back to them, "and this is a very serious situation. A friend of ours'll die unless we intervene, and we can't risk it without a diversion. Now, are you going to help us or what?" he asked, looking the man right in the eye and pointing with his smoke.

"What do I get out of it?" asked Jimmy coyly. He trusted the gruff Scotsman about as far as one could spit an elephant.

"Thirty thousand Euros from the guy we're rescuing," replied McKinley as Jimmy's eyes just about exited his skull. "Five in cash now, the rest when the dust settles."

The Canadian's jaw wasn't on the floor; it had gone through. Maybe he'll be able to buy a real car, thought Carter.

McKinley went on. "That'll be plenty to cover expenses, repairs, any fines and legal fees and leave you enough to buy... err... whatever it is you people buy."

"*You people?!*" blurted Jimmy.

"Sorry," interjected Carter. "He finds it hard to talk properly when his foot's in his mouth."

"Whatever," shrugged McKinley. "We got a deal?"

Jimmy felt fathoms out of his depth, but the money was amazing. He turned to Wilson as if for support. "What say you, hunky chunks?"

Embarrassed down to bedrock, Wilson replied "it'd really help."

"Okay," sang Jimmy, recovering quickly from his astonishment. Winking at Carter but nodding toward Wilson he added "I'll do anything for this one."

They quickly arranged the details and the TDR.12 lads prepared to cram themselves and their gear into the little two door SEAT. Before leaving, Wilson trotted over to the idling Skoda, where Jimmy was standing in the open door and turning the large envelope of cash over in his hands, a look of pleased disbelief on his finely chiselled features.

"Hey, can I ask you someth... about something?"

"What's up sugar dumpling?" replied the Canadian, smiling warmly. His turn of phrase didn't inspire confidence.

"That night we met," started Wilson and paused, feeling sheepish. He genuinely didn't know how to ask, but he had to find out. "I had a bit to drink," he continued, "and I, err... don't remember much. Not even leaving the club. Did we, err, go back to your place?"

"Yup," chuckled Jimmy, a wicked twinkle in his eye.

Oh great, thought Wilson, this just gets better. "Well, did we... err, I mean... umm, you know." Wilson shook his hands in frustration. "Damn it! What *happened?*"

Jimmy smiled a knowing smile and nodded discerningly. "*Nothing* happened. We talked – mostly about *Julia*," he pouted, rolling his eyes exaggeratedly. "We shot the breeze, we joked around, I got you a cab." He took Wilson's wide shoulders in his hands and looked up at him reassuringly. "Nothing happened. You think I'm some kinda date rapist?"

Ah yes, thought Wilson, I'm glad you brought that up. "No. But, umm, didn't you put something into my drink?"

"Yeah," crowed Jimmy, "ten and a half Euros of my hard earned cash! Brent's gotta pay for his Merc somehow; that ain't no cheap cocktail." He nodded toward McKinley. "*And* your dumbass buddy wasted the first one!"

Wilson paused for a moment. "Sorry, it's just that we... I thought I saw some, err, particles floating in it... them."

"You dingbat!" chided Jimmy, grinning. "It's a White Russian. It's kinda like a coffee with vodka and cream. I thought you needed the caffeine. Maybe the cream was a bit off?" He shrugged. "I dunno."

"Oh."

"But I think dumbass wanted to protect you from the scary prairie-fairy," laughed Jimmy, again nodding in the direction of his car. "As if a big tough breeder like you needs protecting!"

"He's just looking after me," rationalised Wilson. "He's okay."

Jimmy bowed his head toward Wilson and lowered his voice, his eyebrows skipping furtively. "Oh, he *is!* He might be an asshole but he can look after *me* any time!"

Wilson couldn't help but laugh out loud. If McKinley heard this conversation he'd run a mile.

Suddenly the Scotsman shouted from the other vehicle. "Oy! Kiss goodbye already!"

"Well then," said Jimmy with a stalwart handshake. "I guess I should header. Don't be a stranger – 'specially if *Julia* don't realise how good she got it. Ciao sweetcakes!" With this he dived into the Skoda and took off at speed.

Wilson crammed his svelte frame into the confines of the *Mii* and Carter started down the hill. The ride was typical of a city car and McKinley grunted unhappily.

"How far is it?"

"Twenty four miles," answered Carter, "down some of the worst roads in Europe. Give or take."

"Brilliant," complained McKinley. "My ass is gonna be sore in the morning."

It could have been worse, thought Wilson, grinning to himself.

The road, although such a moniker hardly qualified, was indeed rough, and more winding than any of them would have imagined. The little vehicle's suspension suffered as they bounced around inside, each bemoaning not being in something more spacious, more powerful and more appropriate to this kind of punishment.

In less than an hour, though, the roads improved as they started descending toward their destination of Puerto de Mogan, another coastal town four miles to the north-west of Puerto Rico.

They passed the junction of the disused road that used to lead to Playa de Veneguera and McKinley looked round at Wilson. "You'd better text 'army of lovers'," he suggested snidely.

Wilson took out Carter's phone. "What does that make us?" he muttered unhappily.

"Ah," declared Carter. "That would be McKinley's barmy army."

The almost cubical basalt formations of the gnarled valley walls started to recede as they rejoined the main road and passed through Lomo Quiebre, noting that this *urbanización* was like a smaller version of Puerto Rico. To their left, the ubiquitous new construction sites jostled with apartment blocks and freshly graded parcels of land. On their right the hill was spattered with more expensive houses and villas, their terraces and decks brightly illuminated. Satellite dishes peered into the southern sky whilst palm trees lined the seaward side of the narrow road.

They continued south, mindful of the speed limits and not wanting to attract attention. Here and there darkened figures graced the sidewalk, some heading down into town and some moving a little more slowly in the opposite direction. Buildings, streetlights and signs multiplied as the road became a little steeper and they saw the narrow stream to their left, its bed mostly a cluster of dry, weed encrusted rocks that would only be submerged during the infrequent rainy spells.

Just as the watercourse widened and deepened several footbridges came into view, and they turned right at the small roundabout by the taxi rank. *Callejon Explanada del Castillete* was the populous and commercial heart of the town, bordering the docks. Restaurants, shops and *tabernas* lined the street, which was still crawling with people.

"Didn't expect it to be this busy," muttered McKinley. He saw no obvious media crews, but hopefully they'd all be in Puerto Rico anyway.

After the *Restaurante Varadero*, the harbour came into view on their left, overshadowed by a colossal wall of grey rock at the corner, towering high above and fading into the night sky. Now they were on the dock itself, heading south again. All manner of little craft were blocked up for repairs in the small boatyard at their left, and to their right the massive sea wall was featureless concrete apart from occasional graffiti and signs in basic English announcing sport fishing trips, the humble offices of which entrepreneurial mariners were housed opposite in rusting yellow intermodal freight containers.

The dock curved left and a row of white buildings with brown accented paintwork obscured the harbour for a moment. When it came back into view there was a two hundred meter long floating pontoon dock on the left to which were moored about twenty sailing yachts and a handful of motorboats. Here there was no-one about, prompting McKinley to say "this is better" as he looked around. They stopped for a second, allowing he and Wilson to exit the vehicle.

Near the furthest, eastern end of the pontoon was a small white vinyl gazebo broadly emblazoned with the words '*U-Boot Submarine Adventure*' in big, bold lettering. Between this and the dock's refuelling station Carter turned Jimmy's *Mii* round, then stopped in one of the many parking spots. He pulled out their gear, locked the car and pocketed the keys.

Carter looked about cautiously, mentally logging every tiny detail. The only people he had to worry about would be in the *Restaurante Snack El Faro*, right at the end of the quay. It was a short, round building like a stubby Martello tower and on its flat roof, replete with seating beneath blue and white umbrellas, was mounted the light that guarded the southern side of the harbour's entrance. Only that and the internal lights were on. The staff were cleaning up before leaving; they wouldn't be a problem.

The black sea looked uninvitingly cold, even in this climate. Across the harbour entrance, late night revellers were partying to a soundtrack of Europop, the reflection of the lights in the water dancing with them. During their journey Carter had studied this harbour in great detail, especially the marine charts.

Around the foot of the quay was strewn a massive cluster of big concrete tetrapods, placed there to stop the relentless ocean from eventually claiming both dock and diner. These sea defences could be terribly hazardous to any vessel venturing too close.

Carter directed his attention to the pontoon dock. There was the tourist submarine, a lozenge-shaped splash of dull yellow and orange against the inky waters. Moored alongside was its tender, a launch used for manoeuvring within the harbour, and to which the submarine was connected by an umbilical cable at all times whilst operating. Looking around again, Carter approached the mooring.

Back along the dock, McKinley and Wilson had broken into several cars and moved them into position to prevent any further vehicular access, just in case. This involved blocking not only the road, but the wide promenade in front of the row of white buildings. Once the five cars were in place they jammed on the parking brakes as hard as possible and slashed the tyres. Then they ran back toward Carter's position.

Carter had found and powered down the submarine's land based battery chargers. He then jumped onto its deck, finding the aft hatch held ajar by the cables just as the operators' manual had said. Translating from Finnish had been a pain in the ass, but he was sure he'd got the important stuff down. Carter quickly clambered onto the conning tower, which was an eight foot shield surrounding the aft hatch. Atop it was a small mast with a pair of cameras. He located the forward-looking one and, using pliers, quickly loosened a couple of bolts and pointed it upwards. He detached the rearward camera from its Subconn connector, plugging in a long cable from his backpack that ended in a waterproof GPS unit. Attached to this was a black plastic float that had a thick polythene bag securely taped to it. He switched on the GPS, dropped the assembly onto the deck and lowered himself and his backpack into the vessel. Carter disconnected the charging cables and threw them ashore just his colleagues neared the mooring.

The submarine was a lot more spacious for its size than its military counterparts, and was an elongated cylinder with a level floor about six feet wide. Outwardly domed portholes lined both sides, each about two feet across, whilst a much larger Plexiglas bubble adorned the bow. Each passenger viewing port had a pair of red vinyl covered seats on small aluminium pedestals, and handrails. Overhead bins like those in a passenger jet lined the roof, the clearance of which was just sufficient for Carter's 5'10", but both his colleagues would have to duck.

Carter threw himself into the pilot's seat and brought all the submarine's systems online. Voltage levels were good, although there was a hydrogen alert because of bringing the sub up to power with its batteries still warm from charging. Carter switched on the battery purge compressor, which would drive the unwanted hydrogen out, and turned his attention to the rest of the systems.

His friends' packs landed through the hatch as Carter booted up his laptop, reaching behind the console and disconnecting the camera cable that now ran to his GPS. He brought out a home made adapter and attached it between the cable and his computer. "Ready!" he shouted as loudly as he could.

On the pontoon dock, having knifed the mooring ropes and cast the tender adrift, McKinley grunted "push!" and he and Wilson started to heave the weighty submarine away from its mooring. The boat's movement was incremental at first, being an object of considerable mass, but inch by inch it receded from the dock. Sitting on the deck, they used the strong muscles in their thighs to get the boat moving, then picked themselves back up. They descended the ladder, closing and locking the hatch securely as the submarine got under way.

Carter revved the electric thrusters hard. McKinley squashed himself into the left hand chair and took the laptop, which was now displaying co-ordinates from the GPS floating above them. The vector maps were superimposed on a montage of satellite images and marine charts.

"Okay," said McKinley, "do your stuff sailor."

"Naval Intelligence isn't *quite* the same thing," said Carter absentmindedly, his eyes fixed on the controls and displays.

Once away from the quayside they steered east, then turned due south, giving a wide berth to those treacherous tetrapods which could lacerate the hull.

"Drive," said Carter once they were on course. "I need to trim the boat."

McKinley reached over the center console to the computer style joystick and concentrated on keeping the sub level and going in the right direction. It was a strange feeling not being able to see anything, but the GPS compass quickly became a firm friend. Nonetheless, McKinley was aware of the length of the cable to which it was attached, creating a significant margin for error that could be influenced by wind or currents. Carter worked knobs and switches, grunting the occasional acknowledgement. Presently he sat back.

"How are we doing?"

"Heading south," replied McKinley. "Depth is—"

"Twelve bloody meters!" yelped Carter. He grabbed the joystick again, working other switches with his spare hand. "Way too deep! We'll hit bottom *and* lose tracking."

Thrusters whined as Wilson felt the submarine rising. "Do you think we're out far enough to put the lights on?" He couldn't get images of wartime submarine movies out of his head and didn't want to end up like so many U-boat crews had, entombed forever in a cold steel coffin.

"From land," Carter regarded the laptop's display, "yes. But any nearby boat'll be able to see us." He rolled his eyes in the direction of the controls. "Up there. Bottom row only."

McKinley threw the switches and immediately the vessel was surrounded by an eerie blue glow. Fish of all kinds twinkled and undulated, weaving in and out of visibility.

Wilson leaned into the pilots' compartment and peered forward. "Oh yeah," he muttered sarcastically, "that's *much* better. How deep's this thing rated anyway?"

"A lot deeper than we need," answered Carter. "Turning south-east," he announced, and the boat rolled minutely.

"What's our ETA?" asked McKinley.

"About forty minutes," replied Carter

McKinley grinned sourly. "Next time let's jack a faster sub."

Kyle Bacon sat in darkness, terrified, traumatised and in a lot of discomfort from being motionless for so long. The Turk had locked him in a cupboard and left him for more than a day now. In the last couple of hours there had been increased activity on board. At least, it *seemed* like a couple of hours. With his hands tied behind his back he couldn't have seen his wristwatch, but one of Erbakan's heavies had claimed it anyway.

He still couldn't believe what the arms dealer had done to him. Bacon felt horribly violated and abused. He tried not to think about the brutal wound because every time he did a wave of nausea threatened to eject what little food he'd been given. Lack of toilet breaks meant that he'd had to make do, and now he was sitting in a pool of his own feculence, to which Erbakan would doubtless react badly.

Bacon was convinced he was going to die – and *soon*. There was no word of whether anyone would cough up for the ransom, and his faithful acolyte Plugger didn't have access to enough of Bacon's own funds. As far as he knew he had been abandoned to his fate. He felt utterly alone and hopeless.

Suddenly the sound of a key in the lock brought him to sharp awareness. His eyes hurt a little as the light touched them. One of Erbakan's men stood silhouetted. "Get up," he said in poor English.

His legs barely co-operating, they manhandled the stiff, aching gadget dealer into the lounge, where Erbakan sat with a drink in his steady left hand. The Turk was smiling, perversely pleased at his guest's suffering.

"I see you have soiled yourself!" laughed Erbakan. "Is this any way to repay my hospitality?"

Bacon just stood there shaking with fear. What answer could he possibly give?

"You will clean that closet before I kill you," ground the Turk. "But for now you will be out here where I can see. I have received news that your friends are back on the island. I hope for your sake that they brought my money."

The tiniest, most feeble glow of optimism ignited in Bacon's gut. Although he didn't know much about McKinley's employment, he knew it was some kind of special forces thing. McKinley had once told him to think of it like MI6 meets the SAS. This meant that McKinley and his colleagues might be able to do something, although Bacon could only imagine what form that might take.

Perhaps there was hope, however small, of rescue.

"This is the tricky bit," said Carter, his teeth gritted.

McKinley knew. They had to work their way around the *Fata Morgana* at some distance, and approach from the landward side. He was hoping with everything he had that Erbakan's impressive yacht didn't have its sonar running, or even a fish finder.

"It's getting freakin' shallow," continued the weapons tech, leaning forward as though he might see something useful through the impenetrable black water. All the lights were now off except for the instrument panels, and the floating GPS, propelled this way and that by every wave, was hardly accurate.

"Willy," said McKinley, switching on a small flashlight as Wilson looked up from one of the passenger positions. "Let's get tooled up."

McKinley extricated himself from the cramped pilot's compartment. He and Wilson opened their packs, removing webbing, weapons and other equipment. They quickly fitted themselves with their gear and started to check each other over.

Suddenly the whole sub jolted as though kicked by a giant and there was a deafening metallic thud. McKinley and Wilson were thrown off their feet. Carter swore, wrestling with the thrusters. The vessel started to roll to starboard, throwing his colleagues against the row of portholes.

"What the hell?!" yelled McKinley, trying to right himself in the angled hull.

"We hit something!" shouted Carter back. "I said it was shallow!"

A dissonant scraping noise like a cacophony of badly played tubas resonated through the submarine.

"Dragging!" reported Carter. The noise stopped as the whole boat rolled to port, back again, and came to rest on a more or less even keel. Suddenly there was a piercing alarm.

"We're leaking," hollered Wilson from near the stern, fear evident in his tone.

"Oh, you think?" rasped Carter through clenched teeth.

McKinley looked around, seeing only vague shapes in the darkness. "Chris, lights!" he ordered over the electronic wailing.

Carter hit the internal lights and McKinley looked back to where Wilson was picking himself up near the ass end of the boat. Sure enough a stream of water like the issue of a garden hose was spraying from the edge of one of the port windows.

"Chris check it out! Are we going to sink?"

Carter craned his neck whilst trying not to accidentally move the controls. He took a moment to gauge the threat then turned back to piloting. "Not for a while, but it's only going to get worse. It'll affect the ballast."

"Shit!" spat McKinley. Manoeuvring was already difficult enough. "Douse the lights and see if you can kill that bloody alarm!" He hoped that the brief illumination hadn't betrayed them to those on the yacht.

"Roger," said Carter and smashed the alarm with the butt of his pistol. He worked at the controls and darkness returned. Everything was suddenly strangely quiet save for the electric whiz of their thrusters and the unnerving splatter of running water.

McKinley ran forward and leaned his head into the pilot's compartment. "Please tell me we can make it to the yacht!"

"Right," said Carter, flicking switches and swivelling his head between various readouts. "But it's going to be hard as hell to surface now!"

McKinley nodded as Wilson arrived at the partition. Accurate buoyancy was essential to his plan. They were low on options and in danger of getting pickled in their own brine barrel.

"Mickey," said Carter, the concentration audible in his voice, "I'm making the turn now. She's becoming unstable. Much more of this and we'll be re-enacting the Titanic."

"How long have we got?" asked Wilson, trying his best not to think about drowning. The mention of that most famous of shipwrecks hadn't helped.

"Bloody hell, I don't know!" snapped Carter. "Let's just get this done. Mickey, watch that monitor. You'll see the hull in a minute. Let me know the instant it appears."

"Roger that," said McKinley and knelt in the doorway. "Willy," he said, "stand by with the hatch."

"On it," answered Wilson, and strode to the ladder. He could hear an increasing amount of sloshing from below the checker-plate floor.

McKinley stared intently at the monitor. The little camera above them had a low light mode, but it was crap compared to something like military issue NVGs. The display was dark green snow with occasional sparkles and he felt like it would be hard to recognise anything on there. Suddenly though, a fuzzy black shape started to intrude diagonally into the field of view from the top right corner.

"Chris!" he barked.

"Got it," said Carter, backing off the thrusters. They heard the revs drop to almost nothing as the screen filled with black. "Right up his jacksie," whispered Carter nervously. "Again, I need to know the moment we start to clear the hull."

McKinley watched the little screen, feeling as though he was being pulled toward it. "Now!" he said.

Carter counted for a second, gave the thrusters a tiny jolt of reverse and brought them approximately to a stop. The black edge of the *Fata Morgana's* hull had now receded to the bottom third of the screen.

"Yawing," whispered Carter, operating the turn thrusters. The boat started to rotate to port as Carter aligned their hull with Erbakan's. A few moments later he said "that's it."

"You sure we're not going to hit it?" called Wilson from half way up the ladder.

"No," snarled Carter, "but if Mickey's right, and I'm right, and there's any truth to this mathematics thing, we're between the port hulls."

McKinley patted Carter on the shoulder. "Hold position and take her up. Slowly."

"I'll try," said Carter, an edge of desperation now audible in his voice, "but don't take all day 'cause we are *so* sinking." Warning lights were multiplying on the console.

"Shit!" grunted McKinley and groped his way to the ladder in the near darkness.

Carter's eyes were pivoting between the depth readout and the camera feed. He was fighting an uncertain battle somewhere between an unavoidably rapid ascent that would hit the *Fata Morgana*, making their presence bloody obvious, and an uncontrolled plunge to the depths of the bay where the chances of surviving would be slim and, even if they did, they'd be cannon fodder upon surfacing.

Taut like an over-wound clockspring, McKinley primed himself on the ladder beneath Wilson, who had his hand braced on the hatch, anticipating the weight of water reducing sufficiently for him to lift it. The moment he felt the pressure on the hatch decreasing, he was to give a signal.

Mindful of how near the yacht they must be, Carter was sweating beads. He tried his best to slow the ascent even further, but the amount of water in their hull wasn't helping. A small but noticeable tilt to stern was escalating and the longer he waited for Wilson's signal the more chance there was of a watery funeral. Grimacing, Carter worked the compressed air controls and vertical thrusters as gently as he could, but the whole sub was becoming increasingly unstable.

"Go, go, go!!" shouted Wilson, pushing the hatch hard. Carter hit a switch in his chest pocket and immediately a monstrous bang like having one's head inside a bass drum shook the sub. Wilson got a face full of cold seawater and the hatch slammed down. He pushed with all his might and opened the hatch again as a torrent of water spilled into the submarine. Fighting against the salty waterfall Wilson heaved himself up the ladder, followed by McKinley.

The submarine was tipping further to stern and slipping away from the yacht. Carter fought the controls as his friends made it out of the hatch, but she was in her death throes.

McKinley and Wilson jumped from the deck of the submarine and grabbed the handrail on the port side of the *Fata Morgana's* central hull as a horrible watery sucking sound like the emptying of a giant bath issued from the hatch below them and the sub started to recede into the shadowy depths.

They worked their way astern on the rail, to where the angular pylons supporting Erbakan's outboard engines joined the main hull. Here Wilson made an acrobatic leap that would have impressed any gymnast, finding the gunwale rail then pulling himself up. Wilson pulled out his silenced Walther P99 and looked about with amazing speed, establishing that he wasn't being observed. Thank God, Carter's floating bomb attached to the GPS receiver had drawn everyone on board to the yacht's starboard side. They probably thought they were being shelled.

He pulled McKinley up and onto the deck. The team leader instantly span round, seeing the prow of the submarine disappearing fast at a scary angle. "Oh shit!" he exclaimed. A huge plume off bubbles foamed and frothed, and then she was gone.

"Go!" snapped McKinley, and Wilson raced to the stern where a narrow staircase would take him below. He descended with haste, pistol held out in front.

McKinley entered the lounge, crouching low. He scanned the room, and the first thing he noticed was a very unhappy Kyle Bacon sitting on one of the couches. There seemed to be nobody else there. Bacon caught sight of McKinley and his eyes widened.

Suddenly, the lounge's side door opened and one of Erbakan's men entered. He looked at Bacon and saw the young man's expression. He was just drawing his own gun when McKinley's single round to his head stopped him in his tracks. McKinley gave Bacon a signal to keep quiet and moved forward.

Wilson was in the bowels of the yacht now, also moving toward the front. He found himself in a utility space which was mostly storage whilst providing access forward. There were lockers of various sizes, ropes and tools, cables and spare parts. He moved ahead carefully, scanning every inch of space.

He sensed movement from behind and whirled, a machete narrowly missing his shoulder. Wilson stumbled against something on the floor and fell. His attacker, a well-built man with a long, black ponytail, turned easily and brought the blade down again. Reacting with lightning speed Wilson kicked the attacker's feet out from under him and, as the man fell, planted a double-tap in his chest. The man's body landed on Wilson, pinning his right arm as another crewman ran in, cocking a pistol.

Hardly thinking but reacting instinctively, Wilson grabbed the big machete and hurled it in the man's direction, at the same time throwing off the heavy body. The man dodged, but before he could raise his weapon Wilson felled him.

In the trapped air at the bow of the sub, Carter filled his pack with everything he could carry. His laptop had already fallen into the rising water at the stern of the vessel. It was a toughened military spec model and valuable to him, but of even greater value was the highly useful software it contained. Yet despite this the pitch blackness and the rapid ingress of water made him unwilling to risk the hunt. The flooding had slowed a little, but only because the hatch was designed to be lifted forward in its normal orientation, and its weight had almost closed it. The pressure of the water from outside would make it impossible to open until the interior was completely flooded. He quickly took the small scuba kit they'd brought and shoved the regulator's mouthpiece in. Pushing gently on the purge button he established that airflow was good, then dropped his body from the pilots' compartment, not knowing how far up the flooding had reached.

With an intense, stabbing pain in his right shin that made him yell, Carter found out. The water was at the level of the ladder to the aft hatch, the side of which his leg had just impacted on. He held on to the cold metal for a moment, eyes clenched shut, trying desperately to compartmentalise the agony. Come on brain, he thought, put it aside.

In the few moments it had taken Carter to rebuff his discomfort sufficiently the water was reaching his chin. Time to go, he thought, and then the sixty ton submarine *thudded* onto the ocean floor as though being hammered into it. Carter froze for a moment, terrified as to which way the hull might tip.

On the yacht, McKinley climbed the short steps into the *Fata Morgana's* wheelhouse, FN Five-seveN held steadily ahead. How many hired hands did Erbakan have on board? On that point, where the heck was the Turk?

"Don't move," said a gruff voice behind and to his left. McKinley froze. Damn it to hell, how had he not checked in that corner? "Hands up," ordered the unseen man.

Cursing his luck, McKinley lifted his hands. He heard movement on the steps from the lounge, then another man approached from behind and took his pistol. The second man yelled something in Turkish and undoubtedly to Erbakan.

Two pistol rounds whizzed into the bridge and a grunt of pain came from behind. McKinley used the momentary diversion to throw himself behind the big pilot's chair. With a sharp *crack* a round followed him, slicing through the leather and sending out a small explosion of stuffing. The shooter quickly marched to the chair and peered over, snarling at McKinley from behind his Smith and Wesson revolver. He looked away for a moment to see what was going on in the lounge, then back at McKinley. The man, a thin, gawkish looking specimen with closely cropped dark hair, raised the weapon and took aim.

There was the *cough* of a silenced pistol and the man's head snapped to his left, his body crumpling to the deck. Wilson climbed into the wheelhouse, covering the man in case he was still kicking.

McKinley got to his feet and looked down at the bodies. The one that had his gun was lying in a pool of blood, eyes looking blankly through the ceiling. McKinley collected his weapon, saying "all quiet below?"

"Roger," affirmed Wilson. "If Erbakan's down there he's well hidden."

"Bollocks. How's Bacon looking?"

Wilson frowned, raising an eyebrow. "I didn't see him."

"Damn!" spat McKinley. "He was back there. Let's head forward."

Many meters below, the submarine came to rest on the ocean floor and Carter found himself disoriented. It was pitch black and, though he could breathe via his mask, horribly claustrophobic. He didn't know which way was up.

Reaching to his webbing, Carter pulled out a waterproof flashlight and switched it on. The beam danced through the chilly water and Carter realised his head was in a pocket of air. He directed the light upwards and saw the rubber of the floor above him, the seat pedestals either side looking like an inverted grove of silver trees. Damn it! The submarine had tipped onto its deck making for the worst possible scenario because the hatches could be jammed shut. The Perspex of the viewing ports would be far too thick to break. Any use of explosives in water would turn his guts into a meat smoothie and even a bullet impact wouldn't be enough, especially submerged. If Carter couldn't get out soon he would definitely be sleeping with the fishes.

He duck-dived and found the four foot wide aft hatch partially open. He tried pushing, then kicking at it, but it was solid. Piercingly aware of how little compressed air his tiny scuba kit contained, Carter swam for the bow, thumping his head soundly on an inverted seat. The forward hatch was similarly solid. Suddenly there was a deep, echoing moan of grinding metal from aft. Breast-stroking for the middle of the boat, Carter swallowed his growing fear and took another, closer look at the hatch there. The gap might be just wide enough without his gear, so Carter undid his webbing, tying it carefully to his pack, and propped his flashlight up so that he could see.

He wriggled into the opening and tried to push his body through the gap. It was tight, and being upside down was particularly difficult. Carter heard the noise again right on top of him, leading to his realisation of what it was. The conning tower was collapsing! If the submarine crushed it now the hatch would bite down on his abdomen and he'd be cut in half. Carter wriggled his body, trying to find purchase on anything he could. He could detect tiny creaks and snapping sounds coming from the tortured metal housing through which he was trying to squeeze. His stomach passed through the gap and with the force of pushing he rammed his pelvis hard on the hatch rim, bringing an involuntary grunt into the scuba mouthpiece. Suddenly he was free, and he quickly turned in the water, pulling his legs out behind him. He had to get that pack!

Just as Carter reached back in, the agony of metal under enormous strain rang through the black water again. Reacting without thinking, he thrust his left arm hard into the vessel and groped desperately for his gear, feeling the hull tilting inexorably down upon him. He found the edge of his pack and tugged with all his might, unable to see anything but a tiny glow from the flashlight, which had fallen somewhere. He pulled hard, straining as the gap started to close on his shoulder. The pack came free and popped out with his webbing just as the hatch slammed shut like an alligator's jaw and the heavy hull flattened its conning tower like a discarded beer can.

Carter knelt on the sandy ocean floor, thanking his stars as he donned his webbing. Although he'd lost the computer and all his clandestine software tools, he'd got the pack, its shape barely visible in the minute glow from the flashlight still shining through the sub's windows. Sinking the boat hadn't been part of the plan, but things seldom went completely to plan.

Weapons held in front of them, McKinley and Wilson convened on the foredeck from either side of the wheelhouse. As they expected, there was Erbakan, his arm looped around Bacon's neck from behind and his gold plated Para-Ordnance *Warthog* pistol held to the Londoner's temple.

"Stop there and come no closer!" demanded the Turk. "This hand is not so steady. Drop your guns or he dies!"

"And then what d'you think's going to happen to *you?*" said McKinley, his weapon trained steadily on the arms dealer's head.

"Nothing is going to happen to me! You want him alive? You do what I tell!" The furious Turk wobbled the gun against Bacon's head, who moaned in fear.

"Willy," said McKinley, "do it."

"Roger that," replied Wilson, retracting his Walther toward his chest.

McKinley started to lower his own pistol. "I thought you wanted the money," he taunted.

The instant that Erbakan's face registered consternation, McKinley fired, his Five-seveN neatly aimed at the Turk's thigh. Erbakan screamed as the second shot, fired by Wilson, knocked the gun right out of his hand. The arms dealer fell to the deck, as did Bacon.

With Wilson covering Erbakan, McKinley helped their friend up. Bacon looked—and smelled—as rough as hell, but at least he was alive.

"You alright pal?" asked McKinley.

Bacon cursed loudly. "*Do I bloody look alright?!*" He scowled down at Erbakan for a moment without word, then spat on him – a great round globule of sputum right in the Turk's outraged dial.

"I ain't a violent man," growled the Londoner, "and I don' believe in killin'. So I ain't gonna do anything to ya. But this lot don' 'ave the same morals as me, innit? So they can do what the 'ell they like wi' ya sorry ass."

Erbakan retorted something in Turkish which none of them assumed to be complimentary.

McKinley nodded toward the wheelhouse. "Get yourself back in the lounge and lie down. We'll take care of you. Can you do that?"

"Yes I can," nodded Bacon uncertainly, and headed inside.

"This is all very well McKittrick," gasped the fallen arms dealer through his pain, "but the boat is nearly here with my men. I do not know how you came on board, but how do you think you are going to make it to the shore?"

Wilson looked out over the port quarter. Sure enough waterborne lights were approaching fast.

McKinley dropped to one knee by Erbakan. "You really are an arrogant cock aren't you?"

Erbakan grimaced hatefully back.

"But you're wrong, see," smiled McKinley. "We're not going ashore."

Eyes popping and mouth agape, the surprised arms dealer started swearing in his native tongue and beating the wooden deck with his hands. How can you be so dumb that you didn't see *that* coming, thought McKinley. "Corporal," he ordered, "take this bag of shit aft."

"Yes sir," said Wilson enthusiastically, easily lifting the Turk despite his struggles. He started to frog-march the limping, swearing arms dealer toward the stern, passing a sodden Weapons and Equipment Technician coming forward.

"Looks like I missed the fun," said Carter, water running from his clothes.

"There's more on the way," said McKinley. "Get in that wheelhouse and let's motor!"

Carter planted his soaking body in the big chair and for the second time that night prepared to pilot an unfamiliar vessel in mission-critical circumstances. He scanned the control surfaces. Everything seemed straightforward apart from the Turkish nomenclature, and he quickly got the layout and hit what he believed to be the engine start.

A throaty, satisfying rumble vibrated the hull for just a second and settled down to a powerful hum. As McKinley watched, Carter retracted the anchor, bringing up the running lights, navigational aids, computerised charts, sonar, radar and the big floodlights on the bow. If nothing else, he thought, I'm getting a lesson in Turkish seafaring terminology. "Good to go," Carter shouted.

"Take us out Chris," ordered McKinley. "U-turn to port then a slow pass close by the other boat. Once they've got the message we head for Gando."

"Aye aye skipper," said Carter, gripping throttle levers and wheel. McKinley went back on deck to join Wilson.

Carter started to put pressure on the middle throttle lever. Gently to start with, he thought. The yacht responded smoothly, giving the impression of huge power under perfect control. He went a bit further and she was off, accelerating toward the black cliffs of the bay. "Like shit off a shovel!" grinned Carter. He took the boat in a wide, graceful turn, seeing the lights of the other boat come into view from his left.

The two boats neared in the darkness. Carter slowed the *Fata Morgana* and steered to within a close but safe distance of the approaching launch, seeing armed men on board.

In fear for his employer's safety—and his own if Erbakan was harmed—
Shurik Skumarovsky took out his pistol as Erbakan's huge boat approached
theirs. The *Fata Morgana* rose out of the night majestically, her streamlined
shape slicing through the ocean water with barely any disturbance. Three
figures were visible on deck. As they drew abeam, Scum's expression turned
from determination to shocked surprise.

McKinley and Wilson flanked Erbakan, each with a pistol glued to the Turk's
skull.

"Drop your guns overboard!" commanded McKinley in Spanish, "or he dies!
Right now!" With this he deliberately cocked his pistol and once again planted it
on Erbakan's skull.

They watched Scum turn to his companions in the launch. They didn't seem
to be discarding their firearms so McKinley nodded to Wilson. The combat
specialist sighted up a man on the launch and shot him through the heart.

"Guns over the side *now!*" shouted McKinley. Shocked at Wilson's amazing
pistol marksmanship, hands started to reach for the sky and guns disappeared
into the black sea. Once it seemed that the launch was weapons free, McKinley
retracted his Five-seveN from the Turk's head and took an object from his
webbing. "Time for your bath!" he shouted, and lobbed Carter's improvised
grenade into the launch.

Their horrified faces reflecting desperate panic, everyone on the launch
instantly scrambled to leave it. Just as the last occupant flung himself over the
side, the block of C4 detonated, blasting the little boat's hull apart with a
thunderous *wallop* that echoed off the coastline. The *Fata Morgana* left Scum
and his cronies in her wake.

010: The Voyage

They rounded Gran Canaria's southernmost point, Punta de Maspalomas, where the sixty meter tall lighthouse marked the resort village of Meloneras and the beginning of the two mile wide Maspalomas dune field. Carter kept the yacht ploughing through the waves at a brisk pace, yet far from approaching Erbakan's claimed performance, whilst McKinley and Wilson secured the extremely unhappy arms dealer in the same stinky cupboard that Bacon had been forced to endure.

They passed the power plant near Castillo del Romeral and turned north by north-east, working their way back toward the airport so that they could dock at Punta del Gando and enter the military airbase where Valenciano was expecting them. Whilst passing the massive industrial terminal at Puerto de Arinaga, Carter shouted to McKinley and the team leader made his way to the bridge.

"See that?" said Carter, tapping on the radar display. "We've got a situation."

McKinley saw a pair of radar contacts astern. "The Dibble?"

"Only if they've got a Cockney accent," said Carter, turning up the radio.

"...not be harmed. Repeat; heave to and turn Kyle Bacon over to us and you will not be harmed. Our weapons are trained on you and we will not hesitate to fire. Fata Morgana do you read me?"

McKinley quickly glanced at Carter. "Bounty hunters!"

"That's what I thought."

"Heh." McKinley grinned. "We got there first." A tiny fragment of wariness surfaced in the back of his mind, as though something wasn't quite right. That someone wanted a reward for Bacon's recovery wasn't unusual, but there was something about the timing...

"What's the play?" asked Carter.

McKinley came back to the moment. His official capacity was definitely the best approach. "I guess pull over. I'll get rid of them."

Carter reduced the revs and they felt the yacht settle into the sea. He picked up the microphone and signalled that they were slowing.

Pistol hidden in the back of his belt, McKinley went to the stern. The approaching vessels were private yachts as well. Certainly not as unique or advanced as the *Fata Morgana*, they were nonetheless impressive and undoubtedly expensive. The yacht nearing the port side was long and low as if built for speed whilst the other had a more conventional look like a floating holiday home.

The faster looking yacht came alongside as Wilson joined McKinley, the waves chopping and slapping between their hulls. On its bobbing deck were several men looking back at them. One, a tall, bull-like figure with a blond flat-top and light yellow jumper, stepped forward and shouted.

"Who are you?" The accent was indeed obvious.

This struck McKinley as an odd question and he wouldn't normally have countenanced such a demand, but it was important that these people thought they were dealing with someone official. "My name's McKittrick, Security Intelligence Service."

"Oh!" The man's eyes widened in surprise. "Where's Erbakan? Is Bacon okay?"

"I've arrested Erbakan and we're taking care of Bacon. He's safe and we're returning him to the UK."

Even in the darkness McKinley could see the man's face fall. Yeah, sorry pal. No reward money for you. The man turned to his companions and McKinley watched them discuss this new development. Then the man came back to the side of his boat.

"Can I say hello to Kyle please? I was a friend of his dad's and I'd just like to make sure he's okay."

Really, thought McKinley. Let's find out. He pondered for a moment. "So tell me; what date did Len Bacon die?"

"May tenth, four years ago. And the funeral was May fourteenth."

"Fair enough," shouted McKinley. "I'll be back in a moment."

He strode forward and into the lounge, finding Wilson and Bacon sitting together, the former examining the horrible wound on the gadget dealer's head.

Bacon looked up. "What's going on?"

McKinley helped him up from the couch. "We've got your would-be saviour alongside. He wants to see you're okay. Reckons he was a friend of your dad's."

"Oh nice," said Bacon as they headed back to the stern with Wilson in tow.

They exited into the night air and approached the port side. McKinley quickly scanned the deck of the other boat for weapons. There, on the bench seat at the far side and wrapped in a towel, was Scum. *What?*

Suddenly several things happened at once. Bacon screamed, the men on the other yacht started pulling out rifles and the *Fata Morgana* accelerated hard, throwing them all to the deck. Carter was shouting something from the wheelhouse as the crackle of gunfire accompanied rounds slamming into the yacht's superstructure.

Bacon landed on McKinley. "What the hell?!" yelled the latter.

"*You moron!*" shouted Bacon in distress. "You stupid berk! That's Frank Farmer!"

Before McKinley had time to register this there was a flash of light and a horribly loud noise like radio static being tuned through a big guitar amplifier. The bastards were firing rockets! Thank God, that first one had flown past. The sound of an explosion came from somewhere ahead.

Although the yacht was rocking and bounding through the waves they got themselves inside. McKinley and Bacon made for the bridge, where Carter was trying to steer and work the console at the same time. Gunfire continued and lead peppered the stern. Wilson had fired back a couple of times, but a pistol against rifles was something of a joke, so he turned and ran, keeping low, to the bridge.

"That was an RPG!" yelled Carter. "I saw it just before they fired!"

Hence the sudden acceleration that caused it to miss, thought McKinley. Thank heavens for Chris' speedy reaction. He turned to Bacon. "Who the hell is that?!"

"That's the guy who killed my dad!"

"Bloody—!"

Another lurch of the boat sent them all falling to the right except Carter, who swore as an explosion off the starboard bow shattered a window, spraying him with glass and seawater.

McKinley was picking himself up, shouting "hit the gas! Outrun 'em!"

Carter slammed the main engine control forward as McKinley grabbed the side of the pilot's chair.

"All the engines!" snapped McKinley.

"No good! Those two won't start. They're on a different system!"

"Shit!" snapped McKinley. "You've got ninety seconds to sort it. I'm gonna slow them down."

Wilson came up behind the chair. "How?"

McKinley frowned. "Feed them Bacon," he grunted.

Frank Farmer was determined to get Kyle Bacon. Whoever these James Bond wannabe SIS guys thought they were, he wasn't afraid of them. Not only did he want his share of the two and a half million Euro reward, but to settle a few old scores.

He was standing on the bridge of his boat, watching as his pilot guided their craft expertly through the night. Mister Erbakan's yacht was fast, for sure, but they were gaining on it. They'd left their other boat far behind.

Suddenly the radio burst into life. "Farmer!" it squawked, "slow down! We're going to drop Bacon overboard! He's all yours."

Surprised, Farmer looked at his pilot. What the hell?

The pilot shrugged. "Want me to do it?"

The gangster grinned unpleasantly. "If those pansy bastards don't want him, I'll take him." Visions of reward money titillated his mind.

"Yes sir," said the pilot, dropping the engine revolutions. He acknowledged the transmission as his boss exited the bridge.

Farmer grabbed his binoculars and ran out onto the foredeck. "Searchlights!" he shouted to his crew.

Ahead they could see the *Fata Morgana*. Two men were on deck, manhandling a third, blond-haired figure. Farmer lifted his binoculars to see them tipping the guy over the side.

"Slower!" he yelled to his pilot as his men raked the waves with their lights.

McKinley and Wilson dashed back in to the bridge. "You got it?" demanded the team leader.

"Think so," muttered Carter, scrolling between different touch screens. "The outer engines have to be primed from here, then the main engine needs to be synchronised to a certain RPM. You can't just—"

"Not with the science lesson!" barked McKinley. "Just make this tub fly!"

Carter looked round at him, a devilish gleam in his eye. "Hold on to your ass."

He brought the main engine up to speed, watching the displays carefully. Once it seemed right, Carter hit a couple of switches and a high pitched whine could be heard from outside. Then he pushed the outer throttles. The *Fata Morgana* took off like a rocket, tipping both McKinley and Wilson over. Wilson held on to the chart table whilst the massive surge of power rolled McKinley down the steps back into the lounge.

"Tried to warn you!" called Carter.

The sodden figure in the lifebelt was about as sorry a sight as Farmer had ever seen. Not as sorry as you're *going* to be though, he thought, as his yacht came to a halt by the man.

Farmer looked over the side and stopped there, terrified.

"You stupid British *değersiz salak!*" snarled Erbakan, absolutely livid, tearing off the swatch of cushion fabric which had been duct-taped to his head.

Colour drained from the London gangster's face. "Oh blimey... *I'm so sorry!*" he stammered.

The *Fata Morgana* was no more than a rapidly shrinking cluster of lights.

McKinley threw his butt onto the couch at the chart table. Wilson and Bacon were already there. He held on to the table's edge, feeling the amazing power of the *Fata Morgana* vibrating through her whole hull. The boat was travelling incredibly fast, but maybe not fast enough.

"So what about this Farmer?" McKinley held a palm upward. "Who the hell's he?"

"Gangster, isn't 'e?" replied Bacon, whose pulse rate was starting to descend to normal levels. "One of the Bushies."

McKinley nodded. *That* was where he'd heard the name. The Bushy Boys were a London gang whose manor was the Sherpherd's Bush area of the city. They were into some nasty business.

"What's he want with you?" asked Wilson.

"The reward, *obviously*," retorted Bacon. "That and screwing me over I bet."

"I thought your dad's murder was never solved."

"Not *officially*, but everyone knows it's Farmer did it. He 'ated my ol' man."

McKinley sighed, turning away for a moment. This shit, he thought, just gets deeper. Now TDR.12 were on the run from a murderous Turkish arms dealer, a bunch of London gangsters with a fast boat, and probably their own unit too. He rotated back to Bacon as Wilson voiced another thought.

"I suppose he does business with Erbakan?"

Bacon nodded. "Lot longer 'n me, too. But they ain't friends."

That could change, thought McKinley, but first the gangster would have a lot of ass kissing to do. He and Wilson looked at each other. That was why Farmer and his pals were in Gran Canaria. Erbakan had doubtless offered to split the reward with them, probably not wanting the complication of delivering Bacon back to the UK. But on rescuing the bedraggled Scum, and learning that a government agent had control of the arms dealer's vessel, they'd obviously decided to ingratiate themselves with the Turk by taking both it and his hostage back. The pieces were falling into place and McKinley didn't much like the picture they were forming. He got up and carefully stepped over to Carter's position. "Report."

"One boat in pursuit."

"I thought we're outrunning them."

"We are," said Carter, "but you can't outrun radar. As long as we can see them, they can see us."

"They can't catch us though, can they?"

Carter scowled. "They can see where we're heading. When we dock they'll be all over us."

"Reception committee," murmured McKinley, nodding. The pursuers would undoubtedly have primed their people on the island, making the COAST lads' survival unlikely and their return to the Gando airbase impossible. Even if they tried to dock somewhere else, both Erbakan's and Farmer's people could get there ahead. They had no choice now but to find another route back to the UK and it looked like Plugger would have some explaining to do at the air charter company. McKinley was starting to feel worried and it pissed him off. The odds were stacking up against them. What to do? He rubbed his face tiredly. This was his party, and he had to make it work.

He dumped himself back down at the chart table next to Bacon. Like everything on the *Fata Morgana,* it was a high-tech version of its typical maritime counterpart: a large touchscreen monitor lying on its back, currently displaying their GPS position, radar contacts and the surrounding seas. Its surface radiated the warmth of its underlying electronics.

McKinley zoomed the display out, noting that the interface bore some similarity to the mapping application on his new phone. There was Gran Canaria's coastline as a misshapen brown lump up the left hand side of the image. They were travelling north at speed and were still a couple of miles out from Gando.

He widened the image even further, bringing the other Canarian islands into view. There was Tenerife to the west, and to the north-east Fuerteventura and Lanzarote. Even if they ran for it they'd still be on radar, and Erbakan knew where they were going. The Turk might even be talking to his contacts in the UK already, but TDR.12 would burn that bridge if and when they reached it.

He found the scale indicator which, as he touched it, became a moveable circular measuring tool. Intrigued, McKinley started to plot the distances to the various islands, half his mind still desperately hunting for a solution.

Horribly fatigued, Carter stared into the darkness, aware that at this speed disaster could overtake them with no warning. If they hit anything, even something as mundane as a piece of driftwood, it could be catastrophic. His energy drink was wearing off and he felt like shit, having not slept at all since the night his car was borrowed by McKinley, whose sudden exclamation startled him.

"Chris! I've got an idea! Turn north-east and increase speed as far as you like."

Carter's brow furrowed. "Maximum?"

"Enough to lose them."

Carter sighed, making the course correction. "You know how dangerous this is in the dark, right? Not to mention stuff like safety tolerances and fuel usage."

"I know. We got plenty?"

Carter nodded, watching the GPS compass carefully. "Oddly enough we're loaded."

"Heh... If we have to outrun the coastguard," quoted McKinley.

Carter yawned. "I suppose you want me to nobble our ID too?"

McKinley nodded. "That's my next question."

"If someone else drives. I'll try to mod the AIS and anything else I can."

"Can you have a look at his ear first?"

Carter leaned, showing McKinley his left hand, which was shaking. "Mate, it's not getting any worse, and you don't want me doing medical stuff without sleep."

McKinley nodded. "Okay." He turned to Wilson. "Willy!"

Wilson looked over from the chart table. "What's up?"

"Time for your shift at the wheel." Out of their team, Wilson was the only one to have slept on the flight. He was also a little fitter, a decade younger and the new boy. Naturally it was his turn.

"Roger," affirmed Wilson, rising. McKinley turned back to Carter.

"Now, the distance to Fuerteventura is about a hundred miles. Once we get over the horizon they won't be able to see us on radar, will they?"

"Right, I see what you're doing. But they'll know which way we went."

"Aye," said McKinley. "I'm counting on it."

Forty minutes and a lot of bone rattling later, McKinley finally told Wilson to back off the power. It had been a hell of a ride, even with he and Bacon lying on the floor, which was the safest place. Bacon had already heaved his guts up twice and was looking like a repeat performance could be forthcoming. Carter in the meantime had been in the lounge, trying to master the yacht's computerised systems. So far he had at least got the software to talk English, making his next tasks a little easier.

Wilson dropped the revs with relief, mindful of the danger of such high speed dashes at night, but by now a warm glow was spreading through the sky from behind Fuerteventura, making life considerably easier.

McKinley strode through to the lounge, finding his friend looking wrecked but still glued to the computer screen, muttering frustratedly and configuring.

Carter looked up and blinked a bit. "I *wish* I hadn't lost that laptop," he drawled tiredly. "What do you want to call this thing? Boat's gotta have a name."

McKinley rolled his eyes. "I don't care. Think of something. As long as I can paint it on the bow."

"Okay then," said Carter. "*Ghost Rocket.*" He typed into the computer and hit 'return'.

McKinley found the name oddly appropriate, a slight smile tweaking the corner of his mouth. "*Ghost Rocket?*"

"*Spökeraket,*" replied Carter. "Old Swedish term for a UFO."

"So it's all set up then? We're good?"

"I *really* need the software to do this properly, so it's a bodge for now." Carter swiped a few touch keys with a dramatic flourish. "But *Fata Morgana* no longer exists; *Ghost Rocket* is on her maiden voyage."

"Good work," said McKinley. "Get some doss. We'll see you in a couple of hours."

He climbed back through to the wheelhouse, where Wilson was carefully paralleling the north coast of Fuerteventura, turning from the Bocayna Strait into the El Rio channel, between the main island and its little northern neighbour. The horizon was a plane of lurid incandescence with a growing nodule of intense, unwatchable brightness at its center. The whole ocean seemed to have changed colour from a forbidding black to a rippling orange as fierce as a nearby bonfire.

"This is deep enough, right?" asked Bacon.

"Definitely," said McKinley. He reached to the console and pointed to the depth of water beneath their hull, which was fluctuating around the eleven meter mark.

"I guess I'd just rather we went around that island," said Bacon.

McKinley turned toward him. "We want to look like local traffic," he explained, and rotated back to Wilson. "On that point, keep the speed down from now eh?"

"So where *are* we going?" said Wilson, watching the town of Corralejo slip past on their starboard beam, a vista of ancient, cyclopean volcanoes towering beyond it. To port, the single, half-eroded cone of Isla de Lobos seemed isolated and forlorn by comparison.

McKinley could now understand the boat's operating system much better thanks to the language change, and he reached past Wilson to bring up the chart on one of the screens. "South-south-east," he said, zooming the display out. He pulled the image back far enough to reveal the Moroccan coastline, then focused on a point just above the disputed border of Western Sahara. Several pinch-zooms later a tiny village became visible right on the coast. The coastline was labelled *Playa de las Negritas*.

Right, thought Wilson, Beach of the Bold. You'd have to be bold—or mad—to live somewhere as bleak as that. "There's nothing there," he observed.

"*Tah*, it's called," said McKinley, "and no, nothing apart from some fishermen's huts. Just use the place as your bearing, then we'll follow the coast south."

"Because they think we'll be going north? Makes sense."

"Aye. The boat's got a new ID, and this island," McKinley nodded to their right, "hides us from their radar. It's a big ocean; hard to find something you're not looking for."

Carter woke up on Erbakan's big bed and looked at his watch. He'd been asleep for nearly three hours—an uncharacteristically long stretch for him—and bright sunlight was streaming into the cabin. He got up and found the toilet facilities.

Carter looked around as he sat. It sure was a nice dunny, all pure white porcelain with detailing in natural granite. He found the flush, which was a small button on the wall to his right. But when he pressed it a sudden draft of cold, damp air assailed Carter's nether regions accompanied by the sound of the yacht's engines. Surprised, he nearly jumped off the throne.

Intrigued, Carter washed his hands and pulled his pants back on. He found a skin moisturiser bottle and, whilst pressing the flush, jammed it into the opening. Sure enough there was a gust of wind, motor noise and a continuous rushing sound. He smelled seawater. Looking down the pipe he could see a dim glow of what appeared to be daylight. So, the dirty bastard was sending his sewage straight into the ocean. Carter considered this discovery for a moment. Wilson the environmentalist nature nut would be a storm of umbrage upon learning this. But for the moment he filed the information away and headed for the shower.

In the cubicle Carter refreshed his body with Erbakan's expensive toiletries. We might be killed by the Turk, the Bushies, the Spanish navy or even our own people, mused Carter, but at least I'll go out smelling posh. He found some of Erbakan's clothes and tried them on. The trousers were a couple of inches wide and too long in the leg but he turned up the ankles, pulling the waist in with his own belt. The shirts, though, were pretty good, if far more fashionable than Carter was used to. Donning his cap, he put his own clothes in the sink and gave them something of a wash, then took them up to the foredeck, tying them securely to the railings to dry. He leaned for a moment on the port siding, drinking in the bright sunshine and admiring the seascape rushing past.

"You look like a twit," commented McKinley as he joined Carter, scanning him up and down and smirking at the incongruity of a well used COAST crew cap crowning a Turkish arms dealer's ostentatious apparel.

"I don't care," smiled the weapons tech. "Better than stinking."

McKinley took his smoke from his mouth and lowered his nose toward his own armpit for a moment, grimacing. "S'pose."

Carter looked down at his friend's hands, splotched with grey. "Painting?"

"Covered up the old lettering. I fillered some of the bullet holes too." He turned his back to the railing, leaning over the speeding water and groaning with satisfaction as several vertebrae popped into better alignment. McKinley stood upright again. "D'you wanna come inside? We need to discus stuff before I get my rack."

They returned to the bridge, where Wilson was still manning the wheel. It looked quite different in the daylight, as though all the shiny high-tech gadgetry was overwhelmed by the rays of the sun. Every surface gleamed and the blue light from the various controls seemed muted. Carter noted that his friends had secured some kind of plastic over the broken window, and it was flapping like a piece of paper caught in a fan. Apart from this, though, the soundproofing in *Ghost Rocket's* cockpit was surprisingly good and conversation would be easy. McKinley, Carter and Bacon sat at the chart table, the latter still looking a bit green.

"Kyle," began McKinley, "we'd like to talk about the reward."

Bacon's eyes narrowed. "You ain't getting' it, if that's what ya think," he griped. "It were you what got me 'eld 'ostage in the first place!"

McKinley had expected this response. "*You* wanted to stay behind! And as to being kidnapped, we could've turned a deaf... Sorry, blind eye. I meant a blind eye."

"No you couldn't." Bacon shook his head, frowning unhappily. "The 'ole thing were your fault. See I *know* you Mickey. You got a conscience."

"Rarely," said Carter under his breath.

"All the same," continued McKinley, throwing Carter the dog-eye, "we want *some* reward. If someone else'd sprung you you'd be playing air Stylophone already."

Bacon was frank, shaking his head. "Not gonna happen."

McKinley pulled out his trump card, shrugging. "That was your chance to offer, but the deal we made with Plugger was for half the money, minus any expenses."

"Bollocks!" spat Bacon in disbelief.

"Chris, can I use your phone mate?" said McKinley. Carter passed it across and McKinley started finding Plugger's number.

"What's wrong wi' your phone?" asked Bacon, trying to stall McKinley.

"Ah," interjected Carter. "The new ones are all tied in to our employer's databases. So if we even switch 'em on they'll know where we are. My old phone – which I was sensible enough to keep," he looked pointedly at McKinley, "doesn't have that problem... yet. I've changed the number and ESN, but it's still fully functional."

"Oh yeah?" said the gadget dealer. "Don't ya want the new one? I could use a phone like that."

"What, you want to reverse engineer it? Well you can't. I'm keeping it."

"Shit," muttered Bacon.

"Plugger!" sang McKinley cheerfully as his call connected. "Good news; Kyle's safe." He paused as the other party tried to exclaim loudly but instead produced a short series of staccato yelps. "Now, I wonder if you could please advise him of our agreement?"

Plugger must have got an 'okay' out between stutters because McKinley passed the phone to Bacon, grinning faithlessly. After assuring Plugger of his reasonable health, Bacon listened and made occasional grunts of acknowledgement that increased in unhappiness for about a minute before he swore crudely and hung up.

Bacon looked about as happy as a man that had repeatedly poked himself in the eye. "So let's get this right," he grated, "*you* got me into this bloody mess and you want me to pay for *you* getting me out of it?!"

Carter nodded. McKinley said "yes exactly."

"So I just piss away a million quid because of you? And I don't get nothin' out of it?!"

McKinley shrugged. "You're alive, aren't you? *And* free. And it's already agreed with Plugger."

"You bloody assholes!" Bacon spat. "Half minus expenses? You bastards took advantage of him, didn't you?!"

"No, I don't think so." McKinley shook his head. "He offered it."

"I'll deal wi' that twat later," frowned Bacon. "But..." his eyes narrowed, "I got a *better* deal for us both."

Wilson looked over at them with a raised eyebrow. McKinley and Carter glanced at each other suspiciously.

Bacon sat back smirking despite his pallid complexion, as though he was about to royal flush a poker opponent into bankruptcy. "Now I've 'ad a look round the rest of this thing," he said, motioning around them with his hand, "it's nice. Really nice. A man like me should 'ave a boat like this."

McKinley groaned inside, certain as to what would come next.

"So I'll tell ya what," continued the Londoner. "I'll give you the *whole* reward, *if* I get the yacht. Then I *do* get something for going through all this shit."

"You're talking bollocks," said Wilson, looking over at him. "Where on earth would you hide it? He'll have people looking for it. It'd be like we rescued you just so he could find you and kill you."

"I'll get it remodelled," answered Bacon. "It'll cost a bomb, but it'll still be a fraction of buying one of these things. Like where...?" he trailed off in thought. "Hmm. I'm thinking the Med. Always liked Corsica, me."

McKinley had also been thinking. "Lads," he said, "we could definitely use the money. If we're going after Heinmarsh that sort of cash would grease the wheels. As long as we're done with this tub."

Carter shrugged and sat back, indicating his acquiescence to whatever decision McKinley and Wilson made. McKinley turned across to Wilson. "What d'you think Willy?"

Wilson's eyes stayed on the horizon despite their furious tiredness. "Well, once it's out of our hands it's not our problem, is it?"

"One... *small* caveat," interjected Carter, raising a finger. "Our science department gets to examine the systems, engines, all that stuff."

"They can get in line," quipped Bacon.

So, thought Carter, it's not *just* going to be a rich man's plaything. He admired the Londoner's enterprising mindset.

"But yeah, okay," finished the tech dealer.

"Kyle," smiled McKinley, "you just bought yourself a yacht. It's yours as soon as we're done with it. That'll be two and half million Euros, please."

They shook hands. "Deal?" said McKinley.

"Deal," answered Bacon, smiling widely and showing off his whitened teeth in the evident belief that he'd got the bargain of the century. "Just don't wreck it, eh?"

"Okay," said McKinley, his tone becoming more serious, "next question. We've got transport and now we've even got funds. Are we going after Heinmarsh or what?"

"Or should we just split the money and retire?" said Carter, smiling impudently. McKinley regarded him with contempt.

Wilson sighed heavily. He'd been dreading the moment in which the Heinmarsh question was posited. Here on the wide blue ocean, batting along in this amazing yacht, he'd almost forgotten about young women tragically blowing themselves to pieces for some stupid cause. But now the subject and the disturbance it caused him stabbed back into his conscience with force. He *did* want to do something about it, whether that involved bagging Heinmarsh or not; he wanted to stop the suicide bombers.

"There's just one more thing first," said Bacon, pointing to the side of his head.

"Oh, right," said Carter. "Yes, I'll get that looked at. There should be a decent first aid kit on board. Let's have a gozzie."

Bacon leaned over to better reveal the awful wound.

"Ruddy Ada!" exclaimed Carter, closely scrutinising the gap formerly occupied by Bacon's auricle, "that must have *hurt.*"

Bacon's eyes squeezed shut as he remembered, then snapped open again as the motion of the boat got to him. "You ain't bloody kidding! Worst thing ever 'appen' to me." He shuddered. "Anything you can do?"

"Prosthetics are scarce round here, but I can tidy it up a bit," nodded Carter. "Clean out any infection."

McKinley hung his nose over them. "What about anaesthetic?"

Bacon scowled in emotional stress, swearing. "That bastard didn't use any did 'e?! They just 'eld me down while 'e did it!" Tears started to run from his eyes and his breathing sped up as he shook again. "I ain't never goin' through nothin' like that again!" He involuntarily raised his hand to the side of his head, trembling.

"It's okay chap," smiled Carter, placing his hand gently on Bacon's arm. "Won't be a problem. You ever been hypnotised?"

The gadget dealer's eyes widened. "You're kiddin' me? Always wanted to, but not on one of them stage shows, cluckin' like a bleedin' chicken, innit? You can do it?"

"Absolutely," smiled Carter. "hypnosis training is mandatory for Weapons and Equipment Techs."

Wilson was getting interested in the conversation and turned, carefully holding the wheel steady. "Slight change of subject," he started. "D'you think these suicide bombers are under hypnosis Chris?"

Carter winked at Wilson, making sure that Bacon wouldn't see. Turning back to the Londoner, he said "look, Kyle, go lie down and we'll get this sorted, okay?"

"Heck yeah," responded Bacon enthusiastically, getting up. "Can you do somethin' wi' sea sickness 'n' all?"

Carter nodded politely, smiling. "Consider it done."

Bacon's face split into a wide grin. "Monster! Thanks mate." He got up and left, carefully descending the stairwell toward the master bedroom.

Carter turned to Wilson again. "You were asking?"

"Are these suicide bombers hypnotised, d'you think? I mean, no-one in their right mind would blow themselves up for a cause, would they?"

Carter shook his head firmly. "No. Humans have a strong instinct for self preservation. But if you call it the power of *belief* then we're on the same page."

"Explain," prodded McKinley

"Well," aired Carter, "hypnosis, *I think*, is just the power of belief and imagination, coupled with an altered state of consciousness. People *believe* they're going to quit smoking, so they do. Or they imagine barking like a dog, so it happens right?" He waited for McKinley's nod before continuing. "It's kinda the same with a religious cult. So if someone's belief is strong enough, they'll make themselves do anything." Carter nodded sideways at the stairs. "That's why I asked him to go below. Didn't want him to hear this."

"Aye, *right*," answered McKinley, rubbing his chin thoughtfully. "It would have changed his *belief* about being hypnotised. Clever."

Carter's finger shook toward McKinley. "Ten out of ten. He *believes* he's going to get hypnotised and I'll stitch up his ear and fix his motion sickness. Because he *believes* it, it'll work."

Wilson was scanning the chart again as he replied from the wheel. "But don't some people blow themselves up because they think it guarantees a place in heaven?"

"Aye," said McKinley, frowning angrily. "Jem mentioned that. And I've read the intel; that's what they teach in some of these ideologies."

"Well," frowned Carter, "God's hard to argue with, if you believe, right? But the *problem* is that people put their faith in religious leaders as God's voice, if you like, and do whatever they say."

McKinley nodded slowly. "So it's down to rhetoric?"

Carter spread his palms. "Yes. You make your followers feel special, set apart, one of the elect—"

"The elect!" burst McKinley. "She used that exact phrase."

"Of course," said Carter. "Anyway, you tell them *your* teachings come straight from God and they're more radical than anyone else's. Introduce the fear of divine punishment so nobody disobeys. To finance your empire you promise prosperity to givers. Create jealousy in the majority who give the least by rewarding the few who give the most. It's quite simple."

"I'm just guessing you researched this," deadpanned Wilson. Blimey, he thought, you're *such* a bloody nerd.

McKinley was following Carter's explanation with interest. "So that's what this Makaru's doing then?"

"Probably, but there's something more. Witness Jem's behaviour on those videos."

"Right," exclaimed McKinley. "She didn't remember who she was at first, and then it came and went. What's with that?"

Carter sat back and linked his hands, his lower lip covering its upper twin and his eyes raised toward the roof. They could almost hear the cogs grinding. After a moment he came back to them.

"I don't know. It's neither hypnosis nor the usual kind of cult mind control. The memory loss is the clue."

"To what?" asked Wilson.

"Still trying to figure that out," said Carter. "Leave it with me. I'm off to mess with Bacon's head."

It was the same room, straddling a line between traditional and sterile, and a little colder than he might have preferred. There wasn't much to look at on the whitewashed walls save for a couple of small portraits of long departed dignitaries and an ancient carved coat of arms that looked to have suffered more from cleaning than it had the ravage of ages.

General Sutton had been waiting a long time. As a busy man he wasn't used to waiting. When he issued an order he expected it to be carried out with all due promptness plus interest, but that was at the COAST headquarters. Here he was forced to dance to the politicians' tune in all its pomposity and time-honoured rigmarole. But Sutton was a patient man and capable of keeping his mind occupied with all kinds of intelligence related questions.

After twenty eight minutes, subcommittee chairman Clifton Cambion-Dawkins and his group finally made their grand entrance. They could have been wearing exactly the same clothes save for the woman, who was now attired in dark blue. They sat in the same positions as before and got down to business quickly.

"You know why you're here General," simpered the politician without even looking up from his papers. "We're correct in understanding that your operative Tripod and his team-mates Hazard and Shadow have disappeared, aren't we?"

"Minister," began Sutton, immediately on the counter offensive, "*disappeared* isn't the appropriate term, but we're not currently monitoring their whereabouts."

"Oh General!" The minister's face looked like he'd just stepped in shit. "Don't play the semantics game! They've disappeared, vanished, gone off the grid, done a runner. They're *renegades!*" Cambion-Dawkins calmed quickly, adjusting his tie. "I'm led to believe they travelled from Birmingham airport to Copenhagen yesterday evening. What, may I ask, are they doing in Denmark?"

Caught between a rock and a hard place, Sutton answered flatly. "I wouldn't know sir."

Cambion-Dawkins' mouth turned down at the corners. "Are they even in Denmark, General?"

Sutton sighed. "I'm not monitoring their location sir," he affirmed. "Furthermore, I cannot agree that they've gone AWOL without evidence."

"You'll get it," sneered the politico. "Now, this operative Tripod; as we touched on last time, I'm right in saying that going AWOL wouldn't be entirely out of character, aren't I? That he's something of a loose cannon? Doesn't always follow orders or adhere to prescribed methodologies?"

Sutton sighed inwardly, but duty demanded he answer. "His methods are sometimes unusual—"

"Unusual?!"

"Unusual. Perhaps unorthodox—"

"*Highly questionable!*" barked the civil servant, looking as though a bad smell was under his nose. He shrugged exaggeratedly. "At *least*, highly questionable!"

Sutton cleared his throat. "Sir, Tripod and his team have always delivered. He gets the job done, sir, and I mean no disrespect when I say that most of us in this room have no idea how much TDR.12 have already saved thousands of British citizens and others from."

"But now they've gone rogue, haven't they General? Can't we just agree that Tripod's got his own plans – as have his team-mates, apparently?"

"Sir, they're not our enemy and this isn't the problem you think it is. COAST has procedures in place to deal with any possible renegade operatives. I'll give the order as soon as we're done here."

"Whilst we definitely support that decision, General, it won't be necessary," smirked Cambion-Dawkins. "I've already appointed a contractor to take control of this matter. He will be exclusively concerned to seek, capture and—if it becomes necessary—*dispose* of Tripod and his team."

General Sutton assumed his impenetrable poker face and surveyed the cocksure Cambion-Dawkins. The slimy politician bore the expression of a cat which had just wolfed down the canary... and really enjoyed it. "May I ask to which contractor you're referring, minister?" he asked.

"I'm sure you're aware of him General; Roger Jolley."

Sutton nodded slowly. "I understood that Mister Jolley's employment was on indefinite hold, subject to an inquiry into certain indiscretions in the Irish Republic."

"And the members of this subcommittee are satisfied," spat Cambion-Dawkins, "that these circumstances demand Jolley's attention. Furthermore, the evidence appears to demonstrate that the casualties were unavoidable in the instance to which you're referring."

"Civilian casualties, sir, just to clarify," replied Sutton, "and there are other incidents on record as well – for example those in Suriname and Croatia. Mister Jolley's outfit's been an embarrassment to Her Majesty's Government several times and I find it odd that you'd send someone of such questionable methods after those whose own practices you just called questionable. In dealing with even minor incidents Jolley's been..." Sutton paused in hope of hitting the right note. "More than over zealous," he concluded. Sutton knew more about Jolley's operation than Cambion-Dawkins could have guessed and, whilst he didn't like the man, his crew or his methods, if he was honest with himself, Ian McKinley and Roger Jolley were cut from similar cloth.

Cambion-Dawkins gave a sickly smile. "The word you're looking for might be 'ruthless', General Sutton. His commitment to his contractual duty is laudable. He has no concern whatsoever with superficial loyalties, niceties and fair play. To use your own phrasing, he gets the job done and that's what we need right now. We need to reign in these renegades before they do something *really* embarrassing."

Sutton was angry at that. "*Alleged* renegades, Minister!"

Cambion-Dawkins waved a dismissive hand in the air. "Whatever, General, whatever. Either way, the retrieval team's been deployed and this subcommittee will do everything to ensure that Tripod and his accomplices are apprehended in short order."

Sutton set his expression to neutral with considerable difficulty. "I'm sure you've made the right choice in your judgement, Minister. Let the record state that I recognise the sense of duty with which you're clearly taking personal responsibility for Roger Jolley, his staff and his actions."

Cambion-Dawkins glared at Sutton's logic. "Responsibility, General, is something I've never avoided!"

"Good," said Sutton. "May I report to my military superiors your assurance that this issue will soon be resolved?"

Sutton could see that the man opposite was getting upset yet trying his utmost not to let it show. Cambion-Dawkins' left hand was scrunched into such a tight ball that it looked as though it might collapse in on itself.

"You may tell them, if you wish, to draft a press release announcing that three renegade British operatives have been caught and *brought to justice*," he snarled, heavily emphasising the last phrase. "Before this meeting I myself composed a release drawing attention to the problem. We must do all in our power to limit their damage."

Damn it, thought Sutton, you stupid fool. He nodded politely, making sure that everyone in the room heard him. "Thank you, sir, for your assurances," he replied, his words as smooth as cream yet bitter with sarcasm.

Once the subcommittee had filed out, General Sutton sat in silence for a while. He was dutifully willing to accommodate the politicians; that was imperative. In his position he couldn't possibly be seen to be overlooking, much less *condoning* independent action by his men. He had no choice but to go after McKinley. What the hell are you doing, Corporal, he thought.

"There may be an additional problem," growled Carter, climbing back into the bridge, a pack of Erbakan's beer swinging from his hand. He'd been gone a bit more than an hour, and the seascape looked exactly the same.

"What, you can't hypnotise him?" grinned McKinley, catching his cigarette deftly as the smile caused its fall from his lips. "I was hoping you were gonna get us more money."

"Ah, no," said Carter, sliding into the L-shaped couch smoothly despite the movement of the boat. "He's done. Turned out to be a perfect subject. No pain. He's resting now."

"Blimey," said McKinley, quite impressed. "So what's the problem?"

Carter slid his fingers about on the chart table. "Watch this." He hit a control and a video monitor opened, showing a London background and a figure surrounded by the press. The man had a handsome bearing but his dark grey suit didn't fit well and his hair looked too black, as though freshly dyed. He had a rounded nose like Carter's, high temples, and jowls which seemed just a little too full, like he was recovering from mumps.

McKinley wanted to punch that fleshy face. "Slimy little shit," he snarled.

Carter pulled himself out of the seat and leaned in front of Wilson, bringing up the same frame on the pilot's monitors. "The Right Honourable Clifton Cambion-Dawkins," read Wilson. "So that's him."

McKinley grunted something inaudible but undoubtedly inappropriate for polite company.

Carter slid his finger up the right hand edge of the image and the volume reached an audible level.

"*...situation to be allowed to happen is a disgrace,*" said the televised politician, "*and a full inquiry will be set up into this incident. But I'll say this for now; not only will these rogue agents be apprehended, but as criminals they will be brought swiftly to justice.*"

McKinley's heart sank. Carter cancelled the video feed.

"It was just a matter of time," said Wilson pessimistically.

Carter sat again, pointing his finger at McKinley and speaking with an optimistic tone. "We still have the edge. They don't know where we are."

"We're beyond the Spanish coastal radar now, aren't we?" McKinley was thinking tactically.

"Yes," nodded Carter, "but remember that huge radar we saw at Pico de Las Nieves? We might be in range of that."

"Think they'd be interested in us? They're about planes and ICBMs aren't they?"

"No and yes."

"Our passports are gonna be flagged," said the team leader. "Both sets. Uncle Victor'll be doing that right now. We're already down to one phone."

"Borders, ports and airports are gonna be a no fly zone," observed Wilson. "No pun intended."

"They're only going to see Gran Canaria," responded Carter, spreading his palms wide. "They've no idea we've got this boat."

"Aye," said McKinley, nodding slowly. "So, begs the question: where are we going?"

"In for a penny," said Carter, winking at his Scottish friend.

Wilson turned in annoyance. "You're so damn predictable!" he complained. "If he said jump off a bridge you'd bloody do it, wouldn't you?" He shook his head.

"That would depend on what's beneath the bridge," frowned Carter.

"Look Willy," snapped McKinley, "Chris and I have been doing this for a bit. We've got what's called a *working relationship*. So don't bloody moan about him being a team player! What about you?"

Wilson wasn't giving much ground. "The idea was to *discuss* this after getting Bacon back."

"Right!" growled McKinley, "so we're discussing it!"

"Discussing what?" asked Bacon, appearing from below with more of the Turk's beer. "What'd I miss?"

The wind fell out of McKinley's sales. He was frustrated and uncertain – not a situation in which he was used to finding himself. He felt like he was treading water of unknown depth, but he was glad to see Bacon looking better. "How are you doing?" he asked.

"Great," smiled Bacon, pushing himself behind the chart table. He turned to Carter. "I dunno how you do that whizzy voodoo but it worked, innit? I ain't seasick no more, either. I feel great!"

"Good," replied Carter. "Let's keep an eye on that ear and see how we get on, okay?"

"Roger dodger," grinned the Londoner.

Carter faced McKinley. "Getting back on track," he said, "practical issues; if we do this, how are we going to get to Indonesia... or wherever the hell we end up?"

"Boat," said McKinley flatly, pointing his finger about.

"My yacht?" said Bacon.

McKinley ignored the arms dealer. "We'll go round the Cape," he continued.

"Around Cape Agulhas?" exclaimed Wilson.

"Cape Horn," corrected McKinley as he looked up.

"Cape Agulhas," re-affirmed Wilson, "is the actual boundary of the oceans. Those waters are lethal. We'll drown."

"Not to mention *my yacht*," added Bacon.

"You're gonna need a bigger boat," muttered Wilson sarcastically.

Carter shook his head. "We can't go round the Cape in this *toy*, Mickey. That's one of the most dangerous stretches of ocean in the world. Supertankers *die* there."

McKinley nodded slowly. "Aye but then it's the Suez, right?"

"And that would be a problem," replied Wilson. "Security, regulations, piloting, passports. We'd get picked up in no time. What the heck are you thinking?"

"Do they even allow private vessels through the canal?" asked Carter.

"Don't know," responded McKinley. "Can you go online and find out please mate?"

"On it," said Carter and went looking for another computer terminal, hoping they were still in a decent satellite footprint.

Carter's instant willingness to research this improbable venture unsettled Wilson all the more. Was Carter buying into McKinley's apparent insanity? He stared angrily out at the stark but nonetheless beautiful seascape around them for a moment. The weather seemed to have calmed somewhat and *Ghost Rocket* was slicing through the waves even more smoothly than before. "So what if we can't?" he asked.

McKinley shrugged. "We'll jump ship at Port Said."

Wilson rolled his eyes. "This is bonkers! Onto what? A bloody banana boat?!"

"I dunno!" barked McKinley. "I'm making this up as we go along, aye? Maybe see if we can get passage on a cargo ship or something."

Wilson sighed heavily. This plan sounded so hyperbolically far from plausible that he would have been willing to wager a generous sum on it never happening. "Then? There's still the freakin' Indian Ocean to cross."

McKinley thought for a moment. "We exit the canal into the Red Sea. We could buy another boat. Actually, if we could just take this thing through the Suez then hug the coastline, that would make life easier."

Bacon looked concerned.

Shaking his head, Wilson snarled. "What do you mean 'easier'?! For a start we're on a bloody stolen yacht." He tilted his head to the right, back toward Gran Canaria. "I don't think someone like him'll just take it on the chin. Oh and, BTW, the Suez Canal's that way," Wilson asserted, pointing over his shoulder in the direction of the vessel's wake.

He'd been trying to identify some kind of positive aspect to this malaise of impossibility and simultaneously toying with the boat's computerised navigation system. It was straightforward and, thanks to Carter, talking excellent English. "You know if we stay on this boat, assuming we can pass through the Suez, we're still talking about ten thousand nautical miles?"

"Ten thousand?!" blurted Bacon.

"Gonna take a while then," replied McKinley, leaning back on the couch, pulling his cap down over his eyes and folding his arms behind his head. "There'd better be plenty of that beer on board."

011: The Port

Carter fought with the computer. It was a capable system and he expected nothing less of Erbakan. Apparently, though, its internet connectivity had been designed for optimum function when moored.

Despite this he'd made a synopsis of the available information and printed it out. Indeed, private boats were allowed through the Suez and could move somewhat freely although vessels of greater than three hundred gross tons having to travel in convoys and be steered by an official pilot of the Canal. There were numerous legal hoops through which to jump, but it seemed that transiting the famous waterway was possible. Carter grinned to himself at the imagined conversation with Suez Canal officials: "Yes, we're three renegade British agents and he deals spy gadgets. We're on a stolen yacht and we're hunting an insane billionaire who's involved with a cult of suicide bombers and got a nuclear warhead or two." The most that the truth could possibly gain would be a good laugh on the part of the customs officials followed by incarceration in some filthy foreign slam – or sanatorium.

General Sutton would have nobbled their passports, MOD90s, phones, credit cards and probably their own bank accounts. More than likely he'd got at least one TDR team working to track them. Carter was praying that his old phone would continue to work.

Mickey was probably bloody mad, as was he for following the Scottish twit. How the hell could they hope to pull all this off? They'd need navigation certificates, ship's records, insurance... and the list went on. Carter made a mental note to create an inventory of everything that would be required at any port of call. He thought about fuel, food, toilet paper, all kinds of consumables. The whole endeavour looked nearly impossible, although he had to accede two things to McKinley: one, that the crazed audacity of his idea was admirable; and two, that travelling by sea made more sense than trying to board planes. Airports were studded with security cameras and they'd be tagged the moment they walked into the foyer. If they could travel by sea they *might just* make it to Indonesia. Carter leaned over the computer, resting his brow in his palm and rubbing his scalp under the rim of his cap, noticing the constant bumping of the waves through his elbow. The internet connection was frustrating him and he was concerned that they could be tracked through it. Perhaps he should walk away for half an hour. Topside was bright sunshine, fresh air and company.

Then Carter had another thought. Bacon wanted the yacht. Fine; let him take care of the details.

Carter stepped up to the bridge where McKinley and Bacon were having an animated conversation. Each swung a bottle of Efes Pilsen about whilst Wilson, looking overly tired, hung on to the wheel and kept his reddened eyes on the surrounding ocean.

"Can I interrupt?" started Carter.

McKinley settled down. "Righto," he said. "What've you got?"

"Yes, we can go through the Suez. It'll shave two thousand miles off the trip and save us all from an early bath. Plus it means we're near land for most of the journey and I'm fine with that in case anything goes funny. But here's the fly: we need paperwork; lots of it."

McKinley rolled his eyes. "Yup. Knew there'd be wrinkles."

Carter looked pointedly at Bacon, who wiggled uncomfortably for a moment; then his face brightened with the usual wide, disingenuous grin. "Reckon I can 'elp wi' that."

Carter nodded. "We've got no choice if you want to keep the yacht. You must know a cobbler, surely?"

"Passports? Me? I... *no!*" Bacon's face was full of pique. "I wouldn't do nothin' like that, innit?"

"Obviously we'll need one each and one for you," continued Carter, indifferent to Bacon's denial. "See if you can get the details at least close."

"No, really mate, no—" stuttered Bacon.

"Because," Carter added, "if you want this yacht you'll need some kind of transport licence and you don't want your *own* name on it, do you?"

Bacon thought for a second. "Okay," he said quietly.

"Thanks." Carter turned his gaze back to McKinley, who raised his bottle and clinked it against Bacon's. "Good lad," he said appreciatively, downing a gulp of the drink.

Carter took a breath. "There's something else," he said a little nervously.

"What now?" sighed McKinley, wiping a dribble of beer from his chin.

"I think the fuel monitoring system's buggered. We're reading way too much in the tank. We could be running on empty and we wouldn't know."

"Shit!" exclaimed McKinley. "Can you fix it?"

"Probably, but I don't even know what's wrong yet and he won't have spares for *everything* on board. But I can inspect the fuel level. That's my next little job."

McKinley nodded thoughtfully. "Aye. Where's the nearest place we can bunker?"

"Already got it." Carter called up a satellite image on the chart table. The western portion of the image was mostly desert through which buildings poked like weeds. To the east there were homes, industrial areas, a respectable airport and endless hectares of sand.

He looked up at McKinley. "Nouadhibou," he stated.

"Noo-whatwhat?"

Carter leaned back from the display. "Noo-wa-dee-boo," he said, running the first pair of syllables together and emphasising the last. "AKA Shipwreck Central. It's right on the tip of Mauritania, and we're heading toward it. There's food, supplies, fuel... the works."

McKinley was quiet for a few seconds. They'd already lost all the privileges which The Team afforded them. This was even starting to sound like some kind of perverse holiday. But it was the only practical route he could imagine.

"Are we mad?" he asked. "I mean, going to all this trouble to nail Heinmarsh?"

Carter gave a matter-of-fact frown. "Someone's got to. Might as well be us mate, not to mention that we owe him a slapping."

McKinley looked up at Carter appreciatively, whose eyebrows raised to emphasise the question lodged in both their minds. As usual the weapons tech was both dutifully practical and fiercely loyal to their team. But what about Wilson? He'd been clear about his intent to rescue Bacon, but would he appear in the sequel?

"Gimme a second," said McKinley and got up, striding to the pilot's station. He told Wilson to let the gadget dealer steer *his* boat for a while, then join his team-mates below.

A few moments later they sat underneath the bridge in the lower part of the hull. This section of the vessel was nowhere near as ostentatious as the rest, yet it wasn't without its comforts. There was even a small bar in the corner stocked with mostly unrecognisable bottles that clinked slightly as *Ghost Rocket* drove through the Atlantic swells.

"Willy," began McKinley, "what do you really think about all this? About going renegade to get Heinmarsh?"

Wilson chewed it over for a long moment before replying. "Goodness knows what'll happen to us if we ever get home. Uncle Victor'll kick our asses into next week." Wilson held up his hands with an exaggerated shrug. "So... I think we're mad to be taking this thing all the way to Indonesia but there's probably no other way. Is that what you wanted to hear?"

McKinley was a little surprised by this last question. "I'm trying to find out if your heart's in it, if you see what I mean. After all, it was you who wanted to save all the poor little suicide bombers."

"What was I thinking?" Wilson smiled emptily.

McKinley pressed the point. "Your motivation's fine. I just want to know... how you really feel about committing to the mission all the way."

"Mission?" Wilson huffed. "Yes, I want to rescue the suicide bombers and I want to see Heinmarsh brought down. And it's the only thing on my dance card since I just wasted my frikkin' job."

Carter felt he should clarify things a bit. "I think what Mickey's asking is whether we can *rely* on you to do this without second thoughts. Whether you're committed to this course... to this team. So are you reaching for your flexible friend or just kicking the tyres?"

Wilson fell silent, a silence that McKinley found more worrying as it continued. It was an uncomfortable few seconds before Wilson spoke again and this time his countenance lifted somewhat.

"Yeah, I'm on board," affirmed the tall combat specialist. "We've got to. And I don't blame you for asking. So," he grinned conspiratorially, "let's do this thing."

"Thanks," said McKinley. "Now, go get some shut-eye for goodness' sake. Chris, keep an eye on that idiot," he rolled his eyes toward the bridge. "And stop shaving. Heinmarsh saw us, so we need beards. Willy, you're our ace in the hole 'cause he's never eyeballed you."

"Roger that," affirmed Wilson.

"Right then," said McKinley, yawning, "I'm going to doss 'n' all."

"Rise and shine!" effervesced Carter.

McKinley's eyes opened and he yawned, feeling resentful that his sleep had been interrupted. The motion of the boat had been as soporific as a rocking chair, and McKinley had slept more soundly than he could remember for a while.

"We're at the isthmus," said Carter.

"Huh?"

Carter sighed good-naturedly. "You wanted waking up when we're at the narrow bit before the headland."

McKinley sat. "Already?"

"You've been asleep for nearly five hours."

"Blimey." Feeling like the period of blissful unconsciousness had been fleeting and he deserved more, McKinley rolled off the Turk's expansive bed and did several jumping-jacks to get his blood pumping. "Is Willy awake?"

"Yes I am," grunted Wilson unhappily, his 6'2" frame emerging from the cramped smaller bedroom, the door of which was just outside that of the main one. McKinley had been adamant that, despite its more than sufficient size, sharing Erbakan's bed was not appropriate.

They ascended to the bridge and Carter took over piloting duties from Bacon. He turned east, toward the shore, continuing until the surf was visible then setting the autopilot to station-keeping. McKinley sparked up a cigarette and asked him about the fuel situation.

"Ah," said the weapons tech, waving his left index finger in the air, "*really* interesting, but I won't know for sure until I can dive the hull."

How typical, thought McKinley, mentally bemoaning Carter's penchant for wanting his mini-lectures encouraged through interaction. "What's interesting?" he asked.

Carter smiled. "As you know the fuel's still reading about eighty percent," he answered, "but I dipped the tank and sure enough there's not much in there. So out of curiosity I calculated the tank's capacity against the fuel economy figures and there's a *massive* difference. So big, I smelled one standard issue rat."

Wilson raised an eyebrow. McKinley was intrigued. "Go on," he prompted.

"I figured out the size of the other tanks too, and the combined volume is only two hundred liters more than a full tank."

"Uh, so what's going on?" asked Wilson, a little confused. "You're not saying there are extra fuel tanks, are you?"

"Not exactly." Carter turned toward him, eyebrows raised. "An incident in the dunny tipped me off to this. He's using both the fresh water and sewage tanks for fuel."

"So what the heck's coming out the taps?" asked Bacon, his face screwed up in consternation.

"Seawater." Carter shrugged. "There's a little desalination and filtering plant in the bow. Really neat tech."

"How about that?" said McKinley, his mouth turned down at the corners.

Bacon grimaced. "Seawater?" he gasped. "That's gross. Fish have sex in it."

Wilson's face was clouding over. "What about the sewage?" he asked.

"Sorry mate," said Carter apologetically. "I checked that and there's only a thin layer of nasty stuff; enough to fool a nominal inspection, like the fresh water. Whenever you use the bog it's going straight in the sea."

"Bloody hell!" snapped Wilson. "That's *criminal!* What about the environment?!"

"Erbakan don't care," shrugged McKinley.

"We can't be part of that," said Wilson, shaking his head. "We've got to be responsible."

"Right on," agreed Bacon. "No jobbies in the sea. It's wrong, innit?"

"Well I'll tell you what then," frowned McKinley. "You two can keep your bloody legs crossed until you get into town. Time to work."

The sun was sinking from behind, a suitable arrangement that might allow them to remain inconspicuous from land. Bacon helped McKinley and Wilson unpack and inflate the dinghy from its storage below decks, and they attached its small outboard motor. Lowering the big hatch which, when closed, formed the yacht's transom, Wilson and Bacon set off in the little boat to make landfall and head into Nouadhibou, preparing the way for *Ghost Rocket* to moor after the twenty one mile journey around Cap Blanc. McKinley grinned when he saw that Carter had used a marker to scrawl *SS Toilet Terror* on the bright yellow rubber.

The yacht's capable engines once again pressed them into the leather as McKinley and Carter turned south toward the cape. They passed the ruins of La Güera on their port side, its abandoned buildings gradually being subsumed by the reddish desert, its inherent hue brought beautifully to life by the sunset.

As they rounded Cap Blanc the sand grew an even deeper red and McKinley felt like he was watching a ghost emerging from behind the rocky headland.

"Will you look at *that*," he marvelled.

Facing them from the shoreline almost exactly stern-on, the corroding hull of a huge vessel sat on the sand, listing slightly to starboard. It gave McKinley a melancholy feeling to see this mechanised spectre loom out of the dusk. He wondered how it came to be there.

"*United Malika*," announced Carter as though hearing his thoughts. "Been there since '03. All crew rescued."

"Aye, you said there were shipwrecks."

"You'll see."

Wilson and Bacon hit the shore of Western Sahara, all of which both Morocco and the Sahrawi Arab Democratic Republic were laying claim to, and started trudging east-by-north-east toward the Mauritanian border. Their destination lay about one and a half miles away, on the opposite coast of the Ras Nouadhibou Peninsula, a forty mile spit of land bisected by the international border.

The powdery sand, known in Arabic as *fesh-fesh*, made walking difficult. It seemed like every step required twice as much effort yet covered half the normal distance. They left plumes of fine dust behind them, which were whipped about by the coastal winds and sometimes came back at them head on, obscuring the way ahead even further in the deepening dusk and causing the unpleasantness of grit in their mouths.

The border was unmarked, but they knew that if they crossed first a smaller, almost disused road and then the RN2 highway, that they were definitely in Mauritanian territory. Soon, low walls started to come into view, as did the city of Nouadhibou beyond.

Wilson was amazed by his first look at a west African town. Although there were paved, straight roads, the buildings seemed random and haphazard. Next to a small modern office block would be a hut with junk for a fence, or an unfinished building the foundations of which had been converted into stopgap accommodation by the locals using corrugated iron and plastic sheets held down with rocks. Tiny shops of bare brick frontage had expensive cars parked outside whilst billboards advertised internet connectivity via USB in French. Mohammed would have turned in his grave and denounced it as witchcraft.

Carter had brought up all *Ghost Rocket's* lights, illuminating a wide swathe of choppy sea around the yacht. McKinley stepped out on to the foredeck, the wind lashing his face and bringing unusual smells to his nostrils. Suddenly he saw what Carter had meant.

Marine wraiths loomed from the dark. These spectres appeared first as low lying, angular clusters of deeper darkness against the horizon. Once his eyes adjusted, McKinley saw ships of all kinds rusting, rotting and dissolving gradually into the sea – scores of them. The yacht was surrounded by dozens of dead boats, abandoned to gradual disintegration in the shallow bay.

The combination of decay and relative silence felt cold and uncomfortable. It was profoundly eerie to sail through this phantom fleet slowly turning into iron oxide around them. Were it not for the lights of the city ahead this would've been one of the spookiest places McKinley had ever seen. Where did these extinct craft come from? Who had deserted them to ruin?

They passed close by one of the corroding hulks and McKinley saw fresh oxyacetylene torch marks amidst the crusty orange. So the locals *were* salvaging these forgotten boats, bit by bit. He tried to make out the boat's name but its paint was long gone, consumed by the voracious rust. She listed heavily to port and was down at the bow, allowing McKinley to see dark green water sloshing within. What had been pristine steel was now scabbed in brown encrustation as though afflicted by some leprous marine disease.

Most of the derelicts appeared to be trawlers or other fishing vessels, but there were freighters too. Some were gathered together in haphazard groups; others were grounded alone. Many were listing; some had capsized completely. None were as big as the impressive *United Malika*, but nearly all were in a greater state of decay, some being mere skeletons of girders to which hull plating had once been riveted. Few looked to have arrived recently.

As they neared the town they radioed Wilson for directions and soon made their way to a mooring. Once *Ghost Rocket* was securely tied up under the fluorescent glow of the dock they ate a functional part-Turkish meal that Carter threw together, and McKinley decided that an early night was a good idea for all of them. Wilson and Bacon went off in search of toilet facilities whilst McKinley and Carter shared a knowing glance and claimed that they didn't need to go.

Feeling refreshed, McKinley strode onto the aft deck with a cigarette and a cup of the Turk's coffee, which came across more like coffee-flavoured creosote.

An amorphous and constantly changing crowd of dark-skinned onlookers stood by the mooring, all captivated by the amazing yacht. The dock itself was a monstrous cement slab poured into the sea between dark iron caissons, typical of its kind. Red and white concrete barriers ran the length of the huge hockey stick shaped construction, at the far end of which a large ship was craning containers off its deck, their battle-scarred sides labelled with Maersk, P&O and other familiar logos. On the opposite side of the quay, blue and white coastguard launches were moored together in a friendly huddle and, beyond these, a huge new port was under construction, producing echoing sounds of heavy machinery. The air smelled fresh and salty, but there were more than hints of iron oxide and the pulveratricious landscape.

Seaward, a linear flotilla of brightly painted Senegalese canoes was heading out to fish, weaving their way between the rusty derelicts that littered the bay. It was only now that McKinley saw just how many dead ships were lying there like hundreds of little brown islands.

He was looking in the direction of the unbearably bright sunlight, so he turned back to the dock, sipping on the coffee.

"Do you realise how popular we are?" asked Carter through his breathing mask as he waddled up from behind, an air tank on his back, nothing but underwear and weight belt around his waist, and dark black diving fins for footwear.

McKinley looked him up and down in mocking distaste. "Bloody hell, it's the Loch Ness Monster! Need a hand?" Some of their observers started to point and laugh at the bizarre marine lifeform.

"Please."

They opened the yacht's transom hatch—again to the crowd's amazement—and McKinley helped Carter on to the short white plastic ladder. The weapons tech disappeared into the waters of the bay with a splash.

McKinley noticed Wilson's figure up in the bridge and called to him, discarding the last of the coffee over the side and heading in that direction. "Willy! Where's Bacon?"

"Gone to get the money," answered Wilson, his body in the pilot's chair and angled over the screens.

McKinley entered the bridge. "Oh man I *hope* he's not using his real name."

Wilson huffed, smiling. "With the number of times you hammered it into his head last night even he couldn't screw that up. At least he *has* anonymous accounts."

"Aye, go figure," muttered McKinley. He waved his hand at the controls. "What're you doing?"

"Chris has a theory," replied Wilson, "that there's a hatch down there that we can open via the software."

"He's got a lot of theories," said McKinley cynically, just as Carter's yell came from the stern. McKinley quickly trotted down there.

"I was right," spluttered Carter, shaking seawater from his face as he held on to the ladder with one hand and plucked the mask off with the other. He beckoned his friend closer and spoke quietly. "There's some kind of join in the hull right below the sewage tank."

McKinley was getting more interested now. "Got any ideas about opening it?"

"Well, try the sewage system. That's where *we'd* hide it."

"I guess." McKinley went back to the bridge and, pushing Wilson aside, called up the utilities section of the yacht's software. He hit the submenu for sanitation. Nothing was immediately obvious amongst the many menu items.

"Tools," suggested Wilson, pointing. Upon actuating it another submenu popped up.

"Mechanical?" hummed McKinley. Wilson pressed it.

"Heh," said McKinley as the page appeared. "Emergency sewage dump!" He tentatively pressed the highlighted area and a message appeared. '*Are you sure? Yes / No.*'

McKinley reached towards the '*yes*' but Wilson's hand grabbed his arm. "We can *not* dump that stuff in the sea," he insisted.

"Push off," said McKinley. "I want to know what's going on down there. Besides, I doubt there's any turds. Otherwise why would the crapper feed straight into the sea?"

"Sorry chief," said Wilson, shaking his head firmly, "we can't risk it."

"Aye, you're right." McKinley shook his head sadly. "Shame though."

"I know," said Wilson, withdrawing his arm. McKinley immediately pressed 'yes'.

"You bloody—!" began Wilson, then saw the screen change again. "Ah! That's pissed on your little box of fireworks." A dialogue box had appeared with the phrase '*input password now*'.

McKinley looked at his younger colleague with contempt. "I wonder what it is," he said snidely, and typed four-four-five-six-six.

Immediately there was a loud, bass-heavy *clunk* from below and the yacht seemed to leap slightly in her moorings. Almost instantaneously she settled down again and rocked a bit.

"How did you—?!" gasped Wilson at McKinley's retreating figure. He got up and followed the team leader out onto the aft deck.

As they reached the stern, Carter's masked head surfaced. "Guys," he said excitedly in nasal tones, "can you go to the starboard engine pod?"

McKinley looked at Wilson, who shrugged, and they both headed forward and away from the dockside.

"How d'you know Erbakan's password?" asked the younger man as they arrived at the gunwale.

McKinley started climbing the short ladder that led out onto the engine pylon. "He gave it away," he said.

Wilson heaved himself onto the pylon's flat upper surface, a geometric pattern of roughened strips lending purchase to his feet. "How?"

McKinley spat into the sea. "Don't they teach you anything in the BC regiment these days?"

A small splash from beyond the engine nacelle alerted them to Carter's position and they carefully lowered themselves onto its housing.

"Check *this* out," said Carter proudly, looking around then holding up a long narrow block of what looked like translucent candle wax.

McKinley's eyebrows knitted. "What the hell's that?"

Carter was smiling. "Look closer."

"Holy shit!" said Wilson.

McKinley frowned and peered into the waxy object. There was a shape within, a slightly blurry but nonetheless familiar shape, from its wedge shaped stock to its short, blunt muzzle. It was a Heinmarsh rifle, packed in some kind of acrylic material to prevent the ingress of moisture.

"My bastard scissors!" he exclaimed. "*They're* in the sewage tank?"

"Fourteen of 'em," nodded Carter, "loads of ammo *and*," he grinned, "a sizeable stash of grenades. When you did whatever you did, the damn tank dropped out on levers – just missed me. Anyway, that's where he's keeping all this. No-one'd look in the sewage, would they?"

McKinley grinned. "You would. Anyway, put it back and let's keep this on the down-low. The last thing we need's a customs inspection because Bacon's blabbed his mouth off."

"Righto," said Carter and, squashing the mask back onto his face, disappeared again.

"Willy, go see how to pull that tank back up."

"Roger that," said Wilson, turning and climbing back up the pylon.

"One more thing," said McKinley.

Wilson looked back. "What?"

"No turds in the sea. Happy now?"

Wilson smiled. "Mother nature thanks you for your co-operation."

Once the sewage tank was retracted securely into the hull and Carter had changed, they discussed their 'to do' list and waited for Bacon's return. The gadget dealer soon arrived in a taxi and, much to McKinley's annoyance, seemed to be enjoying the notoriety of having the sexiest boat around. He did at least bear an attaché case full US dollars, Mauritanian Ouguiya and Euros, as well as a number of well-loaded prepaid credit cards. The four of them locked up *Ghost Rocket* and headed into town. Carter had done his usual investigation and steered them in the direction of an electronics shop.

The weapons tech's research also yielded some troubling news. McKinley had started to feel isolated from their world of clandestine warfare, espionage and violence, leading to a fleeting sense of purposelessness, but Carter's dour announcement reminded him that they were indeed pursuing a most serious matter. There had been two more incidents of suicide bombing with sniper support, again at the hearts of their respective governments, but this time in Azerbaijan and India. With interest McKinley noted the latter in view of General Sutton's mention of Pakistan, the two countries being infamous for their mutual animosity. Apart from the UK, these were the first nuclear weapons states to be attacked in this way and could feasibly blame each other, leading to renewed tensions. As they made their way through Nouadhibou under the blazing sun, McKinley discussed this development with his colleagues, re-affirming their commitment to act when their own government wouldn't.

The streets were awash with people. Women sported brightly coloured *jilbabs* and *hijabs*, leaving visible only their cheap foam rubber sandals and faces of the deepest, most beautiful brown. Men were similarly cloaked but mostly with either a *taqiya* embroidered skullcap or *keffiyeh* headscarf adorning their cranium. Some men, perhaps less zealous devotees of their prophet, were attired in western dress.

The dusty streets rang with the clip-clop of donkeys pulling makeshift carts fabricated from vehicle axles, differential gear housing and all. This seemed to be the *de facto* mode of cargo transport in Nouadhibou. Shining Mercedes saloons wove between them and dilapidated Renaults and Fiats struggled to keep up. Temperatures were scorching, but the sea breeze stopped the heat from becoming oppressive. The sun, on the other hand, was an unrelenting demon of despicable brilliance that made every reflective surface blinding.

Carter, with Bacon's enthusiastic connivance, insisted on picking up toiletries so the two spent some time in a drugstore trying different brands of cologne. McKinley and Wilson stayed outside, the former getting through two whole cigarettes whilst waiting.

When Carter and the gadget dealer reappeared, Bacon smelled predictably expensive whilst Carter's scent of choice seemed both a little too regional and too intense for McKinley's tastes.

"You smell like a bloody curry house," complained the Scotsman.

"What's wrong with that?" asked Carter, disappointed that his choice was being impugned.

"It's not that bad of a smell," said Wilson, "just really strong."

"So what?" said Carter. "It's better than stinking."

McKinley shook his head. "Laptop!" he growled.

The electronics store was less of a shop front and more of a blue-washed cinderblock construction surrounding a narrow wooden door. A hand painted sign read '*Ordinateur Électronique Radio Et Chaîne Stéréd*' with what must have been the Hassaniya Arabic equivalent underneath. Once inside, though, things became more familiar, with dusty glass cabinets containing electronic equipment, and big flat screen televisions on the yellowed beige walls.

The shopkeeper, who seemed to be mostly comprised of a huge smile surrounded by black beard and shining little eyes, leaned across his counter and rubbed gold-adorned fingers back across his balding pate. "Oui monsieur?" he began.

Though perfectly comfortable with French, Carter asked "parlez-vous anglais?", feeling that their own tongue would be more appropriate if technical details needed to be conveyed.

The salesman's smile twisted a little. "Yes, yes, I speak the English sir," he beamed, extending his hand. "My name, Mahmoud."

"Nice to meet you," said Carter pleasantly, reciprocating the handshake as McKinley, Wilson and Bacon perused the shelves, talking between themselves. "I need a laptop. What's the best that you've got?"

"Yes, I will get you best laptop. You English sir?"

Carter hesitated for just a moment. How much harm could it do? The guy was right, anyway. It was pointless trying to hide it. "Yes."

The man nodded vigorously. "Ahh, you want BBC! I have BBC News on BADR4 satellite, very good picture sir! I watch all the day." He indicated one of the televisions, the screen of which was indeed displaying a news broadcast with the The Beeb's familiar logo at the bottom.

"That's great," said Carter. "But I'm just here for *a laptop*."

Mahmoud rubbed his hands together. "I will do this, because I like you sir. You buy satellite system and I will make very good price with laptop. You like?"

Carter was getting a little frustrated. "Well Mahmoud, that's kind of you but we're just passing through so I only want the laptop."

"BBC!" implored Mahmoud, his eyes pleading for the sale.

"Just a bloody laptop!" snapped McKinley as he joined Carter at the counter. "No satellite system, no stereo, nothing. We just want a damn good laptop."

Mahmoud seemed undeterred, wagging his finger. "You not an Englishman, sir?"

"No," said Carter nonchalantly, "he works for a living."

McKinley scowled. "A laptop, *now*, please," he grunted.

Finally registering the hostility evident in McKinley's refusal, Mahmoud scurried into the back of his little shop and they heard things being moved around. When the Mauritanian returned there was a laptop sized box under his arm. "This is best laptop, yes?"

Carter read the specifications off the side of the box. "Yes, fine. Thank you Mahmoud." He turned to Bacon, saying "cough up."

The TDR.12 boys turned away as Bacon started to make the deal. "Is that alright?" asked McKinley.

"It'll do the job," answered Carter.

"So come on then," interjected Wilson, "how d'you figure out Erbakan's password?"

McKinley huffed, but Carter started to explain. "Elementary my dear Wilson. Fact; Erbakan doesn't trust his right hand because it shakes so much. Fact; when he went to the safe the glass was in his left hand and we heard him put it down, so he's using his left hand to enter the combination."

"But that was—"

"Stay with me okay? The keystrokes gave away three things: one, there were two double digits because we heard dit-dit-da-dit-dit." Carter wiggled his fingers as though miming the code. "Two, the sequence was fast so it must have formed a simple shape. Three, the fastest way to type with your left hand is from left to right because you'd start on the least dextrous finger."

"The fourth."

Carter smiled. "Right. So he was typing from the left in a straight line, making it probable that the sequence was either one-one-two-three-three or its equivalent on a different row. We just punched those in until it opened. We tried it on other systems and thankfully it was the same."

"Bloody hell," gasped Wilson, impressed. "Remind me not to tell you which bank I'm with."

"Well," frowned Carter, "in fairness it *was* a very simple code, and that's his fault."

"But you figured it out just from hearing it? That's... amazing."

"Mickey figured it out and, again, it *was* an easy one," continued Carter. "We learned something though. If you put the wrong code in the safe a hatch opens and everything goes in the drink, just like the crapper. So that rifle he showed us is on the seabed somewhere and whatever secrets were in there are still secret."

Bacon joined them, asking if the laptop was what Carter wanted.

"It's not perfect," responded the weapons tech, "but I'm sure you can get me a better one in time."

"We need to talk about that, too," added McKinley, scratching his beard, "but not here."

They exited the tiny shop to the sound of Mahmoud offering them munificent blessings and thanking them for their custom. McKinley, though, couldn't help noticing the vulpine look in his eyes.

Back on board the yacht, Carter started the long process of downloading and installing the software they needed whilst McKinley figured out additional requirements. Because of Erbakan's illicit cargo they now had weapons, but If they were going to achieve their goals without COAST's resources they'd need a lot more gear. McKinley had an extensive shopping list for their gadget dealer friend, who in the meantime was almost continually talking to Plugger, running his empire by proxy and asking about the latest football scores.

Using a spoofed internet connection and a Voice-Over-IP service, Wilson placed a call to Julia Bridgewell and was surprised to discover that his rival Kendal Gundersen had inexplicably lost all interest in her overnight. Whilst it was an unexpected turn of events, it was nonetheless welcome and Wilson felt more confident than ever about the future of their relationship – if he somehow made it through McKinley's crazy out-of-hours activity.

After a lot of arguing with Bacon and trimming lists somewhat, it was decided that Plugger would join them in a couple of days, bringing the stores they needed. He would also arrange transport for the yacht.

Nouadhibou airport wasn't the most attractive of its kind, and neither was Maurice 'Plugger' Broadwick, the strange character who was Bacon's right hand man. Plugger was a throwback to the sixties who religiously wore tight, dark grey flannel trousers and a Dartmouth green tank top over a white shirt with grey tie. His attire was entirely inappropriate for the heat of Mauritania, but Plugger bore it stoically, huge blossoms of perspiration quickly forming on the starchy shirt.

In his mid fifties, Broadwick was even taller than Wilson and had eyes which appeared to protrude from their sockets as though about to pop out. His thinning dark brown hair was plastered into the classic seventies comb-over and his sharp, pointed nose jutted like an inverted ship's prow above an almost nonexistent chin. He'd been Len Bacon's right hand man for decades, and Bacon Junior had inherited Plugger along with the lucrative gadget business.

Long before Plugger was within earshot, Carter turned subversively to his colleagues. "Blimey," he exclaimed, "saying he looks like a deformed armadillo will really offend deformed armadillos."

Bacon laughed hoarsely then quickly calmed himself as Plugger approached, waving a long, gangly arm with mad exuberance.

Bacon seemed to do all the talking which, in view of Plugger's terrible stutter, was not a surprise. In fact the only time he could be described as vocal was when first meeting his boss alive and well, missing auricle notwithstanding. Tears welled in Plugger's extrusive eyes and he fussed like an old lady, yet without going as far as showing overt affection for Bacon.

The gadget dealer had explained that Plugger, despite his first officer's odd bearing, was in fact highly intelligent with an agile mind and amazing memory. He was fiercely loyal to the Bacon clan and had always been a laudably diligent manager of their affairs. Bacon also remarked that Plugger's social skills weren't that great, conjuring a humorous comparison with Carter in Wilson's mind.

It was whilst loading Plugger's yellow cargo cases into their rented van that Wilson spotted an old aircraft at the southern end of the apron. The plane was within the airport's perimeter, close to where a thin strip of land devoid of buildings save a prestigious hotel joined Nouadhibou to Port-Étienne, previously the name of the whole area. He asked Bacon and Plugger to excuse him and wandered down there in curiosity.

The plane was big, about a hundred feet long, with a towering tailplane and rudder assembly that looked too much for it. It had four engines from which dark carbon deposits trailed like badly sprayed racing stripes across the massive wings. Most intriguingly, the fuselage bore lettering, ineptly hand painted in something approximating English.

4-SALE DOUGLAS DC4
BILT IN CANADA VERY GOOD AIRWORTHY
FEULED UP + READY TO FLY
PLEASE CONTACT OWENER

There was a local telephone number that Wilson memorised before returning to his colleagues. They left the airport and made their way through the sand-saturated city back to the dock.

With it being some weeks shy of Christmas, Carter looked as though his had arrived early as he inventoried the equipment that Plugger had brought them, thoughtfully housed in tough, waterproof Pelican cases. He ticked off GPS units, radio equipment, two more laptops, electronic tools and components. There were also binoculars, knives of several different kinds, torches, clothing and boots, an inflatable dinghy, survival kits and plenty of espionage and surveillance tech.

"You should see him drooling over the RS Components catalogue," McKinley confided to Bacon and Plugger. "Honestly, it's like porn."

"It's all here," said Carter. "Thanks, Kyle, I'm *really* grateful."

"Well you're payin' for it, ain't ya?" said Bacon. "But I'm glad I could 'elp."

Wilson hadn't told McKinley about the aircraft yet, but he decided this was as good an opportunity as any. "How about we make the rest of the journey by air?" he asked.

"No good," said Carter dismissively. "Airports are full of cameras, plus there'll be passport checks at the major ones."

"Agreed," added McKinley, "but what's brought this on?"

"What if we had our own plane?"

McKinley and Carter looked at each other. "Explain yourself," demanded the Scot.

"What if we had our own plane," repeated Wilson, "and avoided major airports? What if we just flew over sparsely populated areas? It'd be a lot quicker than sailing, even with this yacht and," he raised a finger, "no Suez Canal."

"Can I just point out," said Carter, "that we don't know exactly where we're going yet?"

"Indonesia," said Wilson. "We fly down to Singapore and start searching there."

"I'd love to fly," nodded McKinley, "but there's one small detail missing: a plane."

"That may not be the case," smirked Wilson.

"Well," said Carter, hands on hips, leaning back to regard the aircraft. "Mister... what's his name?"

"Salek," said McKinley, reading the name from Carter's telephone.

"Mister Salek doesn't know what he's got here. It's not a DC-4; it's a Canadair C54-GM, also known as a North Star. Rare as rocking horse poo."

They stood in a loose group under the glaring sun, on the sand of the airport's southern reaches, looking up at the huge aeroplane. In appearance it wasn't unlike the C-47 Skytrain—known as the Dakota to the RAF—which itself was the military variant of the famous DC-3 airliner. The C54-GM, however, was appreciably wider and fifty percent longer with twice as many props. Her cigar shaped fuselage was a paint-flaking white and silver sandwich of a thin red line along the side. It was remarkable that an airworthy example of the rare aircraft could just be sitting here on Africa's west coast yet here she was, all nineteen forties curves and wartime attitude.

"What's the difference then?" asked Bacon.

"Engines," said Carter, gesturing at the nacelles. "They're Rolls-Royce Merlins, like in a Spitfire or a Lanc."

Wilson whistled in awe. "This thing's got the power of a Lancaster bomber?"

Carter smiled. "Yup."

"Neat," nodded Bacon, almost understanding the benefit of such things.

"So let me get this straight," said McKinley. "A Canadian-built American plane with British engines is for sale right here in Mauritania?"

"That's about it," answered Wilson.

McKinley turned to him. "There's a small chance you might redeem yourself," he said derisively, "eventually." With this he rotated away leaving Wilson feeling like he couldn't win.

Mister Salek had informed McKinley that it was alright to board his aircraft, but without a ladder McKinley had to give Carter a boost up so that their tame mechanical nerd could check Salek's claim of airworthiness. The owner had said that he'd started the engines once a month or so for at least seven years and that the North Star was regularly maintained. This McKinley found hard to swallow, but reasoned that the maintenance intervals might indeed be long in this part of the world.

McKinley was three smokes into waiting for Salek when Carter came to the aircraft's forward hatch and advised them to step away from the propellers. Thirty seconds later the enormous 27-liter V-12s were coughing into life with deafening vitality and McKinley was starting to prefer the idea of flying. This was wholeheartedly supported by Bacon, knowing that he'd get his yacht sooner.

Rahim Salek arrived in another shining Mercedes, glowing with pride that his asseveration of good engine function had been proven. The dumpy middle-aged African had brought a ladder and, once they'd all had a good look around the inside of the C-54GM, kindly helped Carter with his inspection. Salek explained that the aircraft was his father's, who was now too old to fly, but for years had run a profitable cargo operation between Nouadhibou and the Mediterranean port of Algiers, making the round trip on a single fill of avgas and forming a useful air bridge between the seas.

A half hour of heated discussion and debate later Mister Salek was the happiest and probably wealthiest man in Nouadhibou, whilst TDR.12 were forty five million Ouguiya lighter and the unlikely owners of a septuagenarian cargo plane. But, as Carter explained, a hundred and sixty thousand US Dollars was still about a hundred grand under par for such a find.

Bacon and Plugger arranged to transport the yacht, which was about as long as the North Star and thus not a cheap thing to rent a floating dry dock for. To ship it back to the UK for remodelling, Vladimir Kholitczyn put them in touch with a Ukrainian cargo airline and an Antonov AN-124 *Ruslan* was soon en route. Without the accommodation of the luxurious yacht, TDR.12 located a garage, the owner of which was happy to let them use his workshop for a week or so. Under cover of night they retrieved the stash of weapons from *Ghost Rocket* and buried it behind the building, moving an abandoned truck over the patch for security.

McKinley asked Wilson to start loading their gear onto the North Star and the younger man took the van back to the airport, filled with the cases Plugger had brought.

It was just after Wilson had finished securing the equipment in the belly of the C-54GM and was about to drive off the airport property that he noticed an aircraft coming in to land. It was a familiar model of four jet regional airliner and, curiously, had a British registration. Wilson drove the van to where it couldn't be seen from the apron, jumped out and took a look round the corner at the dark red visitor.

Arriving from the north, the small plane came to rest on the 2.6 kilometer runway not far from Wilson's position. But rather than head for the terminal to disgorge passengers, it started taxiing across the hard sand to the far side of the runway, near a massive salt deposit. This was unusual, and Wilson gave it ten minutes to see what would happen. When nothing did, he carefully left the airport and drove at speed back to the workshop, his mind alive with questions.

Carter was busy as usual, soldering together some computer modifications when Wilson ran into the workshop. "Chris," he coughed, "need a favour."

Carter swung round on the squeaky old chair, the tip of his soldering iron trailing curls of grey vapour. "What can I do you for?"

"Can you check to see if there are any scheduled flights from the UK today?"

Carter's mouth dipped at the corners. "Why?"

"It's quicker if you just do it, please."

"Okay," sang Carter, tugging out his phone.

Wilson took a second to catch his breath and allow his pulse to steady. The workshop smelled of soldering layered with the musty dryness of the dust. Carter was prodding away at the tiny keyboard and muttering.

"Umm, nothing so far," he said. "What kind of plane?"

"BAe 146 I think," answered Wilson. The adrenaline was starting to decrease and he could feel minute particles invading his nose. A sneeze would follow shortly. "Just a little guy," he continued, "short, sharp nose, high wing and T-tail, four engines, kinda like a maroon colour."

"Sounds like a 146... or an Avro RJ. Got a tail number?"

"R, J, A, C."

Carter worked the phone. "Hold on."

Wilson waited patiently but the uneasy feeling made it hard. If it was a commercial flight, why would it just taxi to the outer edge of the apron and sit there? It wasn't a military flight; not with a G prefix tail number. If it was a privately owned aircraft it would be on record. There was something strange about it and Wilson wanted to know what that was.

Carter looked round with a puzzled expression. "G-RJAC? You sure?"

"Certain," nodded Wilson vigorously. "You find it?"

"Details withheld. Digging deeper." Carter's fingers performed a manic Riverdance on the diminutive keys. Suddenly he stopped and grunted.

Wilson's curiosity was near the top of the scale. "What?"

"Okay," said Carter in a tone indicating that it was anything but, "let's find Mickey."

"Why? What is it?"

"Garbage men." Carter frowned, his head tilting apologetically. "Could be."

"You what?"

"A retrieval crew. Target: *us.*"

012: The Flight

Sixteen hundred meters away, the skinny man swaggered off the Avro RJ wearing DPM combat trousers tucked into army boots, his hands stuffed firmly into the pockets of a black bomber jacket, looking like he owned Nouadhibou and had come to make sure it was performing its duties appropriately. Surrounding him, his subordinates glanced fervently about, adopting a defensive formation and seeking any potential targets for their automatic rifles. Through the ever present heat haze of the runway, a closer look at the main character revealed a tall head and pinched nose riding above a cocksure smile. His dark, curly hair surrounded only the top of his high cranium, looking like the cap of some implausible mushroom.

"*Bloody Roger Jolley!*" barked McKinley, adding more swears for good measure. "I might have guessed." He lowered the binoculars from his eyes, crestfallen and pissed off.

"Yes," murmured Carter, scratching at his beard, "it takes a special kind of ego to have the model of your plane *and* its tail number match your initials."

They were hiding in the small industrial area near the southern end of the runway, where new buildings of bright blue and white housed start-up businesses mostly based on foreign money and marine salvage. The TDR.12 lads were against the airport's perimeter fence, hunkered down behind a row of old wooden crates. It wasn't the best vantage point, but with Jolley's crew spreading out toward the terminal buildings it provided some cover.

"How the hell did they find us?" asked Wilson.

McKinley shook his head. "Doesn't matter. They're parked across from *our* exit strategy." With this he produced another stream of blue language.

Wilson sighed. "We'll have to stay mobile now."

"Aye," said McKinley. "Kyle, these guys are here for us. They're not interested in you at all, which means I have to ask you a favour."

Bacon looked worried but nonetheless a bit enthusiastic at this request. "They gonna shoot me?" he asked.

McKinley looked him right in the eye. "Probably not."

"*Probably* not?!"

"They don't care about you," interjected Carter. "It's possible they don't even know who you are."

"Aye," growled McKinley, "and pigs might fly."

Bacon thought for a moment, his eyes pivoting between them. "What's the favour?"

McKinley turned away from the object of their surveillance and lowered himself to the ground, his back sliding down the crate. "Watching *them*. We'll disguise you and hide you on the North Star. You've got facilities in there: bed, toilet, food and water. We'll give you a radio. We talk in Spanish and you tell us everything they do. Get the idea?"

"What's in it for me?"

McKinley winced. "We already got you a bloody private yacht. What do you want? The Moon on a stick?"

Bacon did not respond well to having his blond hair dyed black, nor his skin bronzed with tanning lotion. The fact that tanning lotion should even be *available* in Mauritania, he argued, was stupid. But once the rough disguise was in place, Bacon cheered up, enjoying the charade and finding the African garb comfortable. He took a taxi to the airport and made his way onto the C-54GM, passing near several of Jolley's men and managing to look nonchalant despite nearly soiling himself with fear.

Sitting in the rental van, McKinley received Bacon's first transmission. The radios that Plugger had supplied were of excellent quality, providing clear reception. Additionally, Carter had specified that they must have encryption, a Morse code facility and be waterproof, and McKinley was grateful for the weapons tech's foresight. These radios were seriously mil-spec.

"They're dressed up in some kind of uniform," reported Bacon in Spanish. "Desert camo with a bright green beret, and they're carrying Ay-Kays."

"Roger, thanks," radioed McKinley. "We'll be in touch, but call if anything changes."

"Yeah, I will," replied Bacon.

McKinley turned to his colleagues. Wilson was in the passenger seat whilst Carter, being slightly shorter, was crammed into the back with the remaining gear and the excavated weapons, where the terrible Mauritanian aftershave was marginally less offensive. McKinley switched back to English.

"Mauritanian army getup," he said. "Playing soldiers so nobody gets suspicious."

"Means we'll spot 'em easier," said Wilson.

"Aye." McKinley passed his friend the radio so that he could concentrate on driving.

They circulated through the city, looking out for Mauritanian military uniforms, but McKinley was keenly aware that Jolley's retrieval crew could just as easily be looking for—and finding—them. A greater worry, though, was how they were going to get out of Nouadhibou. Their plane was off limits, the yacht's engine pylons were already being dismantled for transport and Jolley's people would be covering the two roads and railway line, probably at the point where they converged at the northern end of the city. To all intents and purposes, TDR.12 were trapped like rats in a barrel.

Using a scanner, Carter picked up the radio chatter from Jolley's outfit. His crew of mercenaries were identified by numbers whilst Jolley was using the callsign 'Control'. They counted twelve on Jolley's crew. The mercs were systematically grid-searching the town and checking off areas one-by-one. This made TDR.12's strategy of remaining mobile all the more necessary, although the retrieval crew appeared to have acquired vehicles as well. It was a deadly game of cat-and-mouse with at least twelve highly mobile, armed cats and just a trio of mice.

Around eight thirty in the evening Bacon's frequency buzzed into action, and they were unhappily surprised to hear English with an Oxford accent.

"Hello! Hello there Ian McKinley! Are you there chap? This is Roger Jolley."

McKinley's heart fell. Jolley had found Bacon. He knew about the plane! Could this get any more screwed up?

"Don't answer!" said Wilson urgently.

McKinley looked sideways in contempt. "D'you think I'm—"

"Listen!" hissed Carter.

"Well," said the radio, "I think you're being quite ignorant, but if you're not going to talk to me I suppose I can carry the conversation. I know you can hear me." Jolley paused for breath. "So look, here we are in this godforsaken shithole and it's my job to arrest you... or get rid of you. I'm cool either way, so it's up to you. But just to prove I'm serious..." The sound clicked off for a moment.

McKinley looked around at his friends, his face tensed between anger and fear.

"I'm going to kill the one-eared Spic with the bad hairdo," said Jolley. The little speaker crackled with a bang that was far beyond the SPL tolerances of the transmitting microphone.

"By the way," said Jolley's mocking voice, "there's a TV repairman somewhere round here who just earned himself a nice little packet. Bad form, old boy, very bad form." The radio fell silent.

Head lowered and mouth agape, McKinley swore profusely, enraged and horrified. Bacon was *gone*. An innocent man, a *friend* who was caught up in this ridiculous drama by their actions and was just trying to help, had been murdered in cold blood. McKinley knew of Jolley's reputation and this thoroughly underscored everything he'd heard. He looked around, trying to get a grip on this tragedy. His chest seemed filled with ice whilst his neck and shoulders prickled with heat. After wresting the Londoner from the clutches of the evil Turk, he'd betrayed Bacon to his death.

"Holy shit," breathed Carter, removing his cap. Wilson did the same.

McKinley tried to compartmentalise it, to get his head straight in this terrible moment. He had to focus. Moreover, he had to motivate his brain, against a sweeping tide of grief, to do its job and find them a way out.

Retrieval Operative Nine was patrolling in the Port-Étienne area, south of Nouadhibou proper and next to the local satellite earth station, an under-impressive affair with just two dishes sprouting like big, white cacti from the sand.

Nine had studied their quarry. He knew what they looked like, how they spoke – the works. Like all Jolley's crew he was thoroughly up-to-speed on this job. The men they were hunting—renegades from some highly secret special ops unit—were intelligent and dangerous. That was why the boss, despite their mandate from Her Majesty's Government, was taking no chances. He'd ordered their crew to shoot to kill on sight.

Having reported the area around the satellite station clear, Nine turned toward the city, advancing east-south-east along a dilapidated street where many of the buildings didn't have roofs. How do people live in this filthy place, he asked himself.

Suddenly he heard Roger Jolley's voice nearby, as though through the radio. He couldn't make out what was being said.

"Nine to Control, are you squawking me, over?"

"Negative Nine, carry on."

"Wilco."

Operative Nine turned about, aware that these spec-ops whackos could be almost anywhere. The brilliant full moon made visibility easy, giving the sand a purplish cast and producing deep pools of jet black shadow beside the neglected buildings. This part of Nouadhibou was quiet. The few party-goers were in the other end of town.

There was Jolley's voice again, somewhere nearby. "Control to Nine."

He stood still. "Nine here."

"What is it Nine, over?"

Nine frowned. "Did you call me, over?" He tapped on his radio. Perhaps it was faulty.

Jolley sounded pissed off. "*Negative* Nine, what's going on?"

Nine looked around again. Remain vigilant, he thought. "Control, I'm hearing spurious radio chatter from somewhere, over."

"Understood Nine. Be careful. This lot could be tricky bastards, over."

"Wilco Control, Nine out."

Operative Nine dropped his AK-47 on its butt and used it to steady himself as he scratched at his long goatee beard and rubbed his tired eyes. When he opened them, a tall white man was lunging at him with a length of wood. With barely enough time to register the image, Nine took it in the face, his nose smashed.

McKinley and Carter appeared like ghosts from out of the ruins, the latter catching the falling man and laying him in the sand. Wilson threw the two-by-four away.

"D'you have to hit him that hard?" said McKinley. Wilson ignored it.

Carter returned the scanner to his pocket. Its record and playback function sure was a good idea.

"Bring him round," ordered McKinley. Carter leaned over the man and gave him a quick, sharp bite on the earlobe, bringing about sudden wakefulness and a surprisingly energetic cry of pain. The yell soon turned into a series of profane phrases, most of which began with 'F' and 'C'.

"Shut your bloody trap," said McKinley. "You're going to radio Jolley for me."

The guy's response was also more than ill-tempered so McKinley rolled him over, yanking his right arm up behind his back. He blocked its return with his knee while Carter and Wilson immobilised the mercenary.

"If that's how you want it," snarled the Scot, "that's fine. This is for our friend that your boss just capped." With this he snapped the man's little finger, triggering another yell of agony.

"You've only got nine more," ground McKinley like the snarl of a wolf. "But I can get cruel and unusual if you want."

He broke the next finger and Nine's wailing climbed a few semitones in pitch. Carter and Wilson were having some trouble holding him down as he kicked and writhed in the sand. Goodness knows how much of it was getting in his eyes and mouth.

"That was for..." McKinley paused for a moment. "Oh, I dunno... what about those poor bastards in North Korea? They've got it pretty bad." He gripped the middle finger and felt the man's body tense.

Snap! Nine moaned like he was giving birth, his head beating at the sandy ground.

"That was for the nurses," growled McKinley. "They *definitely* don't get paid enough." He advanced to the index finger.

"*No, no, no!!*" hollered Operative Nine. "I'll do it!"

"Alright," said McKinley. "No tricks or I'll cut your knackers off. *After* I break the rest of your fingers and knock your teeth out."

In considerable pain and fear of McKinley's brutality, the man nodded. "Okay!"

"Here's what you say," ordered McKinley. "There's something going on at the docks and the police are there. That's all. Now pull yourself together and don't try anything because I *will* slice you!"

Feeling something through his trousers that was undoubtedly a blade at his perineum, Nine nodded again. Carter released Nine's left arm and the merc keyed his radio. "Nine to Control," he groaned, the pain yet evident in his tone.

"Go ahead Nine," said the radio.

"There's something going on at the docks and the cops are there, over."

"Nine, what's happening, over?" asked Jolley, concern in his voice.

McKinley mouthed "commotion."

"Some sort of commotion, over."

"Received and understood, Nine; Control out."

"Thanks," said McKinley. "Willy, tape him up tight. Chris, get everything useful."

McKinley stood up and walked a few paces away. Ten minutes ago he'd dialled 17—the local police emergency number—from Carter's phone and, in French, had alerted the Mauritanian cops to a big drug and arms deal going on at the docks. It would probably piss Plugger off, but the big ugly geek was in no real danger. Now McKinley heard sirens. Good.

McKinley brought his own radio up to his face. "Hey Jolley, are you there?"

Even through the radio, the returning call resonated with surprise. "Ian McKinley!" said Jolley in his haughty private schoolboy inflection. "How good to hear from you. Have you decided to play nicely, over?"

"No chance," replied McKinley. "I'm at the docks. Come and get me. 'Cept you'd best be quick 'cause I've got hostages."

"You realise," transmitted Jolley, "you're just making things ten times worse, don't you, over?"

"Ask me if I give a shit," responded McKinley. "I just want to see if you've got the balls."

"You'll find my testicles quite formidable," sneered Jolley. "Over and out!"

The rental van barrelled through the dusty streets, taking a fast but serpentine route toward the airport. They'd seen one vehicle heading the other way at speed containing Mauritanian army look-a-likes, but there was no way of telling how many of Jolley's crew were left behind.

At a corner of the airport's fence, by the Hotel Al Jazira, there was a dusty track that led south-east by a filthy come-and-go lake. Here they stopped, the van's lights already extinguished. Wilson and Carter jumped from the vehicle and started to crop the links of the fence. It wasn't a substantial barrier, but trying to drive right through it would have attracted attention.

"Come on," snapped McKinley as his colleagues worked madly. Carter had a pair of sturdy pliers whilst Wilson was using an Eickhorn KM4000 combat knife that formed a pair of wire cutters when linked with its polyamide sheath. It wasn't the most dexterous of tools, but it was working.

Finally they tore the separated section of the fence away and drove onto the airport property. There was their plane and, only five hundred meters further ahead, Jolley's Avro RJ. Wilson raised a pair of night vision binoculars to his eyes.

"One guy by our forward landing gear, rifle, no NVGs," he reported.

"Can you take him?" asked McKinley.

"Yes," said Wilson, "if I can get as close as we said."

"Okay. Proceed as planned."

"Got it," replied Wilson. He gave the bins to Carter then threw himself out of the vehicle's door. He rolled upright as McKinley and Carter headed east.

Wilson heard the vehicle receding. The brightness of the full moon could be both a curse and a blessing, allowing them to see more but providing much less cover. He quickly sprinted north, putting a building between him and the C-54GM.

McKinley and Carter turned the vehicle toward their plane and proceeded slowly. Carter watched through the binos. He saw the guard raise a hand toward his radio.

"Now!" snapped Carter.

McKinley flipped the full beam headlights on as Carter quickly turned the stereo up, ramming the microphone of Operative Nine's radio into the speaker. Hopefully this would disrupt communications between the guard in front and Control. A couple of rounds cracked into the van's bodywork.

Wilson pistol-whipped the man's neck hard and the guard stumbled forward with a grunt. But at that moment there was a gunshot and Wilson felt air as a bullet tore past him. It came from their plane.

McKinley turned hard as another round shattered their windscreen. Bright muzzle flashes could be seen from the area where Jolley's aircraft was standing. The reception committee was bigger than they thought.

Wilson's mark rotated quickly, bringing his AK-47 to bear on Wilson, but the combat specialist grabbed the barrel as the man fired, unleashing several shots into the Mauritanian night. Without even thinking Wilson yanked on the weapon and pulled himself behind and below the man, who was now between Wilson and the forward hatch of their plane. Several rounds slapped into the guard, giving Wilson time to fire back with his Walther P99. All he heard was the sound of lead shredding aluminium. Not good.

Killing the stereo, McKinley and Carter heard radio chatter. It was Jolley, ordering everyone back to the airport, stat. They had only minutes!

Carter leaped from the vehicle and hit the dirt, firing back toward the Avro RJ with one of their Heinmarsh rifles. It was impossible to see if he was doing any damage but he kept an eye on the answering muzzle flashes and tried to aim where the shooter's body would be.

Wilson ran for the C-54GM's port side, knowing that this would shield him from the fire that was coming from the forward hatch. McKinley drew up beside him.

"Ready?!" he shouted.

Wilson bounded onto the vehicle's engine compartment, and then to the roof. "Let's go!"

McKinley floored it, the van transcribing a big semicircle counterclockwise; then he turned directly toward the North Star's huge rear cargo door, which was still open just as they'd told Bacon to leave it. The silver belly of the aircraft approached all too quickly but McKinley dared to wait a few milliseconds before slamming on the brakes. Even so, the roof of his van knocked into the plane.

Wilson leaped with everything that was in him, feeling weightless for a split second. With a resounding, bone-jarring bang he hit the interior starboard side. No time to hurt; he had to survive! Ringing metallically in the fuselage, automatic fire followed him as he rolled behind the extra drums of avgas they'd brought on board earlier. He shot back, fiercely aware that with every round he risked starting a catastrophic fuel fire. Several more loud bangs later there was a body fall and his opponent's gun fell silent. Wilson raced forward, switching on a torch, and found the man breathing his last by the forward hatch. The man died as Wilson started to remove all his useful equipment.

McKinley in the meantime was heaving cases of gear through the cargo hatch as Carter tried to dissuade any more fire from Jolley's jet. At last it appeared to stop.

McKinley shouted at Carter. "Get your ass up here!"

Carter ran to the van, leaping up like Wilson had and entering the fuselage of their plane. The first thing he noticed was the overpowering reek of aviation fuel. He and Wilson quickly swapped places. Carter saw Bacon's body, wrist still cuffed to the ribs of the fuselage. He threw himself into the cockpit, bringing up the ignition systems. The engines slowly started to come on line.

McKinley and Wilson pulled a record number of muscles heaving the crates up from the van and into the C-54GM's fuselage, but neither had time to think of such things. Already, vehicle lights were bouncing up and down as they raced toward them from beyond the perimeter fence.

McKinley dived down to the van and reversed it as hard as he could away from the plane. Where it had impacted there was a big dent in the aluminium fuselage, but nothing that would prevent the aged aircraft from flying. McKinley stopped the vehicle behind the C-54GM and ran back to the cargo hatch, leaping as Wilson caught his arm and heaved him aboard. Together they pulled the doors, shutting the big aft one firmly. Its smaller companion wouldn't quite shut, its progress impeded by the damage the vehicle had caused, but they pulled hard and managed to latch its locking mechanism nonetheless.

McKinley ran forward and dumped himself into the pilot's seat. As the best aviator of TDR.12, it was his job to coax the old bird into the air. His hand instinctively found the throttles and brought the starboard pair up. He saw that lights were dancing around at the airport, doubtless belonging to security personnel. McKinley reached down the left hand side of the control pedestal and released the parking brakes.

Amidst the thunder of engines, the big old bird started to rotate. It seemed to take an age, but when the C-54GM was pointing in the right direction McKinley gave more power to the port engines and she started to crawl toward the runway. Carter was checking the instruments whilst Wilson bent over Bacon. The gadget dealer's body was limp, but oddly warm. Wilson pulled away the *keffiyeh* that had been placed over the gadget dealer's face and at that moment Bacon's eyes opened. His mouth was covered by a fat swatch of silver tape.

"Holy shit!" exclaimed Wilson, nearly losing his footing. "He's alive! He's awake!"

"What?" yelled Carter over the monster-roar of the Merlins.

"Bacon's alive!"

McKinley took his eyes off the runway lights for just a second to look at Carter with immense relief.

Wilson knelt for a second by Bacon, looking him over in the insipid interior lights. He didn't appear to have any ballistic impact wounds, but he'd taken a bit of a beating.

Just at that moment the heavy metallic pitter-patter of lead hail reached them from the back of the plane. There was nothing they could do but wait for her to reach the runway. The seconds stretched out as the COAST lads *willed* the ageing airframe toward the smooth concrete.

Suddenly McKinley snapped "screw this!" and rammed the throttle levers forward, all the way to takeoff power. He knew that if they hit some bad ground they could take out the undercarriage, but he needed to get to that runway.

"Don't!" yelled Carter, knowing that this could happen. Suddenly the whole aircraft rattled and bumped. Wilson fell on top of Bacon. Carter reached over to try and back the power off but McKinley's hand was rock solid. If they stopped now, they'd be done for. Gritting his teeth and pleading with the universe to allow the plane to keep rolling, McKinley channelled his concentration into the nose wheel steering control. With every jolt the smaller cargo door rattled like it would fall off.

With a final lurch they joined the runway. McKinley had to act fast on the power to avoid going across it and ending up ramming the retrieval crew's aircraft. Vehicles were approaching fast from the terminal, their blue flashes reflecting from the cockpit walls like lightning. Doubtless the rest of Jolley's crew were now inside the airport's perimeter and heading for them. McKinley quickly modulated the revs on the port engines to align the North Star with the runway, then powered all the juice back on.

They felt the acceleration as the aircraft began to move, but it was frustratingly slow.

"Come on!" yelled Carter, his hands balled tight.

The aircraft was picking up speed, moderately at first then faster and faster, gradually reaching takeoff speed. Suddenly McKinley saw bright lights ahead.

Another plane was coming down at them to land! Carter's jaw dropped. Wilson could only stare in horror at the rapidly expanding cluster of lights. Will this be it?

Just when it seemed like there was no escape the lights peeled off to port with a deafening rasp of engines under punishment. Their whole airframe vibrated with its passage as the ground speed continued to gain.

"Let there be flight!" grunted McKinley. He pulled back hard on the yoke, and with a shudder like an unbalanced spin dryer the elderly North Star broke her earthly bonds and ascended into her natural environment.

McKinley breathed again, only now becoming aware that he'd forgotten to. Wilson laughed like a maniac in relief and Carter yelled "you're getting the cleaning bill for my underwear!"

The C-54GM climbed slowly and noisily for a moment before the radio burst into life.

"Impressive!" Jolley crowed. "Very impressive McKinley! And bloody lucky too."

McKinley took the radio from Carter's outstretched hand. "Don't tell me you're pleased."

"Only because I've left you a present. Once you're clear of the town I'm going to give you a surprise."

McKinley looked across at Carter, his eyes wide. Mirroring McKinley's expression, Carter dived into the cargo compartment to search. McKinley regained his composure a bit and replied.

"I thought you liked civilian casualties," he said.

"Not on this scale," replied Jolley. "But if it gets the job done then I'm fine. Goodbye, Mister McKinley!" The radio went silent.

McKinley turned to port, shouting "going around!" He was so low that it looked as though they might brush the lights of the sleeping town, but he had to remain near civilisation because of the chance that Jolley *might not* detonate under those conditions. "Find the bloody thing!" he yelled, reaching down to the bottom of the central control pedestal and lifting the lever which would raise the landing gear. Don't want her dragging at this altitude...

Carter and Wilson were scrambling about, the latter heading toward the rear of the plane. There were a hundred different places a bomb could be hidden. Where the hell could it be?

Northern Nouadhibou raced by underneath as McKinley tried to stay over the town, his arms shaking with the effort of manoeuvring the behemoth. Suddenly there was darkness below. Without lights down there, he couldn't even tell whether it was land or sea. McKinley kept turning to port, knowing that the town had to come back around eventually. Where were the local transmitter masts? Where were the towering minarets? If he even touched one it was all over!

Bacon was moaning. McKinley wished he would shut up. Bacon's moans got louder as the gadget dealer tore the tape away from his face.

"Bomb!" he croaked, pointing with his free hand around the bulkhead.

Spotting the lights of the town to his left, McKinley risked a momentary glance back. "Chris!"

Carter jumped over several cases that had come loose, heading for where Bacon was pointing. It was behind the second bulkhead and aft of the forward hatch. Here they'd secured a whole load of cases.

"Willy!" shouted Carter, "gimme a hand!" He pulled his knife and started to slice through cargo straps as Wilson ran up from the back of the plane where he'd been searching.

On the ground, Jolley could hear the noisy engines phasing in and out with the Doppler effect as the C-54GM circumnavigated the town at impertinently low altitude. I've got to hand it to these boys, he thought, they've got some spunk. His index finger hovered just above the remote trigger.

"Err, boss?" said a voice next to him. "You don't want another inquiry, do you?"

Jolley looked around at his executive officer, Rafferty. "No," he smiled, "I suppose not."

The big aircraft started to approach again from their south, its navigation lights appearing like bright stars over the silhouetted roofs. The engine noise was getting louder and louder.

"Just send him some lead," said Jolley. Rafferty spread the word to their remaining men.

McKinley saw the runway lights and tiny flashes of gunfire. Impacts started to rattle around the aircraft.

Carter pulled the last of the cases out of the way to discover a grey ABS plastic box a bit smaller than a shoebox sitting on the floor where it joined the cylindrical fuselage, a single red LED glowing on its end panel. The cheeky bastards had buried it under the cases, which were now strewn haphazardly about the North Star's cargo compartment.

In the shifting G-forces Carter passed unsteadily between the bulkheads and into the cockpit. "Got it," he puffed. Twanging, tearing sounds of bullet-meets-aluminium continued. Carter saw that two of the cockpit windows had taken a hit. Thank God they were Plexiglass.

"One more circuit," grunted McKinley, "then gasoline stir-fry!"

"Roger that," said Carter, grabbing Wilson and running for the back of the plane.

When they got there, Carter saw what a sorry state they were in. Several of their fuel drums had been punctured, leaking avgas all over the plane's interior and creating a suffocating petrochemical stink. It was a wonder they'd not burst into flame. The partially unseated cargo door was rattling like a shopping trolley travelling along a pebble beach.

Roger Jolley heard the aircraft turning away again in a wide arc. How long are you going to keep this up, he wondered. "Number One," he said, turning to Rafferty, "bring me that M72."

"Yes boss," said Rafferty and ran across the runway to their plane. Most of their men were now concerned with keeping airport security at bay and it looked as though things would turn ugly.

It took Rafferty no more than a minute to get back with the shoulder-launched Light Anti-tank Weapon in his hand. By the time he passed it to Jolley they could hear the increasing rumble of the C-54GM's engines again as it approached from the south. The huge droning noise bounced and echoed from the buildings as it became more fierce.

Jolley looked around at his XO. "This should be good," he sneered.

They listened to the engine noise getting louder and louder. But where the heck was the plane?

"What's going on?" said Rafferty. Jolley glanced at him, wondering the same.

The roar of the four V-12s suddenly increased by an order of magnitude and the lights of the North Star exploded into view above the town, barely skimming the rooftops and flying directly at Jolley and his crew.

Looking through the M72's sight, Jolley was aghast. How could the bastards be flying that low? "Holy bloody shit!" he exclaimed, realising that if he shot down the aircraft it would not only flatten civilian buildings but the plane's wreckage might just bury him and his men.

The ground shook as the enormous plane tore across the airport perimeter and bore down on them at zero feet and full speed. Just before the C-54GM passed over the retrieval crew's plane, a large object dropped from her rear and there was a grating crash of destroyed aluminium as it struck the RJ, smashing the central fuselage and shunting the ruined aircraft a couple of meters. Both the RJ's wings collapsed as though relaxing after a long, final flight.

Jolley gaped at the catastrophic damage, cursing profusely. "*MY PLANE!!*" he screamed. "*You bastards!!*"

In insane, vengeful anger he dropped the M72, grabbed his detonator and mashed the trigger.

The Avro RJ blasted into a million pieces in a huge fireball.

After the violent *kick* that the shockwave gave them, shaking the C–54 like a small but intense earthquake, the radio started going nuts, pouring forth swearing and cursing. Carter switched it off. McKinley looked round at him with a knowing eye, about to make the turn to starboard. Carter slapped him on the shoulder.

"Keep going north!" said the weapons tech.

"What?"

"You don't want him to think we're heading east."

"Okay. Let's get some altitude." McKinley kept on his heading and brought the Merlins up to maximum power.

"Not too high mate," said Carter. "Radar low down is patchy."

McKinley nodded. "I know. Just want to get away from the bloody sand."

Carter could understand. He'd certainly never been in as big an aircraft at as low an altitude in such dark conditions. What McKinley had just done required both ridiculous flying skills and the audacity of a raving lunatic. But there was no chance of pursuit by Jolley's plane now. That bird had definitely flown its last.

"Willy's looking after Bacon," said Carter. "I'm going to check out these systems."

"Roger that."

Reasonably assured that the gadget dealer was going to be alright, Wilson was using a hacksaw on the handcuffs. It was going to take a while thanks to their hardened steel, but he was working vigorously.

"Willy," said Bacon, "Sorry I let ya down, innit."

"Nothing you could do," grunted Wilson, his efforts directed to the saw.

"I kept talkin' Spanish, didn't say nothin' in English, like. Didn't fool 'im though."

Wilson raised his eyebrows. "We'll make an operative out of you yet."

"No," said Bacon firmly. "No you won't. I nearly shit meself when he shot that gun at me."

"Happens to me all the time," smiled Wilson.

Carter left the instruments alone for a moment and leaned toward McKinley.

"Just a thought," he posed. "Wouldn't Uncle Victor normally send COAST crewies?"

McKinley kept his attention on the flying. "Aye, *he* would. It's the JIC."

Wilson called from behind the bulkhead, his voice almost inaudible over the engines. "Bloody Cambion-Dawkins!"

"Aye," scowled McKinley. He risked a quick turn of his head toward Wilson. "If that bastard pisses me off any more this stork's going to deliver him a lead baby with a brass afterbirth."

Turning back, McKinley doggedly clung to the yoke, his movements as gentle as he dared yet firmly coaxing the elderly airframe into even flight. Despite the C-54GM's age, she seemed to be responding adequately. There was some stiffness—hardly unexpected—and it was no aerobatic flyer, but he could feel the reassuring power of those noisy Rolls-Royce engines. The instruments, however, were operating at less than peak efficiency and several remained dead, their needles bouncing languidly with every slight course correction or bump of turbulence.

Once they'd flown about ninety miles north, McKinley executed a 112 degree starboard turn, changing heading to east-south-east, and they settled in for the long flight to their planned destination of Berbera, a town of less than a quarter of a million souls in northern Somalia on the Gulf of Aden coast. There was a barely used but serviceable airport with a thirteen thousand foot runway where they would be able to refuel for their next leg around the Arabian Sea and down to southern India.

Unable to see the desert beneath him, McKinley instructed Wilson to keep a watchful eye on the GPS software on one of the new laptops and guide him away from or around any areas of high ground or other potential hazards. He wanted to climb to greater altitudes but Carter's logic was sound; staying low would help to keep them out of trouble.

Carter had been working in the bowels of the plane. Now he pushed past Wilson and Bacon, and returned to the co-pilot's chair. He waved a finger at the right hand extremity of the panel.

"What?" said McKinley, his eyes still scanning the darkness outside.

"Sorry bro; bad news one, and this really is a pig: landing gear hydraulics are *dead*." Carter emphasised his report with a downturned thumb. "Must've taken a round."

McKinley chanced a look at the gauge. "You sure?"

"Yes mate. We can fly fine but we can't lower the gear."

"What the frikkin' hell?!" spat Bacon. "You mean we can't bloody land?"

Carter looked round and nodded with almost tangible unhappiness.

"Holy *shit!*" breathed Wilson.

"Fine," growled McKinley with angry sarcasm, "we'll just stay up here. What else?"

"Bad news two: we're not going to make it."

McKinley roared in angst. "Bloody hell! Always with the pessimism!"

"Sorry pal," shrugged Carter, pointing at the fuel gauges. "We started off with about thirty eight hundred miles in the tanks. Our extra fuel would've got us there no probs but most of it got pissed away, not to mention we dropped a barrel on those wankers."

"I don't believe you lot!" burst Bacon. "You couldn't organise a piss-up in a bloody brewery!"

McKinley ignored him. "Shit," he breathed. "Got an alternate?"

"Djibouti," said Carter. "More populous, bit more civilised, three hundred miles closer. The main international airport would be a problem 'cause of passport control, video cameras, military presence, etcetera, so we'll have to put her in the sea. Either way we'll need to declare an emergency and we'll be under the microscope."

McKinley cursed. The increasingly sisyphean circumstances made him feel that for every step forward they were being pushed two back. "Nowhere closer? Nowhere at all?"

"Not with the runway length and facilities we'd need."

"Runway length don't matter. If we belly-flop this crate it'll never fly again."

"I know. There aren't *any* good options, but I think we can make it to Djibouti."

"You *think?*"

Carter raised his palms to the roof. "Bloody hell Mickey, we know *nothing* about this thing's fuel usage. Not to mention we've got to burn more climbing over a massive mountain range in Ethiopia! I'm giving you the best intel I can."

"Aye, alright," said McKinley, trying to keep his head clear. "Settle down. We'll head for Djibouti. Unless you can fix that gear we've got no choice; we'll have to ditch."

"Agreed," grunted Carter dourly. "I'm on it."

The blackness of night was turning into a dark blue ahead and soon there was a hint of coral pink as they flew toward the rising sun. But for the next hour, as the sky blazed into spectacular fire and then brilliant dawn, there was just one sound as constant as the deep, throbbing drone of the four engines: the irritating, nasal drone of Bacon's complaining. The Londoner was annoyingly vocal in the opinion that his presence on the C-54GM was unnecessary and that he should have remained in Nouadhibou to oversee the shipping of his beloved yacht.

At the controls, McKinley didn't need as much effort to tune Bacon out, but he could see that both Carter and Wilson were getting irritated. Carter would probably just punch Bacon's lights out or threaten his life, either of which McKinley wouldn't have minded much, but what about the new boy? McKinley had never seen Wilson in this kind of situation—heck, none of them had ever been through this bloody nonsense—and he didn't know how his new colleague would react.

A few minutes later, though, it was Carter who addressed the gadget dealer with surprisingly restrained words.

"Kyle," he began, raising his voice to overbear the engine noise. "You know complaining always makes everything better, right?"

"Complaining?!" scowled Bacon. "Who's complaining? I shouldn't bloody be here! I should be on the ground makin' me way back 'ome, not in a flying coffin that can't land! Who's bloody complaining?"

"Okay," said Carter, turning away to end their exchange, "you can either shut up or we'll put you on the ground to make your way back home. A parachute may not be part of the deal."

Bacon swore and was about to launch another barrage when Wilson lunged and grabbed his collar with more ferocity than either of his team-mates would have expected, yanking Bacon toward him with no perceivable effort. Bacon's eyes took on the roundness of saucers as Wilson grunted viscerally, grinding the words out methodically through clenched teeth. "Be *quiet!*"

With this he propelled Bacon back across the cabin, where the arms dealer landed in his own seat with a thump. Shocked down to bedrock, Bacon stared at Wilson for a split second, then composed himself a little and turned to the front, peering keenly forward as though the view ahead had suddenly become the most fascinating and necessary thing in the world.

The day wore on in heat, brightness and occasional points of interest. The flight time was, in theory, seventeen hours and the GPS seemed to agree with that. McKinley and Wilson took turns flying whilst Carter buried himself in the mechanics and tried to fix the landing gear issue. The archetypal Scot, McKinley couldn't help thinking what a ghastly waste of money it would be if they totalled the North Star.

The sun quickly rose above their eye line, bringing the Sahara into glorious panorama before them. Whilst the scenery changed slowly from the air, the desert wasn't as uninteresting as any of them had expected. There was a surprising amount of colour and, here and there, amazing rock formations. As they crossed the border from Mali into the southern tip of Algeria, the horizon became rocky, with a spread of low but rugged dark grey peaks, and they increased altitude before the landscape flattened out again. They entered Niger's air space and found the relief increasing more sharply. This huge range, Wilson found out, was called the Aïr Mountains, and was volcanic in origin.

As if to rub salt in the wound, Carter emerged from the guts of the aircraft with further bad news; the manual mechanism for lowering the landing gear had several essential parts missing. A thorough search failed to locate them. McKinley tried to take this in his stride and went through mental rehearsals of putting her in the drink, but it was clear that any return to earth they now made would be far from ideal.

The flight continued, long, arduous and hot. As the sun slowly worked its way around and behind them, they crossed Chad and Sudan, passing over the River Nile south of Khartoum, and McKinley started to worry about the fuel situation. As they flew into Ethiopia the land became imbued with a more fertile appearance and the geography changed from flat desert to rolling hills and then towering, rocky peaks. They climbed above ten thousand feet as the landscape below started to look like the lunar surface.

While Wilson was taking a turn at the controls McKinley made his way behind the second bulkhead where Carter had the floor panels up and had been tracing the hydraulic lines in an effort to improve the situation.

"We're getting close mate," said McKinley. "What's the news?"

Carter pulled his head and arms out of the hole. "I've made a patch between the hydraulic systems, but I can't bleed them so it won't stand really high pressures. Might not work at all. Thing is, I can't find where the fault is. It could be before the hydraulic pumps, or after them. Front, back or anywhere."

There's only one way to find out, thought McKinley. "We should try lowering the gear."

"Okay."

They returned to the cockpit and McKinley relieved Wilson. As he took his seat he realised he was becoming attached to this old plane. He'd actually enjoyed the legs of the journey that he'd piloted. Carter secured himself in the co-pilot's chair and watched the gauges.

"Okay," announced McKinley, "here goes nothing." He pushed the landing gear control on the central pedestal down. Two thirds of the way there it became stiff. McKinley pushed harder. No go. He looked at Carter nervously.

"Let me have a go," said the weapons tech, whose physical strength was envied throughout The Team. He brought the lever up again and tried to push it smoothly but firmly down. It became jammed at the same point.

Unleashing his safety harness, Carter threw himself onto the floor between their seats and unscrewed the panel, hunting for any obvious impediment to the control's operation. Not finding any, he quickly pushed the panel back into place to avoid obstructing other controls.

Lifting himself, Carter said "we have a situation."

"Oh you think?" grumbled McKinley. "Just do what you can – and quick! Willy!"

"What?"

"How far until the coast?"

Wilson quickly tinkered with the GPS as Carter pushed past him again. "Two hundred miles, give or take."

McKinley checked the fuel gauges. They'd already put all their additional fuel into the system and used up the reserve. It hadn't made much difference. McKinley did some mental maths and came out with a shitty answer. They weren't going to make it as far as the coast.

"Willy, get up here," he ordered. Wilson climbed into the co-pilot's chair.

Bacon said "what's going on?"

"Right," grunted McKinley, "we're going to have to put her down in the desert. Without undercarriage. I need the flattest bit you can find." McKinley was getting desperate. All he could see ahead was a huge expanse of volcanic mountains.

"On it!" Wilson played with the laptop.

"Chris!" shouted McKinley. "No news?"

"Yeah, we're screwed!" shouted Carter from somewhere in the cargo compartment.

Holy bloody shit, thought McKinley, this is going to be a new experience. Despite the innumerable flying hours he'd logged, he'd certainly never pancaked a vintage airliner into a desert. There was no right way to do it.

"Got this valley," said Wilson, rotating the lappy. "It's the flattest thing anywhere near, and it's three miles wide."

"Right," said McKinley, quickly taking a look at the screen. "Give me directions."

"Roger that," said Wilson, and brought up the navigation tools. "In about twelve minutes we'll see it starboard. When we do, turn south-east dead. That should line us up."

"Got it," affirmed McKinley. "Chris!" he shouted, "secure everything you can. We're going to land in the desert."

"Roger!" came Carter's shout from behind. Bacon ran to help him.

The interval until they saw the valley seemed like an eternity to McKinley, especially whilst watching those fuel gauges. He wasn't sure how the engines were still guzzling their avgas, but as long as they did there was hope. They passed over a deep river valley, a thin strip of green and shadow in the pinkish beige of the landscape, then climbed over a ridge of bleak, brown hills.

"There!" said Wilson, pointing. McKinley started to turn the aircraft and saw the valley many meters below. Shitty death; that was a hell of a steep descent. He began to edge the nose lower, completing the starboard turn. A huge conical peak passed by to port and then the valley spread before them as though opening its welcoming arms. The airframe started to buck and shake with the turbulence coming off the mountains.

Carter poked his head into the cockpit. "We're good; all tied down," he gasped.

"Okay lads, strap in," instructed McKinley. "This is going to be rough."

Turning briefly, he caught site of Bacon's terrified mug. The poor lad was about to face death again, as were they all. McKinley looked around for the flaps control. There it was, just to the right of the landing gear lever. He grabbed it and said "deploying flaps." The aircraft's decrease in speed was noticeable and their passage became even more turbulent, like driving over the dried out ruts of a mud road. The airframe started to complain audibly, low pitched thuds and groans issuing from its members.

Suddenly there was a sharp, mechanical coughing sound from outside. McKinley craned his neck left and saw that the nearest engine was winding down. Damnit! He feathered the propeller to cut drag and draw as much usable power as possible from the other engines.

As the mountains stretched upward around them, McKinley saw that this valley floor wasn't as level as expected. Though it had looked flat from higher altitude, it was easy to see now that the whole expanse was strewn with boulders ranging in size from cars to houses.

"We can't land here!" gasped McKinley.

"Lake!" said Wilson. "Big lake at ten o'clock!"

McKinley looked across. There it was, only just visible through the haze, about thirty miles away. They had no choice. He retracted the flaps. Goodness only knew how much height, airspeed and fuel they'd wasted with them.

"Rig for ditching!" shouted McKinley. "Lifejackets on!" Carter dashed back into the cargo compartment, knowing that everything he and Bacon had just done had to be undone, and at emergency speed.

Lips parted and teeth gritted, McKinley steered toward the lake. The whole fuselage tipped left as she turned. McKinley fought the rudder to avoid side-slip. He had to maintain altitude for as long as possible!

"Lake Abbe," reported Wilson, rapidly donning his life preserver as he read from the laptop. "Straddles the border. Salt lake. Make for the far side if you can."

"No shit!"

The ground was getting horribly close so McKinley dared a tiny forward push of the throttles and pulled back on the yoke slightly. But how much fuel was left?

Ahead was a gateway of volcanoes. That to the right was of dark rock and low down. It looked extinct. Its twin was a narrower but higher cone made of much lighter rock and somewhat further away. The lake started to become clearer as they left the first volcano behind.

"How far now?" yelled McKinley as an engine on the right started to chug and choke.

"Eighteen miles!"

I can't glide for eighteen bloody miles, thought McKinley. Still, with only two engines sucking fuel, there's more to go around. He looked at the airspeed. It had slowed drastically and their height was only about four thousand feet. The second volcano whizzed past to port and now they saw that, even though massive in itself, the cone was only a secondary feature on a gargantuan volcano beyond it, its enormous summit vanishing into the distant haze.

"Chris!" yelled McKinley. "How we lookin'?

Carter's voice came from behind the bulkhead. "About as ready as we'll ever be."

"Everyone strap in!" ordered McKinley.

They flew over what must have been an ancient lava flow, the western edge of which had been undercut by a river, forming an escarpment. It vanished quickly into their propwash. Trees, outcrops and valleys were becoming frighteningly clear as the plane descended for what would be her last time.

McKinley checked their height. Twenty two hundred feet. Shit.

A diminutive volcanic cone passed underneath as they saw yet another on the approaching shore. These geographical features were *flashing* past beneath the C-54GM now, indicating how low they were getting. It felt like they could see every rock and fissure. The third engine spluttered and died. McKinley swore.

Suddenly they were over the beach. He caught sight of an isolated, low hill on the right and then they were over water. The dark green lake stretched out ahead and to each side.

With six miles of lake to go until Djiboutian territory and eight hundred feet between them and the wet stuff, McKinley prepared to give the North Star her bath. He trimmed the plane as best he could and reduced airspeed by tiny fractions. He tried to keep the nose up so that the tail would drag on the water's surface. With any luck the ground effect would help him keep her in the air for a bit, but it would also create drag. If he allowed the nose to drop and it hit first, the whole aircraft would somersault and be torn to pieces. Three hundred feet and holy shit, the water's surface looked terrifyingly close. Ahead, a huge flock of big, bright pink birds could be seen exploding from the surface to take refuge in flight.

One hundred and sixty feet.

"*Everyone brace!*" shouted Carter.

Fifty feet.

McKinley shook his head, his fingers white like bone as they gripped the flight yoke. "Don't try this at home kiddies!"

013: The Desert

A jarring, *wrenching* deceleration like being shaken by the claw of some Lovecraftian deity jolted the old airframe as its underbelly slashed the glistening surface of Lake Abbe, slamming them harshly into their safety harnesses.

McKinley made one last, desperate effort to keep the nose up, and then there was nothing he could do. With a mammoth concussive impact the C-54GM belly-flopped into the lake sending thousands of gallons of water flying in a tsunami of spray. She pitched forward under nineteen tonnes of her own inertia and came approximately to rest, rocking and slewing like a fairground ride.

Before the oscillations even began to settle Carter was on his feet and racing toward the tail. Already the sounds of sloshing, gurgling water could be heard from below. The weapons tech snapped open the largest case and yanked hard on a long cord. With a bang like a vehicle airbag followed by a metallic hiss, a black dinghy started to inflate, its burgeoning form rapidly filling with CO_2.

"Get the doors open!" shouted McKinley, knowing that they had mere seconds before the weight of water made this impossible. Wilson and Bacon ran past Carter to the wide double cargo hatch and, unlatching the doors, started to push. As soon as they did, lake water rushed into the opening and around their ankles. Wilson got between the doors and heaved with all he had, forcing them against the inflow. As the gap widened the pressure started to abate and they were finally able to latch the doors back against the fuselage.

Bacon slipped and yelled. Wilson grasped the door's top edge and lunged for the gadget dealer, snatching a grip onto Bacon's belt. The Londoner caught the rear of the door frame and heaved himself upright, holding on to the aircraft's ribbing, his eyes looking desperately into the flooding plane and yearning for the dinghy. Now they were irreversibly sinking.

"Not again!" grunted Wilson as he helped Carter heave the inflatable boat to the doors. They started to pack it with their cases as the aircraft's nose dipped dramatically.

"Hey what about me?" yelled Bacon, seeing that the dinghy was filling up. Joining them in the desperate deplaning of their cargo, McKinley snapped "you can *swim!*" Bacon took a deep breath and pulled himself outside, swimming hard to retreat from the suction.

Deepening water rushed around their calves and the disconcerting sounds of dying airframe under strain got louder. The fuselage was filling up fast and already the cockpit was completely awash. Carter was waist deep, retrieving floating Pelican cases.

"Leave it!" shouted McKinley.

Wilson was ready to go and pull Carter out of the flood when McKinley told him to get out. He reached and grabbed the sill at the top of the door as his body started to float in the tide flooding into the increasingly diagonal aircraft. Suddenly the foaming outrush of air under pressure was at his back and Wilson's head popped out of the plane and into daylight. He reached to the edge of the big rear door and pulled himself further away from the inrush of water. He saw that the front half of the North Star was already submerged.

"Chris!" roared the team leader, still inside the fuselage, his head in the rapidly shrinking bubble of trapped air. With a gigantic gurgle and sheets of spray, the old aircraft slipped below the lake surface.

"Holy shit!" yelled Wilson and attempted to duck-dive and return for his friends. But as soon as his eyes opened in the water they stung with such ferocity that he involuntarily closed them. Barely able to detect which way was up, Wilson struggled until his head broke the surface. Spitting acrid water and coughing, he tried to open his eyes but the biting pain was unbearable.

McKinley and Carter had both discovered the same. The former found himself in sudden gloom, floating inside the descending wreck. A pelican case found its way to his chin, giving him a nasty knock. With his eyes hurting like hell, McKinley suddenly realised that he was only moments from drowning. The ancient life preserver strapped around his torso appeared to be largely useless.

Wilson felt Bacon's hand on his shoulder, pulling, then he felt the firm, reassuring slickness of air-filled vinyl and held on to the dinghy's side rope as he tried to open his stinging eyes. He could feel them issuing profuse amounts of tears as his body tried to clear the invading bitterness.

McKinley was in deepening darkness and pain, his stored breath running out and his left foot trapped hard at a very uncomfortable angle between unyielding objects. He shook and rotated his body, putting great strain on his knee joint as he tried to free it, but it was useless. He was stuck fast and he didn't even know how. He bent his leg and body, reaching for the obstruction, then felt something wrapping round the trapped ankle and pressure increasing. He was snagged on a rope!

Suddenly whatever it was tugged hard and with a shock of stabbing agony his foot became free. He lost whatever breath he had to an involuntary cry. Someone grabbed his collar and pulled.

Several agonising and unbelievably long seconds later, McKinley felt his head break the surface and he gasped air, retching with the sharp, sour taste of the lake salt. It was like brine mixed with vinegar. This led to alternate coughing and trying to catch his breath whilst his throat spasmed, reacting to the strong chemicals. He heard bubbling like a gigantic pot on a fast boil.

"Let me do yours," said Wilson's voice. He heard splashing, then Carter gasping in discomfort.

"You 'right mate?" came Bacon's distinctive voice nearby. McKinley tried to open his eyes. All he saw was a bright blur, then they snapped shut again. His ankle, too, was screaming torture.

"This water's... my bloody eyes!"

"We know," said Carter's voice, sounding similarly pained. "We're going to deal with it right now. Calm down and float on your back."

Unable to even perceive where he was, McKinley did as he was told, feeling the brush of tiny bubbles all over his body as the drowned aircraft gave up her last breath somewhere below. He felt Carter's hand guiding his arm, then wet nylon rope between his fingers. He held on tight, calming somewhat, and allowed buoyancy to lift his body until he felt his chest break water. All his stinging eyes could see was the bright red, mottled glow of sunshine through his eyelids.

"I'm going to pour clean water on you," said Carter. "Try to open your eyes and we'll flush this shit out."

McKinley felt cold wetness descending, as though he was being waterboarded without the cloth. It splashed around his eyes and nose. He tried to blink and it hurt again. He persevered and the pain receded a little. With a bit more blinking he felt like he could maybe get his eyes open for a bit. Not wanting to be blinded by the sunlight, he turned his body again to an upright position. His eyes still hurt like mad, but with more blinking McKinley started to be able to keep them open for longer periods.

They were by the inflatable dinghy amidst a wide field of bubbles from the wreck, as though they were floating in fizzy pop. The light seemed too much and he was fighting the urge to close his eyes again and leave them that way. Through blinks he noticed that Carter and Wilson's eyes looked fiercely red. Bacon's eyes were clear; obviously he'd kept his head up. McKinley wished he could have done the same. His ankle was transmitting horrible shafts of misery.

"What happened to my leg?" he asked, feeling stupid because he didn't know.

"Your foot was caught at the hinge between the cargo door and the fuselage," said Carter. "I bloody hope I didn't break your ankle."

"I don't know. Hurts like hell."

"Sorry mate, it was that or drowned haggis."

McKinley coughed. "Okay."

"Let's get to the shore," said Wilson, "and figure out where the heck we are."

"Shit street," muttered Bacon.

"Right," nodded McKinley, bitter water still running off his noggin. He joined in as they swam east, the inflatable in tow with its cargo. "How the hell d'you find me with your eyes like this?"

"You kicked me in the head on the way out."

McKinley spat phlegm into the lake. "Sorry."

"Don't be sorry," said Carter. "That's how I found you."

They fell into silence as they swam beyond the expanding circle of foam. The acrid water gave their skin a soapy feeling. Ahead, the low, mostly brown mountains were turning red. With their eyes still stinging, they were all glad that the sun was behind. At the base of the mountains, heat haze turned the shore into a shimmering blur, making it impossible to see how far away they were. Through the distortion, McKinley saw tiny blobs of light orange moving around, but it was only when members of their colony took to the air that he realised they were flamingos. Countless numbers of the aquatic birds were gathered at the shore, feeding on the brine shrimp and algae that imparted the distinctive colour to their plumage.

Presently the lake bottom rose up to meet them and they waded the rest of the distance to dry land, under constant observation by the suspicious birds. Once there, Carter insisted on flushing their eyes again, admitting that this otherwise unnecessary use of potable water was a concern in these desert conditions. He took a good look at McKinley's ankle and established that it was a sprain, albeit a very painful one. They built a fire from driftwood that seemed mostly unwilling to burn, shared some rations that had been salvaged from the North Star, and elected to take watches through the night, guarding the equipment.

The morning brought visions of an alien landscape across which winds whipped the sand into something like a low lying mist and through which nomadic herdsmen were slowly passing with their beasts. Around them, towering chimneys of limestone rose like the set constructions of an overly-imaginative production designer on a sci-fi movie. These weird geological structures, some tens of meters tall, had a texture that engendered images of the *rusticles* on sunken ships. They were ugly and gnarled like gigantic termite colonies. Apart from these, the desert was flat and almost featureless, although they could see hills rising to the south and east.

McKinley rubbed copious deposits of goo from the corners of his eyes. Just as Carter had predicted, his tear ducts had worked a vigorous night shift to remove the remaining haline contaminants. He scraped the gluey lumps from his eyelashes with a gentle fingernail and used his palm to rub the dried salt from his beard. The encrustation around his lips tasted harshly bitter.

The first order of the day was to take stock of what had been rescued from the aircraft and McKinley was pleased that Carter's list was about two thirds complete. The plane itself was a total loss though, as the salt of the lake would eat its aluminium skin in no time, and even if a salvage operation could be rushed into this desolate environment, it would be phenomenally expensive. McKinley thrust his affection for the C-54GM to the back of his mind and concentrated on their next move.

"There's this place," said Carter, perusing the mapping software. "Kouta Bouyya — I don't know how to pronounce it. About twelve miles SE. The road starts there."

"We're not going to walk twelve miles with all *this* shit," grumbled McKinley, gesturing at the equipment. There was too much for four to carry, and Bacon would doubtless prefer not to participate.

"There are vehicle tracks here," observed Wilson, "but I'm sure we're not on a bus route."

"Screw this," said Carter, rising to his feet. "They're supposed to speak French here. I'm just going to collar one of these shepherd guys." He took off at a run toward a distant group of tents that looked like domed fungi sprouting from the salt flats.

McKinley and Wilson were preparing a list of the kind of gear to leave behind if necessary, but within ten minutes Carter was back, announcing that a convoy of tourist Land Rovers would arrive in the early afternoon and would be able to help. True to form, the weapons tech had even got a name and contacted the organisers from his satellite-enabled smartphone. They rigged simple sun shelters from the gear and inflatable boat and settled down to wait.

The tour organisers were nothing if not helpful, but it still took all of the rest of that day to cover the seventy or so miles to Abi Salieh, a town of forty five thousand, where there was at least a hotel with functional showers.

The next day McKinley gladly replenished his cigarette supply and reluctantly bought a high sided cargo truck in which they could transport their equipment. It was old, perhaps from the seventies, but in running order and with four reasonably good tyres. Its cab was wide enough that all of them could sit on its single bench seat, and had been painted a murky yellowed green through which crusty iron oxide was visible.

They headed for Djibouti city, passing through a landscape that appeared both strikingly similar and diametrically different to what they'd seen in Mauritania. On one hand it was desert—dry, hot and unbearably dusty like Nouadhibou—yet on the other the geography here was undulating, with hills and valleys, volcanic peaks and dry river beds. Some of the lowlands were even carpeted with lush vegetation.

They travelled slowly east along National Highway Five, although the term 'highway' was loose indeed, there being not a square inch of tarmac anywhere. The next populous place they encountered was Ali Adde, where the track descended to cross the valley and they were surrounded by diminutive dwellings clinging to the hillsides. The scenery was spectacular yet harsh and it was hard to believe that over three thousand resided there.

Heading north, their next waypoint was Holhol—immediately renamed 'Hell Hole' by Bacon—a smaller town at the confluence of two *wadis* that would become raging torrents of flash-flooding during the infrequent periods of heavy rainfall. Over one of the dry watercourses an impressive stone viaduct carried the railway at a height of nearly thirty meters. Its architecture was a peculiar sight, reminding them of the Elan Valley dams that they'd seen during the summer. They continued toward the coast, their path criss-crossing the railway several times as both wound through the varying terrain. The sun continued its path toward the west and it didn't seem long before the shadows were starting to elongate.

Shortly before entering Djibouti city the N5 finally became a paved road and their surroundings segued into more familiar fare with a huge, modern livestock market on their left, yet surrounded by mud huts and improvised shelters. On the right, a clearly defined road junction appeared to lead directly onto the long runway of an airfield, but Carter explained that it was a race track and parade ground.

Again the wide dynamic of societal strata was clearly evident. Shacks stood side by side with gleaming office blocks, and new houses next to empty lots that lay peppered with scrub, garbage and evidence of human habitation. Djibouti City was bisected by a winding, sparsely populated tract of *wadi* half a mile wide through which ran the Ambouli River on its course to the nearby delta. To the west was the sprawling suburb of Balbala, at least as large as the city center but containing only about thirteen percent of the population. A wide, modern bridge carried them over the Ambouli and into the heart of the port city, where lights were already on.

McKinley and Carter dropped Bacon and Wilson near the airport and looked for some kind of property management company with an out-of-hours number. There were just three listed, two of which had answering machines. At the third, French with a very strong African accent was a minor stumbling block but they managed to convey their interest and arrange a meeting. With the kind of money they were offering it was easy but time-consuming to rent a small warehouse without too many questions being asked. Once the company's agent had driven away, they stashed the truck in the old building, making sure that both were tightly secured. Their colleagues had returned with a rental car, a little white Toyota Yaris, because McKinley was still in considerable pain from his twisted ankle.

The city bustled with life, colour and vibrancy, even at this hour. The atmosphere was markedly different than in Mauritania, and it seemed like Djibouti was a lively mixture between Nouadhibou and a typical British city, with the culture of the former and the busy lifestyle of the latter. The architecture was different though, with almost no high-rise buildings. Of course there was the endless sand which invaded their footwear, clothes and noses.

"Right," said Carter as they drove, squashed into the little Yaris, to the center of town. "First order of the day: find the bloody rubber."

"It's ninety four percent Islamic here," observed Wilson, handing back Carter's phone with which he'd been having a VOIP chat with Julia. "I doubt there's a pub."

"I don't care if it's a shed made of camel bones," replied Carter, "as long as they serve beer."

His throat dry, McKinley agreed with the suggested beverage whilst remaining adamant about security. "Aye, but let's try *not* to get the attention of Djibouti Five-O, shall we?"

"Do they even have cops here?" asked Bacon ingenuously, grinning like an idiot as he imagined a dromedary with a blue flashing light on its hump.

McKinley frowned good-naturedly. "Let's not force the issue."

"Really Mickey," griped Carter. "We're off the radar, AWOL, extracurricular, out-of-office-hours. We're not bloody accountable out here. No MDTs!" he shrugged. "We can drink, drop, shoot or snort whatever we like."

McKinley laughed at the mental image. "If I find you with your sniffer buried in bleaching powder or something I may have to use harsh language."

The wind seemed to be blowing them toward the harbour and they were all sick of seeing sand in every direction so, thanks to Carter's penchant for on-the-go research, they made their way onto a fishing quay and parked, locating a small whitewashed restaurant that served both alcohol and western food. Finding that they were nearly the only customers, they ordered drinks and perused the menu.

A lone figure observed the quartet from the shadowy recess behind a beaded curtain as they awaited their food. He was puzzled at the lack of stealth in their movements, the obvious nonchalance of their behaviour. He'd first tagged them at the city limits via his small network of informers. Even if recognisable solely from a curiously sparse dossier placed briefly in his hands a few months ago and in which the beards were absent from two, they were undoubtedly the same covert team that had been deployed to recover those missing warheads. Presumably that operation was now concluded and they'd been assigned another duty, which being to locate and retrieve *him*. Despite their casual demeanour, that was surely the reason for their presence in Djibouti. Why else would a spec-ops crew from the UK be in this unremarkable dump of a port city? But their unconcerned attitude made him wonder nonetheless.

Who was the fourth man? He didn't act the same way. The first three, despite their genial behaviour, had 'that' look about them; he was well acquainted with their kind. He could almost smell their training from where he watched. There was the one that appeared to be the leader: wiry of frame but with broad shoulders, broken nose and straggly fair hair and beard. His eyes took in almost everything; a trained observer. The man next to him, the one with whom the first was obviously good friends, was built like a tank. A bit shorter, but very muscular. He smiled more than the others, but his eyes bore deep pain. The third was tall, lean and ripped, clean shaven and bursting with energy, clearly younger than the first pair by minimum five years. He looked like the kind of man you wouldn't want to get in a fight with, an improbable chimera of marathon runner, martial arts champion and trained assassin.

The fourth character wasn't the same; he acted like a civilian. Who could he be? Surely not an overseer? No; they certainly weren't affording him due deference for that position. A trainee? Not possible. But why would a three man team of secret operatives be joined by an apparent civilian whose blond hair had been so obviously dyed black and whose left ear was bandaged? His body language seemed to convey that he was an addition to their group. Was he a contact? He wasn't local; that much was certain. An informant? Some kind of advisor maybe? Why had he arrived with this team? There was something peculiar about this turn of events.

It didn't matter. Their removal would be quick, clean and cost-effective. Thank God I'm just passing through, he thought.

Wilson tried a sip of his coffee. Its cup was small and ornate and the contents were as black as midnight in a coal cellar. The aroma was beautiful, enchanting and exotic, the taste potent and aromatic, imparting a rich, warm sensation to the back of his tongue. He could tell it was much stronger than what he was used to.

"What's it like?" asked McKinley, taking a slug of beer and making a face which suggested that the uniqueness of its flavour was unexpected.

"Jump leads," replied Wilson. "I don't think I could drink more than one."

McKinley huffed. "As long as it's not made from cat turds you'll be alright."

Wilson's eyes expanded and he involuntarily returned the tiny cup to its saucer with a clink. "Cat... turds?"

"Aye, coffee that's made from moggy poo. They drink it round here." McKinley leaned forward with a concerned yet patronising expression, nodding as he spoke. "Does it smell... funny?"

Wilson opened his mouth, his tongue partially out, an increasing mask of disgust stretching across his youthful face. He didn't want to smell the coffee again.

"Actually," interjected Carter with an air of authority, "A, it's not made from shit; B, it's not from a cat; and C, we're in the wrong part of the world anyway."

"Bloody hell," complained McKinley, throwing himself backward in the chair. "You'd rather be a freakin' know-all than support your best mate on a perfectly good wind-up." He made a sour looking face and a gesture of resignation.

"Oops, my bad," replied Carter, smirking.

"Another wasted opportunity." McKinley winked at Bacon.

"So, err, what about this crap coffee, then?" asked Wilson, still uncertain.

"It's called Kopi Luwak," said Carter, "and it's not crap. It's supposed to be the best coffee in the world. The beans pass through a Palm Civet's guts, then they wash 'em, roast 'em and grind 'em."

"Nice," said Bacon sarcastically, sitting back and stretching.

Wilson's mouth turned down at the corners. "But it's still come out of an animal's bum?"

"Well, yes. By the way, Kopi Luwak comes from Indonesia, so you still might get to try it. Costs a fortune though."

"I'll remember... not to," said Wilson, looking with a little animosity at his existing cup.

Bacon blinked hard and yawned. "Bugger me, this beer's a bit bloody strong, innit?"

"I find it mild." Carter turned down his mouth in distaste. "Pansy pop at best."

McKinley grinned. "Aye but you could drink meths and get nay more than a mild buzz."

Carter feigned umbrage through sly eyes. "I resent the accusation that I'd get a buzz."

Wilson looked across the table at Bacon. He was still blinking, but appeared as though he was about to spew. He seemed a little pale.

"You tired pal?" asked McKinley. "Don't go screensaver on us."

"I... I don' feel great," stammered Bacon, his eyes rolling.

Carter leaned closer, studying their friend's face with growing concern. "What the hell?"

McKinley put a hand out to Bacon. "What's wrong?" He'd barely touched the latter's arm when their colleague's torso toppled forward, his face slamming onto his plate.

"Don't drink any more!" exclaimed McKinley pushing his chair back and leaping to his feet.

Carter pulled Bacon's limp form up by its shoulder whilst glancing nervously at his own half empty glass. The tech dealer was out cold.

Wilson surveyed their table as McKinley and Carter held Bacon upright in his chair, trying to wake him. Of course: there were four glasses but a single plate. Bacon had been alone in ordering an appetiser.

"The starter," he said. "It's in his grub!"

McKinley instantly scanned the room. Seeing no present threats he addressed Carter. "Any ideas?"

Carter was urgently checking Bacon over. "Chloral, barbs, roofies, something like that. Too early to tell but we've got to get him to hospital."

"Lethal dose?"

"Time's a factor!"

"Right." McKinley helped Carter to heave the unconscious Londoner to shoulder level and, as Wilson grabbed their jackets, drag him to the door. As the other occupants of the eatery watched in stunned surprise, they rammed the door open and lugged Bacon out into the tropical night. Wilson and Carter took Bacon's weight whilst McKinley moved ahead.

"Get him in the car," ordered McKinley as he looked around. It was quiet – the kind of quiet that raised his suspicions a good ten notches.

They hurriedly rounded the corner of the building and there, standing between them and their car were five African guys. Four were holding firearms and the other was unarmed – perhaps the leader. As the COAST operatives came to a halt with their unconscious friend, the armed men moved to surround them, leaving their colleague in front. The man produced a pistol, which he held out at McKinley.

"Come to pull me in?" he said in an unmistakably English accent. "Think again."

"Who the hell are you?" replied McKinley. His instant gut reaction was that the stranger was one of Roger Jolley's crew, but the man's reference to being pulled in cast doubt on that. McKinley quickly analysed the situation, seeing a rough cruciform of men, two with the well known Russian AK-47 assault rifle and the other pair with pistols of unknown manufacture. They didn't look professional but they did appear to mean business.

"Don't insult my intelligence," said the stranger derisively. "Let me tell you what's going to happen now. These blokes are going to bury you in the desert. I'm *not* going back, and neither will you."

There it was again. This man was afraid of the very thing McKinley's mind had flitted to. McKinley considered several options before answering.

"Alright," he began slowly, "this is what *I* think's going to happen. First I'll disarm you. My friend here," he indicated Carter, "is going to clip these two, and *he's*," He tipped his head toward Wilson, "going to deal with those." The gunmen weren't phased—maybe they didn't understand too much English—but McKinley detected a tiny change in their stances.

"Oh, you reckon?" said the stranger, sneering. "We've got the guns."

In a fraction of a second and before anyone could have reacted, Wilson threw their jackets toward the leader. McKinley ducked and rolled toward him, flipping himself up as he came out of the roll. At the same time Carter used Bacon's body as leverage and launched himself into the air, kicking hard at an African neck. Wilson, dropping Bacon, used the diversion to pull his closest assailant toward him and hold him whilst the other fired his pistol right at him. Wilson felt the impacts through the man's body.

McKinley kicked the leader right in the solar plexus as the man fired, knocking him backwards and sending the bullet far into the African sky. McKinley came down and his ankle fired a debilitating shock of pain into his body. Carter's boot broke the neck with a shattering impact and he grabbed the man's rifle, pointing it at the next figure and squirting three rounds into his chest. Wilson leap-frogged his dead Djiboutian and came down hard on the other, pinning his arms. With the heel of his hand he planted a solid blow on the man's jaw, knocking him out cold.

Whilst McKinley was recovering from the pain of his landing the English-accented black guy did a remarkably acrobatic back flip, turned tail and ran along the dock to a Land Rover. He threw himself in before McKinley could even get up and took off in a cloud of dust.

"Get rid of the mess," shouted McKinley, limping toward their car. He dropped his body into the Toyota, cursing its economical specification and automatic gearbox. He fired up the motor and raced after the 'Drover.

The other vehicle was nearly at the end of the quay so McKinley punished the little engine. The Land Rover turned at the roundabout, racing off along the *Route de Venice*, a long straight stretch that divided the sea from the lagoons behind it. Land Rover, thought McKinley. Very tough, but not built for speed. I might *just* be able to outrun him.

Not waiting for other traffic, McKinley threw the Toyota across the roundabout to the sound of horns blaring. So much for not alerting the cops, he thought, but I need to nail this bastard and find out who he is. He saw the Land Rover leave the road ahead. The scumbag was trying to make this a cross-country thing and thereby waylay McKinley's pursuit.

McKinley turned onto a street that looked like it would take him in approximately the same direction as the 'Drover. If he could stay on paved roads his speed would still be better. Once he left the road he'd be screwed, just as the occupant of the other vehicle clearly intended.

Racing through the darkened streets, McKinley tugged his Five-seveN from his belt behind his back. He clicked the safety off, concerned that he'd have to shoot left handed if necessary.

City blocks flashed by in a regular rhythm, editing his view of the space beyond. He'd lost sight of the Land Rover yet he could still see its dust. McKinley slowed, taking longer to peer between the buildings. He couldn't see the other vehicle at all. Damn it!

He got on the radio and called Carter. There was no reply. Holy crap, don't tell me they've been arrested! He pulled up behind a minivan, not sure how to proceed.

Just then McKinley looked ahead and saw the Land Rover's nose peeking out from between buildings. He quickly switched off the little car's lights. Had he been seen?

No! The Land Rover inched out, its occupant looking around warily. It turned slowly onto the street, toward McKinley.

Damn, how to stop it? McKinley didn't want to use his firearm and attract any more attention. The situation was already uncertain and he was worried about Carter's lack of response.

The LR was getting closer. Its occupant appeared to be driving sensibly, trying to play it cool. McKinley had an idea. It was a stupid idea, but it would bring the scenario under control rapidly. Keeping his left foot on the brake, he selected reverse, turned the wheel hard and manoeuvred his body into the passenger seat, unlatching the door as he did.

The other vehicle was almost upon him when McKinley smashed his foot onto the gas pedal. With a surge of acceleration the little car bounced into the road, reversing in a mad semicircle and smacking into the front of the Land Rover with a crunch. At the same time McKinley allowed the momentum to throw him out of the car. He rolled, carefully letting his right leg take the strain, and came up by the Drover's right hand front wheel, pistol held out threateningly in front. The occupant was trying to select reverse but as soon as he saw McKinley he raised his hands, looking pissed off. He might be a decent driver, but at this range there was no escape from a bullet.

McKinley yanked open the passenger door and jumped in. They needed to have a serious conversation, but not here. And McKinley needed to know what was happening with his team-mates. "Drive," he instructed, "back toward the harbour." The man complied, his weather-beaten face sour.

On the way there, McKinley's radio sparked up and a familiar voice rang from its little speaker.

"Hazard to Tripod."

"Tripod here, report."

"The cops are crawling all over the quay," replied Carter. "We're at the landward end of the other one. What's your status?"

"I'm on the way there," said McKinley, his face adopting a puzzled frown. "How did you get off the quay?"

"Borrowed a boat."

"Righto. See you in five." He turned to the driver, who looked back, angry but uncertain. "You heard the man," said McKinley. "Let's go."

"See, that's what *I* thought would happen," grunted McKinley. "Looks like I was closest so you owe me a pint. Now, I'll ask again; who the hell are you?"

They were on the dry portion of the *wadi* under the bridge, having used the Land Rover's renowned off-road capabilities to reach the isolated spot which appeared to be Djibouti City's unofficial garbage dump. The place was covered in unwanted toys, dead televisions, mattresses and every kind of plastic container. It was a disgusting location and they were unlikely to be disturbed.

The stranger was face down on the ground, his hands behind his head and the muzzle of McKinley's pistol at the back of his neck.

Fearful yet still defiant, the man answered McKinley. "You *know* who I am!"

"We haven't been introduced," said McKinley. "Try *again!*"

A worried look crossed the man's dark face. "Middleton!"

"Why should I know you?" asked McKinley.

"You weren't sent to bring me in?"

McKinley cast a glance to his colleagues. "I don't think so."

The man paused for a second, gasping frantically. "Look I'm sorry, okay? I thought you were the frikkin' retrieval crew!"

Wilson had come to stand at McKinley's side and touched his friend on the shoulder. "We should find a more secure location."

McKinley nodded and dug with the Five-seveN. "Name again?"

"Blake Middleton! I'm SIS! MI6 if you like."

McKinley raised an eyebrow. "Wallet," he said to Wilson, beckoning with his index finger.

Wilson reached into the man's hip pocket and pulled out the leather pouch. "Chris!" he barked and Carter came to join them, all the while looking around, an AK-47 at the ready.

Together they flicked rapidly through the contents of Middleton's wallet and soon found what they were hunting for: an innocent looking business card for *Mission Global Development Consultants*. No Security Intelligence Service agent would carry anything identifying them as such, but all COAST operatives knew the covers under which government agencies operated. The card bore the name Blake Harwood Middleton and announced his area of expertise as 'Management Information Systems, Power Generation and Distribution'. They looked at each other, then Carter handed the ID to McKinley.

McKinley quickly scanned the card. "You'd better get up," he ordered Middleton, backing away.

The man lifted his frame clumsily and dusted himself down a bit. "You swear you weren't sent to pull me in?" he asked.

"We should find somewhere to lie low," suggested Wilson again. "The warehouse, maybe?"

"Look," said McKinley to Middleton, "we're on the same team; I buy that. And you're on the run. We need to talk."

"What about him?" asked Carter, looking in the direction of the Land Rover, where the unconscious Londoner was spread out across the back seat.

"He'll be okay," stammered Middleton, turning toward the vehicle. "It's just a sedative, I promise. It'll wear off by morning." He paused, looking back at McKinley. "I've got somewhere we can go."

"You'd best show us then," ordered McKinley, gesturing at the big black man with his pistol. He waved toward the driver's side and Middleton hesitantly got in. McKinley climbed in the passenger side, his gun never wavering, whilst Carter and Wilson sat carefully on the supine Bacon.

"Now drive," said McKinley, "and don't try anything."

"I'm cool," deadpanned Middleton frustratedly as he started the car. "I'm not a threat."

"You'd better not be," responded McKinley then turned his head round to his friends, looking down at Bacon. "And you two; *try* not to fart on him... although goodness knows he deserves it."

"I own everyone here," explained Middleton, spreading his hands wide to indicate the whole bar. "They're all on my payroll."

The Casablanca Lounge was more of an upstairs bedroom that had been converted into a tiny drinking establishment, thus somewhat neutering Middleton's grand asseveration. Atop an office supplies retailer in the heart of Djibouti, it provided an out-of-the-way venue for any Anglophone desirous of a quiet drink. They served several European beers as well as a brace of spirits that were African approximations of their better known counterparts, even down to plagiaristic labels. The little enterprise had only eight tables and the bar was barely two meters long, but the place was diligently decorated in black vinyl and imitation walnut with gold painted accents. The chairs and tables were rickety and worn, and the stereo seemed to be receiving signals from the early nineties.

Their host's face seemed built around a frown, or was perhaps made of viscoelastic rubber that had gradually surrendered to gravity's influence, bringing to mind the old adage about a bulldog chewing on a wasps' nest. Middleton's lower lip protruded a little, giving the impression that he was constantly pouting, whilst deep lines dwelled in the leather folds of his skin, making his cleft chin look like an action figure's ass. Although receding at the temples, his curly black hair was long and thick, and pulled back into a ponytail that lent him the appearance of some hippie musician born a bit too late to appreciate what the seventies were about. So tightly was the ponytail bound that it looked like a plastic moulding adorning his cranium. The nearly spent cigarette drooped from his mouth as though glued there.

Blake Harwood Middleton was about five feet eight inches tall and, whilst he couldn't be called fat, was not a skinny man. His clothes—white shirt mostly concealed by a navy blue sweatshirt, and beige slacks—looked a little too big. His physical appearance wasn't unusual, but his eyes told another tale. They were of the darkest brown and their depth was underscored by the pronounced concavity of the sockets in which they lay, as though another person were hidden inside, watching from his concealment. Those eyes took in everything, measuring and analysing all their gaze touched. Here was a man who would be hard to fool, whose pessimism and aloofness were not so much character traits as they were merit badges, the award of which he'd laboured furiously to attain.

Middleton looked like he belonged in the Horn of Africa. There was something about him that indicated comfort in these surroundings and a pragmatism with which he'd quickly adapted to the local culture; he possessed an easygoing stance of understated confidence. Presumably he was—as an experienced SIS operative—adept at making use of any and all resources with which his situation presented him. This was obviously why he was untroubled at the idea of hiring Somalian ne'erdowells. To them, Middleton had perhaps been an archetype of the British secret agent despite the colour of his skin. Maybe they held him in the same kind of respect one would a gangster who had just rolled into town and forcibly staked his claim. But whilst Middleton wasn't a gangster, he was definitely a man on his own mission.

He lifted both hands in a gesture of peaceable intent then, keeping his right hand in that position, he carefully reached with his left into a capacious pocket and withdrew a packet of locally branded cigarettes that he then opened and held toward the team.

"Smoke?"

McKinley leaned slowly forward, reaching to extract one. "Aye, cheers."

Wilson looked round at McKinley then at Middleton. "No secret ingredients in that?" he asked cynically. McKinley's eyes momentarily flickered to Wilson.

Middleton huffed, allowing the vaguest echo of a friendly expression to momentarily emerge, followed by mild umbrage. "What, waste a good durry? You want one?"

"No, thanks."

Middleton held the packet toward Carter with a questioning leap of the eyebrows. Carter lifted his hand and shook his head politely.

"Typical," noted Middleton, spitting the used butt onto the floor and inserting a fresh cigarette. "No-one smokes anymore; not even a spook. Can't even pick up a woman with a fag these days."

"Oh, I dunno," replied McKinley, for whom this methodology had struck gold several times. "Depends on the woman."

"Depends what's in her glass," muttered Carter with a wink. Wilson frowned unhappily and McKinley gave Carter a look that Middleton would interpret as a reference to Bacon's drugging even though it wasn't.

Middleton took a pull, sucked in his breath sharply and leaned back, his left hand resting on the edge of the table with the cigarette prodding from between his fingers. "So the company didn't send you, eh? But you've got to admit arriving out of the desert looks odd. So tell me; how and why are you here?"

"Just passing through," replied McKinley carefully. "As to how, there's a busted propliner on the bottom of Lake Abbe. What's your story?"

Middleton leaned forward and rubbed his hands together, the cigarette assuming its habitual placement at the corner of his mouth. He looked left and right, apparently for effect, then spoke.

"Got into some trouble in the Iranian desert near Konari. Made a run for it. Glover—the other agent—shot dead, poor bugger. Managed to get away in the mountains, but it looked like I'd be dead soon too. So I decided—if I was dead— it was time to go off the reservation."

McKinley raised a finger. "What were you doing in Iran?"

Middleton rolled his eyes. "With the Ayatollah on his way to a weaponisable bomb?"

"Intel then."

He nodded. "Standard business cover; posh hotels, money to flash around, flawless back-story. 'Course the IRGC were watching us. Didn't make it easier."

"And you ended up in the desert how?"

"Somebody shopped me. Can you believe it? Someone in the company ratted us out! We had to split."

There was silence for a moment.

"Interesting," said McKinley with narrowed eyes. To learn of another possible double agent somewhere in British intelligence was troubling indeed. "So we're actually in the same kinda situation."

Middleton's eyes widened slightly and his voice ground out a whisper. "Really?!"

"We don't exist," added Carter. "We're *personae non grata*, AWOL, disavowed."

"Yes, thank you," said McKinley pointedly. "Actually we're..." He thought for a moment, rephrasing his explanation. "Look, Chris is right; this is out-of-hours work for us. We're shit-screwed if we get caught, but we're trying to tie up some serious loose ends that the JIC have washed their hands of."

Middleton nodded in understanding. "Anything I'd know about?"

Now it was McKinley's turn to look around carefully. "You been briefed on *Operation Copper Burial*?"

"No."

McKinley frowned. "I guess our codenames don't make it to the SIS. But maybe you know about a couple of missing Trident warheads a few months ago, right?"

Middleton gestured with the cigarette. "Right, yeah, I know about that. That's how I tagged you. I knew your faces from the file."

Carter smiled. "Lead team on the investigation."

"Whose lead team?" Middleton looked suspicious.

McKinley sighed. He felt like he was bearing his soul, but in view of the fact that Middleton was seemingly willing to do the same, he decided to play it straight. "We're COAST."

Alive with thought, Middleton's narrowed eyes panned slowly around the group again. "I've heard rumours. What is COAST?"

"Covert Operations And Surveillance Team. General Clive Sutton's unit. Operationally we're supposed to overlap with your lot and the SAS. Blimey I could get shot for saying all this."

Middleton spread his hands, smiling. "We could all get shot mate. Look, we're on the lam in the middle of bloody Africa. Nobody cares."

"He's got a point," observed Carter quietly.

"Aye," replied McKinley, "I suppose so. Anyway, the JIC held an enquiry and cancelled the gig; put a stop to us chasing the perp." McKinley paused for a second. "Well, as you can imagine there's more to it, but the point is: here *we* are, trying to nail him to the ground because Her Madge's Government won't."

Their new associate appeared highly sceptical of this information and shook his head in disbelief. "So why're you doing it? And why'd they stop you anyway?"

McKinley glanced at this colleagues before answering. "The latter, we don't know – yet. The former, we have our reasons. Chris," he indicated Carter, "wants to stop the nuclear threat."

Middleton's eyes popped. "They're still in the wind? Shitty death mate!"

McKinley held up a finger and shook his head. "One is."

"And the JIC *stopped* you going after it?!"

Carter threw his hands up. "I know, right? Unbelievable."

Middleton scrunched up his face and swore. "We live in dangerous times!"

"You can say that again," nodded McKinley. "Anyway, Willy wants to save the suicide bombers this guy has."

Middleton's wide mouth sank at the corners. "Suicide bombers?"

McKinley nodded. "You been keeping up with the news?"

"Woah! They're *linked*... I mean, your target's behind it? That's mad!" gasped Middleton in disbelief.

"We've got intel," continued McKinley with an indifferent glance at Wilson, "that uses the words 'army of suicide bombers'."

Middleton blasphemed, spitting on the floor. He leaned back and gestured at McKinley. "Okay. What about you?"

"Me?" McKinley tipped his thumb back at himself. "The above plus settling the score. I want to take this bastard down. Someone's got to. He killed a lot of our mates."

"Your sense of duty," observed Middleton with undisguised sarcasm, "is admirable. Me, I'm just passing through too. I ain't in it for queen and country no more; I'm in it for me. I've earned a fresh start."

McKinley exhaled smoke. "Where?"

"Oz."

Wagging his finger knowingly, Carter said "yes, I thought you were an aboriginal guy. No wonder you got a Middle Eastern gig."

"Just another black face," smiled Middleton.

"And relocating to Australia," continued Carter, "well, obviously you were born there."

"Yup. Dead easy."

"Aye, right," responded McKinley dubiously. "So, begs the question, what are you doing in *this* delightful little corner of paradise?"

"I came here to earn some pocket money. Now, I've got a ship."

"Really?"

"I'm just trying to pull a crew together. I'll cross the Indian Ocean to get down there. Avoid... you know, formalities."

McKinley leaned back, pointing with his smoke. "She'd better be big enough... and seaworthy."

"She's both," replied Middleton. "An ocean going motor vessel. Cost me a fortune too, but I think it's worth it. Once she's moored in Sydney Harbour I can just live aboard. Saves buying a house, right?"

Wilson butted in. "How on earth d'you afford a boat like that?"

"My savings," answered Middleton, "plus the out-of-hours work I've had here. But I'm buggered without a bloody crew." He turned away and sucked unhappily on his cigarette.

McKinley judged Middleton's behaviour as that of desperation. He wanted to get to the southern hemisphere and, like themselves, he didn't dare go through an airport. So he'd looked to waterborne transport instead. But Middleton needed manpower to operate his vessel.

McKinley thought quickly but carefully before positing his suggestion. "We could travel together," he said quietly.

Middleton turned back. "Come again?"

McKinley also took a puff before answering. "You want to get to Australia, we need to get to Indonesia. We *all* want to avoid formalities."

Middleton was trying not to look interested but McKinley sensed that he'd taken the bait.

"Why Indonesia?" asked Middleton airily.

"Our bad guy. That's where he is. And it's pretty much en route to Oz, isn't it?"

The MI6 agent nodded. "So you're offering to crew for me until Indonesia. What about after that? It's still a ways to Oz and I can't run the boat on my own."

"Well, that's up to you. But it's ninety percent of the journey covered at no cost. You should think about it."

"*I'd* like the luxury of thinking about it," murmured Wilson unhappily.

McKinley turned to him. "What's to think about? This is ideal. It'll pay to have a much bigger boat."

Wilson shrugged his shoulders wearily. "Whatever you say chief; as long as we get there I'm good... I'm happy."

McKinley shook his head sarcastically. "No you're not."

"I'm fine with it," interjected Carter, indicating no deviation from his policy of usually being fine with most things.

McKinley rotated back toward Middleton and pointed with his cigarette. "What about it then?"

"Makes sense," replied Middleton nonchalantly.

They shook hands and Middleton said "I'll get you that pint now." He reached back into his pocket and extracted another rectangular object. "Then we play cards," he grinned vulturously.

014: The Ocean

Wilson stood at the edge of the dock as the hordes of Africans went about their business, his foot nudging the heavy iron ring into which the rope from *Priscilla* was looped. The water below him was somewhat clearer than he would have expected for a harbour and, in the unyielding heat, looked thoroughly inviting. Nevertheless there was an unusual smell in the air which carried elements of both a salty sea breeze and rotting meat. Wilson's suspicion that the source of the reek was the water itself firmly deflected the notion of recreational swimming.

The vessels moored here were a random assortment which, Wilson surmised, could only assemble in a place like this. Tiny rowing boats floated alongside fishing vessels and tugs whilst, across the bay, huge container ships and military craft could be seen. There seemed neither rhyme nor reason to the haphazard flotilla other than variety. Some boats were well maintained; others appeared about a pint away from vanishing into the depths. The one in which Wilson was most interested lay close by, the ripples gently lapping against her tired old hull as though to caress a partially healed wound.

Although Middleton had referred to her as a ship Wilson now realised that this was far too grand a portrayal. My goodness, he thought, what a tub. The phrase 'tramp steamer' floated into Wilson's mind and he found himself recalling the lyrics of a folk song he'd learned as a child, Stan Rogers' 'Barrett's Privateers':

"Oh the Antelope sloop was a sickening sight,
How I wish I was in Sherbrooke now,
She'd a list to the port and her sails in rags,
And the cook in the scuppers with the staggers and jags..."

The *Priscilla* looked for all the world like a maritime version of the horrible old green and silver busses which were sufficiently cheap that his school would hire them for canoeing trips. With a mixture of nostalgia and dismay he remembered bare seats, barer wires and Perspex windows still covered with protective metal grilles in case another miners' strike kicked off or which someone simply hadn't been bothered to remove. He recalled grumpy, chain smoking drivers, faded banners announcing long forgotten football victories and a lingering reek which straddled a triangular gap between Jeyes' Fluid, nicotine and vomit. It wasn't a delightful memory.

But now one of those dishevelled vehicles had, it seemed, returned from its scrapyard grave to haunt Wilson, albeit in seafaring form. There were the drab plastic windows, the dull chrome, the green paint which might have been a more vibrant shade before constant exposure to sunlight and salt spray. More evident than the paint, however, was the ubiquitous rust. From her gunwales hung perished car tyres like cheap earrings from a former movie star whose career had abandoned her half a century ago.

With a manly pat on the shoulder, Middleton's figure came into his field of view, the ever-present whiff of smouldering tobacco providing a last recollection of those vile busses. Bacon was with him, the two having struck up something of an unlikely friendship despite the incident with the appetiser.

"She don't look very pretty," he started, puffing smoke like the Cannonball Express, "but she's a good 'un. She's got it where it counts."

Wilson turned his head inland. "I'll take your word for it."

"It was me grandmother's name," revealed Middleton, pointing toward the tarnished brass lettering with his cigarette. "She was an ugly old boot with a heart of gold." Middleton laughed, patted again and headed for the gangplank.

Bacon lowered his voice and leaned toward Wilson. "Bloody glad I ain't going with ya." He strode off after Middleton.

Another memory raised itself into Wilson's consciousness; the motion picture 'King Kong'. *Priscilla* appeared not unlike the Venture, the steamship in the film. True, it was certainly a more modern version but in terms of dilapidation Middleton's boat was the clear winner. Wilson imagined himself running about inside that dingy hull, frantically operating pumps and fighting incessant leaks under Middleton's dubious command. If they were to plunge forever into the abyss and be lost to Davy Jones' locker, he could not imagine a more fittingly shabby vessel in which to so do. The *Priscilla* was a floating coffin.

Wilson spoke quietly to himself. "We should have kept the yacht."

They loaded their gear at night, using Middleton's Land Rover to move the cases from the warehouse to the dock. The next day Middleton bought as much fuel and supplies as he possibly could using their funds. Carter thoroughly checked the mechanical condition of the vessel and declared it somewhat seaworthy, although the two big marine diesels would need plenty of TLC on a seven thousand mile voyage.

Bacon found a hair salon and got his mop returned to something approximating his natural shade. The gadget dealer admitted a certain sadness at leaving TDR.12 behind, but it was clear that he'd had more than enough of being drugged, threatened, kidnapped, brutalised, mutilated and scared shitless. He was eager to get back to the UK, where the yacht was due to arrive the following week, but would linger in Djibouti for a couple of days following the *Priscilla's* sailing. The aim of the delay was to waylay interception, as Bacon would now have to use his own passport.

They plotted their route to Indonesia carefully, mostly staying within a relatively safe distance of the coast but with two oceanic legs; the Arabian Sea and the Bay of Bengal. These intercontinental stages would take them hundreds of miles from land. Wilson expressed more concern than either McKinley or Carter would have expected and seemed to have a deep-seated fear of drowning, but his team-mates' merciless joking dissuaded him from saying anything further.

"Obviously I'm the captain," asserted Middleton on the morning of their departure. "It's my boat."

"Chris should be captain really," answered McKinley. "He's ex-navy."

"Thanks mate," smiled Carter, understanding the reason for his friend's slight inaccuracy, "but the engineer's going to be essential to this trip."

"Right," said Middleton. "That's settled then." He nodded at McKinley. "What about you?"

"I don't bloody know. Deck hand, bosun, chief cook and bottle washer... whatever."

Carter cracked a grin. "With beards like these I think we qualify as pirates."

"Huh... Blackbeard, that's you," grunted Middleton to McKinley, and rotated to Wilson. "You?"

"I'll just do stuff that needs doing," said Wilson. "I don't know much about sailing."

"No worries mate." Middleton nodded, the left hand side of his face twisting into something which might have been mistaken for a smile under bad lighting conditions. "We'll figure it out as we go."

With Carter fussing round them like a mother hen the big diesels turned over and started to rev up, their vibration coursing through the hull like an infant earthquake. Once up to speed the shaking died away and they sounded like the distant rumble of jet engines, a constant atonal growl which would accompany them for a month.

With McKinley taking first turn as the pilot, Carter in the engine room and Wilson on watch duty they said goodbye to Bacon and sailed out into the Gulf of Tadjoura, dodging between supertankers and huge container ships; maritime monsters that dwarfed *Priscilla*. Once through the melee of enormous vessels transiting between the Red Sea and the Gulf of Aden, Djibouti City receded into the haze and nothing lay between them and the horizon ahead.

They followed the coast of Yemen for the first five days until turning east near the tiny Omani island of Al-Qibliyah, their last sight of land for eleven hundred miles and another six days. Astern, the breathtaking sunset poured forth fire and amber brilliance over Al-Qibliyah as the mouth of a mighty furnace might issue molten glass, until the sun was consumed by the black horizon and the clouds became soaked in the richest crimson like towers of smoke above a burning city. Inexorable darkness followed, cloaking them ever tighter, surrounding them on all sides until its chilling touch stroked the hull and their minute iron husk seemed suspended as though on a rippling monolayer film between the utterly black, abyssal deep below and the coruscant yet infinitely deeper abyss above. Alone in the night save for each other, they were further from fellowship and the comfort of communication than the ants which crawl on the skin of an elephant.

Life aboard the *Priscilla* soon settled into a regular routine which mostly involved Middleton being an arrogant dick and thrashing them at poker, McKinley arguing and grudgingly handing over the winnings, Carter hiding in the bowels of the boat nursing its engines and Wilson sensibly maintaining a low profile, all the time worrying about the distance from any possible source of rescue and the proximity of the ocean floor.

Meals were lonely affairs, usually comprising a pair of *Priscilla's* crew at most. Middleton had sensibly filled the galley with non-perishables although Wilson bemoaned the lack of fresh fruit and vegetables. He unhappily asked if anyone had ever heard of scurvy, to which Middleton adopted the habit of referring to him as 'Pommy'.

Pasta, condensed soups, biscuits, endless tins of tuna and other easily stored items formed the bulk of the culinary fare whilst several racks of African spices with weird names provided a little variety. Hot drinks were made with bottled water and UHT milk, and their Australian colleague had a least sourced some alcoholic beverages. Several bottles of cheap rum disappeared a little too quickly, not only through indulgence but because nobody wanted to crack one of the bottles of Algerian scotch that presented the only alternative in the spirits department. Beer was plentiful though and Middleton had loaded up several different brands. All of the mediocre brews tasted basically the same, leading Carter to term them 'generic almost-beer.'

A couple of days after bunkering at the unbelievably congested port of Mumbai in India, McKinley realised that he hadn't seen his weapons tech for a while and headed aft of the wheelhouse to where an enclosed stairwell led down to the engine room. He passed the lower deck as even the lights became less powerful, fading to a dirty yellow as though he was entering a goblin's lair. He opened the bulkhead door. There were the twin heavy lumps, chugging away, blistered with pipes and gauges and surrounded by support equipment. Around the hull were tool cabinets and benches. Near the stern, he saw that a camp bed had been built on one of the latter. The air in this noisy grotto was thick and foul but nonetheless he could still detect Carter's potently spicy cologne through the all-pervading scent of machinery, and something much worse.

Hearing McKinley's approach echoing from the metal steps, Carter shouted. "Hey, would you tell Captain Australia to keep the revs steady if possible? Just let 'em run nice and easy, like."

McKinley raised his voice to reply. "Roger wilco. How are you doing?"

"I'm... anyway," continued Carter, his body rising from underneath one of the big diesels like a spider extracting itself from a matchbox. "That's the problem: If you want the ratio of water outside versus water inside to remain in its more-or-less favourable condition I've got to keep these pumps running smoothly, so a steady engine speed is good."

"Aye, well, I'll pass it on." McKinley nodded, wondering why Carter hadn't answered his question. "Why does it smell like a shithouse?"

"Ah yes," replied his friend, grimacing with embarrassment. "Delhi Belly, Bombay Bum, whatever; I've got it and there's no bog down here."

McKinley looked in the direction Carter's head was angled to see a suspicious looking bucket. "*Oh!* That's disgusting! You never said you were sick."

"What's the point? I'll get better. I've got to keep the pumps going unless we want to set up shop on the Goodwin Sands. Can't leave 'em unattended... you know."

"What about at night?" McKinley was starting to feel more concerned.

Carter shrugged looking around the noisy space. "Sleep's not really an option."

"That's nothing new, though, aye?" McKinley was well aware that his friend was the worst insomniac he'd ever known.

Carter looked down at the filthy water swashing around his feet. "I'd like the chance sometimes. Anyway, I rigged an alarm. It sets off my phone if one of the pumps goes bozwonk."

"Would there be enough time to join us on deck for a beer?" McKinley winced the moment the phrase exited his head. The words 'deck' and 'beer' sounded way too cheerful in this dour environment, way too hopeful to even be expressed in this filthy iron sarcophagus. He hoped that the diametric difference between Carter's situation and the lifestyle topside wouldn't hit his friend too hard, but Carter appeared to have latched onto that second word.

"We still have beer?" The Weapons and Equipment Technician appeared both surprised and delighted at the same time.

"Some."

Carter's face took on an apologetic look which, in the near dark, was hard to detect through his blossoming growth of beard. "It'd be easier if you sent some down here... just in case, like."

"Roger mate, will do."

"Thanks." Carter turned back to the grimy old diesel engine, lifting a wrench.

McKinley was so sorry for Carter at that moment that there was a tiny chance of him feeling something emotional but he brushed it off before that could happen. The guy was doing a great job keeping the elderly vessel sailing and, after all, someone had to. Carter was as reliable as a Swiss watch; never moaning, never quitting, always playing for the team. It was McKinley who felt like something of a scumbag now. His own orders had brought them to the middle of this godforsaken watery wilderness; his commands had torn them away from the familiarity of their COAST duties and launched them on this bizarre odyssey. But, just as Carter had to sustain the mechanics of this floating joke, someone had to tackle the Heinmarsh situation. Unfinished business never sat right with McKinley. True, he'd made his way out of the obsessive amarulence and tunnel vision of *Operation Copper Burial* but there was still a score to be settled, an enemy to be countered and a potential threat to be nullified.

"Seeya later." McKinley turned and made his way back up the rusty steps.

Time seemed to pass with unusual sluggishness as *Priscilla* sailed south-south-west down the coast of the Indian subcontinent, passing Mangalore, Kozhikode and Kochi, and thereby clocking another eight hundred miles before heading further out into the Laccadive Sea and rounding the cape near Nagercoil. They navigated around the southern tip of Sri Lanka to cross the Bay of Bengal, a deep ocean jag that would take them about five hundred miles from land but was the most efficient route to the Andaman Sea. After several days of nothing more than water and sky they passed between the Nicobar Islands to port and, to starboard, the tiny island of Pulau Rondo—the northernmost point of Indonesia—its nearby formation of huge monolithic rocks, the Geulanteau Stones, forewarning their anticipated entrance to the Malacca Strait.

It turned out that Carter wasn't just maintaining their forward motion down in the engine room and a short while later he asked if Middleton wouldn't mind watching the pumps whilst he had a discussion with McKinley and Wilson, and enjoyed some fresh air and sunlight. Apparently not considering mutiny by his crew to be a serious risk, the cynical *Koorie* agreed and descended to the bowels of the ship for a quick lesson in running the machinery.

They stood in the wheelhouse around Wilson as he took steering duties and McKinley kept watch. The old radar set, though, was clear of traffic for the moment, giving them an opportunity to relax a little. The room itself looked more like a museum exhibit with yellowed oak panelling and vintage instruments with their infrequently-polished brass and thick, black gloss paint. It was obvious that the *Priscilla* had been partially modernised and she bore the scars, with cables poking through roughly drilled holes in the bulkheads and screws driven at odd angles into the ancient wood.

"Makaru," started Carter, turning the laptop he was holding to face McKinley, "is... a slippery bugger. He's been very careful not to build up an online presence, but I found him."

"How?" inquired Wilson.

"Hours in foreign chat rooms," answered Carter, "Activity logs, religious bulletin boards, clues here and there. Thank God he's got such a unique name."

"He's the only Makaru?" asked McKinley with raised eyebrow.

"Not quite. There's a mountain on the China-Tibet border, a village near the Caspian Sea in Iran, a dive site in the Maldives, a computer game character, a place referred to but not mentioned in the Bible and a couple of verses in the Quran – it's actually an Arabic word. But there's only one *Pastor Abel Makaru* who holds revival meetings in Singapore."

McKinley frowned. "That's a church thing, Right?"

Carter nodded. "You bet."

"Can you get us in there?"

"It's a free for all," shrugged Carter. "We can just turn up."

"Alright!" said McKinley. He turned toward the wheel. "Willy, Heinmarsh never saw your face, so you're going to infiltrate this cult. You alright with that?"

"Heck yeah," enthused Wilson, eager to get the mission moving and perhaps score points with McKinley.

"You and me," continued McKinley, wobbling his finger back and forth between Carter and himself, "let's keep on with the beards."

"Righto."

The team leader rubbed for a moment at the kink in his nose, misshapen since an accident at eleven years of age. "We know anything else about this Makaru?"

"Less than you'd hope," frowned Carter. "But I picked up on the chatter. He's well respected, well liked and supposed to have a degree in every field they've got a name for. There are people online beaking-off about what a man of God he is."

Great, thought McKinley, here we go again with the religious crap. "Picture?"

"Yes." Carter turned the computer back toward himself and worked for a moment. "This is the best I could find. He's been unusually thorough to cover his tracks."

"That's interesting."

Carter grinned. "Well, as I always say, if you don't want to get caught doing something bad then don't be seen doing bad things. *Ergo*, he's up to something." He flipped the laptop round to McKinley.

The first outstanding thing about the image was the crazily gleeful expression on the faces of the two young women captured in the foreground of the 'selfie'. The deliriously happy girls appeared to be standing in front of a stage, surrounded by many worshippers. Behind them a small sea of hands was lifted to heaven. Up on the stage, near the corner of the picture, was a lectern and standing beside it was the man they presumed to be Makaru. It was hard to make him out at this level of detail, but McKinley saw a middle-aged East Asian man whose face seemed expressionless yet whose mouth turned down at the corners, making his lip jut proudly. Makaru had piercing little eyes surrounded by almost feminine features and a thick mop of well groomed, shiny black hair. His glasses were possibly the biggest McKinley had ever seen and he wore a beige dress shirt, wide open at the collar, upon which sat some kind of ceremonial robe in dark brown with the wide sleeves of the archetypal wizard. His left hand was held out toward what must have been the rest of the auditorium as if beckoning his congregants.

McKinley looked closer. There was another man, a larger figure, right at the edge of the image and almost obscured by the celebrant's arm. Although it was impossible to tell for definite, the big man looked like Heinmarsh.

"Yeah," acknowledge Carter upon seeing his friend's reaction. "Wanna know the date?"

McKinley looked up. Just tell me already, you idiot. Why did Carter always do that? "Aye," he said.

"April fourteenth."

McKinley took that on board. Wilson said "hey, wouldn't that mean—"

"Aye!" interrupted McKinley. "He was involved with this Makaru guy before *Operation Copper Burial.*"

"The plot thickens," added Carter.

"Well that's all we need," spouted McKinley, "Heinmarsh and a religious nut in charge."

"But it's not as though he's really in charge of anything big," replied Carter. "It's just a congregation."

Wilson raised an eyebrow. "That's probably not very many."

"Enough for a private army," answered McKinley.

Wilson held out a finger. "*If* they're trained and have the kit."

McKinley looked down his nose at Wilson. "You were the one who wanted to rescue all the poor little suicide bombers. If they're armed, they're an army."

Wilson huffed. Carter said "it's a fair point."

"And I'll say this;" added McKinley, "If Heinmarsh's got the warheads with him, that's a credible threat. Not that the JIC'd notice," he added, muttering sourly.

"But a nuke needs a delivery system," offered Wilson. "What about that?"

McKinley shook his head. "What about a ruddy great rocket in Canada? Don't you think he can find a way to do it?"

"Alright then," said Wilson, giving up the debate. "Makaru's cult has the potential to be very dangerous. The thought of suicide bombers in every major city is terrifying. But why do they do it?"

"Like I said before," nodded Carter, "making your followers do your shit is easy. Believe me, I've studied this in some depth."

He prodded at the laptop screen. "This Makaru's a demagogue. You know, a religious fraud, a snake oil salesman, but with the charisma to attract followers. From what I gather he's mixed his own religious cocktail; bit of Islam here, some Catholicism there, a bit of New Age and a dash of Buddhism, humanism, I dunno. He's an ecumenist."

McKinley was new to that term. "What's that?"

Carter turned and smiled humourlessly. "All roads lead to Rome... or God or, well, whatever you want. Ecumenism says all religions are the same, equal, all about the same thing. They've really been hyping it up for the last thirty years or so. The idea is that no single faith has all the answers and they need to unite to figure it out. Yeah, I could see Makaru falling right in with that crowd."

"Wow," said Wilson flatly. All this talk of God and religion was getting weird. It would, however, likely become an increasingly necessary evil the more they examined the strange case of Pastor Abel Makaru.

"I'm not afraid of death!" she cried. "I'll be welcomed into paradise!"

She was just a child. She looked like Jem, but not the same age. She reminded him of Jem and he felt it from his head to his loins.

"Don't do it!" pleaded McKinley. He wanted to get away, but the handcuffs held fast. She seemed unusually strong.

"You can't save me!"

It was tearing his heart to pieces, despite his own plight. "Just don't light the fuse," he begged.

She pressed the button and the cable started to burn down toward her middle. McKinley tried to grab it, to extinguish it, but his hand wouldn't move. His arms felt lethargic, heavy and as though glued in place.

"It'll be alright," she said, giving a melancholic smile. "We'll be married when you get to heaven."

How can wire be burning, McKinley asked himself vaguely. The explosion was milliseconds away. He made a last, desperate lunge at the fizzing cable.

He exhaled sharply as his left arm twitched and his eyes opened. Sudden departure from the dream world was disorienting yet there was a definite sense of relief too. He was back on the boat, the bloody rotten old boat, in his bunk. Those ancient engines were still drumming like the sound of a distant military march and there was a peach glow pouring through the porthole like a spotlight.

McKinley lifted his arm and flexed his numbed fingers. He'd been lying on it, leaving a pattern of flattened sheet ripples impressed in his skin. He thought back for a moment. It had seemed so real and vivid, but the puzzling thing was his reaction to the girl. Somehow he'd known that he'd be okay, but his deep, desperate weight of concern had been for her. He'd wanted so badly to save Jem... *her* from everything. He shook his head; stupid bloody dream.

He looked at his watch, dangling on a rubber band from a nail in the wooden bulkhead. It was 06:12. His alarm had been set for 06:30 and his shift at the wheel would start half an hour later.

Sitting up, McKinley rubbed his face, his palms sliding down the unfamiliar hair of his cheeks, and fingers massaging the corners of his eyes, crumbling away crystalline deposits of rheum. The dream was already becoming indistinct and coffee was calling, or at least that excuse for coffee which Middleton had inexplicably stocked up on. He headed for the galley with little enthusiasm.

Eggs or porridge? McKinley chose the former. Not that he, as a Scotsman, didn't like porridge, but it wasn't the top brand. Actually it *was* like the top brand of wallpaper paste. Well, he mused, these Sri Lankan eggs are about the same grade, but I can camouflage their fishy taste with ketchup. He quickly fried three which he choked down accompanied by dry bread plastered with tasteless, cheap margarine. Oh, a life on the ocean wave, he thought sarcastically. This ain't no pleasure cruise.

Wilson and Middleton were in the *Priscilla's* wheelhouse, both looking like death warmed over. McKinley smelled that horrible coffee, machine oil and old sweat. The little bridge itself was somewhat more inviting in the warm glow of the fresh sunrise, which seemed to distract from the dents and imperfections in the woodwork, the ever present dust and the few tiny nodules lying around on the floor which were undoubtedly rodent turds. Ever the musophobe, Carter had insisted on the acquisition of poison but it looked like their furry travelling companions weren't taking the hint.

Wilson was about to retire after eight hours piloting followed by eight on watch. Middleton had just finished his shift at the wheel and would stay on watch with McKinley until 15:00. These long shifts were working, but with three weeks of this regimen already under his belt McKinley couldn't help but wish for a proper crew.

"The Strait of Malacca," announced Middleton tiredly. "Only three days till Singapore, Blackbeard."

"Glad to hear it," said McKinley, taking a slurp of coffee and spilling a drop down his hairy chin. He looked round at Wilson. "You alright?"

"Yeah, fine," returned Wilson without conviction.

"On the left," continued Middleton, "Malaysia.   On the right, Indonesia. Where's that chart?"

He rummaged in a wooden pigeonhole which was screwed to the side of a console and brought out a folded sheet which he flapped until it opened.   He threw the chart over the console as though it was a dust cover.

"Here's where we are now," indicated Middleton with his finger.   "This is one of the busiest waterways in the world so we gotta follow their Traffic Separation Scheme, *capeesh?*"

"Roger that," muttered McKinley, his tongue curling against an unpleasantly metallic taste.   Bloody hell, he thought, is this coffee ever rank.   He gulped the last of it with a shudder.

"Morning all," announced Carter, stumbling through the door with a laptop.

"How's the troglodyte this morning?" asked McKinley.

Carter ignored it.   "There's news," he said gravely.

McKinley and Wilson looked at each other.   "I've got a bad feeling about this," said the latter.

Carter backed himself between the wheel console and the windows so that Wilson could see the screen without taking his attention too far from the binoculars.   He held the laptop so that it faced his friends.   Middleton looked on from across the bridge.

"This was all over the news last night," said the weapons tech.   "I'll translate."   He pressed the spacebar.

An internet video of the Russian premier in front of his parliament started playing and Carter narrated.

"We are warning the west not to interfere in our internal affairs," intoned Carter spasmodically.   "Any interference will provoke a strong military response. It is clear that these incidents are related and the Russian Federation will rise to the challenge of neutralising this cowardly threat."

"Them's fightin' words," said McKinley in a fake North American accent. "What's brought this on?" he asked, a strong suspicion that he already knew tugging at his consciousness.

Carter turned the laptop to face himself, clicked a few times, and turned it back.   "You won't need a commentary."

The scene was familiar to anyone with more than a passing interest in matters Russian.   It was Red Square in Moscow.   There was the Goum department store on the right and the State Historical Museum in the background.   A large crowd was gathered, stirred by something.   Suddenly, the viewpoint changed, panning rapidly left toward Lenin's mausoleum and The Kremlin behind it.   The picture became even more familiar as the camera zoomed in, and it wasn't good.

"Not again," groaned Wilson.

"When was this?" asked McKinley.

"Also yesterday," replied Carter.   "But zero on regular news services.   It's locked down tighter than a duck's ass."

The cameraman zoomed in again with his longest focal length, to where a group of people were holding hands between the tomb and the Kremlin's wall, where the busts of former leaders formed a row behind Lenin's final repose.

McKinley nodded at the screen.   "How d'you find it?"

"I'll get to that."

McKinley continued watching.   If this was going to be just the same as before...

It wasn't. There were four young women and a man. The male was in the middle holding a megaphone and there were two girls on each side, frighteningly pregnant. There was no sound, but Cyrillic subtitles scrolled across the bottom of the picture. Before McKinley could read and translate them, the girl to the man's immediate left started to cry. She withdrew her hands and started to tug on thin cables which linked her to the other women.

"Second thoughts," said Carter quietly.

"Aye..."

The girl's chest exploded red and her body flopped instantly to the ground as though jerked down by wires. The crowd started looking around, some running frantically.

The other four figures seemed oblivious to their companion's demise. The girl on the extreme left of the group was even checking the wires around the body to make sure they were still connected. Wilson was horrified.

Suddenly the man stopped talking and dropped his megaphone to the ground with the same unearthly smile that they'd seen before. He looked round at the girl on his far right and said something. She held up the detonator switch and instantly the picture was obliterated by a bright flash and chaotic destruction. Even the camera, distant though it was, rocked violently. Then a second blast shook the camera, hurling debris, and the video reached its end.

McKinley looked up. "They're getting bolder," he observed. "How'd you find it?"

"I followed a link posted in a chat room. They were already censored, but I found a server that had backups. So I grabbed 'em while I could."

"Hold on," said McKinley, raising his finger. "*Religious* chat room?"

"Spot on," nodded Carter. "And there's the link. This particular propaganda's called *dominionism*. They've been trying to flog it to the church since the forties. It means taking over the world via this *kingdom* they all talk about – that's what the subtitles say, by the way. Look, I didn't manage to grab the data logs; sorry, but the videos are more important. Anyway, the same people who were celebrating this incident are *definitely* the bunch that follow Makaru."

McKinley nodded. "Aye so if I'm reading you right, he's probably behind censoring the videos and stuff, for anonymity."

"Like you said," agreed Wilson, "very thorough."

"Right," said Carter, getting a bit more animated. "But both those videos were filmed by *Perviy Kanal.*"

"So?" shrugged Wilson.

Carter grunted in frustration, scrunching up his face and shaking his head. "Don't you get it?"

"I do," nodded McKinley unhappily. "Either he's running the Russian news people, or he's got an influential pal on the inside, or they've got the same agenda... *and* he's in bed with Heinmarsh."

The approach to Singapore, the only place in the world which falls into the brackets of both 'city-state' and 'island nation', and among the world's busiest ports, was a forest of ships. Myriad vessels were both moored in and transiting the Singapore Strait; tankers, container ships, cruise liners, liquid natural gas carriers and freighters in such numbers that they looked like an invasion flotilla.

They reached the port's outer limit and were obliged by the Singapore Maritime and Port Authority's rules to take on a pilot. They radioed the harbourmaster's office, hoisted the blue and yellow signal flag 'G' indicating need of a pilot, and waited.

After half an hour the pilot arrived on a powerful launch and took over. He was a much older man, well fed and short at about five foot five, with a perfect tonsure of white hair like a slipped pair of headphones around his dark skinned head. He seemed pleasant, but spoke only when necessary. They changed their signal flag to the red and white 'H'; pilot on board.

At their pilot's skilled hands, *Priscilla* wove through the maze of floating steel, dwarfed by her much larger kin, making her way toward the port. Singapore was laid out like a fantastical landscape before them with legions of cranes like tall, clawed insects and, beyond, shining skyscrapers probing for the heavens with fingers of silver and grey. Huge petrochemical plants of stubby white cylinders with domed roofs guarded the harbour on crowded, flat islands, and giant flares of excess gas burning brought to mind the futurism of 'Blade Runner'.

The island of Singapore itself was largely level, with just a few low lying hills to the east, near the border with Malaysia, and one bigger hill in the center. It was hard to believe that this gateway between east and west, smaller than the area of Greater London, housed so much heavy industry and was home to more than five million people of diverse ethnicities.

Passing docks occupied by tankers which made *Priscilla* look like a scale model, the pilot followed radio instructions from the harbourmaster's office and found their way to a mooring. Here the grandeur of the enormous port was absent and they docked at an ill-kempt, dusty wharf between vessels which were even more run down than theirs. Sounds of huge machinery, boat engines and the distantly thunderous tone of a busy metropolis greeted their ears.

It was warm; very warm, and terribly humid. Despite having crossed Africa and sailed an ocean there was nothing which could have prepared them for the muggy, hazy conditions in Singapore at this time of year. The heat itself was alright but, for British men unused to it, the humidity was choking. They found themselves sweating profusely and their clothes quickly became damp.

Singapore was a mesmerising flurry of activity despite the unusual paucity of private vehicles. There was an infestation of the human kind, with people walking rapidly or cycling everywhere. Apart from these the wide, modern roads were filled with commercial vehicles, many of which must have been associated with the business of the enormous port. Although an industrialised city, Singapore was blessed with green foliage everywhere, grass lining the roadsides and lush palms and deciduous trees the central reservations.

They didn't see a single house although there must have been some. At least, there was nothing to compare with the British idiom. The concrete canyons were bounded by endless apartment buildings, underscoring the old adage about how, if one cannot spread out, one must build up. Singaporeans seemed content to live on top of and in close proximity to each other. Unlike Nouadhibou and Djibouti, everything in the commercial and residential areas seemed laudably clean and cared for.

Middleton was happy to stay on board the boat whilst TDR.12 conducted their business, so they took care of a few details. Wilson, of course, contacted his ladyfriend from an internet café. McKinley acquired several packets of cigarettes and Carter complained that he couldn't source a proper beer anywhere. An hour later they set about finding the venue where Makaru held his meetings.

Locating the church, however, proved to be more challenging than expected as Singapore was flooded with places of worship; temples, shrines, mosques, synagogues and churches of every persuasion. They'd made enquiries about Makaru with eight churches and met with blank stares before even hearing about the 'Ecumenical Assembly of the Kingdom', a name which ticked all the right boxes. The Presbyterian minister who spoke of it did so with disdain, dourly commenting that its leadership and in particular the visiting preacher Abel Makaru were departing orthodoxy and promoting every heresy under the sun.

"How do you keep *this* secret?" frowned Carter, staring up at the impressive building. It was a tall beige edifice, artfully decorated with religious symbols of every tradition they knew and many they'd never heard of. Built in the style of an old, traditional church but with modern adornment and facilities, the Assembly bore towering stained glass windows, the pattern of which was impossible to discern from outside, and the heavy oak doors one might expect to find on a British stately home. It sat in an unlikely position at the junction of two relatively small streets, surrounded by the omnipresent apartment complexes.

A young East Asian man approached with a smile and eager eyes. It was impossible to tell whether he was of Chinese, Indonesian or Malay origin, but his enthusiasm for the Assembly was crystal clear.

"You want to come along?" he asked in excellent English with only a trace of accent.

"Aye," said McKinley. "When's the next meeting?"

"We have meetings every evening. Tonight's is at seven o'clock. Prophet Bellegarde will be speaking."

"How about Pastor Makaru?" asked Carter. "We've heard good things."

The young man's face bulged with joy, his eyes expanding. "Oh, he is a *man of God!*" he exclaimed, emphasising the last three words as though the Vatican leadership would look to Makaru for counsel.

Carter smiled. "That's what we heard. What are his services like?"

The guy laughed ebulliently. "You have to be here! I just can't describe it. The spirit *moves*. Miracles, impartation, healings... *he* is the one who will usher in the Kingdom!" His face fell a little. "Well, in my opinion."

"That sounds like our guy," said Wilson.

The man nodded, his jet black hair bouncing. "Well Pastor Makaru will be here tomorrow night, but you should come see Prophet Bellegarde as well. Then next week we have Bishop Tan from South Korea."

"Thanks pal," said McKinley, steering his group back toward the docks. They had more than a day to prepare, and he was in want of a good, civilised meal.

When they returned to the Ecumenical Assembly of the Kingdom the next evening it was already getting dark and there was a queue three blocks long to get into the place. Ushers were busy marshalling the attendees into an orderly line under the watchful eyes of two police officers. With half an hour to go before the service, the doors finally swung wide and the crowd flooded in.

"We all set then?" McKinley asked Carter as they approached from a couple of streets away.

"Good to go," replied the weapons tech, patting the laptop under his arm.

"Ready as I'll ever be," said Wilson. He was dressed in brightly coloured clothes with the intent of fitting in. Brown canvas sneakers and lightweight blue jeans adorned his lower half whilst his torso bore a red and yellow tie-dye T-shirt. Around his neck were a couple of inexpensive silver chains and a purple braid whilst his right wrist carried the archetypal WWJD bracelet.

"Aye, okay," acknowledge McKinley. "You'd best hop to it."

"Roger that," said Wilson, and sprinted off.

"Hey Willy," called Carter. Wilson stopped and turned back.

"Don't drink the Kool Aid!" smiled Carter. Wilson gave them a thumbs up and headed off.

"And remember," added McKinley, "what kills you doesn't make you stronger!"

Wilson's running figure waved a hand.

McKinley and Carter made their way to the back of the lineup at a leisurely pace and didn't even look in Wilson's direction. Playing the 'grey man', they wore plain clothes in muted colours and did their best to be unnoticeable.

"You ever been to something like this?" asked McKinley quietly.

"Once or twice," said Carter. "It's not really my thing."

McKinley huffed. "What should I expect?"

"You've been to church before?"

"Aye, 'course I have."

"Well imagine that but with a few hundred percent more lunacy. It's what they used to call a revival service. There'll be people speaking in funny languages, falling down... all sorts of oddness."

McKinley rolled his eyes. "Great."

They filed inside the huge church, surrounded by many eager believers. The roof was much higher than it had looked from outside and huge cylindrical light clusters hung from it like weights from a grandfather clock mechanism. Whilst the architect had obviously done their best to honour tradition, pews had been supplanted by rows of comfortable chairs of maroon fabric and honey-hued wood which were arranged in graceful curves around the stage, to which the dividing aisles pointed like the spokes of a wheel.

The interior of the impressive building was roughly circular, with the smaller but no less impressive circle of the stage at the opposite side from the big front doors. The stage was raised by about five feet and covered by the same plush, dull pink carpet as the rest of the auditorium. At its front was the same pulpit they'd seen in the photograph and behind, in prime position to attract the eye, was an enormous stained glass window, its multicoloured panes radiating from a central geometric motif. Angels and human beings were depicted in worship around the periphery of the window, and across the bottom was the Latin inscription 'Nam Libertatem'.

"See that?" asked Carter, having to raise his voice a little over the crowd's expectant hubbub.

"Something about liberty, obviously."

Carter smirked humourlessly. "Literally, 'For Freedom'."

"No shit!" remarked McKinley, casting his mind back to their visit to Strood, where he'd acquired a pen with the very same motto from Martin McCulloch's houseboat. They'd later found an identical pen in Heinmarsh's home office.

"Let's sit here," McKinley suggested, indicating a row which was to the rear. They took their seats near one of the diverging aisles. Wilson, they saw, was front and center as planned.

McKinley noticed that the logo from the window appeared in a number of places; the lectern, posters, the back panel of the keyboard player's instrument and several of the pillars. The ushers all had it on their badges and clearly it was a central theme. "What's with this symbol, d'you think?" he asked.

The logo was circular, its lower half resembling part of a doubled solar wheel but with the rim widening at its center to form a crescent moon. The semicircular top half contained a smaller circle which itself surrounded a five pointed star based on the geometry of an equilateral triangle. Through the center of the star was a small circular hole which McKinley quickly realised was the radial center of the design.

"It'd be hard to make it more inter-religious," murmured Carter.

"Explain," demanded McKinley.

"The bulging rim and star? That's the crescent and star of Islam. The horizontal and vertical bars and the medium circle? That's an ankh, and there's your pyramid, which is why the star's not a perfect pentagram. The diagonal bars are like a so-called Nero's cross AKA the peace symbol, and you can make the bottom half of a Roman cross with the rest. Not to mention the top circle looks like the all-seeing eye."

A large projection screen descended from above the stage, displaying lyrics, and the service kicked off with some loud and energetic songs. The band was admirably well rehearsed, sounding as good as any pop record. After about twenty minutes of dancing and clapping though, the tempo decreased into more reflective, worshipful music. McKinley noticed Carter trying to join in on some of the songs, whilst he himself just stood there feeling like a pork pie at a *bar mitzvah*. This 'fitting in' lark was overrated.

"Just a small point," whispered Carter during one of the slower numbers, "notice how the words don't mention any deity specifically."

"I hadn't noticed," confessed McKinley, to whom the lyrics were a cross between syrupy love songs and the Nuremberg Rallies.

At the end of the music everyone sat down and a minister gave a long talk about supporting the work of The Assembly. Ushers moved through the congregation like a maritime grid search and McKinley and Carter each donated twenty Singapore dollars so as not to appear out-of-the-ordinary.

The minister led a short prayer and then introduced the guest speaker to a rapturous welcome.

"Religious superstar," declared Carter, leaning toward his friend. "Joseph and his Technicolor coat; he could recite the phone book and everyone'd hoist their Bic."

Pastor Abel Makaru appeared from a door at the back of the stage, walking slowly toward the lectern, his head bowed in apparent humility as the applause surged even louder. He wasn't an especially striking figure, being about level with Carter's 5'10", but he certainly had a *presence* about him. His entrance was accompanied by some pomp and circumstance from the band and a change in the stage lighting to focus attention on the central lectern. The pastor wore the same outfit that they'd seen in the photograph; dark robe over expensive shirt – neither starchy like a suit nor too casual, but definitely ceremonial. His left breast pocket bore the circular logo, embroidered in bold scarlet.

Behind the pastor four men filed onto the stage and spread out in a line behind him. They were strapping lads dressed in purple tunics which made them look like priests, and each had a large, gold version of the symbol on a chain around their neck. Obviously they were bodyguards.

The applause went on for a good couple of minutes, during which the man under the spotlight bowed politely to every quadrant of the room. When he did speak, though, the whole sanctum fell to silence, leaving only the whine of air conditioning and, beyond, the unending murmur of traffic.

McKinley leaned forward, his chin on his folded hands, curious to hear what the speaker would say and how it might pertain to their mission. Greater yet was his curiosity as to how rhetoric might convince people to blow themselves up. But before long McKinley found himself lost in the religiosity. There were so many terms he didn't understand that the context was wasted on him. Carter, on the other hand, paid rapt attention, even to the extent of making notes on his laptop.

McKinley heard a few things, though, which made him raise an eyebrow. The idea of laying oneself aside for this 'kingdom' that they were touting was brought to the fore, even to the extent that it sounded communist; absolute self denial in favour of the body politic. But McKinley knew that communism had always derailed itself through one thing; the various appetites—money, power and status—of those in charge. Yet as communism and atheism were best friends, this was diametrically different. There was considerable mention of the 'Universal Spirit' and how he, she or it wanted to enter the world through The Ambassadors Of The Godhead and their supposed kingdom. There was a big deal made of 'the mission field', and how the missionary's purpose was the most profound obligation. The whole spiel was clearly targeted at those who already had a religious background.

Carter turned to him. "You see what I mean?" he whispered. "It's all straw man arguments and circular reasoning. It's like Hegelian dialectics except the synthesis *always* underscores his dogma."

McKinley had no idea what Carter meant by that so he nodded as though he did.

Carter raised an eyebrow slyly and explained. "Everything he says is designed to create dissatisfaction in the listener and sets his religion up as the answer."

"Could be dangerous."

"You see how the crowd are hanging on every word? I think he's about ready for the altar call."

"Hmm." McKinley nodded. Now their Trojan horse would enter the city gate.

In the front row, Wilson couldn't deny that Makaru's preaching was powerful. Although his mind was firmly set on his mission, some of the sentiments expressed resonated deeply with him. Care for nature, respect for all, equality – all these were fine and admirable. But to think that this eloquent Asian man was behind a cult of suicide bombers brought him sharply down to Earth.

Wilson could feel the anticipation in the room rising. There was something intangible going on; a vibe, a chemistry, a feeling that was touching everyone around. Whether he wanted to or not, Wilson started to think of himself as part of this crowd of worshippers. These people—mostly younger than himself although there were some older—were caught up in something *special*. Whether it was truly divine or some psychological thing, Wilson could feel it. This troubled him, but he was there with purpose; he had a job to do. Then the altar call came.

"The most serious disciples will make this leap of faith," said Makaru from the lectern, his voice having descended to a deep tenor, "because you will allow the Universal Spirit to erase your past. You will abandon your old, earthly life. When you put your hand to the plough you must *never* turn back. To do so would make you an enemy of the Universal Spirit, a blasphemer. But! Now that you feel led to give your life alongside me in the service of the Kingdom, I adjure you to come up here!"

The preacher nodded to the band, who began playing something which sounded like an old hymn. Wilson couldn't place it. He felt unpleasantly self conscious but, as arranged, he moved out of his row and ascended the steps. Only when he reached the top and looked back, the spotlights blinding him a little, did he realise how full the place was. An usher took him gently by the arm and guided him.

Makaru continued his appealing from the front whilst Wilson realised he was the first of a growing line near the back of the stage. Then there were two rows forming, and then three. The band stopped playing when it seemed like no more would make their way up to the stage, and an expectant hush fell over the sanctum.

Just do what everyone else does, thought Wilson. That was Carter's advice. But it seemed that he'd been a little too hasty in his approach and, whatever happened, he was going to be first.

A Herculean bull of a man approached, about the same height as Wilson and smiling disingenuously. His name badge said 'Prophet Luis Bellegarde'. His square jaw bore a distinct five o'clock shadow although his head was almost completely bald with just a narrow band of dark grey travelling around the back from one ear to another, and his skin was rough as though he worked outside. Bellegarde's deeply set grey eyes were somehow dead, like an animal's, and Wilson felt uncomfortable in his presence. Stay on mission Willy, he told himself.

Wilson tried to look excited. Bellegarde leaned toward him and spoke in an American accent with more than a hint of French.

"You will serve the Kingdom Brother?"

"Yes," said Wilson. "I want to build the Kingdom!"

"You want the Universal Spirit to take away your past and give you a new life?"

"Yes sir, with all my heart." Crikey, this religious pretence was hard work.

"Then I will pray for you," grinned Bellegarde, showing teeth, "and the spirit will give you a new life!" He placed his shovel-like left hand gently on Wilson's head, lodging the thumb of his right in his belt.

Wilson felt something cold spray across his eyes, and out went the lights.

015: The Island

McKinley and Carter saw Wilson's body fall limply backwards into the hands of a waiting usher who laid him carefully on the floor. As Makaru's balding colleague went down the line of converts, each was overcome the same way.

"Is this supposed to happen?" asked McKinley, concerned.

"Uh, it's kinda normal," answered Carter, his face doubtful. "Except that... looked a bit more real than I'd like. We should be ready to intervene."

"This is what we wanted," McKinley reminded him. "Someone on the inside. He's just playing the part."

Carter grimaced. "We hope," he murmured.

They stayed until the end of the service, when ushers became busy asking attendees to leave. All in all it had been a weird experience for McKinley and reinforced his dislike of all things religious. Some of the bizarre things he'd seen didn't seem to belong in a church but then, he reasoned, neither did he.

Carter prodded the arm of an usher whose name badge said 'Sister Drusilla' and asked what was going to happen to those knocked out by the supposed supernatural force.

"The Universal Spirit will minister to them," said the cheerful Indian girl with huge earrings, beguiling eyes and a gold dress which revealed such a generosity of cleavage that Carter considered it irreverent in these surroundings but nonetheless hot. "Then they join Pastor Makaru's assembly to serve the Kingdom."

"Oh yeah?" replied Carter enthusiastically. "Where's that?"

"I don't know," she smiled, "but Pastor Makaru, peace be upon him, will bless their comings and goings."

"Right... great," said Carter, unconvinced. "Hey, one more question; what's the symbol?"

"It is the *Basmolet!*" she gasped deferentially, lowering her eyes fearfully as though to even speak of it invited divine retribution. "It draws together and focuses our lives. It gives us a visible truth to meditate on."

"That's... interesting," said Carter, more to himself than anyone else.

"May you be blessed to see the Kingdom," she chirped, and went back to her duties. Carter wandered outside the building to see something which could hardly be more familiar: McKinley lighting up. Once they'd moved away from the thinning crowd the team leader spoke.

"Tracking good?"

"Yes of course *at this range*," Carter frowned. "This is easy." He opened the laptop and checked. Sure enough, Wilson's beacon was pulsating just a few hundred feet away.

"See?"

"Okay," muttered McKinley between puffs. "I guess we wait."

Nearly an hour later, as they sat in a small coffee shop near The Assembly, Carter slapped McKinley on the arm. "He's moving!"

"Let's go!" said McKinley. They rose from the table leaving a handful of Singapore dollars and set out into the night.

"Definitely motorised," said Carter. The tracking dot was following the streets exactly.

McKinley thrust out his hand to hail a cab.

"Going south," announced Carter.

A minivan with a black body, yellow roof and blue topsign screeched to a halt right by them and they jumped in, Carter issuing rapid fire directions to the confused driver. When McKinley waved a wad of money at him his confusion seemed to be replaced by determination and he started driving like he meant it.

They joined a major route heading west. Wilson's tracker was only a mile or so ahead.

"Must go faster!" McKinley instructed the cabbie. The man eagerly toed the pedal.

It only took minutes to catch up with the large bus that contained Wilson and the other converts. They stayed back about thirty meters and in a different lane. The bus was marked with the logo of The Ecumenical Assembly Of The Kingdom, the same curious mixture of different religious symbols. Curtains were drawn across the windows. McKinley and Carter shared a look. Something odd was going on.

They followed the vehicle west for more than fourteen miles, then the coach turned south toward the docks. Keeping their distance carefully, they observed it reaching a gated road, one of many leading into the world's largest and busiest port. After a guard spoke to the driver, the gate opened and the bus drove in.

McKinley jumped out as the cab came up to the gate and ran to the guardhouse, its approach encircled by the bland green of fluorescent lighting.

"Can you open the gate please?"

The guard smiled, reaching for a clipboard to which was attached a very long list. "You have a pass?"

"Here's my pass," answered McKinley, displaying a handful of money.

The guard, his eyes having retreated back into their sockets, looked tempted. He wiggled his fingers toward the cash for just a moment then shook his head.

"I'm sorry sir, I think you came to the wrong gate."

Damn, thought McKinley, where's a dishonest man when you need one? He got back into the cab.

"Are there other ways onto this dock?"

"No sir, sorry," replied their driver.

He took them back to the main road and McKinley signalled Carter to get out.

"Thanks," said McKinley quickly. "Here, this is yours. Get out of here." He handed the money to the taxi driver. It was at least ten times their fare. The man drove off with appreciative hollers.

McKinley looked back at the dock. Whilst trying to negotiate with the guard he'd noticed a long and somewhat dilapidated fence around the property, bordering a small drainage canal.

"This way," he said to Carter, and disappeared into the undergrowth by the little watercourse. They forded the stream and, breaking a couple of panels off the fence, were in.

"Hard hat area," said Carter, pointing to his head, "and coveralls."

McKinley spat. If they looked out of place there'd be questions. "Let's find some," he ordered. They set off walking quickly in the direction the coach had taken.

McKinley saw what he needed: a gentlemen's bathroom. They entered to find one man washing his hands. At McKinley's signal Carter quickly jumped the man, putting his neck in a blood choke hold and squeezing hard. Just at that moment another man walked in, looked wide-eyed at the scene and made a run for it.

McKinley dashed after him as the man ran back toward the guardhouse. With extra exertion McKinley caught up with the worker as he passed a row of parked cars. The man yelled, but McKinley quickly snatched at his jacket and wrapped a hand round his mouth. He dragged the man down between two cars, punched him soundly in the face to disorient him and quickly applied the same kind of sleeper hold as Carter had done.

Dressed as a dock worker in a yellow hard hat and dull beige coveralls with reflective strips on the knees, elbows and shoulders, McKinley joined Carter at the entrance to the bathroom. Their borrowed outfits were almost identical.

"Snap." said Carter.

McKinley ignored it. "Where's your mark?" he asked.

Carter angled his head toward a cubicle. "Tied to the throne."

"Let's move."

Carter took a quick look at the laptop screen and said "this way." They set off at jogging pace.

In fifteen minutes they'd found the coach, parked and empty. It was on the quay by several moderately sized ships, the nearest of which appeared to be making preparations to sail. Looking from the cover of a building's corner they saw men carrying stretchers up the gangplank of a modern vessel that was about twice the size of *Priscilla*. With a hull of bright blue and pristine white superstructure she looked like a freighter, but what was being loaded would seem to suggest otherwise. The ship's name was *Dhul-Nun*.

"Bloody hell!" gasped McKinley. "They're still knocked out!"

"So that's his game," said Carter. "Cart 'em off while they're insensible. That's how he keeps his location secret." He looked at the screen. "Willy's definitely aboard."

McKinley ducked back into cover, thinking hard. He decided that their only option was to follow the vessel in Middleton's *Priscilla*. Even if the tracker went out of its thirty five mile range they'd still be able to see *Dhul-Nun* on radar for some distance.

He cursed and they took off.

Having stripped themselves of the unfortunate dockers' attire, McKinley and Carter grabbed another taxi back toward their own mooring, both keenly aware of the urgency of their situation. The *Dhul-Nun* would be sailing soon, so McKinley told Carter to call Middleton. There was no answer.

They reached their dock quickly and again McKinley made the cabbie's day. He felt like a traitor to his Scottish traditions, but these guys needed *incentive*, and on the *Priscilla* there was more money than they knew what to do with.

Before they reached their mooring they realised that something was wrong. The reflection of blue flashing lights was their first clue.

"Hold on," said McKinley as they reached the last corner before the quay, and they came to a stop by some stacked shipping containers. They cautiously looked round at *Priscilla* and McKinley swore a small city back to the stone age.

There were four police cars arranged in a semicircle around *Priscilla's* mooring as well as vehicles from the port authority. Officers with automatic weapons patrolled the boat's decks and a very unhappy looking Blake Middleton was kneeling by the water's edge, two rifles held to his head and his hands cuffed behind his back.

"Oh my freakin'... *this is SO NOT GOOD!*" ground Carter as his hopes took a sound beating. "The gear!"

McKinley looked like he'd just heard about the passing of a close relative. "The money! The weapons."

He closed his eyes and breathed deeply for a few seconds. The light of their mission had just been snuffed out. Everything they'd acquired to reach their objectives had been on that boat and was now in the hands of the Singaporean authorities. The vessel itself, computers, tools, gadgets, ammunition... all was lost. McKinley lifted his hands to cover his face, deep stress tearing at his professional composure. What the hell would they do now? Their mission was dead in the water, as thoroughly sunk as a lead balloon.

Carter was also kicked in the crotch by this unbelievable circumstance, but he had the presence of mind to say "let's leave" in a whisper filled with tension and bitter discouragement.

The sense of loss and failure was threatening to crush McKinley, but he kept telling himself that he was a fighter. There was another option, somewhere. He just had to get over this ultra-disappointment and try to think something out. It's like a Rubik's Cube, he told himself. You *know* the answer's in there somewhere; you just have to keep twisting until you see how to reach it.

The other massive problem this shitty luck created was that an unconscious Wilson was steaming away from them to heck-knows-where with no tactical support and no option to pursue. Damn everything, thought McKinley. They should have sneaked aboard that bloody ship when they found it. Either way they'd have had no kitnology.

What *did* they have left? Carter had that laptop and his phones, the newer of which he hadn't even switched on. McKinley had a few hundred Singapore dollars and they both had knives. Holy shit it wasn't much. They were absolutely back to square one. DAMN EVERYTHING!

He was about to have to stop and breathe again when Carter suddenly caught his arm.

"Pilotage!" he exclaimed.

"What?" said McKinley in a voice so perturbed that it sounded alien to his own ears.

They stopped by the entrance to a floating dock for private vessels and Carter turned toward him. "They're under pilotage! There's a Singapore pilot aboard who's got to get off sometime."

"Will they slow down or stop?"

"Probably not, but there's going to be a launch heading for them. We could be on it."

The most feeble spark of hope re-ignited in McKinley's gut. Yes, maybe they could get to the *Dhul-Nun*, and maybe they could even find a way on board. They had no gear at all, but they couldn't leave Wilson to whatever fate might befall him.

McKinley raised the obvious objection. "We don't know where it leaves from."

"*Shit!* We are so screwed."

McKinley looked beyond his friend, the tiny spark growing imperceptibly. "Not necessarily."

Ahead they saw the bulk of the *Dhul-Nun* and, between them, the pilot launch. It was racing, as were they, to catch the much bigger vessel so that the expert navigator could disembark.

Stealing this motorboat had been a pain in the ass and Carter had cut his hand badly bypassing the ignition but they were back in the game, if by the skin of their teeth. Now they just had to get on board. McKinley had tied a big socket wrench to the motorboat's mooring line which, thankfully, looked about twice as long as they'd need.

As Carter steered, they saw the pilot launch draw alongside *Dhul-Nun* and then it was their turn. Controlling the engine speed as carefully as he could, Carter brought them alongside the vessel's stern. Their little motorboat started to shake and sway in the turbulence created by *Dhul-Nun's* powerful propellers.

They had to move quickly. The *Dhul-Nun* may or may not slow down to transfer the pilot, but either way it would be the only time her crew might be distracted. Carter threw McKinley a hand signal and the latter readied his rope.

Suddenly the turbulence rocked them violently, sending McKinley sprawling on the foredeck. Landing on his side, he realised that they'd have to back away from the propwash and he'd have to throw harder. Clearly Carter understood this too and, as McKinley picked himself up, Carter tried to steer a fine line between the ship's massive wake and being too far away.

Gathering his strength and concentrating on his aim, McKinley threw the socket wrench hard. It clattered off the side of the ship and came back down at him, landing in the water between them and the *Dhul-Nun's* hull plating. McKinley quickly grabbed it and pulled, fearing that it might get caught in the bigger vessel's screws. He raised the soaking rope again and steeled himself for another try.

Same result, damn it! McKinley swore, gathering up the line to go again. The third attempt went over the gunwales, but didn't catch on anything. Getting desperate, knowing that the diversion of the pilot launch would soon become irrelevant, McKinley turned to Carter and motioned with his hand, indicating that Carter should swing toward the wall of steel as he threw.

Carter obliged, steering their little boat dangerously close to the speeding vessel, and McKinley thrust the socket wrench upward with all his might. It disappeared over the side of the *Dhul-Nun* just as their boat tipped way over to port. McKinley lost his footing and slid straight down into the dark harbour water.

Just before he went under, McKinley felt a tug on the rope and he gripped like mad, his hand tightening like a vice around the soggy cord. As cold seawater rushed over his body, he felt lifted up and realised that their boat was rolling the other way now, toward the *Dhul-Nun's* hull. Through blurry eyes he saw water flooding into their hull and Carter struggling at the controls then leaping up toward the foredeck.

Their boat passed down and from under McKinley and he managed to get a second hand on the rope. His body slammed against the big vessel's hull, then he was dangling with his feet raking the surface of the violently moving water. Eyes wide with dismay, he saw their boat going under, dragged into the depths by the enormous suction of the ship's propellers.

Carter leaped with everything in him as their boat was sucked into oblivion and caught McKinley's leg. McKinley grunted with the pain. He was lifting them now, both of whom were being dragged toward those murderous propellers. About four hundred pounds of spec ops personnel were in his soaking cold yet burning hands. He was about to slide off the rope, and there was nothing he could do!

There was a ghastly rumble from underneath them and McKinley saw smashed pieces of white fibreglass being ejected into the *Dhul-Nun's* wake. The props had chewed up the motorboat and spat it out.

Suddenly he felt movement. Carter was pulling himself up McKinley's body.

"*Just don't let go!*" shouted his friend.

McKinley renewed his grip, feeling intense pain as the rope dug fiercely into his palms. Carter, a terrible expression of agonised determination on his face, reached McKinley's level. "My turn," he growled, and kept moving upward. "Grab my belt!"

Carter pulled McKinley up about eight feet, and the team leader was incredibly grateful for his friend's enormous strength. Carter was probably the only person he knew who could have pulled off this feat of power lifting.

McKinley wound his legs around the rope as Carter did the same from above, dripping saltwater onto his friend. They climbed with intense difficulty, but once Carter had made it to the deck he pulled McKinley up again.

They lay on the deck in a soggy pile, unendingly thankful to be on the ship. McKinley felt completely spent and he couldn't imagine how much pain Carter was in.

"Lost the lappy," choked Carter.

McKinley replied through fatigue. "Still got your phone?"

Carter thrust an inquiring hand to his breast pocket. "Yeah, both."

"Okay. We should hide," McKinley gurgled, rolling over to his front.

"You no hide! You go captain now!" ordered a high pitched voice from above.

They looked up to see a young man standing above them, holding a rifle as if it was a broom with which he was pretending. Indeed, he looked possessed of much more experience with the latter than the former. His brown face with sunken cheeks was pock-marked, yet his eyes were fierce under an unruly mop of jet black hair. He looked terrified and this was doubtless his first incident with pirates, stowaways, or whatever he thought they were.

Carter picked himself up, slowly raising his hands. His left palm had a giant gouge in it and was bleeding profusely. That horrible climb had exacerbated the wound.

"You hurt!" said the gunman, pointing with his jaw.

"Brother," groaned Carter, smiling as best he could. "Please don't think badly of us; we just want to see the Kingdom."

"You no see Kingdom! You see captain!" The rifle-broom waved threateningly.

"We missed the bus," explained Carter, turning on the charm through his pain. "We're disciples of the Kingdom too. I'm Brother Christian and this is Brother Ioannes. What's your name please?"

The man hesitated. "Brother Jokshan."

"Jokshan, Jokshan," repeated Carter, chewing it over. "It's a godly name. Well Brother Jokshan, we were so excited to get to the island that when we missed the bus we had to get aboard somehow. We've got important mission work to continue for Pastor Makaru when we get there."

"You never been before?"

"No," smiled Carter. "We were recruited and trained in Europe. This is our first chance to go to the island and meet the leaders."

My bastard scissors, thought McKinley, this kid's actually buying into Carter's bullshit.

"Heh!" chuckled Jokshan, lowering the weapon, "you fighter!"

"Yes!" affirmed Carter. "We're Pastor's special forces for the Kingdom. I know we shouldn't be aboard, and even a faithful servant like you shouldn't know we exist, but please can you help us? We'll be able to get you a special commendation from Pastor. Remember; in as much as you did it for the least of these, you did it for the Universal Spirit."

"I... don't know." Jokshan looked around nervously.

McKinley pulled a soggy note from his pocket, feeling complaint from numerous pulled muscles. "This'll grease the wheels," he smiled.

Seeing the money Jokshan's eyes took on a pleasing greed. "You call me Joko," he beamed.

Joko the deckhand turned out to be better than helpful once money had been exchanged and, convinced of their need for secrecy, quickly found McKinley and Carter an unused storage locker in which they could hide for the voyage. It wasn't much, being a rusty, dusty little metal room in the bowels of the *Dhul-Nun*, but under the circumstances nobody was likely to complain. Joko left them alone for about half an hour, but when he came back he'd raided the ship's stores and brought with him a first aid kit and some food and canned pop. Carter cleaned and bound his wound carefully, answering McKinley's question of whether it would need stitches with an unhappy nod.

They learned that the voyage to the island would take six days, so they settled in for the long haul as best they could, lining their 'state room' with sacks and sharing the space with a spare chemical toilet that Joko had found them. Their Indonesian friend was an absolute diamond, becoming a welcome sight whenever he thought he wouldn't be missed, and he appeared to be one of few that ever ventured into this part of the ship. With each visit, McKinley paid Joko, and it appeared that he was enjoying bucking the system for profit. His cheerful visits became an eagerly anticipated relief from the humdrum.

Starting to feel a weight of concern, they needed to establish Wilson's status other than simply being on the same ship, and asked Joko where the new converts were.

"They learning," answered the Indonesian, nodding like the dog toy one sometimes sees on the parcel shelf of the car in front. "They sleep and learn. Mostly."

McKinley looked at Carter and sensed those wheels grinding into action again. The weapons tech was casting his eyes around thoughtfully in typical style.

"How do they learn, Brother?" asked Carter.

"Like you do. Like I do. Magnetic headset." Joko lifted his hands and pointed to his ears. "Pastor talk to them while they sleep."

"Oh," said Carter. "Is he on board?"

"No, it recorded. Pastor—peace on him—already on island. He gots seaplane."

McKinley looked round at Carter. "Hypnosis?"

Carter pursed his lips in thought for a moment. "Not *exactly*. This is more what they call 'sleep teaching' I think. It's not a proven methodology. Joko, what did you mean by 'magnetic headset'?"

"It gots magnetic fields," nodded Joko as though feeling cleverer than usual. "Magnetic fields change you brain." He raised his hands and tapped his index fingers on his temples.

McKinley saw Carter's eyes take on *that* look. Something had fired his imagination.

"You no remember learn?" said Joko. "Me too. Nobody do. That how it work."

McKinley thanked Joko, who went about his business. Once their helpful friend was sufficiently distant, the Scotsman spoke. "Aye then," he said, "what's on your mind?"

"Magnetic fields," answered Carter. "You know what they can do to you?"

"Not unless you tell me."

Having got his preferred response, Carter continued. "They can mess with your brain. Stimulate growth, cause seizures, change your speech, induce emotions, etcetera, etcetera. But the fascinating thing is that your brain can get so relaxed that it doesn't really think." Leaning back on the dirty steel, Carter held out his hands and shrugged. "Imagine the damage *that* could do."

McKinley didn't think he could imagine it, but it sounded bad. As they consumed the spam sandwiches that Joko had made, he wondered what this latest revelation could mean, especially for Wilson.

The days passed with withering slowness and increasing concern for the absent third of their team. Seeing nothing but the inside of a dreary locker and listening to the constant guttural drone of the huge engines was hard even on the most determined soul. There was no daylight and even the electric light that peeped through the louvers in the door was pallid and weak. Temperatures were high even at night and McKinley found himself sympathising with Carter's insomnia. The air wasn't too bad, but they both suspected that they'd become used to it and that after the voyage their first taste of fresh air would be like the best thing in the world.

McKinley tried to use the time to plan ahead but there was so little known about the situation, their destination or anything else that to scheme thus was hard. It occurred to him that to most people this adventure would appear far more trouble than its worth, and that they were certainly going the long way around to secure their quarry. Nonetheless, McKinley was committed. Heinmarsh could still detonate a nuke any day, and that *had* to be prevented.

Despite its proven design, Carter's old smartphone refused to work this far below deck, the hull of the *Dhul-Nun* forming an effective Faraday cage that blocked signals, and they didn't want to activate his new model for fear of being tracked. It was far safer to stay incommunicado, but the lack of contact with anyone except each other and the cheerfully ingenuous deckhand was torture in itself. Carter's left fingers were starting to stiffen and he expressed concern that the wound was becoming inflamed.

And so the hours of near-darkness stretched out like the miles of an endless road, each the same as the last.

A day before their supposed arrival at the island, Joko brought something really useful: a chart.

"This island," he declared, pointing with a stubby, grimy and black-nailed finger as he sat on top of the chemical toilet, chewing on a chocolate and peanut bar. "I only find out soon."

Carter smiled. "Recently."

"Yeah, that what I say." Joko seemed a little resentful that his terrible English was being impugned.

McKinley looked closer at the island, which was tiny at this scale. It was shaped like a fat sausage but with a broken coastline and many smaller islands around it. "Rubakang," he read.

"I'm no wiser," said Carter, whose geographical knowledge was usually excellent. "Never heard of it."

Joko grinned. "It nice place. Lot of nice bird, jungle, mountain. We dock at Hosao."

"Aye," said McKinley, looking closer with the magnifying glass on Carter's Swiss Army knife. "I see it. Where's Wolf River?"

"West and north." Joko's finger prodded in the direction of the coastline diametrically opposite Hosao. "Not on map. Hosao east, Wolf River west." The young deckhand finished his snack, made his excuses and left them again.

"First thing we need to do," said McKinley, "is fix up that hand."

"I'm not going to argue," said Carter. "You'd think they've got medical facilities."

"I guess we'll find out. Anyway, next job: recon. We have to know this place inside out. Our primary target is that warhead, *if* it's here. We need eyes on Heinmarsh—again, *if* he's here—and we need to gauge the suicide bombing threat."

"Agreed."

"Thirdly: supplies. The guards have guns. I'd like to lay our hands on some."

"And any tech we can grab."

"Aye."

Carter addressed the analogical elephant in the room. "What about Willy?"

McKinley looked round, a tiny hint of uncertainty in his eyes. "We'll contact him when it's safe. He knows what to do."

"Try not to make it worse," griped Carter as McKinley inexpertly attempted to stitch his wound.

They sat in the darkened doctor's surgery in the village of Hosao, the only featured point on the map of Rubakang. The building was a small, whitewashed cube with a little reception-cum-waiting room, a simple bathroom and the doctor's office, with an examination table and just enough equipment to treat smaller injuries and provide basic birthing facilities. More serious situations were presumably sailed to another island.

Having held back until disembarkation of the 'converts' was complete, the TDR.12 lads elected to further stay their own egress until nightfall and, to avoid any confrontations, jumped over the seaward side of the *Dhul-Nun*, swimming ashore well away from the dock and hiding in the undergrowth by the beach until they dried out.

Hosao was in darkness apart from the lights around the quay, leaving the little town somewhat mysterious but making their task easier. They'd quickly located and broken into the doctor's office where, thankfully, there was the equipment needed to clean and sew up the ugly gash in Carter's left palm.

"If you'd shut up and hold still it'd be a lot easier," replied McKinley, casting his eyes momentarily to the torch that Carter held above their heads.

"Well don't take all night then. I want it done *before* the anaesthetic wears off."

"Nearly there."

After a couple more strokes, McKinley stood up from his work. "How's that?" he asked.

Carter looked down and flexed the wound a couple of times. "Hey," he said, in a surprised tone, "not bad for an amateur. Thanks mate."

"Aye. Let's douse that light, get whatever you need and blow this joint. It's a long way to Wolf River."

"Roger that," answered Carter, re-wrapping the wound.

They stuffed a bag with what amounted to a roughly-compiled field medical kit, grabbed as much bottled water and other supplies as they could carry and exited the building by the ill-secured window into the pleasant warmth of the tropical night. The doctor's premises were on their own little driveway with its single solitary streetlight, away from the haphazard cluster of lesser-illuminated cabins and huts that formed the bulk of Hosao. From the crossroads at the end of the drive, the mud road descended south to where they could make out the *Dhul-Nun* moored to the tubular steel and wood dock, on the other side of which a small knot of slender canoes with wooden outriggers was roped together, indicating that Hosao was a fishing town but not mechanised. They estimated there to be less than fifty dwellings, with a tiny mosque, a disused church and a general store. The narrow beach where the waves licked languidly sported several huts built on stilts with what looked like palm frond roofs. In the opposite direction the road rose north-by-north-west into the darkness of the surrounding jungle, from the dense canopy of which emanated peculiar animalian sounds. Fresh tyre tracks betrayed the transport of Makaru's presumably still somnolent neophytes to Wolf River, so McKinley figured that the road must be at least half-decent.

They left all trace of Hosao's anaemic lighting behind and trudged up the road, following the eastern side of a mile long inlet at the mouth of which the village was located. According to Carter's mapping application, the road crossed the low hills of the island's eastern end and was barely visible even with the latest satellite imagery. It meandered a winding route, mostly following coastal lowlands but occasionally rising to crest one of the many arêtes descending from where a spine of mountains straddled the island, their height increasing dramatically to the west.

All in all they had just over twenty seven kilometers to walk. Night was their friend, hiding them, and therefore so was the phone's GPS receiver. Nebulous starlight diffusing through thin clouds enabled them to distinguish approximately between very dark and utterly black.

McKinley listened with curiosity to the ambience of the rainforest. There was a constant melange of chirping sounds like crickets and frogs, interspersed occasionally with echoing howls, whistles and growls. Suddenly, movement in the undergrowth nearby made him jump.

"Bloody hell," he snarled as Carter chuckled. "Look, is there anything on this island big enough to hurt us?"

"Not really," replied Carter, stifling his mirth. "Wild boars, marsupials, some interesting birds, some rodents—mostly rats, urgh," he shuddered, "—and hordes of different bats. No man-eaters."

"Wild boars are dangerous."

"Yeah, we should watch out for those buggers."

McKinley looked away for a moment, wanting to preserve his night vision as Carter consulted the sat-nav. "What else do we know about this place?"

"Forty six K long, ten and a half at the widest point. Maximum elevation about fourteen hundred meters—"

"That's forty five hundred feet. Pretty high."

"Yeah. Papua Province, Indonesia. Climate, equatorial as you can tell; environment, tropical rainforest; geology, volcanic with historical activity."

"Aye. Nothing else? Nothing tactical?"

Carter huffed. "Geez, what do you expect? Blueprints of their missile silos?"

McKinley didn't acknowledge as much, but he conceded internally that it was a bit of a daft question after all. "What about Wolf River?"

"Nothing. Not a sausage. Like the rest of Makaru's doings."

"Okay." McKinley looked at his watch, the Tritium tubes of its tiny hands indicating nearly eleven thirty. "We'll walk another three hours then get some rest. How about that?"

"Works for me."

Carter opened his eyes to the sounds of the jungle coming alive. Brilliant blades of sunlight sliced through the verdant canopy, speckling the underbrush with glowing dots and incandescing the thin mist which clung to the ground like a growth of mould.

They were camped on a mountainside several hundred meters from the road, overlooking it. Spread out before Carter was an amazing landscape of lush green and rolling hills, beyond which the beautiful blue ocean was dotted with islands bathed in sunshine. After six days in a metal box and a few hours of walking in near total darkness, his eyes drank in this wonderful vista with gusto.

Carter gently probed his cheek with two fingers. Just below his right eye was a lesion, a rounded swelling that itched as he touched it. Apparently the insect repellent they'd acquired from Hosao's doctor wasn't a hundred percent effective. He quickly checked his wounded hand and was relieved to see the little crawling sods hadn't got in there. He flicked at the bottom and sides of his beard, eager to remove any unwanted passengers.

McKinley was still sleeping so Carter went some distance away to void his bowels, marvelling at the lush jungle and the relief of the landscape. He estimated that they were about a hundred and twenty meters above sea level. Around him, countless organic spires yearned for the sky before bursting into verdurous foliage and arcing back down, trailing vines to the forest floor. Everywhere was green, greener and more green.

Carter was tucking into the last of Joko's spam sandwiches when McKinley rolled over and reached for his lighter. "Morning," he grunted, sparking up a smoke and inhaling deeply. "Bloody hell," he coughed, looking at the cigarette with deep displeasure, "these are shite."

"Indeed," smiled Carter. "You'd think a doctor would smoke better."

They moved out, working their way abreast of the road rather than along it. At the next ridge, Carter plotted a route that would take them even further away from the road but reduce the horizontal travel considerably. The other side of this coin was that it required some climbing, but would lead them to high ground where they could observe Wolf River before making their infil.

The going was tough due to the thickness of the undergrowth and the constantly changing slope. Who knew if human feet had ever trodden this same path before? They were further impeded by ravines and watercourses that were too small to appear in the satellite images, but with determination they pressed ahead. By mid-morning they were approaching their planned vantage point.

"Well, you don't see that every day," said Carter.

The glittering township of Wolf River was centered in the cusp of the bay, three and a half kilometers to their north-west and about four hundred meters below them, and was radically different from Hosao. Whereas the south-eastern settlement was comprised of roughly built houses and huts with reed roofs, Wolf River was like a tiny high-tech city sprouting incongruously from the rainforest.

Tall antennae with microwave and satellite dishes rose over the site like masts over a flotilla of sailing ships. Beneath these towers the buildings were geometrically arranged on a grid of pristine, modern roads. Most seemed of concrete construction, but here and there bright colours belied the use of more modern materials. Two were outstanding for their scale. The biggest was a huge round central block neither of concrete nor advanced composites but what appeared to be dark stone, with enormous windows that curved into the glass roof supported on a web of girders, with a tall, angled spire leaning over it like the gnomon of a sundial. At the top of the spire was a giant golden version of the *Basmolet* they'd observed in Singapore. The other noteworthy building was further away, perhaps another seven hundred meters, around the curve of the bay and forming a straight line with the township from where they were. It was a large concrete and steel cylinder of about the same width to height ratio as an oil drum, with many windows on three of its six floors. The roof was again replete with communications devices. Between the imposing cylinder and the township was a huge, flat greenhouse that sparkled in the sun as wisps of steam rose above it. Beyond the cylinder and partly obscured by it was a smaller structure that might be a garage or boathouse.

Lining the curve of the beach were four concrete pads with helicopters on them. So, thought McKinley, Makaru's even got his own airforce, probably with equipment supplied by his American friend. Near the helicopters were big stacks of fuel containers, several small all-wheel-drive vehicles and a bus; no doubt that was used to ferry the new converts from Hosao.

The beach itself was bisected by the town's eponymous watercourse, an unimpressive trickle no bigger than the tiny drainage canal they'd had to negotiate in Singapore. To call it a river was to lend it prestige that it didn't deserve. Its source unseen somewhere up the mountain, the stream snaked through the compound, barely visible from their altitude. It only asserted its existence at the beach, where it formed a small, fan shaped delta, displacing sand but leaving rocks undisturbed as it emptied placidly into the bay.

The modernity of Wolf River was glaringly inconsistent with its surroundings. It was a tiny enclave of technological progress in the primal jungle. It looked like the sort of base that scientists might establish when first exploring an alien world, but bigger and probably with a lot more budget behind it than any cash-starved space program.

Just under two kilometres up the mountainside south of Wolf River, a towering volcanic cone belched white cloud out across the jungle, overshadowing the town.

"That's never an active volcano?" exclaimed McKinley, who didn't much fancy being caught in an eruption.

"No. Have to be stupid to build this close," said Carter.

"What d'you think then, geothermal power? She mentioned a power plant."

Carter wagged a finger at his friend. "That's steam, not smoke, so yes, more than likely."

Suddenly a crashing in the undergrowth not far away gave them a start. McKinley tipped his head back toward the thicket they'd emerged from. Moving with great stealth, they retreated into cover.

A thin East Asian man came into view, carrying a Heinmarsh rifle. McKinley and Carter glanced at each other, hardly daring to breathe. Whilst it might seem ridiculous that a supposedly peaceful organisation would employ armed guards, the question of Heinmarsh's involvement with Makaru was definitely settled. The man stopped near where they'd been standing and looked around, listening.

This was obviously one of the compound's guards because, apart from the familiar advanced firearm, he wore the weird symbol on the left pocket of his beige shirt, which looked as though it had come from some down-on-its-luck military surplus store. Lower down he wore faded khaki shorts, hanging from the belt of which was a small megaphone, and his feet were embedded in tall camo-pattern hunting boots.

Shouldering his weapon, the guard raised the megaphone and spoke.

"You cannot leave! To turn back from your mission is sin! If you try to leave, we are under divine mandate to hunt you down and destroy you as an infidel. Repent now and return to The Ambassadors!"

He swapped megaphone and rifle again. The guard waited some long minutes, by the end of which McKinley was toying with murderous thoughts, but a missing guard would be a dead giveaway. Besides, he might have friends nearby. But eventually the guard seemed satisfied that there were neither intruders nor escapees in his vicinity and turned downhill, talking in an Asian sounding language on his radio.

When they couldn't hear the guard's movements anymore, McKinley gave voice to what they were both thinking. "Motion detectors? Cameras?"

"If they'd *seen* us he'd be a lot more determined," murmured Carter. "If we're not escaping then they probably think we're the wildlife."

"Agreed," nodded McKinley, "so let's do this slowly. I'll go first; you take a different route. We go down in short random movements."

"Got it."

McKinley raised himself out of the foliage. "See that area to the south-east?" He pointed to where a small field was full of colourful clothes drying on lines. "We'll meet in the trees near there."

"Roger that," replied Carter. "Try and steal something that fits this time."

He opened his eyes as if from a year-long dream. Where was he? The room was built of wood and he was lying on a metal framed bed that was positioned against the wall under the window. It was warm and there were bird sounds. He felt comfortable enough to lie there all day, yet energised as though ready for some exhilarating activity.

A face swam into his field of view, a mature man composed mostly of muscle with a long but squarish, almost bald head and grey eyes.

"Brother Dawoud, are you okay?" The gravelly voice lay somewhere between French and North American.

Brother Dawoud? That sounded familiar. "Yes, I'm alright. Where am I?"

The man helped him prop himself up on his elbows. Behind the bald guy a pair of ashen faced men in purple jackets stood as though ready to intervene.

"The Universal Spirit ministered to you for a long time, my brother," announced the older man. "I suppose you don't remember."

Dawoud looked into his memories and was shocked to the core at not finding any. He panicked with a yell, trying to jump off the bed. The man gently but firmly held him down.

"It's okay, it's okay!" he insisted. "It's a normal reaction. Your old, sinful life is gone. You've been given a new life, a spiritual life. This happens to every convert."

This assertion calmed Dawoud a little, yet he was deeply alarmed that he didn't know who he was. "I... don't remember *anything!*"

He tried to concentrate for a moment, forcing himself to look deeper inside, yet there was a void. He simply couldn't find a single memory from his past. It didn't feel like he'd just forgotten; it felt like there was nothing to remember in the first place. Where did he come from? Did he have a family? Where did he live? How old was he? The myriad questions ricocheted around his mind like pinballs in an arcade game. There was no past; there was just the now. It was deeply troubling and yet *wonderfully* liberating. Apart from the continuing explosion of questions, he felt as light as a feather.

"Do you remember your training?"

"Training?" Dawoud was way past confused. "I don't know..." He paused, then resigned himself to the stupid sounding question. "Who am I?"

The man nodded to himself, smiling. "You're mightily blessed, my brother. The Universal Spirit has taken your old, earthly life away. You've been given a fresh start. You're Brother Dawoud of The Ambassadors Of The Godhead."

Brother Dawoud's eyes narrowed. Yes, he knew about the Ambassadors. To be called to be a member of that assembly was a great blessing.

The man tapped his badge. "I'm Prophet Bellegarde. Louis Bellegarde. I minister to all the new converts once the Universal Spirit allows them to wake up."

"Hi," said Dawoud uncertainly.

"It's the accent, isn't it?" smiled Bellegarde. "I was born in France but lived in the US most of my adult life." Bellegarde looked around at his companions and nodded. Without a word they filed outside.

Dawoud started to look around more, taking in the details. He was in a hut. There was bright sunshine outside and the sounds of voices.

There were principles he could remember. Absolute obedience to the cause. Surrender of one's selfish will. Somewhere deep in his mind he knew this stuff, knew what he had to do. He *knew* that he was a divine warrior with great purpose, on a mission to usher in the Kingdom. He felt thoroughly secure in this knowledge despite not knowing himself. The principles felt *right*, undergirded by the inner witness of his heart. It was *truth*. It was freedom. Yet there was a definite sense of having lost his identity. How could this be?

Bellegarde smiled widely. "I wish you could see your face."

Dawoud swung his legs to the wooden floor. "Where are we?"

"Brother, we're in the most blessed place on Earth. We're in Pastor Makaru's community of Wolf River."

Dawoud tried again to look into his memories but came up with a blank.

Bellegarde caught the look. "Don't try to dig up the past, Brother. Let it all go. You don't want all that sinful garbage back in your life, do you?"

Dawoud felt compelled to agree. "No, I don't."

Bellegarde jerked a thumb back over his shoulder. "Why don't you have a look in the mirror?"

"Sure." Dawoud got off the bed and went to the other side of the room. Framed in the glass over the sink was a man in his mid-twenties with auburn hair and innocent looking eyes. He was about six feet two and possessed of a lean, fit body. Dawoud looked down at his hands. He didn't recognise them at all, yet he could see that they'd worked hard. What did I do with these hands, he wondered.

Bellegarde came up behind him. "Ready for the tour?"

Brother Dawoud felt a surge of joy. It was a visceral, deep explosion of peace and happiness right in the depths of his heart. To be a disciple of these holy men was more blessing than he knew what to do with. Something deep inside wanted to please Prophet Bellegarde with every fibre of his being.

"Yes, sir, I am!"

Having skilfully acquired a fresh wardrobe of used yet freshly washed clothes, McKinley and Carter decided to walk round the Wolf River compound and reconnoiter the place.

The township was bigger than it looked from above, and replete with facilities. There were dormitories, kitchens, classrooms and workshops, making the village analogous to any small town in the outside world. When they approached the north-western end of Wolf River, though, further progress was discouraged by a barred road, fences and a pair of armed guards complete with guard houses barely bigger than a telephone booth. This, they saw, was the track to the greenhouses and Makaru's personal living quarters, which was apparently what Jem had referred to as 'the Citadel'. They noticed that the Citadel had a long, narrow floating dock stretching into the bay, at which was moored a powerful looking boat, the only vessel in sight. It was a large cabin cruiser, or maybe a tiny private yacht. Either way its two huge outboards looked like they meant business.

This caught McKinley's attention. He'd been wondering why the *Dhul-Nun* docked on the other side of the island, necessitating the long journey. It might be the much smaller dock here or the depth of the water, but McKinley knew these were inconsequential problems that the technology that built Wolf River could have neutralised with ease. Which made it all the more interesting.

McKinley and Carter turned and paralleled the beach, making their way back to the center of town. When they reached the tiny river delta they turned south-west and found themselves on the main street, if it could be called that. They worked their way further into the township, observing everything.

"Wow," said Carter, "there are some cuties round here."

They were walking past a group of smiling females of various ethnicities, several of whom were chubby enough to fit Carter's parameters for attractive.

"I thought you and Hughie were getting serious," grumbled McKinley.

Carter paused for a second. "Admiring the flowers ain't the same as picking 'em." Carter turned and walked backwards for a moment to survey an outstandingly bathykolpian member of the group. "Blimey," he whispered, "you don't get many of those to the pound."

"If Hughie finds out, your privates'll be in the frying pan."

Carter said "is that concern I hear?"

"*Bésame culo,*" replied McKinley.

"I dunno Mickey, I think you're getting soft in your old age." Carter shook his head slowly. "Maybe there's a chance you'll find love yet."

McKinley faced his friend, jabbing with a finger. "There's an absolute certainty of my boot up your arse if you don't clamp your bloody snack-hatch."

They strode on and, despite his complaining, McKinley found himself agreeing with Carter's observation. There were indeed lots of attractive young women in Wolf River. Attractive young women who were hopelessly under Makaru's influence, not in their right minds and on the way to being suicide bombers. What a horrible thought.

His attention was captured by one girl and he realised it was because of her similarity to Jem. She was about the same height and build, but her hair was a darker shade. She read from a book—a Quran, Bible, Tripiṭaka or other sacred tome—whilst a group of her friends stood around listening. The girl's attention strayed from the text for a moment and she looked up at McKinley. Their eyes met and the operative found himself assailed by opposite emotions. On one hand she was intensely beautiful, creating a drive within McKinley to get closer. On the other, he was disgusted by the kind of fate which Makaru had probably planned for her. He was starting to understand Wilson's drive to save them all.

Carter noticed McKinley's lingering gaze and sighed. Despite the remonstrations of a moment ago, his friend was still a career lizard. The woman smiled at McKinley, whose head was rotating like an owl's as they walked on.

Carter leaned in and lowered his voice. "Mate, I've got socks older than that."

"Hey, just leave it..."

Before he could finish his sentence, there was an echoing ping of high frequency sound and a voice burst from speakers that they couldn't see but which were obviously installed all over the compound.

"The tour for new converts starts in five minutes. Please go to the parade ground where Pastor Makaru will lead you. May you be blessed to see the Kingdom!"

As the reverberation died away McKinley turned to Carter. "Let's do it," he said. "We wanted a look round; this is ideal."

"I'd still rather have some hardware," mumbled Carter, turning to follow after his friend.

The route to the parade ground was clearly signed and they were there within minutes. Carter spotted Wilson across from them, looking cheerfully wide-eyed; there were also several faces they recognised from the service in Singapore.

"Friendly on your three," said Carter quietly.

"Aye. Looks like he's fitting in."

Shortly, Makaru arrived, driven in a jeep by one of his purple jacketed bodyguards and flanked by two more, as the crowd exploded with anticipation and delight. The preacher was in a similar garb to their last encounter, but this was yellow and white, and very lightweight. He stood in the back seat of the vehicle and motioned the crowd to silence, which came like the flicking of a switch. McKinley was a bit unnerved by the degree of control Makaru wielded.

"My children," began the pastor, producing a ripple of approving adoration in the crowd, "I welcome and love you all!"

Again the crowd broke out in adulation whilst McKinley rolled his eyes sourly. Carter caught the expression.

"Play the part," he hummed. With difficulty, McKinley switched to a smile.

"I thank you from the bottom of my heart," continued Makaru, "for you have given yourselves to the service of this ministry. May you be blessed to see the Kingdom!"

The applause was even louder now, yet Makaru's gesture brought it to a close with equal suddenness.

"As you are new to our faith community," he said, "you will enjoy a tour of our facilities here. We will start with our main meeting hall. You will follow me."

The jeep moved off slowly as Makaru sat again, and the crowd dutifully fell in behind. They filed like sheep toward the center of Wolf River, where the biggest building stood, asserting its presence over all that surrounded it. It was the same temple as they'd seen earlier from up on the mountainside, but it looked a lot bigger close up.

Whilst they saw Wilson going on ahead, McKinley and Carter stayed back to see what was going to happen. The column went through a set of ornate but substantial double doors which were carved with the same *Basmolet* symbol that adorned the building's spire.

Walking through, McKinley was impressed by the grandness of the architecture. Cyclopean blocks of black lava rock, polished to a high gloss, formed the horseshoe shaped base of the building, between the horns of which was the now familiar stage with podium, Plexiglass lectern and choir stalls. Directly above this was a projection screen to rival most cinemas and, above that, massively sturdy wooden beams radiated down to become pillars lining the outer walls. Behind and above them the glass roof which covered half of the building was supported by similar beams and he realised that on the outside these were the gigantic steel girders they'd observed earlier.

The auditorium itself wasn't dissimilar to the church in Singapore, with plush dark yellow upholstered pews in rows above a stone floor. The pews were bisected by a wide central aisle leading from the doors by which they'd just entered to a large carpeted area in front of the stage.

McKinley and Carter took their seats as Makaru announced that there would be a video presentation. The lights went out and Carter looked up to see the wide panes of roof glass becoming dark and more opaque.

"Impressive," he muttered.

"What is?"

"Those are huge liquid crystal panels if I'm not mistaken," answered Carter, pointing upward. "Rude money."

"Aye, well, I think he can afford it." McKinley folded his arms as the show began.

The video was a religious propaganda movie about the wonders of the coming kingdom and the merits of laying one's life down for Makaru. McKinley again tuned out, looking around the expansive auditorium, trying to learn useful information. He saw Wilson up front in a pew by himself and decided it was time to make contact. McKinley got up and walked down the aisle toward the stage, taking a seat next to his colleague.

Wilson looked round and smiled innocently.

"How are you doing?" asked McKinley quietly, pretending to watch the movie.

"I'm deeply blessed Brother," answered Wilson. "How are you?"

"Cut the religious crap," said McKinley, "or you'll get blessed with a clown's nose."

Wilson's face took on a sad, apologetic look. "Brother," he smiled, "there's no need to be so hostile."

McKinley started to feel like the rug was being pulled from beneath him. "I said cut the act Willy," he muttered sternly.

Wilson looked puzzled. "Willy?"

Holy *SHIT!*

016: The Cult

A horrible suspicion was overtaking McKinley and he felt blood draining from his face. He thought for a moment then warily asked "what's your name?"

Wilson's right hand popped up like a trafficator. "I'm Brother Dawoud," he said, "and you?"

McKinley struggled to answer. "Umm... I'm Brother..." What was that name they used on the ship? Damn it, he was blanking. He fought for a mythical sounding name, starting to unconsciously back away. "Polaris," he blurted. Oh blimey that was pathetic!

"That's an odd name for a disciple," smiled Wilson emptily, not the faintest hint of recognition in his eyes.

McKinley dumped himself back in his own pew next to Carter, who looked round.

"Bloody hell Mickey, you look like you've seen a ghost," he whispered hoarsely.

McKinley panted, steadying his pulse rate. "Ugh... you ain't far wrong. Willy's compromised."

Now it was Carter's turn to be shocked. "*What?!*"

Shaking his head disconsolately, McKinley gestured toward the front. "He got brainwashed like the rest of 'em. Didn't recognise me. Didn't even know his own name."

Carter went silent, his hand over his mouth, thinking.

"Come on Brains," hissed McKinley, "I need options."

Carter shook his head. "This is different. I'm gonna have to figure it out."

McKinley had neither time nor patience for out-figuring. "We need—"

At that moment the video presentation ended and the lights came up. Peals of applause rang throughout the huge building as Makaru returned to the stage.

"Thank you," he said, leaning toward the lectern's microphone. "Now you will go outside in an orderly manner to continue the tour."

Sure enough the new disciples did exactly as they were told. McKinley was sickened to his stomach. His view of Wolf River and The Ambassadors Of The Godhead had just changed radically. Now he understood the confusion that Jem had demonstrated. These weren't even people any more; they were deceived robots, seduced and programmed into thinking they were the happiest company on Earth as their Pied Piper plotted their doom. Now Wilson was one of them.

He watched the line as it passed him. Previously cheerful smiles now appeared like clown faces to a coulrophobe. These grins were not real joy, but were joyful looking masks. McKinley realised that these converts had been made to love and obey Makaru entirely separately from their own volition. Yes, the Asian was a gifted speaker; of this McKinley had no doubt. Yes, he was charismatic and intelligent. Yes, he had clear leadership skills and academic qualifications up the wazoo. But this was something else: a horror dark and insidious. *Somehow*, these young people—and Wilson—had been brainwashed to believe and do anything Makaru told them. McKinley felt like he'd been para-dropped into the Twilight Zone.

His system still in shock, McKinley slapped Carter on the arm and they joined the line, trying hard to look as buoyant as the others.

Following a thorough look around the kitchens, accommodations and other utilities, the pastor announced that they would be going through the security cordon into the hydroponics area. McKinley and Carter glanced at each other, wondering why greenhouses would be so well guarded. Perhaps it was for the presence of the laboratories that Jem had mentioned, a large and almost featureless block behind the greenhouses being a prime suspect for their location. Perhaps it was because of Makaru's 'Citadel' beyond.

The cordon was a waist height barbed wire fence supported by electrical insulators on hammered-in posts with small yellow warning decals. The gate was a simple two-barred affair like the entrance to a field, made of steel and painted bright orange. Each guard had their own kiosk, slightly larger than a telephone booth, set a couple of meters back from the gate. Behind the fence there was a deep trench.

"Wonder why they need the cover," whispered McKinley. Carter nodded.

The beige clothed guards stood aside, bowing as Makaru's jeep approached. The column snaked through the gateway, approaching the first greenhouse. Carter nudged McKinley. "See that?" He pointed to their left.

McKinley looked. Almost hidden within the boundary of the forest several meters beyond the western corner of the greenhouse block was a tall, robust fence of rigid steel wire. McKinley couldn't see it beyond the point where it vanished into the canopy, but estimated a height of twenty feet. More warning notices were scattered along it and they looked a lot more threatening than the plastic signage of the security cordon, featuring skulls and threatening text with many exclamation marks.

McKinley observed that the area between the fences was a long, convex quadrilateral of which the beach formed the only curved side. The two fences started to diverge from a point about twenty meters to his left. The security cordon stretched behind them to the beach and, between there and the other, bigger fence, the area was at its widest, accommodating the greenhouses. Beyond this the beach and the treeline started to draw together again, encompassing the hidden garage/boathouse and presumably joining at an unseen point beyond the cylindrical Citadel, where the jungle met the sea directly.

The leader's jeep stopped and the group came to a halt behind it. Makaru stood in the back of the vehicle and spoke in a most serious tone, making McKinley wonder if the preacher had somehow read his mind.

"You will never, ever go beyond the fence," commanded Makaru, pointing. "To even approach that fence is a grave transgression. *Never* sin in this manner, for the wrath of the Universal Spirit will surely find you in short order. Promise me now that you will never consider going near that fence!"

Several shouts of "yes Pastor" and "I promise" went up. Makaru looked menacingly from side to side, making sure to capture everyone's attention.

"All of you! Do you promise?"

McKinley and Carter joined in as the whole group chorused "yes Pastor!"

The Asian nodded as if the response was no more than satisfactory then stepped carefully out of the jeep and started walking toward the greenhouse.

As they approached they saw that it was considerably taller than it had appeared earlier and the glass was obscured from the inside by condensation through which narrow trickles of water carved roughly vertical paths.

Makaru boldly pushed aside the huge steel doors that looked as though they were meant to be kept locked at all other times. The preacher swept into the space beyond, which seemed devoid of artificial light, having an emerald cast to its ambience. As they entered, the cause of this was revealed to be sunlight reflecting from the many climbing plants that hung like festive decorations near the lofty glass roof. A network of support cables kept the greenery in place away from many large acrylic glass cabinets at chest height, in which were beds of rocks, moss, soil and other materials. The cabinets were supported on dark cubical bases which themselves stood on adjustable feet a few inches high.

The air inside the enormous greenhouse was thick with humidity and, up near the suspended flora, wisps of vapour faded in and out around maintenance gantries. The moisture and warmth made clothes feel even more sticky and uncomfortable but the air carried a pleasing smell not unlike freshly mown grass or the *must* of woodland.

"This is my mycoculture and hydroponics department," announced Makaru, his arms spread wide as though he was lapping up applause in a television singing contest. "The study of mycology yields many benefits to our holy assembly. Fungi are so misunderstood by the world, yet they are a tremendous resource of biochemical blessings. With the substances derived from mycological organisms, we can perform medical miracles."

"Yeah I bet," whispered McKinley tensely. His dismay at Wilson's fate was starting to give way to anger.

Carter nodded but was busy turning this way and that, his eyes consuming every aspect of this fascinating enclosure. He considered himself something of an amateur mycologist and this department was thoroughly feeding that fire.

They continued in procession behind Makaru as he strolled down the central aisle of the massive conservatory. All around them many kinds of mushrooms and fungi were growing in their own sealed environmental cabinets, some cold, some dark, others bright and warm. Some were saturated with moisture while others appeared as dry as a desert. A worker disciple scurried away at Makaru's approach, after whom the preacher sent a radiant but condescending smile.

In the middle of the huge building, encircled by a flowerbed and sturdy railings, there was a single towering tree growing from floor to ceiling, its slender trunk enshrouded by clinging vines and mosses. An artificial waterfall, the source of which was hidden from view somewhere in the lofty canopy, poured from above, parallel to the tree. With flow carefully governed, its waters splashed around the tree's base and made their way neatly into three small, kidney shaped ponds containing *nishikigoi* that circulated indifferently. Their tour guide stopped at the railing and turned toward his group.

Makaru launched into a well-rehearsed speech about how his faithfulness and obedience had led him into these supposed blessings, but Carter's gaze had fallen on a particular cabinet to their left and several rows from the center. Giving McKinley a wink, he wandered nonchalantly in that direction, made a rapid inspection and drifted back, continuing the impression of polite but guileless curiosity at their surroundings.

"Something interesting?" muttered McKinley under his breath.

Carter whispered back. "I'd question the medicinal value of *Amanita virosa*."

"Sounds dangerous."

"The Destroying Angel. One of the most poisonous toadstools in the world."

His curiosity piqued, McKinley started slowly moving in the other direction, toward a large glass case opposite the one Carter had examined. He drew closer to a leafy shrub in the enclosure, its upper regions dotted with thorns. What's the purpose of this, wondered McKinley.

As he approached it became apparent that each thorn had a hard, dark lump at its base, and that the thorns weren't coming from the plant's stems. They appeared to be projecting directly from the lumps. McKinley was no botanist, but even he knew there was something odd about this. He peered through the glass and condensation, trying to make out what was in there. Tilting his head slightly, McKinley observed a striated formation at the base of a close spike. He rubbed the glass, but all the water vapour deposition appeared to be on the inside. Squinting, he started to make out detail. Holy cow! The brown lump was an ant, and the thorn was poking from its head. McKinley started to feel creepy. There was something disturbing about an obviously parasitic fungus using an animal like that, and images from Ridley Scott's *Alien* came to mind.

"*Ophiocordyceps,*" announced Makaru suddenly, standing only inches behind McKinley who jumped, whipped around and was instantly ready to give the man a sound beating. Makaru stepped daintily back with consummate control of his limbs. McKinley caught himself before acting, but no excuse came to his mind.

"W... what?!" he stuttered instead.

"*Ophiocordyceps unilateralis,*" repeated Makaru, smiling. "You were wondering what this species of fungus is."

"Right... Pastor." McKinley looked around at the rest of their party. Everyone was focussed on him except for Carter, who was walking calmly away, making noisy footsteps and trying to create a distraction for his colleague.

Makaru's body relaxed beneath the robes. His eyes gave nothing away, but it was apparent that he'd gauged any threat presented by McKinley and discounted it.

"A fascinating organism," continued the Asian, leaning forward and staring into the cabinet as though taking note. "It infects ants, mostly this *Camponotus* variety, and gains control over them. Once the spores have infected the creature's body, it is driven to climb to a certain height on the plant and anchor itself. The fungus kills it, takes over its whole form and sprouts fruiting bodies from its head within a few days." Makaru turned back to the rest of the group. "*Fascinating,*" he reiterated, shaking his head in wonder. "You will move on."

The group obediently turned to follow the leader and Carter made his way back to where McKinley loitered at the rear of the procession, feeling like an idiot.

"Little jumpy today?" hummed Carter. McKinley scowled and they made their way after the group.

Shortly, Makaru turned and faced his attendees. "In the kingdom of fungi," he pontificated, "we see order, not chaos. There are millions of different species, but there is unity. Each species performs both specific and general functions. They work together by similarity and work on their own by diversity. It is a remarkable model through which the Universal Spirit has spoken to me many times."

"And here we go again," whispered Carter. "Indoctrination time."

Makaru looked snidely at Carter, having noticed the turn of his head, but continued anyway. "Make no mistake my friends, a new kingdom is being birthed! This Kingdom is not a natural kingdom of this world, but a *supernatural* kingdom, an earthly shadow of the divine realm. It is a kingdom, if you like, of religion, but let us not be mired in that term. I prefer to call it a kingdom of *faith*, where each different belief system brings its own value. In the new Kingdom, believers will not be bogged down in the terminology of individual faiths; it will be a *communion* where each believer will find fulfillment in both their own specific calling and through the common ground of our faith-conversation."

The religious babble was wasted on McKinley. He preferred to concentrate his mind on new priorities: one, learning as much about this place as possible; and two, figuring out what to do about his brainwashed team-mate. These were aside from reconnaissance of the nukes, pegging Heinmarsh, acquiring weapons and stopping the suicide bombers. Right now it looked like a hill to climb of such steepness as to be near vertical.

After more spiel from Makaru, the preacher led the group out of the greenhouse and back through the security cordon, where his vehicle stopped and he ordered his followers to mingle and learn about the place. He adjured them all to return to the central meeting hall for the evening's service, advising them that they would be assigned tasks in the next few days.

McKinley and Carter spent the rest of the day trying to harvest intelligence, but their efforts were thwarted at every turn. Much as there seemed to be an amazing freedom in the township to do whatever you wanted at whatever time and with whomever you wanted to, not a single soul would betray any details beyond what was obvious to the eye. Even amongst his zombies, Makaru had covered his tracks thoroughly.

They found their way to the dining hall to take advantage of the free catering. Sitting on long benches at equally long tables, surrounded by effervescent disciples, McKinley and Carter ate their better than average tuna salads in virtual silence, feeling like aliens.

The population of the dining hall started to thin down and when he felt like there were few enough people about, McKinley addressed Carter.

"So, you're the expert. How's he done this to them?"

Carter bit his lower lip for a moment then shook his head. "I still don't know. Remember me saying the memory loss was the key?"

"Aye."

"No-one remembers anything before coming here. It's like their old lives *did* get erased, just like he says."

McKinley shoved a final piece of dressing-enrobed lettuce into his mouth. "But that's bollocks."

Carter nodded. "So either it *is* some kind of hypnotic process—the sleep teaching on the boat—or chemical. Or magnetic. Maybe a bit of all three. I can think of a few countries that'd pay real money to know about this."

"No shit. How's it possible to erase memories?"

"Well, there are drugs that screw with your memory. Like, benzodiazepines cause memory loss in some people. Then there are so-called truth drugs that can do the same."

McKinley licked his fork. "Right. But that's all short term, isn't it?"

"Yes. So the jury's still out."

McKinley's mind went to his mission. "What about Willy? Please tell me we can get him back."

Carter sighed, a worried look in his eyes. "I bloody hope so."

At that moment an attractive young woman approached their table. Her curly black hair cascaded around her hazel eyes and boyish smile, which seemed almost wide enough to warrant the installation of a second face. Her well-defined cheekbones were spattered with freckles and her rounded face with its small, almost triangular chin bore the attractive elongated dimples of a soul that enjoyed laughter often.

"Hey fellas," she started in the broadest Australian accent. "Can I get your washups?"

McKinley was still having difficulty enacting the fake happiness, so Carter answered, holding up his plate. "Thanks."

"I'm Sister Miriam," she announced, then lowered her head, winking. "Isabella any other day of the week," she whispered.

Carter found that most interesting. "That's your old name, right? How did you remember it?"

She continued with the humorously conspiratorial tone, holding up her hand to her face as if to shield her speech. "I remember loads of stuff," she said. "Lots of us do. Only don't tell anyone; wouldn't want any divine judgement up me rear end."

McKinley raised a quizzical eyebrow at Carter, and Isabella went on.

"You guys are new, so if you need anything just let me know. I'm nearly always in the kitchen 'cept if I'm cleaning Pastor's apartment. I love cooking. Cheers!" With this jolly valediction she whisked their plates away and vanished into the kitchens.

"So," mulled Carter thoughtfully, "it's not a hundred percent effective."

"Right," said McKinley, wagging his finger at his colleague. "But she's still scared of punishment if she gets found out."

Carter opened his mouth to speak but the public address system cut him off. A speaker above them in the corner of the dining hall blared its announcement.

"The evening service will start in ten minutes. Make your way to the main meeting hall. May you be blessed to see the Kingdom!"

"Let's go," said McKinley. "I hate to admit it, but we need to fit in."

They sat at the back of the huge sanctuary, near one of several sets of smaller doors. The auditorium was packed almost to capacity and they estimated that the whole population of Wolf River was there save, perhaps, for the guards. It was, after all, an ideal time for anyone to escape.

The crowd thronged around them and McKinley was once again assailed by the horror of Makaru's programming. The sheer joy of the crowd was the hardest thing to bear, knowing that many of them could face a future explosion. Their faces were full of camaraderie and glad expectation. Perhaps that's what you get if your past is stripped away, McKinley mused. He wondered what it might feel like for a moment, but his repugnance at the thought of being manipulated like that tore him back to the now.

After the band had played through their set, Makaru arrived to the usual rapturous welcome, two purple jacketed bodyguards on either side. As the crowd continued their adulation, he positioned himself at the lectern and McKinley and Carter saw him reach into the folds of his robes, extracting his telephone. Makaru typed something into the device as they watched.

Carter nudged McKinley. "That's interesting!"

"What?"

"You didn't see the cameras?"

McKinley looked up and around. At various points surrounding the stage, small television cameras were mounted on the walls and the overhead beams. A central camera was suspended on cables from the lofty ceiling, focused directly on the speaker's position. On the rear and top of each, glowing red lights were visible.

"Aye, of course."

"They all came on at once," said Carter. "He's using his phone as a remote."

"Aye," replied McKinley, not appreciating Carter's excitement, as the applause and yelling died down.

The imposing Asian stared out over his congregation, every minute gesture and hint of expression designed to captivate, to command their loyal attention. Once he appeared to have satisfied himself that all eyes were trained on him, he took a deep breath, raised himself up and spoke.

"My children," began Makaru in a voice both smooth like rich chocolate and full of deadly authority, "we are The Ambassadors Of The Godhead. We are a chosen people, a priesthood of destiny, a royal nation of prophets with a divine mission. We are mandated of the Universal Spirit to build a new kingdom by taking dominion over this world; only then can we be blessed with the promised saviour."

"Familiar?" asked McKinley quietly.

"Same old story," replied his friend. Noting McKinley's curious expression, he added "you might want to take notes."

The leader continued, his speech fiery and ripe with unyielding confidence. "Our masters' Kingdom will be one of freedom and righteousness. Each individual who has entered into our communion through whatever faith—and the spirit of the godhead within them—will be valued most highly and esteemed as each soul should rightly be. But for those who go against our heavenly law, punishment will be swift and sure.

"As the Universal Spirit blesses us with the power to manifest..." the preacher paused to give his next words even more weight, "...the *presence* in our lives, we will become the very sons and daughters of the Universal Spirit, revealed in the flesh. What privilege! What destiny!"

"What dysentery," added Carter quietly.

"We will show this filthy world a new way of worshipping the deity of our varied understandings. As we conquer this world by our holy war, our *jihad*, we will unite all religions under one universal divinity, all nations under one divinely-appointed government and all humanity will come to share in a common wealth. We will turn this world into one that is fit for the manifestation of the godhead to come unto!"

Cheers were starting to erupt from around the packed auditorium. Shouts of "*namaste!*", "yes Pastor!", "amen!" and "*allāhu akbar!*" echoed from the rock walls. McKinley and Carter shared a glance as Makaru went on.

"But my children! There may be those for whom the going is too tough, those who are still in love with the filth of their godless earthly life. There may be those who, having dishonestly put their hands to the plough, turn again to the sinful pleasures of this world."

Suddenly the preacher shouted angrily, making a few people jump. "*There is no place for them among us!* They are against this anointing! They are antichrist; they are *shaitan!* They are *haram!* When they question or disobey your pastor they are not fit to enter into our new Kingdom! Doubters! Cowards! Backsliders! They must be expelled from among us!"

Silence had dropped like a lead weight over the assembled believers. Not one dared utter a sound in the face of Makaru's forthright fury. Now that he held them in the palm of his hand, Makaru went on in a more subdued, intimate tone.

"My dear children, hear me now. Have nothing to do with the deeds of darkness nor those who commit sin. If you see a brother or sister falling away, entertaining doubts, questioning our doctrine or disobeying our instructions you must report them. All of you must be in absolute accountability to this pastorate, confessing all things so that we can help you. We seek not to judge or punish, but to nurture and guide. If our manner sometimes seems strong, it is because you *need* strong leaders, men of holy faith who will not back down in the hour of testing. Trust and obey your divinely appointed pastor! Let not the smallest stain of dissension be found in this sacred city, for that would dishonour the Universal Spirit in every way possible."

"Blimey," breathed Carter, almost in awe, "he *really* knows his stuff. See how they're taking it in?"

"Aye," replied McKinley, "this kinda control scares me."

Carter hummed his agreement whilst the Asian continued, his voice measured, slow and steady.

"When you pray, center yourselves on the Universal Spirit within you. Speak the name of your deity—whatever name you choose—and repeat it as a mantra to shut out the clamour of the world. This will be your exercise of spiritual formation. There, in that hidden, sacred place, find your truth and commit again to our way; receive the Spirit's instruction. When you go deep, deep inside yourselves, remember... my... words. Remember my words and feed on them."

Makaru was almost down to a whisper now. "Let them nourish the spirit of the godhead in your inner being. Seek the divine within as you contemplate my teaching. Believe and obey as righteous followers; believe... and obey."

"See?" whispered Carter. "Classic hypnosis techniques. This is mind control one-oh-one."

"Alright, I get it," admitted McKinley. Maybe there's something to this stuff after all, he thought.

Then Makaru came to perhaps the most predictable part of his message and Carter smiled wryly.

"Do not hold back in your generosity to our mission. Give now and you will receive thirty, sixty or a hundred times more! Your seed-faith offering has mighty power to break strongholds in the heavenly realms. When the people of this world see the prosperity of your pastor, they know the Universal Spirit blesses my faithfulness! That's what my name means, from the Greek *makarios*, meaning blessed! Become like me as I become like the divinity within me!

"We come now to the offering. The Universal Spirit knows your hearts; hold up your offering and speak the future!"

All over the sanctuary hands darted into the air, each holding an envelope. The murmur of many voices could be heard reciting a collective spell for blessing, their magic wands of cash waving. Then, somehow subtly cued by Makaru, the band started playing again.

As people started to stream toward the platform, McKinley turned to Carter. "I think it's about time we left, don't you?"

"Not yet," hissed Carter. "You want to see if Heinmarsh appears, don't you?"

McKinley's voice betrayed a hint of nervousness. "It's too much of a risk."

"Not with these chin rugs." Carter pointed to his face.

"Let's go."

"Look, just wait a bit. Did you spot Willy anywhere?"

McKinley shook his head, frowning.

After a few more minutes of singing and filling buckets with money, Makaru approached the lectern again and the music subsided. Once again he allowed his gaze to pass over everyone in his congregation, making each focus their attention.

"Bless you my children," he cooed. For the first time the preacher seemed to notice the others on stage with him. "And now Elder Heinmarsh, our true son of the gods, will minister in the spirit."

"Our true...?!" Carter was flabbergasted at the phrase. "He... what the *hell?!*"

"Steady on," hissed McKinley.

Carter lowered his voice. "Sorry. I should have expected it."

"Why?"

Carter wriggled his fingers, making a sour expression. "He's hexadactyl, isn't he? Remember at his party in Wales?"

McKinley cast his mind back to the summer and his discomfiture at shaking a hand with an extra digit. "Oh... yeah... urgh."

"Well, the *nephilim* were supposed to have six fingers and they were descended from the so-called *sons of god*, fallen angels."

McKinley was momentarily torn between telling Carter that he came out with too much bullshit or acknowledging this explanation. Instead he held his tongue as a familiar figure took to the stage.

Kurt Heinmarsh was a touch under six feet tall and big of frame. His black hair hung in lank curtains around his full face with its rounded nose but angular chin. He was dressed in a dark grey suit of excellent manufacture with white shirt and purple tie.

As Makaru disappeared from the back of the stage, Heinmarsh spoke.

"Dear children," he growled in his strong American accent, "we live in exciting times! The spirit manifests in us to make us divine sons and daughters. If you need a fresh infilling, if doubts affect you, if you feel the going's getting too tough, then come forward now and be touched by the Spirit!"

"Okay, *now* it's time to go," intoned Carter, elbowing his friend.

"Why?"

"He's probably going to start calling people down for the blessing or the impartation or something. They'll go up to the front and get prayed for. There'll be more falling over, maybe writhing, glossolalia... You don't wanna get picked, right?"

"Hell no. Let's blow."

The operatives walked as casually as possible to the back of the massive chamber where there was an encircling colonnade, and made their way toward the nearest exit door, incongruously brown and wooden in this dark stone edifice. They were just about to open it and make their way out when one of Makaru's ushers, a tall young man with almost jet black skin, stepped up to them from the end of an aisle. He was strikingly handsome and in another setting, without the ridiculous ceremonial robes that made him look like a choirboy, could easily have been a prince or diplomatic dignitary.

"*Salaam*, my brothers," he said, smiling broadly and with a strong hint of equatorial African—perhaps Cameroon or Nigeria—in his accent. "Why are you leaving now? Don't you want to receive a touch from Elder Heinmarsh?"

Several thoughts flashed through McKinley's mind, only one of which was non-lethal, but Carter came to the rescue again.

"*Salaam* Brother," he responded, "we both felt it would be presumptuous to stay when we were given such a powerful word after last night's meeting. We're going to the other side of the island to tell them about the Kingdom!" Carter's affected enthusiasm was almost tangible.

The thin African's smile seemed to expand a full thirty percent. "May the Universal Spirit bless your efforts!" he beamed. "Pastor Makaru will surely honour you. May I come with you when the meeting is over?"

Bloody hell, thought McKinley. Well done Chris, now we've got a cling-on. But Carter seemed ready for this latest question.

"My brother," he said, nodding reverentially, "I mean no disrespect, especially to one of Pastor's faithful ushers, but I don't recall you being there when Pastor Makaru spoke the Spirit's mandate over us. We're just obeying what we've been given. Perhaps you should seek the Spirit's direction for yourself? Elder Heinmarsh could be calling you forward right at this moment! You wouldn't want to be seen as disobedient, would you?"

With a shocked expression, his eyes suddenly wide in realisation, the young man mumbled "bless you" and turned on his heel, almost stumbling as he hastened back to the seating in his eagerness. Carter grinned at McKinley as they exited the auditorium. They took a left down the corridor and, via the big central set of double doors, found themselves back in the open air of the compound.

"Thanks," said McKinley. "I don't know where you picked up all that BS but it worked."

"Judging by the look on your dial he was seconds away from a broken neck."

"That obvious, huh?"

Carter grinned. "We need to work on your religious face."

"Aye. Look, let's keep an eye out for Willy. I want you to see if you can get through to him."

It was a peaceful, deeply beautiful evening as Brother Dawoud stood on the beach, pondering the amazing blessing with which he was bestowed. The evening meeting had been wonderful, thoroughly inspiring him to do his part in spreading Pastor Makaru's message and building the Kingdom.

Beyond the powdery sand, the steady surge of waves evoked a giant creature drawing breath. The regular crash, followed at a lazy interval by the swish and patter of pebbles and shells in the backwash, was to Brother Dawoud like the calming melody of a lullaby. He felt serenity and wonder. All his past sins, his mistakes, his regrets... every bad memory associated with his past life was gone, dissolved painlessly away by the divine energy that flowed through Pastor Makaru. Dawoud sighed with incredible relief. What a blessing on one so unworthy. But such was the nature of redemption.

In the absence of artificial illumination from Wolf River, which was around the headland to the west, the shore was bright with moonlight, allowing Dawoud to view the delightful scene comfortably. His excellent eyesight could even make out the white hull of a boat, far out beyond the intertidal zone and the reef. They were probably fishing, but Dawoud would keep an eye on it. He estimated the distance to the boat at three thousand meters and made note of the wind conditions: roughly five kilometers west-south-west.

He caught himself. What was he thinking? That must be behaviour associated with his old, earthly life. The past must be allowed to die. Nonetheless he found himself maintaining a proportion of his attention on that boat, a habit the origin of which was forgotten now. Perhaps it was time to head back.

Rubakang's fine sand squeaked beneath Dawoud's feet as he dawdled toward the narrow valley—no more than a big crack in the rocks—that led to

Wolf River. The tide was near its low mark so he walked on the damp swathe of beach, his feet making evenly paced impressions. Something bothered him about that and he moved himself back over the line of desiccated seaweed to where his footprints would be less distinguishable. Something deep in his mind was arguing for watchfulness, but Dawoud shook his head and dismissed it. He was under Pastor Makaru's covering; divine protection was assured.

Despite this, he felt a sense of latent readiness, an awareness that he should be prepared. It was an odd feeling: a tingling in his spine, a slight over-alertness of his mind despite the tranquillity of the beach. He looked at the arc of trees surrounding the sandy crescent, then up and down the stretch of shoreline. He sniffed the air, noting that the wind speed had increased by a few KPH. Dawoud found himself measuring distances again, counting how many strides it would take to reach cover. Not far away, a piece of driftwood was being tickled by the uppermost curls of the surf. He calculated its weight, reasoning it substantial enough that a sound blow to someone's cranium would be sufficient to render their attack harmless. It was just about long enough to form an improvised *hanbō*.

Dawoud looked to the gully, his route back home. He was stupid! That fissure was too easily defensible and any enemy would know this. He should have maintained a defensive posture and used the available cover.

Suddenly Dawoud grunted in angst, his hands forming frustrated claws in the air. He'd allowed it to happen again! He'd given in to the vagaries of his old life, a life he should be rejecting. He hung his head for a moment, seeking solace in prayer, but a tiny sound of movement from the trees brought him instantly back to complete alertness. Ready once again for an enthusiastic defence, he found his eyes seeking out the tiniest detail, looking for something that would clue him in...

...That he was being watched!

Dawoud's body jerked, suddenly striking a fighting pose and instantly ready for action. This was beyond strange! How the past life refused to lie down and die. Despite the alarms going off in his head, Dawoud forced himself to relax, but there came a cry.

"Hey!"

Dawoud's sharp eyes made out a marginally stocky, muscular man appearing from the treeline. The man's attire made him look like he'd just stepped out of a campsite frequented by those in a lower income bracket, with baseball boots, a loose, black sweatshirt and canvas trousers cut off at the knees. Despite his dishevelled wardrobe, the man was built like a tank, all testosterone and years of pumping iron. Dawoud was wary, but the man held up a friendly hand in greeting as he approached. So *this* explained Dawoud's feeling of being under observation!

"How you doin'?" asked the man, a County Durham accent emerging through his bushy beard that in daylight would have been the most drab shade of barely brown.

Dawoud blinked a couple of times. "Who are you?" he demanded sharply.

"Steady on Brother," said the stranger, holding his open palms forward. "I'm not a threat."

"Sorry." Dawoud looked stupidly at his feet for a moment. "I just... I thought I knew you. Have we met?" He reasoned with himself that the man's use of the term 'brother' must mean that he was a fellow believer. If so, the odd sense of familiarity must be the Universal Spirit's way of telling him. How amazing! I'm going to take a while getting used to this, marvelled Dawoud.

The man looked bemused. "You what?"

"I thought we might know each other. Are you an ambassador for the Kingdom?"

"Oh, no." The man shook his head, smiling wistfully. "I'm just here for the scenery."

"The scenery?"

The man grinned through his mass of facial hair, leaning a little closer. "I'm a tourist."

Dawoud sensed the opportunity for some evangelism. "You're not staying at Wolf River?"

"I was there earlier today," nodded the stranger. "You might have seen me on the tour."

Dawoud nodded enthusiastically, his own face splitting into a huge smile. "Ah, right. Isn't Pastor Makaru wonderful?"

The man ruminated on the question for a moment, his eyes piercing Dawoud's. "He's a remarkable chap, I'll give him that."

"Oh, but he's so much more," gushed Dawoud. The potential of making a convert had ignited a fire in his breast. "He's a messenger from heaven, from the gods themselves. He brings a divine word that'll transform our world!"

His companion nodded. "Awesome!"

Not wanting to believe badly of a new friend, Dawoud took the response at face value but found himself reading the tiny muscle movements around the man's eyes and mouth. The motion of the man's eyebrows made him suspicious. There was something odd going on here.

The conversation lapsed for a second and they both looked out to sea. The blackness of the ocean, spotted here and there with whitecaps, mirrored the mantle of night through which stars were showing. It was warm despite the breeze, and the beach felt like the most comfortable place to be. The troubles of the world could be a million miles away, but something was nagging at Dawoud's mind. It was a deep, deep familiarity that he just couldn't bring to mind. Half his consciousness fell into the exploration of this peculiar knowing-yet-not-knowing. It was as though it was a memory from his childhood, like a well loved plaything that had long been absent from his life. Dawoud had almost drifted away from the present when the stranger spoke.

"Can I ask you something?"

Dawoud looked warily at the man. "Uh... sure."

"I've got a friend at Wolf River. Paul Wilson. D'you know him?"

Dawoud shook his head. Again that weird sense of cognisance stirred his guts. He felt irresistibly drawn to that name for some weird reason, yet was also a little afraid of it. "I... haven't met him, but I wouldn't know him by his old name anyway. We all get new names, see."

The man nodded. "Yes. What's your name then? If you don't mind me asking."

"I'm Brother Dawoud."

"Interesting name," replied the man as though soliciting an explanation.

"It's the form of David that would have been used in ancient Babylon. It means 'beloved'."

"Sounds good," nodded the stranger. "So you don't know Wilson at all?"

"No, sorry." *But why do I feel like I do?*

The man nodded as if this news was painful. What a strange reaction, thought Dawoud.

"Well look," the stranger continued after a moment. "If you run into him, tell him I said hi."

"May I ask your name please?"

"Carter. Chris Carter."

Dawoud was struck by another peculiar, intangible sort of recollection. *Chris Carter* was also a terribly familiar sounding name. He felt as though he should know where he remembered it from. It was an annoyingly evasive feeling that unsettled him at a primal level. He understood that he had a clear choice: either ignore this weirdness before it stole his peace, or pursue the elusive and obscured memory until he resolved it. Even the tension between these alternatives was enough to make him feel shaky and uncertain. If Pastor Makaru were here, he would have told Dawoud just to forget the things of the past; move on, live your new life, build the Kingdom. But wasn't self-discovery just as important? Dawoud was getting confused.

Carter turned away. "Well," he said over his shoulder, "seeya."

Dawoud remembered his duty. "May you be blessed to see the Kingdom," he parroted. The man trudged back toward the treeline and Dawoud, feeling uncomfortable and somewhat disoriented, ran up the beach toward the gully and Wolf River. He needed to seek counsel from an elder, to get the advice of someone who was travelling the way ahead of him. Perhaps he could even get to see Pastor Makaru, who would undoubtedly know the answer to this troubling feeling.

Carter ducked into the trees and watched the other figure enter the gully. He smiled humourlessly to himself; that had been the weirdest experience of his life.

One thing was certain; they no longer had a man on the inside. TDR Corporal Paul Wilson was gone, his personality and memories now lost somewhere within another man who called himself Brother Dawoud, this fabricated doppelganger that was Makaru's willing servant. Carter shuddered at the disturbing thought. To see a colleague, a friend, made to forget who they were was fundamentally wrong in more ways than he could number. It was just another horribly difficult item on their to-do list. Not only had they to neutralise Heinmarsh, stop the suicide bombers and locate the nukes, but now they had to rescue their team-mate and *if possible* return him to his right mind. All of this without the undergirding of assistance by General Sutton, Maddocks, Captain Chrimes, fourteen other TDR teams, a regiment of BCs and everyone else at HQ. On top of this they had to remain vigilant in case the retrieval crew could have tracked them somehow. Carter felt like Atlas, son of Iapetus, bearing the weight of planet Earth on his shoulders. He couldn't imagine how much this was affecting McKinley.

Taking a last glance around just in case, Carter turned away from the beach and started to walk up the hill, thinking hard.

"You're new, Brother," crooned Bellegarde. "You've been through a lot, and I understand." He smiled warmly, but his eyes seemed to be windows through which a red flag fluttered.

Dawoud closed his eyes tightly for a moment. Bellegarde caught it.

"Happening again?"

Dawoud nodded.

"Brother, let me tell you something," purred Bellegarde. "You are blessed, *blessed*. You have been given great gifts of the Universal Spirit with which to serve the Kingdom. Your former life was nothing like what you imagine, nothing at all."

"Really?"

"You imagine these things are remnants of your previous life, but how could they be? You were an office worker in London. Do you remember that name?"

Dawoud nodded. "Yes Prophet. Was that where I came from?"

Bellegarde held up a cautionary finger. "Be careful, my young brother. Do *nothing* to resurrect the ways of your old, worldly life."

"Yes." Dawoud shook his head to dismiss the thought. "Sorry."

Bellegarde continued. "I mustn't say too much, but you were a nobody, a pen pusher, a bean counter. How could you possibly have the abilities of a soldier? But!" His eyes widened. "It's obvious that the Universal Spirit has imparted these gifts upon your conversion! It's an amazing blessing." Bellegarde looked down sadly. "I wish I could share in such gifts."

"So, you mean, I could be a soldier in the Kingdom?"

Bellegarde's face exploded into a huge grin. "Why wait? Be a soldier now! Pastor Makaru needs you now to usher in the Kingdom. You could be instrumental in creating the new age. You could even become a member of his personal guard."

"Really?" asked Dawoud breathlessly. Such an honour felt far beyond him.

"Why not?" smiled Bellegarde. "But look Brother, it's late, and you've come a long way in a very short time. This man on the beach; who was he?"

"He said he was a tourist."

"Did you get his name?"

"Chris Carter."

Bellegarde shook his head, his lips curling down at their corners. "Never heard of him. He probably is just a tourist. They pass through from time to time. I wouldn't worry about it Brother."

The French-American patted Dawoud gently on the back and continued. "Go get a good night's sleep. We'll cover you in prayer, just as you pray for us. You'll feel better in the morning, I promise."

Dawoud smiled. "Thanks, Prophet." He got up and headed for the door. "May you be blessed to see the Kingdom."

Bellegarde dipped his head in a respectful manner and Dawoud left the bungalow. It was generous of Brother Bellegarde to give him so much time this late at night. He certainly felt a lot better. Perhaps that fella on the beach had been sent by the enemy of their souls to plant these worrying thoughts in Dawoud's mind. Or maybe he really was there for the scenery. Either way, Dawoud was comforted by the prophet's words, resolving to put any concerns out of his mind and pray. Brother Louis was right; he *would* feel better in the morning. Dawoud smiled and headed for the dormitories, humming worshipfully.

Bellegarde watched from his window as the figure disappeared along the track. To be sure, he waited a full minute more before picking up the telephone and dialling. The other party answered almost instantly.

"Yes?" said Makaru's voice.

"We might've been infiltrated," reported Bellegarde.

"How so?" The Asian's voice was pinched and curt.

"Dawoud—new convert—reported meeting a man on the beach who *claimed* to be a tourist."

"Did you get any details?"

"Just a name for now. I'll look into it.'"

There was silence for a moment. "Interesting. How about Dawoud? Is he responsive to the programming?"

"Better than average. He's loyal and subservient. Ideal material."

"Very well," replied Makaru. "Watch him anyway. You judge what to do, but I'll get him emotionally involved. Inducting him into my personal guard would be prudent."

Bellegarde allowed himself a mental pat on the back. "Enemies closer? I already suggested it."

"Keep me updated."

The phone went dead.

017: The Betrayal

McKinley gently lifted Sister Sheba's arm so that he could roll away from her. Her dark brown skin felt so smooth and delicate, as though even his touch risked damaging its fragility. She stirred a little, but didn't wake.

He sat up on the edge of her bed and rubbed the sleep from his eyes. By thunder, it was going to be a beautiful day in this beautiful place. McKinley could understand the appeal of living on Rubakang, insulated from the world. Even though the converts' minds were no longer their own, their existence here was, for a time, enviably pleasurable.

Dazzling sunshine glowed through the slats of the blind as McKinley got up and stretched. He gathered his clothes, taking another look at the delicious female with whom he'd spent the night. What was it they said about never going back? He grinned to himself. Sheba could have been Beyonce Knowles' darker sister. She was spectacular, with long, perfectly black, straightened hair, rich full lips, high but rounded cheekbones and sumptuous dark brown eyes that, when open, just invited him to fall in. Her understated curves were as perfect as an ebony carving and her rear view was one of the best he'd even seen.

McKinley was amazed by the liberal attitudes of Wolf River. The surprising freedoms afforded Makaru's disciples were something his traditional Scottish family would have frowned upon. Whilst being a highly religious community in appearance, sexual promiscuity was rife, as was smoking certain recreational pharmaceuticals. The only thing that seemed marginally controlled was the use of alcohol, but McKinley suspected that this was a supply issue. It seemed that, although obedience to the leadership was an absolute duty, there were no moral absolutes. It made a certain sense; how better to control than through the endowment of multiple pleasures and then the threat of losing such hedonistic delights if you happened to piss 'god' off by disobedience or going AWOL. The fear of divine retribution was a powerful motivator. Makaru's really got this figured out, he thought.

He found Carter munching on a banana in the dining hall, which they shortly left to do the morning's reconnaissance: a look inside Wolf River's power plant. McKinley had learned from his ladyfriend that inside the steaming mountain was a viewing gallery to which access was unrestricted. Carter had found the narrow road that led up the hill away from the township and McKinley decided to explore it.

The road, which was more of a mud path, ascended steeply from the compound and was about wide enough for a single vehicle. It appeared to have been cut directly through the forest and nowhere was there evidence of additional utilities such as pipelines and cables, leading them to deduce that such things must be underground.

As the sun climbed it became hotter and more humid. They gradually became used to the constant ambience of myriad creatures in the foliage, accepting it as the normal soundtrack of Rubakang. The gradient was steep, making the climb seem more like two miles than two kilometers.

Eventually they found themselves in a wide, flattened area next to the rock wall of the cone which, as Carter explained, wasn't a volcano in itself but a subsidiary thermal vent called a fumarole. There was a spectacular view of the township and the bay from this point, and again they were struck by the beauty of the island landscape. Looking north-west, they could see that the fence that

Makaru had so vehemently warned against approaching also reached this height and skirted that side of the fumarole.

A concrete staircase with orange painted railings rose to a substantial steel door through which they passed, finding themselves in a long corridor carved through the solid rock. At the end a similar door opened into the viewing gallery. Inside, the humidity went up by at least ten points and the sounds of working machinery echoed around, mixed with the hissing of pressurised steam.

The observation platform was a huge concrete shelf built into the side of the fumarole's throat measuring about forty feet across. Its ceiling was a fantastic collection of stalactites and other rock formations that would have made a geologist swoon. There was another door at the opposite end and, built right across the front, a concrete safety barrier sprouted more orange railings on which they could lean to look into the bowels of the power plant.

McKinley turned to his friend. "You know what we're going to do?"

Carter was leaning right over, probing the steamy depths. "What?"

"Five decades ago, a bunch of farmers with improvised weapons maintained a campaign of harassment that kept the mechanised might of the world's most powerful nation on its toes. That's what we're going to do; we're going to be the Victor Charlie of Rubakang to Makaru and his bully-boys."

"Right; the dirty tricks brigade. Consider it done."

McKinley nodded to himself. If they acted clever, they could divert Makaru's toy soldiers from actually looking *for* them. They'd blend in, gain as much access as they needed, and bring the Asian's whole empire crashing down around his ears. Yeah, thought McKinley, we can make this happen.

"This is neat," said Carter, reading an information sign, several of which lined the barrier. "They're taking superheated water from way down near the magma chamber and using it for heat and power in the plant down there," he stabbed over the railing and downward with a finger. "This acts like a cooling tower."

McKinley bent to look over the railings. Stretching away below him were tiers of silver cooling vanes that looked at first like the backs of rows and rows of chairs. They continued downward until they faded into the yellow tinged steam, below which he could make out nothing at all. He rotated his head and, above, saw the glow of daylight through the ascending cloud.

Carter was still reading the information panels. "Clever, clever stuff," he acknowledged. "They're using giant chemical heat capacitors to store the geothermal energy. I'd die to get a look at the tech."

"You can do that another time," answered McKinley. "I wanna get sucking the *real* secrets out of this place."

Brother Dawoud could not believe the extent of the morning's blessing.

"You will meet with Pastor Makaru," said the usher, a short, blond-haired fella with rough complexion and more than a hint of Eastern Europe in his scratchy voice.

Dawoud was a bit lost for words. "Wow... I mean, yes absolutely! Do you know what Pastor wants?"

"I don't," replied the young man, "but it must be important. Very few are summoned for a personal audience."

"Wow," repeated Dawoud.

The usher led Dawoud to a waiting jeep and drove them up to the security cordon where the pair of guards gave them a thorough looking over. As they passed through the gate, Dawoud noticed another jeep approaching from behind. It too was let through.

The jeeps drove past the greenhouses and parked together by Pastor Makaru's Citadel, an impressive residence in the shape of a cylinder with six visible levels, each of which was slightly smaller in circumference than its lower, creating a series of tall, narrow steps. Three floors had windows of floor to ceiling height and some were wide, the biggest being at the top level where it wrapped around half the cylinder and faced the bay. Parked next to their vehicles was the pastor's Rolls-Royce, a handsome conveyance in a very dark red.

The occupants of the other jeep were a female usher and a cute young woman with long black, curly locks flowing down to her shoulders. She smiled at Dawoud, revealing perfect teeth and emphasising her cute dimples.

"Hi," she beamed. Dawoud smiled back.

"Go in here," said Dawoud's usher. "Sit down. Pastor will call you."

He swiped a security card at the door's lock and with a click and hum it slid open. Beyond was a well lit concrete corridor about ten feet wide, lined with two leather couches and with an elevator door at the far end. Other than these and the impressively polished floor tiles with their myriad fossils, it was featureless. Dawoud and Miriam walked in and the door slid shut behind them. They sat on the couches facing each other.

"You haven't been in here before, have you?" she inquired.

Dawoud struggled a little to find an answer. "This is all new to me. I only got here—"

"I'm in here a lot," she announced. "I clean Pastor's apartment sometimes."

A little bemused by the charming arrogance with which she expressed her privilege, Dawoud smiled. "That's a tremendous blessing."

"I'm Sister Miriam," she announced, holding out a thin fingered, willowy palm. "Isabella any other day of the week."

He shook her hand. "Brother Dawoud. Nice to meet you."

"You too."

Dawoud was a little puzzled. "Why did you say Isabella?"

"That's me old name," she grinned, "only don't tell anyone, eh?"

"I think you should be more careful not to dig up your old life."

She was about to remonstrate when Pastor Makaru's voice echoed eerily in the corridor.

"Please step into the elevator," he said.

"Yes Pastor!" they choroused.

The readout in the elevator indicated that they were ascending to the top of the building and when the doors opened they found themselves stepping into what was clearly Pastor Makaru's office.

The panoramic window that they'd seen from below provided a wonderfully impressive view out over the bay. They could see the whole township and everything else in a one hundred and eighty degree arc to the north.

The office was enormous. Its centerpiece was a huge mahogany desk with rich red leather inlay bearing a gilded serpentine pattern. Behind this a big, winged chair in the same red leather had its back to the center of the glass expanse. Opposite the window, the straight wall of the office was formed entirely of bookcases apart from the central elevator door, another door next to this on their left, and the top of a circular stairwell on their far right, beyond the end of the window. Around the room, artifacts from all over the world were presented as ornaments. Here was a model pagoda, there an African carving of a hunter with spear raised in a fearsome pose. They saw a pottery hippopotamus statue painted with colourful flowers next to an intricately carved chest inlaid with gold. There were several ethnic and antique musical instruments and, near the desk, a tall, narrow glass case, containing roughly eighty entomological specimens.

There were three skylights. One was above the main chair and the others in triangular juxtaposition with it, closer to where the long window met the wall. The floor was covered with a thick carpet of deep, luxuriant brown.

Their pastor, leader, apostle, the Universal Spirit's earthly representative and the man for whom they would gladly surrender their lives faced away from them, looking out over his domain, hands linked behind his back.

Dawoud and Miriam didn't know what to do, so they just stood there outside the elevator. Its doors slid shut and this sound appeared to arouse the pastor from his reverie.

He turned his head slightly to the right and said "come in. Sit down." His voice was quiet, yet its tone instantly commanded obedient respect.

Casting a nervous look at each other, they sat in front of the mammoth desk. The pastor continued to stare out over the bay.

"There is such great beauty here," he rumbled. "Such great beauty. We are so blessed, you and I."

Dawoud and Miriam didn't know what to say, so they maintained their silence.

"I feel that I have the greatest blessing of all, though," continued Makaru, "because I get to see the faces of you beautiful disciples."

What an amazing honour to be so described by the holy apostle! Dawoud and Miriam were blown away.

Makaru turned slowly, his head somewhat bowed. As he faced them, he lifted his head and said "you are so beautiful. I love your obedience."

Overwhelmed by this heavenly vote of confidence, Sister Miriam started to weep. Dawoud could appreciate her feelings, but he was having trouble making an emotional connection. It felt wrong that he couldn't also cry tears of joy, but it somehow felt equally wrong that he *should*. Dawoud chided himself and returned to the moment.

"Sister Miriam," said the pastor, "you are a young woman of quiet but steady faith and service."

"Thank you," she whispered, the tears now flowing openly.

Makaru spoke a little more softly. "Your work in the kitchens has not gone unnoticed. You have kept my humble dwelling in immaculate condition. Your life of joy has affected many around you."

Miriam's head was in her hands, weeping freely as she was overwhelmed by love for her pastor.

The Asian turned to Dawoud. "Brother Dawoud," he said.

"Yes, Pastor?" Dawoud couldn't believe he was here. Could he possibly be so blessed as to hear the same kind of approval as Sister Miriam? He'd only been in Wolf River a couple of days! It was too much to ask.

"The Universal Spirit has spoken to me deeply of you." Makaru fixed his eyes on the young man. Dawoud's heart started to melt.

"You have received blessings of strength and skill, of courage and resourcefulness. I sense the Spirit leading me to advance you way beyond our other new disciples. I feel that the two of you can become leaders in our assembly."

His eyes wide, Dawoud sneaked a quick glance at Sister Miriam, surprised to find her tear-drenched and reddened face also looking keenly back at him, her eyes almost popping with emotion.

"Yes," said the Pastor, catching their shared look. "The Spirit bears witness in your inner being. You know it to be true."

Dawoud could have fallen through the floor. This was the greatest and most exciting experience he could possibly imagine. What a ridiculous blessing on one so unworthy!

The minister regarded him with such a long glance that Dawoud became uncomfortable, but then the Asian spoke.

"You will become a member of my personal guard. You will wear the amethyst uniform that signifies your sacrificial obedience, and the gold *Basmolet* of rank."

Dawoud was having trouble taking all this in. His excitement at hearing such words from the pastor was almost sexual in its intensity. He felt like he was floating on the Universal Spirit.

Makaru slowly walked around the desk until he was standing behind and between them. He placed his hands gently on their heads. "Close your eyes," he murmured, "and I will impart a blessing upon you."

They bowed their heads in obedience.

Makaru's voice became a soothing bass drone. "As you concentrate on my words, take them deep into your inner being. Forget everything else and focus on my voice. Hear my voice deep inside your soul. Listen and obey. You will feel the spirit's fire igniting flames of affection for each other. Let yourself go into that wonderful place and allow those feelings to flourish. They will grow into a huge blaze of love for each other. Love each other deeply, without inhibition, and obey your leadership as you follow the call. Be all you can be for your leaders as we love and guide you. When you open your eyes as I say 'amen', may it be fully so. You don't have to remember my words, but your heart will always gladly obey."

He looked down at his disciples. They were completely still. Even their breathing was slow and regular.

"Amen!" he snapped, clapping his hands.

Dawoud opened his eyes with a start. He'd allowed himself to drift off and missed the blessing, but he certainly wasn't going to admit to it; that would look terribly disrespectful. He felt peaceful and yet energised. He shook his head a bit and looked round at Miriam. Maybe he just hadn't noticed before, but she was incredibly beautiful and he felt the most wonderful attraction to her at that moment. Judging by the look on her face, the magnetism was mutual.

Makaru had returned to his side of the desk. He pushed a switch to open the elevator doors and held his hand toward it, making it clear that it was time to leave. "We'll talk more," he said, smiling peacefully. "May you be blessed to see the Kingdom."

Having repeated the standard valediction, Dawoud and Miriam entered the elevator feeling like they were awash with love in paradise. As the doors swished together, they looked longingly into each other's eyes, all inhibitions gone. There were no words, for no words could suffice. As they surrendered themselves to each other in a deeply passionate kiss they became each other's world.

Makaru watched the video feed from the elevator. Dumb peasants, he thought, this is just too easy. Their hormones would do the rest.

Dawoud saw the herculean figure of Bellegarde waiting for them as they passed through the security cordon. Their jeeps pulled up right next to him and Bellegarde leaned toward Dawoud. The prophet had a brown paper parcel in his hand.

"Brother Dawoud," he announced with a great big smile, "this is for you."

Still overawed, Dawoud took the offered package and opened it. He saw shiny metal and violet fabric. Pulling back the wrapping, he found a *Basmolet* that was nearly the size of a Compact Disc, its lustrous gold glinting in the bright sunshine. The medallion and its chain were cushioned on a jacket which he quickly unfolded. Sister Miriam took the scrap paper as Dawoud held up the garment and let it hang before his eyes. It was a wonderfully handsome piece of clothing which couldn't have looked more ecclesiastical, with its high, white sown-in collar. It was cut in a thoroughly modern style, yet reminded him of something that a cardinal in the Vatican might wear. Its colour had the depth of a fine wine, a rich Palatinate purple that seemed uncommon to his eye.

"Yeah," said Bellegarde, nodding. "That's it. You're in Pastor's personal guard now."

Dawoud shook his head. "I... I'm... I don't know what to say!"

"Wear it with pride, son," added Bellegarde. "It's a position of great responsibility. Very few receive this honour."

Still as high as a music executive in a cocaine factory, Dawoud simply said "I *will*."

The musclebound prophet seemed to have something else on his mind. "Your training will start soon, but I must speak about another matter with you Brother. Walk with me."

Could this be *more* blessing? Dawoud gave Sister Miriam a tender kiss then eagerly jumped from the vehicle and followed Bellegarde onto the beach.

The tide was low, exposing a wide swath of drying sand and clusters of seashells. The warm air was filled with the moist aroma of seawater: hints of ionisation, fish and the sulphurous whiff of decomposing seaweed. Dawoud fell into step alongside the leader and listened.

"The man you met on the beach," started Bellegarde gravely, "is an enemy of the Kingdom."

Dawoud was shocked. There was no way he could have known!

"I'm so sorry, Prophet," he quaked. "I had no idea!"

Bellegarde turned and gave him a somewhat twisted smile. "It's not your fault. The enemy specialises in trickery and deception."

"Still, I'm sorry."

"I know. You'll remember him if you see him again, won't you?"

"Yes sir. I'll tell you straight away."

Bellegarde turned suddenly, bringing Dawoud to a halt facing him. He lifted a stalwart finger for emphasis. "He's dangerous; *extremely* dangerous. He's a trained killer for the old world order. He and his people already caused terrible trouble for us in the Canary Islands and... other places." Bellegarde's face hardened further. "His presence here means that his organisation plans to destroy us."

Dawoud gasped. "No way!"

"Now you're in Pastor's personal guard you might be called upon to dispose of him. Can you do that Brother?"

"I'll do what I have to," nodded Dawoud. He would rather die than let such a man impede the mission of The Ambassadors or threaten their pastor, but there was something puzzling about the information that Prophet Bellegarde had relayed. His mention of those Spanish islands had the most tantalising ring of familiarity, and Dawoud wondered why.

McKinley and Carter were circumnavigating Wolf River, keeping their eyes peeled for anything they'd missed before. Heinmarsh was here and all their worst suspicions about the American were coming true. But where was he hiding and, more to the point, where were the nuclear materials?

"Have you wondered about the dock?" asked McKinley as they skirted the buildings, walking north in the margin between the compound and the edge of the jungle.

"What about it?" said Carter.

"Why didn't the ship bring us straight here?"

Carter shrugged. "The dock's too small, obviously, and the bay's too shallow."

"Exactly. But why have it moor all the way on the other side of the island?"

"I see what you're thinking," nodded Carter. "If they built all this stuff, why not a decent sized dock?"

"Aye," nodded McKinley. "Something's hidden. From both land and sea."

"So Makaru needs that boat to get to it?"

"Reckon. Whatever it is, it's important."

"Hence the serious warning. We should check it out."

McKinley winked. "Tonight."

Carter nudged him. "There's... Willy." It felt peculiar to use their colleague's nickname, knowing what had happened to him.

McKinley followed Carter's gaze between the row of buildings and saw Wilson—or that which used to be Wilson—having what appeared to be a serious conversation with one of the leaders. The older man was speaking animatedly and Wilson, holding a purple-coloured bundle, nodded every now and then. Suddenly, he looked up and right at them. His eyes widened and he pointed.

"*That's him!*" shouted Wilson.

Bellegarde yanked a pistol out of his pocket and started running at them, yelling "*guards!*" at the top of his voice.

McKinley and Carter took off running, heading north-west toward the security cordon near the greenhouses. But there were guards there! McKinley's first thought was to get to the beach somehow, but they'd been caught in almost the worst place imaginable. They heard sounds of panicked voices in the compound. As they came into site of the barrier, the guards at the gate dashed towards Bellegarde's shout and McKinley saw their opportunity.

"Weapons!" snapped McKinley and, rounding the corner of another building, they chased the guards. McKinley caught the first, sweeping him down at the shoulders and punching him soundly in the face. He relieved the man of his Heinmarsh rifle as the other stopped, turning to see what had happened to his colleague. A mighty blow from Carter sent the guard flying backward into a garbage skip. Moving like lightning, Carter slammed the man's head against the metal. His body hadn't even hit the ground before Carter was tearing away with both rifle and bandolier.

McKinley hurdled the security barrier as the first shots came. So much for a peaceful paradise, he thought, as he dropped behind the left-hand guard kiosk. He saw Carter throw himself over the gate, roll and quickly disappear into the other.

Cocking the weapon, McKinley grudgingly admired its efficient design. A round tore into the sand near his feet, sending a cloud into the air. Okay, thought McKinley, my turn. He leaned round the corner of the little guardhouse and fired once, catching a guard in the leg. The man fell with a sharp cry.

McKinley ducked back into cover, counting their assailants from the snapshot image his eyes had captured. There were six coming from various angles, minus the guy he'd shot, plus any he couldn't see. Holy *shit* why did they always have to deal with these odds?! He leaned out and took two more shots, being careful not to kill but wound.

Carter was firing too, toward the beach. McKinley heard the screams of the crowd, running away from the gunfire. He chanced another look. More guards.

"You're surrounded," yelled Bellegarde's distinctive voice. "Drop the weapons and come out with your hands behind your heads!"

McKinley wasn't ready to capitulate. There had to be another way.

"Look what I found," hissed Carter.

McKinley quickly shuffled his body to be able to see his colleague across the track. Carter was winking at him from inside the other kiosk, pointing to a box labelled 'GRENADES H.E.'. McKinley rolled his eyes. Only Carter could dive into a random bit of cover and find such a useful thing. Now that explained the trenches, which were for blast protection, but what on earth were *grenades* doing in a religious cult?

"Cover me," grated Carter as he pulled a 'pineapple' out of the top of the case.

McKinley made ready, selecting automatic and positioning himself on one knee, but further back from the booth so that he could see what his friend was doing.

"Now!" shouted Carter, breaking cover and heaving the box with all his might into the air and toward their assailants. McKinley quickly sprayed a hail of lead in the same direction. They both broke cover and threw themselves toward the trench.

Bellegarde's face took on an expression of abject shock as he turned tail and fled. His guards fell into confusion as the case tumbled onto the ground in their midst.

McKinley's body crashed into the bottom of the sandy trench as the grenades went off. The detonation was terrific, kicking him in the lungs and sending a shower of sand from the walls of the cutting. But instantly he was getting up, knowing that they'd only bought a few seconds.

As McKinley rolled out of the trench he saw Carter doing the same. On a whim he threw himself into the guardhouse behind which he'd hidden. Paydirt! There was another case of grenades and a bandolier. McKinley grabbed both and he and Carter ran like men possessed, behind the greenhouses and toward the Citadel. The jungle was their only possible refuge.

They looked at each other. "Down," ordered McKinley as he pulled a grenade, plucking the safety pin out with his teeth and throwing it toward the base of the tall fence. They both dropped to the ground and sheltered their heads as well as possible.

Bang! The shockwave from the explosion smacked them both against the greenhouse wall as it tore a hole in the steel mesh. Without thinking twice McKinley jumped to his feet and fled through the gap, being careful not to touch the metal, which would still be live. They heard sounds of pursuit and orders being shouted. McKinley heard yells about helicopters.

"Hit the choppers!" he barked.

Carter ran to the edge of the greenhouse where he could see the beach with its four helicopter pads. McKinley threw him a grenade. Using all the strength he could muster, Carter propelled the little bomb as far as he could toward the aircraft. Without waiting, McKinley passed another.

The first grenade exploded as Carter was throwing the second. It didn't have much of an impact other than dissuading the guards from approaching the helos. The second was better, smashing the second nearest aircraft. Carter threw another and managed to get it right under the nearest. It exploded in a ball of fire as bullets started to twang around him again.

"Let's go!" snarled McKinley. Carter dived through the gap in the fence.

The undergrowth was just as dense as before but, propelled as they were by urgency, it seemed so much thicker. They tore north, passing behind the Citadel and into unknown and untamed territory.

McKinley held his hand out, stopping Carter's progress. "Listen!"

Sure enough the sound of 'copter rotors munching on air could be heard like the roar of distant automatic fire. Then they were joined by another sound: dogs!

"Move it!" snapped McKinley and they headed inland, tearing through everything they could to create a passage through the tightly packed rainforest. They climbed higher and higher as they left behind the bay, causing their muscles to ache. They swapped the box of grenades between them from time to time to share the load.

Suddenly the loud thrashing of a helicopter ripped through the sky above the canopy, bringing them to a halt. They were surrounded by undergrowth and probably invisible from up there. McKinley listened again. Something was amiss.

"Those dogs aren't getting any closer," he panted.

"Maybe they didn't find the gap," suggested Carter, his breath also heaving.

"Bollocks," refuted McKinley. He quickly jumped and caught a low hanging bow. Swinging his legs up, he got himself on top of it and sought a view through the foliage. McKinley had to move back and forth on this precarious perch, but he finally found a position where he could see the compound clearly enough to make out what was happening.

"You're right," he gasped. "The purple bodyguard guys with the dogs are waiting at the fence. Makaru *really* doesn't want anyone out here."

"Down!" snapped Carter as the helicopter tore overhead again.

McKinley jumped off the branch and rolled, coming to rest in some bushes and swearing. "Let's go!" he said, picking himself up.

Keeping away from the ridge, where their cover would be patchy, they cut back south-west, heading further and further inland. A second chopper joined the search and both pilots were getting bolder, swerving low in their hunt for the fugitives.

"What's the plan, boss?" coughed Carter.

"Right now? Stay alive," said McKinley, looking up as one of the choppers made a low pass.

Suddenly an ear-splitting crack came from nearby. The explosion shredded the thicket and knocked both men off their feet. It was clear what had happened.

McKinley wiped dirt off his face. "Now who's got grenades?" he complained.

They picked themselves up and ran, trying to out-think the pilots, who were closing in, getting a better idea of their location with each flypast.

Another grenade blew a hole in the forest just downhill from them and McKinley swore again. A third blast hit them from ahead. It was obvious that a lucky throw on the part of the pilots could be bad news.

"See that clearing down there?" said McKinley.

"Got it."

The team leader braced himself on the trunk of a sturdy tree. "Get over there then on my mark wave your arms or something."

"Roger... that," said Carter uncertainly, as he started crawling through the undergrowth in the indicated direction.

McKinley climbed hard, but the biggest impedance was the moisture. The tree was covered in a lime green moss that felt like damp sponge. Several times his hands and feet slipped and McKinley found himself being too cautious to climb with necessary speed. The trainers he was wearing were next to useless, unable to penetrate the thick bark for a foothold, and his shirt was tearing on the many woody protrusions. Cursing his idea, McKinley finally got some height and straddled a bouncy branch, hoping it wasn't suddenly going to let him down.

"Chris!" he yelled.

Carter heard McKinley's call just as one of the aircraft barrelled deafeningly overhead at almost zero feet, shaking the foliage with its downwash. As it was flying away from him, though, Carter used the opportunity to stand, finding his way to what was roughly the center of the clearing. As soon as the chopper swung round for another pass, he put up his hands as though in surrender.

The chopper pilot had obviously seen him as it turned because the aircraft stabilised on a dead heading toward him and its front dipped hard as it accelerated. That was when both Carter and McKinley realised that the aircraft was armed. Two dark stalks projected from its belly. Suddenly they started to flash and Carter felt impacts around him. He threw himself to the ground as it shook with the ballistic force.

McKinley cursed. He'd expected the chopper to come to a hover near Carter, but this guy was on the attack! There was only one thing he could do so McKinley took aim and squeezed the trigger. The recoil knocked him right off the branch.

Like a vehicular impact, McKinley's insides were pummelled as he crashed into the undergrowth, the rifle still in his hands. It smacked him right in the face and McKinley tasted blood. He couldn't breathe because his thoracic diaphragm was still in spasm from having the wind knocked out of it. He rolled, thankful that by some miracle nothing appeared to be broken. He could hear the automatic fire of the onrushing helicopter, then the sound of Carter's rifle joined it.

In the clearing, strafed by debris, torn leaves and shit from the forest floor yet somehow having been missed by actual rounds, Carter desperately fired into the aircraft, registering vaguely that this situation was familiar. He saw the canopy starred with bullet impacts; then it was upon him. The helo dropped and ploughed into the mountainside just above his position, where it exploded with a huge hot *thump*, sending rivers of burning fuel down toward him and a great mushroom of fire back up into the sky. Caught for a second in his own shock like the proverbial rabbit in the headlights, Carter looked agape at the aircraft's carcass, which groaned metallically and started to roll down the hill, spilling more fuel. He was going to be crushed and fried at the same time!

Carter threw his arm up reflexively, expecting burning agony, but suddenly a strong hand yanked him to his feet and propelled him out of the path of the rolling inferno. Carter landed in the bush at the edge of the clearing and

McKinley landed next to him. Passing within a foot of them, the dead helicopter continued its crazy somersaulting, crushing and scorching an incandescent path through the rainforest. Terrified birds erupted into the air in a cacophony of screeches and cries. The smell of burning fuel filled their lungs.

"We need to move," said McKinley, but Carter didn't register it. He looked into McKinley's face.

"What happened to you?"

The lower half of McKinley's face, daubed in blood that was soaking into his beard, opened to speak. "Shared a kiss with the rifle."

Grimacing, Carter thumbed in the direction of the chopper's descent. "I think they know where we are now."

As if in answer, the second chopper burst into view over the ridge and started to circle their position. They would be covered for now by the smoke cloud, but mobility was everything. McKinley and Carter jumped into action, crawling desperately back uphill and under the arboreal canopy.

They ran when they could, jumped over what they could and scrambled through everything else. The helicopter kept buzzing them. A wide ravine predicated that they turn south and they accelerated their pace, knowing how close this could take them to Wolf River's boundaries. The going was exhausting and painful. Their clothes ran with sweat and their hearts beat loudly in their ears, bringing their breath in choking bursts.

Suddenly Carter pulled up and McKinley slid to a halt beside him.

"Your call," panted Carter.

McKinley stared at the big fence, which towered above them. They could blow another hole in it and be found out, or they could turn right and climb again, not knowing where the hell they would end up. Either way their pursuers were closing in. Damn it!

"Right," heaved McKinley, his hands resting on his knees, trying to get his breath. Carter was still panting hard and tucking his shirt into the top of his shorts.

"What're you doing?" asked McKinley.

"I'm fed up with carrying this case," Carter said. He took four grenades and threw them to McKinley. "Put 'em down your shirt, in your pockets, whatever."

"Good idea." McKinley followed suit.

Carter discarded the box and slowly, with great difficulty, they forced themselves to move again. Keeping in sight of the fence, they clambered back up the slope.

McKinley looked above. They were by the base of the fumarole, its dense output overshadowing the forest and bringing a little relief from the constant heat.

"Chris," he gasped, "see that?"

Up ahead was the entrance of a tunnel in the rock wall. McKinley bounded over and looked into the gap. A couple of meters in there was a door much like that which led to the viewing gallery. He cast a questioning glance at Carter. Somewhere to hide? Could they be that lucky?

Prepared for disappointment, McKinley pushed on the substantial handle and to his surprised it moved. The door swung open to reveal a vertical shaft beyond, containing a stairwell built from steel I-beams with mesh steps, all painted in the ubiquitous orange and illuminated by electric light.

Carter trotted in behind him, looking up the stairs to see where they led.

Opposite the entrance was another, much more substantial door. Its sign bore a downward pointing arrow and the words 'GEOTHERMAL PLANT'.

McKinley dashed across and tried the door. The moment he touched the handle a loud klaxon blared its warning and the door through which they'd entered slammed shut. McKinley swore, throwing himself at the outer door, but to no avail. It was locked solid.

The only option was up and McKinley felt trapped. Indeed, if this *was* a trap, he'd fallen for it hook, line and sinker. But what were they to do? Wait for their pursuers to find them? Better to move than no progress at all. He started to leap up the stairs and Carter followed.

His heart pounding mercilessly, McKinley counted eight reciprocal flights of steps before seeing any way out. There was another door on the right and he slapped his hand down on the handle in hope.

It opened and McKinley ran into the space beyond, recognising it instantly.

Carter followed him, saying "oh, we're back here" between gasps.

They were on the viewing platform of the cooling tower. Once again they found themselves in what must have been a huge lava bubble or other natural cavity, until Makaru's people created this impressively engineered gallery. Again the humidity soared because of the massive volume of steam that was rushing skyward to their right. It felt like Makaru's greenhouse yet much, much hotter.

McKinley allowed himself to fall to the ground, his back against the point where the lava wall met the concrete. He was bloody knackered, yet pressured by his instinct for survival to keep going. Carter looked the same, but was busily checking his rifle.

"Here," croaked McKinley, and tossed Carter the bandolier he'd liberated from the guard's little gatehouse.

"Thanks," said Carter, as he started to pull the extra ammunition from its pouches.

Just as he was feeding the precious rounds into the Heinmarsh rifle, there came an ominous mechanical clunk from behind. Carter turned back to find that the door was locked.

"Trapped!" he exclaimed.

McKinley was fresh out of options. The only way out was the other door and Makaru's guards would undoubtedly be coming through it at any moment. The only possible alternative could be to jump over the balcony's edge, but that was suicidal.

"Chris," he said slowly, "we're going to have to fight."

"There's no cover."

"I know."

They looked at each other, both knowing that their capture was more than probable and their survival even less likely.

"We shouldn't have come inside," said McKinley. "Sorry."

"Too late," smiled Carter dryly. "Don't get your knickers in a twist."

McKinley jumped as the door at the other end of the galley opened. He readied the rifle, as did Carter, who fell into a sniper position on the floor, supporting the weapon on his crooked left arm. Four guards walked in, taking position either side of the door, and more were visible in the corridor beyond. McKinley vaguely noticed a metallic tinkle from the floor near him.

Bellegarde swaggered in as if he owned the mountain. McKinley toyed with the idea of plugging him right then and there, but that would assure their demise. Unless this turned into a shit-fight of its own accord—and a very brief and one-sided shit-fight it would be—surrender was the only option that could possibly keep them in the game.

The big French-American stood there with hands on hips holding his jacket back, and turned around.

"Nowhere to hide McKinley," he mocked. "Thought you could maybe do better."

"I'm having a bad day," said McKinley. *Wait a moment, how the heck does this bastard know my name?!*

"It's about to get worse," replied Bellegarde, an evil leer parting his lips. "This is the part where you surrender and I don't order these guys to open fire."

McKinley decided to gamble. "I'm aiming right for your heart."

Bellegarde huffed, turning to his men. He spoke in an Asian sounding tongue and they all brought their weapons to eye level. McKinley realised what Bellegarde had said as the big man gave voice to it.

"They're aiming right for your buddy's head."

McKinley sighed heavily. There was no way they could stare Bellegarde down. The odds were too well stacked against them. If he pegged Bellegarde, Carter's death would be instant and there'd be nothing in the world he could do to prevent it. It was time to accept the odds and try to figure something else out.

"Okay," said McKinley. He looked down at Carter. "Stand down."

Carter backed away from the weapon and started to get to his knees. McKinley laid his own gun down and stood, putting his hands behind his head.

"What's up with your hand?!" demanded Bellegarde.

McKinley looked at Carter. "Nothing," said the latter. "It's injured."

Bellegarde growled angrily. "What's *in* your hand?!"

"Oh," replied Carter, as if he'd realised what he was holding. "Just this."

He threw the grenade forward, its handle spinning away with a *ping*. Instantly he dropped to the concrete again. McKinley, shocked to see what was happening, also dropped, covering his head with his hands.

The grenade sailed past Bellegarde, whose eyes followed it with horror, whilst the guards panicked and dived for cover. It clattered into the corridor through the open door. There was a second of screams, then it exploded with a bright flash of light, blowing the door off its hinges and pulverising everyone in the corridor. Bellegarde was blown forward toward the COAST men, his legs flailing.

McKinley grabbed his rifle and started to fire. Bellegarde rolled into Carter and the two of them grappled. Shots cracked into the rock and concrete, creating tiny explosions of shards. Carter and Bellegarde were circling each other. The guards were trying to shoot McKinley without hitting their leader. A ricochet hit McKinley on the top of his right shoulder, bringing stinging pain. Carter got in a flying kick at Bellegarde and the big man recovered quickly, punching him in the face sharply. McKinley shot one of the guards in the stomach. He saw Carter and Bellegarde viciously punching it out like boxers without rules. Another round passed his ear with a whip-like crack, its bow-wave smacking his head. One of the grenades in his shirt fell out so McKinley grabbed it, plucked the pin between his teeth and threw it across the smooth floor beneath Carter and Bellegarde, who were slugging it out nastily. He took up his rifle again as the grenade clunked against the far wall. A gut-punching shockwave hit McKinley as it detonated, killing two of the guards instantly. The last guard fell forward toward McKinley, who shot him between the eyes. He looked up to see Bellegarde physically lifting Carter from behind with an inhuman roar.

McKinley jumped to his feet but it was too late. With a guttural bellow of victory, Bellegarde heaved Carter over the wall and down into the guts of the power plant. Carter gave a terrible, fearful cry that was cut off as suddenly as an audio tape being snipped.

In shock and rage McKinley screamed "*NO!*"

Bellegarde, his face a twisted mask of brutality, turned toward McKinley in time to get whacked right in his dial by the butt of McKinley's rifle. He bent double in agony but started to get back up immediately. McKinley swung the rifle from behind him with all his might down onto Bellegarde's exposed neck. The big man hit the ground, his legs splaying out from under him.

McKinley hit again. And again. He kept slamming the solid firearm down on Bellegarde's head and muscular shoulders in a ferocious rhythm driven by rage, pounding repeatedly until his hands started to lose their grip on the weapon.

Suddenly there was a sharp bang nearby and McKinley felt the passage of a round in front of his face. He turned to see the guard he'd wounded in the stomach shakily holding up a pistol. McKinley turned the rifle round and shot the man through the head without even thinking.

Filled with rage and terror, McKinley ran through the corridor, ignoring the ghastly carnage it contained. Swinging over the handrails one after another, he spiralled down the stairwell and headed outside in a confused panic. There was something nagging at his mind but survival was his first priority. He had the rifle and a pair of grenades. He must find shelter and something to eat! McKinley ran east, giving the path that led to Wolf River a wide birth. Come on, remember your training! Find a watercourse! Set up a shelter! Concentrate on your priorities! Don't think about...

The ground vanished beneath him and McKinley was weightless for a second, tumbling helplessly. With a cold, jarring impact he came to rest in a gully. He'd found a watercourse. Cold wetness washed over him, chilling his battered body and bringing some clarity to his mind.

Carter!

He'd seen Carter thrown over the wall.

Carter was...

McKinley felt himself being pulled by the current. The cold made him piss and he couldn't stop it. His body flopped over slimy rocks and he felt himself falling again although now he seemed to accept it.

With a great splash McKinley dropped into the plunge-pool at the bottom of the waterfall. He knew it was time to act, to get up and move, to *fight*. He didn't want to. He didn't feel like he could.

A terrible sense of aloneness gripped McKinley. He was cold on both the outside and the inside. Hope had been extinguished. He was alone. His job was gone. His team-mates were gone. The unit was gone. Even the rifle and grenades had left him for the bottom of the stream. He was brutally isolated on a cult-controlled island eight thousand miles from home and all his grand plans were screwed to shit.

Carter was ... gone.

A light went out inside McKinley, leaving just the training. He didn't know what the hell he was doing but he pushed himself along the stream, slipping and stumbling on the rocks, his mind fighting to make sense of this galactic level shitstorm. He crouched low, seeing guards running up the path toward the fumarole.

McKinley heaved himself out of the stream near where they'd first infiltrated the township. He found where the washing was hanging and quickly stole himself some dry clothes, making sure to grab a cap off a nearby picnic table. He got some kind of vegetable curry with rice at the kitchen serving hatch but avoided the dining area, knowing that Wilson could be there. He walked around the camp in a daze, pushing the food mechanically into his face.

Chris. Dea... gone. The 'D' word was unthinkable.

His heart was still beating at twenty-to-the-dozen. His nerves were alive as if running with electricity and his mind was in overdrive, trying to work out what to do next. Did he really see what he saw? Carter, arms and legs flailing, plunging to his... plunging over that precipice?

"You look *terrible!*"

McKinley started, the delightful voice puncturing the vortex of thought in which he found himself. He looked up, the fork hanging from his mouth.

Her gorgeously dark, round face formed a grin. It was Sister Sheba, the girl with whom he'd spent the night. He looked at her stupidly for a moment.

With an echoing crackle the compound's PA system came to life, blaring a message.

"Because of recent events, there will be a special service in ten minutes. Come for an important and life changing message! Come to the meeting hall in ten minutes!"

McKinley vaguely heard it. He was too busy looking into the eyes of Sheba's friendly face, seeking solace, seeking redemption, forgiveness and peace. The comfort with which he had satiated his desire during their night of passion *yearned* to take hold of him, to wrap him in its seductive forgetfulness, to absolve him of his sins, to tell him that everything would be okay, and he *yearned* to be thus taken.

She put her arm in his. "Come to the meeting with me," she smiled, patting his hand. He dropped the plate without noticing. She reached up to his mouth and gently pulled the fork out. "You won't need this," she chuckled, casting the utensil aside. "What on earth happened to you?"

McKinley didn't answer, simply letting her pull him along. Twenty different voices were clamouring for attention in his mind. Carter's was asking why. General Sutton's was issuing the sternest admonishment ever. Wilson's was talking like someone else. Maddocks' was getting stressed out about the logistics. In the midst of all of them came the accusing tone of Clifton Cambion-Dawkins, thrusting semantic phrases like knives. McKinley was in a mental whirlwind. Thank God for the peaceable guide at his side, beautiful and caring. Her tenderness was as the sweetness of honey to a tongue steeped in wormwood. For the first time in his remembrance McKinley willingly deferred control to another.

Sister Sheba kindly and gently brought him to the main meeting hall. They found a pew and sat down, waiting for the service to begin. She stroked his now blood free beard, whispering gentle kindnesses as the crowd settled around them.

McKinley mostly missed the music, much more enthusiastic than before though it was. He was distracted by a deathly cry echoing from the interior of a steam-filled volcanic vent, and a recurring image of arms and legs flailing, disappearing into the cloud.

He was still tuned out when Makaru started the propaganda, but something about this particular message caught McKinley's attention. Makaru was talking about the end of the world.

"This is just their first attack," yelled the preacher, reminding McKinley of videos he'd seen of extremist political rallies. "The end of all things is upon us, and we must fight with our lives for the Kingdom! They want to defeat us in the apocalypse they have created, but they can never stand in the way of the Universal Spirit, and they can never stop you, dear children, the many-membered manchild, our victorious end time army!"

Choruses of approving shouts reverberated in the hall. Makaru ploughed ahead. "You are all ready to lay down your lives, are you not?"

The room burst with a deafening shout. "*Yes Pastor!*"

"If you have the tiniest doubt," shouted Makaru, "you will come forward now and let Elder Heinmarsh impart the Universal Spirit to refresh you, revive you, renew and equip you!"

"Go forward," suggested Sheba. "You *need* the impartation."

"No... no... I'm fine," mumbled McKinley. Hell, could he *ever* use a smoke right now.

"Go forward," she murmured seductively, "and I will love you forever. You'll never be alone again. You'll never know fear or sadness. You'll be at peace, and my body will be your Garden of Eden, freely given."

Despite what was left of his better judgement, Sheba's voice seemed to be turning a key in his soul and McKinley felt a definite twitch in his nether regions. Could he give it all up? Forget everything and melt away? Lose himself to the charms of this African princess and succumb to her spell? It would be *so easy...*

"You should go forward," said a nearby young woman with the blondest hair, deep brown eyes and braces in her teeth. "You look so lost. We'll take you." Smiling, she grabbed his right arm whilst Sister Sheba held onto his left. McKinley felt like things were going way too fast. He saw Heinmarsh come to the platform as several of the young Ambassadors ran up the steps to the stage.

"Don't fight it, my handsome white man," soothed Sheba. Her tone was mesmerising. His loins savoured the sexual promise in each syllable. His Stepford Wife was offering all of herself as a bribe, and part of him wanted to surrender to it.

McKinley felt drawn, like there was some invisible force propelling him to the front. But I don't believe this stuff, he told himself. Others patted him on the back and shoulders. "You're doing the right thing; may you be blessed to see the Kingdom!" said a man's voice.

McKinley realised that he'd allowed himself to be guided to the aisle. People flooded around him in a sea of religious fervour. His mind was in a fog. If he went up there what would happen? He didn't believe this nonsense, and somewhere deep inside him there was a voice demanding what the effing hell he was doing. But if he refused he'd stand out like a biker in pink leathers.

Suddenly there was another male behind him, a man with a terribly familiar voice.

"Go on up," came Dawoud's words from Wilson's mouth. "Even *you* can be forgiven and receive a new life."

Forgiveness? Through the onslaught of confusing emotions McKinley felt like he understood how he could use some of that. He wanted Chris to forgive him *so badly...*

Wilson-Dawoud was marching him up to the front now. In a moment of lucidity McKinley pulled the brow of his cap down further. They were on the carpeted area. The crowd was going wild with exuberance. Waves of hyped-up spiritual enthusiasm crashed forth from the throng.

"May you be blessed to see the Kingdom!" yelled Sheba's cheery voice, receding behind him, disappearing into the chanting of the herd.

He climbed the steps. *What am I doing here? If I run, it's all over. If I go through with it... will I be like Wilson? I don't believe this stuff! Where's Chris...? Gotta play the part. Holy shit I'm stressed.*

Passing around the deeply shiny grand piano that was near the top of the steps, his reflection following its lustrous curves, McKinley lined up with the others who had responded to the altar call. *I need to find a way to get out of here,* he thought. The band were going crazy, breaking all musical performance records to keep the gathering excited. Suddenly they stopped playing and silence fell over the hall. *What the hell am I doing here,* thought McKinley.

He looked down at the floor, trying to be invisible. He saw Heinmarsh's expensive shoes, shiny turtleshell leather adorned with a wisp of Rubakang's sand. The American wasn't going to the end of the line; he was coming straight toward McKinley.

The big man stopped in front of him and McKinley smelled aftershave. He kept looking down as though the floor was demanding every ounce of his attention.

Heinmarsh leaned forward, bringing his name badge right in front of McKinley's face. "Got any relatives in Kirriemuir?" he quietly snarled, putting his right hand in his pocket.

What?

Something cold sprayed across McKinley's eyes and out went the lights.

018: The Beach

McKinley came round in considerable discomfort.

His shoulders seemed numb, yet his arms hurt like hell, as did his wrists. He opened his eyes to see why.

He was bound at his wrists, hanging from them in a hut. He knew he was still at Wolf River because he could hear the sounds of the compound and jungle outside. As his eyes came into focus he saw an armed guard sitting in the corner nearest the window, which had shutters across it.

Feeling like death warmed over, McKinley tried to look around. The room was quite big, perhaps four hundred square feet, and appeared to be an office. Opposite the darkened window was a desk with a computer, above which a bookshelf held a few volumes and some folders. In the corner, to the desk's right, was the door, and to the desk's left was what appeared to be a medical cabinet.

McKinley tried to look upward, hard though it was with his head sandwiched between his arms. He saw a thick wooden beam and a single, naked light bulb around which insects circulated.

Seeing that his charge was conscious, the guard dipped his head to a microphone on his chest and spoke in the same Asian sounding language that they'd heard before. His report made, the guard sat back. He seemed satisfied that McKinley was helpless.

Hello square one, thought McKinley, we meet again. In some respects he did feel better for the period of unconsciousness. The debilitating confusion was gone from his mind. He was perhaps able to enumerate his tactical position with clarity.

Holy shit. This was bad. He wasn't at square one; this square was in bloody negative figures.

Carter was *gone!*

He remembered with horror, a deeply cold sensation blooming in his guts. He tried to force his mind away from it, to work on his options, but he had none. He was at the mercy of Makaru, Heinmarsh and whomever else.

Hold on, thought McKinley, I appear to be in my right mind. He tried to probe his feelings, to see if there was any undue affection for the cult leaders, but couldn't find any. He did the thirteen times table in his head, then the alphabet backwards. He didn't believe any of that religious stuff; a good sign. He still felt passion for his cause. Memory loss was the key, someone had said. McKinley thought back to his childhood, to his dad, to his dad's half-brother Brennan. I remember killing that scumbag, thought McKinley. I remember my first kiss with that drippy girl from the college. Terrorising the other kids in our village. I remember setting up that fake company when I was thirteen and getting arrested. Joining the army and basic training. I remember my sister Iona. *I remember my past!*

It was clear that whatever Makaru had done to Wilson hadn't been done to him. Why? Why didn't they just turn him into a brainwashed slave?

He heard the door unlocking and it swung inward to reveal Bellegarde. Bellegarde with bandages around his head, a look of the utmost vengeful anger on his long face.

Oh that's right. I gave that shitbag a thrashing. Guess I'm going to get it back now. Yep, another cold day in hell.

Bellegarde walked slowly over until he was only a foot away and swung a mighty right hook into McKinley's face. The impact was so hard that McKinley started to swing from the rafter. He blinked hard, a searing pain burning his left cheek. Bloody hell, Bellegarde could sure throw a punch.

McKinley opened his eyes properly to see Bellegarde's murderous face leering even closer. Suddenly the ugly head shot forward, head-butting McKinley soundly in the lower half of his face. The wounds he'd sustained from getting a rifle slapped into his kisser started to bleed again.

Rubbing his forehead, Bellegarde moved behind and instantly there was a sharp blow to McKinley's kidneys. He felt it all the way through his body. A second brutal impact in the same area caused McKinley to gasp, spraying blood.

Bellegarde came back to face him. "You like that?"

McKinley said nothing. Bellegarde leaned his head sideways toward McKinley as though listening intently.

"What's that?" he nodded, as though not hearing a response properly. "You want to really *feel* it? Okay," taunted the French American, stepping back. In an instant he launched a powerful high-kick into McKinley's stomach. The pain hitting him like a train, McKinley coughed more blood. He wanted to puke.

Bellegarde moved in again, smashing a hail of fists fall into every part of McKinley's torso. McKinley's frame shook with each agonising impact as Bellegarde continued his attack.

The big man slowed down somewhat, breathing hard. The blows stopped. McKinley could do nothing but hang there in agony. His whole body was shouting out in torment and felt like it would fall to pieces.

"That's better," panted Bellegarde. "If I weren't hurtin' I'd have ripped your head off."

McKinley croaked his answer through a bloody dribble. "Don't... beat yourself up about it."

"Funny," Bellegarde smirked. He looked at his wristwatch then approached again. "Time for your nap."

"Hey," gasped McKinley. "Why didn't that stuff make me..." he paused to catch his breath, "forget everything?"

"This stuff?" Bellegarde tapped a finger on his name badge, raising his eyebrows. "It's just a sedative. We don't give them the serum till they're on the boat."

Again there was a cold spray and McKinley's mind dropped into bottomless blackness.

When McKinley next awoke, he was strapped to a metal chair in a claustrophobic prison cell. The first thing he noticed was aching pain in almost every part of his body. McKinley closed his eyes for a second to try and muster his thoughts. Had he not been tied he could probably have taken Bellegarde to pieces in a fair fight. McKinley told himself that the French American was a coward and tried to feel pity for him. Despite the circumstances and the continuing pain from Bellegarde's assault, he had to foster a positive mental attitude.

The next thing McKinley noticed was the smell of the room. Dusty and rank, the odour was of old concrete, years of neglect, rodents, and bathrooms whose encounters with disinfectant were few and far between. He looked around. In front of him was a strong steel door on substantial hinges. The pale blue walls were streaked with dirt, especially below the tiny, barred window up near the ceiling to his left, where cobwebs enshrouded the opening. In the corner to his right and in front of him there was a table containing some unidentified boxes. Listening, McKinley could hear only the birds of Rubakang, strangely dull through that little opening.

Twisting his head painfully, McKinley could make out a low wattage lamp above him; the only source of illumination in the dingy room. The metal chair to which he was bound wasn't unlike a dentist's chair but McKinley was sure that whoever might visit him in this filthy hole would hardly be the bearer of a pleasant bedside manner.

Experimenting with his bonds, McKinley found the straps unyielding. Clearly it was intended that he shouldn't move at all; someone was making sure of that. He looked around for anything that might help him in some way, anything within reach of his painful hands, but there was nothing. All he could do was sit there getting hungrier and thirstier.

With nothing else to usefully occupy his mind, McKinley went to work reviewing The Team's anti-torture procedures. He'd been through the psychological training and knew the principles well, but he'd never had occasion to put them into practice before. Heck, he couldn't guarantee that torture was even his captors' intent. Maybe they'd left him here to die. He wanted to use the time to think but, try as he might, he kept seeing a friend falling like a discarded rag doll down some vapour-shrouded pit. It was a constant battle to thrust the morbid image—and the question of what might have been done to prevent it—from his mind.

And so the hours rolled past like a slow and seemingly endless North American freight train.

Lapsing in and out of an exhausted, haunted sleep, McKinley felt like a good portion of the day had been and gone when there was noise beyond the door. Suddenly he roused himself to full wakefulness and prepared his mind, breathing fast to oxygenate his system. Craning his neck to look at the diminutive window he observed that the ambient light had changed, a clear indicator of the passage of time. Whilst he had to protect his psyche against torture he must, nonetheless, try to retain any and all details. If – no, *when* he got out of this, that information might prove important.

McKinley heard keys in the lock and the door swung inward, the rusty hinges scraping and shrieking in protest like fingernails on some infernal blackboard. Silhouetted by a source of illumination behind them, two of Wolf River's guards stood with Heinmarsh rifles at the ready. Then they moved back from the door, parting deferentially to let someone through. McKinley guessed who was coming.

Pastor Makaru glided across the threshold of the cell, his long robe making it look like he was on wheels. McKinley was suddenly struck by how suitable Makaru would have looked in a vampire movie, all robes and expressionless yet malevolent visage. The cult leader stopped in front of McKinley a few feet back, looking intently down his nose at his captive. Although spooked by Makaru's strange silence, McKinley tried to look steadily back, to impress upon Makaru his immunity from fear. But Makaru's eyes, behind those big, round, owl-like glasses, betrayed nothing. McKinley started to wonder whether Makaru was trying to hypnotise him or something. It wouldn't work; of that he was determined. Makaru's physical presence, however, seemed to radiate both a superior confidence and total disdain for McKinley.

The silent stare-out continued for at least twenty seconds: men of diverse character and position trying both to size each other up and gain some psychological advantage over their opposite. To McKinley this seemed ridiculous given his current state, but he had to retain what ground he could in the psychological battle.

Without warning Makaru broke eye contact and turned back toward the door, rotating as if he was on a turntable. He slid soundlessly out, apparently having got as much measure of McKinley as he needed. A guard pulled the door shut and McKinley was alone again. He heard muffled voices but couldn't perceive the details.

Then the door opened to reveal a familiar silhouette, wider than the East Asian demagogue. Kurt Heinmarsh stepped into the cell, looked arrogantly at McKinley and, hands in jacket pockets, started to pace round the room. A guard swung the door back into its frame and there was a dull clank as it found its mountings, but no sound of keys. The situation was obvious. Makaru had made McKinley Heinmarsh's problem.

"You're a long way from Kirriemuir, Mister McKinley." Heinmarsh slowly circumnavigated the cell, passing in and out of McKinley's field of view. Would he strike while behind? Would he do something despicable from where McKinley's eyes couldn't reach? McKinley steeled himself against the pain, all the time desperately chanting the anti-torture mantra in his head.

Heinmarsh's voice came from directly behind. "So, Brennan McKinley had a nephew in COAST," started Heinmarsh. "What a freakin' coincidence. Who knew?" He went silent for a few moments.

McKinley stared straight ahead, mentally immunising himself against Heinmarsh's goading. If the industrialist had nothing better to talk about than McKinley's family background, this would get boring quickly. Of course, Heinmarsh would have information on himself and Carter through their former colleague.

As if responding to McKinley's thought, Heinmarsh spoke again. "Actually, I regret not usin' you 'stead of Brook. Things might've gone down better. But 's'all yesterday's news now, ain't it Tripod? Or should I call you Ian?"

The large American appeared on the left extremity of McKinley's vision, stooping a little to better observe the captive Briton. "I'm... kinda disappointed," he announced quietly to McKinley's ear.

"So's your mother," replied McKinley through gritted teeth.

Heinmarsh curled his lip in a sneer, then chuckled. "I'm disappointed you got caught s'easily. See, you're supposed to be, like, some kinda kick-ass secret agent... but we catch you in a revival meeting? What, you get religion or something?" He laughed again. "Let's be honest; *you* need absolution a lot more than most folks."

Heinmarsh paced, McKinley waited. The American paused somewhere behind him.

"I'm *still* pissed off about my jeep. You smashed the roof in, then you forced me to leave it in your shitty little country? That ain't cool."

McKinley stayed silent. He knew Heinmarsh was enjoying this. The Team's profile on the billionaire suggested he was a psychopath who received satisfaction from inflicting pain and who could be expected to act both randomly and violently. McKinley tested his bonds again, proving that they were as solid as before and causing his battered limbs to ache.

"Ain't there s'posed to be three of ya?" Heinmarsh started circulating again, dysfunctionally cheerful as he considered the operative at his mercy. McKinley kept schtum.

Heinmarsh sneered through his ugly gash of a mouth. "Bellegarde flushed your geek buddy down the cooling tower; too bad, so sad. Where's the third guy? Replaced Brook. Tall fella; code name Shadow, last name Wilson. Reckon it was him shot me." He stopped right in front of McKinley and leaned over him. "I mean, a freakin' *rifle round* in my shoulder?! Son of a *BITCH!* D'ya know how much it cost to get that fixed up?! It's still keepin' me awake!" The adversary lowered his voice to a sinister growl. "He's here, ain't he? Reckon it's him's been stealin' the fertiliser. I'm gonna find him and I'm *so* gonna hurt him. I'm gonna make him feel pain he didn't know were possible! He's gonna rue the day he was born."

For a second McKinley considered answering, but thought better of it. To say there were just the two of them would sound both unbelievable and predictable; to confirm Wilson's presence on Rubakang would be very unwise. Better to play the grey man and leave Heinmarsh guessing. He knew one thing: his enemy still didn't have a visual ID on Wilson. Be thankful for small mercies, he thought. But *how the hell* did Heinmarsh know Wilson's name?

At McKinley's stony silence Heinmarsh shrugged off the question with a frown and raised an eyebrow as though the subject wasn't that important. "Okay." He started to pace slowly around the room again, his voice taking on different tones as it reverberated from the angles of the dirty little cell.

"I guess you're wonderin' what we're goin' do to ya. See, I'd a plan, which I kinda liked, but Makaru reckons it can't be done. I wanted to pump your ass full of his serum and order you to strangle your General Sutton or whatever, all *Manchurian Candidate* like."

McKinley thought about that. Holy shit, what if he could have done it? But Heinmarsh had already given away that it wasn't an option for whatever reason. Move on, McKinley told himself; don't think about what *might* have been.

Heinmarsh waved a hand dismissively. "Ah, it ain't gonna happen. Makaru's smart; he's made some real advances in mind control. But it ain't perfect yet so we couldn't rely on you, could we? Might be a mistake. We could make you talk though."

McKinley felt cold inside. He was already worn down; the bashing from Makaru's henchman had left him in such pain that part of him just wanted it to end. But he had a duty, even if just to his colleagues back in The Team. And he had to prove a point to an uncaring, dismissive government: *someone* had to try to stop Heinmarsh. Hope could not be allowed to die because if it did he would give up and become no more than a tool in Heinmarsh's creepy six-fingered hand. McKinley strengthened his resolve.

The punch to his face came without warning, twisting McKinley's cranium painfully hard on his neck and causing him to see stars. As his head swam he noticed a fresh rip inside his cheek and he tasted blood again. Blinking against the pain, McKinley tried to look defiant as he turned back, straight into Heinmarsh's maddened eyes.

"*I need information!*" shouted the American, tiny droplets of saliva spraying into McKinley's face. "I need to know what you know 'bout us!"

Through the pain McKinley sensed the opportunity to gain a slight tactical advantage. "We know it's not just you and Makaru," he croaked.

Heinmarsh threw his arms up. "Oh you *know* huh? Well big shittin' deal! You think anyone could set this up on their own? You think I was ever actin' alone? Or Makaru? You stupid Limey bastard!"

Outwardly McKinley turned his face to stone. Inwardly he was satisfied to have proven the thing he had suspected for some time: Heinmarsh and Makaru were part of something much bigger. It gave McKinley new motivation to find the head of the serpent and cut it off. If only there was some way out of this hell hole. If only Carter wasn't... was around. If only Wilson was in his right mind and could come kicking the door in, guns blazing, just about now.

Another punch exploded in his belly and McKinley roared with the pain. Still so tender from being used as a punch bag, McKinley's stomach lurched with such ferocity that he started to retch. There wasn't anything to bring up, but his guts heaved anyway. It hurt like hell. Dizziness invaded his brain as Heinmarsh shouted again.

"You WILL freakin' tell me! How many o' you're on this island? And where they hidin'?!"

McKinley moaned; he didn't want to let the sign of weakness out but he was in so much pain that he couldn't help it.

"Oh, hurts does it?" Heinmarsh leered scarily at his prey. "You don't damn well know the trouble you've caused me! You and your damn unit!" He moved back, perhaps done, perhaps to ready himself for another harsh blow.

From between the waves of confusing thoughts and the shards of pain that pierced his mind, McKinley formulated a question. It was an absurdly simple question, neither intelligently thought out nor terribly relevant, yet McKinley felt a need to ask it in the indistinct hope not of a clear answer, but of what *any* response might tell him. It was hard to keep his tear-filled eyes open, but he looked straight at his attacker and spoke as clearly as he could under the circumstances.

"Who do you work for?"

Heinmarsh shot back toward McKinley, the fat index finger of his weird hand shaking in the latter's face. "*Don't ask that!* It don't matter who I work for! You ain't asking the questions here!"

So, thought McKinley, you're definitely working for someone... and you're scared of them. And you're not a very good interrogator. A tiny glimmer of satisfaction boosted his ragged attempt to stay positive.

Heinmarsh stepped back, breathing hard. Loosening his tie, he pulled open his shirt collar and took a couple more breaths to calm himself.

"Like I said," he grunted, "we can make you talk." The large figure moved to the corner table where he opened a grey metal box and took out a syringe. He held it in front of McKinley's face, so close as to make him go cross-eyed, had he been able to focus.

"This stuff... ain't the same as what Makaru uses. It don't block your memory. See, I *need* you to remember stuff for me. I need you to tell me shit."

Heinmarsh's powerful grip rotated McKinley's forearm, twisting it ungracefully and sending a burst of pain up through his shoulder. McKinley looked wearily down at where Heinmarsh was trying to aim the needle.

McKinley smiled, thinking of Carter's quirky sense of humour. "No MDTs for a while," he breathed, barely able to form the words.

Heinmarsh looked up, bemused by the statement, and their eyes met for a second. At this moment the blazing madness had retired from the windows of the American's soul, but McKinley knew and had seen just how fast his enemy could go from one extreme to another. Now Heinmarsh looked like a caged animal. There was genuine fear in those eyes. Desperation. McKinley knew it and Heinmarsh knew he could see it. The big man looked away again, his eyes darting anywhere but toward McKinley. The needle went in and McKinley felt cold starting to travel up his arm. I hope it has analgesic properties, he thought vaguely.

"Be over soon," said Heinmarsh menacingly as he withdrew the empty syringe. "Once we've had our heart-to-heart you're going to the seaside. That's my idea too." He nodded slowly, eyebrows raised. "You know, there're quicker ways, but they ain't nowhere near so cruel."

The unusual threat hardly reached McKinley. Damn, he thought as his mind slipped sideways, this stuff does work fast. The lateral motion seemed to continue as the room tilted at a rakish angle and McKinley asked himself why Heinmarsh wasn't falling over. The inanity of it seemed insanely funny for a second and McKinley might have giggled. His vision became fluid and unfocused, his body seemed to melt warmly away as the faint, concrete-filtered sounds of the Indonesian jungle started to echo, echo, echo into nothingness, and a deep luxuriant blackness welcomed him with open arms.

A sharp, painful pinch on the top of his head roused McKinley to consciousness. He opened his eyes to beach and sea, mostly obscured by something fluffy near his head. It was moving.

Startled, McKinley suddenly realised that he was immobile. His arms and legs seemed to be locked solidly in place, but he could turn his head. He looked up at the fluffy thing.

With a loud squawk the bedraggled seabird hopped onto a ridge of sand to the left of his head. Its carrion was disappointingly alive.

"Piss off!" grunted McKinley. The bird didn't move much so he spat at it, causing it to run away with another raucous noise, dirty brown wings outstretched. He lost sight of it.

McKinley took stock of his surroundings. He was buried throat deep in the beach. He tried to look round, his movements impeded by the weight of sand. Well, this wasn't Wolf River. Judging from the angle of the setting sun this deserted beach was on the south facing side of the island, probably about five miles and a lot of vertical travel from the township.

What did I tell Heinmarsh? The thought suddenly hit McKinley like a train. What secrets did I spill? What can those bastards do with my intel? A deep sickness invaded McKinley's guts as he realised that *he* was now the traitor. For anything that the double-crossing Corporal Brook had given away months before, this was the icing on the cake.

An insect *pinged* off McKinley's hairline, switching him back to matters current. I'll deal with that issue later, he thought.

McKinley knew that Rubakang didn't have a huge tidal range, but someone—doubtless at Heinmarsh's pleasure—had created a U-shaped channel in the sand about eighteen inches deep, in the center of which McKinley was buried. This ensured that his head was below both the high water mark and the level of the beach. So that's what Heinmarsh meant about cruelty. It would be death and burial in one act.

It's only sand, thought McKinley, and tried to move his shoulders. If he could get an arm out he'd be able to dig at the rest of it. But his shoulders and arms were stuck firmly. Despite the pain he still felt throughout his body McKinley tried even harder, to no avail. He might as well have been glued in.

The lapping seawater wasn't far away. At this point McKinley didn't know on which part of the tidal cycle he was, but he could make an educated guess.

The daylight was waning as McKinley continued to try and work his shoulders free. The waves kept approaching and the bird came with them incrementally, as though waiting for him to expire. McKinley was exhausted and the waves were starting to wash away the sides of the depression.

Maybe once the sand became wet he could work his way loose. McKinley allowed himself a short period of rest, feeling the cold dampness spreading round his shoulders. Once the sand became more plastic he could move them a little, but his arms remained immobile. He tried to wiggle his shoulders harder, but quickly realised that his movements were helping to demolish the edges of his crater. The seawater was already up to his chin.

A wave slapped him in the face and McKinley spluttered sand out of his mouth. The intensity of aquatic assault was steadily increasing as the waves encroached higher and higher up the beach. The water was at the level of his mouth. McKinley tipped his head back, but just at that moment a bigger wave sent salty water up his nose. He coughed and gagged, realising that this was going to be the end.

He'd scuttled his career, lost the support of The Team, pissed off the British government, sunk a submarine, crashed their aircraft, let a good man get arrested, lost a shit-ton of money and gear, caused a team-mate to lose his mind and watched another die. It was the worst imaginable epitaph. Ian David McKinley, thirty four, former secret operative and multiple loser, was about to drown. It had all come to *nothing*.

McKinley threw his head back in desperation, trying not to panic. He needed to remain calm and preserve his body's supply of oxygen as long as possible. Even with his head back the water was about to crest his chin. One more big wave would do it. He knew that holding his breath was useless, as his body would begin to scream its warning about increasing carbon dioxide in his bloodstream, which would get stronger and stronger until he reached the so-called breath-hold breakpoint, when his body's reflexes would ensure a last big inhalation of water. With any luck he'd go into laryngospasm and be unconscious by the time the water fully covered him. Then...

Holy shit, I really am going to die!

The wave came, squirting seawater down his nasal passages and bringing on uncontrollable coughing. He felt the water pouring into his airways as he struggled to get one last breath of air. Despite the coughing he tried to slam his mouth shut tight, but it was no good. Stored air burst out through his nose and McKinley prepared to take his last ever breath. He steeled himself against the inevitable moment, wondering if all that religious business was true after all. No amount of training could have prepared him for these final, fleeting moments.

Suddenly there was a thump and his world seemed to shrink down to almost nothing. Water slopped around his neck but his head was in air – perhaps the most rotten, fishy air ever. McKinley choked out water, sensing acoustics like his head was in a washing machine. His nose was registering the stink of decomposition, as though someone was trying to suffocate him in a dead whale. The sickening malodour made him cough and retch, but it was *breathable*.

He blinked. It was completely black. *What the hell is going on?!*

Someone was digging out his right arm! He could feel a hand scooping sand away from his shoulder, which was starting to loosen. He heard waves against a hard surface. Suddenly McKinley realised that his head was in some kind of container and its inverted orientation formed the bubble of horribly stinky but life giving air. Buoyed by this incredible knowledge, McKinley started to work with whoever it was, levering his shoulder around painfully, allowing water to pass down his torso.

His arm was coming loose! Waggling his shoulder through such a wide range of movement was painful—at least in part thanks to Mister Bellegarde—but McKinley didn't care.

He was on the point of giving his arm a tug when suddenly the container lurched off his head and he was again submerged. He could hear the waves rolling over him. The stranger was trying to free his right arm, tugging at his shoulder with great strength. It felt like tearing his muscles but McKinley was so thrilled to have a chance that he had no difficulty ignoring the pain. His torso was becoming free as the sand was plasticised by the water.

Suddenly the stranger let go. McKinley was aware of the person's legs moving about in the swells. Filtered through the liquid environment he could hear their splashing.

Whatever the filthy container was, it was pushed back down over his head again. In a flash McKinley understood what this meant; the stranger was giving him a chance to take breath! The rotten air made him want to puke, but he started to hyperventilate, flushing carbon dioxide from his bloodstream. He could feel the stranger fighting against the container's buoyancy, then it lifted again and he was under water.

The strong hands resumed their war against the cloying sand and McKinley felt a tiny upward movement. To preserve his breath with its vital oxygen he tried to let the stranger do most of the work. If they had any sense at all they would understand why. McKinley found he could bend slightly at the waist, feeling the effects of Bellegarde's assault again.

The stranger pulled harder until McKinley felt like his shoulder would be dislocated. His breath was running out. Another few seconds and he'd need air again! He could work his legs, but the urge to breathe was getting uncontrollable. Precious seconds left him behind as McKinley and the stranger fought the grip of the sand. Time to breathe, shouted McKinley in his head. I need to breathe NOW!

As if the universe in its enormity had heard him, the sand suddenly relinquished its grip and McKinley burst upward feeling as light as a feather. His head broke the surface and he gulped down air, coughing and choking but relishing the fact that the water level was now beneath him. The fishy smell was gone, replaced by a faint odour of familiarity. He felt strong arms encircling his chest, then he was dragged from the water and dropped unceremoniously onto the damp sand just below the high water mark.

McKinley opened his eyes and at last beheld the face of his rescuer in the dusk.

"Hi!" crooned Carter cheerfully, his sand-daubed palm raised in greeting and its fingers splayed like the petals of a partially denuded sunflower.

"I knew it was you," grunted McKinley as a wave stole over his legs. "Even after all the shit we've been through I can still smell that stupid aftershave."

"You're welcome," replied Carter, his smile quickly melting from cheer to disillusionment. "Oh no, it's no trouble at all, you'd do the same for me, of course, granted, my pleasure, yeah I know you missed me, it's great to see you again mate, so glad you're alive."

McKinley let his head drop back onto the sand, sighing. He rolled over and saw a man's legs lying there, as still as stone. So they'd left someone to watch him, but Carter had neutered the problem. They needed to hide that body.

He looked to his right. A blue plastic barrel was bobbing in the surf, making its way down the beach, caught in the longshore drift. So that was what Carter had shoved over his head. I'm just guessing, thought McKinley, but it probably contained *long-time-no-sea* fish somewhere along the line. Either way, it and Carter's resourcefulness had saved him. Yet there was no way on God's earth he was about to betray his *unspeakable* relief at seeing his best friend's face, despite the depth of his gratitude. Instead he gave voice to the obvious.

"I thought you were dead."

Carter shrugged. "All the best heroes get a resurrection."

"You weren't *actually* dead."

"You nearly were."

McKinley raised himself to a sitting position. "D'you know how much grief I wasted on you?" he sputtered.

Carter's face looked expressionless. "So little as to be of no consequence?"

"Not even that much. Now let's disappear before something horrible hits the fan. You got anywhere we can hide?"

"Oh yes."

"So what the hell's your story?" asked McKinley, climbing hard and losing his breath. The humidity didn't help and neither did the remaining wet sand. Every member ached from his last meeting with Bellegarde. Clouds were starting to settle around the island, their westernmost lower layers imbued with the coral pink of the dying sun. He sensed that a storm was coming.

Carter paused for just a second to look down at his friend. "Well, I survived, apparently."

Inwardly McKinley cursed Carter's archetypal British penchant for stating the bleeding obvious. But rather than snap back at his friend who had, after all, just saved him from drowning, McKinley kept his peace.

"You know those horizontal cooling vanes we saw going down the shaft? I didn't fall all the way to the bottom; I came round on one of those things. Must've caught something on the way down."

McKinley tried to picture it in his head. He remembered the devices to which Carter was referring; they were radiators of a sort. Cold water would be run through them so that the steam from the geothermal plant would shed its heat and condense. But the rows of metal fins were assembled together up the shaft wall almost vertically; it was only by some kind of miracle that Carter had landed between them and not been splattered like bird shit at the base.

Carter continued. "Holy shit was it ever hot there. But I guess I was K-O'd for a while. When I came to I was sweating bullets. But I couldn't climb back up in case Emperor Ming's goons were still there and, I'll be honest, down was a lot easier. Just hotter, that's all."

McKinley lost his grip on a piece of rock and slid backward for a second, regaining his footing and thrusting ahead determinedly. He thought he detected an early flash of lightning from miles away. "What's down there?"

"The guts of the geothermal plant. It's interesting actually but hot – hot as hell. No wonder it's all run remotely."

"How'd you find your way out?"

Carter looked around for a moment. They were out of the thickest part of the trees and in more rocky surroundings. Their destination was only a few more minutes' climb.

"I found the duct that leads to the camp."

McKinley thought for a second. "But that's, like, two kilometers."

Carter didn't look back. "Yeah."

As he ascended, half climbing, half stumbling, McKinley pondered the idea of Carter crawling through some godforsaken ductwork for a full two thousand meters. He noted Carter's obvious resolve to escape, which meant that there must have been no other way out. He didn't want to think about how hot it must have been down there, but...

"Didn't you get burned or anything? I mean, with all that damn steam and stuff?"

Again Carter talked more to the darkening mountain than to his friend. "Doesn't matter. Point is, I got out alive and so did you. We're back in the game. Oh, and I collected a few things from Wolf River."

This news cheered McKinley just a little. "Like what?"

"Like anything I could find, you know? It's all hidden, don't worry. I mean, we gotta eat, right?"

"Aye." Despite fatigue and pain, McKinley was thankful for Carter's initiative. Not only had he managed to escape from—figuratively speaking—the pit of hell, but he'd skilfully acquired some supplies. But then the thought occurred to McKinley that whilst Carter had been 'shopping' at Wolf River, he himself had been under torture by those bastards. He was about to ask why Carter hadn't come after him, but thought better of it; if Carter had risked his own safety there might not have been anyone to dig McKinley out half an hour ago. Things had worked out how they'd worked out and he felt incredibly relieved, regardless of anything else. McKinley set his mind to the task of ascending the rocky slope ahead of him to where Carter had promised a hideaway.

The dull plum clouds were surrounding them steadily with a fine mist and they heard thunder. A tropical storm could go on for days and McKinley wanted to be under cover by the time the heavens opened. They'd made some ground and, he estimated, were about three hundred meters up, maybe more. "How much further?" he asked breathlessly.

"We're here. Welcome to Carter's Cavern."

Through the thickening mist there was a dark, onion bulb shaped opening just ahead, looking like a gaping mouth frozen in a moment of shock. McKinley hauled himself up the last bit of the slope and stood with Carter on the tiny ledge, barely big enough for both of them. Carter heaved his body over the lip of the shelter and held a hand out to his friend.

Once inside, McKinley's eyes adjusted and he could see a bit better, taking in their surroundings. The place was roughly conical, about ten feet high at the apex, and presumably started life as no more than a fissure in the rock before being enlarged by centuries of dripping water. What could be loosely described as the floor was earthy with, as McKinley observed, too many angles to allow a man of his size to lie straight. Further into the cavity a ledge at the back gave way to a small tunnel which was probably a continuance of the original fault in the rock. It looked perilously narrow. To one side was Carter's stash of goodies comprised of a black dustbin bag and some other items shrouded in filthy old blankets.

Despite the smallness of the dirt floor, the cave was about eight feet wide and maybe twenty five deep, its walls rising at an angle until they curved back upon themselves to complete the sharp triangle of the roof. Most of all McKinley felt comforted that the place was dry. With a sense of irony he thought about the COAST base back in Nottingham, where he and his colleagues lived and worked in an environment that had once been caves like this. What he wouldn't give to be there now, surrounded by the welcoming familiarity of the boys from other TDR teams, the command staff, the computers, Carol Hewins mothering

Carter and the simple security of being in and part of something terribly meaningful.

How that sense of purpose had become twisted, warped and ultimately almost torn away by their current circumstances! How had he allowed himself to make those decisions? Or to lead Carter and Wilson into this ridiculous mess? Suddenly McKinley realised how extraordinarily distant he was from everything he was accustomed to. They'd deserted their jobs, their unit and everything that was now behind them for the sake of... *what?* To rescue Kyle Bacon? To hit Heinmarsh? To save the poor suicide bombers? To find themselves here, making it up as they went along, in a shitty mountain cave instead of pursuing a defined mission with planning, support and resources?

McKinley sat down, his back to the knobbly, angled rock wall and let out a heavy sigh. His training and innate mental discipline told him to regain what determination he could, to forbid himself from wallowing in the dourness of this almost hopeless state of affairs, but it was too much. Inside, he started to fall...

Suddenly McKinley snapped himself back to normal. What the hell was he thinking? He was indulging himself stupidly. Taking a good, deep breath, McKinley turned his thoughts to planning, back to the daily regimen of calculating answers to tactical problems. That was familiarity; that was security. That was what he did best and by crikey he was going to do it – despite that inner voice of hopelessness taunting him.

The first and most notable item in Carter's collection was familiar. The guard that had been left to oversee McKinley's demise had carried no more than a machine pistol—a Velocity Arms VMAC9—which had become so wedged with sand that, in the absence of cleaning materials, they'd buried it with its owner. But from elsewhere Carter had obtained something far more useful: a Heinmarsh rifle. With it was a set of webbing that McKinley judged to contain about sixty rounds of the caseless ammunition.

"Nice," murmured McKinley. "Who'd you borrow it off?"

Carter shrugged. "He won't need it back."

McKinley expressed a concern. "Body?"

"Fish fodder."

"Anything else on him?"

Carter held up something partially translucent. "Map, radio that got busted in the fight, knife, some personal items." He tossed a small bag to his friend.

McKinley caught the polythene bag deftly and looked at its contents as the storm growled again, closer this time. There were Indonesian *rupiah* notes and coins, a lighter, a geek stick and a gold St. Christopher medallion. McKinley shoved the bag into a pocket of his moist fatigues and tried to look nonchalant. His retirement fund—assuming he ever got out of this shit-show, never mind reaching the appropriate age—was still growing.

McKinley turned his attention to Carter's collection of stolen goods. He opened the neck of the garbage sack to inspect its contents, pulling the plastic wide apart so that they could both see in. He wanted to make sure Carter's acquisitions were of some use. There were small items in there: a couple of screwdrivers and some electrical bits and bobs, a couple of keycards—probably useless now—a flashlight, a calculator, pens, ruler and compass, nail polish remover, batteries of various sizes and several chemiluminescent glow sticks. But the first thing that his hand found was a bottle. He looked at it somewhat incredulously. It was about seven inches long and the label, whilst indecipherably Indonesian for the most part, clearly said 'Surgical Spirits' in English text at the bottom.

McKinley shook his head, glancing around their rocky accommodations. It was little better than a dusty hole in the mountainside that offered some meagre protection from wind and rain, but certainly not from anything poisonous or injurious enough to be worried about. Snakes, spiders and larger, perhaps dangerous fauna would find them an easy target. Makaru's men probably knew this area anyway, but erecting some kind of barrier was mandatory, both to keep the critters out and any light source from being visible at distance.

He put down the bottle and continued to inventorise Carter's acquired hoard beyond the bag, noting a huge box of biscuits, gravy granules, some cooking utensils, several packets of spaghetti, a jar of tomato chutney, a catering size drum of coffee creamer and a sack of weed killer. McKinley's eyes rolled. "What the heck were you thinking?" he asked.

Carter frowned defensively. "Hey, I got whatever I could. It wasn't easy you know."

Despite the pain from every member of his physique McKinley smirked. "You forgot the lobster thermidor."

"Darn it."

McKinley pointed to the sodium chlorate. "Weed killer?"

Carter's eyes turned conspiratorial. "It has its uses."

McKinley could imagine. His mind briefly hovered over a scenario in which he and Carter would poison the whole settlement by liberally dosing their water supply with the weed killer. But that was the kind of indiscriminate guerrilla warfare he'd been taught to avoid and, anyway, what would Wilson say if he were here? The outspoken conscience of their team would never allow them to do it; such an act placed them on the same level as someone who would send suicide bombers out into the world.

McKinley continued surveying the haphazard collection and mentally ticked off vitamin pills, curry powder, a bulk pack of sugar that looked as though it should take two to carry, three tubes of toothpaste, powdered parmesan cheese, a sack of fertiliser, chocolate, a couple of bottles of hydrogen peroxide sterilising fluid, about twenty cheap looking cans of vegetables and, somewhat conspicuously, a two liter bottle of cooking cider.

"Cider?"

"You drink it," offered Carter innocently.

Bloody hell! McKinley managed to divert his annoyance at the pointless comment and not bark at his friend. He did, after all, owe the man an enormous debt of gratitude. Carter was right; this stuff, none of it, would have been easy to come by. Not with armed guards patrolling Makaru's camp and now more than likely roaming the island, hunting them down. Beggars can't be choosers. I suppose I should congratulate him, thought McKinley, but a lot of this stuff isn't exactly useful.

"You could always make a 'white lady'," suggested Carter from the gloom at the back of the cave.

"A what?"

"With the surgical spirits. Inch in the bottom, inch in the top. Just the right amount to get blind drunk without *going* blind. It's what nesbits drink."

McKinley actually laughed. There they were; renegade agents and hunted men sitting isolated in a filthy cave in the middle of an Indonesian jungle, and Carter was jovially using Nottinghamian patter as if he were still on the streets of that very town, observing the inebriated vagrants around the famous market square who had been kicked out of the Salvation Army hostel for the day. The bizarre contextual dichotomy was so ridiculous as to be insanely funny.

The humour was so impossible to ignore, in fact, that something snapped and the laughter started to get manic, then turned into gasping, grunting and finally teeth-gritted moaning, rising up from inside him like a geyser. The weight of having been captured, brutalised and then, unbelievably, rescued almost at the point of death was far too much to contain any more. McKinley bent forward, his head in his hands, as the agony of recent events made its tormenting passage back into his thoughts.

Carter crouched in the darkening hollow like some kind of troglodytic gnome, flash-photographed by intermittent lightning, watching McKinley's silhouette release days of pent-up emotional pressure. He knew much better than to intervene. McKinley's displays of what the Scotsman would term 'weakness' were so infrequent that they held considerable importance in Carter's eyes. This was only the fourth he'd ever seen, the occasional alcohol fuelled pity-party or shouting match notwithstanding. Let it out, thought Carter. Let it all come out and then we'll try to sleep in this grotty hole. Tomorrow's a brand new day. New challenges, new opportunities ... same old threats.

A couple of minutes later McKinley was calming a bit. Acknowledging the pain was a healthy thing to do, he reasoned. Better than holding it in and having to carry it for however long. Holy crap, he thought, I have been through some shit. McKinley shook himself as though to clear away the remains of the 'weak' moment and looked back at Carter with eyes that conveyed in no uncertain terms that the last few moments would never, ever be spoken of, just like the other times. Carter's discretion in such matters was a fact on which McKinley knew he could rely.

"Never mind the fancy cocktail," suggested Carter gently. "Let's just drink the cider and be done with it."

"I won't argue."

The lightning, much closer now, flashed around their hideaway and peals of thunder buffeted their ears. The cave seemed to funnel each booming report in toward them, exaggerating the percussion of its passage. In a few minutes the rain started to fall, at first no more than tiny globules bursting like minuscule fireworks on the outer edges of the cave walls. But soon these gave way to speeding rivulets which arced and undulated, splitting into countless droplets as they relinquished their grip on the grey rock. The rain seemed to be voicing its own sorrowful threnody as the streamers of water became torrents and the full weight of the tropical thunderstorm bore down on their stony shelter. The stroboscopic dazzle of almost constant lightning and the incessant impact of crackling thunder made it feel like an artillery barrage.

As he lay on the cold hard floor, his mind slightly numbed by the cider and his belly stuffed with biscuits, McKinley thought about one more detail.

"Hey, what's the date?"

"Twenty fourth," grunted Carter tiredly.

Shock overcame McKinley. "*What?!* You're bloody kidding!" Could it be true?

"Two and four; twenty four."

"So I was... knocked out for *three days?*"

Carter's reply reverberated from the back of the cave. "Mostly."

McKinley felt puzzled and disorientated. Apart from the periods of wakefulness he could recall, what the hell else had happened in that time? It was a peculiar feeling, as though a part of his life that he naturally assumed was there had been stolen away in some unearthly time warp. In reality, this was almost the case from a certain perspective. McKinley had lost days of his life to unconsciousness and he felt violated, but wasn't sure how. The uncertainty was deeply unnerving.

As he grappled with this revelation, another question occurred to him. "Aye, well, what the heck were *you* doing then?"

"G'night."

McKinley resigned himself to a later pursuance of this question as he turned over on the rock and pulled the stiff, scratchy blanket around him. The COAST agents were cold, damp and horribly fatigued, with nothing more comforting on which to sleep than unyielding bare rock, in the heart of the violent storm. It would be a long night.

019: The Discovery

By the time McKinley woke up, Carter had already been busy.

The violent storm had beaten the night into a fragmented collage of sleep and wakefulness that seemed to go on far too long. But once dawn came the tempest had blown itself out, leaving the jungle sodden but aromatic and the cave feeling much more homely than it should.

He was stiff and aching, but the fresh air of the rain-washed island was invigorating. McKinley lifted himself from the compacted dirt and performed a few stretches, feeling tension from several muscle groups. He put his back to the rock wall and used his knees to lever himself up and down like a bear scratching itself against a tree. Twisting his head to one side, he heard a distinct double crack from his neck. McKinley rubbed his face and eyes, then stretched his jaw with a huge yawn.

After sucking down his nicotine hit, McKinley stuffed himself with more biscuits and parmesan cheese, feeling bruises and aching in his body. During the last few days—most of which he didn't even remember—he'd been drugged, hung up, kicked, punched, tied up, interrogated and buried. No wonder he felt so rough. He dropped a couple of vitamin pills, made a quick visit to the undergrowth and then turned his attention to what Carter was doing. He found his friend using a penknife to poke the stems of leaves into the fabric of a blanket.

"I hope that's yours," began McKinley.

"'Course it is," said Carter without looking up. "Just about done."

McKinley could see that Carter was creating some kind of makeshift camouflage and soon learned why as the sound of a helicopter echoed from far away. Clearly Makaru's security guards were still on some sort of alert.

"What are we going to see?"

Carter reached into his breast pocket and pulled out his old phone. It looked shabby, but McKinley knew how tough the little devices were, having used one himself for two and a half years.

"Thank goodness you've still got that thing," said McKinley.

"Still got 'em both. I've been trying to hack Fu Manchu's systems except they seem to be the Newland Comtech variety. But anyway, look at this."

McKinley received the phone from his friend's hand and held it up. The little display showed a satellite image of coastline, presumably Rubakang. The picture was essentially two shades: lush mottled green for land and dark green, almost black, for the ocean.

McKinley studied the image carefully. Whilst there was nothing outstanding about it, the coastline was noteworthy, with an L-shaped promontory forming what could be a useful natural harbour.

"What am I looking for?" he asked.

Carter continued with his handiwork. "That image was sixteen months ago," he said. "Scroll right."

The next image was almost identical, but where the hook of the 'L' had previously bounded a rectangular bay it was now connected to the land by more jungle, creating an elongated lobe of foliage against the dark water.

McKinley cocked an eyebrow. "That's interesting."

Carter looked round. "That's the latest image. Islands do not just grow like that."

"Where is this?"

"Pretty much due north. Cross the valley, over the next ridge and downhill."

"Think this is what he's trying to hide?"

Carter grinned. "I bet."

"That's better!" roared Bellegarde as he got back up off the gymnasium's wooden floor. "Boy, you got some skills! Bless the Universal Spirit!"

If he was completely honest with himself, Brother Dawoud was getting a bit fed up with the constant, mandatory insertion of religiosity into every conversation. We all know this stuff, he thought. We're all here for the same reason. We don't have to bang on about it *all* the time.

He pulled the *obi* tighter about his waste and watched for Bellegarde's move. The muscular French American was a challenging contender, but *somehow* Dawoud knew how to foil his assaults, to rebuff his advances, to counter and neutralise his attacks. It was ingrained in his brain as if second nature and he was starting to suspect that his old life may have been something other than just a pen pusher.

Instantly Bellegarde was upon him, leaping with amazing speed. Dawoud blocked his flying punch, catching Bellegarde's arm and twisting it, using the big man's momentum to propel him into a roll. The leader hit the mat with a loud thump, lay there for a moment and then turned over.

"Dawoud, you got the gift," he said. "There ain't many people can do that to *me*."

Dawoud offered his hand. "I hope I didn't hurt you," he said.

"No, no." Bellegarde shook his head. He took Wilson's hand and got up. They bowed to each other in the traditional manner.

"I'm off to get showered," said Bellegarde, heading toward the door. "Good training session Dawoud. Same time tomorrow?"

"Yes sir!" answered Dawoud enthusiastically. He felt uncomfortably constrained to offer the typical valediction. "May you be blessed to see the Kingdom!"

Sister Miriam ran into Dawoud's arms as the prophet left the gym. She slapped her lover playfully on the chest.

"You're not allowed to leave without a kiss!" she giggled, planting a huge snog right on his surprised face. He returned the gesture and they embraced for a while, lost in the moment. Dawoud felt his body responding to her affections, as it had done many times recently.

Eventually their lips parted and he said "I didn't want to wake you up."

"You can wake me up anytime, silly," she smirked, her eyebrow lifting seductively. She tugged on his arm. "Let's get some tucker before breakfast's over. It's a mushroom omelette today; Brother Sanjaya made it."

"We'd better be quick or there'll be none left."

Dawoud allowed himself to be pulled toward the dining hall by the giggling, winsome girl. What a blessing, what a privilege, he thought. She's amazing. So full of life, love, and the love of life.

The breakfast period was ending but thankfully there was plenty of Sanjaya's amazing food left. Dawoud chose a big portion of the omelette with some toast and orange juice. Miriam got herself a bowl of fruit accompanied by coffee.

They sat under the cheerful decorations and made small talk for a couple of minutes, but Dawoud's heart was heavy. There was something he needed to speak about, and his girlfriend was probably the only person in the universe who could understand.

"Sister—"

"Izzie!" she grinned, her eyes wide. "It's okay to use my real name when we're..." she looked around carefully, "alone."

"Well," said Dawoud, "I'd like to talk about that. Is it the only thing you remember from your old life?"

"'Course not," she smiled. "Isabella Conroy from Dowling Street, Colac, Victoria, in the good ol' land of Oz. I remember it all. I had a red Ford Mondeo called Pipkin."

Dawoud was puzzled indeed. "Why would the Universal Spirit allow you to remember all that?"

Miriam lowered her voice. "I'm not the only one. By a long way. There are a lot of grey areas."

His eyes narrowed questioningly. "But... but don't you *believe*?"

"Yeah, of course. Most of it. There's a lot of questions that don't have answers."

Dawoud found himself agreeing with this assessment, yet the idea seemed so antithetical to what he'd learned. He didn't like grey areas. He liked clear information. "Such as?"

"Well, okay," she nodded, holding up a finger. "Such as, why doesn't anyone sent to the mission field ever come back home?"

"I don't know."

"No-one does," she hissed. "We never hear a word. They just disappear. It's creepy."

Dawoud considered this for a moment. People like themselves were constantly being commissioned by Pastor Makaru or Prophet Bellegarde for the mission field, but they just left and were gone. Come to think of it, it did seem a little strange. What the heck did 'the mission field' mean anyway?

"And what about the elders? A lot of people think Pastor's paying them to watch us. The band and some of the ushers too, never mind his personal guard. That lot are brainwashed or something."

Dawoud looked about nervously, eager to remain unheard by others. "I don't think we should be talking like—"

"How about Sister Zulayka?" she continued undeterred. "She had a *right* meltdown; all the way to bedrock. Said her name was Juanita something and insisted she'd been kidnapped from Brazil and all sorts. So then she goes forward in tears at the meeting and disappears for a couple of days like they all do. When she comes back she don't remember nothin' again. Totally changed, like she was a different person. That's *weird!*"

"I think *my* memory's coming back," admitted Dawoud. It felt conspiratorial to give it voice, but he couldn't deny it any longer. To deny a clear and obvious truth would be... *sinful*.

Her eyes widened. "Really?"

"That guy on the beach the other night," he said, his voice almost a whisper. "I knew him. I don't know how, but I *knew him* from somewhere. The more I think about it the more I know it. Chris Carter, he said his name was. I remember something about him being involved with computers. And he mentioned another name; Paul Wilson."

"That's the other spy they killed?"

"No." His eyes were full of confusion. "I think *I'm* Paul Wilson."

The climb was tough, but once McKinley and Carter were at the island's peak the view was beyond spectacular. It felt like flying over all the Earth or looking down from a space station. The beautiful geography of Rubakang stretched away east and west to their sides, and dropped steeply down to the sea ahead and behind. They could see to the south that the island was part of a group of several, where clusters of rocky islets and bigger mounts punctured the surface of the sea like stubby claws through blue fabric, each bearing the same colour gradient from white to green to dark grey as their altitude increased. Rubakang was—as far as they could tell—the biggest, but through the binoculars there were indistinct hints of a much larger land mass on the south-eastern horizon.

To the north, the view was clear apart from a single big, low island in the middle distance. Aided by his phone's GPS function, Carter had found out that they were at a point near where the Pacific Ocean meets the Celebes Sea. It was a part of the globe typified by lofty volcanoes above and abyssal maritime trenches below.

Toward the north-east was the massive rocky ridge, like the spine of some long-deceased *kaiju*, which crossed half the island and separated Wolf River from the western portion of Rubakang and Makaru's presumed machinations. From behind the ridge the ever-present steam plume of the fumarole with its geothermal plant towered high above the rainforest. A deep valley lay before them and, beyond that, a lower, secondary ridge would have to be negotiated to reach their objective.

Here the arboreal cover was sparse and Carter's blanket would come into its own, providing a leafy hide under which they could hopefully avoid observance by the persistent helicopter flights. Whether Makaru's minions had discovered that neither the beach nor the power plant contained a Brit's body was unknown, but they must surely be aware that someone had 'retired' two of their number.

Upon leaving the cover of the treeline, they spread the blanket wide and crawled underneath, lying where weathered rock, moss and short, tough grass met in chaotically mingled patches, their odours exotic yet somehow familiar, like a walk in a botanical garden.

Trying not to prod himself in the eye, McKinley brought the binoculars up to his face. They weren't of the caliber he was used to, but they were quite good. At least they had a good zoom range from ten to twenty two times magnification, and respectably useful sixty millimeter objective lenses letting in plenty of light.

It was two and a half miles to the intriguing coastal feature, and more than these bins were good for, but McKinley could make out some detail. The foliage was continuous over the area, but somehow it didn't look right. The trunks of the trees seemed much taller than those around and it looked as though they sprouted directly from the sea. McKinley swept the binos along the formation. It just seemed a little too *geometrical* to be part of the forest.

McKinley caught movement and squinted, trying to squeeze as much information out of the limited view as he could. He saw what appeared to be a small boat emerging from within the trees, moving between the trunks. The view was frustratingly unclear, but it looked at though the people on the boat were hosing down the trees.

Something registered at the limit of McKinley's perception. Something wasn't right about the light. Knowing that the edges of his vision could be more sensitive to such things, McKinley rotated his eyes to the right a little, looking not at the anomaly but into the sides of the binoculars. Sure enough, something was flickering between the trees, bright and faintly bluish. How interesting.

McKinley put the bins down. "Welding," he said. "There's welding going on in there."

Gravity became their friend on the way down, but neither were looking forward to the return journey. More careful than before to move stealthily, McKinley and Carter negotiated the terrain until they were in sight of their objective, and it was now apparent that it wasn't a natural formation at all.

They hid at the edge of the water across the bay from the site. Here Rubakang wore a different face. There was no beach, and the water around the mangroves looked black and viscous, like the living slime of some stagnant alien pool. Large boulders formed the boundary between sea and jungle, so the COAST lads hid behind an example that was sufficiently sizeable as to obscure them from view. Carter leaned the rifle on the big, rounded dark grey rock.

The L-shaped spit of land had been covered by a huge construction of steel more than three hundred meters long. Trees grew out of the top and sides, providing both camouflage and shade for whatever was in there. Whilst the roof was solid, the side wall appeared to be a substantial steel curtain from which trees and other flora sprouted at angles. McKinley nodded to himself. The boat he'd seen earlier was irrigating the camouflage, using fresh water from an unseen source.

There was the sound of a marine motor from around the headland to their right and McKinley saw Makaru's launch come into view, heading for the massive steel canopy. He brought the binoculars up to his eyes and looked carefully. In the boat were Makaru, Bellegarde and Heinmarsh. He handed the bins to Carter.

Seconds went by and the sound of the launch was joined by another, marginally more harmonious tone. Carter was *singing*.

"I saw three shits a-sailing by, on Christmas day, on Christmas day. I saw three shits a-sailing by on Christmas day in the morning..."

McKinley grinned despite himself. Those men were indeed as Carter described them with the traditional melody. But what about the date? Oh blimey yes! Yesterday was December twenty fourth, of course.

"Chris," said McKinley quietly, holding out his right hand, "merry Christmas."

Carter's head quickly snapped from the binoculars to McKinley's hand, his face, and back to the hand again, which he shook. "Right, yes mate. Seasonal greetings to you too."

"Seasonal...? What's wrong with merry Christmas?"

"Well," started Carter as McKinley felt a lecture coming on, "Jesus wasn't born on December twenty fifth, was He? The research indicates September. Anyway, I hate Christmas. It's *supposed* to be His birthday, yet everyone *else* gets presents? It's commercialised, shallow and ninety nine percent meaningless."

McKinley was becoming bored already. "So I should return your gift?" he drawled.

"Sure," said Carter. "Unless it's one of those disavowed Chinese subs. If it's good enough for Heinmarsh, it's good enough for my Christmas box."

In a rare moment McKinley regarded his friend with appreciation. The man's face was filthy with mud and jungle slime. His beard was bushy and unkempt and his eyes bore a terrible weariness. And, whilst Carter was an adept pianist, he just couldn't sing to save his life. Yet despite all this, despite the adversity of their circumstances and the distance by which they were separated from the familiar, Carter somehow remained buoyant. Yes, he was coming out with stupid stuff as he sometimes did, but this little flavour of the normal was tremendously encouraging to McKinley. Whilst he would usually have disabused Carter's joviality as totally unnecessary, right now it was the most welcome breath of fresh air.

Smiling, he turned back to the unusual construct. "Looks like the Three Stooges don't celebrate it either."

"Yes." Carter patted the rifle. "We could, you know, just hit 'em right now."

"Aye. It's tempting." If only our sharpshooter team-mate was here, thought McKinley.

They heard the engine note of the launch drop a few tones and turned back to look. Carter held out the bins to McKinley, but he could see what was happening without them. The launch had slowed upon approach to the side of the covered area. The center section was being drawn aside as though it was indeed a huge curtain, allowing passage of the boat within. The trees and shrubs that lined the sides wobbled and swung with the lateral movement but soon came to rest.

"We *so* need to get in there," whispered McKinley, "once those bastards have left."

They waited nearly two hours, but sure enough Makaru, Bellegarde and Heinmarsh eventually departed on the launch, presumably returning to Wolf River.

McKinley and Carter lowered themselves carefully into the dark water and prepared for a long subsurface swim. It was the only way into the mysterious enclosure that was imbued with some element of secrecy.

They could see nothing in the deep water, but before long their hands made contact with the steel curtain and they cautiously surfaced, keeping under cover of the foliage which hung down to the water.

They were looking up into a rectangular space like an aircraft hanger, but much longer. Its length was about five times its width, the former being approximately three hundred meters. They could clearly see how the roof, about twenty five meters above them, had been constructed with giant troughs into which forest trees had been transplanted. This partial cover allowed through enough daylight to facilitate work, but would block the view of any satellite surveillance. To their left a concrete dock ran all the way along the enclosure. Further along it there was a crane, which doubtless ran along the quay on rails, leaning over the water. But none of this impressive engineering could hold a candle to the object in the immediate foreground.

The biggest bloody submarine McKinley had ever set eyes on rose from the water before them. It was wide—twice as broad as any he'd seen before—and, he estimated, nearly double the length of the Royal Navy's new Astute Class boats. They'd surfaced right at its monstrous stern, where the huge dorsal fin towered about fifteen meters above them, and the tops of the propeller shrouds were clearing the waterline by three meters. Way overhead and about seventy meters away, the enormous sail barely had clearance under the roof's matrix of girders, even with its snort, periscope and other masts retracted.

Heck, thought McKinley, this thing could *eat* a Trafalgar Class sub and wouldn't even ask for a toothpick. "Holy shit," he breathed.

"Russian Akula," stated Carter. "NATO reporting name Typhoon. Biggest ever built."

"I know. I thought they were being scrapped."

Carter shrugged. "Yet here it is." He nodded forward left, sending droplets flying. "Look over there."

"Santa must've heard you," said McKinley in awe.

Moored between the dock and the enormous Typhoon was the hijacked Chinese Type 091 *Han* Class submarine they'd last seen crash-diving off the coast of Mallory Island, carrying Heinmarsh and at least one functional nuclear warhead. It was dwarfed by the gigantic Russian *podvodnaya lodka* but was itself a hundred meters long. They knew that its Chinese owners had disavowed all responsibility, which proved that the UK wasn't the only nation deploying submarines that didn't officially exist.

"Well," murmured Carter, "now we know how he got here."

To their extreme left the roughly poured concrete of the dock's southern end met with the rocky shoreline so they swam over, staying within the cover of the drooping boughs and vines. They heaved themselves from the water and looked along the dock.

Workers milled about, carrying out various maintenance operations on the submarines. They were in two distinct groups: red coveralls and orange. The former seemed to be concerned with the vessels whilst the latter, less in number, looked as though they were in charge. Perhaps they were the subs' crews.

Of particular note was the forward section of the Typhoon, where one of the missile hatches was open and a couple of meters of shining steel cylinder projected from below. It wouldn't take a genius to figure out what was going on.

"Feeling daring?" asked McKinley.

Carter raised an eyebrow.

McKinley nodded. "Let's find some of those uniforms."

Off the dock's landward side were a number of doors of various sizes and designs, and at its far end could be seen something resembling an apartment building. McKinley surmised that this was accommodation for the workers, who obviously couldn't be housed at Wolf River. He and Carter had to get to the other end of the dock.

They descended again into the dark water and carefully swam to the stern of the Typhoon. If those giant engines came online now, they'd be mincemeat. Their most appropriate methodology was to swim along the huge curtain, surfacing only when necessary and staying below the foliage.

McKinley took a good breath and pulled himself down to the bottom of the barrier, which ended a couple of meters below the surface with big, cylindrical weights, the welded joints of which to the curtain provided useful handholds. He worked his way north, only coming up whenever his breath was running out. McKinley started to wonder if there were any unpleasant and/or hungry fish in this neighbourhood, but he was committed now. To infil the dock from its northern, seaward end made a lot more sense.

Brother Dawoud knelt in the sanctuary shortly after lunch, bemused and alone. It was so strange to see this expansive building empty, especially on Christmas Day, but the Ambassadors didn't seem to officially celebrate any of the traditional religious holidays, the merry decorations in the dining hall notwithstanding. The unusual degree of silence was oppressive and every tiny sound from outside was lost in the echoes of the hall. He was trying to pray, to seek divine guidance, but his mind was abuzz with distracting questions.

Who is Paul Wilson? Am I Paul Wilson? Darn it, that name seemed *glued* to him somehow.

Chris Carter was one of the spies that had been caught and executed. Pastor had spoken of the men's demise with great relish, drawing the analogy of skin lesions that needed to be radically excised. But maybe *Carter* could have explained all this. Dawoud understood that their leadership would eradicate any threat to the Ambassadors' mission, but to just *murder* those spies without mercy horrified Dawoud. Where was their regard for the sanctity of human life? It was especially troubling as they *might* have borne some answers to Dawoud's multiplying questions. Dawoud felt robbed of something intrinsically important, yet as to the reason for its significance he could but guess.

Dawoud felt guilty; he was questioning the pastor. That too was wrong.

Why shouldn't I question him, came another thought. He's only human.

But he's the holy apostle! He knows the will of the Universal Spirit!

Isn't *God* capable of speaking for Himself?

How do I know if He does?

Dawoud slapped his hands to his face, thrusting his mind away from the debate. This confusion was too much, too frustrating. In that instant he wanted to get away from the whole damn *ecclesia*, from the island, from Makaru and his sinister security people. He wanted to punch through the walls and escape to clarity, to freedom of thought. He didn't believe... no; he didn't know *what* to believe, or whether he believed anything at all.

He *had* to find out the truth!

The accommodation building reminded Carter of his days as a technical college student. It was assertively square and constructed of cinderblock with metal framed doors and windows, all painted black, whilst the windows themselves were inexpensive acrylic.

They worked their way around behind the building, out of sight of the dock, and tried the first keycard at what seemed to be a rear access. It didn't work, but they kept it in case it would be useful elsewhere. The second keycard, however, yielded a *buzz-click* from the lock and they opened the door, looking around carefully. At that moment the place seemed deserted.

They quickly located a stash of uniforms, making the call that orange, whilst more conspicuous, would be less likely to get them questioned. The 'reds', after all, seemed to be the menials. Carter used a handful of socks to briskly clean the rifle down and make it look like it was cared for.

McKinley and Carter walked brazenly out onto the dock, mustering as much conviction as possible. Their training told them that acting confidently or even arrogantly would discourage enquiry, but it was a hard balance to strike. Appearing more confident than necessary would draw attention. Both adopted the most serious of expressions, a spycraft technique used by cold war era soviet agents, who were trained to wear their 'important face' when gaining access to sensitive locations.

The immense enclosure was some remarkable engineering. It must have taken considerable time and manpower to put this thing in place. McKinley and Carter looked at each other with the same sense of shock as they'd shared in Wales a few months before. The scale of the project whose perpetrators they were up against was still awe inspiring.

The grid of the roof, with its tons of trees and soil, seemed to be supported in cantilever with the pivotal point resting on the huge concrete wall that formed the landward side of the dock. Beyond that, significant mass must be holding those enormous girders in a manner not dissimilar to a suspension bridge. If we could sever those supports, thought McKinley, the whole damn thing would come crashing down on its own, right onto those subs. They'd never get them out. He filed this idea away.

There were a couple of small tugboats at this end of the dock, which would be used to manoeuver the submarines in the confines of the bay. Several other boats stood by, including the one they'd seen previously with its spraying equipment. A big roll of what looked like fire hose lay on the dock.

The quay was so long that the bow of the Typhoon was still a hundred meters away, and the bow of the *Han* a further seventy meters beyond, with the crane trundling slowly and noisily by it. They walked past stacks of paletted supplies and parts, looking around constantly for anything more interesting.

It was Carter who spotted the wide tunnel that led away from the dock. They turned right and followed it past several artificially lit workshops and out into an open area that had been deforested and was protected by the same kind of overhead camouflage as the dock. Not wanting to appear as if they were there just to look round, McKinley and Carter headed toward a large central building made of whitewashed concrete and fronted by a wide roller shutter.

Just as they approached the building, the shutter started to clank upward with an electrical whine. Startled, McKinley indicated with his eyes to Carter and they split up, coming to a halt either side of the doorway. A few red clothed workers joined them and McKinley wondered what the heck was going on.

The shutter clanked upwards, revealing his answer. Emerging on a steel trolley pulled by a 'red' and accompanied by two white coated scientists was what could only be a nuclear warhead, emblazoned with radiation warning decals. The workers around them started clapping so McKinley and Carter joined in. As the trolley was ushered out, others came running up to share in this important moment. McKinley noticed Carter studying the machine intently. It was a rounded cylinder about four feet long, strapped in vertical orientation to a circular base. A little over a foot in diameter, it had a domed upper end, and cables ran from its flat bottom to a series of plastic boxes that presumably housed electronics. Looking like a deconstructed MIRV, there could be no doubt as to its identity; it was the British WE82 tactical thermonuclear warhead that Heinmarsh's people had hijacked back in July. They noticed that several of the workers had pulled out their mobile phones to picture this historic occasion, so Carter did the same.

Workers trundled the warhead through the tunnel back to the dock. When they got there, McKinley and Carter saw that a long metal bridge had been laid, spanning the Chinese submarine and reaching the forward casing of the Typhoon to where the sub's large, heavy silo door had been opened.

Carter quietly switched to Spanish, hoping that nobody else around them could speak it. "You see what's going on here, don't you?"

"They're mounting it on the missile."

"Here comes the nose cone." Carter looked upward and McKinley followed. The crane was approaching, its conical cargo raised aloft.

"That's ablative shielding," observed Carter. "So it can re-enter without burning up."

"This is a little too damn familiar," growled McKinley, "and it looks like they're getting ready to launch."

Carter nudged him. "The boat!"

McKinley looked out beyond the submarines. Sure enough the tall steel curtain was retreating and Makaru's launch could be seen beyond.

"Time to leave," hissed McKinley.

They turned north again and headed back toward the accommodation block but soon realised that this was a mistake. Now clear of the barrier, the launch turned right and quickly started gaining on them.

"Stay cool," whispered McKinley. Their only chance was to become as invisible as possible, but then he had a terrible thought; he and Carter were the only people there sporting great big, bushy beards. Oh shit.

The launch passed them, heading toward a ladder on the quayside, and McKinley got that sinking feeling. He heard the sound of multiple footsteps echoing from behind as workers hurried to greet their boss. He nudged Carter and they quickly turned left into a large, square double doorway.

They found themselves in a warehouse. Pallets stood in organised rows on their yellow painted racks, stretching away for forty meters in each direction and illuminated both by skylights and long, colourless fluorescent tubes. Quick as a flash McKinley jumped with all his weight onto a spare wooden pallet, smashing it, then grabbed two of the longer pieces and shoved them through the twin door handles. It wouldn't hold for more than a few seconds but any advantage was good. He and Carter quickly ran down the nearest end of the rows.

"Height!" gasped Carter. "I need open sky!"

McKinley stopped dead and looked up for just a second, then leaped onto a supporting strut. Carter needed no second bidding and started scrambling up the next rack. Dust flew off the stored items, bringing on coughing, but neither had time to think of it. They pushed themselves upward using any handhold they could.

With a crash the doors exploded open and they heard men running into the warehouse. McKinley reached the top tier, wobbling unsteadily for a moment on the narrow girder. He steadied himself on a nearby pallet full of cardboard boxes, then pulled himself up it, his fingers raking the shrink-wrap. He saw that the skylight was made of corrugated plastic which he could probably break. He sensed Carter climbing up behind him.

Without thinking of the calamitous fall that might result, McKinley placed his hands on a nearby electrical conduit and swung his body hard. His flailing legs found the plastic window and smashed a hole in it, shards of plastic raining down on him as shouts came from below. He swung again and managed to get most of his body through the gap. Without even taking the time to steady himself, McKinley reached back with both hands and grabbed Carter's.

The weapons tech was a solid block of muscle and not light, but with the urgency of desperation McKinley pulled hard on Carter, lifting him a couple of feet.

"Got it!" yelled Carter, pushing with his own arms against the skylight's edges. A shot rang out and they felt a burst of air as the round pierced the roof close by. They both flopped onto the tarred surface, rolled and got up.

Dodging tree trunks McKinley ran south, back along the lengthy dock, hoping to distract the guards below as Carter fiddled with his phone. More shots pierced the roof, showering leaf fragments.

Carter staggered between the trees, trying to keep his footing and concentrate on his task as the pummelling of lead continued. Suddenly he stumbled and fell flat on his face, the phone slapping him right in the nose. Carter blinked and shook his head, regaining focus on the tiny screen. There was a connection! Quickly he entered the commands for data transfer, hearing an accusative yell from further along the roof. The progress bar started.

McKinley shouted some profanity at the advancing guards. He had to buy Carter some time! Now there were men approaching from the direction in which McKinley was running. With loud reports several rounds slapped into the trees nearby and McKinley flung his arms round his head, feeling splinters of wood pepper his torso.

Carter thrust the phone under his prone body as the guards surrounded him. He slowly put his hands on the back of his head and lay there, waiting. The black surface of the roof was warm against his face. I hope my body's not a radio insulator, he thought.

A pair of the guards turned Carter over and he looked up into the face of Makaru, whose eyes radiated hatred like he'd never seen. The furious Asian looked from Carter down to where the phone was lying, and gestured to a guard, who picked it up and handed it to his leader.

Makaru regarded the little screen, breathing hard and with his teeth gritted. He seemed to comprehend what was displayed there.

"What are you doing?" he hissed, his voice grating with anger.

Carter saw stars as a rifle butt impacted his head.

"Answer the pastor!" snapped the guard that had hit him. "NOW!"

Carter felt a body drop next to him and opened his eyes to see McKinley, cuffed at the wrists.

"I'll give you one last chance," growled Makaru. "What did you upload?"

Carter looked at McKinley, who nodded his assent.

"Video of your warhead," spat Carter triumphantly, despite the pain. "GPS co-ordinates 'n' all. We just brought Her Majesty's armed forces down on you!"

Eyes ablaze with rage, Makaru kicked Carter in the face, then regained his composure, controlling his breathing carefully. He flicked a stray lock of jet black hair into place.

"Well then," he sneered, "I think you should know that someone else is on the way here. A Turkish associate of mine whom you met in the Canary Islands."

McKinley and Carter looked at each other again, the latter with a thin stream of blood exiting his nose.

"He's anxious to talk to you," concluded Makaru. He turned away, barking an instruction at his guards, who scooped up the COAST lads like two sacks of spuds and manhandled them over to a set of steps and down to the launch.

"Brother Dawoud!" came the now irritatingly familiar voice of Prophet Bellegarde. Dawoud was getting a bit fed up with the constant attention from the leader, yet he instinctively wanted to do right by the man. He turned away from the delightful view of the bay in the early evening sun, brushing grains of wind-blown sand from the pristine purple of his jacket, and met Bellegarde with a smile as he strode up.

"Prophet," he said, squinting, "how can I help you?" It was hard to read the big man's face in silhouette, but he didn't seem cheerful.

"How does it feel to be in Pastor's personal guard?" Bellegarde seemed even more interested than usual.

Dawoud answered warily. He dared not give voice to his doubts. "Great."

"Good, good. You'll be pleased to know that Pastor wants to personally approve you for his service."

Dawoud's eyebrows leaped. "Really?"

"It's nothing unusual," replied Bellegarde in serious tones. "It's a rite of passage, if you like. Separates the men from the boys. A measure of your loyalty. You *are* loyal to Pastor, aren't you Dawoud?"

"Of course," answered Dawoud, not entirely possessed of conviction but nonetheless a little affronted that his devotion was in question.

Bellegarde nodded slowly. "Okay. No training session tomorrow, but you will come to the Citadel at nine o'clock in the morning."

That sounded exciting. "Yes sir," Dawoud replied enthusiastically.

Bellegarde gave him a long look before turning away. "See you there."

"I've got a bitch of a headache," stated Carter.

"Don't worry," said McKinley, staring at the ceiling and trying not to think about cigarettes. "Erbakan'll take care of it."

They sat with their backs to opposite walls in a concrete cell that was a little smaller than a single garage. They'd been there overnight and were horribly uncomfortable, not to mention hungry, thirsty and unbelievably tired. The enclosure was situated at the bottom of Makaru's impressive 'Citadel', and was featureless apart from a light in the center of the ceiling, a drain in the corner and a couple of metal panels in one of the end walls. It smelled strongly of cleaning fluid, leading them to wonder what it had been used for that required such attention. There was no window and even the lone electric bulb was recessed and protected by thick glass.

"Wonder what Uncle Victor's doing now?" mused Carter.

"Like you said; bringing the weight of our forces down on this place."

"Wonder how long it'll take 'em to get here."

McKinley huffed. "I hate to sound pessimistic, but probably longer than Erbakan." He was desperate for a smoke.

"True."

After a couple of minutes of quiet, McKinley spoke again. "Well, that's a couple of items off the list. We rescued Bacon and found the warhead."

Carter sighed, nodding. "Still wanna get Heinmarsh though."

"Aye."

Suddenly their attention was caught by sounds in the corridor. They looked at each other.

"Erbakan?" said Carter nervously.

McKinley steeled himself for the confrontation. "I guess we'll find out," he said dourly.

They listened. Although the heavy architecture deadened sounds from outside the room, it was clear that there was a heated argument going on between at least two parties. McKinley wished he could hear what was being said.

The argument abated and then they heard the door being unlocked; Makaru, Heinmarsh and Bellegarde entered, flanked by two guards. They all looked mighty pissed off and McKinley wondered who had been arguing with whom. He could take a fairly educated guess that Makaru had been browbeating both Heinmarsh and Bellegarde for their failure to kill Carter and himself.

The trio regarded the COAST agents for a moment with varying degrees of hostility, then Makaru gave a signal to the guards. They manhandled McKinley and Carter into kneeling positions with their hands behind their heads and then left the room. Bellegarde followed them to the corridor and spoke what sounded like an order. There was a shout and they heard another door opening, followed by footsteps advancing toward them.

McKinley's eyes nearly popped out of his head with surprise when Wilson walked in. Their tall Combat and Survival Specialist was the last person he expected to see. Wilson appeared just as fit and healthy as usual in the purple tunic that made him look like some kind of priest, but there was an expression of disquiet on his face.

When Wilson saw the prisoners he was also shocked. He turned to Bellegarde, his face a mask of misunderstanding. "Prophet, I thought they were executed," he exclaimed.

"They will be, they will be," explained Bellegarde quickly. "It was a prophetic utterance, a foretelling. Calling things that are not as though they are."

Heinmarsh and Makaru stepped back as Bellegarde put his hand on Wilson's shoulder.

"Brother Dawoud," he said, "we're asking something of you. It'll be difficult, but when you do it you'll be confirmed as a leader in Pastor's personal guard, an extremely important position. D'you think you can do this for me, son?"

Dawoud's heart was beating hard. He was caught between the excitement of the promotion and the urge to find answers for his questions, foremost of which being why they were told that these men were already dead. It didn't make sense and that explanation was just semantics. "What do you want me to do, Prophet?" he asked warily.

Bellegarde brought a Kahr CM45 pistol out of his pocket and held it out by the barrel.

"These men are enemies of Pastor Makaru," he said, "and of the Universal Spirit, and of everything the Ambassadors of the Godhead stand for. Kill them."

"Is that... really necessary?" stammered Dawoud, his brow furrowed.

"Don't question our commands," grunted Bellegarde abrasively. "Think of it as... a test of faith." He pressed the gun into Dawoud's hand and withdrew slightly.

Dawoud took the pistol and it felt oddly apropos. To have a firearm in his hand was comfortable, like it belonged there. He looked at the little black and silver Kahr. It was a relatively ordinary weapon of American manufacture. Simple but effective.

Okay, thought Dawoud, time to man-up and get this thing done. He looked back at Bellegarde with determination in his eyes. The leader nodded, egging him on. "Dawoud, execute these infidels."

"Kill them," echoed Makaru.

McKinley was getting increasingly worried. Why were they doing this when Makaru had already said Erbakan was on the way? Were they going to get murdered by their own team-mate?

"Hey," he snapped, "think what you're bloody doing!"

Wilson angled his head down. "I have just one question for you," he said quietly, bringing the gun to Carter's forehead.

The weapons tech looked up into his eyes but couldn't tell whether Dawoud's or Wilson's soul was looking back. "What?" he breathed, trying his hardest to face death with some measure of dignity.

Wilson pressed the barrel into Carter's skin.

"What's my name?"

020: The Escape

"Brother Dawoud!" commanded Makaru. "*Kill the infidels! Kill them now!*"

"Kill the enemy!" snarled Bellegarde. "Prove you truly serve the Universal Spirit!"

"Obey your leaders!" added Makaru.

McKinley was thinking hard, trying to analyse this horrible new turn of events. If the Brother Dawoud persona remained and was reinforced in Wilson's psyche, they'd die right there. If he or Carter answered Wilson's question truthfully then these three shits would know for sure what they already suspected.

"You're Tactical Corporal Paul Wilson!" blabbed Carter before McKinley could reach a conclusion. Wilson withdrew the pistol and stepped back as Carter continued. "You work for the Covert Operations And Surveillance Team. Your codename—"

Makaru slapped Carter across the face so hard that it made his neck crack.

"BE QUIET!" yelled the Asian, spitting with rage.

"You hit like a little girl," smirked Carter, recovering quickly despite the redness of his face.

His arm moving with staggering speed, Makaru slammed a devastating punch into Carter's skull, knocking the weapons tech to the floor. The demagogue hissed like a vicious lizard. "Is that better?"

Carter groaned in a childish, mocking tone. "Pansy! Lady-boy!"

Enraged, Makaru drew back his foot for a harsh kick to Carter's nether regions. Suddenly, with a blur of speed, Wilson brought the pistol directly to Makaru's head. "Leave him alone!" he snapped.

Makaru turned to face Wilson, bringing the gun's barrel between his eyes. "What's the call, Brother Dawoud?" he said with unexpected calm. "Or should I say Wilson? Are you going to kill the godhead's anointed servant?"

With sudden understanding McKinley realised what was going on. There was a reason why Heinmarsh and Bellegarde were just standing there.

Wilson's answer smouldered with contempt. "No... but I can kill *you*."

Makaru was unruffled. "Then do it. Do it now."

Wilson squeezed the trigger. The pistol clicked and Makaru punched Wilson hard in the face, knocking the lanky young man over both McKinley and Carter. He landed on the floor with a thump, rolled back up again and cycled the weapon's action. A round popped out of the chamber and rattled on the floor. Wilson tried to fire again but was rewarded with no more than another dead click.

McKinley had been knocked over by Wilson's tumble, but now he saw that both Bellegarde and Heinmarsh had weapons drawn. It had been an act. The slimy scumbags had both tested the brainwashing *and* smoked Wilson out with dummy rounds. Neat, thought McKinley.

As the two guards returned to the room Makaru drew a pistol of his own, a little Heckler and Koch P2000 SK, and stood over Wilson, who raised his hands. The Asian kicked away the inert Kahr weapon. It rattled into the corner where Heinmarsh picked it up. Makaru's voice was afire with anger as he glared at Wilson. "*Infidel!*" he spat disgustedly, as though there was no more vituperative insult in the whole world.

Heinmarsh exited the room. Bellegarde grinned cruelly. "And you know what happens to infidels," he rasped, enjoying the implied intimidation. "He's nearly here."

With this he also left, leaving the reunited TDR.12 alone with the sinister figure of Makaru and the guards, who stood with their Heinmarsh rifles at the ready.

Makaru looked between them for a long few moments, gathering his thoughts.

"Here comes the monologue," observed Carter, rolling his eyes.

Makaru snapped. "Shut up! *SHUT UP!! You twisted little puppet!* You filthy lowlife cretin! You damned reprobate insect!" He wiped the spittle from his chin, breathing hard, obviously putting effort into calming himself down. "You haven't changed anything. The submarine is leaving as we speak. You cannot stop it."

"Who're you going to drop it on?" said McKinley.

"How about your capital city?" snarled Makaru. "Eight million victims in *your* honour. Or what about Nottingham? That's where you live, isn't it?"

McKinley shrugged. "Whoever you like then. Guess you've had a re-think since that Yankee idiot blew your last plan."

"Perhaps," said Makaru, having nearly subsided to his usual cool. "Once in orbit we can direct the warhead anywhere."

"That's what I thought," nodded McKinley. "Just another terrorist."

Makaru's face twisted rapidly through a number of different emotions, none of which were nice. After a moment he breathed out a sigh and appeared to change tack.

"You... *you* attacked this community. *You* robbed us of our peace. *You* brought death to this paradise."

McKinley frowned in disbelief. "Well that's rich coming from the silly bastard who sent it everywhere else."

The short, sharp blow of the P2000's butt to McKinley's head knocked him to his knees beside Carter. He felt a wet trickle on his forehead.

"You think you're so clever," growled the Asian.

"*No,*" responded Carter from his prone position. "He's *cunning. I'm* clever." He tilted his head toward Wilson. "And he's confused."

Makaru struck like lightning again, dealing Carter another kick to his face, then turned to Wilson.

"*You,* Brother Dawoud—"

"That's *not* my name!" bellowed Wilson.

Makaru continued as though Wilson hadn't even spoken. "*You* were touched by the Universal Spirit. *You* partook of the age to come. Yet you threw it all away for the sin of this present darkness! You could've been part of *the Kingdom!*"

"Bullshit!" answered Wilson. "It's all bullshit and brainwashing!"

"What's so good about this Kingdom anyway?" grunted Carter, pushing himself up to where he could both kneel and lean on his forearms. Blood had formed several small rivers from a gash to his left cheekbone. "All it does is use innocent kids to blow up politicians!"

"That's just the opening act," Makaru sneered. "This world is full of foetid boils and we are lancing them one-by-one. We will take dominion and replace the corrupt political systems. Ever heard that nature abhors a vacuum?"

"Ever heard of outer space?" quipped Carter.

"The *Communion* is coming," announced Makaru, his eyes ablaze. "This world will be united for the first time, free from the burden of self-seeking futility." The Asian raised his gaze as though looking out at some future utopia. "There will be peace. Chaos will cease; order will reign."

"Order?" said McKinley derisively. "As in *new world?*"

"What you gonna do, chopstick?" mocked Carter. "Unleash *Godzilla?*"

Makaru kicked Carter in the stomach, causing the weapons tech to grunt in pain. He rolled over onto his side.

"Maybe *Rodan* then," coughed Carter.

"Death's too good for you," the Asian snarled. He waved the pistol between them, his hand shaking with frustration. "All of you! When Mister Erbakan gets here you will suffer beyond imagining! Your death will be lonely and meaningless, and I'll be there to watch."

"So will it be lonely or not?" derided McKinley. "'Cause you're not really making yourself clear."

"Mickey," gasped Carter, "I think he's the new Shirō Ishii."

"Yeah," laughed McKinley, "or Jim Jones. How about Mengele? Can I get a starting bid on Mengele?"

Wilson was shocked at the blatant flippancy – McKinley and Carter making irreverent fun of the leader as though he wasn't even present. What the hell were they trying to do? Piss him off even more? Makaru's eyes were nearly popping out of their sockets, his whole body shaking with a hostility that seemed to radiate and pressurise the room. Any moment, thought Wilson, there'll be an explosion.

"Roger that," replied Carter. "Definitely stalker material."

Makaru screamed in frenzied rage and fell upon Carter, smashing three hate-fuelled blows into the Brit's cranium. McKinley hurled himself at Makaru but found himself landing on Carter. At least his friend would be protected. Then there was a rifle muzzle at his forehead. Makaru stood back, his face twisted with furious animosity.

"I think I hurt his feeling," croaked Carter. "Yes, he only has one: arrogance."

As Wilson was again bewildered by Carter's brazen impertinence, Makaru flew from the room in a flurry of furore. Looking freaked out, the guards backed through the door, shutting and locking it.

Wilson was still feeling like a prisoner of two worlds, yet the whole altercation had brought memories back, memories of these men. Yes, he did know them. They were his friends, even though they were jerks. He felt an odd sense of affection for their contumelious effrontery.

"Why did you do that?" he asked. "Why deliberately wind him up?"

McKinley helped Carter up. The latter's face was dripping with blood from his cheek, his nose and his lips, but he sat up with a measure of poise, ignoring the injuries.

"His Achilles' heel," sniffed Carter, wincing at the effort of speaking. "We exposed his weakness."

"You did?"

"Ego." Carter grinned painfully. "I think he believes the crap he comes out with. He really thinks he's something special. Thing is, deception's like a cold; you can't spread it without getting infected."

Wilson was uncertain. "Err, okay."

"Pride comes before a fall," asserted Carter, raising his finger to make the point. "The problem with very clever people is that they usually think they're cleverer than everyone else, so they make mistakes."

McKinley looked round at Carter. "Says someone who just called himself clever," he grunted.

Carter huffed, shrugging dejectedly. "Not really."

"Aye and why not?"

"Well, if I was *really* clever I'd be filthy rich, wouldn't I? Not stuck on this godforsaken island with you two muppets and a deranged clever person."

McKinley shook his head. Carter could be annoyingly irrepressible. "Willy, are you back to normal?" he ventured carefully. "We could really use your help."

Willy. That word again had a tremendous familiarity about it. "Willy as in Wilson?"

"Right," said Carter, leaning his head against the concrete. "You just forgot. It's okay. You've been through some shit."

Wilson allowed himself to drop to the floor, his back sliding down the wall. The memories were emerging as if from a dream that dissipates upon waking, but which one recalls later.

"Can you help me remember?" he asked.

"You're Paul Terrence Wilson," replied McKinley, crouching opposite him. "You're from Long Bennington, Lincolnshire. Your parents are Elizabeth and Jack and you've got younger twin sisters: Kim and Kaitlyn. You live in a flat in Stapleford and you drive a Nissan Pathfinder. You were in the Parachute Regiment then the Special Forces Support Group. Now you work for General Sutton of COAST and you're the Combat and Survival Specialist of Tactical Deployment and Response Team Twelve. I'm Ian McKinley—Tactical and Surveillance—and this is Chris Carter, Weapons and Equipment Technician."

Apart from that last name this all sounded like a foreign language to Wilson, but it was one he was eager to learn as bits of it started to stick to the sides of his mind.

"What happened to me?" he said.

"They drugged you," grated Carter. He wiped his cheek, looking dispassionately at the blood on his palm. "As far as I can tell it blocks long term memories, and while you were knocked out he filled your head with his garbage. Like he said; nature abhors a vacuum. Your hungry brain ate whatever they fed it. That's why you felt such loyalty."

"I did." Wilson was getting confused again. There was a time, not many days ago, that he'd gladly have lain down his life for the pastor. How could he have been so wrong?

"You're remembering, aren't you?" continued Carter. "The more you do the easier it'll get. I think."

Wilson mouthed his name. It tasted *right* on his lips. Hey, he thought, I *am* Paul Wilson. It felt good.

"Is everyone here like me?"

Carter's lips formed a frown for a moment. "More or less."

Wilson had a small revelation. "That's what they do!" he exclaimed. "At the services. The ones that are having doubts go up for the altar call and vanish for a couple of days."

"Right," nodded Carter. "They're getting a top-up."

"And the missionaries! They never come back. What's happening to them?"

McKinley took over. "Suicide bombers."

Suicide...?

Suicide bombers!

A dump truck full of unpleasant memories suddenly unloaded into Wilson's mind like a huge avalanche of rock from a frangible cliff face. They were memories of videos and television news broadcasts, and they all ended the same way. He felt like he was watching afresh as young people, devoid of their own reason through the cult's programming, blew themselves to atoms. Wilson shook with horror.

There was sound in the corridor. McKinley threw Carter a look. It sounded like another argument. There were two loud thumps.

"Is this... Erbakan?" asked Wilson. He could recall who that was.

"If it is," murmured Carter, "we're all gonna have much more in common with Andy Lucas."

"Shut it," growled McKinley. "We need to—"

Someone was outside the door. They looked at each other. What was going on?

"Dawoud! Are you in there?" echoed a female voice, dulled by the metal of the door.

Wilson got up and ran to the door, a look of wide-eyed surprise on his face.

"Izzie!" he shouted, head pressed to the metal. "Yes, it's me. What're you doing here?" McKinley and Carter picked themselves up.

"Hold on," she said and swung the door open. Wilson and the girl embraced like they hadn't seen each other for years. They kissed passionately.

"Get a bloody room," complained McKinley. "Who's this?"

"I'm his girlfriend!" she snapped, her Australian accent roaring to the fore.

"I'm getting that," said Carter, "but what about Ju—"

McKinley prodded him on the shoulder. "She's Willy's *girlfriend*," he nodded, winking.

"Oh, right. Hi. I'm Chris."

She was frowning unhappily, but returned the salutation with a nod. "Izzie."

"Ian," said McKinley, his right thumb jerking back toward his chest.

Wilson blinked a few times. "These guys are my team... guys. I work with them," said Wilson a little slowly. He let forth a heavy sigh. "I'm having a hard time with this shit."

"It's alright," chorused Carter and Izzie, glancing at each other warily.

Wilson drew back from his woman. "How on earth did you get in here?" he asked, still shocked.

She shrugged. "Well there's a ruddy big hole in the fence." McKinley and Carter nodded at each other.

"You went outside the compound? That was a risk."

She smiled. "Fair dinkum, but nobody messes with *my* man."

McKinley came up to them, limping a little. "Aye, well, let's cut the fairytale shit and quit this joint."

They entered the corridor. It was a different one than Wilson had been in before. The walls diverged vertically with a single step, forming two shelves on which stood white ceramic busts of various religious leaders and philosophers with nameplates of black and gold. There were popes, ayatollahs, dalai lamas and rabbis. Zoroaster and Confucius stood alongside Guru Nanak Dev and Paul the Apostle. One of the busts was conspicuously absent from the ordered rows and now surrounded the supine form of a guard, whose head was encrusted with pale fragments. Carter looked down at the nameplate, surprised to see that it was Aleister Crowley lying there in bits.

"D'you do that?" asked Wilson, eyes wide.

"'Course I did," said Izzie. "I wasn't gonna let him stop me!"

McKinley grinned, pleasantly surprised. This young woman had some fire in her belly.

"Mickey!" said Carter. "Here's our stuff." From the shelf he grabbed his telephones and the few other items they'd been carrying. McKinley picked up the unconscious guard's Heinmarsh rifle and—thank goodness—his cigarettes, then they carefully approached the open outer door.

McKinley glanced outside, thrusting his head out and back in the briefest moment. His natural observational skills, enhanced by years of training, instantly captured an image of their surroundings: the back end of the greenhouses, the fence and jungle facing them, the cordon to the left, the neatly laid out township beyond and, further yet, the forest climbing toward the fumarole. All this told him that there was no-one between them and the fence and, if they were sufficiently stealthy, they would evade the view of the little guardhouses. The door was at the western side of the Citadel, offering them a little cover. On McKinley's signal the fugitives quickly escaped into the jungle.

Once they were a few hundred meters away from the fence, McKinley stopped with Carter.

"Get onto Uncle Victor again and tell him the Typhoon's on its way to launch the warhead."

"Roger that," said Carter and unlocked his phone. Suddenly his mouth opened in surprise. "Bloody hell! Paydirt!"

McKinley's face registered bemusement. "You what?"

Carter was grinning. "It's been running in the background since we got here."

"What's going on?" asked Wilson.

"Listen," said Carter excitedly. "I can hack Makaru's phone!"

McKinley scowled. "You can hack any phone. I don't see—"

"No, listen! Their computers are a trinary system; that's why we can't break into 'em. But his phone's a regular mobile OS and I wrote a little program to brute-force his password. Now I can access it."

"Your point?" deadpanned McKinley.

"Bloody hell Mickey. He must have software that handshakes with their Newland computers! So if I can grab his phone, we can too!"

McKinley saw the possibilities in a sudden 'aha' moment. With knitted brow he asked "you'd *have* to physically get it?"

"Yes." Carter nodded energetically, lamenting the action as his headache reasserted its presence. "I can't get in by wireless, just read its data and a couple of little things. If we can jack it I can input this password manually, then *change it*."

"Then it's a priority," replied McKinley firmly. "That'd be a breakthrough. Might even get us off Uncle Victor's shit-list."

Izzie put her hand up to speak, then lowered it, a little embarrassed. "'Scuse me," she said, "but how're you going to get close enough?"

"We'll burn that bridge when we come to it," replied McKinley. "Right now, let's keep moving." He grinned, winking at Carter. "To the batcave."

The hiked west-by-south-west to avoid any traffic to or from the geothermal plant, but this took them perilously close to the submarine dock. Once they'd turned south though, it receded into the distance and they gained altitude.

Looking back, they saw one of the tugboats returning to its mooring, indicating that the Typhoon with its nuclear-tipped missile was long gone.

They crested the first ridge and headed into the valley through which a small river ran west, which then turned north, entering the ocean near the submarine dock. The underbrush became thicker and their going tougher. Both McKinley and Carter took note of Wilson acting like the perfect gentleman toward Isabella, tenderly helping her through the often almost impassable terrain. With a glance, McKinley indicated to Carter to pull ahead, and they left the couple behind a little way.

McKinley lowered his voice. "Do you think he can relapse?"

Carter grunted, heaving himself over a fallen tree trunk. "It's possible, but he's not like the Fox girl. I don't know for certain, but the effects are inconsistent. I don't think this memory drug's very reliable."

"Aye. He seems to be remembering stuff better than her."

"Agreed. And Izzie's different again, like she never even forgot."

McKinley hummed his agreement, ducking a cluster of low hanging branches.

After fording the narrow river, over which Wilson carried his ladyfriend, they slowly climbed to the highest ridge, on the other side of which lay the cave. Uphill the going was even harder, although the gradient had thinned the vegetation somewhat. Finally they prepared to come out into the open and cross the rocky ridge, first checking carefully for aerial activity. Unable to hear the telltale thud-thud of a helicopter, they scrambled out of the trees and down to the earthen slope at the mouth of Carter's cavern.

"Welcome home," said Carter jovially, then suddenly held out his hand. "Wait!"

"What is it?" asked McKinley.

"Someone's been here."

McKinley could see. Carter's carefully piled supplies had been moved around.

Suddenly the forest erupted with shouts. McKinley saw DPM-clothed figures bursting from the undergrowth and brandishing rifles. So swift was the assault that he didn't even have time to raise his own.

"Hands up!" shouted one of the figures, a woman. "Down to your knees! Hands behind heads!"

"Okay, okay!" said McKinley, dropping his weapon. Damn, blast, bugger it and oh shit, he thought, this is all we need.

The COAST operatives knelt quickly, but Izzie hesitated, looking scared. One of the eight men took his rifle butt and knocked her over with a sharp blow to the back of her right leg. She fell in pain, shouting an angry obscenity.

Leaping forth like an uncaged hawk, Wilson flew at the man. Hitting with tremendous force, Wilson used his elbow on the side of the man's head, knocking him flying down the slope. In less time than it took to realise what was going on, the tall combat specialist had relieved the man of his rifle and was standing over him, its muzzle to the guy's head.

The other men reacted instinctively, turning their guns on Wilson, who looked to be an instant from death. But suddenly he spoke, spouting a rapid fire stream of foreign syllables.

"I knew it," said McKinley.

"QBZ-95s," affirmed Carter, recognising the Chinese assault rifle.

The woman held up her hand to halt any firing, indicating that she was the leader. She spoke in the same unfamiliar language. She had wrappings of black cloth around her face, leaving only a narrow slit for her eyes, but otherwise was clothed in fairly typical camouflage combats with webbing for her equipment. Her subordinates lowered their weapons to a standby posture.

Wilson looked round angrily and spoke again.

"Yes, I speak English," said the leader.

Thank heavens for that, thought McKinley. "We're British special forces," he insisted. "We have the same objectives."

Wilson looked up at him. "I just said that."

McKinley shrugged back, his eyes saying 'how was I to know?'

The leader brought her weapon up to McKinley's eye level. "How do I know you are who you claim?"

"Alright," said McKinley. "Your mission is to either retrieve or destroy your government's disavowed North Sea Fleet Type 091 *Han* Class submarine, hull number 407, which was hijacked by its crew under orders from Kurt Heinmarsh."

The Chinese soldier nodded slowly. "Alright. What is *your* mission?"

McKinley lowered his hands. "Officially: nothing. Unofficially: to stop Heinmarsh launching a nuclear warhead, and Makaru sending out more suicide bombers. We're on the same team."

The leader said something in Chinese and her squad slung their weapons. Wilson got up and helped the man he'd knocked down to do the same. They exchanged a few words in Mandarin, apparently putting their altercation behind them, although the Chinese guy seemed bloody unhappy.

"I am Chen Yan Ping," said the leader. "Sub-lieutenant, People's Liberation Army Marine Force." She pointed to another associate, a shorter figure with strikingly thin legs. "This is Sergeant Lee Yi Wu, PLA Navy Submarine Force, my second in command."

McKinley held out his hand. "Ian McKinley, Covert Operations And Surveillance Team. These are my colleagues Chris Carter and Paul Wilson."

They shook hands then Chen frowned. "You mentioned a nuclear warhead?"

"Aye. It's British, stolen earlier this year. They've mounted it on a missile and it's on that Typhoon—the big Russian sub—heading out to launch it. Once it's in orbit they can drop it anywhere on Earth."

Chen's eyes widened so much that they looked like they'd push the mask off. She said something vehement in Chinese that required no translation, then switched back to English. "We must stop them!"

"No kidding." McKinley turned to Carter. "Where do you think they're heading?"

Carter sat back with his ass in the dirt, thinking for a moment. "Somewhere deep 'cause it takes a bit of sting out of the waves. Helps keep the boat stable. And for an orbital shot it should be equatorial."

"But we're almost *on* the equator."

Carter frowned, tipping his head sideways. "Yeah. Hundred miles or so. Assuming she's submerged and under full steam that's..." He drifted off, his eyes losing their focus for a moment. "About three hours' sailing time. But she won't be at flank speed."

"Why not?"

Carter held out his hands as though the answer was obvious. "Remember the *USS San Francisco*? It hit a seamount. The water round here's so shallow it's too risky for a big boat like that to go faster. Plus they've got to navigate the passable channels so they're not going in a straight line, are they?"

Lee barked something at Chen and the latter spoke. "Lee's English is not good, but he's a submarine officer, an expert on the Type 091 boat. He says you're right, and he knows how to stop it."

"I like that," said McKinley. "Can you translate please?"

Chen nodded and her XO came out with a long burst of speech. McKinley looked round at Wilson, intrigued that the combat specialist, despite the modification of his memory, had retained his talent for Mandarin. Hopefully Wilson would tip him the wink if there was any hint of deception.

"I'm getting the idea," said McKinley quietly.

Carter turned to him. "What, *you* speak Chinese now?"

McKinley nodded. "Lee's an expert on the *Han*. We have to stop a submarine. Go figure."

Carter got the picture. "Oh," he nodded, eyebrows raised.

Chen and her colleague seemed to have concluded their exchange, and the former addressed McKinley.

"We have an idea."

"Use the *Han* to go after the Typhoon?"

She cocked an eyebrow, a little surprised. "Yes. My officer agrees. If we can get within torpedo range before they launch, there is a chance of preventing it."

McKinley was gobsmacked at the audacity of the idea, but it seemed plausible. "That sounds... good."

"But," countered Chen, "I'm not authorised to do anything like *that*."

"Well," shrugged McKinley, feeling hope building in his guts, "you can waste time talking to Beijing or you can stop them launching. Either way, *we're* going to try."

They broke into two groups, McKinley and Carter with Chen and three of her subordinates, and Wilson and Isabella with Lee and another three. The choice was logical based on the fact that neither McKinley nor Carter spoke Chinese, but Chen's English was excellent. Wilson and Lee, on the other hand, would have little trouble making themselves understood. McKinley was reticent to allow Wilson into a combat scenario but there was no choice. He was even less inclined to allow the Australian woman to accompany them but what else could he do? If she stayed at the cave she'd more than likely be discovered and shot. McKinley's group headed north toward the dock's accommodation section, whilst Wilson's prepared to infil from the south.

The hidden dock seemed almost deserted. There were a few reds about but their orange clad colleagues were absent, presumably having departed on the Typhoon. Chen gave the order to attack.

Both groups burst onto the dock from their respective ends, heading for the *Han* Class submarine. McKinley's group threw themselves behind the various palletted stores on the dockside for cover as the reds quickly reacted to the assault. Carter had a Chinese Type 77 pistol which in no way made up for the Desert Eagle to which he was accustomed. McKinley used the Heinmarsh rifle.

Wilson's group encountered the heaviest resistance and it seemed almost as though they were expected. Forty or so reds, who were all carrying rifles, offered a spirited defence.

"Stay here!" Wilson ordered Izzie, squeezing her hand. She ducked down behind the rough boulders at the southern end of the long quay as the lead hail started.

Wilson threw himself down against a long, low crate. Splinters of wood cascaded around him. He rolled left, taking a quick glance round the bottom of the object, where he'd be least likely to attract fire. He pulled himself back up, readying the Chinese assault rifle he'd been given.

In a sudden fog of confusion, Wilson wondered what the hell he was doing. Here he was in a gun battle with not the slightest clue of what he was fighting for. All his motivation for following McKinley's lead had instantly evaporated. What about the divine mission? What about Pastor Makaru and all the disciples? Wilson was light-years out of his depth and terrified. With a sharp crack and outburst of fragments, a round exploded through the container next to his head.

He dropped the rifle, but the instant it left his hands something felt wrong. He should be fighting! What happened? He'd forgotten for a moment. Now he remembered the unit, McKinley, Carter, General Sutton and their new Chinese friends. Yet for a harrowing few seconds all these things had been absent from his cognition. Now he felt back on track, but horribly vulnerable. What if he had another flashback?

At the other end of the dock, McKinley's group were advancing, slowly but surely taking out the reds and pushing toward the conning tower of the sub. If they could get that far, the battle was essentially won.

McKinley threw himself down next to Chen as a spray of automatic fire sought them. These Chinese marines were bloody good fighters, yet two were already down. The reds were amateurs by comparison, but they had numbers. A Chinese marine shouted something and McKinley saw two grenades sailing through the air toward their opponents.

Despite scattering, several reds were caught in the staccato double blast and fell along the quay. McKinley jumped up and ran forward again, crouching behind the next available bit of cover, a palette with a tarpaulin strapped around it. It wasn't even a meter high and far less than ideal. McKinley looked up to see that the reds were throwing grenades as well.

In an instant of heart-seizing fear, a grenade clattered to the ground not two feet away from McKinley. Instinctively he rolled to the left, knowing that mere rotation couldn't get him far enough away. He closed his eyes against the blast and suddenly felt nothingness below him. His vision span between quayside, roof and submarine hull.

The two bangs came almost simultaneously. The grenade exploded with a tearing impact that made his ears ring and then, separated by an infinitesimal heartbeat, the air was knocked from McKinley's lungs as his body slammed into the bottom of a rowing boat moored next to the tugs.

Disoriented, McKinley shook his head. He'd broken the lateral plank that formed the oarsman's seat and both his back and his head were screaming in pain. Better than getting chewed up by a grenade though, he thought. One of the Chinese soldiers looked down from the quayside, his expression black.

McKinley realised what had happened. Chen had been following him and was caught in the blast. He didn't need a degree in Mandarin to figure out that the squad's leader was dead. McKinley looked about. His rifle had disappeared.

Wilson's group were still pinned down at the southern end of the quay. The reds were fierce and tenacious in their defence and their numbers seemed to be holding despite losses.

Suddenly there was a shout from behind. "Hold your fire or she dies!"

Wilson closed his eyes tightly for a second as a horrible dread invaded his inner being. He turned slowly, knowing exactly what he would see.

Izzie was pressed down to the rock by a rifle barrel at the back of her neck, her eyes pleading for survival. The Asian man behind her was thin yet sturdy, breathing hard, and clearly surprised at having gained this unexpected advantage.

"Drop your weapons!" he ordered. Laying down his rifle, Wilson translated for his colleagues.

They allowed their guns to drop to the concrete. The man pulled his Heinmarsh weapon back from Isabella's head to cover them.

Suddenly she roared and grabbed the weapon's barrel, swinging it in the direction of the water. "I've got him!" she yelled.

Wilson fell to the floor and retrieved his rifle as his woman clung to the end of the other. It's owner, enraged, was trying to shake the woman off, after which he would doubtless use it on her. Wilson brought his rifle to bear and squeezed the trigger once.

The man's chest exploded from front to back and his body collapsed on top of Izzie. Instantly she rolled from under him and picked up his rifle. Holding it like one does a shotgun, she yanked on the trigger and spattered the man's brains all over the rocks. The recoil nearly knocked her flying and she stumbled on the rough boulders.

"Woah! Hey!" said Wilson, running over. "You didn't have to do that!" They both ducked down behind the concrete edge as their Chinese colleagues resumed the fight.

"I told you," she snarled with a determination that shocked Wilson, "nobody messes with *my* man! *Or me!*"

"All the same," he said, "don't go too hard with this thing."

"What?" she frowned. "Because I'm a woman?"

"Hell no," grinned Wilson. "Because it's freakin' dangerous."

"Duly noted," she smiled.

McKinley rolled over the side of the rowboat to get closer to the sub and surfaced, as planned, level with the Han's sail. The swim from the rowing boat had been time consuming but if he could get up to the bridge hatch it would be worth it. He looked both ways, seeing a mooring rope off to his right. It must have been attached to the huge Typhoon. McKinley hauled himself up the rope, trying to keep low and not attract attention. It was soaking wet, and his hands hurt, but before long he reached a point on the curvature of the hull where he could let go and gravity would keep him in place.

Unseen from the dockside, McKinley quickly climbed the sail's side ladder. Reaching the top, he looked around to make sure no-one could peg him from the quay, then jumped and heaved himself over the rim. He landed in the bridge and found what he was looking for. Suddenly a round tore through the left leg of his coveralls, narrowly missing flesh. McKinley stumbled and fell on the deck. That shot had come through the hatch. There was someone on board.

McKinley pressed himself to the wall and quickly crawled behind the hatch cover. Then he let out a moan as though in pain. "Help!"

There was no response, so he waited about five seconds and did it again. He heard movement from below. "Help!" grunted McKinley.

He watched as a pair of shoulders came into view behind the hatch. Quick as a flash McKinley kicked it with all his might. There was a dull thud and he felt a slight tremor in the deck. McKinley levered himself up and saw the man, another red, knocked out cold. In his unmoving hand was a standard Model 1911 pistol of the kind that virtually every major gunsmith had manufactured at some point. McKinley grinned. Now at least he had some personal firepower. He let the unlucky red drop down the ladder and got back onto his objective.

The sub's main gun, welded roughly to the deck as an after-market modification, was a potent affair in fifty cal. McKinley pulled back on the cocking handle, checked what he hoped was the safety and lit up the dock.

With a slightly lower rate of fire than expected, the machine gun spat a thunderous stream of lead at the quay, destroying everything in its path. Men, crates and concrete were pulverised by the heavy rounds, showering the area with fragments and blood. McKinley only raked the area for about fifteen seconds, but it was clear that he'd won the battle; the surviving reds all adopted a surrendering posture.

He made it back to the dock as the Chinese marines were locking the prisoners up in the storage area, tying them securely to the racking. Carter was coaching the group as quickly as he could on submarine warfare as Wilson occasionally shared a comment in mandarin with Lee, who nodded a lot and expanded on the information for his remaining men.

"We push the engines to the limit to catch that thing," said Carter, "but this is the PLA's first nuclear boat so it ain't very fault tolerant. We can't risk overheating or over-pressuring the reactor or we'll end up dead. It's kinda sub-standard."

"Got it," said Wilson robotically. His head was spinning with all this new information.

Carter held up a chart. "We pass through the shallows here," he said, pointing. "The Typhoon's too big so she'll have gone round. This is our main advantage, but we'll have a bum-scraper if we dive too deep. If we have to stay surfaced we'll be slower."

"When we get close," interjected McKinley, "we'll contact them."

"Agreed," murmured Carter.

Wilson raised an eyebrow. "Isn't it better to stay silent?"

"Normally yes," answered McKinley. "But we'll order them to stand down. Maybe they will, *maybe* they'll speed up."

"Hey guys," came a shout from Izzie, who was in one of the rooms off the dock.

"What is it?" called Wilson, concern for his partner suddenly leaping to the top of his consciousness.

McKinley and Carter looked at each other. They didn't have time for distractions.

"You need to see this," she shouted back. "It's frightening!"

Wilson ran over to the room, which was a small office. High on the wall was mounted a television screen and it appeared to be showing a feed from Wolf River's main meeting hall.

"He's telling them to kill themselves," wailed Izzie.

Wilson pecked repeatedly at the volume up button. They needed to hear this clearly.

"...not be afraid of death! You will be welcomed into the afterlife as both believers and martyrs!" preached Makaru. "Our lives will not be taken from us, but we will lay them down of our own accord just like Jesus said! Now I urge you, I command you my children, you will first of all defend our *ecclesia*! Then, when you have destroyed every infidel invader, you will go out into the world and bring about their apocalypse!"

The demagogue raised his hands to terrifyingly enthusiastic applause.

McKinley had entered the room, his jaw dropping at what he was hearing. Carter came in behind him.

"We enter into the birth pains of our Kingdom!" yelled the imposing Asian to more clapping and cheering. "Say it with me! We lay down our lives for the Kingdom! We lay down our lives for the Kingdom!"

As the chanting started, Carter turned away from the screen, a morose look on his face.

"This is Jonestown all over. There's nothing we can do. We need to stop that sub." He reached back and switched the television off.

McKinley leaned on a desk, Makaru's words ringing in his ears. He was deeply troubled at the depths to which the cult leader would descend. At least half those kids would probably blow themselves sky high. But Carter was right: what the hell could they do? These poor people were *programmed* to obey.

"I've got an idea," said Izzie. McKinley looked up. Rather than disabuse her lack of military and tactical experience, he was willing to hear anything right now.

"We split up," she continued. "Daw… Paul and I go with the sub. You two go and get that chinger bastard."

"You've changed your tune," muttered Carter.

"Yeah, I have!" she scalded. "Big bloody deal. I ain't gonna stand by and watch my friends blow 'emselves up! If that don't work for ya, then you take the sub and I'll go back there to *save people!*"

McKinley almost laughed. He raised an eyebrow at Wilson. "She's a keeper."

"I know. And she's right. I have to be translator."

McKinley shook his head. "*No.* Chris is the navy guy."

"Err…" Carter raised a finger. "Naval *intelligence*. Told you I'm not a sailor. And I definitely don't speak bloody Mandarin."

McKinley sighed angrily. There was no good answer, so he opted for the least bad one. This doesn't feel right, he thought.

"Willy, you're on the sub."

"Got it," answered Wilson.

"Begs the question," added Carter, "how are we going to stay in contact?"

"There must be a radio around here somewhere," said McKinley. "Can you go find?"

"On it," said Carter as he exited the little room.

McKinley turned back to Wilson. "He should be on the sub. You *know* that. But I can't send you both."

Wilson frowned. "You're probably gonna need his bomb disposal skills."

McKinley backed down, forced to agree. He turned to Izzie, pointing.

"Right you; consider yourself drafted. You look after Willy; support him, back him up and make sure he's alright. I need him a hundred percent functional so that's your job now. Is that clear?"

"Right on," she responded. "Take this." She reached into her pocket and pulled out a key card, handing it to McKinley. "It'll get you into the Citadel."

"Thanks!" said McKinley, more than impressed with the girl's willing attitude. We could do with a few more like her in The Team, he thought. Maybe it's an Australian thing.

Lee ran in from outside and squirted a string of Asian syllables at Wilson, then disappeared again.

"They've got the sub moving," said Wilson, "so we need to go."

"Go, go!" ordered McKinley, waving his hands as if to hurry them outside. "Take the marines."

Wilson and Izzie ran hand-in-hand. "*All* of them?" he asked over his shoulder.

"That sub normally has a crew of seventy," explained McKinley, catching up.

"But what about you guys?" asked Izzie.

McKinley grunted. "We'll figure it out," he said, worried that they wouldn't, but unwilling to let any doubt show. The most important thing was to stop that missile from being launched. As to stemming the flood of human bombs and nailing Heinmarsh and his cohorts, he was still improvising. They ran onto the dock to see that the submarine was already moving and the huge steel curtains of the camouflaged enclosure were withdrawing.

The front of the sub was already several meters from the dock and receding as one of the tugboats pushed against her bulbous bow. Wilson leaped down to the deck of the stern tug and shouted to his girlfriend to jump. With only a moment's hesitation she also sprang from the quayside and he caught her capably. Wilson shouted some Chinese instructions to Lee, who was at the controls of the further tug, and then he and Izzie jumped over the boat's bow, landing on the sub's hull. They ran forward to a dorsal hatch near the conning tower and McKinley watched them vanish down the ladder.

"Good hunting," he whispered.

The aft tug revved his engines and the whole submarine started to slide out of its mooring, passing under the huge steel canopy with plenty of clearance. Full daylight sunshine graced her hull, perhaps for the first time in months, betraying how dishevelled she had become under Heinmarsh's illegal ownership. McKinley could see how her anechoic rubber tiles were patchy in their dilapidation, and the paint obscuring her original Chinese hull number was peeling off. She was four decades old, and looked it.

Lee and the other marine set their tugboats adrift and leaped onto the sub's casing, flinging themselves with haste through the hatches and slamming them down.

Carter ran up. "Radio, good," he said. "Bulky, but it works."

"Right," said McKinley. "Let's find something else to wear then grab all the weapons, explosives and tech we can carry and get out of here. Priorities are Heinmarsh and Makaru, but we've got to minimise the suicide bombing threat by the time our lads get here. If we can."

They worked their way back through the jungle, loaded down with weapons, ammunition, various supplies and the all important radio by which they'd be keeping in touch with Wilson. The going was hard with all that weight and both were terribly tired as well as thoroughly bruised. Carter's head still hurt whilst McKinley remained tender all over from having been used as Bellegarde's punch bag. They were in bad shape, but they were determined.

McKinley was worried. There was no standard procedure in place to deal with a burgeoning crowd of suicide bombers. All he knew was that, somehow, they had to locate Heinmarsh, gather whatever intel they could from him and then either send him back to the UK as a prisoner or end his career right there. Back in August McKinley had been about to execute the American, but had been prevented from doing so by priority orders to locate the warhead before it turned Mallory Island incandescent. Now he was uncertain about carrying through with the 'retirement'. Orders notwithstanding, Heinmarsh was corpulent with valuable intel. It had already become clear that the billionaire, his Asian chum, that bastard with the French accent and probably Erbakan too were part of something much bigger and more sinister. They'd already tried to wreck the world's financial systems, and now they were not only sending suicide bombers to attack at the hearts of various governments, but they were going to put a nuke in orbit, ready to plummet down on just about anyone. Had they abandoned the financial coup or was this simply part of it? What the hell was their end goal? The Team had to find out. It was imperative.

Maybe they'd learn more if Carter could get his grubby little paws on Makaru's phone. The demagogue always seemed to carry the device with him so it was clearly important. If it could, as Carter claimed, interface with the peculiar computer systems that Heinmarsh and Makaru used, it was just as valuable as any other piece of evidence.

According to their exchanges with Wilson, the *Han* was working her way through the shallow waters to a point north where the Typhoon could be intercepted. They'd identified a probable launch location: a narrow, abyssal tract of ocean called the Qurahai Trench. Straddling the equator, not only did it fit the technical requirements for a launch, but it was the only marine geophysical feature within a reasonable sailing distance that did. The Chinese submarine was making progress, but the difficulty of navigation in the region was a constant concern.

McKinley had an idea, disliked by Carter, that they could infil Wolf River using the subterranean conduit by which the latter had escaped the geothermal plant. Carter's doubts notwithstanding, they made their way in the direction of the fumarole with the intent of establishing whether this course of action was feasible. They approached the steaming mountain from the south; the terrain was much tougher there and they'd be less liable to interception by Wolf River's guards.

As they came in sight of the rocky saddle between the billowing cone and its huge, dormant parent volcano, McKinley held up a hand signal to Carter, who stopped, breathing hard from the climb.

"What?" said Carter quietly.

"No birds." McKinley turned, his eyes scanning everything.

Carter's expression said that he understood. They both peered around. Downhill there was nothing, just the expansive jungle shifting in and out of the shadow from the enormous cloud of vapour. Ahead was the almost flat ground between the slopes, its covering mostly grasses, smaller shrubs and the pervasive moss.

"Mickey," murmured Carter, his voice low and cautionary.

McKinley turned to Carter as the weapons tech looked pointedly toward the Scott's chest, then slung his rifle to the ground and raised his hands. McKinley looked down to see a dot of red laser light glowing brightly from the fabric over his heart.

He sighed heavily and let his own rifle fall, also reaching for the sky. "This is starting to feel like a regular thing," he growled.

021: The Team

"Ahoy shipmates!" echoed a familiar voice. "Not getting into any trouble are you?" The laser targeting dots vanished simultaneously.

"Oh," sighed Carter with relief, "it's the attack-hobbit."

McKinley couldn't help grinning as the speaker strolled from the treeline. Captain Mike Dexter was a slight figure who seemed to style himself for a more innocent age, with an overly sensible haircut and trim little moustache that looked like it had been stuck on. His pointed chin made his face look longer than a man of 5'3" should own. Dexter was dressed in lightweight black combats that were clearly appropriate to the equatorial climate. McKinley noticed that the captain's webbing bore one of the unit's PF70 pistols, a stealthily quiet gas powered weapon that they'd used before.

Dexter smirked at McKinley, who was visibly relieved through the filter of his customary cynicism. "How are you doing?"

"Aye, better now, thanks. How about you?"

"Strong, healthy, handsome and virile," replied Dexter, smiling, "and unusually tall for my height. I turned fifty last month. Not bad, eh?"

"Not bad at all," replied McKinley.

Dexter rotated to Carter. "How about you sport?"

"I'll take all yours apart from fifty."

Dexter pointed an approving digit at Carter. "Check!"

"How did you get here?" asked McKinley, feeling that he would already know the answer.

"We flew, naturally," replied Dexter, "with a little known airline called Black Falcon Two." He gave a knowing wink.

"Right," said McKinley. TDR.12 were familiar with the modernised Vulcan Bomber that their unit and other secret services used for covert para-insertions.

"Hell of a long flight, though," frowned Dexter, "and those chemical toilets are... small."

"So," ventured McKinley, "we're back in play?"

Dexter blinked a couple of times as though not expecting the question. "*Officially*, I'm here to cart your asses back to Nottingham. *Unofficially—*"

That was what McKinley was waiting to hear. "We're cool with Uncle Victor?"

"Well, I don't know how 'cool' you beardy-wierdies could be, but I must say getting that little phone to him via the Fox girl was a smart idea. And your report moved some mountains. So here we are."

McKinley breathed out a relieved sigh. It had been a hell of a risk, but he'd played the odds and the tide finally seemed to be turning in his favour. They'd been to the brink of defeat and were fighting back. Now all they had to do was win the game.

"Brief me," ordered Dexter. "Just the bones."

McKinley summed his thoughts for a moment before speaking. "Okay. We put Corporal Wilson on the inside but he was compromised. They use mind control techniques to make people forget who they are and tow the party line. Wilson exposed us—not his fault—so we had to escape and hide in a cave. Then we located a hidden dock and found both Heinmarsh's Chinese boat and a Russian Typhoon..."

Dexter's face popped. "*You what?!*"

"Yes sir. They have a Typhoon."

"It's the only sub big enough for an orbital launch," added Carter.

"Orbital...? Wow!" said Dexter. "*That* wasn't in your report. But no matter; go on."

McKinley nodded. "We infiltrated the dock and managed to get those images. Then we got taken. They tried to make Willy execute us but he was getting his memory back. So they locked us up together and his girlfriend broke us out. We ran into a bunch of Chinese marines, joined forces and attacked the dock, but the Typhoon'd already sailed for its launch point. Because Willy speaks Mandarin we decided to send him and the PLA marines in the *Han* to sink the Typhoon before it can launch. Now Makaru's ordering the cult member to commit mass suicide. That brings us up to date."

"Blimey!" Dexter was shaking his head incredulously. "Never do things by halves, do you?" He paused. "Think Wilson's... fit for duty?"

McKinley had been anticipating that. "Not really, but I expect him to do his job."

"There's more," interjected Carter. "Turns out Heinmarsh and Makaru are working with Süleyman Erbakan. They're part of the same organisation. Last we heard Erbakan's on his way here and heads will roll; ours in particular."

Dexter raised an eyebrow. "That's just one of your problems."

"Oh?" chorused McKinley and Carter simultaneously.

"We've been *ordered* to stop the suicide bombers somehow. Intel says they're all over the world, dozens of 'em just waiting to go. Since you jokers dropped off the radar there's been nineteen incidents, and that's just the start. Same M.O. as ever with sniper support. The UN's alive with accusations and suspicion."

McKinley spread his hands out. "And we're supposed to do that how?"

Carter placed his hand on McKinley's shoulder. "Think about it mate; they're getting orders from somewhere."

McKinley looked round at him, nodding. "Okay. Communications? That's what we're looking for?"

"Exactly," affirmed Dexter. "That's your primary objective. Let us worry about apprehending Heinmarsh and Makaru."

McKinley smiled dryly. "Us?"

Dexter grinned back and raised his voice. "Let's move, shipmates." Lifting his gloved hand high in the air, he rotated his finger in a circle.

Causing barely a rustle of leaves, six figures in black COAST fatigues with camo wrapped faces seemed to materialise as if out of nowhere and approached, grouping around them. One was instantly recognisable by her figure and stance.

"Cumberland!" exclaimed Carter. "Blimey!" He paused, raising an eyebrow. The front of her combat fatigues was plastered with residue. "You know how we hate each other?"

"Yes...?" she answered defensively.

"Well right now," continued Carter, "you're a sight for sore eyes. Despite the spew." He realised that she'd vomited during either the flight or the drop and found himself feeling bad for her. Embarrassed, Cumberland held her normally ill mannered tongue in check.

"Hello there... sirs," said another of the figures, still obviously struggling with that last word.

"*How strange the change from major to minor*," sang Carter, quoting Cole Porter for the umpteenth time but not hitting the notes.

"Atkinson?" frowned McKinley.

"Oh for goodness' sake," complained the former army major. "Yes, it's me, and those jokes are getting a *little* old... sir."

"I don't know," smirked Dexter. "I think it's still a *minor* source of amusement."

Atkinson's resentment was almost visible beneath the fabric.

"Masks off chaps," said Dexter.

McKinley and Carter couldn't have been more grateful to see familiar faces as they headed south and back under cover of the jungle. Apart from Cumberland and Atkinson, both of whom were in the Tactical and Surveillance discipline, there were Jason Nash and Jed Thornhill, Combat and Survival trainees, and two Weapons and Equipment Technicians. Of the latter, Carter was pleased to see his young friend Graham Payne, who he'd been mentoring for the last year or so. Dexter told them that these six BCs comprised two future TDR teams. The other WET was Christina Judkins, a very fresh-faced young lady whose dubious claim to fame was hacking into Her Majesty's Treasury.

The group made their way to a vantage point not far from where McKinley and Carter had first overlooked Wolf River. Heavy with undergrowth, it was a break in the trees which offered near optimal cover. The magnificent, breathtaking view was still a pleasure to the eyes, and seemed horribly at odds with the island's sinister purpose. Here the captain and his team had hidden a stash of equipment.

"This is for you," announced Dexter, bringing out an FN Herstal Five-seveN.

McKinley took the offered firearm, pleased with its familiarity. "Thanks."

"And as for you," said Dexter to Carter, "say hello to your little friend."

Carter took the Desert Eagle and rotated it in front of his face. "Nice," he said. "Still the best point-and-click interface."

"And the rest," said Dexter, opening a large pack that Atkinson handed to him.

McKinley and Carter took the offered weapons eagerly. In addition to the Five-seveN, McKinley received his trusted M4A1 Carbine assault rifle and FN P90 submachine gun. Dexter handed Carter an IMI TAR-21 'Tavor', and a Brugger and Thomet MP9. These were weapons they'd chosen for themselves, just as each new TDR team member received the same privilege. In the unit it was seen as a badge of merit upon being placed in a TDR team. Dexter issued them both with new radios, and McKinley with a new telephone. He passed out four grenades, two demolition charges with a radio detonator and a small pair of binoculars.

"It's great," muttered McKinley, "to have shooters I can rely on."

"And that's all very well," said Dexter, "but I should mention that we've got specific orders not to harm civilians."

Carter didn't look up from checking his weapons. "Even if they've got exploding baby bumps?"

"Not unless *directly* threatened," said Dexter. He patted the skeletal aluminium PF70 in his webbing. "Tranquillisers."

"That'll nay work," said McKinley, also inspecting his pistol. "They've got dead man's switches."

"I understand," shrugged Dexter, "but what the hell can I do? I must admit it's causing me some concern. But we're here to get Heinmarsh and Makaru. You have to tackle the comms."

"Which reminds me," nodded McKinley, "we should check in with Willy. He'll be just about on top of the Typhoon by now."

Wilson hung the microphone back on its clip. He was encouraged to learn of Captain Dexter's arrival, but was still having trouble processing all of this information which, to him, felt like new data.

Despite his discomfort with deep water and *especially* the thought of being under it, Wilson couldn't help but be even more worried about the radiation that undoubtedly saturated the entire hull. Both Carter and Lee had explained that the Type 091 was China's first nuclear-powered boat and that the forty year old technology was inefficient in the area of reactor shielding. Wilson didn't know much about nuclear radiation other than it was bad. Becoming sterile or contracting leukaemia didn't sound too great either.

'Sub-standard,' Carter had quipped. Yeah, thought Wilson, *no pun intended*. And here we are stealing another bloody submarine that doesn't belong to us. Let's hope this one stays afloat.

The submarine's control center was claustrophobic, not so much by being small as by being stuffed with the equipment required to control the boat's many systems. Around the periphery were intricate consoles bristling with controls and indicator lights, and between them snaked pipes, conduits and cables. There was a constant hiss of steam over the humming of machinery and the rumble of the vessel's massive turbines. Wilson wondered how the PLA Navy sailors could ever get used to such an environment.

In the center of the area, like a pole dancer's set piece, was the periscope, and behind it a ladder and ceiling hatch which led through the double hull to the sail. Lee had assumed his command position at a tall, narrow desk by the periscope, a microphone on its long, coiled cable never leaving his hand.

Wilson smiled to himself. He'd first met Dexter in the basement of a factory in Wales immediately following his promotion to TDR status. The unlikely little captain wasn't the sort of character one would expect to find in COAST, but his career demonstrated that he was a perfect fit. He was also the kind of man you couldn't help but like, with his constantly upbeat positivity and total commitment to their cause. Now he was on Rubakang with a team of operatives and suddenly the odds didn't seem quite as steep.

Wilson was starting to feel somewhat like his old self and diverse memories were popping into his mind at random intervals. He could clearly remember his first car, a clapped-out gold Austin Rover Montego that he'd paid just a hundred pounds for. No wonder it had descended to vehicular hell in only six weeks.

He recalled his family; he could hear the sounds of their voices, remember their birthdays, visualise their habits. He remembered his sisters' penchant for never wearing matching outfits, because they were identical twins. He knew where he'd grown up: the modern house in Long Bennington with its double garage and brown window sills and eaves.

Wilson remembered his training as a BC and his frustration whenever he was passed over for TDR selection. He remembered being somewhat in awe of his TDR.12 predecessor, and could still feel the shocking iconoclasm of learning that Corporal Brook was the only traitor The Team had ever employed.

He and Izzie stood together near Lee's position. She held Wilson's arm as though afraid to let go. Around them, Lee's men were operating the boat with laudable efficiency despite their lean numbers and lack of training. Their officer was constantly barking orders and would dash from man to man, overseeing their duties and explaining things they didn't know.

Their submarine was passing through an area to the north of Rubakang known as the *Misqu Shoals*. Here the topography of the seabed was highly variable, mostly shallow and full of hazards such as small islands seeming to appear as if out of nowhere. There was no choice but to stay on the surface, and the depth of water that *wasn't* beneath their keel did nothing to help Wilson's composure. He remembered that terrifying grinding noise as the tourist submarine had scraped along the reef and sprung her fatal leak.

Lee had been operating a small netbook computer at the communications station and turned to Wilson. Whilst not smiling, his expression looked positive.

"Good news," said the Chinese officer. "I've downloaded new charts. They're much more accurate than the ones on this boat."

"Okay."

Lee pointed to a multicoloured display that was slowly creeping down the monitor. "I'd prefer to be submerged but we'll have to stay surfaced until here. We have no choice."

Wilson looked at the contours on the map where Lee was pointing. Even surfaced it was tight, but once through these shallows they'd only be a matter of miles from the Qurahai Trench. With any luck they'd beat the Typhoon to its presumed launch point. "How long until we're out of the shoals?" he asked, half for the mission and half for his nerves.

"About half an hour," answered Lee, "but we might be able to hear the Typhoon before that. We'll try to get a bearing."

"Okay," said Wilson. He looked down at the beautiful girl on his arm and she stared back with eyes full of love that, with all her heart, transmitted courage into his own.

"Oh. That's quite the reception committee," observed Dexter, lowering the binoculars. He passed them to McKinley.

A human chain of suicide bombers surrounded the Wolf River compound, all the way from the tall, western fence to the far eastern end of the township's beach. They stood several meters apart, holding onto their trigger switches, but no swellings of fake pregnancy were in evidence. Instead, each had a wide belt on which was taped what appeared to be a small electronics housing and a recognisable demolition charge. From each belt hung the familiar set of handcuffs that had ensnared previous targets. McKinley gave the bins to Carter.

"C4," he said. "Standard M112 package. Five hundred and sixty seven grams. Some of them have several." He pointed with his thumb over his shoulder to his backpack. "Same stuff as you brought."

"Right," responded Dexter. "What's the difference with what we've seen on the news?"

"A lot," answered the weapons tech. "C4 detonates at about eight thousand meters per second. It's way more powerful."

"Lethal radius?"

"Twelve meters, maybe more, times the number of blocks they have. If they're near structures there'll be fragmentation issues. Shrapnel effect."

Dexter rolled his eyes. "Great. How are we going to get past without killing them all?"

McKinley spoke. "Well, Chris don't like the idea, because he already did it, but we thought about the conduit from the power plant."

Dexter looked from one to the other. "Carter?"

"The plant's secured at ground level. There's no other way out and the tunnel's a bit of a nightmare. But there's a maintenance hatch about halfway along."

"Is it outside the perimeter?" asked Dexter.

Carter raised his eyebrows. "Indeed."

"Sir, we're going to clear the shoals in about ten minutes," announced one of Lee's men.

"Good," said Lee, and turned to Wilson. "It's still shallow, but when we submerge we can go faster. It's a straight line to the trench now, and we're probably close enough that we can shoot." He nodded toward the comms. "Time to call."

Wilson, Izzie and Lee met at the communications station. "I hope her listen," said the latter, approximately in English, handing Wilson the microphone.

Wilson spoke in his native tongue. "Typhoon Class submarine, this is Corporal Paul Wilson of Her Majesty's Special Forces. You are within range of our torpedoes. You are ordered to stand down and surrender your vessel. Over." He repeated the transmission in Russian, just in case any of the vessel's original compliment were aboard her.

The radio crackled its response in quiet static. Wilson and Lee looked at each other.

"Typhoon Class submarine, this is Corporal Paul Wilson of Her Majesty's Special Forces. Do you read me? Over."

"Do you think their radio's switched off?" asked Izzie.

"Unlikely," said Wilson, and keyed the mic again. "Typhoon Class submarine, do you read me? Over."

The radio speaker above them was still fizzing quietly like a bowl of Rice Krispies.

"What do you think?" said Lee.

"They're not going to answer," replied Wilson, switching back to Mandarin. Izzie clutched his arm tighter.

Suddenly Lee's man on the sonar spoke excitedly, Wilson's grasp of Mandarin being just enough for him to catch up.

"I have propeller noise," announced the marine, "I think."

Lee strode to the other side of the conn and took the headphones, listening intently. "Good work," he said, patting the man on his shoulder but speaking to Wilson. "She's... what's your word? Making more propeller noise than she should. Your team leader was right."

"Cavitating," said Wilson in English. Lee nodded enthusiastically.

Mickey, you clever son-of-a-gun, thought Wilson. Of course an inexperienced sub driver would accelerate to get away. Heinmarsh's amateur crew would be ignorant of how pockets of vacuum would form on the trailing edges of the blades at high revs and how much noise they'd create.

"I need to be on the weapons station," announced Lee.

"Can you be accurate at this range?" asked Wilson.

"With all that noise," grinned Lee, "I could hit her in the dark with a .22 pistol!"

The sonar operator spoke again. "Sir, I think she's turning toward us."

In the horribly cramped confines of the rectangular tunnel, McKinley was sweating like a pig. So was everyone else.

Their progress was unbearably slow, making the team leader wonder how on earth Carter had managed to do this journey perhaps several times. His elbows and knees hurt from tiger-crawling along the harsh concrete surface, and he ached for relief from the incessant heat. McKinley steeled his mind; if he got too anxious now it could lead to the onset of claustrophobia followed by panic. That would do no good at all. He'd never suffered from a fear of enclosed spaces, but this was a special kind of tight squeeze. His body and equipment barely fit the horizontal width of the conduit, and the space above him was filled with supply lines, pipes and cables of all sorts, leaving only about a two foot gap. Below, his hands and arms had endured several squishy moments as they came down on large but unseen insects. Behind him, Dexter and his team could be heard grunting with effort. Ahead, Carter's boots and ass were barely visible in the flashlight's glow. There was no sign of a light at the end of this tunnel, although Carter had assured him that it wasn't far now. The air smelled like sour milk mixed with garbage, and was irritatingly humid.

McKinley's face nearly rammed into Carter's footwear as the latter suddenly stopped without warning.

"What's up?" demanded McKinley.

Carter waved a dirt encrusted hand. "Just listen for a moment, will you?"

"Hey," said Dexter, almost rear-ending McKinley, "what's the hold-up?"

McKinley rotated his head back in the near darkness. "We're supposed to listen..."

A dull thump vibrated the tunnel. "That was an explosion," said Carter.

"Bloody hell," answered McKinley. "They've started."

Wilson and two of the marines scrambled into the torpedo room near the sub's bow. It was a long, narrow space dominated at the forward end by the six twenty one inch tubes. Around them were clustered the controls of the operating mechanisms. Lining the sides of the chamber were long horizontal racks, on each of which would be stowed a 'fish'. It was poorly lit, with water sloshing about under the decking. The air smelled strongly of oil.

Wilson came to an abrupt halt, his face aghast.

"*Two?!* That's all we've got? There should be bloody twenty!"

One of the marines turned, his face an apologetic mask, but the intercom system pinged loudly and Lee's voice came over it. "Corporal Wilson, the Typhoon is probably attacking. We heard her bow doors opening."

Bloody hell! Wilson threw himself at the intercom. "Can we even fire when we're surfaced?"

"Yes we can! But we have not got much manoeuvring room here."

Wilson looked up at the hoist. He grabbed the chain, swinging the mechanism toward the nearest torpedo. "Is the first tube clear?" he demanded.

Whilst one of the marines checked, Wilson and the second guy manhandled the enormous steel cylinder onto the hoist, keenly aware of time running out and never having fired one of these things before. The torpedo had a lot of weight to it, and its inertia made it hard to move.

"I think the tube is clear!"

Wilson put his back into the work. "You think?!"

"I am... pretty sure."

"Carry on," Wilson told his helpmate, knowing that singlehanded manoeuvring of the heavy weapon was probably nigh-on impossible. He ducked under it and clambered forward.

His colleague at the launcher looked at him with worried eyes, finger gently stroking the tiny copper tube that would indicate the presence of seawater beyond the breech door. It seemed dry.

This is it, thought Wilson. If I crack this tube and it's already open to the sea, we're dead. We're all dead. He turned the handle.

Bang! The sudden release of air nearly caused a release of another kind in Wilson's underwear. He scrunched his eyes closed and fought to control his emotions. His heart had probably doubled its pace. Opening his eyes again and panting, Wilson continued to turn the handle until the hatch unlocked.

The audio system rang again with a distorted electronic chime. "They have launched a torpedo," yelled Lee. "I am taking evasive action. Hold on!"

Instantly the *Han* started to roll to starboard. The angle increased rapidly, sending Wilson overbalancing into the Chinese guy and swinging their torpedo terrifyingly. If that warhead clunked too hard on something it would be game over. Warning alarms sounded.

Wilson and the man landed in a pile on the inner hull. They could feel their boat accelerating, the rumble of its engines swelling and ringing the vessel like a bell. Wilson got up and helped the other guy to his feet as the boat stabilised. With great effort they tried to control the swinging torpedo and line it up with the tube. Eventually the deadly cylinder settled enough, and with difficulty they slid it into the launcher. The PLA marine connected some cables inside the tube.

Wilson shut the breech door, turning the geared handle several times to lock it. Now what?

"We have to get power to it," said his companion.

"Where's the switch?"

The man pointed to a panel at Wilson's left.

"*Prepare for impact!*" clamoured the intercom.

Impact? *What the frikkin' hell?!*

A roaring bang of such sudden loudness that he'd not have believed it possible slapped Wilson around his head and he dropped to his knees. The submarine shook and loose components rattled about. His ears ringing, Wilson opened his eyes again and looked around. Were they sinking? The lack of alarms hopefully meant otherwise.

"That was close!" said the nearest man, who'd also fallen to the floor. He levered himself up and leaned over Wilson to operate the arming panel. "We have power," he announced, his voice shaking. "Flooding the tube!"

The whole submarine rolled again, this time to port. They must be lining up for the shot, thought Wilson.

By the time McKinley, Carter and Dexter's group reached the tunnel's end, it was clear that there was a battle in progress. Sweating profusely, they climbed from a hatch that was little more than a manhole surrounded by electrical panels and large pipes with numerous valves and control systems. This was obviously where the geothermal heat and power were distributed to other parts of the Wolf River compound. It was a twenty foot concrete cube with a roller shutter door and windows on two of the other sides, one of which faced south. McKinley and Dexter ran to it. By heavens did it ever feel good to be out of that damned conduit.

The crackle of small arms echoed from the jungle, into which the township's guards were firing. McKinley saw a man take a round and face-plant the forest floor. Closer, just beyond the security cordon, there was a sharp explosion, reverberating from the surrounding jungle.

McKinley wheeled to Dexter. "Your backup?"

The captain's features conveyed a degree of confusion. "We haven't requested backup."

"Then what?"

Carter stepped to the window. "Erbakan?"

McKinley frowned, thinking. "Why'd he be fighting Makaru?"

Carter tipped his head sideways. "Indonesian army then?"

Another explosion rattled the window.

"Maybe," said Dexter. "Either way, this might have saved us some trouble."

"Unless we're on their shit list," countered McKinley.

"Yes," nodded Dexter. "That could become a problem. For now, we'll stay on mission."

"Roger that," answered McKinley, as he and Carter made for the roller shutter. On a steel box by the right hand side of the big door there was a substantial lever switch, which Carter operated. With an electric whine, the shutters started to crank upwards. Sounds of jungle warfare emanated from the expanding aperture, then there was the tearing roar of a fighter jet at low altitude. The harsh thunder of a mil-spec turbojet at high power seemed to split the sky and echoed around Wolf River's bay.

McKinley and Carter looked at each other in consternation.

Wilson's ears again took a pounding as their torpedo fired. With a thump and a painfully loud metallic hiss the fish shot from its tube and left them behind as it raced to its target.

"Let's load the next one," said Wilson. The Chinese guys rushed to comply.

"Torpedo launched and homing!" blared the intercom.

Operating the torpedo hoist, Wilson cringed inside. The last shot had been a close miss. Would the next hit? Out of all the ways he could die, drowning was that which he dreaded most.

Wilson felt the boat accelerating and turning. This time he held on to the chain and it kept him upright. Lee must be punishing those turbines, he thought.

Suddenly a jarring *rap-rap-rap* echoed through the top of the hull. It was a rapid series of percussive impacts like some idiot trying to open a gasometer with a jackhammer.

"What the hell?" said Wilson, looking up at the ceiling. He gave the chain to a marine and found his way to the intercom.

"Torpedo room to con," he said in Mandarin, "was that something to be worried about?"

"Paul it's me," said Izzie's voice. "Speak English!"

"What was that banging?"

"Lee thinks we're being attacked from the air!" she gasped.

As if a bloody great torpedo up our ass isn't enough, thought Wilson, what the hell's this? "By who?!"

"They're going up the ladder to take a look," she replied. "Oh wait! Lee just said "torpedo go quick-quick". He wants you to load another one!"

Wilson had grasped that fact. "Thanks!" he snapped, and went back to the fish.

The sub continued to turn, its engine noise becoming uncomfortably loud even at the bow. The Typhoon's torpedo would be approaching fast. Could they somehow sidestep it?

Wilson's group finished loading the fish and flooded the tube. "Torpedo ready!" he shouted through the intercom. "Let's void the warranty on that spam tin!"

Barely a second went past before Lee loosed it into the ocean.

Having gained entry with Izzie's keycard, McKinley and Carter found some suspicious facilities in the Citadel's ground level, including the cell in which they'd previously been held, the smaller cell in which Heinmarsh had drugged McKinley and a pair of small but well equipped operating theaters. There were several utility and storage rooms, an emergency generator and a modest HVAC plant. Finally, a garage housed Makaru's impressive Rolls-Royce Ghost Series II with its gleaming Deep Carnelian paintwork. The beautiful vehicle seemed not only thoroughly out of place on the island, but a shameless extravagance considering that the township's paved roads totalled less than a couple of miles.

Carter closed the garage door behind him, a question on his mind. "What do you think about that jet?"

"Fighter-bomber, for a guess," answered McKinley.

Carter's eyebrows knitted and his face formed a lopsided frown. "I meant, what's it doing here?"

"Indonesian Air Force? Reconnaissance?

"Air cover for ground forces?"

McKinley shrugged. "Not our pigeon. Let's check out the next level."

Understanding how easily one could become entrapped in an elevator, they climbed the fire escape stairs. Like every other stairwell they'd seen at Wolf River the metalwork was painted orange. The fire escape was a square shaft of stark concrete that seemed glued to the Citadel's cylindrical exterior as though a modification. The stairs zigzagged back and forth with small landings of diamond plate on and between the floors, at each of which there were lights in bulkhead style housings.

The next level was a surprise. It was twice as high as the other levels and without internal walls, apart from the ubiquitous central elevator shaft and a wedge shaped windowed booth adjoining it and meeting the outer wall. Opposite this, about a third of the curving wall was draped with a lurid green curtain. The cameras with their sturdy tripods and intricate controls said as much as the suspended lighting gantries did.

"TV," said Carter. "He broadcasts from here."

"Well, we found the comms," shrugged McKinley. "That was a bit of an anticlimax."

"Not just this," said Carter, wagging a finger as he looked round. "It's the whole deal: satellite, TV, radio, internet... you name it."

"What about that?" said McKinley, nodding in the direction of the booth. They strode over and found the room unlocked.

McKinley saw video equipment like he'd expected in the darkened room. There were monitors, switching units, a sound mixer and racks of disk drives. It appeared like a professional television station but much smaller. He switched on the lights.

"Oh, that explains that." Carter pointed to a large wireless router, its green LEDs blinking with the arrival and departure of each data packet. Across its front panel was a length of tape bearing the scribbled legend 'P.M. PHONE – DO NOT DISCONNECT'.

"I need to make notes," said Carter, pulling out his telephone and pecking at its tiny keyboard.

"'Pastor Makaru's phone'," guessed McKinley. "He was controlling those cameras from it."

"Exactly."

The booth's three windows were soundproof, triple-glazed panels of the type one would find in a recording studio, and a large flatscreen monitor obscured the top half of the middle one. What was disconcerting was the material that was playing on it. In high definition and brilliant colour, it was the playback of Makaru's sermon that they'd caught part of at the submarine dock. Carter pocketed his phone and turned up the volume on the sound mixer.

"...unforgivable sin is *not* heeding the Universal Spirit's call," pontificated their Asian enemy, "and both it and I command you now to lay your lives down. It is not only ushering in the Kingdom; it is a global revolutionary act against this corrupt world system! We will fight fire with holy fire..."

Carter killed the sound and leaned over the video console, noting the settings of the controls. "It's on repeat," he said, "going out online."

McKinley breathed out a horrified sigh. "They'll attack," he said. "All over the bloody world!"

Carter shook his head. "All hell's gonna kick off."

"Let's check out the next floor," ordered McKinley. "Shut it down."

Carter nodded, reaching for his phone. "I can do better than that."

A series of rapid, regular bangs rang through the hull again. If it's an aerial attack, thought Wilson, who the hell's doing it? With both their torpedoes used up, his presence in the bow wasn't needed, so Wilson quickly dived through the hatch to head back to the control room. The machine noise increased dramatically as he made his way aft.

Lee glanced at Wilson with desperate eyes as he entered and Izzie ran to his side. The man on the radio was shouting like mad. Although his delivery was rapid with panic, Wilson heard "break off your attack."

"It is our air force!" Lee shouted over the cacophony. "They must think our mission failed so they are trying to destroy us!"

"Why aren't they answering?"

"I do not think we have the right frequencies!"

Ah, thought Wilson. Maybe we *should* have taken the time to check in with Beijing. He translated for Izzie.

The man on the sonar screamed "*impact!*" and tore his headphones off.

Wilson braced himself, his woman hanging on to his torso like a limpet. Maybe there was a chance he'd get Izzie out through the sail if the explosion didn't finish them.

The next violent instant they were on the deck. Izzie was screaming and Wilson's head was ringing like a bell although his hearing seemed to have lost three quarters of its volume. The explosion was so loud it had somehow bypassed his consciousness... or maybe he'd passed out for a second. Alarms sprang to life, filling the cramped hull with even more noise. Wilson jumped to his feet, lifting Izzie up by her hand. She looked terrified, her eyes wide and her dark hair plastered to her face. Wilson looked at her clothing. It was soaked. Only then did he realise that a cold spray of water was issuing from an overhead pipe. Tugging on Wilson's shoulder, Lee reached past him and turned a small wheel. The spray subsided as the valve closed.

"Damage aft!" shouted one of Lee's men. "Engine room reports flooding!"

"Get him out of there!" yelled Lee, pushing himself into the middle of the con, "and secure all the hatches!" A nasty gash on his forehead issued a trickle of blood down his nose.

Oh my freakin' stars, thought Wilson, *we're bloody well sinking!*

The fourth level of Makaru's Citadel was even more up Carter's alley than the two-level television studio below it. Banks of mainframe computers lined three quarters of the circular perimeter whilst the last quarter circle was painted grey and had grids of small digital cameras lining it. Near the elevator shaft was a bank of terminals with huge flat screen monitors and behind it was a clothes rack with garments hanging from it.

"What on earth is this?" asked McKinley, eyebrow arched.

Carter went to the clothes rack and pulled out a hanger. From it was draped a grey jumpsuit, along the limbs of which small fluorescent yellow balls had been attached. With his free hand Carter lifted up some kind of fabric headpiece with similar markers and also a small camera that would face the wearer head-on from its little stalk-like mount.

"I'm no expert," Carter frowned, "but this is a performance-capture rig."

"In English?"

"It's how they make creatures in movies. Like Gollum in 'Lord Of The Rings'." He pointed to one of the yellow markers. "This setup captures three-dimensional co-ordinates—"

McKinley rolled his eyes. "You're a bloody geek. What's it for?"

Carter looked about, his eyebrows twitching as his brain cells fired. "Blimey, I dunno... He's not a filmmaker."

McKinley shrugged, overawed by the technology. "Maybe he is."

"There's a thought," said Carter, "I wonder if he's making a virtual copy of himself."

"Go on."

Carter lifted a finger. "Well, think about it. What if he could issue individual orders to all his people all over the world? But there aren't enough hours in the day, are there? So, what if he's created a digital copy of himself and *anyone* can work it?"

McKinley raised his eyebrow, considering Carter's idea.

"'Course, it could work the other way round," frowned Carter.

Out of the corner of his eye McKinley saw movement. He glanced round to see that the elevator was operating. Framed by a panel above its double doors, numbers illuminated in yellow were counting up.

"Hide!" he snapped, and they dived into cover behind the workstations, weapons at the ready.

The Chinese officer slammed his hands down on the chart, pairs of fingers turning this way and that to figure out their course.

"Steer three-three-seven and increase speed!" shouted Lee. He looked up at dive control, barking "emergency blow all forward tanks!"

What the hell is he trying to do, thought Wilson. It's so bloody shallow here we haven't even got hydroplanes.

"Reactor's at one hundred and four percent!" bellowed a crew member. "We can't hold it there!"

Lee marched to the helm position. "Engines, maximum revolutions! Flank speed!" he commanded.

The noise increased by another factor of ten as Wilson's hearing continued to settle down, causing him to wince and wish for earplugs.

"Hit!" shouted sonar man. "We hit the Typhoon!"

Wilson blinked. You're kidding, right? *We actually nailed that big fat thing with our last fish?*

Lee rushed back to his command position, speaking as he passed Wilson. "By my ancestors, I hope this works!"

"What?!" demanded Wilson.

"Hold on to something," grunted Lee. "We are beaching!"

Rap-rap-rap-rap!! The cannon rounds rattled their world again. Izzie ducked.

"Another torpedo!" shouted the man at sonar.

Without warning an unbelievable, *grating* deceleration of the huge vessel sent Wilson and Izzie sprawling forward. Wilson hit the bulkhead first and somewhat cushioned her impact. It felt like the whole damn submarine was suddenly heaved up from underneath. The steel hull was moaning and grinding, reminding Wilson of the underwater collision in Gran Canaria but twenty times more powerful. The vessel shook and groaned.

Suddenly the enormous shaking dropped away, leaving only the clamouring machine noise. Wilson noticed that the submarine wasn't level. Her bow was way up and she had a slight list to starboard, but he could tell that she wasn't accelerating now. In fact she seemed perfectly still.

Lee keyed the mic on the intercom. "Reactor scram!" he ordered sternly. "Kill the engines!" The overbearing rumble of power started to die, slowly at first, its diminution barely perceivable. But as thirty seconds or so crawled by the machines resigned their tortured whine and relative silence descended.

"Sir," said the marine who was manning both the radio and the station next to it, "listen!" He cranked the volume control. Lee strode over to stand at the man's shoulder. Is that the sound of singing I can hear in the background, wondered Wilson.

"...us into an uncontrolled dive in the trench," came the English speech of whoever was in command of the enormous Typhoon. "Our sub will implode, but we won't die in vain."

"What is happen?" demanded Lee in English.

Wilson came to stand next to him. "They're sinking!"

The radio continued to blare forth speech and a faint chorus of sacred melody. "We lay down our lives for the glory of the Universal Spirit and Pastor Makaru, who's given us the ultimate suicide weapon!"

"Strewth!" said Izzie, her eyes blazing with horror.

"Oh my bloody..." gasped Wilson. He switched back to Mandarin. "They're going to detonate the nuke!"

Lee looked back, terrified, his jaw slowly dropping open. "How?!"

Wilson looked at him in puzzlement. "Damned if I know!"

"How far away..." started Izzie, but Wilson held up his hand to silence her.

"You cannot stop the Kingdom!" continued the voice from the Typhoon, dripping with insanity, and the radio cut off.

Lee snatched the microphone from the radio operator and thrust it at Wilson. "You talk talk!" he shouted in English.

Wilson brought the little black wedge to his mouth. "Typhoon, you are ordered to stand down! I repeat, stand down! Do not detonate the warhead. I repeat, do not detonate the warhead!"

He released the transmit key and, still holding the mic, pressed the back of his hand to his mouth, waiting and breathing hard. His eyes rotated to Lee.

The radio remained inert.

"They don't care," grunted Wilson angrily, shaking his head. "They'll die anyway!"

Lee pushed past Wilson and said "come with me." Wilson turned and joined his colleague at the base of the sail where Lee was opening the hatch, and they climbed the ladder. Izzie followed and Lee unhooked two pairs of binoculars as he climbed.

Wilson blinked in the bright sunlight as it stung his eyes. He'd become used to the interior of the *Han* and hadn't realised it was so dark. The three of them crowded into the sub's bridge, which was almost dry. They were surrounded by bright cyan, clear shallow sea across which was spread a smattering of tiny islands.

It was only then that Wilson fully realised what an amazing feat of navigation Lee had achieved. The boat was tilted several degrees to starboard and lying on a sandbank like a beached whale. Looking over the edge, Wilson estimated there was still about four meters of water sloshing around their hull, meaning that Lee's beaching had raised the boat by more than three meters. Behind, he saw that the vessel's stern was still under the water, which showed evidence of recent violent disturbance with a wide, murky cloud of suspended silt and a circle of foam around the *Han's* hindquarters. The clever officer had driven her up onto the sand bar to save them from both foundering and further torpedo attack, but she would never sail again.

Wilson scanned the sky, worried. Where was that bloody jet?

The ascending elevator slowly passed by the fourth floor and McKinley breathed a sigh of relief. Moving soundlessly, he dashed across to the shaft and brought his ear to the doors. He heard the machinery of the elevator's passage and then clunking as it stopped. The doors opened with an almost inaudible swish, and he detected conversation from above: Makaru and Heinmarsh.

Carter walked over, rifle in hand and puzzled expression on his face. "What's up?" he asked quietly.

McKinley indicated the next level with a quick upward glance. "Lovers' tiff."

Carter looked slyly at his friend. "We could... you know."

McKinley raised an eyebrow as an evil grin twisted his face. It wasn't as though the idea hadn't occurred to him. "Aye."

Moving carefully to avoid creating the slightest disturbance, McKinley triggered his radio. "Tripod to August."

"August here, go ahead Tripod," came Dexter's voice in his earbud, tinny and slightly distorted.

Looking quickly over his shoulder, McKinley said "we've got Heinmarsh and Makaru right where we can take 'em out. Can you authorise, over?"

Dexter's response was instant. "Negative Tripod; do not engage targets. I have orders to capture and interrogate, over."

"Aye, roger," said McKinley, a little disappointed.

"I mean it, Tripod. Makaru'd be more dangerous as a martyr. You know that. August out."

McKinley shook his head at Carter, who shrugged. The Scotsman nodded toward the fire escape. "One more floor."

"Sure?"

"Just keep quiet. They got out at the top."

Assault rifles held out in front, McKinley and Carter carefully ascended the fire escape again, treading lightly and creating as little sound as possible, although everything seemed louder than it should in the reverberant stairwell. They arrived at the fifth floor landing and McKinley took a peek through the door's wired glass window.

McKinley dropped like a stone, crouching quickly down. He was wrong; Heinmarsh and Makaru weren't on the top floor. He quickly closed his eyes, bringing back to mind a snapshot of what he'd seen.

"What?" asked Carter, whispering.

"Heinmarsh and Makaru. Six bodyguards, MGs. Some kind of military facility," replied McKinley. "Gimme a sec."

He raised himself cautiously again.

Holy shit! Now bloody Heinmarsh was standing right by the doorway! His eyes wide with the electricity in his nerves, McKinley ducked like lightning and motioned for Carter to retreat down the stairs. McKinley followed, moving ever so carefully backwards with his weapon trained on the door. If they were discovered they'd be trapped. Yes, they could dash down the fire escape, but where from there? Makaru would doubtless alert more guards.

McKinley could hear Heinmarsh and Makaru discussing something passionately. He came to rest at the first landing down from the door, his finger caressing the trigger. Now he could see the big American's brown jacket partially obscuring the view through the glass. The upper body of a moustached, Hispanic bodyguard with a shaved head and plenty of piercings filled the rest of the little window. Thankfully the man's attention seemed to be on his bosses.

Heinmarsh's figure disappeared to the left, followed by the guard, and they heard the muted clanking of footsteps ascending another metal staircase with its deep, atonal ringing. Waiting for a few seconds to be sure, McKinley and Carter looked at each other then McKinley gave the signal to advance back up to the door.

Once again outside the fourth floor entrance, McKinley took another look. Now the room appeared empty.

"Hope this don't make any noise," whispered McKinley as he swiped Izzie's keycard. With a tiny *click-whine* the lock actuated. McKinley gave a quiet sigh of relief, winking at his friend, and twisted the handle as smoothly as he could. He opened the door, weapon held out in front.

Carter had to concede that the space beyond did indeed look like some kind of tactical facility. This impression was reinforced by the lighting, which was noticeably reduced compared to the other levels of the Citadel. Instead of overall illumination, the consoles bore small lights on gooseneck mounts, highlighting just what was required, and the only window had a blind drawn over it. The mechanical susurration of cooling fans filled the room. Carter noted the ubiquitous computers but also radio equipment, a radar set and, near the central elevator shaft, a large table that was built from a flat screen, much like what they'd seen on board *Ghost Rocket*. It was displaying a global map.

Moving as silently as a cat and piercingly aware of the proximity of Heinmarsh and Makaru, McKinley listened at the bottom of the spiral staircase next to the fire escape door. The bad guys were having a more than heated discussion. Like an old married couple, thought McKinley. Makaru was talking about delaying the launch, whilst his American chum was arguing vehemently for the reverse.

McKinley quickly surveyed the room and affirmed his earlier conclusion. It looked to him like this would be the place from which Makaru would control the army of his supposed kingdom. This kind of tech was so familiar, in fact, that McKinley felt like he could have operated it without training – apart from the nomenclature which, with a few English exceptions, was in East Asian logograms of some kind.

Suddenly the stairs rang with heavy footfalls and, heart in his mouth, McKinley sprinted to the other side of the room, throwing himself down behind a pair of tall, grey racks of television monitors. His last furtive glance told him that Carter had similarly ensconced himself, but he couldn't tell where. His hands and knees came to rest on bundles of snaking cables. McKinley froze, his forehead against the side of some other equipment, making further forward movement impossible. Damn it, he should have backed in!

Whoever had descended the stairs was coming toward him! Had they detected his urgent dash for cover? The many cables snaking beneath McKinley formed ridges that pressed painfully into his kneecaps. He bit his bottom lip, stilling his breathing, concentrating on trying to be both invisible and inaudible. He noticed his heartbeat in his ears over the electronic humming which filled the room. He heard a second person coming down the circular stairwell.

It was then that McKinley realised his cover wasn't great. Between the tall racks was a gap of about an inch, which McKinley's head was too far from to be able to see through without kneeling up. He could hear keypresses and switches clicking. The figure on the operating panel side of the equipment was working its controls. He listened as the other person approached and the first stepped aside.

McKinley heard Makaru's growling voice. Boy, did he ever sound pissed off.

"Who are they?!" the Asian demanded.

The other speaker, obviously a bodyguard, sounded decorous and apologetic. "Pastor, I'm sorry; they're not wearing known uniforms."

"Terrorists?" snapped Makaru.

"Yes Pastor, or maybe mercenaries."

Terribly aware that his midriff was entirely visible between the racks and that *bloody Makaru* was a meter away, McKinley could imagine the cogs grinding in the pastor's head. His tortured knees were killing him and he had to clamp his jaw against the pain.

"Why here, Brother Chellis?" mused the demagogue irately. "Why now? It's not the British."

"No Pastor."

McKinley heard Makaru's robes swish as the preacher turned away, walking back to the stairwell. "Keep at it." Suddenly the voice ramped up in timbre, becoming a furious shout. "I want to know *who they are!*"

"Yes Pastor," murmured Brother Chellis pessimistically, returning to his video monitors as Makaru disappeared, clanking up the stairs again.

The pain in McKinley's knees was starting to become more than he could ignore. In fact, it was screaming for his attention. It didn't help that he was sweating profusely. His right leg was worse and it felt like something sharp was being dug unrelentingly into a nerve just beneath his kneecap with all the persistence of a bad toothache. McKinley closed his eyes, trying to get his mind away from the multiplying torment, but the more he tried the greater the suffering became. It felt as though the rest of his body was turning numb, leaving only the intense, nagging discomfort. If this agony had come on suddenly it would have elicited a yelp of distress from even the most stalwart, but its inexorable increase had already passed that threshold and McKinley knew that if it didn't stop he'd give himself away.

If he shifted his weight onto his left leg it might offer a little relief if not comfort. Millimeter by millimeter, McKinley moved to adjust his body's center of gravity. The pain started to recede minutely and McKinley became aware of his right toes again.

Suddenly something gave way under McKinley's left leg and at least one of the cables there went slack. Unable to arrest his momentum, McKinley's body thumped against the back of the racks. He heard cooling fans starting to wind down.

"Oh... *What?!*" exclaimed Chellis.

Bloody hell, thought McKinley, I've cut the power!

He heard Chellis come up behind him. There he was, defenceless, his ass and back facing the bodyguard. He couldn't move forward, he couldn't fight. He felt Chellis leaning over him.

Suddenly there was a ruffle of clothing and he felt the bodyguard straighten up. There was the sound of a short but strenuous scuffle, two simultaneous groans struggling with intense effort, and a sickly, bone-popping *crunch* followed by the morbid exhalation of a death rattle.

McKinley rotated his head until his neck started to hurt, seeing Chellis' collapsing and oddly *naked* legs at the edge of his vision. McKinley quickly got up and shuffled his body backwards, fighting the cathartic complaint of sudden relief from his legs. Gasping as the feeling returned, McKinley looked down at the dead bodyguard, whose neck was clearly broken and whose trousers were around his ankles. Carter was standing over the corpse, panting a little.

Soundlessly, McKinley braced himself against the side of the rack and lifted his right leg, rubbing at the kneecap. He could hardly feel the motion of his fingers. "What the hell?" he gasped.

"Couldn't reach his neck," shrugged Carter. "I improvised."

McKinley suddenly had a comedic mental image of his colleague yanking down the bodyguard's trousers and the latter instantly standing bolt upright in fatal embarrassment. Reality's stranger than fiction, he thought, looking up at Carter.

"That's going in the combat training manual," McKinley sneered. "Now grab the poor bastard's keycard and let's get the hell—"

"One more thing," interrupted Carter, snapping the digital key from around Chellis' neck. Walking silently back toward the consoles at the other side of the room, Carter motioned for McKinley to join him and, looking quickly about, the team leader crept to where his friend was hovering over one. The weapons tech was scratching his beard, a thoughtful gleam in his eye.

This particular console bore a red lever. It was a larger control with just two positions.

"Know what this is?" said Carter, grinning conspiratorially, his voice only just above a whisper.

McKinley's eyes widened. "Kill it and pull the knob off," he instructed. "Then let's de-ass this joint and find Dex."

022: The Battle

"Qurahai Trench nine miles," reported Lee, slinging a pair of binos around his neck. "We must not look at it," he said. "It will blind us." He pointed north, which was a few degrees off their starboard bow.

A tiny smile tweaked Wilson's lips. Not only was he recalling swathes of his previously buried memories, but he was remembering some of Carter's techno-bullshit. He shook his head. "She's too deep for that."

Lee looked unconvinced. "How big is the warhead?!"

Wilson grimaced. "Unknown," he answered, "but the last one they modified was nine megatons."

"*We're too close!*" gasped Lee in horror. "There will be waves, seismic shock, fallout...!"

They heard voices from below and, looking down the hatchway, saw something red being pushed up and through it. Lee took hold of the object and lifted it, revealing a Chinese naval flag.

"Sir, we can wave this when the aircraft approaches," said the man who was following it up the ladder.

"Good," said Lee. "Now deploy the masts!"

There was a deafening bang and flash in front of them, knocking the air out of their lungs. Wilson ducked instinctively as they were showered with salty spray. His ears rang. That was close. Wilson blinked the water from his eyes. That was powerful, but *absolutely nothing* compared to what was coming. He noticed a deep electrical hum and saw that several tall, thin columns were rising from the top of the bridge.

"What the effing hell was that?!" snapped Izzie.

"Their last torpedo," nodded Lee.

Wilson switched to English. "Just before we beached, sonar reported another torpedo. It just hit this sand bar."

"Bloody hell!" she groaned, seawater dripping from her raven hair. Wilson was forced to concede that despite her admirable spirit, she probably wasn't having the greatest day.

A thunderous roar like a colossal piece of paper being ripped suddenly hammered them from above as the Chinese jet tore the sky asunder. Wilson winced against the terrible, ear-crackling sound and Izzie issued an involuntary scream, slapping her hands to her ears.

Lee unfolded his body and shook his head as if to clear his hearing, lifting his bins and studying the rapidly receding aircraft.

"Chengdu J-10," he reported. "Your people call it 'Vigorous Dragon'." He turned to his men and barked "get that flag up!"

Lee's on the money as usual, thought Wilson. That pilot's just doing a recon pass, but he'll be back round in no time and either riddle us with holes or, with luck, spot the pennant. More likely the first option. Wilson started to help Lee's men tie the flag to some mountings which were clearly intended for that purpose. A crew member climbed onto the sail's upper surface and stretched as high as he could, holding the ensign out horizontally.

Turning forward again, Wilson grabbed the second set of binoculars, then realised he wouldn't need them. He thought about the nuclear test footage he'd seen. This could be a thousand times bigger!

Suddenly Wilson felt as though someone had walked over his grave.

An enormous white circle of spray miles wide instantly flashed outward across the distant surface and continued to expand. Even at this range Wilson thought it would overwhelm them. Beyond the shockwave, the ocean seemed to shimmer, changing between different shades of blue from horizon to horizon. Shitty death, thought Wilson, we *are* too close!

Several seconds went by during which the white water faded, then an immense plume blasted violently through the horizon. Roughly conical at first but quickly expanding into a sheer sided column that must have been a mile wide, it thrust its monstrous limbs skyward. Seemingly unstoppable, it reared upward and continued to rise several kilometers into the sky. It looked like the behemoth would never stop growing and they lost sight of its peak. But, long moments later, the gargantuan column reached its zenith and slowly started to collapse. Plumes of water that could have engulfed whole fleets curved away from the colossal geyser, creating an enormous base surge of spray and vapour like an impenetrable white fog bank hundreds of meters tall. Wilson realised that the whole submarine was vibrating.

"Get below!" shouted Lee and all of them raced down the ladder to the base of the sail. Lee strode to the intercom and started issuing rapid fire instructions. Several of the men who were seated at consoles strapped themselves in.

Barely thinking, Wilson pushed Izzie toward the periscope. "Hug this hard!" he ordered her. "Do *not* let go!"

He dropped his ass to the deck on the opposite side of the tall steel cylinder, paying no heed to the dirty, dark brown swathes of lubricant which covered its surface. Intertwining his legs with hers, Wilson held Izzie as tightly as he could without constricting her breathing.

The tremor in the deck became a shudder and then a violent shaking. The submarine's internal components rattled and clacked about. Items fell to the deck and sparks flew from fractured power lines. Izzie cried out in fear, her scream almost drowned by the noise.

Just as the shaking started to subside, a force so great it might have been a kick from a giant *threw* the submarine backward. All the lights went out and Wilson felt his hands fighting the terrible acceleration, losing their grip on Izzie's clothing. There was a sound like jet engines. He wrapped his legs even tighter around her abdomen, pulling muscles. Some of the Chinese marines were yelling and Izzie screamed. Wilson felt the boat rolling powerfully further to starboard, so that the periscope to which they clung was heading for horizontal.

Wilson blinked a couple of times and opened his eyes to the emergency lighting. There was Izzie staring back at him in the red gloom. Around them, Chinese voices were speaking in urgent tones and he could hear the sounds of them moving around carefully, trying to help each other. Wilson realised that his arms and legs were incredibly fatigued and stiff from holding onto her. The periscope was about thirty degrees off horizontal and he'd slid round to what was now the bottom side of the cylinder. Wilson tried to look down in the half light. There were control racks beneath him. They would stand his weight, but the rakish angle was a concern.

"I'm going to get you down," he said, and she nodded. In this lurid red glow she looked as though filmed for some highly stylised science fiction movie.

Wilson held on to Izzie's arms and let go with his legs. His body swung down and, with both their arms at full extension, his feet connected with the solid surface. He heard the cracking of plastic components. "Tip yourself over," he told her. "I've got you."

Despite the dingy, blood red lighting and the weird orientation of the control center, Wilson managed to catch Izzie and set her down next to him. She slid her bottom down the racking and stood with difficulty in the asymmetrical valley created by it and the deck. Lee's face appeared from the shadows.

"You must go quick-quick!" he said in English. "Back at island!"

Wilson helped Lee retrieve a packed inflatable boat whilst the marines prepared two powerful outboard motors that had been stored in racks near the sail. Their climb through the tower with the boat was slightly uphill, but manoeuvring those big engines and the fuel tank via the hull's larger hatches would be even more difficult for Lee's men. When they reached the bridge Wilson and Lee crouched down as the latter unpacked the boat and inflated it from a cylinder of compressed gas.

Wilson took a look around the previously horizontal bridge. Because the sub had both tipped further to starboard and lurched backwards there was now a steadily draining pool of seawater within, whilst the ocean was sloshing below. Wilson turned his eyes skyward. Towering above him to the north was a vast wall of boiling whiteness against the blue. The cloud seemed to hang in the sky like an approaching supercell. It was so huge that it appeared as though it was right on top of them yet Wilson could see that it was still at least a kilometer away. However, it was expanding fast, engulfing all in its path.

Lee abandoned his attempt at English. "That cloud's poisonous, radioactive. We will shelter here inside but you need to go back to your team. This boat is fast; you can outrun it."

With difficulty they worked the inflatable around the edge of the sail to the hull, where the open hatch was allowing the submarine to flood. Mindful of this dangerous complication, Lee's men quickly secured the bulky motors to the inflatable's transom. Each outboard weighed at least a hundred pounds and heaving them and their collapsible fuel tank about in these conditions was agonizing work. Lee's men filled the tank with fuel pumped from somewhere within the bowels of the sub and got the motors started whilst Wilson lifted Izzie aboard. Soaking and frightened, she wasn't saying much now.

Lee gave Wilson a rifle, GPS unit, portable radio set and two flasks of water, making the tall combat specialist deeply grateful. Lee had proven his mettle in some excruciatingly difficult circumstances and Wilson had learned incredible respect for the Chinese submariner. He hated to leave these brave marines behind but they'd be safe in their spam tin. Their government would rescue them, vanish the disavowed sub and all would return to something which for the sake of most of the world looked like normal.

After having shaken hands, Wilson gave Lee a heartfelt salute and brought the outboards' power up. Lee slammed the hatch and they heard its mechanism cycling as Wilson took the outboards' controls. The boat's acceleration forced both he and Izzie back against the fuel container as they raced south, only just ahead of the encroaching cloud.

"Alright then!" roared Basic Commando Cumberland in her most intimidating voice. "Who wants to die?!"

The group of suicide bombers looked at each other with varying degrees of puzzlement.

"We all do," said a young, long-haired Filipino man, shrugging.

Cumberland glanced at Dexter. "Did you have to do that?" glared the latter, shaking his head. "D'you think you're like freakin' Bruce Willis or something?"

Cumberland looked like she didn't quite understand the reprimand. "Sorry sir," she conceded.

Idiot, thought Dexter. That's definitely *not* the way up the promotion ladder.

Up the hill to the south of the compound, the battle was still going on. There didn't appear to have been any suicidal explosions for a while but the sporadic gunfire continued. The unidentified combatants that were trying to work their way down the hill into the township were tenacious and well armed. But who the hell were they?

For nearly half an hour Dexter's team had been pinned down in the blistering heat, crowded behind some refuse containers that they'd quickly positioned near the junction of two of Wolf River's many streets. At any second the suicide bombers might rush them but whether they did or not it was a most unequal stand-off. Dexter had orders to avoid civilian casualties and therefore use the tranquiliser darts. They had suicide bombs with dead man's triggers and a religious death wish. Why the group of disciples were just standing there and not levelling the area was something Dexter didn't know, and the only sensible recourse left open to him had been dialogue. That approach had failed so far because he wasn't talking to the people, but to the brainwashing.

Dexter resigned himself to the non-sensible. The only weapons they carried that might scatter a crowd were their 'pineapples'.

"Ready grenades," said Dexter with regret. He didn't want to create any offensive action. These weren't professional soldiers. Neither were they necessarily terrorists. They were mostly average folks somewhere between their late teens and mid twenties, and not in their right minds. He didn't want to be the cause of their deaths.

He was about to give the order to deploy when his radio came to life.

Dexter grabbed the mic. "August here, report!" he barked.

"We've got a QTH on Heinmarsh and Makaru," replied McKinley. "They're both in the Citadel."

"Acknowledged," replied Dexter. "We're surrounded by suicide bombers and pinned down in the center of town."

"What about grenades?" asked McKinley.

Dexter huffed frustratedly. "How did I manage five decades without you?"

"On the way," said McKinley. "Tripod out."

A spurt of automatic fire ricocheted off the side of a nearby building, spraying concrete shards and causing the suicide bombers to duck.

Poor bastards, thought Dexter. Still, it's the only way now. He raised his head a little and shouted.

"We don't want to hurt you but if you don't retreat we're going to use grenades. Clear the area now because if you're anywhere near it could both injure you *and* set off your suicide belt. So *get out of here now!*'

They weren't moving. Dexter closed his eyes for a moment. "Hit 'em!" he ordered, feeling the hopelessness of a man who'd just condemned a litter of cute puppies to death.

Five grenades sailed outward toward their young antagonists. Suddenly one ran, then another, then the whole group was scattering. Dexter felt a tiny, momentary relief.

BOOM! A deafening multiple thunderclap of shockwaves pummelled Dexter's head like blows from thugs wielding Louisville Sluggers as the buildings and bins around him shook. Dirt and debris rained down on his squad.

Dexter poked his head out as the report clattered from the surrounding jungle. Through the clearing greyish smoke it looked like the suicide bombers had indeed run away. Dexter was gratified both that he'd apparently not killed any and that they could still respond to a lethal threat despite the brainwashing.

"Now you'll *die!*" rasped a voice at his shoulder. Dexter's head span round to meet eyes of craziness looking out from the manic, braid rimmed face of a disciple, pale with fear but hardened in determination. He was young – *really* young. A thin, fair starter moustache lined the boundary of his pierced top lip and the wisp of a goatee hung from his chin. Leaning over Dexter, the suicide bomber brought his clenched right fist up between their faces. Dexter felt icy cold all the way down to his ass.

Suddenly the young man's face turned to shocked pain at the sound of a gunshot. As his body started to fall, Dexter moved like lightning to clasp his hands around the lad's grip but saw the switch fly loose.

Dexter grunted involuntarily, shuddering. The man fell on him like a sack of spuds, his last expression mirroring Dexter's fear and confusion. Then his eyes closed in the unnerving silence of no bomb blast.

A harsh tingling swept over the captain's body. Dexter shook himself and looked up, his eyes coming to focus on a pair of familiar figures running toward him between the buildings. Not knowing what to say, Dexter's mouth hung open a little.

McKinley grabbed the body by its shoulder and thrust it aside. "You okay?" he grunted.

"I... I'm... Yes," croaked Dexter and blinked a few times, anger suddenly igniting in his chest. "*What the hell are you doing?!*" he demanded. "*You could've killed me...* us!"

As if to profane his righteous indignation, McKinley and Carter looked at each other with dry smirks.

McKinley thrust out his hand. "Aye." His face returned to its usual hardness. "If we hadn't disarmed all the bomb belts."

Dexter took the offered hand and allowed McKinley to help him up. "You *what?*" he muttered angrily.

"They won't stay that way," urged McKinley. "You've got maybe a few minutes before he finds out and switches 'em back on!"

Dexter regained his professionalism instantly. "Squad, spread out!" he ordered. "Tranquilise anyone with a suicide belt and defuse them as quickly as you can! Retrieve the charges!"

"Sir...?" started Cumberland.

"That's an order, Commando!" snapped Dexter. "They're disarmed, but not for long!"

"Yes sir," affirmed Cumberland as she ran off. The rest of the BCs took off in other directions. The suicide bombers realised what was coming and also ran. McKinley and Carter heard the distinctive *pop-fizz* of several PF70s discharging.

"I want to recon those greenhouses," said McKinley. "For intel."

Regaining a little more of his composure, Dexter nodded. "Do it."

"I'll need some C4," said Carter. "Once we're done we'll blow the place."

Dexter's eyes narrowed. "Why?"

"It ain't *all* greenhouse. If you look from behind the fence, at the other side, that's his lab."

"Aye," said McKinley. "The *serum*. Let's cut it off at source."

"Yes," nodded Dexter, getting shakily to his feet. "This sounds good. Get samples too. We need to understand the chemistry behind that stuff."

"Roger that," affirmed Carter.

"August to squad," radioed Dexter. "Bring me some of those charges."

Three minutes later McKinley and Carter were running for the north-western end of Wolf River, the latter with an additional pack of explosives. They dashed back through the township's alleys and streets, meeting no resistance as all the guards were busy engaging whoever was attacking from the south. Any disciple not suicide-belted kept well out of the way.

The shockwaves of several large detonations suddenly clobbered them from behind and rattled around between the buildings in a deafening noise. McKinley and Carter dropped to the ground.

"*Bastard!*" shouted Carter.

McKinley didn't need to ask. Makaru had re-enabled the suicide belts, killing whomever of their COAST colleagues were close enough. Spitting into the dust in anger, McKinley helped Carter to his feet and they ran on.

McKinley stopped at the point where the buildings gave way to the open area at the west of which was the beach, opposite where Makaru's security cordon met the main fence. There were the greenhouses diagonally to their left. McKinley looked toward the sea.

A boat about the same size as Middleton's *Priscilla* was steaming into the bay at irresponsibly high speed. But McKinley immediately understood what it was doing by the shape of the vessel's prow which, rather than being an approximately triangular wedge in the typical style, was flat. The expanse of metal spanned the whole bow and lifted the hull above the massive waves that it thrust to each side. McKinley could hear the motors roaring with power.

"A car ferry?" gasped Carter.

"Not exactly," said McKinley. "Guess who's coming to dinner."

At the vessel's stern rose its bridge, a square, grey-painted structure encrusted with ladders and railings. Leaning on the latter, on a platform in front of the wheelhouse, was the familiar figure of Süleyman Erbakan, a red kerchief fluttering around his neck. There were other figures on the boat, all brandishing rifles.

"Let's go," said McKinley, doubling back on their path. He called Dexter.

"Sir," came the response, "this is BC Payne. Captain Dexter took a round in the calf. He's okay but losing a lot of blood. I'm fixing him up."

Carter flashed a worried glance.

Ignoring protocol, McKinley barked into the little mic. "Put him on!"

"Yes sir. I... Sorry sir. His headset's broken, see. You're on speaker."

There was a moment's silence, then the radio clicked. "Tripod, this is August," grunted Dexter. "Report."

"We've seen Erbakan, the arms dealer. He's at the beach, mob handed."

"Oh great," said Dexter's tormented voice. "Snap. We've got Roger bloody Jolley's crew bearing down on us. That's who's attacking from the south."

McKinley's face twisted as though the radio had told him a bare faced and most offensive lie.

"Figures," said Carter unhappily. Another loud explosion reverberated from the buildings.

"Stay on those greenhouses," crackled Dexter. "We'll deal with Jolley." He paused. McKinley looked at Carter worriedly, sensing what was coming.

"We've taken losses," said Dexter. "Judkins and Nash got blown up. Atkinson's injured. In practical terms we're dead in the water because Payne's tied up with medical stuff and Cumberland's missing. This means you're going after the targets once you've dealt with the greenhouse. Is that clear?"

McKinley looked at Carter for a moment. Carter angled his head, his eyes becoming cynical as if to say 'I don't believe it.'

"Yes sir," said McKinley.

"Any news on Shadow?"

"Negative."

The momentary silence was enough to convey Dexter's dejection. "Roger that Tripod, carry on."

Using the buildings as cover McKinley and Carter worked their way around to where they could reach the greenhouses yet would be in the open for the minimum possible interval. McKinley signalled to Carter to wait.

With a deep groaning, Erbakan's improvised landing craft impacted the beach and started to slide out of the water, its screws churning the seabed and sending dirty sepia fountains into the air.

Seizing the opportunity, McKinley said "now!"

They broke cover and ran for the security cordon. Not caring whether he touched the wire, McKinley leaped the waist high barrier, landed and stopped. Carter halted, removing his pack that contained the explosives. Being careful not to come into contact with the fence in case it actually was electrified, he passed it to McKinley and then, as the team leader headed for the greenhouse, took a run up and jumped the wire himself. Carter chanced a look toward the beach and saw that the car ferry's bow had come to a halt.

They reached the huge double steel doors of the entrance and tried the keycard taken from Brother Chellis' body. The lock cycled successfully.

Once again enshrouded by the humidity of the enclosure, McKinley and Carter looked around for a second before the welcoming committee cracked off at them. Diving to each side, they returned fire. Carter shielded his eyes as one of the cabinets shattered, showering him with glass and plastic. McKinley sprayed in the direction of the hostile fire and heard a grunt followed by a body fall. Pushing as hard as he could, he sprinted along the row of cabinets, throwing himself hard to the floor just before the stream of hot lead found him. Using his momentum McKinley rolled, firing beneath the base of the nearest cabinet. A cry of pain echoed through the greenhouse as one of the cabinets toppled, yielding an electrical flash and a resounding crunch. McKinley stood and advanced, double-tapping the remaining two men on his side of the room.

Suddenly McKinley was sprawling to take shelter, peppered by shards of acrylic. Someone was firing from the gantries up near the roof. The automatic fire rang loudly from the glass walls and ceiling. McKinley tried to return fire but the persistent bastard didn't allow him a window. Another cabinet crashed to the floor, spilling soil and fungi.

Carter's voice rang out. "Cover!" he yelled.

McKinley ducked as the floor tiles shattered around him and ricochets span past his ears. Shards of ceramic tore at his face and hands.

There was a hell of a bang, obviously a grenade, followed by a huge cracking sound and a yell of terror. McKinley risked a look up to see the tall central tree falling toward him, tearing both vines and cables out of the canopy. He rolled his body as hard as he could toward the windows, his head coming into painful contact with the glass. A massive, splintering crash indicated the tree's contact with the ground. Certain that he wasn't in danger from projectile tree limbs, McKinley pressed his advantage. Leaping up, he observed chaos but was too focused to take it in. He strode determinedly to his right, picking out three more guards who were too stunned to act. McKinley took the first pair out whilst the last was cut down before he could target the man.

"Clear!" shouted Carter.

McKinley responded with his own "Clear!" He turned back to the center of the room to survey the devastation. The tree was lying where he'd been hiding, having pulverised all the cabinets along both rows. Diagonally opposite was Carter, IMI Tavor held out front, working his way past the debris toward the large central door that must lead further into the building.

Taking his P90 in his left hand for a second, McKinley vaulted the felled tree and came to a stop. There was a guard's body, the one that had been on the gantry, neatly draped over the pond's railing with its spine split and ribs smashed. It looked like a rag doll from the center of which someone had pulled out the stuffing. That must have *hurt*, thought McKinley.

Carter walked over. "I feel bad for the fish," he said sadly, looking down at the three little ponds, which were full of debris.

"Let's go," grunted McKinley, and they ran through the next door.

"Whoa paydirt!" breathed Carter.

The big room was indeed a laboratory and well equipped at that. Computer terminals shared desk space with racks of glass tubes and reaction vessels, whilst the walls were lined with storage cupboards and great steel cylinders that were presumably chemical hoppers. The far corner to the left was occupied by a secure looking substructure built from cinderblock and with bulky metal doors.

McKinley nodded in its direction. "Weapons vault. See if that keycard gets you in. Then rig the explosives. I'll get the hard disks."

They split in two directions. McKinley started tipping the computers onto the floor and smashing their cases open with his rifle butt. Carter ran to the weapons vault and slid the card through its reader.

Dexter felt nauseous and weak. The rifle slug just above his knee was hurting like hell and the faintness, coupled with the redness smothering Payne's hands, told him that he'd exsanguinated liberally. Thankfully the young BC, who was a competent medic, had bound Dexter's wound and applied a tourniquet to his thigh before things got worrying.

Despite feeling like he could barely maintain the effort to breathe, Dexter spoke.

"You *bloody stupid cock!*" he snarled. "Which one of these dumb bastards shot me?"

"Look," crowed Roger Jolley, bent over Dexter with his hands on his knees, "whoever's little soldier boy you are—and I really don't care—you're in my way. I've got a job to do and I intend to do it." He looked down at Dexter's leg. "Your problems are your own business. Now put down the popgun before things become... regrettable."

"Stand down you cretin," spat Dexter, his resolve fuelled by Jolley's arrogance. "I'm Captain Dexter of the Covert Operations And Surveillance Team. Your targets McKinley, Carter and Wilson are under my command."

"Really? Well you don't look terribly *commanding* old boy," smirked Jolley. "In fact, you're not even in a *bargaining* position, are you?"

Dexter was forced to concede that the mercenary leader was spot on with that assessment. There he lay in a pool of his own blood, unable to move, with Payne held at gunpoint by two of Jolley's disreputables. They were in a narrow alley between two of the village's dormitory units where the BC had thought they might be safer, but Jolley had found them easily, taking Payne by surprise and leaving the captain barely enough time to grab his submachine gun. Dexter could hardly hold the weapon straight.

"So if it's all the same to you," continued the unbearably smug mercenary, "I'll be off now. When I find those punks I'm going to kill them, just so's you know. No job's worth the loss of my plane." He lifted himself to a standing position with a sigh, nodding to a pair of his men who obediently moved the muzzles of their rifles to Dexter's head.

"Hold it!" ordered Dexter, his grip on his Heckler and Koch tightening. Would this strutting peacock have the nerve to kill him over this? He kept his SMG firmly trained on Jolley.

"Can't hear you," grinned Jolley. "Who's to say what happened here? You? 'Fraid not chap. But if it's any comfort, I am sorry about the ol' tent peg."

With this he motioned to his men. "Sic 'em," he ordered, turning away.

"Wait!" stammered Payne, receiving a rifle butt in the stomach for his trouble. The young man bent double and started to heave.

There was a crackle. Dexter's radio burst into life. Jolley turned back, a single eyebrow arched in curiosity.

"Cumberland to August," said a roughly female voice.

"Who the hell's that?" frowned Jolley.

"Go ahead," said Dexter, not feeling able to say much more.

"Got eyes on the leader," reported Cumberland. "Ready to take the shot."

Jolley whirled, looking about. "Where the hell's that bitch?!" he demanded. His men were also turning around, scanning any possible hiding place. "You," snapped Jolley, indicating a pair of mercenaries, "find her!" The men started to move out of the narrow alley, their rifles swivelling like weather vanes in high winds.

Dexter smiled weakly. "Now I have your attention," he coughed, "perhaps you'd like to see something I brought you all the way from home."

Jolley jumped like a rabbit at the *crack* of a round just about grazing his ear and toppling one of his men. Shot in the shoulder above the heart, the man grunted in agony, writhing on the ground.

Jolley screamed a string of profanities. "*What the effing hell is going on?!*"

"That's enough Cumberland," said Dexter. "We need them."

"Yes sir."

Eyebrows rising, Jolley pointed an accusing finger at Dexter. "No no no no no," he said, shaking his head.

"Payne," gurgled Dexter, cutting Jolley off. The young BC immediately dropped to his officer's side. "Yes sir?"

"Would you please get that letter from my inside pocket?"

Payne tore open the fastener and reached in, pulling out a manila envelope on which large type said 'Mr. Roger N. Jolley'. Frowning, Payne looked at Dexter, who nodded in Jolley's direction.

Jolley snatched the letter with the expression of a man who was being handed a very important turd. He tore it open, unfolded the excellent quality paper within, and read.

Dexter waited as Jolley's face morphed from confusion through shock to abject anger. By the time the mercenary leader lowered the letter in defeat he looked like he was about to puke.

"Obviously there was the chance we'd run into your rabble," croaked Dexter, "so we had the JIC write that up. As to your plane, well, if you didn't have insurance... that's a whole 'nother can of worms."

"Guess we'll be going then," Jolley murmured, his voice infused with animosity, disappointment and several other negative emotions.

"Not so fast," said Dexter. "We've got another team of mercenaries—bad guys—combing the township looking for us all. We're going to need your help against them, so I'm hereby commandeering your force – not to mention that you owe me a leg."

Jolley just shrugged. Good, thought Dexter, he's accepted the circumstances. Maybe this'll turn out better. Maybe the silly bastard'll learn some humility eventually.

"Okay, all of you," said Dexter slowly, for fear that he'd black out. "We'll dig in here. Cover all the corners of this block. Be prepared for a strong defence."

Cumberland appeared around the corner of another building with rifle held high just in case. Jolley's mercenaries looked at each other in confusion and then lowered their weapons as she did hers. The BC knelt down by Dexter.

"Where the hell did you get to?" he asked.

"Sorry sir," she frowned. "Guess I got held up."

"Never mind," smiled Dexter. "Better late than never."

McKinley ran back along the neatly organised rows of laboratory tables clutching a bag containing liberated disk drives and tubes of various chemicals. What the hell, he thought, seeing his friend.

"It occurs to me," grinned Carter proudly, "that Dex could use a little help. I have it in mind to divert Erbakan's attention."

McKinley frowned, staring at Carter's acquisition: an American FGM-172 SRAW rocket launcher and two rounds. Once more he was struck by the absurdity that an ostensibly peaceful religious community should have such things in their inventory. He thought about Carter's idea.

"Aye," he nodded. "You ready to blow this joint?"

"You bet."

"Let's go!"

They dashed back into the huge mycoculture enclosure, clambering back over the destroyed tree. Carter made ready with the large weapon. "If you would?" he asked, nodding at the windows.

McKinley turned his P90 toward the glass and gave a liberal spray, shattering one of the big, rectangular panes. Steam flooded from the aperture and dissipated into the island's air as McKinley looked out toward the beach. The repurposed car ferry had its ramp lowered and a ring of men had formed a defensive perimeter on the sand. It looked as though they were preparing to move out. They'd obviously noticed the automatic fire and smashing glass. He turned back to Carter.

"One up the spout?"

"Of course."

The weapons tech read the launcher's nomenclature. Although he was somewhat familiar with it from technical reports, he was used to British gear.

"Wait a bloody minute!" barked McKinley anxiously. "You're not going to fire that thing *in here* are you?!"

"As far as I remember," said Carter with a slightly worried look, "this model's rated for enclosed spaces. All the same, there's going to be a heck of a bang."

"I'll bear that in mind," snarled McKinley, covering his ears with his palms and stepping away to the side.

Carter peered along the sights. All he needed was two seconds for the SRAW's internal guidance to acquire. He counted two and squeezed the trigger.

There was indeed a heck of a bang, sounding not so much like a balloon being popped near one's ear as a balloon bursting *inside one's head*. Grunting sharply, Carter blinked for just a moment and thought he saw the projectile whizzing downrange.

The visible side of Erbakan's landing craft disappeared in a bright orange flash and shrapnel tore up the surface of the water in countless white spurts. Those on the beach not knocked flying by the blast dived to the ground. The shockwave hit the greenhouse and several more panes of glass cracked.

Carter looked round at McKinley. "More?"

The team leader lifted the next rocket. "Abso-bloody-lutely!" He carefully fed the round into the back of the SRAW and patted Carter quickly on the shoulder, then stepped back.

Seeing at least ten armed men running toward the greenhouse, Carter fired at the beach in front of them. With the gut-punching thump of the rocket's detonation the sand erupted in a spectacular cloud, killing several of Erbakan's men and shooting a dusty blast wave outward for a hundred feet.

"Last round," said Carter as McKinley reloaded. "Where d'you want it?"

"Can you hit the Citadel?"

Carter grinned dryly. "I can try."

McKinley patted his friend's shoulder and backed away to Carter's left, heading for the middle of the wrecked greenhouse.

Carter positioned himself at an oblique angle to the glass, which wasn't easy because the rocket launcher's muzzle was protected by a wide, conical rim. He took the weapon away from his shoulder and smashed out some of the remaining glass. That's better, thought Carter as he sighted up the citadel's main door and fired.

With a shuddering explosion that demolished the rest of the greenhouse's windows, the front of Makaru's residence instantly vanished in a cloud of pulverised concrete and steel. Carter reeled away from the torrent of sharp fragments, dropping the launcher. He heard automatic fire and the impacts of bullets nearby. Those bastards were getting closer! Carter hurdled the fallen tree and followed McKinley back into the laboratory, the swarm of lead chasing them and causing particulate debris to fly around their heads.

"Over there!" shouted the Scot, pointing in the direction of the lab's northernmost corner where there was an emergency exit. They ran along and between the rows, knowing that Erbakan's men were hot on their heels.

Something caught Carter's attention. He grabbed McKinley's shoulder and stopped. The team leader looked round in horror; they had but seconds left.

"Look!" snapped Carter.

A monitor on the nearest bench was showing a television programme. It seemed that Makaru's broadcasting network was still active. There was no sound, but subtitles straddled the broadcast's split screen picture, which looked like a professionally created programme rather than the recording of a service. The first phrase they saw was 'Die with dignity!'

"He's back on the air," said Carter.

"So?!" McKinley started running again. Carter took another quick glance at the monitor and followed him.

McKinley rammed the door with his body, slamming it open. A wailing alarm rang out. They burst back into the bright sunlight, kicking the door shut and turning right, heading for the gap where they'd first breached the fence. There was a shrubbery of some kind here, its foliage providing just enough cover that Erbakan's men might not see them.

First Carter then McKinley threw themselves between the torn and twisted wires, heading up the hill and deep into the trees. Finally McKinley stopped at a point where they could see just about all of Wolf River.

"This'll do," he panted, leaning on his knees.

"Better get down," answered Carter, lifting the remote detonator that Dexter had given him from his pocket. Rounds started to hit the trees around them as the hostile fire continued.

They dropped down in the undergrowth, watching as Erbakan's men flooded through the greenhouse and laboratory building. Some had broken ranks and were running around the sides.

"Do it," said McKinley.

Carter squeezed the detonator's trigger and the whole building disintegrated in a blinding explosion that shook the ground and sent loose leaves cascading from the jungle canopy. A great pall of dirty smoke rose above the trees.

"Think we got Erbakan?" asked Carter as his ears rang and the thunder of the huge blast died away.

"I can but hope," growled McKinley.

Lumps of concrete were dropping through the leafy canopy, creating a strange swishing, splattering noise that sounded a bit like heavy rain. The shadow of the smoke started to clear their position. McKinley looked toward the building. It was thoroughly demolished. Carter had, as usual, created maximum destruction. I suppose it didn't hurt, mused McKinley, that the weapons vault was probably where the rest of the C4 was.

Carter saw movement to his right and turned to look. "Gimme those bins."

Getting up, McKinley passed the binoculars and Carter brought them up to his eyes. He quickly focussed them and brought the center of the township into view. He saw disciples, maybe a hundred of them, converging on the massive central temple. What the hell's going on, thought Carter.

As if in response, Payne's voice burst from their radios. "Payne to Tripod."

McKinley keyed his mic. "Tripod here, go ahead."

"Sir, there's an audio message being played in the compound. It's like a call to prayer... but with more doom and gloom."

"The broadcast," mouthed Carter, passing the binos back to his friend.

Payne continued. "We think they're going to... umm, commit mass suicide."

McKinley followed Carter's outstretched finger with the optics. Many disciples were indeed streaming toward the impressive edifice.

"They're all going to that big round church," finished Payne.

"Have we got new orders or what?" asked McKinley frustratedly. Payne, he thought, you're not the greatest communicator. That was something the lad would have to work on if he expected to be promoted to a TDR team... and made it alive through this shit-show.

Dexter's voice suddenly came on the radio. He still sounded like crap. "Tripod for goodness' sake can you stop this damned French bloke? He wants them all to commit suicide!"

So it was Bellegarde that was instructing the poor, lost, terrified young men and women to converge at the main meeting hall. Was he brewing up a batch of poisonous soft drinks?

"We'll look into it," said McKinley dourly. "Stand by." He released the radio's push-to-talk switch and turned to Carter. "Obviously it's a diversion."

"Right," said Carter. "Peking Duck's going to leg it."

"Aye." McKinley thought for a long moment. "Chris, we can't let all those bloody kids just die. We have to at least try."

Carter blinked, his eyes wide. "Blimey Mickey, you really *are* getting soft in your old age."

"We *have* to intervene."

"Okay," said Carter. My goodness I never won an easier debate, thought McKinley. Carter would usually argue his corner a little more fiercely. Unless he wanted to dash in like Errol Flynn and compete with Wilson for politically correct benevolence. Either way, that settled it.

"Tripod to August," said McKinley on the air.

"August here."

"I'm still a man down, but we're going to intervene at the temple. We'll do what we can."

Dexter still sounded crappy. "Good job Tripod. By the way, have you heard from Shadow *at all?*"

McKinley looked at Carter, who mirrored his concerned frown. "Nothing."

"Okay," said Dexter. "We have no choice but to carry on. Do what you can at the temple then report."

"Yes sir."

"And Tripod? Roger Jolley's here. The JIC's cancelled his contract and I've commandered his crew. But I still don't trust the slimy bugger."

From its backside the temple looked like the rear of a huge motorcycle helmet. Here there were no windows, just an encompassing expanse of rough, brown lava rock with two double fire escape doors and a central roller shutter for loading in and out. McKinley couldn't help thinking that it was like the kind of venue your favourite rock band might play, and that Makaru almost enjoyed pop star status.

Carter managed to get his hands under the roller shutter, but it was secured from the other side. There appeared to be no way in.

"I've got to get in there," he said.

"Aye, I know," replied McKinley, wondering why Carter was so keen. He tipped his head back over his shoulder. "Ram it."

Carter looked round to where a couple of Makaru's open topped jeeps were parked side by side, then ran over to the nearest.

Keys? No keys. Carter gripped the steering column's plastic surround and pulled it off. Discarding the cowl, he located the rear of the ignition switch and, being careful not to get a nasty jolt off the battery, tugged the wiring loom free. Then he pulled the wheel round until the steering lock arrested its rotation. Bracing himself against the jeep's small half door, Carter pushed his leg into the angle where the wheel's single spoke joined its surround and pushed hard. With a dull crack the steering lock broke. Carter hotwired the ignition.

"Ready!" he reported as the little vehicle revved up.

McKinley stepped back. This was thick steel, not wood or some other light material. Ram-raiding such barriers was never going to be an easy thing.

Carter took the jeep out of its parking space and disappeared down the nearest street. McKinley heard the engine sound disappear for a moment then swell in both power and volume as Carter turned back onto the street that led to the temple's rear and built up speed.

Engine screaming, the little jeep burst from behind the nearest building, speeding crazily at the shutter. It impacted with a crashing, shattering collision that was much louder than McKinley would have expected. As bits of roller shutter rang from the loading bay's concrete apron a cloud of steam erupted from the vehicle's smashed radiator, obscuring its driver.

Weapon at the ready, McKinley quickly jogged over to the vehicle, which was thoroughly wrecked. He saw Carter's face. The weapons tech was holding onto the wheel with both hands, his mug twisted in pain.

"What's up?" demanded McKinley.

Carter carefully pushed himself upright. "Ribs," he grunted.

Lowering his arms, Carter's hand went to his sternum, on which he gently pushed. "Yeah," he gasped. Making further grunts he gingerly applied pressure to his ribcage. "Ahh, yes," he said hoarsely, "one each side, and I think I've got a floating bit."

Hell, thought McKinley, I'm *two* men down. "Can you walk?" he asked.

"I've got to," groaned the weapons tech. "It's only a couple of ribs. You need me in there. Just get bloody Bellegarde out of the way. I'll do the rest."

Frowning curiously, McKinley said "*what* are you going to do?"

"Talk them down."

What the...? McKinley blinked in consternation. What was the bloody idiot thinking? "Okay," he said, resigning himself to Carter's absurdity, "let's go."

With Carter gasping in pain, they worked their way around the twisted, bent steel and into the loading bay. It was separate from the main auditorium and had a large sliding door to each side. McKinley found a switch and opened the left hand door. Thankfully the noise of its passage was thoroughly damped by its inbuilt technology, which had doubtless absorbed the noise of the vehicular impact as well. Sounds of French-accented public speaking reached him.

McKinley thought about Carter's odd request. Sure, he could just shoot Bellegarde in the back. McKinley had no moral problem with that. But then how would the disciples react? He had to remove the French American before Carter did... well, whatever it was the daft bugger was planning to do. Talk them down? What on earth does that mean? McKinley sighed. We're going to die.

He whispered to Carter, who was holding himself upright against the scaffolding that supported the lighting gantries above the stage. The tubular metalwork was obscured from the audience's view by two thick black curtains of fine velvet. Picking up a short unused scaffolding spar and hanging it from his belt, McKinley started to climb, moving with great care.

He could easily hear Bellegarde's rhetoric as he ascended. The big man was majoring on their failure, guilt inducing the disciples into suicide. He heard Bellegarde speak of the supposed kingdom again and again, saying how only a revolutionary act of mass suicide would bring it into the world now. Interestingly, he also mentioned that Makaru's specially recorded message was going out to the four corners of the earth to anyone who would listen, adjuring those receiving it to also take their own lives. I *really* hate religion, thought McKinley.

Having finished programming his phone, Carter listened from behind and below the stage, thinking how he didn't hate religion so much as *bad religion*. When idiots like Makaru and Bellegarde abused and manipulated others' beliefs this was the result: chaos and destruction. Much as he was a killer by trade Carter's own beliefs advocated the path of peace. Not that he'd ever admit such convictions to McKinley, though, as he'd be laughed out of town. Still, Carter told himself, if I'm going to do this I'd better bloody well remember those sacred texts I read. He looked up. There was McKinley, making his way carefully along the gantry toward the middle of the stage.

McKinley crept toward the center of the wide expanse of curtain. There was only one way to make this work and it was a bloody long shot at best. Reaching the seam of the drapes he prised them apart with his finger and peeked through.

The temple was packed, the neatly arranged rows of seating seemingly bulging with disciples who looked ready to accept the ignominious fate that Bellegarde was selling them. They looked to the leader with eyes of excitement, expectation, adoration and fear. McKinley could see that they were hanging on the prophet's every word, unwittingly lapping up his lust for their demise. Bellegarde was pouring it on thick, emphasising every word with a powerful gesture. He would point, shake his fist or raise his hands. It was a horrible mockery of theater, a badly acted drama for the doomed.

The good news was that Bellegarde wasn't stationed at the front of the stage behind the Plexiglass lectern. The bad news, though, was that the big brute was marching around as he pumped out his blarney. There you are you bastard, thought McKinley. I kicked the shit out of you, then you kicked the shit out of me, so I guess we're even... but I've got no intention of letting it lie.

"Prophet!" came a weak voice from the back of the stage. "Prophet Bellegarde!"

Bellegarde didn't notice at first. He continued plodding around the stage, wearing out his microphone with a constant stream of propaganda.

"Prophet, I have a message from Pastor Makaru!" said the voice.

McKinley took out his knife and quickly slit through several fasteners at the top of the left curtain.

Bellegarde stopped treading the boards, ceased preaching and started to look round, clearly suspicious. "Yes?" he said.

"Prophet, Pastor sent me with a message," continued Carter. "I must deliver it personally!"

Bellegarde turned back to the assembled disciples and waved an apologetic hand. "Excuse me for just a moment."

The temple echoed with subdued vocalisations of assent. Bellegarde walked to the back of the stage.

McKinley jumped, holding onto the curtain. He fell like a stone, tearing a wide strip in the fabric behind him.

At the back of the stage Bellegarde looked up to see nothing but blackness enveloping him.

McKinley landed on Bellegarde like a bolt from the blue, still dragging the black drape behind him. The big French American slammed to the floor beneath McKinley's accelerated weight and was covered in the fabric. Hurting, McKinley rolled off the back of the stage to loud cries of consternation from the auditorium. He landed by Carter and Bellegarde fell beside him, cursing crazily. To the assembled disciples it would look as though part of the curtain had simply fallen and obscured Bellegarde.

Quick as a flash McKinley stood, reached to his belt, whipped off the piece of scaffolding and, swinging it as hard as he could, brought it down soundly on the prophet's black wrapped head. The writhing body went limp instantly.

Carter pulled away the now damp fabric, grabbing the preacher's microphone. With his chest radiating constant pain, Carter snapped the clip over his own ear and with some difficulty climbed the short steps up to the stage.

He looked out across the big hall. A sea of shocked faces greeted him. They had no idea what to expect next. Their beloved prophet had disappeared. Okay, thought Carter, it's going to be now or it really will be never. I have to make this work. He looked behind and above to the projection screen. There was a giant image of Makaru, still silently broadcasting his evil message with its subtitles.

At the back of the stage, McKinley typed four zeros into Carter's phone and hit return. Then he did the same thing twice more. Finally he dragged a tiny text document into an upload folder and hit 'send'. McKinley didn't know what this would do, but he trusted Carter's tech skills.

In the Citadel, Heinmarsh looked round at his Asian colleague. "What's that?" he asked, eyebrows knitted.

Makaru's hand dived into his robe and came back out again with his phone, an expression of angry confusion on his face. "What the hell?"

His telephone was playing '*Jingle Bells*'. And he was locked out.

In the main meeting hall Makaru's broadcast suddenly went blank and a little window appeared in the middle of the screen. 'NO SIGNAL,' it said in foot high letters. Then the stage and pulpit flashed across the screen.

Blimey, thought Carter, casting a confirmatory glance at his enormous digital double, meters above. I never had a *global* audience before!

He waited a few moments to be certain his hack was solid, then cleared his throat nervously. "My brothers!" he began. "My sisters!"

Angry shouts were coming from the pews. Carter noticed several weapons being brought to bear on him. He walked slowly and deliberately toward the slightly raised podium, trying to look as though he belonged there.

Holding up his hands in an effort to quell the rapidly rising tide of discontent Carter spoke again. "I ask you to please listen to me!"

Shouts of "no way!" and other increasingly malevolent phrases came back like ricocheting balls in a squash court.

Carter breathed hard, feeling resistance and complaint from his torso. Okay, this is it. He took a deep breath, steadied his nerves and spoke.

"Pastor Makaru, Prophet Bellegarde and Elder Heinmarsh have been *lying to you!*"

A gunshot rang out and Carter fell.

023: The Citadel

Shocked, McKinley leaped up the steps and ran onto the stage as Carter's body hit the deck. He scanned the temple desperately. Where the hell did that shot come from? Using both his FN P90 and Carter's IMI Tavor to sweep the hostile crowd, McKinley saw several rifles coming to bear on him and prepared to shoot. He realised that some disciples were still wearing their C4 loaded suicide belts. Included among them and standing near the front was Sister Sheba, her beautiful eyes so wide that it looked like someone had just done something unpleasantly electrical to her.

"Wait all!" came a loud cry. McKinley paused. That voice sounded familiar.

Joko, the helpful deckhand from the *Dhul-Nun*, was hoisting himself onto the front of the stage like a swimmer making an inelegant egress from the pool. Standing, he raised his hands in front of the crowd and shouted again. "Wait you all!"

The auditorium quietened by just a few decibels. McKinley was amazed. They wanted to hear what Joko had to say. It was not an opportunity McKinley would waste.

He shouldered the weapons and crouched down by Carter. Feeling a sharp sting in the palm of his outstretched hand, he looked down to see tiny shards of broken Plexiglass from the lectern.

"Help me up mate," said the weapons tech. His voice rang hollowly throughout the temple, so Carter switched the mic off. Its disconnection produced a dull thump through the powerful PA system.

You cheeky bastard, thought McKinley, but thank God it's not worse. He started to lift his friend, mindful of the broken ribs and a potential ballistic wound.

"I'm okay," gasped Carter. "The lectern took the round."

McKinley glanced at it. Sure enough, the tough acrylic glass was cracked and striated. The bullet had smashed its way through the furniture but had been sufficiently slowed and deflected as to save Carter from a potentially fatal wound.

"Please!" shouted Joko to his brethren. "Listen to Brother Christian; don't hurt! He my friend."

Amazingly, quiet started to wash over the throng. McKinley could almost see the question mark hovering above each head. *Can what Joko's saying be true? Is this bearded, dishevelled figure of a military type one of us?*

"Yes, good," called Joko nervously, lowering his hands a little as if to further reduce the volume level in the hall. Joko looked left and right to make sure people were attentive. "Him and Brother Ioannes are good. They special forces for Pastor; want see Kingdom as much as you!"

I'm not too sure about those last two claims, thought McKinley, but if it buys more time then what the heck?

He helped Carter up to the lectern again. Groaning in pain, Carter gripped the cracked structure with his right hand, balancing his weight with it, and extended his left to McKinley.

"Phone," he grunted. McKinley passed the little device over. Carter placed it on the lectern and switched the microphone's little transmitter on again. Another thump and a slight ping of acoustic feedback rang out. McKinley stood back, behind Carter's left shoulder. His weapons were slung but he was still ready to intervene if necessary. Part of him wanted to shoot everyone in sight. Part of him knew that was a ridiculous idea. Part of him didn't have a clue what to do except to take his lead from his team-mate, bonkers though this idea was.

"Hi everyone," said Carter. Holy cow, he thought, I am *so* not this guy. He gave a moment for the answer that he didn't expect and, indeed, it wasn't forthcoming. He cast a glance at Joko, whose uplifted thumb urged him to proceed.

"I'm Brother Christian," he said, feeling about as deceitful as he ever had. "Chris; everyone calls me Chris. Prophet Bellegarde's been... called away for a moment. So... as to what I said just now, I'd like to show you something."

He tinkered with his phone for a moment, finding it hard to input information with just his left hand. But if he let go of the lectern he would probably fall again. He could feel warm blood soaking into his shirt but he knew the round had just grazed him. The ribs he could try to ignore. Carter typed carefully. This little phone, declared obsolete by The Team's science guy Stuart Crossman and his lab rats, would prove its worth.

Above, the video screen came to life. In blurry, still-frame video it showed a familiar scene.

"Here in Wolf River," said Carter, "you're in a cocoon. You don't know what's happening in the outside world. Well, this is what's happening."

Carter hit 'play'. McKinley turned and looked up, realising that the clip they were watching was the suicidal drama they'd seen played out in Red Square.

"See anyone you recognise?" asked Carter.

A hundred pairs of eyes were watching the tragic video intently. There were the five Ambassadors of the Godhead delivering their apocalyptic message. There was the young girl having second thoughts. An instant later she was cut down by the sniper's bullet. The center figure dropped his loudhailer and turned to his companion just as before. Then the group were blasted to atoms, closely followed by their sniper.

"There's more," said Carter gently, and advanced to the next video. The same tragedy played out in front of the Bulgarian parliament with the same results.

Carter pressed 'stop' on his smartphone. When he looked up, everyone was looking back at him. *Everyone.* He had their attention, but not in a good way.

"This's happened more than twenty times now," said Carter. "It's always the same – our brothers and sisters killing themselves and others. They always have sniper support in case they change their minds like you saw in the first video. I don't know who she was, but you do. She didn't want to die and I'm sure, deep down, that you don't."

As the echo of Carter's voice died away, McKinley was quietly impressed, seeing that his friend's audience was raptly attentive. You could've heard a mosquito farting. But it was clear that they looked far from kindly on the one who was vilifying their idols.

"This is what Makaru's been making you do!" continued Carter. "He's been using you as walking bombs to destabilise world politics. He's told you lies in the name of truth, and that's the worst lie of all! Don't you know what *Makaru* means in Arabic, the language of Al Quran?" Carter paused, breathing hard.

"It means *deceiver*!"

A shocked murmur spread throughout the assembly like a ripple expanding from the center of a pond.

Does what it says on the label, mused McKinley.

"Who remembers Sister Patricia from England?" asked Carter. A couple of hands rose tentatively into the air.

At the mention of that name McKinley looked round again at the screen. Carter played the video of Jem's distressed confession of how Makaru, Bellegarde and Heinmarsh had lied.

Blimey, thought McKinley, I'd forgotten how hot she is. He turned back to the crowd, observing that expressions of fear and confusion were spreading temple-wide. Some of them were starting to get it.

"They've deceived your brothers and sisters into murdering even themselves! How can a perfect God accept a murderer?" yelled Carter. "And that's what you were about to become: self murderers! You all thought you were children of Makaru's supposed kingdom but you're *orphans of chaos!*"

McKinley could barely believe what he was hearing. Could his weapons tech have rehearsed this religious nonsense? No way... But obviously neither was he making this stuff up, nor his hastily edited videos.

Carter went on, perhaps imperceptibly warming to his forced role. "You don't *think* like the Creator thinks; you think like the world thinks! He doesn't need to fly planes into skyscrapers to make His point. That's what stupid, misguided human beings do! They think power means destruction! But God doesn't want to destroy; He wants to create. That's *real* power! He demonstrates this all the time because, even though He's got the power to destroy you, He doesn't. He'd be justified in wiping you murderers off the face of the Earth but He doesn't do it! He acts like He expects *you* to act! In *peace*, without violence. A *good* god would never use violence and bloodshed. God wants you to show your enemies a better way!"

Well Chris, thought McKinley, this is a side to you I certainly *never* saw before. But at least they're listening. Putting the wrong password into Makaru's phone enough times to lock the pastor out, and then hijacking his broadcast feed had been a genius move. But how long could it last?

"This *ecclesia*," cried Carter, stabbing the air with his finger, "is a breeding ground of evil! Your leaders deceived you and misrepresented the Creator! This place stands in judgement..."

His voiced dropped down hoarsely as he leaned forward a little. "*And now God will judge it!*"

Whoa, Chris! What?! McKinley looked on in disbelief as Carter carefully pecked at his smartphone's tiny keyboard. What the hell was the bloody idiot doing now? What on earth did he mean by that judgement business? Had the fool lost the plot? McKinley scanned the audience. Every single eye in the place was trained on Carter like a heat seeking missile on a blast furnace. Maybe three quarters of them hated him with everything in them.

"They're not buying it," whispered McKinley.

Carter looked round at him, winking exhaustedly. "Now," he said, covering the microphone, "witness the shitness!" With this he hit 'send'.

McKinley was about to ask what the effing hell Carter was thinking when he felt something through the stage. The disciples all felt it too as their eyes widened even further. The earth had *jumped*.

A second sun burst into the sky to the south, blazing unearthly bright amber light and throwing deep, angular shadows into the temple. McKinley gaped up as did everyone else, the whole crowd rotating as one. It was almost too bright to look at.

With the loudest detonation McKinley had ever heard, the shockwave atomised the huge glass windows of the temple and knocked the audience flying.

McKinley found himself flung down on the stage as myriad glass particles shot-blasted him. The terrific noise thundered into the center of his being, rattling his brain around in his skull. The blast tore the tall black curtains from their mountings.

The ground was shaking violently. Ears ringing, McKinley chanced a look up to see an avalanche of monstrous boulders rolling down the mountainside into the village. Rocks started to drop from the sky, smashing everything they touched. The disciples were in chaos, some screaming, others trying to run. A huge rock like an infant mountain rolled into town, flattening several buildings to the west of the temple. McKinley had never seen destruction on this scale in his life apart from televised earthquakes and volcanic eruptions. *What the hell did Carter do?!*

Lying in a sea of debris and feeling as thoroughly pummelled as a deer with which a speeding juggernaut collides, McKinley cautiously opened his eyes. Almost filling the sky was a radiant fireball. A crazy, *gigantic* fireball that was rising like an atomic mushroom above the mountains. Bloody hell... Wolf River's powerplant had literally blown itself sky high. McKinley squinted up the mountain, through the smoke and dust. The silhouette of the enormous fumarole was smashed, truncated like a broken piece of bamboo. McKinley found himself wondering whether this really could be the *hand of God*.

Joko's face appeared at the edge of the stage like Mr. Chad, looking in astonishment at Carter. Indeed the lad appeared like he was about to fall on his face in worship. He carefully lifted himself onto the stage, walked reverently past the Weapons and Equipment Technician, and took a microphone from its stand at the front of the band area. Joko switched it on with the usual thump and handling noise.

"*He speak with voice of God!*" announced Joko, his voice trembling in awe.

As the rumble subsided and the titanic cloud rose far, far above Rubakang, Carter raised his body a little and blinked a couple of times.

"That was surprisingly effective," he stated.

"But not as rewarding as this," hissed Bellegarde, a swathe of blood descending the side of his head, eyes filled with hatred as he raised a pistol to Carter's temple.

Snick.

It wasn't the metallic click of a dry-fire. Bellegarde looked round behind him in panic to find his left wrist firmly entrapped by Sister Sheba's shining steel handcuffs. He tore the gun away from Carter and slammed it to the center of her forehead. Terror immediately filled his eyes as the realisation that he was in a no-win scenario gripped his heart. Her right thumb was on the dead man's switch.

Carter desperately scrambled away, hurting his busted ribs. McKinley rugby-tackled Joko and hurled them both off the stage. Nearby disciples started to run.

"Of all people," said Sister Sheba with eerie cool, "*you* should know not to raise your hand against God's chosen servant."

She opened her fist.

Bellegarde instantly disappeared in a brilliant flash and a supersonic *CRACK* of mil-spec explosive. Shielding Joko's body, McKinley was hammered by pieces of stage.

The disciples were scattering in chaos, all pretence of religiosity long gone. Now they were no more than frightened kids with the urgency of self preservation uppermost in their minds.

Joko was coughing up a storm. McKinley lifted him to a sitting position and patted him on the back a couple of times. Weakly, Joko raised a thumb as McKinley stood up in the cloud of bluish smoke and blinked, looking around.

The stage was an ugly crater of smashed wood and shredded carpet that looked as though someone had excavated it with a giant ice cream scoop. Shattered wood fragments were still falling from the roof and whatever remained of the windows had already dropped out of their frames. The band's instruments had been scattered like seeds in the wind and even the piano had been knocked off two of its legs, its previously lustrous varnish cracked and punctured by a spray of shrapnel.

"Chris?" McKinley said.

"Over here," came Carter's voice in strained tones from the direction of the piano.

McKinley saw a leg wriggling under the felled instrument. "Gimme a hand!" he shouted. Joko and a couple of the nearest men came to help.

The piano was heavier than McKinley would have thought—not knowing anything at all about music, never mind the devices that produced it—but the four of them managed to half lift, half slide the beast off Carter's prone form.

There the weapons tech lay, spreadeagled like a fly on a windshield.

"How are you?" asked McKinley, concerned.

"I... be flat, obviously," joked Carter with the spectre of a smile. The piano had probably protected him from falling debris and its remaining leg had stopped it from crushing Carter's wounded torso.

"Aye," said McKinley cynically. "What about those ribs?"

"It only hurts when I breathe."

McKinley rolled his eyes in exasperation. "So you're fit?"

Carter sat up, pain registering on his face. He ran his hands over his chest and webbing. "Pistol, phone one, phone two... I'm okay. Takes a lickin' and—"

"Never shuts up," interrupted McKinley. "Now, *what the hell did you do?*" He cast annoyed eyes toward the devastated power plant.

"*You* wanted the dirty tricks brigade."

"*Aye?!*" McKinley's eyebrows were knitted and his brow furrowed.

Carter shrugged. "Well, being dead was no fun, so I decided to wreck some stuff."

McKinley shook his head in disbelief. In inimitable style Carter had set the whole show up and never said a word. Normally the lack of prior information would have elicited a sharp rebuke from McKinley, but he couldn't deny it; the normally humble, socially awkward Carter had a spectacular sense of showmanship. McKinley started to think about how the hell Carter had made all that work, but then he realised they had other priorities.

"Let's get to the Citadel," he said, helping Carter to his feet.

It was only then that Sister Sheba's death hit him. Her sacrifice had saved Carter's life, but she was dead; gone forever. It hit McKinley hard in the guts. His beautiful African princess was lost, vaporised by her own choice. *She was protecting us*, he thought. McKinley felt the sting of moisture at the inside corners of his eyes. He immediately blinked the response away and pulled his emotions back from the threshold. There would be time to mourn later.

The front of the Citadel, smashed as it was by their rocket fire, was surrounded by eight purple clad figures who looked ready to lay down their lives for their pastor. They hid behind pieces of the demagogue's residence, from which their rifle barrels poked like antennae.

There had been no small radio conversation with Captain Dexter after the mighty explosion of the power plant and he was sending Roger Jolley's men as backup. McKinley and Carter were at the corner of one of the buildings. Carter was sitting there in pain whilst, crouching beside him, McKinley couldn't do anything without additional personnel.

"It's over!" shouted McKinley. "Makaru's nothing but a murderer! Drop the guns now and you'll be treated fairly!"

He and Carter looked at each grimly. There was no response.

"Surrender now!" yelled McKinley.

Crack! The impact of a round sprayed them with concrete dust.

"There's your answer," grunted Carter.

"McKinley!" hissed a voice.

McKinley looked back for a moment to see Roger Jolley and several of his men creeping along the concrete wall toward them. Well, thought McKinley, he may be a blithering idiot but more firepower is better than less.

"Let's get this quite clear," said Jolley, "I'm not very fond of you and I'm especially unhappy about my aeroplane."

"We can get into that later," murmured McKinley without turning. A jab of cold steel at the base of his cranium brought him sharply back into focus. Jolley's crew member Nine leaned over and looked right into McKinley's face, so close that McKinley could smell his tobacco breath. The big man leered at McKinley with a crazy grin that said 'I've been looking forward to this'.

"So I decided to swap sides," continued Jolley in his absurd public schoolboy tone.

Despite the rifle barrel, McKinley's head span round. "Jolley you freakin' moron!" he spat. "You're bloody miles out of your depth! You've got no idea what you're getting into."

Jolley gave a superior smirk. "A great big load of money," he nodded.

"Jolley, seriously," groaned Carter, "you're being a complete dickhead. This is the big boys' league."

"You and your toy soldiers are going to get eaten up," added McKinley.

Jolley shrugged and shook his head tiredly, as though reading an article from some salacious magazine whose stories were fabricated. "Just be quiet," he said.

His hands tied behind his back, Carter fell onto the plush carpet face first, grunting as his wounded ribcage felt the sharp impression of his equipment and fiery shots of painful discomfort blazed into his brain. The rich chestnut carpet smelled new.

McKinley landed beside him. Here we are again, thought Carter.

They looked up to see the unholy trinity of Heinmarsh, Makaru and Erbakan standing before them.

"All the rotten eggs in one basket," murmured McKinley quietly.

It was undoubtedly the room they'd seen before from outside and must have been part of Makaru's personal apartment. The huge office was fronted by a wide, curved window that looked out over the whole community. A chair the size of a throne sat behind the pastor's desk beneath a large skylight, one of three. On the desk were several open filing boxes, and around the room empty tables and stands seemed as though they'd just been cleared. The exception to this was a tall glass display case by the desk which was full of insect species. Behind was a wall of bookcases surrounding the elevator door from which they'd just been thrown. To the right was the top of the spiral staircase that they'd seen during their earlier reconnoiter of the floor below.

Makaru spoke, doubtless to a minion. "Is the warhead aboard my ekranoplan?"

"Yes Pastor."

"Good. Go to the boathouse. We'll be leaving shortly."

"Yes Pastor."

They heard two sets of feet retreating down the spiral steps.

The *warhead*, thought McKinley as his insides went cold. *They still have Heinmarsh's warhead.*

With weary eyes Carter looked sideways at his friend, thinking the same thing. Despite everything, there was still a potentially viable nuclear weapon on the game board.

"There's just one more thing we need, Mister Jolley," said Makaru in a pleasant tone. "If you would please be so kind as to return with my guards and defend the Citadel until we've left I would be most grateful, thank you."

"Can do," said Jolley. McKinley heard a group getting into the elevator whilst others exited via the stairs and presumably descended the fire escape. There was silence for a few long moments.

"So," said Erbakan finally. "Mister McKittrick, Mister Carver..."

"McKinley and Carter," interjected Heinmarsh.

"We meet again," continued the Turk. "You know, I knew of you from the start. I should have killed you as soon as we met but you know what they say about fouling your own doorstep. But I was curious about—"

"Is this going to be a *long* lecture?" said McKinley.

Erbakan didn't reply but must have nodded to the four remaining guards as McKinley was hoisted up by his shoulders and dragged kicking to a low bench by the window. A pair of them turned him face up and laid his head and shoulders on the narrow table, holding him firmly. McKinley continued to kick, but these were big strong fellas. One moved behind, gripping McKinley's hair whilst the second immobilised his legs and the third covered him from in front with a pistol. Their colleague remained by Carter, weapon drawn. McKinley looked up at the ceiling's white tiles. Is this the last thing I'm going to see? The hair-holder's big Basmolet dangled from his collar, clunking on McKinley's forehead.

The ugly face of the arms dealer hove into view, jerkily reflected in the polished metal. "I will cut from the front," he growled, "because it is much more suffering for you. The blade will not go all the way the first time. Maybe one third; we will see."

Oh my effing goodness, thought McKinley, this is going to be a whole new kind of agony. I never thought I'd go out like this. He started to feel cold inside despite Rubakang's warmth. Carter was swearing in the background. McKinley chanced a look into Erbakan's eyes and saw only his own damnation.

There were muted gunshots from outside and below, echoing through the jungle.

"Your mercenaries have received their reward," said Erbakan. He turned away, speaking to someone else. "May I?"

"Of course sir," said Makaru's voice and there was the sound of sliding metal. McKinley tried to move his head to see what was going on but the guards' stalwart grips refused to yield.

Erbakan held the weapon in front of McKinley's face. Holy shit; it was a bloody Samurai sword!

"This *Katana* has been in Pastor Makaru's family for generations," grated the weapons dealer. "It is a beautifully crafted artifact, eleven hundred years old." He shrugged. "It is a shame to use such a fine blade on worthless filth like you, but I seem to have mislaid my *Kilij*. Oh!" The Turk acted as though surprised. "That reminds me; *where is my yacht?*"

McKinley was about to tell Erbakan to go forth and multiply when Carter spoke.

"At the bottom of the Atlantic," announced the weapons tech.

Erbakan held the Katana not even an inch over McKinley's throat, sheer murder resident on his face. In a sick display of psychopathia he looked as though he was about to relish the tastiest morsel, his anticipated catharsis as obvious as his crooked nose.

"I will ask again, one more time," he growled in Carter's direction. "You have this chance to save him. For now."

"I told you," yelled Carter. "We scuttled it!"

Erbakan looked at Carter, nodding slowly, his lips pursed. "This is not an answer I was hoping to hear." He lowered the blade to rest on McKinley's throat, stinging him as the acute sharpness made its first tiny cut.

"Screw you asshole!" grunted McKinley, launching a blob of spit up into Erbakan's face and getting most of it back on his own. The weight of the blade pushed a little further and McKinley felt a drop of blood tracing the contours of his neck. He was beyond desperate, his breathing and heart rates soaring. He felt unbearable tendrils of terror piercing his heart and he prepared to face death. Erbakan started to slide the blade across McKinley's windpipe, cutting flesh.

Something caught Carter's eye. "Hey Turkish Delight!" he yelled. "Look right!"

Lifting the sword, Erbakan glanced round.

The huge semicircular window shattered with an almighty report, exploding a dense storm of transparent fragments into the room as though the whole top floor was being grit-blasted by a giant. Face lashed by glass, Erbakan fell to his left. The guard that was holding McKinley's hair suddenly let go and lurched forward over his captive, shot from behind. The body collapsed onto his colleague, who rolled off McKinley's legs in shock. Heinmarsh yelled. Makaru and the fourth guard were knocked down by the blast.

Two figures, one tall and thin, the other shorter and slightly stout, swung on ropes into the gap where the window had been, kicking away what was left of the glass.

Lifting his leg sharply McKinley kicked the armed guard in front of him in the nuts. The guy fell forward grunting and McKinley's other boot smashed him soundly in the face, knocking him senseless.

Erbakan recovered quickly and, as McKinley tried to get up, brought the lethally sharp blade around again in a powerful swing. McKinley saw it slice through the air toward his chest with ridiculous velocity.

Clank! The sword stopped dead, its travel instantly arrested by the rifle that seemed to appear out of thin air in front of it.

"Sorry I'm late," gasped Wilson as he pushed hard against the sword, throwing the arms dealer off balance. Drawing a knife he cut McKinley's bonds with a single sharp tug as Erbakan roared.

The guard that had been holding McKinley's legs high-kicked Wilson and McKinley threw a hammer of a right hook into the man's jaw. As his body span to the floor Wilson's companion Cumberland blasted him through the heart.

Heinmarsh was firing. The gun spat at McKinley but he grabbed the recovering third guard and swung himself behind the purple clad man, who was just getting up. As the rounds found the guard, McKinley rolled over and fell behind the wooden bench that had been about to become a chopping block. Heinmarsh fired again and Cumberland cried in pain. Wilson threw a small chair at Heinmarsh then dropped down beside McKinley.

The fourth guard had been disoriented by the sudden explosion, but now he started to get up. Carter quickly rolled and tried to kick the man's legs, but he leaped over the weapons tech toward McKinley and Wilson's cover.

Wilson hurriedly tried to cycle the rifle's action but it had been broken by the sword impact.

"Damn!" said Wilson.

Like an attacking beast Erbakan flew at McKinley and Wilson with both arms holding the sword over his head. The remaining guard appeared above them with his weapon trained. Erbakan sliced down with every ounce of strength he had. McKinley kicked hard at the guard's shins. He overbalanced and the Katana cleaved his torso in half from left shoulder to right pelvis, the blade becoming lodged in the bench.

Pebbledashed by the guard's innards, Wilson scrambled over to Carter as Erbakan screamed in rage, trying to free the sword. Makaru was getting up.

The elevator door started to open. Recovering, Heinmarsh blasted several panicked rounds at it. The figure inside threw themselves into the lift car's nearest corner. Wilson and Carter rolled together out of the way.

Carter, arms now free, jumped to his feet as best he could, blocking Makaru's exit. Makaru flew at him in rage and they grappled, stumbling toward the spiral stairs.

Under fire from Heinmarsh, McKinley crawled around the curve of the window, keeping low behind the massive desk. The big American dodged from side to side, trying to find a shot.

Erbakan was swinging the sword again, trying to hit Wilson. He swung like lightning, just missing the lanky combat specialist, who was too busy not getting in its way to use his busted rifle defensively. Wilson jumped back, avoiding another slice, but tripped backwards over some boxes and fell, his back slamming painfully down on to the edge of the former window and his head over the drop. As Wilson roared from the pain of sharp glass lacerating his back, Erbakan drew back the sword for a piercing thrust.

Suddenly someone with black hair smashed into the big Turk from the side just as Erbakan pushed the sword. The blade skimmed the side of Wilson's chest and dug into the carpet. Erbakan threw his attacker off without any trouble.

"*Nobody messes with my man!*" screamed Izzie as she flew right back at the Turk with the ferocity of an enraged tiger. Her nails scratched viciously at his scarred face, cutting red furrows, and she thrust her knee hard into his crotch.

Erbakan yelped fiercely in pain. "*Kahrolası küçük orospu!*" He flailed madly with the sword, losing his grip. It flew from his hand, tumbling end-over-end and narrowly missing Izzie, and shattered the glass cabinet, spreading dead bugs and razor sharp fragments. He grabbed her arm and threw her hard toward the broken window. Izzie screamed in terror as her body sailed through the gap, bursting some of the remaining glass into a cloud of fragments.

Like lightning Wilson thrust his right hand up and grabbed the fabric of her jeans. Her weight tugged his body round until his arm was pointing down and his chest was cut on the edge. Something gave way in his shoulder and he yelped in pain but somehow held on. Izzie slammed into the Citadel's wall below the window ledge with a cry, upside down and nearly crapping herself with fear.

McKinley had Heinmarsh cornered on the other side of the room where the window was still mostly whole. In a Mexican stand-off the two's pistols covered each other.

"Drop it," said McKinley. "It's over."

Face running blood, Erbakan pushed past Carter and Makaru and threw himself down the stairwell. Makaru tried to heave Carter off but the Brit's grip was firm. Makaru started using martial arts moves but Carter doggedly refused to budge. Twisting hard, Makaru slammed his elbow back into Carter's face, who finally let go. Makaru jumped down the steps but Carter had his Desert Eagle out in an instant.

Suffering horrible pain, he trained the big pistol on Makaru's head. "No no no!" he commanded loudly. "You're not going anywhere shitbag!" Makaru stopped and turned slowly toward him.

Izzie had clambered back up with Wilson's help and now knelt by her man, who had turned over again and was gasping in pain. They heard Erbakan's rushed footsteps descending the fire escape, then its door swung closed.

BC Cumberland, wounded but determined, pulled herself from the floor onto Makaru's chair and joined McKinley in covering Heinmarsh.

Near the top of the spiral stairs Makaru appeared unfazed even though he was breathing hard and fast. "What?" he said, shrugging emphatically. "Are you going to shoot an unarmed man like those two poor souls you sent to hell in Canada?"

His words hit Carter like a punch in the belly. The weapons tech's brow furrowed and his mouth dropped open a little. "How the *hell* do you know—?" he gasped.

Makaru smiled arrogantly. "There are secrets we keep, and secrets that keep us, aren't there Christopher?"

Again Carter was shocked at Makaru using his first name, but he retained his focus. "Well, if you're trying to guilt trip *me*, you're way behind schedule."

"Oh yes, it's all about *you* and how *you* feel isn't it Christopher?" smirked the demagogue. "The only thing you care about is yourself. It's all greed, lust and *self*. You're *pathetic!*" he spat.

"Maybe," replied Carter, frowning as though giving Makaru's asseveration fair regard. "But there again I never claimed to be a good person, did I? So don't get all self-righteous on my ass, 'cause yours is *nothing special.*"

In that instant Makaru jumped with impossible speed. Even from several stairs below his acceleration was inhuman. Carter fired but Makaru was beneath the pistol's axis. Throwing Carter's right arm out of the way the Asian cracked a heavy blow into his gut. As the weapons tech grunted in pain Makaru span like a top, hitting first with a lightning punch to Carter's cheek and then a flying high kick that knocked Carter several feet back. Carter's wounded, pain ridden body slammed to the floor and almost stopped moving. Makaru bent over the weapons tech in a menacingly gentle way, as though one might a delicious meal they were about to relish.

"*Chris?!*" yelled McKinley, turning from Heinmarsh for a moment.

The Asian patted Carter's face. "Now, that's better," he whispered. Carter gurgled and groaned in pain, trying but unable to lift the demagogue from his agonised torso.

"What's *this?*" asked Makaru as though surprised, pulling Carter's Desert Eagle out of his hand.

As Carter tried weakly to retrieve it Makaru levered himself up, pointing the weapon roughly toward McKinley. Seeing it coming, McKinley threw himself down behind the desk as Makaru fired twice. Eyes blazing both anger and surprise, Heinmarsh grunted an F-bomb and dropped like a falling tree.

"That's how The Communion rewards failure, Mister Heinmarsh!" sang the Asian proudly.

McKinley tried to shoot but Makaru sent another of the pulverising fifty cal rounds back at him, smashing a hole in the desk. Cumberland rolled off the chair and landed on the floor by McKinley.

The Asian turned the big gun toward Wilson and Izzie. "*As for you...!*" he yelled.

"*NO!*" shouted Izzie, throwing herself toward her beloved. Instantly Makaru fired again and the round passed through the center of her skull, blowing out her face all over Wilson's. Her body flopped down upon his and Wilson screamed.

Before McKinley could bring his weapon to bear Makaru flew down the circular stairwell, throwing three shots back over his head to discourage pursuit. They heard him drop the empty gun. His movements diminished into silence as he entered the fire escape.

McKinley looked around. The whole damn shit-show had gone down in less than a minute. What a bloody mess! Heinmarsh wasn't moving. Wilson was covered in blood and crying like a peeled baby in a bucket of salt. Cumberland was wounded in the gut and bleeding but showed McKinley a thumbs up. *What about Carter?* McKinley leaped from behind the desk and toward the stairwell, propelled by both fear and worry.

"Hey!" McKinley dropped next to Carter and a bit of stress evaporated when he saw that his friend was breathing. "You alright pal?"

Carter coughed, each eruption bringing more pain. "Yeah," he whispered. "It only hurts when my heart beats. Didn't think he'd be that fast."

McKinley smiled, cradling Carter's head in his hands. "Aye, bloody ninja, eh? If you were alright you'd have kicked his ass. Can you sit up?"

The weapons tech nodded and McKinley carefully lifted him. Carter screwed his eyes up tight with renewed pain from his chest, feeling injuries within. "Oh," he announced, as a rivulet of blood and saliva exited the corner of his lips. "I've got bad news."

McKinley felt more concern than he would have expected. "Huh?"

Carter gave a pained grin. "For him."

"*What?*"

"Well, you know what they say about losing a battle so you can win the war?" Carter opened his bloodied hand, revealing Makaru's cellphone. "He's gonna miss this."

"Hah," sighed McKinley. "You jammy bugger."

He looked up. Cumberland had crawled her way to the distraught Wilson. She was trying to clean the blood off his face with her shirt. McKinley could not imagine how his colleague felt, and didn't want to try.

He walked over to Heinmarsh, pistol ready just in case. The American was lying on his side, a great sucking sound accompanying each breath. McKinley returned the weapon to his webbing and squatted down. The big man was bleeding profusely from a wound in the right hand side of his belly.

"Feel like we been here before," croaked the American.

McKinley huffed. "Bet you didn't expect that."

Heinmarsh's eyes rolled. "I had... an idea. Here." He took McKinley's wrist and guided the Scot's hand down to his jacket pocket. "My... phone," he grunted.

"What about it?"

"Unlock... code is 7, 5, 8, 3... 2."

Steadying himself on the furniture, Carter squatted by McKinley's side. He was breathing hard as every little movement exacerbated his injuries.

Heinmarsh moaned, a deep, guttural ululation in the key of imminent demise. It ended with coughing which sounded like it was going to end the American.

McKinley took Heinmarsh's phone and passed it to Carter. "What *about* your phone?" he demanded.

"Y... you'll see in... in... in a week," grunted Heinmarsh. The billionaire rolled onto his back with another moan.

McKinley brought his pistol to Heinmarsh's forehead. "Better late than never," he grated, and fired once.

Carter's quiet voice sounded as pained as Heinmarsh's. "We're gonna need another bad guy."

Both Makaru's and Heinmarsh's phones suddenly produced five short, loud beeps almost simultaneously. It sounded like a warning.

"What?" gasped McKinley.

"*Number?!*" snapped Carter, pulling Heinmarsh's device from his friend's hand.

"75832," said McKinley. Carter stabbed the digits in and sighed hopelessly.

"We've got to go!"

He turned the phone toward McKinley, who saw 02:52 flash past. He saw 02:51 and that was enough. *I've been down this road before...*

"Bet it's not fake this time!" added Carter.

McKinley jumped to his feet. "Willy!" he shouted, "evacuate! Cumberland, let's go! Help him!"

Carter started hobbling toward the stairwell. McKinley came alongside and hooked his arm around Carter's back, supporting him and urging him along at the same time. He looked round at Wilson, who Cumberland was trying to lift. Their combat specialist wouldn't let go of Izzie's body.

"*Willy!*" screamed McKinley. "She's *gone!* Let her go or you're gonna die!" It looked as though Wilson hadn't heard.

"*WILLY!*"

Wilson's head turned toward his team leader sluggishly, his eyes empty. Slowly he took his hands away from Izzie's body. Looking like a man struggling against the effects of general anaesthetic, Wilson lifted himself to his feet.

"Let's go sir!" urged Cumberland, pulling at his arm.

Suddenly Wilson started to run, grabbing Cumberland in the same kind of configuration as McKinley and Carter. The four of them launched themselves down the clanking spiral staircase, which shook with their descent.

Slamming open the fire escape McKinley and Carter dashed unevenly down the steel steps, hearing the others close behind them. Each floor seemed to take forever. *Clang-clang-clang* rang the steps, echoing crazily up and down the concrete shaft. Carter stumbled, nearly causing Wilson and Cumberland to collide with them. He moaned in pain and forced himself to move.

"*Go! Move it!*" yelled McKinley, pushing Carter as hard as he could.

They burst through the door at the bottom, out into the bright daylight, now tinged red and waning. McKinley could feel Carter dragging him, but where?

As if in answer, Carter grunted "water!"

Right – the density of the ocean might deflect the blast somewhat. Supporting his friend, McKinley ran down the sand as the other two followed.

They splashed into the cold wet surf, pushing themselves deeper and deeper against the water's resistance. Carter dived, turning onto his back, and exhaled. His body started to sink.

McKinley dived forward, raising his legs.

Their world shook with a huge, dull boom and a vibration like a small earth tremor. There was a bright flash of orange light. McKinley dared stick his head above the waves and felt fierce heat on his face.

The Citadel had been consumed by a raging conflagration, a thick, black mushroom cloud roiling and climbing above it. Huge sheets of vivid flame tore into the sky from every window and door as embers and sparks poured forth. Clearly it had been some kind of incendiary device rather than high explosives. Makaru was burning the evidence.

McKinley wiped his hair out of his face. That had been bloody close. Carter surfaced next to him, gasping for air. Wilson and Cumberland were still waist deep and arm in arm.

"Should've brought marshmallows," lamented Carter.

The beach was almost the ideal place for the Indonesians to make landfall and set up a field hospital. Not only was it a respectful distance from the carnage of the township, but the gentle oscillation of the waves was a soothing rhythm that felt needed. The equatorial night had fallen quickly and long rows of rapidly deployed emergency lights adorned the beach like jewelled necklaces.

Lieutenant Colonel Suhardi of the *Tentara Nasional Indonesia*—the Indonesian military—had been helpful indeed, making sure that all the COAST personnel were well looked after. General Sutton had despatched transport from the UK already, and they would probably be flying out in the morning.

Also heading home, but without urgency, were Roger Jolley's people; they had survived because Wilson and Cumberland had ambushed the group and killed the guards, but Jolley's mercenary crew were all under arrest pending extradition. Unless Jolley had *bona fide* miracle workers for lawyers, McKinley and Carter's testimonies of his traitorous infidelity—never mind his eagerness to kill the TDR.12 lads, his antagonism toward Dexter's team, and the amount of Wolf River's disciples that his crew had murdered—would doubtless end his career as the British government's go-to truant officer and more than likely buy him a long stretch at Her Majesty's displeasure.

Teams of infantry soldiers and medics were herding the remaining disciples from all over the island to Hosao, from where they'd be ferried back to the capital Jakarta, on the populous island of Java, and then, presumably, to their countries of origin. There would doubtless be a lengthy process of rehabilitation and counselling for them. Their memories would return and they would see the light at the end of the tunnel.

McKinley hadn't pushed his bereaved colleague too hard, but Wilson's fragmentary report had been staggering to say the least. Further, Suhardi had confirmed the incredible data; a gigantic megaton-range explosion had been monitored in a oceanographical feature called Qurahai Trench. Unusual freak waves had been measured in Papua New Guinea, Micronesia, the New Britain area, Guam and other Pacific locations. Many nations were jumping on the investigation bandwagon whilst others concocted any cover story which would fly. McKinley shook his head. His team had been involved with two of the biggest nuclear explosions ever, and certainly since treaties pushed atmospheric weapons testing underground. This could only happen to me, he thought.

In view of the fact that he'd got off the lightest, McKinley elected to fill his belly with food and then have a walk along the beach. The Indonesians had brought with them generous supplies and McKinley had tucked in heartily to some dish with a central pile of yellow rice surrounded by fried meat. He hadn't even bothered to ask what the meat was; it might as well have been rat or something equally unappetising but to his starved body it tasted like the best thing in the world. He'd cadged a smoke and light off one of the officers and set off in a north-easterly direction, not specifically going anywhere but away from all the fuss.

He looked down at Heinmarsh's phone, it's countdown now stopped at 00:00. '*You'll see in a week*,' the dying billionaire had said. See what in a week? McKinley took another pull on the cigarette and looked out to sea. Screw it. This techy shit was Carter's department and once his friend was up and about, or in a week—whichever was sooner—McKinley would get the geek on the case. There was Makaru's phone to examine as well. Right now it was dead, Carter having pulled the battery to avoid any chance of remote memory erasure. Might as well do the same to this one, thought McKinley, just in case; he prised open the device's back pane. He took out the battery, flipped it through ninety degrees and put it carefully back in.

They'd received reports of Makaru's ekranoplan—not a seaplane as Joko had said, though McKinley could understand the mistake—leaving the island and heading north, presumably with both the Asian and his Turkish colleague nannying the last warhead. Where would they go in a small craft of relatively short range? There were thousands of islands that would need surveying. Being Asian, Makaru could easily disappear into the Indo-Chinese Peninsula, mused McKinley, but he figured that was about two and a half thousand miles away. Erbakan undoubtedly had resources and plenty of places to hide. Would General Sutton go after the bastards? More to the point, did The Team have the support of the JIC now?

Then there was the perplexing manner in which Makaru had addressed Erbakan. He clearly treated the Turk as a superior. Why would an arrogant ass like Makaru show such deference to a weapons dealer – albeit more than a run-of-the-mill ironmonger? And what the *hell* is '*The Communion*'?! Another bloody religious group?

Too many questions, not enough answers. It was getting late, and he was *unbelievably* tired.

McKinley drew deeply on the cigarette and turned back to the south, surveying what he could see of Wolf River in its massive destruction.

Boy, did we *ever* wreck some shit.

024: The Message

I love this car, thought McKinley, but Nottingham really is bloody miserable at this time of year.

A light snow was falling on the brand new Vauxhall VXR8 GTS as McKinley nursed his man-toy through the damp, grey streets. The snow wouldn't settle—it seldom did in this region—but the canopy of colourless cloud suspended over the municipality would probably stay there until March. Pedestrians were going about their business with collars held together round their scarves, walking a little faster than normal in the cold and completely oblivious to the presence of the huge secret complex far beneath the moist pavement.

He slid the Vauxhall carefully into one of the base's hidden entrances and waited as the big elevator with its chipped yellow paint lowered him down at least eighty feet. The base's lights came into view from below.

McKinley twisted the rear view mirror down to look at his reflection. It was much more presentable now that the huge, bushy beard he'd grown had been removed, but his face was uncommonly sensitive. He rubbed at his chin. It felt too smooth now. Still, he thought, I'm looking good.

Driving out of the elevator and into the underground parking bay, McKinley found a TDR section parking space. Killing the ignition, he stroked the black leather and vinyl, relishing the new vehicle's wonderful smell. I've earned this, thought McKinley, reminiscing on the last couple of months. It had been a more than pleasant surprise to arrive back in the UK and find at least a dozen answering service messages from the Vauxhall dealership telling him that his new shag-magnet had been delivered and was waiting there for him. It felt like Christmas, and that was good because his festive season had been spent on that awful bloody island getting hunted, tortured, nearly drowned, beaten and all the other shit.

After signing in with security he navigated the corridors to the medical bay. There was the familiar figure of Doctor Manning sitting inside the med bay's nearly circular central island at his console. Did the guy ever take a day off? Beyond Manning's workstation were a pair of even more familiar figures lying on their beds in convalescence.

Manning was about to say hello when Carter yapped his greeting.

"I see you picked up your car then?"

McKinley laughed. "It's that obvious?"

Carter nodded, coughing a little with a pained expression. "You're walking like a man who just got a brand new motor."

"Corporal Carter," interjected Manning from his desk, a little miffed, "you really should try not to exert your diaphragm."

"Got it," said Carter, holding a thumb toward the medic and smiling, his freshly-trimmed five millimeters of boringly brown stubble rippling upward with the expression.

McKinley turned to Wilson. "Hey big lad."

Wilson barely looked away from the newspaper he was holding with one hand. "How're you doing?"

"Aye, good, thanks." McKinley didn't know what more to say. Wilson himself had hardly spoken since leaving Rubakang. They could *see* the trauma in his eyes.

McKinley turned to Manning. "Doc, where's Cumberland?"

The doctor swivelled on his chair, revealing a sour countenance. "Ms. Cumberland was quite inflexible in her demand for a private room," he deadpanned, looking over his glasses. He turned back to his console and they heard him mutter "bitch." McKinley and Carter winked at each other.

"She didn't do bad though eh?" said Carter. "I reckon she earned that promotion."

"We'll have to see about that," came General Sutton's voice. Wilson dropped his paper, McKinley turned, and the three of them and the doctor saluted their CO.

"At ease," said Sutton and, walking around the island, folded his tall frame onto the empty bed next to Wilson's. He was just as neatly groomed as ever in his pristine uniform, his beard impeccably trimmed, rimming his kindly face from which keen, agile intelligence shone out through his eyes. Under his apparently healed right arm was a clipboard.

"How's that rotator cuff?" he asked Wilson.

Wilson looked up at the boss. "It'll be okay sir, thank you."

"Good." Sutton smiled as though Wilson's reply was lacking conviction and turned to Carter.

"You got roughed up, didn't you?"

"Yes sir, a bit."

Sutton nodded. "Well I'm sure the good doctor's taking care of you."

"Yes sir."

The general waited for a moment. Something's coming, thought McKinley.

"Corporal Carter," continued Sutton with a sigh. "Your report reads like a science fiction story."

There's no way that's a good appraisal, thought Carter. "Sir, it's all true."

Sutton shook his head. "I don't doubt *that*," he groaned. "But I find the extent of your... let's say *technical involvement* rather hard to swallow."

"Sir, I've presented the facts as accurately as possible."

"I know. You're not given to lying; that much is true."

"Yes sir."

Sutton shook his head. "It's just that what I get from these reports is reminiscent of some kind of Hollywood movie. You hacked one of the world's most high-tech yachts, you coaxed a seventy year old aeroplane into flight, you maintained an even older motor vessel, you hacked various computer systems and you used mundane and easily available chemicals to blow up a mountain. And those are just the bullet points."

"Yes sir." Carter was still worried. Where was Uncle Victor heading with this?

Suddenly the general's face cracked a smile. "Well my goodness lad, what on earth are you doing working for us? You should be running some clandestine warfare think-tank full of boffins."

McKinley, Carter and their general laughed. Wilson smiled for the briefest moment and turned away.

The general looked straight into Carter's face. "You know, none of us had any idea you were so religious."

"I'm not sir."

Sutton raised an eyebrow. "You preached a... well I suppose you'd call it a sermon, to those young people."

Carter nodded knowingly. "Yes sir, but it wasn't about religion. It was about saving their lives."

Sutton leaned back a little, taking a moment to consider this idea. Shrugging, he plucked the clipboard from under his arm and summoned his thoughts.

"Okay," he said. "These mobile telephones you recovered. We've got them in the Faraday cage in the lab. As soon as you're fit, Corporal Carter, you can start working on Makaru's. Get into it, find out how he talks to those trinary computers and write us some software that'll do the same. Got it?"

"Yes sir," nodded Carter eagerly, "I can start as soon as you like."

Sutton raised a finger. "No, you can't." He glanced toward Doctor Manning, who didn't look round but shook his head vigorously.

The general turned back. "When *he* gives you the okay; not before."

Carter looked deflated. "Yes sir."

"Now, as to Heinmarsh's device," continued Sutton, "we'll power it up with an external antenna and see what happens. If there's nothing after seven days you can work on that as well. See if it pulls the same tricks, okay?"

"Yes sir."

Sutton took a quick glance at his notes. "Moving on, there's a new drug craze kicking off in Europe, mainly Scandinavia. Seems the kids are taking something called 'Oblivion'. I'm sure you gather by the name what it does."

The TDR.12 lads looked at each other. "Memory modification?" said Carter.

"*Apparently* it makes you forget everything, all your troubles, regrets, bad memories, all that stuff," nodded the general, frowning. "Sound familiar?"

"Yes sir, it does," said McKinley.

"And now to you," said the boss, nodding at him. "You're seeing Jemima Fox later, I understand."

"Yes sir." McKinley had wanted to visit Jem as soon as he got back into the country. He'd missed her. At the moment she was in the unit's detention area.

"Well, this... is an *unusual* request, Corporal," said the general, pointing to the clipboard. "However, in view of the very *unusual* circumstances I'm going to green-light it for now, subject to legal proceedings of course. You're in a good position to supervise until... well, until the courts figure out what to do."

"Yes sir, thank you."

"On a more serious matter," said the general, his face reflecting his tone, "you were given some kind of truth drug by Heinmarsh. I know you don't remember what happened." Sutton saw McKinley's pained look and held up his hand. "Now, this is not to make light of it, but I don't want you to worry. The Command Staff and I have discussed this and we think there's not much you could've added to whatever the late Corporal Brook already gave him."

McKinley was relieved; what Uncle Victor was telling him was probably right. Everything that had happened since Brook's betrayal was related to Heinmarsh and Makaru, so they'd probably already know it. He breathed an internal sigh of relief. He hadn't necessarily sold the unit down the river. But there was still a nagging doubt. It was an ugly, uncomfortable thought – a fleeting impression of a psychological violation that he feared and hated.

"Yes sir," he said.

Sutton nodded slightly. "Which brings us to you, Corporal Wilson," he said. Wilson looked back without expression.

"You've been through a very traumatic time, I know, and clearly it's still raw; it'll take some getting over. Are you certain the cult's programming is behind you?"

Wilson nodded. "Yes sir. I haven't experienced a single flashback."

"Indeed," replied Sutton. "The effects seem to vary from person to person. All the same, I want you to stay away from Miss Fox, in case one of you triggers the other."

Wilson felt discriminated against. *He* knew he was over the Brother Dawoud episode. In fact, Makaru's serum had worn off quickly in his case, maybe due to his energetic metabolism. Paul Wilson was back and Dawoud was gone—as far as he was concerned—forever. Nonetheless, it was true that the general's instruction was a logical precaution. "Yes sir," he said.

"I can't imagine," mused Sutton, "what it must have been like thinking you were someone else."

Wilson shook his head. "But that's it sir; I *didn't* think I was someone else. I was always me, I just couldn't remember my life before."

"Hmm. But you do now, obviously."

"Yes sir, everything."

Sutton paused for just a second. "Okay. Well I'm afraid I have some more... perhaps difficult news."

"Sir?"

"I know you haven't seen each other for a while, but are you still involved with Miss Bridgewell?"

What? Wilson didn't know what to expect. After the pounding his heart had taken recently, he was in dread of what this might be. "Yes sir, as far as I know. We haven't even been in touch since Singapore though."

"You're kidding?" interjected McKinley. Wilson shrugged as if to convey uncertainty.

Sutton frowned. "Okay. Julia Bridgewell's former boyfriend, Kendal Gundersen, was found dead in an apparent suicide last week."

Really? Wilson was surprised. Could it be because of the break up? But that was *weeks* ago.

The general continued. "As you know his father is... the Secretary of the US Treasury. Or was. He was found this morning—"

"Holy shit!" blurted Carter as if troubled. The boss threw him an annoyed look.

"As I was saying, he was found this morning, also an apparent suicide."

"Sir," said Wilson, "do you think he could've just been suffering over his son? I didn't think the split with Julia would've hit him that hard, would it? This isn't some kind of domino effect is it?"

"No," said Sutton, holding up his hands. "Steady on. Gundersen junior broke off all contact with her about the time you lot went AWOL. But here's the thing; in fact, both were poisoned by massive doses of mycotoxins."

There was a moment's silence during which the humming of the computers and other equipment became unusually obvious.

"Makaru," stated McKinley flatly.

"He's got the know-how," said Carter, who still appeared uncomfortable. "I guess that might explain the *Destroying Angel*."

"Yes I saw that in your report," said the general. "What is it?"

"A fungus, sir. It was being cultivated in Makaru's hydroponics department. Extremely toxic."

Sutton nodded. "*Interesting*. Anyway, our American friends are still investigating, but I think it smells highly suspicious, don't you?"

McKinley put voice to the question in all their minds. "Are we going after him sir?"

"That's the plan," answered the CO. "And Erbakan. We've got to get you all back on your feet, and I've got some details to work out, but yes, that's what we're doing. Now," the general stood and raised his voice. "McKinley, attention!"

What on earth, thought McKinley as he jumped up and stood ramrod straight. "Sir, yes sir."

Suddenly gone was the friendly but professional charm. The general's tone was now one hundred percent superior officer, and an angry, hard-as-nails one at that. "Listen to me very carefully. As I predicted, you prosecuted your mission and you came out on top, if by a cat's whisker. But it was definitely *your* mission. The chaos you caused is unthinkable and you've given me several severe headaches to contend with, not to mention somehow convincing the bloody JIC that this was a planned operation. So mark my words well; If you ever, *ever* do unauthorised ops without specific orders again—and this goes for all of you—I'll demote your asses so far down the ladder you'll be saluting the bathroom attendant's dog, and I certainly *will not* cover for you again. Is this perfectly clear?"

"Sir, yes sir!" they chorused.

"There is... one more thing," said the general, returning to his normally calm demeanour. "This SIS man in Singapore, Middleton. You asked me to get involved, and I have a little good news. He'll be released next week. He'll get his boat and his money back, but all that equipment's been confiscated under anti-terror laws. He's a very lucky man, considering how harshly the Singaporean authorities treat these kind of cases."

With this he slung the clipboard back under his arm and said "that's all."

Sutton left the medical bay. Manning looked round at them and raised an eyebrow, a slight lopsided grin on his face.

Once they were sure the general was out of hearing range, McKinley let out a long, deep sigh, his shoulders drooping.

"*Our* money."

"Our *gear*," countered Carter. "What a bloody waste."

"On the other hand," said Wilson, "at least he's not going to be in clink for years and years. And the money'll help when he gets to Australia."

"No shit," said McKinley disconsolately, his imagination conjuring an image of a wealthy Blake Middleton living it up with attractive women, flashy cars and A-list parties. He sat on the edge of Carter's gurney and addressed the combat specialist. "So you're talking again now?"

Wilson hesitated for a second. Suddenly, he looked like he *wanted* to communicate. "Yeah," said the younger man slowly, "I guess so." He paused and took a breath before continuing. McKinley and Carter looked at each other.

"I... I realised something. Don't get me wrong; that Isabella was an absolute diamond." He started to choke up a little but shook his head to get past it. "But I was always about Julia. I just forgot, that's all. Makaru did something to us to make us fall in love; I'm sure of it."

"No kidding." said Carter.

Wilson pointed a finger back at him. "Right. But *that* relationship... kinda wasn't real. It was like a big party balloon: all shiny and colourful on the outside, but inside just empty air. I mean, she was an *amazing* girl. I'll never forget her. Her loss... is..." His lips wobbled a little as he regained emotional control. "Well, it's tragic; it's horrible. I'll be having nightmares for ages, I'm sure. But now I know it's Jules that I really wanted all along."

"Nice to have you back," said McKinley, raising his thumb.

Wilson wagged his finger in the team leader's direction. "D'you remember when we were at Uncle Victor's gaff, and you told me how your heart got all wrecked like stuff in Northern Ireland?"

McKinley cast his mind back. Yes, he'd used that illustration, just as he had many times before.

"Aye. What about it?"

Wilson shrugged, careful to use only his left shoulder. "Well, I think I understand now."

McKinley presented his ID to the Detention Officer and turned out his pockets. Cigarettes, lighter, penknife and a small handful of change fell into the black plastic tray.

The detention area was just like any other prison with drab grey-painted, thick masonry walls, heavy metal doors like a ship's bulkhead hatches, and a lingering odour of disinfectant. It was at least a hundred feet underground and perpetually lit by anaemic fluorescent tubes. Everything there revolved around security procedures, keys, combinations, handcuffs and cameras. McKinley was thankful that he'd never been deemed worthy of its accommodation, even though he'd come close a couple of times.

"Cell three, please."

"Yes sir," replied the officer, making a note in his log. "This way please."

"Thanks."

McKinley followed the man down a short corridor to a massive door equipped with both an electronic lock and a deadlock.

"Turn away please sir."

McKinley turned, hearing the guard's key work the lock and the entry of a numeric code as a series of short beeps. There was the hum of electric motors and a solid *clunk* that echoed from the drab walls. He smiled to himself, remembering Erbakan's password. This key code didn't seem to have such a recognisable pattern and he didn't care to know it anyway.

The officer shut and locked the door behind them as they entered the corridor beyond, which was lined with five identical doors on each side. He steered McKinley toward the second on the left and quickly checked through the peephole. Knocking loudly, he announced "visitor!" The guard unlocked the door and McKinley entered the cell.

Jem threw herself at him in joy, her passionate embrace nearly knocking him over. As the guard locked him in, they hugged as though they hadn't seen each other for decades.

"I knew you'd come," she trilled. "They told me you were back but I didn't know when you'd be able to make it."

McKinley held the girl at arms length admiring her, looking into those deliciously entrancing eyes. Yes, he could stare at them forever, set into that wonderfully ingenuous, smiling face with its cute, pudgy little nose.

"How are you?" he said, smiling broadly.

"I'm okay! Feeling a *lot* better."

That was good news. "No more... you know, Sister P?"

She shook her head, making her gorgeous hair dance. "No, haven't had one for seven weeks now." Jem held up crossed fingers. "I dream about it sometimes."

"Well never mind that then," said McKinley, "it's just great to see you. Look, there's something we need to discuss."

She looked a little wary but he smiled. "It's okay."

Jem sat down on the bed as McKinley set the single dark blue plastic chair beneath him. It's not so bad in here, he thought, looking around. She had a small television and some ornaments, as well as a pile of books on the nightstand. She'd even brightened up the dreary walls with some pencil drawings and magazine cuttings. Clearly nobody in the unit wanted her to have a harder time than necessary. Sure, her bedroom was also her bathroom and toilet, but the cell was still fair accommodation for someone who'd tried to blow up Downing Street. McKinley found himself at odds with that thought. It wasn't Jem who'd been involved with that incident; it was Sister Patricia. How this distinction would play out in court McKinley didn't know, but he was more than willing to be a witness for the defence. He'd seen the changes first hand. He knew that Jemima Fox was innocent, even if she was daft enough to have sought the cult in the first place.

"So what's up?" she said, that amazing smile blinding him again.

"I had a word with General Sutton, you know, my boss," he started, leaning forward, "and I put in a formal request. I asked if I could be your minder."

"What?" she giggled.

"Well, you can't stay here forever. I asked if you could be placed under house arrest with me."

Her smile grew even wider. "You're joking?"

"*If* you want to, you'd live at my place, fitted with an ankle monitor to keep you within a hundred meters of the house or my car. Question is, what do *you* want to do?"

"So I'd be living with you?"

McKinley huffed with a smile. "I think I just said that. I'd look after you, feed you, all that stuff."

"Really?"

He forced a look of cheerful frustration. "*Yes!*"

Her eyes narrowed for a moment. "What's the catch?"

McKinley shook his head. "No catch. Aye, well, there'd be times when I'd be away for a bit, but if you don't mind being on your own it'd be fine. You'd look after my pad, I'd look after you. That's the deal."

"Okay," she replied demurely, looking off to the side. "So what did your boss say?"

McKinley grinned, looking a little embarrassed. "He said it was an awfully complicated way to get a girlfriend."

She got off the bed and sat on his lap, her arms around his neck and her legs straddling his waist.

"In that case," she said beguilingly, "just *kiss* me, you silly haggis!"

A day later McKinley arrived in the same depressing east London street as before, outside the same little box of a house. His head turned for a moment. Had he come to the right place? It was the right number. They all looked the damn same.

This time the door was devoid of graffiti though. In fact it was a different door, a much more modern looking piece of wood painted bright green. That's different, thought McKinley.

But when Geoffrey Fox answered the door, 'different' took on a whole new depth of meaning. There was almost no resemblance to the dishevelled man they'd met last time. McKinley was shocked.

His countenance radiant, Fox smiled broadly. His eyes were bright and his hair was pulled back into a pony tail. A smart but casual burgundy shirt with rolled-up sleeves sat atop new jeans. The apparently rejuvenated man thrust forward his hand.

"Mister McKinley! How are you?"

They shook vigorously and McKinley said "okay, thanks. It looks as though you're doing better."

Fox's smile seemed to escalate impossibly further. "I am! Much better, thank you. Why don't you come in?"

Again McKinley wondered if he'd entered the right house. The room was bright, with newly painted walls and new chairs. Everything else had been cleaned and in the corner was a modern television with a DVD player. The ghastly radiogram had been replaced by Swedish pine shelving holding several flourishing house plants. The air smelled fresh and fragrant and there was music playing from the kitchen.

"If you don't mind me asking," said McKinley, "what changed?"

Fox huffed, turning serious. "You know about Melissa and what happened in Nottingham, don't you?"

"Aye," nodded McKinley disingenuously. "I'm sorry."

Fox's shoulders drooped and McKinley thought the man might be returning to his previous state, but with a sigh Fox took a big breath and continued.

"Thanks. Anyhow, when the cops told me that, well, me 'ead kinda fell off. I lost the plot, like they say these days." Fox, suddenly positive again, threw himself into one of the new chairs and waved a hand for McKinley to sit.

"I hit rock bottom, Mister McKinley. I were at the end o' me rope. Got absolutely smashed that night an' got knocked down by a taxi."

"Blimey," exclaimed McKinley. "Were you alright?"

"Ah well," beamed Fox, "there I was lying in the street outside this gospel hall just down the road from 'ere, bawlin' me eyes out. An' all them Jamaican folks—marvellous people, they are—they come out an' 'elped me. Took me to the quack, looked after me, brought me meals 'n' stuff. Bloody lovely people. Anyway, they got me back on track. I'm a new man, Mister McKinley."

Although he was putting a brave face on it, McKinley was hating this conversation. He thought he knew where it was going and he didn't like it at all. Everything he considered wrong about religion was pushing him toward an angry and inappropriate response. He wanted to make his excuses and leave but he forced a smile. "Aye, no kidding."

"You know, my girls might 'a' been wrong about a lot o' things," continued Fox, his finger shaking in the air, "but they were right about God. 'E can forgive anyone, even a filthy old sinner like me, even though I don't deserve it!"

Fox finished his remarkable account by lifting both hands to heaven in a joyful gesture. "I don't know what you believe, and it ain't none o' my business anyway. But you can see a change in me, and it didn't come outa nothin' *I* done."

McKinley couldn't deny it, and in that moment he had a little epiphany of his own. There was Fox—previously the most depressed person he'd ever seen—ebullient and talkative. He did indeed appear as a new man. Despite the horrible deception of Wolf River, perhaps the cloud had a silver lining. If getting religion could change a man so dramatically and so obviously for the better, maybe it wasn't all bad. It didn't change McKinley's mind or beliefs, but it did come as a most refreshing source of balance. Despite himself, McKinley *could* see the good in what Fox was claiming.

Reaching into his jacket, McKinley pulled out the old airmail letter. "I came to bring this back."

The older man appeared genuinely moved as he took it. "Oh, thank you Mister McKinley, thank you."

"Aye, no worries," said McKinley. "But I'd better get shiftin'. You know; things to do, people to see."

"Well, thanks for comin'," replied Fox. "It's been a pleasure. If you're ever down this way you should stop by and say 'ello. First round's on me."

They shook hands again and Fox closed the green door with a final gracious valediction and a warm but mostly toothless smile.

McKinley got back into his Vauxhall, surrounded by that fabulous new car smell, and smiled. Well, he thought, I'll never believe the stuff you do, but if it's working then great, knock yourself out.

As he drove away, the London cityscape seemed just a little brighter.

Carter was hurting, and more than he'd admit to Manning. But he *had* to see this, so he'd skilfully covered the extent of his discomfort and hoodwinked the doctor into letting him go to the science section.

McKinley was back on base, Wilson was out of the medical section and, apart from Manning's continual check-ups on his ribs, Carter felt that life was almost back to its usual rhythm. General Sutton hadn't handed them any kind of assignment yet and Carter felt that the boss was easing them back into work, but if he was honest he didn't feel ready to take on any more martial arts experts just at the moment. He made a mental note to brush up on his MMA training when his ribs were sufficiently healed.

Carter opened the door and went inside the little room, walking with difficulty. It was darker than the rest of the labs, but there was still more than enough light. There were his team-mates, who could perambulate a little faster than he.

Stuart Crossman, the tall, bearded and unbelievably thin leader of The Team's 'lab rats', was making all the necessary connections to Heinmarsh's telephone. They'd already scanned it, X-rayed it, swabbed it for DNA, taken it to pieces and thoroughly examined it in as many different ways as possible, proving that in the physical sense at least it was no more than a regular mobile phone. Crossman seemed a little disappointed, as though he'd been hoping to contend with and defeat whatever threat it might contain.

Carter stood next to his colleagues inside the Faraday cage with its nested layers of sheet copper and copper mesh wall panels. The floor and ceiling were copper too, the latter a bit lower than standard height, and the floor area was only about ten feet square, making the cage seem a little claustrophobic. It was designed to isolate anything inside from radio waves. Under normal conditions the only cell signals in the base were those transmitted by their own devices and the unit's repeater stations, yet still they were taking no chances.

Crossman was leaning over the bench, his eyes fixed on the phone.

"Oh good, Chris, you're here," he mumbled, his beard moving whilst his mouth remained unseen somewhere within. "I'm just about to power it up."

"Righto," said Carter.

"Care to explain?" asked Wilson.

"In here it can't interact with the outside world," explained the weapons tech, "so we'll just turn it on for a few minutes. You know, make sure it's not going to do something stupid."

"Well, it's booting up," said Crossman. "Looks normal so far."

"Stupid like what?" said Wilson. "Erasing it's memory or something?"

Crossman stuck his thumb in the air. "Exactly. See this?" He pointed to the bench, where the phone's battery was connected via some thin wires and a big push switch to the device itself.

"Yes?"

"If it starts doing anything suspicious this cuts the power."

"Okay," nodded Wilson. "I understand."

Punching in the unlock code, Crossman shook his head. "But I don't think it's going to."

"Good," said McKinley. "I'm itchin' to see what happens."

They waited nearly a minute, all eyes fixed on the little device.

"Let's connect the antenna," suggested Carter.

"Should be safe by now." Crossman pushed past to the door and dragged a thin cable back in with him. He flipped the phone over and screwed the connector into its external antenna socket.

Turning the instrument face up again, Crossman announced "found the network." Suddenly he jumped as the phone emitted a loud chirp. The others chuckled.

"Chris?" said Crossman. Carter walked stiffly over to the bench and picked up the phone. He read the display, which said 'Enter email address for full information'. Carter thought for a moment. If it was going to send them some kind of hostile or invasive software their email system would filter it out and delete it before it spread any further. Surely this was the point of having a *secure* email address, which no-one could find out belonged to COAST? Carter tapped it in and hit 'enter'.

"Now what?" said McKinley a little impatiently.

"Check the mail," shrugged Carter.

Leaving Crossman to make his notes, they headed back down the corridors to the TDR Group 'D' office. It was good to be back in familiar surroundings, as officers and men circulated through the corridors around them. Some greeted them, others were perhaps too busy. They passed the stairs leading to the command section and into their own area.

McKinley slid himself behind a computer terminal and logged in, quickly calling up their email client software. There was a new message. The sender was listed as 'Kurt Heinmarsh'.

He looked around at his friends with an expectant look.

"Well, go on then," urged Wilson.

"This'd better not be adding us to some spammer's list," frowned McKinley. "I already get enough emails trying to sell me Viagra or hook me up with a tart from Eastern Europe."

He clicked on the email, which was wordless, and then double-clicked on the text attachment that arrived with it.

THE SCYTHIAN COMMUNION

My name is Kurt William Heinmarsh, member of the Scythian Communion. This program is to disseminate information via email should I fail to enter a password on the first day of each month. In all probability I have been murdered by other members of the Communion. To receive the rest of this information, CLICK HERE.

"The *Communion*," breathed Carter, scratching his chin. "I wondered what he was talking about."

Wilson nodded. "Makaru preached on it several times. I think it's the name of their cadre."

"This is going to be *priceless*," said McKinley, grinning like an alcoholic in a distillery.

He clicked the link.

Appendix: Glossary Of Terms And Sayings

Words and phrases not in English *italicised*.

ANFO – A low grade explosive mixture of Ammonium Nitrate and Fuel Oil, often used in quarrying.

AWOL – Absent Without Leave.

Ay-Kay – Slang term for the ubiquitous Kalashnikov AK-47 automatic rifle.

Barmy – UK slang; eccentric or mad. Sometimes spelled 'balmy'.

Bésame culo – Spanish; kiss my ass.

Bill, the – UK slang; the Police.

Blues and twos – UK slang; the blue lights and two-tone siren of some British police cars.

Bodge – UK slang; a rough job, a lash-up, an improper repair.

Bog – UK slang; (1) a lavatory. (2) a swamp.

Bonce – UK slang; head.

Bozwonk – UK slang; gone wrong, faulty, broken.

Brown bread – UK Cockney rhyming slang; dead.

Bunker – Generic maritime term for fuel and supplies, and for loading said.

Byesposhudnyi – Russian; deadly, relentless, merciless.

Caked – UK slang; very drunk, inebriated.

Capeesh – Anglophone slang; 'do you understand?' From the Italian *capisce*.

Cavē – UK school slang, now largely defunct. Latin for 'beware'.

Ceverza – Spanish; beer.

Civvie – Military slang; short for civilian.

CNI – Centro Nacional de Inteligencia; the official intelligence agency of Spain.

Cob – UK slang; a type of sandwich made in a round bun or 'bap'.

Cobbler – Espionage slang for someone who makes false passports. See 'Shoe'.

Cocoa-shunter – UK slang; derogatory term for a gay man.

Cook-off – Term for the heat created by a fired round igniting the propellant of the next.

Crim – UK slang; short for criminal. Plural; crims.

Dag – Australian / NZ slang; one who is unfashionable and socially-inept yet amusing and likeable.

Değersiz salak – Turkish; worthless idiot.

Dibble, the – UK Manchester slang; the Police. From the Hanna-Barbera animated series 'Top Cat'.

Dinnae – Scottish slang; didn't, did not.

Dog-eye – UK slang; a nasty look; a harsh, disdainful stare; UK version of the 'stink-eye'.

Dos extranjeros – Spanish; two foreigners.

DPM – Camouflage material; Disruptive Pattern Material.

Dunny – UK / Australian slang; the toilet.

Durry – Australian slang for a cigarette.

Eff Pees – UK abbreviation; f*** pigs; an expression of frustration, disappointment or annoyance.

ESN – Electronic Serial Number. The identifier of the firmware in a cellphone or similar device.

Fag – UK slang for cigarette.

Fair dinkum – Australian slang. The truth, the genuine article, agreement with a fact.

Faraday cage – A metal cage which blocks radio signals.

FGK – UK slang; a f***ing good kicking.

Flexible friend – UK slang for a credit card, from the Access Card television advertising campaign started in 1978.

Fortnight – UK term; two weeks.

Fuzz, the – UK slang; the Police.

Gaff – UK slang; dwelling or home.

Gasometer – Common term for a bulk gas holder, which regulates pressure in gas pipelines.

GCHQ – Government Communications Headquarters, a British security and intelligence agency.

Geek stick – Slang term for a USB memory stick. Also known as a flash drive or thumb drive.

Gib – Computer gaming slang; to reduce an opponent to giblets.

Go off the reservation – Espionage slang for going AWOL. See 'AWOL'

Gorger – A gypsy term for non-gypsies, non-travellers and people who live in buildings.

Gozzie – UK slang; a look, a peek.

Grassing up – UK slang; the practice of informing on someone or betraying them to the authorities.

Greenham Common – former UK nuclear base where protestors chained themselves to the fence.

Grindadráp – The annual Faroese slaughter of cetaceans, which many consider barbaric and unnecessary.

Gurney – Slang, mostly N. American, for a wheeled hospital bed or stretcher.

Haggis – The national dish of Scotland and thus a nickname for a Scottish person. Also 'haggis hunter'.

Hain pislik – Turkish; traitorous filth.

Hanbō – A Japanese martial arts fighting stick. Its name means 'half staff'.

Haram – An Islamic term for that which is sinful and/or prohibited.

H.E. – Military abbreviation; High Explosive.

Header – Canadian slang; to leave, to head out. Sometimes written 'head'er'.

Herashaw – Russian; okay, fine, righto. The 'H' is glottal and sometimes written 'kh'.

HVAC – North American term. Initialisation of 'Heating, Ventilation, Air Conditioning'.

In the pipe – Military slang for being on the right path, heading in the right direction, on target.

IRGC – Iranian Revolutionary Guard Corps.

Jacksie – British slang; a person or animal's rear end or bottom.

Jag – (1) UK slang; to travel, or a journey. Jagging; travelling. (2) A Jaguar motor car.

Jag är så hemskt ledsen, förlåt mig – Swedish; I'm terribly sorry, please forgive me.

Jammy – UK Slang; cheeky but lucky. Having bent the rules yet got away with it.

Jihad – Arabic; struggle. A term used both for warfare to spread Islam and inner spiritual conflict.

Jobby – UK slang; a bowel movement.

Joyeux de vie – French; the joy (or merriment) of life. A cheerful attitude.

Kaiju – Japanese; strange creature. A term used for monsters such as Godzilla, Rodan, Mothra, etc.

Katana – A Japanese sword typically used by a Samurai warrior.

Kilij – A type of traditional Turkish sword, used throughout history.

Kitnology – Special forces slang for equipment, gear or tech.

Knackered – UK slang; extremely tired.

Knackers – UK slang; the testicles.

Koorie – Australian slang for an aboriginal. Originally an aboriginal tribe.

Kort Nozzle – A ducted propeller.

Kahrolası küçük orospu! – Turkish; f***ing little whore!

Lake Abbe – a lake straddling the Ethiopia/Djibouti border with highly concentrated alkali salts.

Lanc – Plane-spotter slang; a Lancaster Bomber.

Lilly, the – London slang, possibly from Polari; Lilly Law; the Police.

Limey – US slang; a British person. In colonial times British sailors prevented scurvy by eating limes.

Linea nigra – A dark line which can appear on the womb during pregnancy. Latin for black line.

Louisville Slugger – A famous brand of baseball bat.

Mandy – Slang term for ecstasy powder, the drug's chemical abbreviation being MDMA.

Maple-sucker – Western slang term for a Canadian.

MDT – Forces abbreviation; Monthly Drug Test, a mandatory screening based on urine samples.

Meths – UK slang; short for methylated spirits, an old term for methyl alcohol.

MG – Forces abbreviation for Machine Gun.

MMA – Mixed Martial Arts.

Mne nuzhen chertov napitok! – Russian; I need a f***ing drink!

MOD90 – An identification card used by British forces personnel.

Mr. Chad – Cartoon man peeking over a wall. Sometimes just 'Chad' or, in N. America, 'Kilroy was here'.

Mycoculture – The study of fungi, mushrooms and molds.

Narked – UK slang; annoyed, pissed off or unhappy.

Nesbit – UK Nottinghamshire slang; a tramp, hobo or vagrant.

Nishikigoi – Japanese; ornamental carp.

No es un problema – Spanish; it's not a problem.

Nonce – UK prison slang; a sex offender.

NVGs – Military abbreviation. Night Vision Goggles.

Obi – A martial arts belt.

Paracetamol – Pain reliever known in North America and Japan as Acetaminophen.

Pedal-bin – UK slang; a hair comb-over, phrase popularised by TV personality Lorraine Kelly.

Percos – Shortened plural of 'percopop'; an anaesthetic lozenge containing fentanyl. Sometimes 'percs'.

Perviy Kanal – Russian; First Channel, the main Russian television network.

Playing air stylophone – Gesture used to indicate that one wishes to write a cheque and thereby pay.

Plod – UK slang; the Police.

Podvodnaya lodka – Russian; submarine.

Pommy – Australian slang for a Brit, from the former use of apples (Fr. *pommes*) to prevent scurvy.

Prevoskhodnyi – Russian; outstandingly good, excellent, superior.

PTSD – Post-Traumatic Stress Disorder.

QTH – Informal usage of the International Telecommunications Union code for location.

Quack – UK slang for a doctor.

Rellies – UK / Australian / NZ slang abbreviation; relatives. Rhymes with 'jellies'.

Roach – Counterculture slang; the remains of a joint. Drug user's equivalent of a cigarette butt.

Roofie colada – Anglophone slang for a drugged drink.

Rosbif – European—but mainly French—slang for the British, who are believed to eat a lot of roast beef.

RPG – Rocket Propelled Grenade.

Rubber – UK Cockney rhyming slang. Rubber-dub-dub; pub.

Rusticle – Contraction of 'rust' and 'icicle'; a rust formation that occurs underwater.

Salaam – A common greeting in Arabic, meaning 'peace'.

Schtum – Yiddish slang; quiet, not speaking.

Set up shop on the Goodwin Sands – Nautical slang; to be shipwrecked.

Shaitan – Arabic name for the devil.

Shoe – Espionage slang for a false passport. See 'Cobbler'.

Shower – UK slang; derogatory term for a group of people.

Silâh tüccarı – Turkish; arms dealer, merchant of death.

Snog – UK slang; a kiss.

Snort – Submariner slang; the snorkel.

Snow – Anglophone slang for cocaine.

Speedo – Anglophone slang for a vehicle's speedometer.

Spic – Western slang; a Spanish person.

SPL – Sound Pressure Level, usually measured in decibels or dBs.

SRAW – Short-Range Assault Weapon, a hand-held rocket launcher.

Stig, the – Anonymous 'tame racing driver' from the BBC TV show 'Top Gear'.

Strewth – Australian slang; a term of exclamation.

Surzhyk – A pidgin combination of Russian and Ukrainian.

Tannoy – UK term for a PA system, in the same manner as 'Hoover' is used for a vacuum cleaner.

Tent peg – UK cockney rhyming slang for leg.

Thuraya – Arabian based satellite telephone provider.

Trafficator – A mechanical arm at the side of a vehicle analogous to the indicator or turn signal.

Tucker – Australian slang; food.

Twaddle – Foolish, meaningless or nonsensical talk.

Up the wazoo – N. American slang to indicate great numbers or fullness; replete, well-filled.

Victor Charlie – US Forces slang for the Việt Cộng or National Liberation Front of Vietnam.

VOIP – Voice Over Internet Protocol. A means of using the internet for telephone service.

You're my wife now, Dave – Catchphrase from BBC TV dark comedy show 'The League Of Gentlemen'.

Zero feet – Aircrew jargon for an almost impossibly low altitude.

Zhestokiy – Russian; cruel, harsh or brutal.

Zoetrope – A rotating cylinder through the slits of which is viewed the illusion of movement.